MW00475518

"Bryan Litfin brings a historian's background to the story he tells about Constantine the conqueror, giving you a feel for the time and actions of a historic figure. This is still fiction, but it tells a good story well. Enjoy."

Darrell Bock, Executive Director for Cultural Engagement, Howard G. Hendricks Center for Christian Leadership and Cultural Engagement; senior research professor of New Testament studies

"With an eye for detail and an engaging fictional story, Dr. Bryan Litfin makes history come alive. If you've ever wondered what life was like for early believers, you will love *The Conqueror*."

Chris Fabry, author and radio host

"*The Conqueror* is a wonderful mix of excellence in storytelling and keen insight into the setting's historical context. This is what you get when a historian crosses over the authorial divide into the world of fiction. Read this book! Read all of Bryan's books! They are enjoyable from beginning to end. This is certainly on my list of Christmas presents for the readers in my family."

Benjamin K. Forrest, author and professor

CONSTANTINE'S EMPIRE

BOOK I

THE CONQUEROR

BRYAN LITFIN

Revell
a division of Baker Publishing Group
Grand Rapids, Michigan

© 2020 by Bryan M. Litfin

Published by Revell
a division of Baker Publishing Group
PO Box 6287, Grand Rapids, MI 49516-6287
www.revellbooks.com

Printed in the United States of America

All rights reserved. No part of this publication may be reproduced, stored in a retrieval system, or transmitted in any form or by any means—for example, electronic, photocopy, recording—without the prior written permission of the publisher. The only exception is brief quotations in printed reviews.

Library of Congress Cataloging-in-Publication Data
Names: Litfin, Bryan M., 1970– author.
Title: The conqueror / Bryan Litfin.
Description: Grand Rapids, Michigan : Revell, a division of Baker Publishing Group, [2020] | Series: Constantine's empire ; 1
Identifiers: LCCN 2020001225 | ISBN 9780800738174 (cloth)
Subjects: LCSH: Church history—Primitive and early church, ca. 30–600—Fiction. | Rome—History—Constantine I, the Great, 306–337—Fiction. | GSAFD: Historical fiction. | Christian fiction.
Classification: LCC PS3612.I865 C66 2020 | DDC 813/.6—dc23
LC record available at https://lccn.loc.gov/2020001225

This is a work of historical reconstruction; the appearances of certain historical figures are therefore inevitable. All other characters, however, are products of the author's imagination, and any resemblance to actual persons, living or dead, is coincidental.

20 21 22 23 24 25 26   7 6 5 4 3 2 1

To the many students whom I have loved and taught
as a professor at Moody Bible Institute.

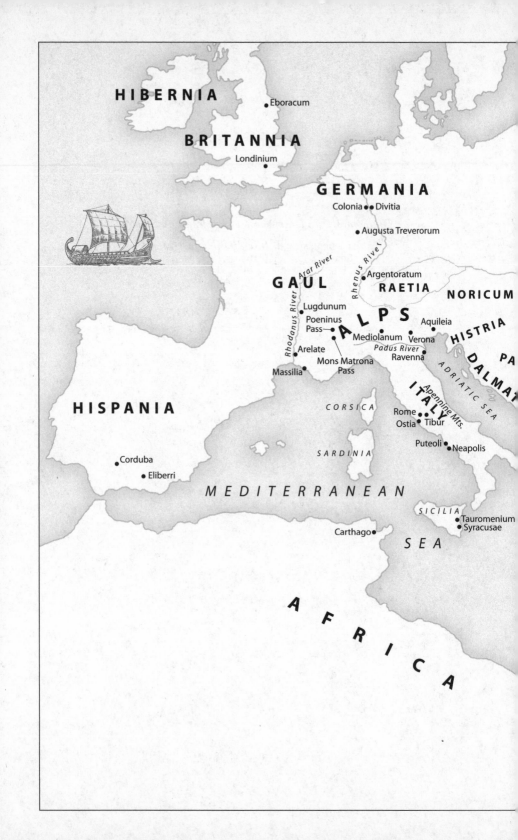

HIBERNIA

Eboracum

BRITANNIA

Londinium

GERMANIA

Colonia • • Divitia

• Augusta Treverorum

Rhenus River

Arar River

GAUL Lugdunum

Argentoratum

RAETIA

NORICUM

Rhodanus River

Poeninus
Pass

ALPS

Mediolanum

Aquileia

HISTRIA

Arelate

Verona

Padus River

Ravenna

PA

DALMAT

Mons Matrona
Pass

Massilia

ADRIATIC SEA

CORSICA

ITALY

Rome

Ostia • Tibur

Apennine Mts.

HISPANIA

SARDINIA

Puteoli • Neapolis

Corduba

• Eliberri

MEDITERRANEAN

SICILIA Tauromenium

Carthago•

Syracusae

SEA

AFRICA

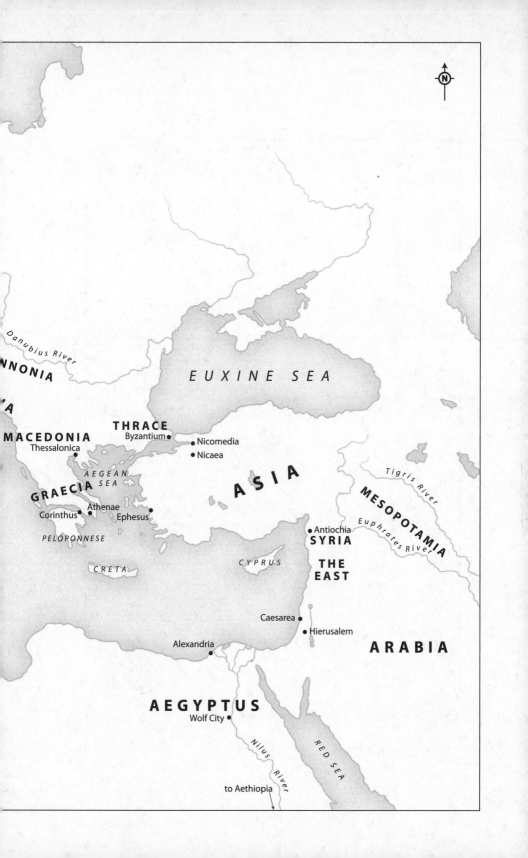

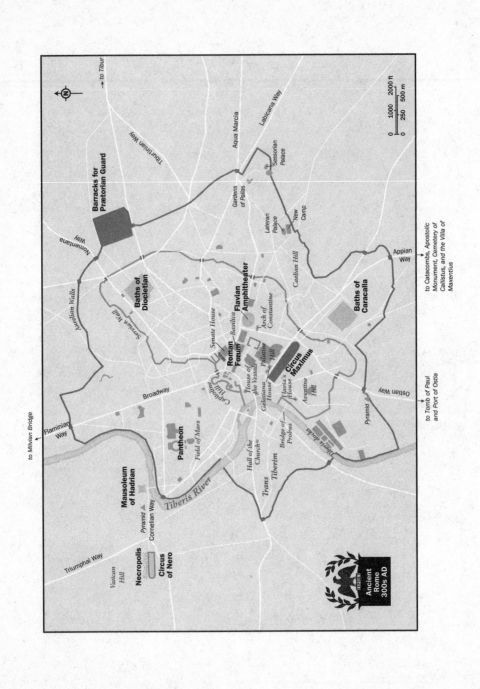

Ancient Rome
300s AD

Contents

Historical Note

THE CONQUEROR IS SET IN THE ANCIENT CHURCH PERIOD, but it isn't a "biblical" novel. Many readers will be familiar with the genre of historical fiction in which a backstory is imagined for the apostles or other characters from Scripture. This isn't such a book. The ancient church period lasted about five hundred years after the birth of Christ, until the Roman world gave way to the Middle Ages. While this novel does take place in the Roman Empire, it isn't the empire of Jesus's day. The events occur three hundred years later, when mighty Rome was learning to bow the knee to Christ. The persecution of Christians was coming to an end. Emperors were taking notice of Christianity—even converting. The age of Christian Rome was dawning.

Historians know quite a bit about this tumultuous era from various written and archaeological sources. As a scholar of that period, I have tried to add a certain realism to my story that reflects the way things really were. The characters are not "evangelicals in togas" who think and act like modern Christians. They were part of the ancient catholic church, not twenty-first-century evangelicalism.

The word *catholic* means "universal." In this novel, the term should not be equated with all the doctrines and practices of today's Roman Catholic Church. At the same time, the faith of the early Christians took a shape different from what today's born-again Christians are familiar with. In some ways, ancient church practices do reflect Roman Catholic belief patterns.

We must remember that this novel takes place twelve hundred years before the Reformation. The characters are neither Roman Catholic nor Protestant. They are the "little-c" catholic Christians of ancient Rome.

Politically, this was the age of what modern historians call the Tetrarchy, which means "rule by four." The ancients referred to it as the Imperial College. This political system, devised by Emperor Diocletian in the late third century, divided the whole Roman Empire into quadrants. Two leading figures, each called an augustus, would rule their halves of the realm, assisted by two caesars who were supposed to take their place in orderly succession. However, this wasn't what happened. The history of the Tetrarchy was tumultuous because many claimants vied to be augusti or caesars, backing up their aspirations by military action. It is safe to say the Tetrarchy led to a lot of civil war, until Emperor Constantine finally defeated all his challengers and united the empire again in AD 324.

Since *The Conqueror* is a historical novel, obviously some of the book's characters are actual figures from history. Rex and Flavia, however, are not real (though there were certainly people like them: a Germanic army recruit, an aristocratic Christian daughter). The main story characters attested in actual history are:

- Neratius Junius Flavianus, the city prefect
- Sophronia (the name Sabina I have attached to her is imaginary)
- Ruricius Pompeianus, the Praetorian prefect
- Alexamenos (nothing is known about this person except his Christian faith)
- Emperor Constantine
- Emperor Maxentius
- Emperor Licinius
- Helena, Constantine's mother
- Fausta, Constantine's wife
- Maximian, Constantine's father-in-law
- Bishop Eusebius of Rome (and Bishop Eusebius of Caesarea is mentioned as well)

- Bishop Miltiades
- Lactantius, professor of rhetoric
- Bishop Ossius of Corduba
- Bishop Chrestus of Syracusae
- King Chrocus of the Alemanni
- Heraclius, the heretic

Of course, we know varying amounts of historical detail about these figures. The best attested is Emperor Constantine. He did indeed witness a solar phenomenon while on a march, interpret it as a sign from the Christian God, mark his soldiers' shields with the cross, and fight Maxentius at the Battle of the Milvian Bridge in AD 312.* Other historical figures require more effort to reconstruct, yet they also grant more latitude to an author's creativity. What I, as a fiction writer who is a church history professor and scholar of early Christianity, have tried to do in *The Conqueror* is spin an entertaining tale that blends real history, accurate context, and exciting drama. May you enjoy the ride. I promise, there is more to come.

Dr. Bryan Litfin

*You can read my academic article about these events at http://www.tinyurl.com/y73bnqy8.

The Dynasty of Constantine

KEY:
+ marriage
↓ children
= siblings
(*not all siblings and relatives are depicted*)

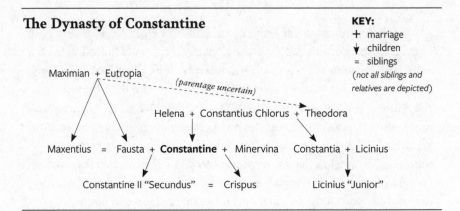

Gazetteer of Ancient and Modern Place Names

Note: the modern names of Rome and Italy are used in this book because of frequent occurrence.

Aegyptus. Egypt

Aethiopia. Ethiopia

Africa. Roman Africa corresponds to Libya, Tunisia, Algeria, and Morocco

Alps. Mountain range across northern Italy and central Europe

Antiochia. Antioch, Turkey

Apostolic Monument. Outdoor dining facility at the original catacombs, believed to contain the relics of Peter and Paul

Apennines. Mountain range down the central spine of the Italian peninsula

Aquileia. Aquileia, Italy

Arar River. Saône River

Arelate. Arles, France

Argentoratum. Strasbourg, France

Athenae. Athens, Greece

Athesis River. Adige River, Italy

Augusta Praetoria. Aosta, Italy

Augusta Treverorum. Trier, Germany

Augusta Taurinorum. Turin, Italy

Baiae. Italian site, near Naples; now submerged under the ocean

Brigantium. Briançon, France

Britannia. Roman Britain corresponds to contemporary England, Wales, and parts of Scotland

Brixia. Brescia, Italy

Campania. Campania region, Italy

Capreae. Isle of Capri, Gulf of Naples, Italy

Carthago. Ancient Carthage, near Tunis, Tunisia

Catacombs, the. Catacombs of San Sebastiano, Rome

Cemetery of Callistus. Catacombs of San Callisto, Rome

Colonia Agrippina. Cologne, Germany

Corduba. Córdoba, Spain

Corsica. Island in the Mediterranean Sea, now a region of France

Dalmatia. Corresponds to parts of contemporary Croatia

Danubius River. Danube River

Divitia. Deutz neighborhood of Cologne, Germany

Duria River. Dora Riparia River, Italy

Eboracum. York, England

Gaul. France, Belgium, Netherlands, and portions of a few other countries

Germania. Areas north of the Rhine and upper Danube, corresponding to parts of Germany, Poland, Czechia, Austria, and other central European countries

Hall of the Church. Basilica of San Crisogono, Rome

Herculaneum. Archaeological site today, near Ercolano, Italy

Hierusalem. Jerusalem, Israel

Hispania. Spain

Histria. Corresponds to parts of contemporary Croatia, Slovenia, and Italy

House of Byzans. Basilica of SS. Giovanni e Paolo, Rome

Lake Benacus. Lago di Garda, Italy

Londinium. London, England

Lugdunum. Lyons, France

Massilia. Marseille, France

Mediolanum. Milan, Italy

Mons Aetna. Mount Etna, Sicily, Italy

Mons Matrona Pass. Col de Montgenèvre, France

Mons Vesuvius. Mount Vesuvius, near Naples, Italy

Mosella River. Moselle River

Neapolis. Naples, Italy

Noricum. Corresponds to parts of contemporary Austria and Slovenia

Octodurus. Martigny, Switzerland

Ostia. Ostia Antica, a contemporary archaeological site

Padus River. Po River, Italy

Poeninus Pass. Great St. Bernard Pass, Switzerland and Italy

Pompeii. Contemporary archaeological site near Naples, Italy

Puteoli. Pozzuoli, Italy

Raetia. Corresponds primarily to contemporary eastern Switzerland

Ravenna. Ravenna, Italy

Rhenus River. Rhine River

Rhodanus River. Rhône River

Saravus Village. Saarbrücken, Germany

Sardinia. Sardinia, Italy

Segusio. Susa, Italy

Sicilia. Sicily, Italy

Sirmio. Sirmione, Italy

Syracusae. Syracuse, Sicily, Italy

Tauromenium. Taormina, Sicily, Italy

Tiberis River. Tiber River, Italy

Tibur. Tivoli, Italy

Trans Tiberim. Trastevere neighborhood, Rome

Tridentum. Trent, Italy

Verona. Verona, Italy

Glossary

argenteus. A silver coin of significant value, though not as much as a solidus or aureus.

augustus. The traditional title for the emperors, used within the Imperial College to designate one of the two highest leaders.

aureus. A pure and very valuable gold coin with a long history, but which was gradually being replaced by the solidus.

ballista. A mechanical weapon for projecting darts and missiles with great force.

balneum. A neighborhood bathing establishment, typically smaller and privately owned, unlike the grand *thermae* constructed by the government.

caesar. The traditional title for the emperors, used within the Imperial College to designate one of the two junior rulers.

caldarium. A hot room in a Roman bath.

cithara. A Greco-Roman stringed musical instrument, like a lyre.

codex. A book of papyrus or parchment pages bound inside covers, readily adopted by Christians to replace the scroll.

colleague. One of the members of the Imperial College.

compluvium. The skylight in a Roman atrium through which rain would fall into a pool.

decanus. The leader of a typical army squad of approximately eight soldiers who shared a tent.

denarius. In late imperial times, it was no longer an actual coin but a monetary unit of low value; e.g., an unskilled laborer would make twenty-five *denarii* per day.

domus. A Roman city house, as opposed to a country villa.

donative. The periodic distribution of large monetary gifts to soldiers to increase their annual pay and keep them loyal.

garum. A salty, savory sauce made from fish intestines allowed to ferment under the hot sun; used as a condiment or recipe ingredient.

genius. The inner spirit (in fact, a kind of deity to be worshiped) that empowered and protected a man or inhabited an everyday place or object.

gustatio. The appetizer course in a Roman meal.

haruspex. A soothsayer or priest performing divination by inspecting animal entrails (pl., *haruspices*).

hippocampus. A mythical creature with a horse's head and an aquatic lower body (pl., *hippocampi*).

impluvium. The pool beneath the compluvium for collecting rainwater in a Roman house.

mile. A Roman mile, equal to a thousand paces, or about 4,860 modern feet (nine-tenths of a modern mile).

nummus. The general name for a coin, including bronze coins of little value, like a penny.

nymphaeum. A decorative fountain dedicated to water spirits (nymphs), usually embellished with mythological and aquatic elements.

ornatrix. A domestic slave specializing in hair and makeup for the lady of the house.

peristyle. The rear garden in a Roman house, surrounded by pillars supporting a shady arcade.

sagittarius. An archer.

solidus. A late imperial gold coin of significant value.

spatha. A long sword that had come into common use by soldiers of the late imperial era, replacing the shorter gladius.

speculator. A Roman special forces agent, like a spy (from *speculor*, to observe, explore, examine, watch).

stadium. A Roman unit of measurement, equivalent to about 607 feet (pl., *stadia*).

strigil. A tool for scraping olive oil from the human body as a means of cleansing.

tepidarium. A warm room in a Roman bath.

thermae. A magnificent imperial bathing establishment, open to the public as a gift from the emperor or other major donor.

tonsor. A barber.

votive. A religious gift given after a sacred vow is fulfilled.

water clock. A Roman timepiece that used a steady flow of water to mark the passage of time.

Prologue

It wasn't the taste of blood that sent me into a rage. It was the dirt.

My lips had been bloodied many times before, of course. We Germani are known for liking to scrap. Even rich boys like me—the illegitimate son of a powerful king—had to fight off bullies. I always made sure to give more than I got.

But now, knocked to the ground and shamed before my father, the urge for vengeance churned inside me like the sulfur springs of my forest homeland. I resolved not to let the fight end with my face in a puddle. As the fat Roman boy forced my head deeper into the mud, grinding me under his sandal while the crowd cheered him on, I decided blackening his eye wouldn't be enough. The centurion's son was going to die.

I came off the ground so fast the crowd was still cheering for the victor when he landed on his back. Writhing in the slick brown earth like the filthy pig he was, the boy no longer had his superior weight as an advantage. The thick limbs and heavy fists that had clubbed me into submission were useless now. I straddled my enemy and began to choke the life from him. *Imagine his shame when he realizes he's about to be killed by a twelve-year-old!*

A boiling lust for revenge gave strength to my fingers wrapped around my enemy's throat. I dismissed the thought of the whipping I would receive. *For a crime like this, I might even get sent to the mines!* But I didn't care. The

21

fat boy's face was red now. His bulging eyes were beginning to hold the distant stare of death. I squeezed harder and felt his larynx pop.

A single authoritative voice rose above the din. "Stop that child!"

"Get him off! Quick!" shouted another voice.

The centurion's vine branch smacked me hard above the ear, knocking me off my opponent. All the mad voices converged into a single roar that echoed inside my skull. I stared at the ground, resting on my hands and knees, trying to control the pulsing ache that threatened to overwhelm me. Though my gut heaved, my breath refused to come. I gasped and coughed. Gobs of blood and grime clogged my throat, blocking the air I so desperately needed.

My arms trembled. My elbows buckled. I toppled into the mud, dimly aware that my father would be proud of what I had done. I had fought well. Having died in combat, I would no doubt be honored in the next life by the hammer-wielding Thor. *But why did no one tell me it would be so dark there?*

A cascade of cold water yanked me back to the world of my birth. Unable to understand what was happening around me, I struggled to regain my bearings. People were shouting. Pushing myself up to a kneeling position, I stared at the ground—no longer mud—and shook my head. At last my surroundings came into focus. I was inside a spacious, marble-lined hall. Sunlight poured through its high windows.

The Fortress Basilica of Eboracum!

The basilica could mean only one thing: this was no longer a back-alley brawl between youths. Death now stared me in the face. I had been dragged inside the judicial hall of Eboracum's legionary fort to be tried before a makeshift tribunal. Normally, the monster of imperial justice slumbered in the background of Roman society. Yet when the mob aroused that beast to action, it could be swift and decisive—and often brutal. Did the mob want me as its next victim? I resolved that if I was sentenced to die today, I would go down fighting.

The scowling centurion, as pig-faced as his dirty offspring, gestured at me with his twisted vine. "Augustus, this murderer must be executed!"

The hubbub in the hall quieted. "Why, soldier?" asked a lone, steady voice.

"That little barbarian throttled my son! A good Roman youth he was! Sixteen years old and newly enrolled as a legionary in your service!"

For a long moment there was no reply, then the voice said, "It seems one of my newest soldiers was just killed by this scrawny child. I fear such a recruit would not have been the kind of warrior the empire needs."

A collective gasp coursed through the crowd at the sharp insult. The centurion clenched his jaw and seethed yet did not dare complain.

Cautiously, I turned my head and gazed from beneath lowered eyes at the only calm person in the basilica. Everyone knew who he was. The handsome man with dark Roman hair and a Mediterranean complexion stood at the base of an imposing statue. The sculpture depicted a rider astride a warhorse: Constantius Herculius Augustus, the senior emperor of the West. Or, at least, that is what he had been until earlier today. Now his spirit was soaring through the heavens like an eagle, while his eldest son, Constantine, just took his place down here on earth. A few hours ago, Constantine was proclaimed the augustus of Britannia, Gaul, and Hispania by the legions of Eboracum, as well as by my father's Germanic mercenaries.

"Stand up, boy," the new emperor said mildly.

I knew I should obey right away, but pride made me delay as long as I dared. I rose slowly, wiping mud from my eyes, shaking water from my hair, straightening my tunic. At last I lifted my chin and met the stare of the augustus with as much dignity as I could muster.

Although I thought at first that Constantine's lips held a faint smile, his tone was harsh. "What is your name?" he demanded. Before I could answer, he followed with, "Speak up! Your life hangs in the balance!"

"I am Brandulf," I declared, "son of King Chrocus of the Alemanni, your blood-sworn confederate."

Constantine's expression changed, though I could not tell if it was to my advantage. "By wife or wench?"

The question made anger flare in my heart. "Neither!" I protested. "My mother is a respectable innkeeper. Beloved she is! More precious to my father than his legal queen in Germania!"

Constantine nodded thoughtfully but did not speak. At last he clasped his hands behind his back and began to approach. I waited with my head bowed and my feet solidly planted so I would not tremble. But inside, my heart was fluttering.

"Why did you kill that boy?" Constantine asked, his voice more measured now.

I did not hesitate, for the insult from earlier today still stung. "He slandered my people, Majesty. Called my father a wild boar of the forest! These Britons were barbarians themselves until just recently. Now they think they're better than us—we Germani who fight for Rome and shed our blood on the empire's borders. We ride into battle like men while they relax behind the walls of Eboracum and Londinium. Who, then, is the truer Roman?"

"Aha," Constantine observed, "it appears you are a rhetorician as well as a warrior."

I fell silent, unsure what to say next. The July sun had warmed the hall, making the air hot and stifling. A bead of sweat trickled into my eyes, and I brushed it away. All around me the hushed crowd waited to see whether I would live or die.

The emperor took a step closer. "Less than two hours ago, your father proclaimed me emperor in this very hall. King Chrocus's warriors and the soldiers of the Victorious Sixth paid me the greatest honor the world has ever known: they crowned my head with the eternal glory of Rome. This action speaks well of your father. It deserves to be rewarded."

I said something surprising then. A powerful emotion rose up within me—from where I know not. Was it love for Constantine? Awe at his majesty? Whatever it was, I blurted out, "When I am of age, Augustus, I will serve you too! I will die for you in the armies of Rome!" A murmur ran through the crowd.

Constantine, however, did not seem impressed. With the sliding metallic sound that a soldier knows all too well, the emperor drew his sword from its sheath. Now his face turned dark, his demeanor hostile.

"Brandulf, son of Chrocus," he thundered, "do not attempt to flatter me! Your quick words will not buy your salvation. You have spilled Roman blood in the precincts of a military fortress. No matter who your father may be, your action was illegal. Our laws declare you must pay for this crime with your life." Raising his sword above his head, Constantine closed the distance between us and towered over me. "On your knees, boy!"

Apparently, it had all come down to this. A swift sword stroke was going to cleave my head from my body and end my short life. Yet now that the great moment had arrived, I did not feel ready to die. And that is why, instead of obeying the direct order of the divine augustus, I looked up at him and said, "Give me a sword, too, Your Majesty, and let's see if you have what it takes to claim me."

The basilica erupted into chaos once more. Everyone shouted their protest at my blasphemous threat—the legionaries screaming loudest of all. Cries of "Treason!" and "Death!" rang out in the tumult. If my life hung in the balance before, now my fate was sealed.

I swallowed the bloody saliva that had gathered in my mouth and awaited the emperor's response. He stared down at me. A stern frown was on his face, though he was not overcome with fury. Slowly he leaned toward me, until he was so close that only I could hear his words.

"Well done, boy," Constantine whispered. "You would make a terrible infantryman. But you have just what it takes to become a great speculator." With that confusing prediction still tumbling in my mind, I glimpsed a flash of metal coming at me. The ruler of the Roman West smashed me across the cheek with the flat of his sword, and for the second time that day my world turned to darkness.

ACT 1

CONVERGENCE

1

OCTOBER 309

All the soldiers said the race to Jupiter's temple on the high pass could be won by only the best. Since Brandulf Rex considered himself the best, he intended to make the climb faster than anyone ever had. By nightfall he would be dining among the gods.

Until then, however, there would be pain.

"It's colder than I expected," Geta complained, warming his hands at his mouth. Wisps of mist trickled between his fingers.

Rex sized up the thick-bodied youth with the bushy mustache and the long braid down his back. Of the ten other cadets milling around the gate of Augusta Praetoria, Geta was the only one Rex considered a threat to beat him. That was something Rex couldn't allow. True, Geta was his fellow countryman and best friend. But it was time to put friendship aside. The race took precedence over all else.

"It is a little chilly," Rex agreed with a shrug, "but it will just make my victory all the more glorious."

Geta swatted his hand at Rex's boast. "Pfft! There's nothing glorious about coming in second."

"You should know. It's a hard lesson you've learned many times since we started our training."

Geta's eyes narrowed. A few paces away, Aratus the centurion called for the men to gather. Geta ignored his commanding officer and approached

Rex instead with a menacing glare. Rex met his rival's gaze and did not break off the stare. The two muscular, athletic warriors stood eye to eye, though Geta was the slightly taller of the two.

For a long moment, each youth scowled at the other, until at last the bond of friendship that undergirded their rivalry couldn't be contained any longer. Smiles spread across their faces as they attempted to stare each other down. Rex clasped Geta's shoulder, and his comrade returned the affectionate gesture.

"May the best man win," Rex said.

"I will," Geta replied, and with shared laughter the pair turned to stand before Aratus.

The route of the race ran twenty-five miles from the low-lying city of Augusta Praetoria to the top of Poeninus Pass, a treacherous yet frequently used crossing over the snowy Alps. Although the road was a good one—*as if the Romans built any other kind,* Rex thought—the hike would be uphill the whole way. At the end of the arduous ascent stood the ancient temple of Jupiter Poeninus, the local expression of the highest and best god. This powerful deity kept watch over one of the main imperial routes through the mountains. Normally Jupiter blessed the pious travelers heading from civilized Italy to the wild Germanic north. Today, however, he would be testing Rome's most elite warriors. Success would prove that their arduous regimen over the past three years—the constant running, sparring, wrestling, and riding—had managed to turn out a soldier worthy to be called a speculator.

"Listen up, cadets," Aratus said when the eleven soldiers had circled around him in the early morning gloom. "The temple that is your destination is the highest sanctuary in the whole expanse of our empire. You Italians should pay special attention. These aren't the little forested mountains that stand behind Rome. The peaks of the Alps are constantly covered in snow and ice. They rise so high that even the hardiest trees can't grow. According to our best geographers, this pass rises more than thirteen stadia above the height of the sea! From here, the road winds up the mountainside to the north. Perhaps you can see it"—Aratus turned and pointed to a snaky track that eventually disappeared into the low-hanging clouds—"right there. No doubt you can appreciate how difficult your journey is going to be."

The trainer's statement elicited a few groans and murmurs. He was known for being demanding and hard-nosed, but today's task seemed to take things to a whole new level. After letting the men mutter a bit, Aratus continued. "Your goal is to reach the temple of the great Jupiter before any of your comrades. There you will infiltrate the temple unseen—or at least uncaptured by rival soldiers trying to thwart you—and retrieve a votive from inside. Anything you can find will do. Just grab something that proves you got in. When you have the item, bring it to the nearby inn and give it to me. Then you shall be declared the winner."

"But, sir," piped up a wiry cadet from Sicilia, "won't that offend the god?"

Aratus gave the man a thoughtful stare, then approached him and stood close. "It might," Aratus agreed, "but that's the difference between a legionary and a speculator. An ordinary soldier fears nothing but the gods. A speculator fears nothing at all." Aratus poked the cadet in the chest. "Perhaps you should consider whether you have what it takes in there."

Chastened, the young man stepped back. Aratus turned to face the rest of the soldiers. "You may take food and water if you wish. Or you may forage for nuts and berries along the way and drink from the streams and puddles you find. Just remember that whatever you take, you'll be hauling it up a colossal mountain."

"And if we win, sir?" Geta asked. "What prize shall we receive?"

"What's the matter, you dirty German? You need something more than the glory of winning?"

"Glory is what I seek most, sir," Geta replied. "I only wish to be propelled up the mountain by the honors I stand to gain."

A chuckle and nod signaled Aratus's approval. "A worthy motivation, Geta—worthy indeed! The prizes of Caesar's army are worth the sacrifice. And judging from your past performance, I believe you may be the one to receive them today." Rex snorted at this assertion but said nothing.

Aratus waved his arms dramatically toward the other men. "Listen to me, cadets! The prize you shall earn from succeeding in this race is more than mere gold—though you will certainly get some of that. But the true prize is better than money or fame or the esteem of your comrades. It is the thing a speculator wants more than anything else."

"Women!" shouted the Sicilian, eliciting an eruption of guffaws.

"Even better than that," Aratus said with an indulgent smile. "Take another guess."

"A warhorse?" someone suggested. "A fine sword?" tried another.

Aratus shook his head, clearly disappointed. "Does no one here know what a speculator craves most?"

Silence fell upon the band of warriors gathered in the gray October fog beneath the walls of Augusta Praetoria. Rex waited until the tension had built to the breaking point. At last he stepped forward. "I know, sir," he said.

"What is it?"

"A mission. An appointment into the greatest army the world has ever known."

Aratus's finger shot toward the heavens. "Exactly right!" he cried. "The true speculator wants nothing more than to serve his emperor on the field of combat, earning honor not just from his brothers-in-arms but from the god who walks on earth." All the other men nodded, and some gave little grunts of agreement.

"That is what is at stake here," Aratus continued. "Whichever cadets I deem worthy will end their training this day. They will be enlisted into the army of Rome as speculators with the Second Italian Legion, based in Divitia. From that post they shall serve the Augustus of the West, the glorious Emperor Constantine."

Rex felt his heartbeat accelerate. *An enlistment into the legions! Today I can earn the right to be finished with my training!* Having reached the age of sixteen, Rex knew he was old enough to enter the army as a foot soldier. But to move straight to the rank of speculator? That was unheard of for someone so young. Even Geta was already eighteen. Rex could see that today's race was his best chance at getting a military post in the emperor's service. It was the only thing he wanted in life. He just wished his father, King Chrocus of the Alemanni, could be there to take pride in his son's success.

"Alright, men," Aratus said, glancing at the overcast sky. "The sun is now above the distant horizon, though it will be several hours before Sol's face clears the crest of the ridge. It is time for your quest to begin. Step up to that chalk line."

The cadets surged forward, each toeing the line and leaning over it as far as possible. Eagerness for glory was written on their faces.

"Are you ready, boys?"

"Ready!" the competitors roared in unison.

"Then with Mercury's wings on your feet . . . I release you!"

Another shout rose from the men as they exploded from their places and charged up the well-paved road. Only Rex remained next to his centurion. After watching the others run for a moment, he started back toward the city gate.

"Brandulf Rex!" Aratus barked, his voice tinged with astonishment. *"You're giving up?"*

Rex spun around to jog backward while facing his commanding officer. "No, sir. Of course not."

"Then what in the name of Priapus are you doing?"

Rex flashed Aratus a confident grin as he continued his backward run. "I'm winning this race like a speculator should," he declared, then turned and darted through the gate of Augusta Praetoria.

The most shocking thing about the dead body was not its pale gray color. It was the crooked condition of the fingers.

Those are the hands of a seventy-year-old, Flavia thought as she waited for the godly Christian priest to finish the funeral rites. *But this man was only forty.*

A little sigh escaped Flavia's lips as she gazed at the corpse. The man's gnarled hands were folded over his breast, and his eyes were closed as his body rested on an oaken table. At last the overworked Roman slave was at peace in the arms of God.

"He looks happy," whispered the slave's widow.

Flavia smiled gently. "I think so too."

A household servant's life was never easy, Flavia knew, even ones with Christian masters like her father. Whips and clubs wouldn't take their toll in a Christian home, but the unceasing labor certainly could. Several times Flavia had ordered the overseers to lighten the burden on the servants. Although she was young—at fifteen, she was just now coming into womanhood—the supervisors still had to listen to the master's only daughter. When she dug in her heels, the overseers would capitulate. For this kindness, the servants would give her secret nods of appreciation.

"Worthy in the sight of the Lord is the death of his saints," the distinguished priest Miltiades intoned from the *Book of Psalms*. At these sacred words, Flavia joined the brethren around the table in signing themselves with the cross. A sweet cloud of incense hung in the air—the prayers of the faithful rising to heaven, as the scriptures clearly declared. Miltiades sprinkled spices into the graveclothes, then folded the shroud over the body. Two deacons came forward to pick it up.

"May you live in God and the Lord Christ," Flavia whispered. "Farewell, dear Pistis."

The deacons carried Pistis's body to a bier outside Flavia's mansion on the crest of the Aventine Hill. Several strong men hoisted the bier to their shoulders. Pistis's immediate family and closest friends had gathered to join the procession to the burial ground outside of Rome. A husky slave bowed to Flavia, then pointed to an elegant litter with curtains of linen.

"You will attend the funeral, Lady Junia?" he asked, using Flavia's family name.

"I shall walk. The tomb of Saint Paul isn't far." The slave bowed again, then beckoned to an assistant, who helped him take the litter away.

The little procession descended the Aventine and made its way past the pyramid that marked the gate onto the Ostian Way. The bier was transferred into a wagon for the remainder of the journey.

About a mile outside the walls, the mourners reached an ancient pagan necropolis. It was here that Saint Paul had been buried after he was beheaded by Nero. Later generations of Christians had put up a memorial to remember the place. But when severe persecution broke out under Emperor Valerian fifty years ago, the remains of both Paul and Peter had been secretly transferred to the Catacombs on the Appian Way for safekeeping. Those holy bones still remained there—but unfortunately, that Christian cemetery was now in the hands of the wicked emperor Maxentius. In these difficult times, the empire had multiple rulers, and few of them favored the catholic church.

The wagon driver pulled up before the tomb of the Junia clan. While the deacons were readying the body for burial, Flavia approached Father Miltiades.

"Pistis was a righteous man," she observed. "He worked hard and never complained."

Miltiades nodded. "It is noble of your father to grant him an honorable burial in your vault."

"The prayers of Saint Paul will comfort his soul," Flavia said, gesturing toward the famous apostolic tomb, which stood a short distance away under a large cypress tree. "Yet the necropolis itself is pagan."

"It is mostly pagan, that is true. Yet many brethren are buried here in remembrance of the great apostle."

"My father's tomb cannot house all the Christian dead, Miltiades. They die by the day in our city—and most of them go to rest among unbelievers."

A long moment passed before Miltiades turned and met Flavia's eyes. "I know what you desire, dear one. Be patient. In time, God may grant our petition."

"You could approach the emperor again," Flavia suggested. "Ask him for a favor."

Miltiades frowned and shook his head. "Maxentius only feigns support for us. He wants to keep our cemeteries as a bargaining coin."

"But the persecutions are over! Our lands should be returned!"

A deacon approached the priest. "We are ready now, Holy Father," he said.

Miltiades put his hand on Flavia's shoulder and leaned close. "Keep praying, dear one," he whispered in her ear, "and I will see what I can do." Turning away, he removed a gospel book from his satchel and proceeded toward the tomb's entrance.

Flavia crossed herself and raised her eyes heavenward as she followed her spiritual mentor. *Lord, your proverbs say, "Like a rush of water, so is the heart of a king in God's hand." Now I ask you to turn that wicked emperor's heart!*

Father Miltiades led the burial rites with gentleness and poise. When the ancient ritual was finished and the body was laid in the tomb, the funeral procession returned to the city. No one wailed or screamed, for Christians did not grieve like those who have no hope. One by one, the mourners dispersed to their homes, until only those who belonged to Flavia's household were left to escort her there.

Upon their arrival, the master of the house met them in the atrium.

35

Senator Neratius Junius Flavianus was a tall, thin man with a spindly neck and a ring of gray hair around the back of his bald head. To the servants he often seemed stern, so they scattered quickly, leaving Flavia alone with him.

"Greetings, Father," she said, offering a bow of respect.

"You walked?"

"It isn't far."

"But is it dignified for a noble girl? Look at your dusty feet."

"Feet can be washed."

Neratius pursed his lips for a moment, then let out a sigh. "Indeed, they can. Come and sit, my daughter." He snapped his fingers toward a hand-maiden standing in the corner of the room. A stool was brought to the edge of the shallow pool beneath the atrium's skylight. After Flavia had seated herself, the servant began to remove her sandals—and with her father standing there, Flavia did not object.

"How was the funeral?" Neratius asked.

"Pistis was given over to God with all dignity. Thank you for granting him a niche in the family vault. That meant a lot to the servants."

"He was a good worker for us."

"And a faithful brother. Yet"—Flavia glanced at Neratius—"he was buried in a pagan necropolis."

The remark made Neratius frown. "A necropolis that once housed the body of Saint Paul! That is no small thing."

"I know. It is certainly a worthy resting place for Pistis. Yet it bothers me that Maxentius still holds the church's rightful lands. He is your childhood friend! Can you not do something?"

"The persecutions only recently ended here, Flavia—and they still continue under the Eastern colleagues. Everything is unstable now. This isn't the time to be making religious requests of a nervous emperor."

"I would do it," Flavia muttered. She noticed the handmaiden who was rinsing her feet suppress a smile.

Neratius snorted. "Oh, I suppose you would snatch the folds of the augustus's toga and shake him until he complied?"

"If that's what it would take, I would!" Flavia replied defiantly, though she knew the statement was ridiculous.

"The Praetorians would run you through before you could take the first step." Neratius craned his neck and gazed at Flavia's feet. "That's clean enough," he told the handmaiden. "Put on her sandals and be gone."

"Yes, master," said the girl. She finished the job and hurried away. The atrium fell silent now, its stillness broken only by the gentle gurgle of the fountain in the middle of the pool. A shaft of sunshine from the lofty skylight made the water sparkle. Flavia stared at the little golden fireflies that seemed to dance on the pool's ruffled surface. At last she stood and faced her father.

"If you were the city prefect," Flavia declared, "Maxentius would listen to you."

"If I were the city prefect, I wouldn't seek trivial favors from the emperor."

"Trivial? You are a Christian! A church even meets in our house. Wouldn't you wish to defend the rights of your brethren?"

Neratius's expression softened. He began to approach, and Flavia smiled as he came. People often said her father looked like a stork, with his long legs and the beak-like nose of his patrician ancestors. *He's awkward, but he's a good man*, Flavia thought, *a man who follows God as best as his high rank will allow.* She let him bend and kiss the top of her head with stiff yet tender affection.

"Will you pray to the Highest God that I might become city prefect?" he asked.

"Of course, Father. I pray for it often."

"I'll make a bargain with you. If God grants that petition, I will ask Maxentius to return the church's properties."

"Not just that. Ask him to favor the Christian religion like Emperor Constantine does. Ask him to be baptized as a believer in Christ."

"Ha! You are worthy of the Junii clan, my daughter! You drive a hard bargain!" Neratius tapped his chin for a moment, then finally threw up his hands and shrugged. "Yet if that is God's price for making me the city prefect, so be it. I shall ask Maxentius about this."

"Do you think he will agree?"

Neratius chuckled and shook his head. "That old pagan? Not a chance." After patting Flavia on the shoulder, he circled around the pool to the far side of the atrium. Pausing at the door, he turned and looked back. "But don't forget to pray for me anyway."

"I will, Father."

Flavia demurely straightened her dress as she watched Neratius disappear into his study. Her father's cavalier dismissal of the bargain disturbed her. Sitting down on the stool again, she glanced up to the skylight. A single puffy cloud adorned the blue rectangle above.

"Can anything ever really change?" Flavia whispered to the cloud.

At that moment the household gardener entered the atrium with a jug and waded into the decorative pool. Flavia watched him cup his hand against the fountain's flow and direct its water into his vessel. When it was filled, the gardener turned and left the room, leaving wet footprints on the marble floor.

"Like a rush of water . . ."

A smile turned up Flavia's lips as she looked back to the skylight again. "Alright, Lord," she said, "I believe."

Rex was halfway up the road to the pass when he heard the first rumble of thunder. Though dark clouds had been gathering in the distance for some time, Rex had hoped the capricious nature of mountain weather might cause the storm to pass by. Now he knew for sure he was going to get wet.

Just keep moving, he told himself. *Embrace the pain and endure.*

Up ahead, two cadets were trotting at a slower pace than his. Soon he would overtake them, just as he had already passed four others. Though the men's head start had seemed like an advantage at first, hunger and thirst were beginning to take their toll. Rex's backpack, in contrast, held the rations, waterskins, and woolen cloak he had retrieved from the urban barracks. He intended to win the race not just with his body but with the careful planning of a sharp mind—like a true speculator should do.

As he trotted uphill, his respiration heavy yet regular, Rex's mind drifted back to one of Aratus's most vivid lessons, an illustration Rex would never forget. The savvy centurion, tested by many battles, had been teaching his young cadets about the importance of the Roman supply chain. "It's what separates us from the barbarians," he had said. "They are mere warriors. We are a field army."

To drive home his point, Aratus had assembled his protégés at the wrestling ground, then ordered a naked Thracian to stand before them. The slave was the most muscular individual Rex had ever seen. His physique was so bulky that he looked like the product of Europa's tryst with the bull. As everyone stood gawking at the giant monster, Aratus pointed to the scrawniest cadet of the bunch and declared, "You shall fight him."

The boy and the Thracian were each given nets like those used by the "fisherman" gladiators. For a long time, the adversaries circled each other under the hot sun—feinting, dodging, throwing their nets, missing, and trying again. The boy was quick and kept his distance, for the Thracian was obviously a superior warrior. Soon, however, it became apparent that the giant's strength was failing. When his throw was errant and his attempt to retrieve the net too slow, the boy managed to entangle his opponent and bring him to the ground. All the other cadets cheered.

Only then did Aratus reveal a secret: the Thracian had been starved for two weeks and deprived of water for two days, making him vulnerable to the skinny trainee. "Your body is like a fire," Aratus said. "Without fuel, it dies to an ember and goes out. A speculator will always supply his flame so it can burn bright." As Rex passed the two men ahead of him on the road, one of whom was staggering like a drunk, he silently thanked Aratus for such a memorable lesson in logistics and resupply.

When the rain finally came, it tumbled from the dark sky as if some aquatic god had decided to empty his pitcher on the sons of men. Rex had already donned his cloak, so he simply pulled up the hood and maintained his slow trot. Though his long blond hair was tied by a thong at the nape of his neck, wet strands hung from his forehead and plastered his cheeks. Water trickled from the hood's edge into his eyes and soaked his tawny beard. Sometimes a cold rivulet would find its way down the collar of his woolen tunic like an icy finger probing his sore muscles. Eventually Rex quit trying to wipe his face and just learned to squint through the ever-present droplets.

"You got another cloak?" the Sicilian cadet called from the base of a larch tree on the side of the road. His arms were crisscrossed over his chest, and he was shivering badly. Rex passed him without reply, for this wasn't a cooperative competition. No man deserved any aid. The winner's prize would not be divided. Only three men were ahead of Rex now. He had seen no sign of Geta, who was likely in the lead.

By late afternoon, Rex's pace had slowed to a steady walk. The rain had not let up and the wind had intensified, sucking the warmth from his body. As the road snaked higher toward the alpine pass, it also turned steeper. Each swing of his leg was an effort, each upward step a victory. Rex longed to huddle under an overhang for a brief respite from the drenching downpour and bone-chilling gale, but such a stop would result in failure. The short breather would become an hour's nap, and then all would be lost. Rex knew his greatest adversary was neither behind nor ahead on the road. His real competition was his own mind. He had to find the iron will to keep going when his body demanded relief.

The attack happened at the place where the road left the tree line. Three legionaries burst from the underbrush with clubs and ropes in their hands. To capture a cadet in this famous race would surely earn the men some leave time or a few coins—and no one would mind if the cadet's nose had to be broken or his teeth were knocked out in the scuffle. Since there was nowhere to run, Rex turned to the attackers and readied himself for a fight. It was time to see whether Aratus's three years of grueling preparation had done their job.

Though the oncoming men were soldiers, troops like these were primarily trained for collective battlefield maneuvers, not hand-to-hand combat. The disciplined ranks of the Roman legionaries, with their stabbing swords and interlocked shields, were more like a consolidated war machine than individual martial artists. But Aratus had taught the cadets the art of *pancratium*, the "all-powerful" method of fighting devised by the Greeks. The techniques included powerful punches, sudden takedowns, stifling chokeholds, and excruciating armlocks. A good pancratist could have an opponent on the ground before he knew what hit him. Most standard legionaries had never seen anything like it.

The first man to reach Rex was a tattooed recruit of Celtic background. He roared like a bull as he swung his club in a wide arc. Instead of taking the force of the blow on his body, Rex stepped into the swing and secured his opponent's elbow and upper arm. Using his hip as a pivot, Rex turned the man's momentum against him and hurled him to the ground. The big Celt screamed as Rex twisted his arm while he wallowed in the mud, forcing him to release the club. A hard whack on the back of the head left the soldier prone in a puddle. Now Rex had a weapon of his own.

The second and third men arrived together, but they hadn't been expecting a confident warrior with a stick in his hand. Rex launched himself at the men with a speed and proficiency they couldn't withstand. Blocking their clumsy strikes, he gave his opponents hard blows to the torso and arms, though he kept the weapon away from their heads, lest he permanently injure a Roman soldier. One of the men—whose hand Rex thought was probably broken—turned and bolted for the forest. A leg sweep took the other assailant to the ground, where Rex put him in a fierce armlock that made him cry for quarter. Rex let up—just a little.

"What's your name, soldier?" the defeated legionary asked, breathing hard through gritted teeth.

"Brandulf Rex, soon to be with the Second Italian."

"Aha! An honorable legion. The she-wolves are great fighters."

"Where are you from?"

"Eighth Augusta out of Argentoratum. The bulls."

"Drop your stick," Rex ordered. The man complied, and Rex released the armlock. He held both clubs while his assailant got to his feet.

"You're just a boy!" the soldier said, inspecting Rex's face.

"Sixteen is old enough to enlist," Rex replied, then added, "and old enough to beat you."

The man laughed good-naturedly. "What's your name again?"

"Brandulf. But everyone calls me Rex because my father was a king of the Alemanni."

"Brandulf Rex," the man mused. "I suppose that might be a name I'll hear someday. You'll make junior centurion within a decade. Good fortune to you, soldier. The house of Jupiter is only a few more miles up the road."

"I know. And I plan to be the first to reach it."

"There are three men ahead of you."

"Not for long," Rex said, then fixed his eyes on the top of Poeninus Pass and left the legionary in the pouring rain.

⟞⟋∿∿⟍⟝

Emperor Maxentius was quite certain that when all was finished, his new suburban villa on the Appian Way would be the most sumptuous dwelling since the infamous Golden House of Nero. It would be the envy of every senator in Rome. Yet even while the palace was under construction, Maxentius intended to present himself in the splendor he deserved. That was precisely what an augustus should do—even if the other imperial colleagues didn't recognize him as such.

"Do you wish to use your full regalia, sire?" the valet asked. The man was new to the house and didn't yet have a feel for the ranking of social occasions.

Maxentius gazed fondly at the royal scepter, which lay on a soft cushion in the valet's case. It was a rod of pure gold shaped like a budding flower, topped by a blue sphere of chalcedony that represented the earth. Such an exceedingly fine piece was far too elegant for a meeting with a mere priest of the catholic church.

"No need for that today. My visitor is hardly so deserving."

"As you wish, Augustus."

Maxentius directed a fatherly smile at the simple valet, who, as a slave, probably didn't know the significance of the term he had just used. "Do you know what that word means?" he asked the ignorant servant.

"*Augustus* means highest and greatest, Augustus," the valet replied, keeping his eyes down.

"Have you ever heard of the Imperial College?"

"No, Augustus," said the valet, though Maxentius suspected the man probably had encountered the term. Slaves were prone to lie. It was their nature.

"The Imperial College is an association of four emperors. The great Diocletian devised it because he realized our empire was too large to be controlled by one man. The four colleagues rule over their own territories in the East or West. Each is a true Roman emperor, though some are more powerful than others. Two augusti take the lead, and two caesars assist them. Four men now govern the realm that a single emperor used to command."

"Yes, my lord. And you are the Augustus of the West. Master of Italy and Africa. Well-deserving of that title."

Maxentius cleared a speck of food from his teeth with his tongue, then spat the bit on the floor. "I *should be* Augustus of the West. But the college doesn't officially recognize me. The augustus who supposedly rules the West is Licinius. Yet Africa is now in rebellion and must be taken back. As for

Italy, it is I who actually hold it. For that reason, I expect Licinius to attack me. He will want to win the prize of Rome."

"May the powers of heaven defeat your enemies, great Augustus! May Licinius and Constantine be destroyed!"

"Ah, Constantine—my dear brother-in-law. He's married to my sister Fausta, you know."

The valet took a step back, his eyes widening. "I did not mean . . . it's just that . . . at times I've heard you say—"

"Be at peace," Maxentius said soothingly. "Just because Constantine is my brother-in-law doesn't mean I can't hate him. I do. And someday I shall also have to defeat him, once I get Licinius out of the way."

"May the powers of heaven—"

"Shut up and bring my toga," Maxentius said, waving the valet away.

The great reception hall at the villa of Maxentius was still under construction, so the heating system that would one day make it comfortable wasn't operational yet. Maxentius found the air unpleasantly cool when he stepped inside. Though he had just finished fussing over the folds of his toga, he was forced to call for his rich purple cape before taking his seat on the throne in the hall's apse. As he sat down, he made a mental note to get the heat working before he entertained any truly important guests.

Two powerful men—Ruricius Pompeianus, commander of the Praetorian Guard; and Senator Neratius Junius Flavianus, an old childhood playmate—had already assembled themselves on either side of the throne. Maxentius greeted them warmly and talked politics for a few moments until the doorkeeper announced the arrival of the day's first appointment. The visitor was Father Miltiades, an official representative from the catholic church of Rome.

The Christian priest was handsome in a middle-aged sort of way. He definitely looked as Greek as his name, with his elegant silver hair oiled and swept back on his head. He wore a full beard that protruded from his chin, a fashion choice Maxentius considered un-Roman—but since when had the followers of that Eastern cult of Christianity ever worried about Roman customs? The emperor decided he ought to be wary about whatever the man had to say.

Miltiades held his palms together and bowed at the waist. "Blessings to you in the name of God, O great Augustus."

It was a respectable enough greeting, so Maxentius welcomed the priest with similar courtesy. When the pleasantries had been exchanged, the emperor urged the visitor to state his business. He hoped the matter wouldn't take long, for he had several more audiences to give, a speech to prepare, numerous documents to sign, and two courtesans waiting in his bedchamber. Today was going to be a busy day, and the emperor couldn't afford to let the affairs of the catholic church occupy too much of his time. "As you know, Your Majesty, there is currently no bishop in Rome," Miltiades said. At this announcement, the so-called "deacons" in the priest's retinue murmured a little, as if it were a matter of grave significance.

"Of course I know that," Maxentius shot back. "I was the one who exiled your bishop for allowing riots to take place. I'll do it again if I have to."

"We had no part in the riots caused by those troublemakers. Yet it explains why I, a mere priest, am standing before you today instead of a bishop."

"I take it you have been sent on behalf of the church. Fine, then. What do you want from me?"

"Your Majesty, you are a friend of the Christians. You put an end to the persecutions in Rome—what is it now? Three years ago? Yes, three years, almost to the day."

"I am a benevolent and tolerant ruler of all my Roman children," Maxentius agreed.

"And yet the properties of the church remain in imperial hands. Do you not wish to gain the appreciation of your Christian subjects by giving them back? We ask only that you apply your long history of generosity to this matter as well." Miltiades smiled gently and gave a slight bow. "If it should please you, O great Augustus."

Maxentius beckoned for Pompeianus and Neratius to bend close as he conferred with them, then turned back to the priest. "To which properties do you refer?"

"I have a list." Miltiades held up a small tablet. "It includes such parcels as the Catacombs, with its banqueting place called the Apostolic Monument, which is just outside your door here on the Appian Way. So, too, are the cemeteries of our former bishop Callistus, and of Domitilla, a woman of holy memory. And we own some urban buildings as well, such as a meeting hall in Trans Tiberim, where many of our people dwell. There is another property on the Caelian Hill—a hall with baths where we perform spiritual washings. It is called the House of Byzans. Our list is not long, but it accurately records what was taken from us and not restored."

Maxentius felt a little peeved at the boldness of the priest's tone. Though he tried to mask his irritation, he could not help but ask, "Do you blame my father, Maximian, for all this? It was he who enforced Diocletian's edicts against the Christians. Is he now your great enemy?"

"We assign blame to no one, whether here or there," Miltiades replied diplomatically. "We merely seek your favor on behalf of the catholic church. It was your own decision to end your father's persecutions. Perhaps you can follow through by returning our properties at last. We hope you will consider it."

Maxentius glanced at the windows in the hall, noting the height of the sun. Enough time had been spent on this matter already. "Leave your list with my steward," he said, "and I will entertain your request."

"Very well. Thank you, Your Eminence."

When Miltiades had taken his leave, Maxentius indicated that Pompeianus and Neratius should come around to stand before him. "What advice do you have for your lord?" he asked.

"These priests disgust me," Pompeianus said. "They reject the gods of our fathers and claim there is only one divinity. It's stupid! We should do something about it."

Maxentius nodded thoughtfully. "Go on."

"The Eastern colleagues still persecute these fools! You could adopt that policy too—your father's policy. Let's rid Rome of these Christian cockroaches scurrying around."

Maxentius turned to Neratius. "What do you think, Senator?"

Neratius started to speak three or four times before he finally found his words. "I'm not sure, Augustus. They are—those Christians, I mean—they are good people, from what I can tell. I hear they are quite popular among the rabble. At least that is what I have discerned from a distance."

"Do you think I should give them back their lands?"

"As you wish. No doubt it would earn you great favor with the masses."

Maxentius inspected Neratius's face, but the man returned only a blank stare. "Perhaps I should convert to this faith myself? What do you think? That would certainly earn me favor in some quarters."

"Never, Your Majesty!" Pompeianus spat.

"How about it, Neratius? Should I convert?" Maxentius rose from his throne and commanded a slave to bring him a jug of water, which he promptly handed to the senator. "Go ahead!" Maxentius urged, extending his bowed head toward his friend. "Baptize me!"

"Your Eminence, I—"

Maxentius snatched the jug and swung it hard at the slave who had brought it. The pottery burst against his skull, knocking the man to the ground in a spray of water and blood. The man put his hand to his head and tried to stand up but could not. Reddened water dribbled down his cheeks and stained his garment.

"Look, a new Christian!" Maxentius exclaimed, then broke into hysterical laughter.

"Now throw him to the lions!" Pompeianus added, laughing along with his lord.

Maxentius made threatening claws with his hands. "Grr! Grr! Grr!" he growled, swiping at the slave on the ground. The man cringed and begged for mercy.

"Alas, he's dead now! Come, let's bury him next to all the others!" Pompeianus raised his eyes skyward and held out his palms in a posture of prayer. "O great God," he intoned, "please welcome this soul into heaven! You will surely like him. He's a torn-up criminal just like your own Son!" Raucous laughter filled the audience hall.

Maxentius clapped Pompeianus on the shoulder, saluting his performance. "That's right, my friend! For some strange reason, those Christians love executed people. They make shrines around the city for little Agnes and all their other martyrs. Each one might as well be inscribed, 'Here Lies the Treachery of Maximian.' See how they continually insult my father!"

"Not while I'm in charge of the Praetorians," Pompeianus said sternly.

"Indeed. Your faithfulness is highly esteemed by your lord." Though Maxentius was self-conscious about his petite stature, he straightened to the fullest height he could muster. Proudly, he extended his hand, which Pompeianus knelt and kissed.

After receiving the honor, Maxentius turned and offered his hand to Neratius. "You, too, Senator?"

Neratius knelt immediately. "Caesar is lord," he said, squinting his eyes as he pressed his lips to the emperor's signet ring.

Maxentius indicated that the two aristocrats could rise. "I believe I shall keep those Christian properties awhile longer," he declared after his friends stood.

A snap of his fingers summoned the doorkeeper. "Take this rebellious slave away," Maxentius said, pointing to the frightened man cowering on the floor. "Have him flogged for dereliction of duty. Then send in my next appointment."

⸙

The sun had gone down by the time Rex crept to the top of the Poeninus Pass. His legs barely seemed to work anymore, their muscles having expended all their energy on the twenty-five-mile ascent. He had surged past the final two racers an hour earlier, leaving only Geta as a possible contender for the prize. But the effort had taken Rex to his limits. Now he begged Hercules for just enough strength to get inside the temple, snatch a votive, and get out—without being seen by the soldiers guarding the pass.

From behind a clump of boulders Rex observed the broken ground before him, which seemed to be deserted. Back in the days when the Romans had not yet conquered the Celts of northern Italy, Poeninus Pass had been a Celtic crossing. But Caesar Augustus had subdued those people and made them take the yoke of Rome. Today Jupiter had replaced their deities, and his modest temple was the most significant building on the pass. The altar of Jupiter was actually a stony outcrop of the mountain itself, uniting the god with the heights upon which he dwelt. A watchtower and two inns also stood nearby for the help of weary travelers—though since it was now October, the inns were about to close for the season. The day's rain had turned to flurries, marking the beginning of an annual snowfall that would suffocate the pass in a white blanket for many months. Even the noses of the best hounds couldn't locate the traveler foolish enough to wander off and succumb to an icy death. As Rex brushed snow from his hood, he vowed not to become one of those fools.

The light from a crescent moon reflected off the new-fallen snow, illuminating the landscape more than Rex would have liked. Yet nothing could be done about that. It was time to move, so he rose from his crouch and darted ahead. Instead of taking a direct route to the temple, he followed a more circuitous path, dodging from boulder to boulder. A final cluster of rocks provided good cover. Only a short open space lay between him and the temple.

A shout from behind made Rex swivel his head, though he didn't leap from his hiding place. A tall man was making a break for the temple, his braid flying behind him. Two soldiers chased the runner, but they were obviously slower. Geta was clearly going to beat them to the goal—until suddenly he slipped in the snow and the men pounced on him with their clubs.

Rex bolted from where he was crouched and sprinted across the uneven landscape, aware that he might twist an ankle yet unwilling to slow down. The soldiers were whacking Geta so furiously that he hadn't regained his footing. Reaching the melee, Rex easily disarmed one of the men from behind and sent him sprawling, then used the stick to parry the other man's attack. The move stretched the legionary's arm wide and out of position. Rex stepped forward and rammed the heel of his hand into his opponent's unprotected torso, knocking him backward into the snow. A much more damaging blow would have been possible, but this wasn't mortal combat, and Rex didn't want to do permanent harm. "Come on," he said to Geta, extending his hand to help up his friend. "Let's make a run for it!"

The two cadets dashed across the moonlit pass, heading for the temple while the pursuers scrambled from the slippery ground and resumed the chase. "Over here! This way!" one of the men yelled, drawing two more soldiers out of the watchtower.

Geta gained the portico first but turned around at the entrance. "You go inside and get something!" he said. "I'll hold them off. Give me your stick!"

Rex tossed the weapon to his friend and darted into the temple. Unlike the portico, which was brightly lit by torches, the interior was illuminated by only two oil lamps in niches on the wall. An oaken table was strewn with votive offerings—mostly bronze plaques inscribed with prayers, but also a small legionary eagle, a couple of coins, and a little statue of Jupiter. Rex grabbed the miniature idol and ran outside.

Geta had reached a stalemate on the portico. He was able to hold off the four men at the bottom of the steps but unable to get past them and escape. Rex came to his side. The attackers crowded close to the base of the stairs, issuing threats, seeking an advantage.

"Warriors of the Eighth Augusta, I salute you!" Rex bellowed. The friendly greeting seemed to catch the men off guard. They fell silent, unsure what to think.

"You are great fighters, I can see that," Rex continued. "But you cannot win against us. To try will only bring injuries you don't want to receive and we don't want to give."

"Not likely, boy!" shouted a swarthy soldier whose foot was poised on the first step of the stairs.

"Do you know what speculators are?"

"We know all about the explorers," the swarthy leader said.

"Speculators and explorers are not the same, my friend." Rex's amicable tone had caught the men's attention, so he decided to take control of their imagination and talk his way out of the impasse. "An explorer is a battlefield scout, a good rider, a soldier trained to operate in forward areas. But a speculator is much more. We operate for months at a time behind enemy lines. We blend into an enemy's society and spy on their ways. We relay coded messages. We know lock picking and poisons and nighttime stealth. We can get inside any building. The best burglars are spared crucifixion so they can teach us how to enter wherever we want and pass by unobserved. Every speculator knows boxing, swordplay, and hand-to-hand combat. During our training we are made to run like Olympic racers, lift sacks of sand above our heads, and go without sleep for days on end. We are fed all the red meat and dark beer we can handle, but our bodies still grow lean and hard. And what about horsemanship? We ride our mounts until our souls are joined to theirs, like a single animal. We are as deadly with the javelin as any cavalryman on the field of war.

"Do you hear me, comrades? We are Rome's most elite soldiers! So now we ask for the respect that only one fighting man can give to another. We ask you to let us pass so we can finish our great quest."

"You make a lot of big talk, boy," the leader said, "but there's four of us and only two of you."

Rex and Geta exchanged grins, then Rex turned back to the man at the bottom of the stairs. "Alright, have it your way. I challenge you to a fight, brother! Come up here and take me if you can. You may keep your club. I will remain unarmed."

With a confident cackle, the swarthy man bounded up the steps and faced Rex from a few paces away. *This is going to be easy*, Rex thought—and it was. As soon as the man drew back his club and began to step into his swing, Rex leapt on him like a lion on its prey. In a continuous motion that was actually a series of well-rehearsed combat moves, Rex disjointed the soldier's shoulder, took away his weapon, slammed him to the ground, and clubbed him twice across the back of the head. Death would have been a simple matter of giving a hard strike to one of the vulnerable spots on the man's body, but Rex had made his point.

The three assailants standing before the temple portico took a step back into the shadows. Their mouths were agape, little murmurs escaping them.

"You see?" Geta said. "It is just as my friend told you. Will you let us pass now?"

Three clubs were pitched into the snow. "Hail, brothers," one of the soldiers said. "You may pass with honor. We fight for the same lord."

"And who would that be?" Rex asked.

"The men of the Eighth serve Constantine."

"And now so do you," said a voice from the darkness.

All heads turned toward the speaker, trying to discern his identity, though Rex already knew who it was. Rex tossed the little statue of Jupiter to the newcomer, who caught it midair. "How was our time, Aratus?"

The centurion held up an hourglass to the light, inspecting its contents. "Best time ever by more than half an hour." Aratus smiled broadly. "Well done, cadets. Well done."

"You sure know how to push us to the limits, sir."

"Ha! You think my training has been hard? Your real work is just about to begin."

The two speculators exchanged glances. *More hiking? More combat? I'm exhausted! But I'll do whatever it takes.*

"You have another trial for us, sir?" Geta inquired.

"We stand ready for whatever it is," Rex added.

Aratus shook his head in amusement. "Yes, I have a great trial for you—but not today. For now, I order you to come inside and get warm. You two won the race together."

Rex and Geta exchanged triumphant glances, clasping each other's hands in congratulation. "Brothers always," Rex said.

"To the death," Geta agreed.

Rex turned back to his commander. "And what of the prize?"

"It belongs to both of you. I'm ending your training tonight."

The announcement brought a whoop from the two young cadets. They beamed at Aratus, and he returned their smile.

"Rex and Geta," the centurion said at last, "you are the newest soldiers of the Second Italian Legion. Welcome to the army of Rome, boys! It's going to take everything you have to give."

2

The air in the Christian meeting hall was comfortably warm, and after what had been an unusually cold winter in Rome, Flavia was glad for the change. The pleasure of the late spring sunshine almost made her forget the most frustrating aspect of the hall, that while it was rightfully owned by the catholic church, the bishop had to pay exorbitant rent to the imperial landlords who had confiscated it as part of a persecution. Not long ago, it was even being used as a granary! Although that travesty had been corrected, Flavia still wanted the property back in the hands of its rightful owners.

She sat next to her mother, Lady Sabina Sophronia, on one of the wooden benches that adorned the Hall of the Church. The service was over now and most of the congregants were leaving, though some had stayed behind to chat. Flavia glanced around the hall, half expecting to see sacks of wheat piled in the corners. *What a job those had been to remove!* She recalled the day well. Flavia had joined the effort alongside the lowborn believers who populated Rome's Trans Tiberim district. Together, they had made the place a church again.

It was Father Miltiades who had gotten the property back into catholic hands by offering a better rent than what the bakeries had been paying. Until the big cleanup a year ago, the Hall of the Church had been filled with grain shipped from Aegyptus and Africa. Instead of offering the Bread of Life, the holy building had been turned into just another warehouse like the many others in this dockside area. But now the name of the Lord was being

52

praised here again—even if it meant that for the time being, the Christians had to pay to do so. The emperor was being stubborn about giving back the property. Silently, Flavia reminded herself of the biblical proverb she often applied to Maxentius: *"Like a rush of water, so is the heart of a king in God's hand."*

"The service today was well attended," Sophronia remarked, her quiet voice snapping Flavia's attention back to her surroundings.

"I thought so too. I've noticed there's always a good crowd here. God's people are found all over Rome, but especially in Trans Tiberim."

Sophronia turned in her seat and regarded her daughter with a gentle smile. "Do you know why?"

Flavia shook her head.

"It is actually quite an interesting story. But I will let someone else explain it to you."

"Who? Father Miltiades?"

Again Sophronia smiled at Flavia, this time with a grin even wider than before. A little twinkle was in her eye as she announced, "No, a very special guest." She pointed to the main entrance, and Flavia let out a gasp.

"Bishop Eusebius!"

Sophronia rose from the bench. "Come. I want you to meet our new shepherd."

The two women crossed the hall, and Miltiades and Eusebius greeted them warmly. Being highborn, Flavia knew how to act in such situations, yet she still felt butterflies in her stomach. It wasn't often that one got to interact with the bishop of Rome.

After introductions were made, a deacon escorted the foursome to a pair of couches beneath a fresco of Abraham offering his son Isaac—the Old Testament prefigurement of Christ's own sacrifice. A glass decanter was brought on a tray with four cups. The elderly bishop poured wine for his friends, then filled the fourth cup with water. When everyone had their drinks, Eusebius directed his attention to Flavia. "Your mother mentioned you were asking about the Christians in Trans Tiberim," he said.

"Yes, Holy Father." The simple affirmation was all Flavia could manage to get out. Though she usually thought of herself as talkative, she found she was a little tongue-tied in the presence of the new catholic bishop.

"Trans Tiberim is one of the oldest Christian districts in Rome. It was here that the Jews first dwelled, long before the time of Christ. Their earliest synagogues go back to the reign of Caesar Augustus. It was only natural that the Jews would congregate here, for the area is across the Tiberis from the original city and outside its earliest walls—a crowded and undesirable place, suitable only for immigrants, slaves, and poor dockworkers from the East. Such were the first Jews to arrive in Rome."

"But what of the Christians?"

Bishop Eusebius motioned for Miltiades to hand him a codex. Flavia craned her neck and saw it was the four Gospels and the *Acts of the Apostles*. Although the book was in the original Greek, not the rough Latin that the common people used, Flavia had no problem reading the title. She considered it a much better use of her aristocratic education than translating the scandalous Greek verses of Sappho.

"Look here," Eusebius said when he found the place he wanted. "Read this text aloud, young lady. Give it to us in Latin."

Translating the Greek in her head, Flavia read aloud the selected portion from the end of *Acts*: "Moreover, having appointed a day for him, many came to his lodging, to whom he preached, testifying fully to the kingdom of God, and persuading them also concerning Jesus, both from the Law of Moses and the prophets, from morning until evening." Flavia lowered the book. Out of the corner of her eye, she noticed Sophronia give her an approving wink and nod.

"The sacred scripture is speaking about Saint Paul's lodging under house arrest," Eusebius observed. "That very house isn't far from here. It is but a short walk, though you would have to cross the river and go back into the city to reach it. What we learn is this: many of the Jews of this neighborhood were converted by the apostle. Such converts made up a good portion of Rome's first Christians. And there have been numerous Christians in Trans Tiberim ever since. For two and a half centuries, the church's faithful believers have been exalting the risen Christ right here."

Flavia felt a twinge of awe as she considered the historic roots of her faith. "What an honor to worship in such an ancient place!" she exclaimed. "I suppose some of those first believers would have been eyewitnesses of the Lord."

"Exactly. We built the Hall of the Church in Trans Tiberim to recognize that legacy. That is why we so earnestly desire to get it back from the hands of Maxentius."

Sophronia nodded gravely. "Then let us pray that—"

A loud crash broke the stillness in the church. Flavia let out a yelp, and all four heads swung around to see a bright orange fire raging in the middle of the floor. A burning amphora of some flammable substance had been heaved through an open door.

Eusebius leapt up and began waving for help. "You men, over here! Put it out, quickly!" Several deacons and lectors dashed toward the flame with heavy cloaks, trying to smother the blaze. The smoke billowing from it was thick and black.

"What is it?" Sophronia cried. "Is it another persecution?"

Persecution? A burst of cold fear shot through Flavia's body. *God help us! Is the age of martyrdom starting up again?*

"It's not persecution," Father Miltiades said, staring out one of the doors. "It's that troublemaker Heraclius."

"Everyone take up a position at an entrance," Bishop Eusebius ordered. "I want five men holding the main door. Bar it tight. Whoever is left, guard the side doors. Try to make sure no one enters this hall. Yet do not risk injury! Your lives are worth more than this building of brick and tile."

Flavia and Sophronia found a spot near a window and peeked out. The scene Flavia saw horrified her. Beefy thugs with sticks and hammers were rioting in the street. Many were hurling rocks at the Hall of the Church. "Stop it!" Flavia cried, but her protest was futile. She was a sixteen-year-old woman, and this was an angry mob of grown men.

The rioters' leader stepped forward. He was a tall fellow with long, spidery arms and stringy white hair that dangled past his ears to his shoulders. "Heraclius," he had been called. Flavia had never heard of him.

"False Bishop Eusebius, show yourself!" Heraclius shouted. "Come forth and step down, lest the judgment of Christ be upon you!"

"The judgment of Christ?" Flavia whispered to her mother. "This man claims to be a Christian?"

"He represents the party of the Lapsed—those who gave in during persecution. They claim they did nothing wrong."

"But, Mother, they denied the Lord. They cursed him and handed over the scriptures for burning. They worshiped demons and swore oaths to them! How can that not be wrong?"

"It is wrong," Sophronia said. "That is why Bishop Eusebius believes in a process of repentance and restoration. But Heraclius calls him a 'false bishop' for this. He denies the martyrs are special heroes. He says they were fools to throw away their lives."

The martyrs are fools? Flavia couldn't believe anyone could think such a wicked thing and call himself a Christian. *Make me that kind of fool,* she prayed, then quickly added, *and give me your grace if you do.*

The rioters were close now. Some of the smaller doors rattled ominously, though the main entrance remained secure.

"Look out!" Sophronia cried—though not quickly enough. A speeding rock clipped Flavia's forehead and sent her stumbling backward. She landed on her rear end, disoriented and confused. The room seemed to spin around her. When she finally collected herself, she felt warm blood trickling into her eye.

"I'm alright, Mother," she said as she was helped up. "Just don't let anyone get in that window!"

"False Bishop Eusebius, this is your last chance!" Heraclius roared from the street. "Come and turn yourself in, or the Lapsed will arrest you by force and confiscate your house of Satan! What say you? Do you dare defy me?"

A hush fell on the mob, and the defenders grew quiet as well. For a long moment, nothing happened. Then, with a slow creak, the door to the church opened and Bishop Eusebius stepped forth. With slow and measured steps, he crossed the space toward Heraclius and stood before him.

"What do you have to say for yourself, you martyr lover?" Heraclius demanded.

Deliberately, the aged bishop of Rome looked Heraclius in the eye and uttered four Latin words that Flavia vowed never to forget: *Semen est sanguis Christianorum.*

"He's quoting the writer Tertullian!" Sophronia whispered. "Eusebius is taking his stand with the martyrs of the Lord!"

Heraclius clenched his fists. His face began to turn a hot shade of red. Seething as he stood in place, he seemed ready to explode, like ancient

Vesuvius. At last the eruption could be held back no longer. "Arrest him!" he screamed. "And ravage this temple of demons!"

The mob broke into a run, surging into the Hall of the Church. Brutish hooligans began striking the deacons and lectors with their sticks or pelting them with stones. They overturned and smashed furniture. Everyone was screaming and wailing. One man began to urinate on the holy altar.

Horrified, Flavia gripped Sophronia's forearm and watched the chaos swirl around her. A scrawny man wearing nothing but a loincloth charged the two women, his club raised high. Sophronia shrieked and pulled Flavia close, sheltering her daughter with her body.

"Back off!" Flavia yelled, thrusting out her palm. The man caught a good look at the women and pulled up, suddenly aware of their lofty social station. The law always favored highborn nobles. Turning aside, the ruffian ran to go destroy something else.

A loud crash signaled the fall of something heavy. Flavia whirled to see that the church's ornate book cabinet had been toppled and broken open. The rioters were pulling out the expensive codices and ripping them apart. "The scriptures!" Flavia cried. She ran to the cabinet, trying to rescue whatever she could. Though she grabbed the *Letters of Paul* in one hand and a Psalter in the other, the books were snatched from her.

"Heraclius forbids you to have these holy books," snarled a burly man with hairy forearms. "To support the martyrs is heresy! The Lapsed have done no wrong!"

"To deny Christ is surely wrong!" Flavia cried. Moisture flooded her eyes, the hot tears of frustration and helplessness. She knew what a pitiful figure she must appear to this big, intimidating man. "Please!" she begged. "Do not destroy the books of God!"

Grinning, the man ripped the Psalter in half. "Heretic!" he spat, then tore the Pauline epistles as well. It was more than Flavia could bear. She fled from the Hall of the Church.

Outside, Sophronia took Flavia's hand, and the two women hurried toward the Bridge of Probus. As soon as they crossed the Tiberis River, they would be back in safer territory on the Aventine Hill.

"Oh, Mother," Flavia groaned when they stopped to catch their breath at the far side of the bridge. "How could anyone do that in the name of Christ?"

"It is truly unworthy of the Savior, and the martyrs who followed in his footsteps. Did Jesus not declare that anyone who comes after him must take up his cross? And he also said, 'The cup that I drink, you shall drink.' Jesus predicted martyrdom!"

"To reject the martyrs is to deny the Lord's own words," Flavia agreed.

"Yet there are many so-called Christians who do just that. And they are violent. That's why we need strong men who can defend us. Brave men, the kind willing to take a stand between us and danger. But such men are in short supply, unfortunately."

"Father Eusebius was very bold, though," Flavia offered. "He looked Heraclius in the eye and quoted Tertullian: 'The blood of Christians is seed.'"

"We may soon find that to be true, I'm afraid."

Flavia's head shot around. "What do you mean? Will there be another persecution?"

"Bishop Eusebius is the head of the catholic church in Rome, so he's responsible for whatever the Christians do. Emperor Maxentius is going to be furious about this riot. The city is already unstable because of the bread shortages, and now this happens. Somebody must bear the blame. The emperor is going to hold Eusebius accountable."

"You mean . . . kill him?"

"It's hard to say. Yet I fear Heraclius has just signed the bishop's death warrant, one way or another."

Flavia put her hand to her forehead and rubbed the sticky mess there. She slowly turned her fingers before her eyes and stared at the dark red smear. Glancing up, she saw her mother's gaze was also fixed on her bloodstained fingertips.

"Mother? What if we had to . . . you know. Could we do it?"

"I don't know, precious," Sophronia said bravely, though with a tremor in her voice. "What I do know is that we should get off these streets. Somebody might be following us to do us harm. And I think enough seed has been planted in the ground for one day."

Rex crept up beside Geta in the underbrush at the crest of a low hill. Spread out before them was a broad meadow filled with tents and busy activity. In the distance, the Rhenus River curved its way through the forests of Germania. On its far side was the civilized empire. Here, though, were only barbarians.

"Look, they're playing games. It's surely a festival," Geta said as he observed the tents below.

"No. Look closer. What's missing that you would always have at any festival?"

"I see a lot of clay jugs. Those Franks aren't short on beer."

Rex shot his friend an amused glance. "Since when are the Germani ever short on beer? It's not that, it's something else—something no party is complete without."

Geta stared at the scene, then turned back toward Rex. "No women. These are all warriors."

"Warriors and carters and blacksmiths. What kind of festival needs that? Not any I'd want to attend. The Franks are telling the Romans they're celebrating a religious holiday. But this is an invasion army. They're going to try to cross the Rhenus."

"I don't see any weapons. We'd need proof before we report back to Aratus."

Rex grinned and nodded. "Of course we need proof! What does he always say? 'Philosophers deal in ideas. Professors deal in theories. But speculators'"—the two spies met each other's gaze and finished their trainer's maxim in unison—"'deal in facts.'"

"I'm going down there," Geta said as he rose from his crouch.

"Meet you at the red tent. Don't talk to anyone. Your Frankish accent sounds like a sow in heat."

Geta flashed Rex a crude gesture as the two men separated. The crowded and busy conditions in the meadow made it easy for Rex to blend in and work his way to the center of the encampment. His clothing was entirely Frankish, and he was carrying no obvious weapon. Fortunately, he was Germanic like those on whom he was spying, so with his shoulder-length blond hair and thick beard, he didn't look out of place. Geta was already waiting at the red tent when Rex arrived.

"It's tied up tight," Geta whispered. "Don't start fiddling with the thongs or someone will get suspicious."

"There's a privy against the rear of the tent. I think I can get inside from back there without being seen."

Rex went around to the wooden shack that had been erected over the latrine hole, finding it ironic that the cultured Romans did their business side by side in a communal toilet, while the so-called barbarians wanted privacy. He started scraping away the dirt of the earthen floor where the privy's wall adjoined the red tent. Soon he had made a shallow ditch that allowed him to wriggle from one structure into the next.

The red tent was filled with crates, leaving little room to stand. Rex opened the lid of one of the boxes, then sucked in his breath when he saw what was inside. He quickly grabbed the object and returned through the ditch and exited the privy.

"Look at this," he said to Geta as they crouched in the shade beneath a wagon. He slipped a well-made dagger into his friend's hand.

Geta ran his thumb along the edge. "Brand new."

"There were ax-heads and spear points too. And arrowheads, a lot of them. Even swords. The barbarians aren't supposed to have access to that much metal."

"This is clearly an invasion army. Let's get back to Aratus."

Night had fallen by the time the two comrades reached the secret camp in the deep woods. Many other speculators had already returned, while others were still trickling in, each with the same report: the Lower Rhenus was seething with Frankish warriors armed with new steel. The pressing concern was where they would converge for an attack.

"Let's plot this out," Aratus said, spreading a map of the Germanic frontier on the table. He held down the map's four corners with olive oil lamps, then placed white beans on each site where troop activity had been observed. One by one, the beans began to form a distinct arrowhead—and its tip pointed directly at Emperor Constantine's new bridge over the Rhenus River.

Aratus looked up at his elite warriors. "There you have it, men! Apparently, it's going to be Colonia. Our home base! The Franks are coming straight at us. The only question is when."

"We still have plenty of time," scoffed one of the spies. "Those Franks are bumbling fools who don't know the first thing about tactics. They won't attack anytime soon."

He's wrong, Rex thought. *The Franks will strike within a week or two.*

Constantine had recently ordered the construction of a bridge at Colonia Agrippina, an important frontier city on the Roman side of the Rhenus. To protect the bridgehead, a fort called Divitia was being built on the eastern bank, the Germanic side. This fort was intended to house a detachment of the Second Italian Legion, along with some other troops. Impressive walls were being raised, to be guarded by fourteen towers and two heavily fortified gates. If the Franks wanted to attack the Roman Empire—not just raid it but move an army across the Rhenus and permanently take some land—they would have to cross at the Colonia bridge. And they'd have to do it soon.

Geta apparently had been thinking the same thing. "I would argue an attack could occur any day, sir," he countered. "The bridge is functional now but still unprotected. The Franks will want to cross it before the Divitia Fortress is finished. We need to prepare for an invasion."

Rex caught his centurion's eye and nodded emphatically to signal his agreement with his friend. "Geta's absolutely right. The Frankish army is large and well supplied. We're in danger without reinforcements. Where is the emperor now? This is urgent news. He needs to know about it so he can decide what to do."

Aratus set his jaw and nodded. "Constantine is at Augusta Treverorum. And I concur, the news is urgent. It's time the emperor had a full report. Get some sleep if you can. We ride out at dawn."

The next morning before the stars had begun to dim, Aratus met Rex, Geta, and two other speculators outside the secret camp. Mounted on their long-legged saddle horses, the men set out in single file, with Aratus in the lead. They followed a game trail to the Rhenus, arriving by midday at Colonia's new bridge, where they crossed back into the empire. From there, the road south was like all Roman roads: wide, smooth, and slightly bowed to allow rainwater to run off into gutters. Rex shook his head as he gazed down at the marvel of engineering. *These people can put an army anywhere they want in a matter of hours. No wonder they conquered the world!*

A hard two-days' ride, switching horses at each of the post stations, brought Aratus's band of spies to the regional capital of Augusta Treverorum. Rex couldn't help but gawk at the size of the city, which dwarfed the other big settlements he had known, such as Colonia or Eboracum. The city's high wall aspired to reach into the clouds, and its circumference seemed capable of embracing the entire population of Gaul. Since the only bridge was under repair, the party was ferried across the Mosella and entered through the northern gate. Rex thought such a massive structure, comprising four stories of pale-gray sandstone, would survive all the wars that humanity could throw at it and still be standing thousands of years in the future.

The imperial residence at Augusta Treverorum was connected to the Palace Hall, a brand-new basilica just put up by Constantine. It had a long nave and a double row of windows with translucent crystal panes. As soon as Rex stepped inside, he felt a rush of heated air—a necessity for the Romans in these far northern lands. The walls were overlaid with white marble and golden mosaics, while impressive statues and luxurious banners made sure everyone knew this was an imperial throne room. At the far end of the hall, in an apse beneath a high arch, sat the emperor himself. Rex approached the great man cautiously, walking down the center of the nave behind a swarm of government functionaries. *He seems so different now*, Rex mused. *This Constantine seems so—what? So much grander than the field general who knocked me in the head four years ago!*

A bureaucrat whispered in Constantine's ear to let the emperor know who was approaching. It had already been made clear to the band of spies that Aratus would do all the talking. The other speculators accompanied him for effect, still wearing dirty clothes to remind their lord that their information was coming straight from the field. If anyone asked, they could provide confirmation of a few tactical details. Otherwise, they served only as decoration. It was the centurion's prerogative alone to speak.

As the party neared the throne, Rex's eyes fell for the first time on the man standing at Constantine's right hand. He was a bulky figure with curly hair and a bushy beard. Though dressed expensively, he wore the garments of a civilian. The expression on his face was placid and unreadable.

"I hear you have important news for us, centurion," the emperor said when the spies were assembled before him. "Clearly, it must be important, since you have come today in the outfit of a barbarian herdsman."

To his credit, Aratus didn't take the comment as an insult, nor did he adopt the whiny tone of a palace sycophant. He was a decorated soldier who knew what he had accomplished and wasn't ashamed to stand before great men.

Aratus had killed enemies in combat just as the man seated on the throne had done. Constantine was famous for respecting courage in battle above all else. Speaking like the commander of men that he was, the centurion stood with his back straight and said, "Your Highness, I salute you in the name of Eternal Rome. I have come to you today not from the safe confines of the empire but from deep in Frankish lands. There we have discovered what can only be described as an invasion army converging on your new bridge at Colonia. We expect an attempt to cross the Rhenus very soon."

Rex noticed the big man at Constantine's side shift his weight, though he said nothing. The emperor stroked his beardless chin. "An invasion, you say. Not just a little sacking and looting by men coming over in boats?"

"An army," Aratus repeated, "equipped with new steel and amassing provisions to take across your bridge for an extended stay. They intend to capture territory and occupy it."

Constantine let out a heavy sigh. "If what you say is true, it appears my summer is going to involve campaigning once again. I shall have to lead some troops to the frontier so I can put down those unruly Franks. But by September, I'll have their chiefs running naked from the leopards in our amphitheater!" The boast elicited laughter and even some cheers from the bureaucrats assembled in the basilica.

Returning his attention to Aratus, Constantine took his measure for a moment, then asked, "How many are there?"

"Twenty thousand at least," Aratus said flatly.

The big man standing next to the throne burst into the conversation. "Twenty thousand? That's impossible! The Franks can't organize an army like that. They're far too fractious. Constantine, you can't listen to this idiot!"

A hush fell on the hall. Slowly, the emperor turned to regard the man at his side. For a short time they talked privately, then Constantine returned his attention to Aratus. "My father-in-law disputes you, centurion. And who among us can doubt that Maximian is experienced in war?" Though Constantine offered a mischievous smile, the remark drew only a smattering of awkward laughter and several nervous glances. Rex sensed the politics here were extremely delicate.

"I would never question the wisdom and experience of an original colleague like the honorable Maximian," Aratus said. "I can only tell you what my men saw in the field. Our observations add up to twenty thousand soldiers, all hungry for battle and glory."

Maximian snorted and swatted his hand. "My sources tell me there's a Frankish rabble of about five thousand up there. Just snatch-and-grabbers, no more than that."

"It is possible our observations were mistaken. Yet to the best of our knowledge, we believe them to be accurate."

With the abrupt authority of an absolute ruler, Constantine settled the matter. "I shall take a quarter of my army across to meet the Franks," he declared. "Maximian will take the rest of my legions down to southern Gaul. Something tells me his clever son Maxentius is getting restless over in Italy. A full-strength army close to Rome will probably do us some good. I'm sure nine thousand will be more than enough to crush the barbarians."

"But sir!" Rex broke in. "I saw those Franks with my own eyes! It's a real army. You'll need a much larger force to defeat them."

A little murmur rippled through the hall. Rex felt his mouth go dry. Swallowing, he stepped back a little.

Constantine eyed Rex closely, inspecting him up and down. "What is your name, soldier?"

"Brandulf Rex."

Will he remember?

The emperor stared at Rex for a long time. At last he announced to the room, "I will take a third of my army to subdue Germania. Twelve thousand. No more than that." He waved his hand at the visitors. "Now be gone."

Rex walked in silence with the rest of the party as they were escorted to the rear of the basilica. Once the men were out in the bright sunlight again, Aratus whirled on Rex. "That was a foolish thing to do!" he said through gritted teeth.

Rex kept his eyes lowered as he stood before his commanding officer. "Yes, I know. I'm sorry, sir."

Aratus grunted like a beast, then stormed away, leaving the four speculators of the traveling squad alone in the courtyard.

"That really was foolish, you idiot," Geta said.

Rex winced and offered a nod of agreement, then glanced up to find Geta giving him an appreciative smile. Though no words were uttered, the two men acknowledged with their eyes the inescapable fact that they both understood: *Constantine is about to face those Franks with only half the men he needs.*

"Maybe he'll change his mind once he thinks it over?" Rex suggested.

Geta swatted his hand dismissively. "There's no use hoping for that. The emperor has decided. Let's forget about it and get something to eat."

"Pfft! What do you know about emperors?"

"More than you might think. Nothing can change the mind of an emperor. It never happens."

Rex shrugged and fell silent. *Someday it might,* he thought as he followed his friends into the streets of Augusta Treverorum. *And when it does, I want to be there to see it.*

———

JUNE 310

The large room in Flavia's house that her father had made available to the Christians was a functional, indeed beautiful, space for worship. Flavia remembered being so excited to watch the workmen knock down a wall to form a spacious hall in which the whole community could gather—about a hundred in all. There was even a decorative nook at one end where the priest would sit and give sermons or receive the faithful at the altar for the distribution of the bread and wine. Every Sunday at dawn, the neighborhood Christians would gather for worship in this homey and intimate setting.

Yet despite its comfortable familiarity, the house church on the Aventine didn't hold the special place in Flavia's heart that the Hall of the Church did. That building was a true house of the Lord, erected for the sole purpose of glorifying Christ. But now, thanks to the terrible riot, the hall was a ravaged shell, locked up by decree of Emperor Maxentius. And to make matters worse, the emperor had just announced that Bishop Eusebius would be banished to the faraway island of Sicilia as punishment for the disturbance.

Flavia shut the double doors of the house church and stepped into the private garden connected to it. Her mother was plucking cherries from a tree that was just now coming into fruit.

"Your face is too lovely to look so sad," Sophronia said.

"How could I not be sad at such terrible news?"

"It could have been worse. Maxentius isn't a persecutor, but he could have considered the riot a civil disorder worthy of capital punishment. We should be glad it was only exile."

"Eusebius is so old," Flavia countered. "Travel will take a toll on him."

Sophronia smiled gently, handing Flavia a bowl of plump cherries. "He's strong for his age. And besides, he's formerly a doctor. He might do just fine."

"I suppose he might. It helps that Father is allowing us to go down to Sicilia ahead of the bishop. We can get everything ready for his arrival. Surely the Christians there will want to care for him."

"Actually, my love . . . I have been meaning to talk to you about that journey."

Flavia swung her head around sharply. "Father isn't reconsidering, is he?"

"No, it's not that. It's just that . . . well, apparently, he wants you to go down to Sicilia with a protector. You know his business partner with the Sicilian estate? The man has a son about your age—"

"Ohhh nooo!" Flavia moaned, clasping her head in her hands.

"What's wrong?"

"I don't need a protector!"

"He's a nice Christian boy. It'll be alright. You'll see."

Flavia could only shake her head in disbelief. She picked up a cherry and popped it into her mouth, then handed the bowl back to her mother. With a sigh of resignation, she retired to her bedroom.

The day of departure dawned bright and sunny, like virtually every other day in a Roman summer. Because Neratius's friend was a wealthy trader, his ships often made the journey between Ostia, Rome's harbor town, and the Sicilian port of Syracusae. The uneventful trip took seven days, during which time Flavia tried her best to avoid Magnus, the "Christian boy" whose tepid personality should have earned him the name Minus instead.

Syracusae, an ancient town that was still much more Greek than Roman, lay on Sicilia's eastern coast. The entire countryside around the port was dotted with vineyards and olive groves. In the distance loomed the smoking bulk of Mons Aetna, an active volcano that sometimes spewed lava down its snowy flanks. According to the *Acts of the Apostles*, Saint Paul spent three days in Syracusae—and as far as Flavia knew, Christians had lived there ever since.

After putting ashore in the harbor, the travelers made their way to the outskirts of the lovely Sicilian town. Bishop Chrestus, a local aristocrat, welcomed the visitors warmly in the atrium of his villa. He was especially delighted to see Magnus. The skinny youth appeared to be well-known to the bishop.

"The scriptures command us to extend hospitality to all the brethren," Chrestus said. "Consider my home yours during the time of your stay."

"Such a warm welcome is greatly appreciated," Sophronia answered with stately decorum. "And it is precisely for the purpose of hospitality that we have traveled to your beautiful island. Our Bishop Eusebius has been exiled here by Emperor Maxentius, never to return to Rome on pain of death. We have come to find a place for him to live out his days. A stipend will be sent from our church to yours for expenses."

Chrestus lowered his head and nodded gravely. "We had heard that awful news." His face was mournful for a moment, yet when he raised his eyes to meet those of his visitors, Flavia could discern the Spirit of God in the man's countenance. "Do not fear, my friends. We think we have found a beautiful place for the esteemed bishop to stay, a nearby cottage. But please—your needs must come first! You have journeyed far and must take your rest. Come, allow my servants to show you to your quarters. Then when you have been refreshed from your travels, we can go see the cottage."

A few hours later, Flavia and her companions were led to a wagon at the villa's gate. They were driven along a country lane to a remote cottage in a picturesque setting: a shady grove of chestnut trees with a brook flowing nearby and a broad view toward the sea. The little house was made of brick and tile. Its porch had a comfortable chair and a book cabinet, a lovely place for the bishop to pass his time reading.

"It's perfect," Flavia said under her breath.

Bishop Chrestus caught her words and smiled broadly. "You like it? Well then, let me show you one more thing."

The energetic priest led his three guests to a small outbuilding, apparently a place to store tools or yard implements. When he opened the door, though, Flavia realized she wasn't looking at a shed but the entrance to an underground crypt. A gaping staircase led down into the gloom.

"Follow me down," Chrestus said, lighting an oil lamp. "There is something I want you to see."

Magnus backed away from the entrance. "I'm staying up here," he declared. "There are underworld shades down there."

Flavia whirled to face the youth. "Shades? We don't believe in ghosts hovering around graves. That's pagan."

"Where are the dead, then? They must go somewhere."

"Have you not been catechized, Magnus?" Chrestus asked gently. "The souls of our departed brethren await the resurrection at the trumpet of Christ. When we visit their tombs, we remember them and fellowship with them until that blessed day when we shall all meet our Savior."

Magnus crossed his arms and took a seat on a fallen log. "I don't know much about theology. All I know is, it's dark down there, and I'm not going."

"I will stay and keep you company," Sophronia offered.

Sure, stay up here with my mother, Flavia thought, although she didn't give voice to her disdain.

"Suit yourself, my friends," Chrestus said. "The choice is yours." He handed Flavia an oil lamp, which he lit from his own before starting down the stairs. "Stay close," he warned, "and watch your step."

The subterranean darkness immediately engulfed the two visitors, yet Flavia did not sense the cemetery was a place of danger. Though the air was close and musty, it did not contain the sickly-sweet smell of rotting flesh, for the burial niches in the walls had been well sealed. At intervals along the way, Chrestus lit more of the clay lamps that rested in tiny nooks.

At last the pair reached a small underground chapel. The bishop beckoned Flavia to a carved arch in the wall—a decoration that everyone called an arch-coffin, because the curved vault sat directly above a burial compartment that was gouged from the bedrock itself. When a martyr's body was placed in the grave beneath the arch, a lid would be sealed over it to provide a flat surface for memorial meals. In this way, the brethren would be feasting with the glorified saint, not celebrating pagan banquets with evil spirits. Typically the rear walls of such arch-coffins were decorated. And indeed, when Chrestus held his lamp close, Flavia saw a glittering mosaic of Jonah bursting from the sea monster.

"It's beautiful," she murmured, running her fingers along the mosaic tiles. "Is it yours?"

"It was going to be. But I am willing to give it to the honorable bishop of Rome."

Flavia glanced at the kindly old man. Though she recognized what a generous gesture this was, something about it didn't feel right. She absently fiddled with the bracelet on her wrist, trying to choose her words. "This doesn't excite you?" Chrestus asked. There was a hint of curiosity in his voice.

"Holy Father, the offer is so incredibly kind, but . . ."

The bishop gave Flavia an appreciative look. "You are a feisty one, my daughter, if you are considering what I think you are."

"Well . . . it's just that Eusebius is the bishop of *Rome*. That is his God-appointed flock. His people are the Romans."

"And yet he has been exiled by the emperor of that city," Chrestus pointed out. "He is never allowed to set foot in the Italian peninsula again, by direct imperial order."

"Surely he will live out his exile in Sicilia. But eventually, he should come home."

"It is possible Eusebius will outlive Maxentius by many years, and by then the political situation might have changed. Yet if something did happen to Eusebius while Maxentius was still in power—would you really defy the emperor and return the bishop's remains?"

Flavia felt jittery, and her heart was beating fast. She was contemplating something that could be considered a capital crime: violating the express will of the augustus by bringing a condemned exile back to Italy for burial. Though it would be done in secret, it would be dangerous nonetheless. It could easily be construed as treason.

A glance at the mosaic steeled Flavia's resolve. *The Good Shepherd lays down his life for his sheep*, she reminded herself, *and so do the church's shepherds—the priests and bishops who pastor the flock. They live with their sheep, face martyrdom with their sheep, and await the resurrection with their sheep. It is how things are done among Christians.*

By the flickering light of her oil lamp, Flavia looked into Bishop Chrestus's eyes. "To honor this worthy man . . . yes, I would defy an emperor," she declared.

Chrestus took Flavia's hand in his, holding it firmly as if to let his courage flow to her. "Then if the need arises," he said, "I will help you."

———— ⟡ ————

Half a wall doesn't make for a very good castle, Constantine thought with a little shake of his head. He stared up at the looming bulk of the Divitia Fortress, with its big, round towers and impressive gate. Unfortunately, the wall ended abrubtly just to the right of the gate's imposing barbican. Anyone who wished could stroll past it and walk up to the troop barracks. It would be another month before the place would be surrounded by a full enclosure. Only then would the bridgehead be secure.

Feeling a little frustrated yet resigned to the realities of construction and architecture, the emperor turned away from the useless wall and gazed across the broad meadow in front of the fort. On the far side of the grassy expanse, just beyond the tree line, a Frankish army was encamped.

"Looks like it's going to be an old-fashioned pitched battle," Constantine said to his general, Vitruvius, who acknowledged with a shrug what both men already knew. Fortifications and sieges and sallies wouldn't decide this engagement. It would be won by manly valor on the field of war, beneath the gods' watching eyes.

Though a steady rain had been falling all day, the Rhenus had not overflowed its banks and the battlefield was relatively dry. Constantine entered the commander's tent with Vitruvius and the other generals, settling in to discuss battle tactics as best they could. They were still waiting on reports from the field scouts. Strangely, it was already late in the afternoon and none had yet returned. What the commanders knew for certain was that the Frankish army facing them across the plain was only about twelve thousand strong, with relatively few cavalry among them. A force of that size numbered the same as Constantine's own, so it would be no match for the superior training and equipment of the legions. This would be yet another Roman rout of the barbarians.

A nervous messenger appeared at the tent door, apologetic yet insistent. He claimed to have just arrived from southern Gaul with intelligence that must be heard right away. When Constantine granted the man leave to speak, the first words out of his mouth hit the emperor like a hard punch to the gut.

"Maximian has taken up the purple—"

Constantine exploded to his feet, overturning the table behind which he had been sitting. "The gods destroy him!"

"Has taken up the purple robe," the messenger went on, "and raided the imperial treasury. Once again, he is claiming to be an augustus. He distributed lavish donatives to buy the loyalty of your troops. Apparently, many of them have gone over. He's barricaded himself in Arelate. And worst of all—he's telling everyone you've been killed by the Franks."

Constantine kicked over the last chair that had managed to evade his wrath. "Killed by this pitiful band of barbarians? That's ridiculous! Nobody would believe that! There aren't enough caval—"

The emperor's abrupt arrest of his words caused a heavy silence to descend on the tent. Even the senior officers dared not move. Slowly, Constantine turned and met Vitruvius's eyes. "Something isn't right here," he said.

The general nodded. "I'll check to see if any scouts have returned." Vitruvius hurried outside.

When Constantine joined his general a short while later, the rain had stopped but the sky was still overcast. Vitruvius was standing next to a spotter, a young man with exceptionally good eyesight.

"Calmer now?" Vitruvius asked.

"First things first. We have these Franks to defeat before I deal with my ungrateful and treasonous father-in-law." Constantine turned to the young soldier. "See anything?"

"Someone's coming from over there," the spotter said, squinting and craning his neck.

"I see him too." Vitruvius pointed toward the far side of the battle plain. "It's a lone rider."

"He's one of ours," Constantine said. "And he's going to die."

The man was galloping at full speed away from the Frankish line. Yet he was still in easy range of the archers, so a hail of arrows was continually falling around him. It was only a matter of time until one of them found its mark.

"What does he have hanging all over himself?" Constantine wondered aloud.

The spotter gave a little laugh. "The guy has enemy shields on both arms and another slung on his back."

"He also seems to be holding one above his head," Vitruvius added.

The three men watched the impossible drama play itself out on the battlefield before them. The arrows kept coming, piercing the shields one after another, yet the horse kept surging ahead.

"I think he's going to make it!" Constantine cried, fully drawn in now. No sooner had the emperor spoken than the horse took an arrow in the rump and went tumbling to the ground. It thrashed in the grass, but the intrepid rider immediately left it behind and began running across the field. Now that he was a much smaller target and had attained some separation, he ditched his shields.

"Uh-oh," the spotter said. "They're sending out a rider."

The enemy horseman gained quickly on the Roman runner. Soon it became obvious the fugitive would be caught before he could reach the safety of his own line. He whirled to face his attacker, but Constantine knew a proficient javelinist in the saddle would easily impale a man on two feet. Even so, the runner raised his arm behind his head, preparing to hurl a knife or some other missile at the oncoming horseman.

Constantine wanted to shout for soldiers to ride out and help the lone Roman, but he knew this confrontation would be decided long before any aid could get there. The galloping spearman drew within range, his javelin poised for the throw.

"God help him!" Constantine cried.

And he did. Above and behind the three spellbound watchers, the gray skies parted, and a golden light washed across the battlefield. It was only a momentary break in the clouds, but the sun's angle was low and full in the face of the rider. He averted his eyes and threw his spear by instinct instead of aim. As it sailed past the runner, the spearman unexpectedly tumbled from the saddle. He writhed on the ground, clutching the knife hilt that protruded from his chest.

But the runner paid him no mind. Before his enemy even hit the soggy turf, he had turned and resumed his run. A few more horsemen were dispatched from the Franks, but they were too late and turned back. At last the runner crossed the final distance to the Roman encampment. Constantine and Vitruvius hurried to meet him at the front line.

The scout was bent over with his hands on his knees, gasping for breath. "Well done, soldier! Well done!" the emperor exclaimed, clapping the man on the back. "Stand up and let me get a look at you!"

When the scout straightened, the emperor recognized him as the young Germanic recruit who had challenged him in the throne room at Augusta Treverorum. He was a well-built youth with the chiseled look of an elite warrior. *These men always look the same*, Constantine thought. Square jaw, strong chin, wide shoulders, muscular arms, narrow waist—just the kind of men the empire needs.

"That was incredibly brave, speculator!" Vitruvius gushed. "What could possibly make you do something so risky?"

With his chest still heaving, the scout could only lift his arm and point to the south. "Eight . . . thousand . . . riders . . ."

Constantine tensed. "What? Eight thousand cavalry? On their way?"

The scout waved his hand. "Delayed. Rain. A bog. Tomorrow . . . earliest."

"It was supposed to be a surprise attack? The footmen to draw us out, the horse to hit our flank?"

A nod from the scout confirmed Constantine's suspicion. He turned and pointed to Vitruvius. "Sound the trumpets," he said. "We fight the Frankish infantry this afternoon. Tomorrow we'll face those cavalry head-on. With their forces divided, they won't stand a chance."

Once some battle plans had been made and Vitruvius had departed, Constantine put his hand on the scout's shoulder. "Good job out there," he said. "Remind me of your name?"

The young speculator had finally regained his breath. He stood at attention and saluted. "Brandulf Rex, sir. From the Second Italian Legion. Based right here at Divitia."

"Brandulf Rex," Constantine mused. "I shall try to remember that name."

The handsome scout with the long blond hair flashed Constantine a fellow warrior's grin. "This is the third time you've heard it, Your Highness. I hope someday to make it unforgettable."

Constantine arched an eyebrow and gave the cocky youth a hard stare. "That's up to you," he said.

"We stop here," General Vitruvius announced. "The augustus is going to pay his vows to the sun god. Everyone else will use the time to eat. We will move out again in one hour."

Rex dropped his pack and rubbed his sore shoulders. "Emperor Constantine sure is religious," he observed to Geta. "He seems to take the gods very seriously."

"Apparently, it's working for him. He's undefeated in battle. The man always finds a way to win."

Geta was right, but he was only giving voice to what all the men had just experienced. The battle with the Franks had turned into yet another massacre, just as Constantine had predicted. Splitting the enemy into two forces had made all the difference. The Frankish footmen were no match for the disciplined and well-armored Roman infantry, much less the cavalry who crashed into them like the waves of the sea. Then when it was time to face the Frankish riders, the barbarians found a battle-ready army waiting for them as their horses pulled their hooves from the rain-soaked bog. The slaughter was complete, and the Rhenus frontier was at rest again.

But the whole empire wasn't at rest. Maximian, a former augustus of the Imperial College and the father of Constantine's wife, Fausta, had taken up the robe of an emperor and was making claims on the Roman West. If he could secure Gaul with his bribed army, then make an alliance with his son Maxentius in Italy, the two would form a power bloc that Constantine would have a hard time breaking. For that reason, the true emperor was moving south from the Germanic line at double time, ready to take out his treacherous father-in-law once and for all. As for Maxentius, that enemy could wait for another day.

Rex's furious dash across the battlefield, carrying the vital intelligence that had turned ambush into victory, had earned him the job of his dreams. The emperor immediately appointed Rex to his personal bodyguard corps—an impressive posting for someone so young. Yet the move was a smart one. In this age of perpetual civil war, emperors needed good protectors even more than they needed battlefield intelligence. Constantine wanted men with Rex's abilities nearby. The first thing Rex did in his new position was finagle an appointment for Geta too. His friend was just as proficient a fighter as he was, maybe even better. It served everyone's interests to have elite warriors in the emperor's retinue.

The day's march had started early and hadn't let up even once. The sun was well past its zenith now, and the troops were grateful that Vitruvius had finally allowed them their first meal since the pork scraps and thick beer they'd scarfed down at dawn. Rex wasn't sure where they were—somewhere in Gaul, no doubt, but exactly where was hard to tell. He knew a famous sanctuary of Apollo was nearby, for Constantine had turned aside to worship there. The holy sacrifice hadn't taken long, and the emperor had returned rather quickly.

Having finished his divine offering, Constantine now made a more earthly request. "Rex, run over to the cook and fetch my soup," he said. Rex dutifully retrieved the bowl and was setting it before the emperor on a flat boulder, along with a stool, when he felt a sudden grip on his forearm.

"Look at that! Up there!"

Rex followed Constantine's gaze and lifted his eyes to the sky. A strange thing had happened: obscured by a haze of high, wispy clouds, the normal roundness of the sun had morphed into a crisscross shape. Rays of light made a kind of X across the sun's face. Two radiant golden arcs glowed on either side of the X. It seemed as if a divine halo had encompassed the heavenly orb. All the men had their heads back, staring up at it.

"What does it mean?" Rex asked, awed by the strange phenomenon.

Constantine tightened his grip on Rex's sleeve, unable to tear his eyes from the sky. "It's a sign—an omen from Apollo in return for my visit to his shrine!"

"What is he saying?"

"He must be adopting me! Ever since I was named emperor, I've been protected by Hercules. Now I'm coming into a new phase, so a new protector is taking me on! It must be Apollo—the Invincible Sun. Think about it, Rex! The sun god helped you escape across the field, right? Then we defeated the Franks in battle. Now we're at a shrine of that same god. I made a sacrifice to him, so he's promising me victory. It's obvious when you put it all together!"

"Maybe those curved rays are victory laurels?" Rex suggested.

"Yes! They must be laurels awarded by Victoria herself! Surely I will defeat Maximian—and Maxentius too, when that time comes."

"The omen is fading," Rex observed, and it was true. A few moments later the sun had returned to normal.

"Let's get on the road as quickly as possible," Constantine said. "I'm all the more eager to reach Arelate now that I know how things will turn out."

This is one of the most religious men I've ever known, Rex thought as he returned the stool to the wagon.

Five days later, the overland expedition met the Arar River, which joined the much swifter Rhodanus at Lugdunum. The soldiers switched to riverboats. However, when they finally arrived at Arelate, they found Maximian had fled to the safer confines of seaside Massilia. Another three days of marching brought the troops to that ancient port city founded by Greek colonists back when Rome was still a tiny collection of shepherds' huts.

Although General Vitruvius predicted Massilia would be difficult to capture, Constantine only smiled in a knowing way and ordered the troops to set a siege. As it turned out, the initial attack was a failure, but a siege proved unnecessary in the end. Even as Maximian was shouting curses from the city walls, his bribed army returned their loyalty to Constantine and threw open the gates. The emperor entered in triumph, and his first action was to strip the purple cloak from Maximian's shoulders. The usurper was remanded to the imperial palace at Arelate, where he was placed under house arrest. His fate, for the time being, was unclear.

The summer weeks passed uneventfully. Slipping into a routine, Rex began to feel more comfortable in his new line of work. His duties included escorting the emperor on official business and controlling access to the private imperial chambers. He was standing watch outside Constantine's bedroom late one night when he heard the door creak open behind him. Rex whirled and was met by Fausta, the emperor's homely, bug-eyed wife. "Come inside," she whispered.

Rex shook his head. He wasn't about to have a tryst with the wife of the augustus.

Behind Fausta, Constantine appeared at the doorway, fully dressed and beckoning Rex urgently. *Something's up,* he realized, and he followed the couple into their bedroom.

"My father is hatching a desperate plot," Fausta said. "He tried to draw me into it. He asked me to leave the bedroom door ajar so he could assassinate Constantine."

Rex turned toward the emperor. "On my life, Your Highness, I would never allow it!"

"I know. But this time we want you to let him in." At Rex's confused look, Constantine unveiled his plan. He gestured across the room. "Look over there at my bed. The man under the blankets is a palace eunuch, a worthless fellow. He's dead drunk. He will be my decoy."

"We want you to catch the murderer in the act." Fausta took her husband's arm in hers. "Then we will have good reason to execute him. For political reasons, we can't execute an original colleague without just cause."

"Go find another soldier to help you," Constantine ordered, "then hide yourselves behind the curtains until Maximian appears. Come get us when you've caught him. And Rex," the emperor added sternly, "we must have absolute proof that this is an assassination. *Absolute proof.* I think you know what I mean."

Rex returned to the sleeping quarters assigned to the bodyguards. After rousing Geta from his cot, the two men went back to the imperial bedchamber and stationed themselves behind the drapes on either side of a tall window. Pale moonlight filtered through the shutters and made a crosshatched pattern on the marble floor. An hour passed in total silence, maybe two.

"I hear footsteps," Geta said at last.

"Stop, sir!" came a voice from the hall. Rex recognized it as one of the other bodyguards.

"I have just had a momentous dream," Maximian announced. "A god visited me in the night with important news, and now I must tell my son-in-law about it. Did not Empress Fausta instruct you to allow such visits from me? Or do you wish to contravene the direct command of your queen?"

"No, sir . . . I mean, yes, sir, she did say that."

"Then let me pass, soldier. You know better than to deny the order of my hot-tempered daughter. She carries the rank of Most Noble Woman of the empire."

"Alright, sir. I beg your pardon. You may proceed."

Gullible fool, Rex thought. *That bodyguard should be executed!*

The footsteps drew nearer, followed by silence. Rex held his breath in his hiding place behind the thick drapes. There was a slow creak as the door eased open. A bulky shadow filled the frame. The big man stood there for a moment—then with a fierce yell, he exploded from the doorway and dashed toward the bed. Geta immediately leapt from behind the curtain, but Rex caught his arm. After holding him back for an instant, he released Geta with the cry, "Let's go!"

Maximian was astride the figure in the bed, stabbing him again and again with a dagger. Geta knocked the attacker to the floor. Although Maximian was a burly man and former street brawler, he was no match for two speculators. Rex had him helpless on his knees in a painful armlock when Constantine and Fausta burst in.

"Traitor!" Fausta accused, snatching up the bloody dagger. "Caught in the act!"

Maximian let out a feral growl yet remained still.

Constantine was calm. He said nothing at first—only placed a basket on the rumpled bed next to the decoy's corpse. Then, in a firm yet dignified tone, he said to Rex, "Stand him up."

Rex moved to a rear chokehold and let Maximian rise. When the prisoner was upright, Constantine drew close and looked him squarely in the eyes. "For old times' sake, I will grant you one final favor."

The emperor spun toward the bed and overturned the basket. Three items tumbled out: a bottle, a sword, and a coil of rope. "Which shall it be?"

No sound disturbed the moonlit bedroom. Fausta stifled a little cry but remained still. At last Maximian uttered a single, raspy word: *rope*.

Constantine picked up the coil and pitched it to Geta. "Make it quick and clean, men," he said, then turned and followed his wife out of the room.

3

AUGUST 310

Sophronia believed the country villa of Maxentius was a spiritual cesspool—a place she hoped she would never have to visit. Hurrying past its monumental gate on the Appian Way, she tried not to catch the eyes of the workers who were busy embellishing the emperor's favorite project. It was the new center of power in suburban Rome—equaling, if not quite replacing, the traditional imperial residence on the Palatine Hill overlooking the Forum. Maxentius split his time between both locales, which was why Sophronia wanted nothing to do with either place. It was unfortunate—at least in some ways—that Neratius was such an influential man, for it meant he had to move in these pagan circles. Sophronia often prayed her husband wouldn't be contaminated by the greed, lust, and violence that came with running an empire.

The ironic thing, though, was that Maxentius had chosen to build his villa right in the middle of a long-standing Christian neighborhood. Did not the *Acts of the Apostles* describe how Saint Paul was met by fellow believers on the Appian Way when he arrived in Rome? Back in those days, during the reign of Nero, it was common for travelers to enter Italy at distant Puteoli and journey by road to the capital instead of landing at nearby Ostia. Ever since the apostle's ministry, the Appian lowlands had been an important Christian area. To this very day, the church's burial grounds lay dotted along the suburban road—although they were still in Maxentius's evil grip. *I bet the revenues from our properties even helped pay for that big circus,* Sophronia thought as she glanced at the racetrack the emperor had recently installed next to his villa. She hoped it wasn't true.

Father Miltiades had asked Sophronia to meet him at the huge, round tomb of Caecilia Metella, a famous landmark on the ancient highway. Most of the pagan burial grounds in the vicinity were the dovecote type in which cremation ashes were stored in urns tucked into wall niches. But Christians didn't dispose of their dead by cremation, preferring instead to let the body sleep intact as it awaited the resurrection at the return of Christ. Father Miltiades had requested Sophronia's presence at the funeral of an important Christian personage whose corpse was being transferred from Ostia for a respectable burial. Though she wasn't sure why she had been invited, she trusted her priest and typically did whatever he requested.

A broad smile came to Miltiades's bearded face when the two friends spotted each other. "Peace to you in the Lord's name, Lady Sabina Sophronia," he said with impeccable politeness. Strangely, he was wearing a plain tunic instead of the more elegant garment he normally donned for a funeral.

"Thank you, Holy Father. The grace of Christ be with you as well. Have I misunderstood something? I thought I was coming for a funeral, but I don't see any mourners."

After a quick glance around, Miltiades took a step closer. "Today is indeed the day of a burial, though it might not be what you expected. Let us walk for a while and speak of other matters. When we have reached our destination, I will explain."

Instead of taking the Appian Way, Miltiades led Sophronia by a country path that meandered back toward the city. He engaged her in casual conversation about the weather and the latest Roman politics. At last they began to approach a mule-drawn cart parked next to a high wall. A slender, dark-haired woman sat in the driver's seat. When she turned her head, Sophronia let out a gasp of surprise.

Flavia!

"Come and greet your daughter," Miltiades said. "I will let her tell you why I have called you here today."

Flavia's expression was animated as she alighted from the cart. Even without makeup or fancy clothing, she still looked dazzling. Her dark hair hung loose in a peasant's style, its auburn highlights glinting in the morn-ing sun. Fresh-faced and innocent, yet certainly a woman now, Flavia had blossomed into a rare beauty. With her high cheekbones, long eyelashes, and delicate chin, she was the kind of girl who would make any man take notice. *Yes, she's a lovely young lady*, Sophronia reminded herself, *but she's also my mischievous little girl—and she's up to something today!*

After greetings were exchanged, Flavia took Sophronia around to the rear of the cart, where it backed up to the brick wall. She pointed to a pinewood casket, then to a narrow crack in the brickwork, partially ob-scured by shrubbery. "We can fit through there, Mother," she said, "even with this coffin. It's only a few steps to the cemetery entrance. In half an hour we can have the body in the tomb and be on our way—no one any the wiser!"

A strange sense of dread took hold of Sophronia. She gripped her daughter's shoulders in both hands. "My precious, what are you doing? You're an aristocrat, not a gravedigger! Why are you sneaking around cemeteries?"

"Don't you see where you are? This is the rear wall of the Callistus burial ground. It rightfully belongs to the catholic church!"

"Flavia!" Sophronia hissed. "This is absolutely illegal! We aren't allowed to bury anyone here, by direct order of Emperor Maxentius. And we're practically on his front doorstep!" She turned toward Miltiades. "Holy Fa-ther, I have to—"

"It's Eusebius's body," he said.

Sophronia stopped short, staring at Miltiades with her mouth open. She glanced back at Flavia, who was nodding emphatically, eyebrows arched, begging for cooperation.

"But . . . we left him in Sicilia . . ."

"Left him sick, if you recall," Flavia said. "There was pestilence in Neapolis when he stopped there. He died not long ago, and Bishop Chrestus arranged to have his remains sent back to Ostia. Eusebius needs to sleep in the midst of his own flock, alongside the previous bishops of Rome."

"It's too dangerous," Sophronia said weakly. "If anyone sees us . . ."

"No one knows us here, Mother. We're anonymous. That's why Miltiades asked you to come. He is too well-known to the groundskeepers. But they wouldn't recognize me. And who can I trust more than you? I can't carry that coffin alone, but we can easily do it together."

Sophronia covered her face with her hands and groaned. After a long moment of uncertainty, she felt Miltiades slip his arm around her shoulders. The gesture was deeply comforting.

"Living in an age of martyrdom is always dangerous, my dear sister," he whispered in her ear. "Sometimes you have to take risks. You have to say to an unjust government, 'Enough! You cannot have this territory. We reclaim it for God.'"

Sophronia nodded, then turned to the pinewood box on the cart. "Alright. Let's do it quickly if we're going to do it."

The two women slipped easily through the crack in the wall and, despite the coffin's weight, hurried across a field toward a shallow depression. They descended into the grassy bowl and found the cemetery door set into an outcrop of tuff stone. Though the official key had been confiscated, Miltiades had secretly made a spare. They set the casket in the grass.

"Ready?" Flavia asked, her hand on the latch.

Sophronia crossed herself. "God be with us."

Flavia yanked open the door and peeked in, then immediately squealed and fell back. An explosion of bats burst from the tombs, darting past her with fluttering wings and high-pitched squeaks.

"That startled me," Flavia said with a little laugh.

The women picked up the coffin by its poles and began to descend the staircase. At the bottom of the steps, Sophronia used a fire striker to light a pile of tinder in a clay pot. From this fire they lit lamps. With two olive oil lamps resting on the top of the coffin, the women proceeded down a dark passageway. Eerie shadows danced on the walls from the tiny flames. The air was damp and cool. After a long walk, they reached a barrel-vaulted chamber decorated with spiral-fluted pillars.

"I have been here before," Sophronia said. "Let's set down the coffin and go in. This is the crypt of the bishops."

Flavia entered the chamber and ran her fingers over a Greek inscription. "Mother, look at this! It says 'Fabian, Bishop and Martyr.' He was killed in the persecution of Decius."

Sophronia held her lamp high. "Yes. There are nine popes buried here. Look—there's Pontian. Sixtus. Anterus. Felix. And others."

"Such great men! It is worth the risk we're taking to lay Eusebius in such holy company."

"Father Miltiades said Eusebius's new tomb is just beyond this chamber. It will be a good place for him to sleep until the Lord's return. Come, we've lingered long enough. We should hurry."

The tomb reserved for Rome's most recently deceased bishop was easy to find, for it was in a small room by itself, and its arch-coffin was decorated with a mosaic of the Good Shepherd between two trees. After maneuvering the heavy marble lid to one side, the women raised Eusebius's body and laid it in the grave. Though the corpse was tightly wrapped in a thick shroud, Sophronia was glad, nonetheless, when the lid was back in place.

"It's not a perfect seal," she said, "but no one will be down here—"

"Shh! Mother! Someone's coming!"

Sophronia froze, suddenly alert. *Yes! Voices! Coming this way!*

"Quick! Put your lamp in the coffin," Flavia urged. "We dare not put them out."

The crypt went dark as the lamps were enclosed in the pine box. Even so, a flickering orange light in the hallway and the sound of footsteps drew nearer. The light paused outside the burial chamber, and the men stopped talking. Nothing moved in the tense stillness.

Sophronia clutched her dress in her fists, trying not to move or even breathe. *Oh God, oh God, oh God . . . help us!*

Two shadowy figures appeared at the door. Suddenly a humpbacked man lurched into the crypt, holding a torch in one hand and a wicked-looking sickle in the other. Behind him was a burly gravedigger wielding a pickax in a double grip. Sophronia couldn't help but shriek as the men barged in.

"What are you women doing here? Don't lie to me, because I saw you go down with a coffin!" The man's voice was stern and uncompromising.

"We're just humble folk who can't afford a burial, so we snuck in!" Sophronia cried. She hoped God would forgive the fib in this circumstance.

The humpbacked groundskeeper stepped closer, studying the women with an appraising eye. "Pagan or Christian?" he demanded.

Sophronia's mouth fell open, and her breath was short as she tried to speak. "Well . . . you see . . ."

"We are followers of the Lord Jesus Christ," Flavia declared.

Silence gripped the little tomb.

At last the humpbacked man spoke into the stillness. "As am I," he said.

———*◈◈◈*———

SEPTEMBER 310

"Rex, wake up," the soldier whispered.

"I'm awake," Rex answered into the darkness. "Speculators sleep light, and always with one eye open. What is it?"

"You've been summoned by the augustus."

The statement snapped Rex to full alertness. He immediately swung his feet from the cot to the floor. After donning his outer tunic, he hurried down a corridor at the imperial palace of Augusta Treverorum, smoothing his disheveled hair and preparing himself for another nocturnal visit to Constantine's private bedroom. *The last time I did this, I ended up hanging a disgraced emperor from the rafters! What now?*

The bedchamber was even more sumptuous than the one in Arelate, where the assassination plot had been exposed. Rex thought back to the night he had hidden behind the curtains with Geta while they awaited Maximian's treachery. Blood had been spilled that night. But here, in this bedroom, there was no hint of violence, only the self-important opulence of a frontier capital city. All was quiet in the room, and Fausta was nowhere to be seen. The emperor stood alone at the window in his linen undertunic, gazing out. He did not turn around when Rex entered but kept staring at the sky.

"How can I serve you, Your Highness?" Rex asked, bowing.

"I have seen a great thing in a dream. It woke me up as if a lightning bolt had passed through me. I believe it is a vision from the world above."

Rex was unsure how to respond to such an assertion, so rather than say the wrong thing, he simply offered a murmur of affirmation.

What does he want from me?

Constantine cleared his throat. "Do you remember when we saw the heavenly sign on the march to Arelate?"

"Yes, sir. My master Aratus trained us in observation and memory. I can still picture it in my mind."

"Tell me—what did we see that day?"

"The rays of the sun formed a cross. On either side of it were bright arcs. The arcs formed a circle of light, like a halo around the sun. We considered it a sign from Apollo and Victoria, offering you victory wreaths."

"Describe the cross. What did it look like, as you remember it?"

"It was composed of two rays—one upright, one crosswise. Like a military standard—a spear pointing to the sky, with a crosspiece holding the banner."

"Yes! A standard!" Constantine turned from the window and faced Rex, clearly excited by this description. "And that upright piece," he said with urgency in his voice, "did it bend around at its top?"

Rex thought for a moment, recalling what he had seen. "I suppose you could say that. There was the curve of the halo, or perhaps a wisp of cloud, or something that curled near the top of the vertical ray. Like the Greek letter rho."

The emperor pounded his fist in his palm in a gesture of triumph.

"Exactly! Like a Greek rho, but with a crossbar like a tau. Two letters superimposed. That is precisely what I saw in my dream! A ρ and a τ, one on top of the other." Constantine beckoned Rex to come close. After breathing on the windowpane, he made a sign in the fog with his finger: ρ.

"Like this, right?" he asked.

Rex felt he had better indulge his lord and agree. "Sure. I think that was it, Your Highness."

Constantine looked Rex in the eye and put a hand on his shoulder, as if the two were sharing a great secret. "Just now, I dreamed I was about to go into battle, but all my men were naked. The enemy laughed at us. They had monsters in their ranks, Rex. Monsters! We were all terrified. I knew it was my end. Then a shining warrior rode up on a horse. He handed me a shield, and I saw the saving sign on it—the tau-rho. Or maybe it was more like a chi-rho. I can't remember the exact shape of the letters. In any case, the shield bore a cross emblem with a curved top, just like we saw in the sky."

"Did you win?"

"Of course I won! The monsters fled, and the troops fell before us. We had armor on now, and we were victorious. Then I woke up."

"Surely it is another sign from Apollo, Your Majesty."

Constantine gave a little laugh and shook his head. "I don't know what to think about the gods anymore. I keep seeing crosses. So I'm starting to think we've had it wrong." He stepped back from Rex, resuming his typically authoritative demeanor once again. "Listen to me now, soldier. I have a job for you. You know my son's tutor, the professor Lactantius? He's a Christian. Have him assemble the most important bishops in Gaul for a meeting in the Palace Hall. I'll pay whatever it costs. Let's do it by the Ides of October. Tell Lactantius to gather all the best theologians, because I have some weighty matters to discuss with them. Go find him right away. It's dawn now, so he's probably awake."

Rex saluted his lord and left the imperial bedchamber. The African rhetorician Lactantius was well-known around the palace, so he wasn't hard to locate after a few inquiries. When Rex told him what the emperor wanted, his face lit up. Lactantius said he would make the conference his foremost priority and that it could certainly happen by the Ides of October. Since the professor had a good relationship with the palace financial secretary, who was likewise a Christian, Rex knew his assignment was complete and the matter was in capable hands. He reported back to Constantine's chamberlain that the conference would take place on time.

As the day approached, Rex was surprised to discover he had been invited to the conference in a ceremonial role. He and several other speculators—the youngest and most handsome ones, he noticed—were given fancy uniforms of luxurious silk, then ordered to hold spears and stand at attention along the sides of the basilica. No cost had been spared in decorating the hall. The windowpanes had been cleaned, silver lampstands brought in, and a fine scarlet rug laid on the floor. The furnace was running at full blast to take away the autumn chill and make the guests comfortable. Apparently, the council was going to be a momentous affair.

When Rex arrived at the basilica, he found chairs had been set up in a semicircle around the imperial throne. The chairs all had placards with the names of the attending bishops: Ossius of Corduba, Maternus of Colonia, Reticius of Augustodunum, Marinus of Arelate, and several others. The lead spokesman was to be Lactantius, who had been given a small lectern off to the side. When all the Christian clergy were in place, a trumpet fanfare announced the emperor's arrival. He seated himself on his throne, welcomed the bishops warmly, and proceeded to describe his heavenly vision and recent dream.

"At first, I focused on those arcs of light," Constantine said. "I assumed they were laurel wreaths promising me victory and long reign. But then I had the dream. The glorious man showed me a shield with a cross on it. Now I realize the vision in the sky was about the cross as much as the laurels. I know the cross is an ancient sign with great magical power. The Aegyptians revered it long before the rise of Rome. Every crossroads is a place of choice, where one path or another can be taken—a mystical moment. The cardinal directions of the earth also make a cross. And of course, I am aware the cross is especially important to the Christians. It is because you are experts in the words of God that I have assembled you today. I wish to learn about what the cross truly means."

The bishops murmured, and some conferred among themselves. Lactantius finally indicated that one of the more senior of them, Ossius of Corduba, should speak. The distinguished Spaniard leaned forward in his seat. "Great Augustus, let it be known to you that the cross is assuredly a saving sign. Yet its power lies not in its magical shape, nor the symbolism it conveys. The power of the cross comes from a historical event—and a shameful one at that! It was on an executioner's cross that the Son of God was put to death, crucified for our transgressions, though innocent of them himself. In weakness and humility, the Savior died the bloody death of a criminal. But what you must understand, O Great Emperor, is that the true Emperor of the cosmos did not stay in the grave—no! He was raised by the power of God, ascended on high, and now sits at the right hand of glory. You are indeed correct that the cross has power, for it offers life beyond death to all who recognize Jesus as Lord."

Rex thought Constantine seemed impressed by this announcement, though it was hard to tell for sure. The books of the Christians were brought forth and a vigorous intellectual discussion ensued. Apparently, the Christians believed in a supreme God in heaven whose Son came down to earth. Though he was crucified during the reign of Tiberius, he did not remain dead but rose up and walked around before returning to heaven. All who chose to follow the Christian way and receive its ritual of washing would go to paradise after death.

And there was much more. The priests seemed eager to explain their faith in detail. After more than two hours of overhearing such weighty matters being discussed, Rex's mind began to drift. His stomach was growling, and he was glancing at the windows to assess the sun's angle when he heard a female whisper behind him.

"Psst! Soldier! Turn around!"

Rex glanced over his shoulder. *The Empress Mother!*

"Come to me," Helena ordered, and Rex did not believe he had the right to disobey. "Give this note to my son," she said, pressing a slip of parchment into his hand.

"You mean—later?" Rex asked hopefully.

Constantine's headstrong mother shook her head. "Do it right away. I will take responsibility."

Rex went back to his place. Yet now, instead of having a guard's calm demeanor, he was wracked with nervous energy. *I'd rather face a Frankish army than interrupt this council!* But the Empress Mother had given him a direct order. Rex took a deep breath, laid his spear on the floor, and walked into the semicircle of chairs.

Lactantius broke off midsentence. "Guardsman! What are you doing?"

Several other speculators immediately closed around Rex, their spears lowered in case he was up to mischief. But far worse than their threats was the look on the emperor's face. Rex could hardly stand the disapproving stare of Constantine, whose fierce eyes seemed to bore holes in him. Tentatively, he stretched out his arm. "A note from your beloved mother, Augustus!"

"Bring it here, Lactantius," Constantine said coldly. Rex bowed his head and remained uneasily in his place.

When the emperor had read the parchment, he ordered the volume of the four Gospels to be brought forward. "My pious mother directs us to read a text in *The Gospel according to John*. Let us now hear the account of the crucifixion in that book."

Lactantius laid the book on his lectern, located the passage, and began to read. He described how Jesus was mocked, flogged, and crowned with thorns, despite being declared innocent by the judge. But when Lactantius recited the words "Crucify him!" he paused uncertainly, then lifted his gaze to look at Constantine. "I think I know what Empress Helena wished you to see," he said.

"Show it to me."

Lactantius carried the book to the emperor, who took it into his lap. After reading it for a few moments, his eyes went wide.

"Keep reading," Lactantius said. "The sign is there many times."

"Rex, come here!" Constantine barked.

Rex ascended the dais and stood at the emperor's side. Though he could not read much Greek, he could at least recognize the mark to which Constantine's finger pointed. It was the saving sign they had discussed earlier: a cross with its head bent around, which they had called the tau-rho.

"This is just like the sign we saw in the sky, is it not?"

"Yes, Your Highness. And also like the one you saw in your dream."

"It appears many times in the manuscripts of our scriptures," Lactantius said, "but only as an abbreviation for one word: *cross*, or its verb, *crucify*."

Constantine wagged his head back and forth, exhaling slowly. "Can there be any doubt, then? This sign was first written in the sky, then on the shield in my dream—and now here it is in the sacred books of the Christian God! This is the mighty sign that gives divine power to mankind. The cross and the crown of victory go together!"

On impulse, Rex did something he couldn't explain, but which seemed right, nonetheless. Recalling his earlier conversation with the emperor, he went to a military standard on the dais, removed the banner from the transverse bar, and lifted the pole from its stand. Constantine craned his neck to see what he was doing. Rex returned and handed him the tall wooden cross, then knelt before his lord.

Seated in his magnificent throne, the emperor raised the standard high and gazed out at the assembly before him.

"In this sign, you shall conquer," Rex declared from his kneeling stance at Constantine's feet.

"In this sign, you shall conquer!" echoed the audience in the hall.

"I surely will," the emperor said.

—⁓⁓—

OCTOBER 310

Flavia sat on a stool in the enclosed garden of her home, trying to hit the right notes on her double flute. Though her tutor was typically a patient man, he was more frustrated today than usual.

"Are you focused on your music, Lady Junia? You seem distracted."

Flavia let out a sigh. "Perhaps another day would be better? My mind is divided."

The slave acquiesced and took his leave, so Flavia wandered from the garden to her father's study, where she found him sorting some books and papers. Neratius's bald head was tipped down as he focused on his work. When she greeted him, he glanced up and welcomed her, though he continued to organize his desk.

"I'm sorry about the city prefect job," Flavia said. "You would have made a good one."

"It still might happen if I bide my time. Volusianus was the obvious choice because he put down the rebellion in Africa. But does he have the grain flowing again? No—and you know as well as I do the people are growing more restless by the day. They won't be happy until the wheat supply is restored. Remember what the *Satires* of Juvenal said the mob really wants?"

"Bread and circuses. And right now, they have neither."

"Maxentius had better provide both very soon or the mob might start calling for a new augustus."

"I knew he was concerned about the bread dole—but circuses too? Is the emperor going to throw some games?"

"Yes, it's part of his strategy. I'm actually headed to a race today at his private circus."

"Perhaps some races will distract everyone from their hunger."

"Ha! Races might help, but to keep the people of this city satisfied, you have to give them more than chariots running in a circle. They want gladiators! Romans crave blood, and they'll get it one way or another. Death in the amphitheater is better than in the streets."

Flavia shivered. "I hate that you have to live in that world. It must be hard for you."

"It's life in the aristocracy," Neratius said with a shrug. "When I'm the city prefect, I'll do what I can to minimize it. So keep praying for me." He paused, collecting his thoughts, then added, "Pray for God's curses to fall on the head of Pompeianus. He is the primary obstacle to my advancement. I have to admit, he worries me sometimes."

Normally Neratius was a stiff and formal man who didn't talk much about his professional life, so Flavia felt honored that he had offered such a personal insight to her in a moment of candor. "Tell me about Pompeianus," she said, hoping to keep the conversation going.

"He's the new Praetorian prefect, which means he runs the army in Rome and all of its police and judicial functions. So it's an extremely powerful position. I think he wants to combine it with the office of city prefect, which is the top political job in the civic bureaucracy. Those are the two highest-ranked offices in the city. If something happened to our augustus, a man occupying both of those positions would be—"

"The next emperor?"

"Well, let's just say he'd be in an excellent position to take over. And that's why Pompeianus sees me as his biggest threat. Emperor Maxentius was my schoolmate back when we were youngsters. I'm a senator from an old, wealthy family. And I've done my time in the course of offices. All that makes me a logical candidate for city prefect."

"I'd like to meet this Pompeianus," Flavia said, "and tell him what a great man you are."

Neratius glanced at his daughter, then looked down and fiddled with a parchment for a moment before finally setting it aside. He rose from his desk and came close to her, as if to speak of conspiratorial things.

"Flavia, how would you like to come to Maxentius's villa today?"

A little gasp escaped Flavia's lips. *That's the last place I should go,* said the rational part of her mind. She was confident no one knew about her secret visit to the underground cemetery, for the Christian groundskeeper had let her and her mother go with nothing but a stiff warning. That was two months ago, and nothing had happened. Still—what good could come of mingling with the cruel and unpredictable Maxentius?

"Uh . . . w-why would I do that, Father?" Flavia asked at last.

"Maxentius always has a bunch of his illegitimate children running around. He really dotes on a couple of them. So I thought if he were to see you playing with them, being so pretty and sweet, it might reflect well on our family. You know how it is! A good girl from ancient Roman stock, taking care of children, doing all the right things. It makes me look respectable."

Despite her reservations, Flavia's desire to serve her father—not to mention her natural curiosity—overwhelmed her better judgment. She agreed to go, then hurried to her bedchamber and called for the ornatrix, who did her hair in the latest fashionable style and helped her put on makeup and a pretty gown. After adding jewelry and an outer wrap, she met her father at the front door and rode with him in the family's most ornate litter down the slope of the Aventine. Though the air in an enclosed litter could be hot and stuffy, today was a beautiful autumn day, so Flavia enjoyed the ride more than she normally would have. At the Appian Gate, they changed to a horse-drawn carriage for the trip into the suburbs under a clear October sky.

The villa of Maxentius consisted of three main sections: the grand tomb of his son Romulus, the imperial residence, and the brand-new circus. Though not so grand as the Circus Maximus in the heart of the city, the oblong track was still plenty big enough to hold chariot races. "It can seat ten thousand spectators," Neratius said. "Though it won't be full today, a lot of important people will be there. Maxentius claims to be reviving the old Augustan Games. Proof of his status as an augustus, you see. He's quite insecure about that."

Flavia filed away the information and rode along in silence. After the second milestone along the Appian Way, they arrived at the villa's gate and entered the complex. Neratius was ushered straight to the imperial viewing box, for his famous name and senatorial toga declared his status even to servants who didn't recognize his face.

The private suite in the circus was connected to the residence by a long, covered walkway. Though the emperor had not arrived yet, a few of his children were playing with ivory figurines, leather balls, and a springy twig.

"Catapult!" they cried as they knocked down the toy soldiers, accompanied by boisterous laughter.

"Can I try?" Flavia asked. Before long, she had joined the little boys in hurling "boulders" at the "enemy troops."

When Maxentius finally arrived, the mood in the box changed immediately. Only the boys seemed oblivious to his presence, while everyone else grew tense. The emperor's aura of power was enough to unsettle anyone who wasn't his illegitimate son. Flavia sized him up from the corner of her eye. He was a short, scrawny fellow in his midthirties, with bangs combed forward and a dimple in his chin. His beard was well maintained, shaved short in good Roman style. Though he was thin in the arms and shoulders, he had the pudgy waistline of a man who ate to excess. *He's homely and unattractive, but he doesn't look like the monster he's been made out to be,* Flavia decided.

Neratius took a place near Maxentius, alongside another man whom Flavia recognized from his description as the Praetorian prefect, Ruricius Pompeianus. In contrast to the mousy emperor, this man was muscular and stocky, with the close-cropped hair of a solider and an aggressive military bearing. A scar on his left cheek proved he had seen combat. Men like that always had a lot of blood on their hands. No wonder her father feared him.

Down on the track, the chariot race in the circus didn't seem particularly competitive, so the aristocrats in the viewing box were using the occasion to play politics rather than enjoy the show. They made no attempt to keep their conversations private, for the slaves and children in the vicinity were nonpersons whose ears were irrelevant. Flavia pretended to play ball with the boys, all the while eavesdropping on the men's exchange.

Maxentius appeared to be in a foul mood, for he had just been informed of his sister's role in the arrest and execution of their father, Maximian. "A donkey take her!" he fumed. "Fausta turned against our family! What kind of Roman girl does that? I'll throw her to the beasts if I ever get hold of her!"

"She has cast her lot with Constantine," Neratius agreed. "No turning back now."

"My spies in Arelate tell me Maximian's death was clean," Pompeianus said. "No torture, no shame. Just a simple hanging at the hands of a couple of speculators."

"An execution by a speculator is the death of a criminal. Curse my sister for her treachery!"

Flavia didn't know the word *speculator*, but she could tell the mood in the suite was souring. Gradually, under the pretense of playing with the boys, she scooted farther from the huddled men.

"I hate Constantine," Maxentius growled. "Someday that son of a stable-maid is going to feel my blade in his gut."

Neratius folded his arms across his chest in a posture of mature sagacity. "Be careful here, Your Majesty. Constantine is popular in certain circles. You mustn't underestimate his appeal to the masses. We want the people to love you and turn against him. Open war might not be our best option. A propaganda campaign might work better."

"You could use his Christian policy against him," Pompeianus suggested.

Flavia's ears perked up. *Christian policy? What does that mean?*

"He recently took up Apollo as his patron," Pompeianus went on, "but I hear he is switching to Jesus—another sun god. Constantine respects this superstition because Helena is a Christian. Apparently, his lowborn mama appoints his divine protector! They say Constantine has been openly consorting with the church's bishops. It's a shameful departure from the religion of our ancestors. Something ought to be done about it."

"Are you recommending I start up the persecution again, Pompeianus? You certainly have been persistent in that request."

"It's for the good of the empire, Your Highness. You should do it."

Flavia felt her forehead go sweaty as a wave of anxiety ran through her. She fanned the collar of her dress, trying to cool herself. It seemed as if the lives of thousands of Christians—perhaps even her own—hung on whatever words would be uttered next. *Father!* she silently pleaded. *Now is the time! Say something!*

But Neratius was mute, his head down, while Maxentius nodded thoughtfully at Pompeianus's urgings. Horrified by what might be about to happen, Flavia intervened the only way she could. After showing the leather ball to one of the toddlers, she whispered "Go get it!" then rolled it toward the emperor's feet. The little mop-headed boy giggled and started after it. When he had caught the men's attention, Flavia scooped him up from behind and steered him back to his playmates. "Forgive me, sirs," she said, bowing respectfully.

"Who are you?" Maxentius demanded.

"Lady Junia Flavia, Your Majesty."

"Aha! The daughter of Neratius!" The emperor stared at her for longer than seemed necessary. Flavia sensed, in the way women always can, that she was being gazed upon with desire. "Well, Neratius," said Maxentius with a snicker, "your girl is just as fetching as her mother."

Ignoring the sleaze, Flavia took her opportunity to speak, fully aware it was now or never. "I'm sorry to disturb your important discussions, Your Majesty. I suppose the Highest God ordained the interruption through the innocence of a child." She began to edge away.

The emperor's eyes narrowed. "Wait a moment! Stop right there. What do you mean by that, little pretty?"

"I . . . I overheard you discussing the Christians. It made me think of the Highest God. May that God never be angry at the great augustus but always help him become a wise and just ruler, loved by all." Flavia thought that was something she could legitimately say.

But Maxentius frowned. "And who is that Highest God, may I ask, since you are so well informed about religious matters?"

"Surely there must be a god more powerful than all the rest, no? That is the Highest God. And isn't he the one the Christians claim to worship? If that is true, I would want you, our appointed ruler, to be the instrument of his holy hand—to be turned here and there by him like a stream of rushing water." Flavia looked up and met Maxentius's stare. "I often pray for you," she said earnestly.

A sly smile crept across the emperor's face. He turned to look at Pompeianus, then at Neratius, whose expression was apprehensive. Rising from his seat, Maxentius came and towered over Flavia. She held her breath, unable to move.

Slowly, the most powerful man in Rome reached out and cradled her face in his hand, stroking her cheek with his thumb. "Such a pious girl," he said in a breathy voice. "I like that. More than you know." Bending low, he kissed Flavia softly on the cheek. "Pray often for your emperor, my little pretty. Pray that I make the right decision about the Christians. Run along now and leave religious matters to the grown men."

Trembling, Flavia slowly backed away. Before she turned to leave, she remembered to give a courteous nod to the emperor and the two men at his side. Though she wasn't surprised to see relief on her father's face, the more startling expression from the other man nearly took her breath away. The last thing Flavia saw as she left the emperor's box was an image she would never forget.

A glare of sheer hatred in the turbulent eyes of Ruricius Pompeianus.

JULY 311

Flavia peeked from the vestibule of her house for the third time, yet still saw no sign of the young man she awaited. It was a hot day, for it was high summer now and Rome was broiling. She stepped back into the vestibule's shade, grateful for its relief. Not many things would get her outside on a stifling day like this. But an ordination service was one of them.

Though Flavia didn't want to attend the ordination with Magnus as her protector, she had decided it beat the alternative: showing up at the Hall of the Church in an ornate litter carried by slaves. To do that would be to lord her wealth over the impoverished Christian brethren in direct violation of the scriptural warning of James, the Lord's brother, who wrote, "Has God not chosen the poor of the world to be rich in faith? But you have dishonored the poor." Therefore Flavia had resigned herself to walking to church with Magnus today, for her father had given her only those two options.

"The streets of Rome can be rough," he had said.

As if going with Magnus would make any difference, Flavia had thought, though she didn't voice that disrespectful reply. Yet she couldn't help but wonder, *Why are the males around me so weak?*

Nevertheless, despite her unwelcome escort, Flavia believed the day was going to be glorious. *Father Miltiades is being ordained Bishop of Rome!* It was one of the many things that had been going well for the catholic church recently. Earlier in the spring, Emperor Maxentius unexpectedly ended his ban on bishops, which he had instituted when Eusebius was exiled for the riot. The local presbyters wasted no time electing Miltiades the next pope. Flavia considered this a direct answer to prayer. When coupled with the Edict of Toleration that had just come down from one of the most vicious persecutors among the Eastern colleagues—the demon-worshiper Galerius—it seemed God's hand of blessing had been abundant upon the Christians. *Now if we could just get our properties back!*

Magnus finally showed up, sweaty and out of breath from his hike up the Aventine. "Ready, Lady Junia?" he asked, mopping his brow with a silk hanky.

Flavia nodded graciously and joined him in the street, making polite conversation as they descended the hill and crossed the river into Trans

Tiberim. The Hall of the Church had been cleaned and repaired after the terrible riot that had resulted in Eusebius's exile. Now the place looked even nicer than before. It was decked out with beautiful lampstands and a fine woolen runner down the middle of the nave. The bishop's throne had been restored to its place of honor on a raised platform. It was there, in his special seat called a "cathedra," that Miltiades would sit to preach sermons from the sacred scriptures.

Flavia took her leave from Magnus as the service was about to begin and assumed her place on the women's side of the church. The liturgy of ordination was somber and holy, as was only proper on such a momentous occasion. Three bishops were normally required to legitimize an ordination. For an event as special as the installation of a Roman metropolitan, the guests had come from quite a distance. The Tuscan bishops Felix of Florentia and Gaudentius of Pisae, along with the Sicilian bishop Chrestus of Syracusae, were the three designated pastors who laid hands on Miltiades and invoked the Spirit's empowerment of his ministry. When this portion of the service was finished, Miltiades called for a copy of the *Epistle to the Hebrews*, which the Eastern church claimed was by Saint Paul, though the Romans doubted it. After an hour's exposition of the ways a bishop should make Christ's priestly ministry present in the lives of the faithful, Miltiades turned his attention to recent developments in the life of the church.

"As you all know by now," he said, "the wicked emperor of the East, Galerius, was horribly infested by worms in his bowels and died a shameful death. Does not holy scripture likewise say of King Herod, 'An angel of the Lord struck him, for he did not give glory to God; and having been eaten by worms, he breathed his last'? Nevertheless, my children, I find that the very portion of *Hebrews* open in my lap reminds us, 'Vengeance is mine, I will repay.' And since 'it is a fearful thing to fall into the hands of the living God,' we shall not glory in the death of Galerius. But let it be known that a deacon from Rome will be traveling to Antiochia and Caesarea with an offering for our Eastern brethren who have been tested in the same fires of persecution that we ourselves experienced not long ago under Maximian. And now we know that this man was executed by Constantine for treason. Nevertheless, my children, let us not wallow in hatred toward these evil rulers who have recently been struck down, but only rejoice in the justice of God—the God who avenges the blood of the martyrs. Whether by disease or by the hand of Constantine, it is the Lord who delivers judgment on the wicked."

Miltiades offered a few more exhortations along these lines, reminding the gathered believers about the importance of confessing Christ alone and letting no pagan worship infect the faith. As Flavia listened to Miltiades speak, she thought he was the perfect picture of a godly bishop: dignified as he sat in his chair, dressed in a stylish yet modest tunic, his silver hair oiled and swept back, the Word of God open in his lap, exhorting the church to persevere in righteousness. *The Lord has blessed us abundantly*, Flavia decided—and then, as if to confirm that blessing, the bishop declared he had an important announcement.

Miltiades raised a parchment so all could see. "My children, before we depart, there is one more thing I must show you." Unexpectedly, he ripped the document in two. "Behold the rental contract for the Hall of the Church. I have destroyed it because it is no longer needed—for Maxentius has restored our properties in full!"

Flavia, along with many others in the room, uttered an exultant gasp.

The properties are ours again! Praise be to God!

The celebratory atmosphere remained in the hall long after the service had ended. Instead of dispersing, the believers stayed as long as they could to rejoice in the favor the Almighty had shown to the church of Rome. Though Magnus was anxious to get home, Flavia put him off, reluctant to leave until she got a chance to speak with Miltiades. Finally, she was able to approach him.

"Holy Father, I wish to give the church a gift," she told the bishop.

"Your piety is a sufficient gift, daughter."

"But piety must result in charitable actions. That is why I wish to provide, out of my own dowry, a banquet to feed the needy. Might we have it at the Apostolic Monument at the Catacombs?"

Miltiades folded his arms in his sleeves and gave a slight bow from the waist. "Yes, indeed, that is a fine idea. For the rich and poor alike to feast as equals in the company of the martyrs seems a fitting way to celebrate the restoration of the properties. I will coordinate this with your mother. Thank you, Lady Junia, for your generosity."

The bishop had several other people waiting to see him, so with the matter of the banquet settled, Flavia excused herself and left the church at last. Even Magnus's awkward presence on the walk home wasn't enough to dampen her spirits. They were nearing the Bridge of Probus when Magnus suddenly said, "I think we should step into this pottery shop."

"It's rather late for shopping, Magnus. I thought you wanted to go straight home."

"There's a man following us. He stands out because he's a dark Aethiops. I have seen him behind us since we left the church. He turns whenever we do."

"I noticed him too. Perhaps he is going our same way by chance?"

"I think he's following us. What should we do?"

"You are the son of a knight, Magnus. You decide."

The youth stared at his feet for a moment, then slyly glanced around before suggesting, "How about if we go into the shop, then go out the back?"

Flavia agreed, so they tried it. After exiting into an alley, they hurried to the bridge. The dark-skinned man, however, was waiting in the vicinity.

"He knew we had to cross the bridge," Flavia said.

Magnus picked up his pace. "Let's just hurry."

The pair ascended the Aventine to the mansion on the crest. As Flavia neared her home, she looked over her shoulder. The Aethiops had stopped downhill at a public fountain on a branch of the aqueduct. He averted his eyes and turned away when Flavia glanced back.

Magnus beckoned Flavia into the vestibule of her house. "We lost him!" he said gleefully.

"He followed us all the way home, though."

"It matters not. I got you home safely."

"Yes, you did. I honor you, Magnus, for your courtesy today. Thank you for walking with me as my protector."

"But of course! It was my pleasure. So then . . . um . . ." Magnus fiddled with the hem of his toga, which he had only recently started wearing now that he had reached the age of manhood. "Lady Junia . . . er, Flavia . . . it was most pleasant today . . . I mean, thank you for going to the church with me." Suddenly the youth closed his eyes and leaned forward, his lips slightly parted.

Ack! He's trying to kiss me!

99

Flavia distanced herself from her incoming suitor. Sensing her withdrawal, Magnus opened his eyes. "Oh! Perhaps I misunderstood . . ." His words trailed off, creating an uncomfortable silence in the little vestibule.

"Yes, I think you did, Magnus," Flavia said gently. With a final farewell, she retreated into her house and closed the door, glad to be home at last. She kicked off her sandals in the atrium and flopped onto a plush divan, putting all thoughts of romance from her mind.

Father Miltiades is the bishop now! she reminded herself, focusing on the real significance of the day. *And the properties are back in Christian hands!* Flavia smiled broadly at the thought. *It was a beautiful ordination service. The age of persecution is over. At last, the church's best times are ahead!*

⸺◦◦◦⸺

The steaming, glistening liver still throbbed in the soothsayer's blood-drenched hand. He had just yanked it from the belly of a live goat, which bleated and thrashed in agony. No doubt its suffering was immense. Yet that was the price the spirits demanded to divulge their sacred knowledge. They always hungered for blood and pain—the more innocent and precious, the better.

"This is not how the old ritual was done," Maxentius said.

"No. But there is a far more powerful magic at work in this." Pompeianus gave Maxentius a sly look. "Just wait. You will see."

The secret room deep within the imperial residence was lit only by candles, making it hard for Pompeianus to see exactly what the soothsayer was doing. The veiled man turned the goat's liver this way and that in the candlelight, inspecting it for holy signs. Suddenly his eyes went wide, and he pulled the liver close to his face. Extending the tip of his tongue, he tasted the blood, then spat it out. He approached the emperor. "You must declare war on Constantine, my lord," he announced. "He is the enemy of the god who empowers you. You must oppose Constantine's faith in the god of the cross."

Pompeianus wanted to utter a victory cry, though of course he could not do such a thing during the arcane ritual. Instead, he urged the soothsayer, "Say it plainly, priest! We should restart the persecution, yes?"

The wrinkled old man stared down at the liver for a moment, then raised his gaze to Maxentius and shook his head. "The omens say no blood of Christians should be spilled. Keep the peace in Rome for now. Focus all your attention on Constantine! He is the real threat to your god. It is he whom you must defeat in war! Otherwise he will change everything, and the cross will triumph."

Now Pompeianus found himself wanting to utter a curse, but since he couldn't do that either, he contained his fury in silence. *I can find a way around this!*

"I have one more question for you," Maxentius said. "Please seek an answer, for I have given the spirits the gift of innocent blood and pain."

The soothsayer nodded. "Indeed, their hunger has been satiated. You may ask."

"Who is my special patron? Constantine has chosen his god, the ridiculous Jesus. Now I need to know—which god favors me most? Who will give me victory?"

A smile came to the soothsayer's face, then he broke into a cackle that seemed impious in the quiet room. At last he pointed with his long fingernail to a bulging ridge of yellow fat in the liver. "See here? This declares plainly who it is."

"Tell me!" Maxentius cried.

The soothsayer leaned over and whispered in his master's ear. Pompeianus strained to hear but could not move any closer without being obvious. The emperor's mouth fell open, then he whirled and rushed to confer with a servant in the shadows. After the man listened to Maxentius's instructions, he bolted from the room.

"We shall assemble in the circus at the ninth hour," Maxentius decreed to the assembled aristocrats who had been gathered for the sacred divination. "There you will discover my special patron. Until then, the services of my palace are yours for the enjoying. Just ask the slaves for whatever you need. You may go."

The dark room quickly emptied. Pompeianus passed the intervening time with a lunch of olives, cheese, and bread, followed by an afternoon fling with the girl who had brought it. When the sundial indicated the ninth hour was near, he made his way along the covered sidewalk to the new circus at Maxentius's villa.

Only a few people were gathered in the imperial box, among them Neratius Junius Flavianus, the ambitious fool who was always angling for the city prefect job that Pompeianus felt should be his. The rest of the guests were sitting in the stands. All of them were aristocrats, for Maxentius had arranged a special exhibition today, not a scheduled race for the masses.

Pompeianus gazed down at the oblong track. Twelve starting gates stood at the western end, flanked by a pair of impressive three-story towers. The long marble spine, decorated with statues, pools, and an Aegyptian obelisk, divided the track in two. At each end of the spine stood the conical turning posts around which the chariots ran. Columns along its length held dolphins and eggs that could be moved to count the laps. In the distance, through a perfectly situated arch, the ancient tomb of Caecilia Metella was framed like a portrait of a bygone age. Everything about the scene was normal except for one thing: a large, cloth-covered crate lay on the track, directly in front of the imperial viewing platform.

The emperor arrived on the sandy floor of the circus dressed in golden armor, with a sword belted to his waist and a plumed helmet on his head. Around him were several gladiators of the "huntsman" type, armed with whips, nets, and spears. Bringing up the rear were two Praetorian guardsmen, each wheeling a small ballista that could shoot heavy darts made of lead. The machines had been known to pierce oaken city gates.

Once the fighters had assembled in a semicircle around the mysterious crate, Maxentius turned to face his audience. "Watch now, my friends, as I bind myself to an old patron of my family! Behold the god indwelling me!"

Maxentius spun toward the crate and took up a position behind one of the ballistae. The hunters yanked the cloth from the box, revealing it instead as a cage. Another man opened its door. The audience gasped as a thick-maned lion emerged into the bright sunlight.

Pompeianus immediately understood the significance of the fearsome cat. *Maxentius is binding himself to Hercules, the slayer of lions!* It made perfect sense. His father, Maximian, had been declared a Herculean by Emperor Diocletian, the founder of the Imperial College. Now Maxentius was claiming that same Herculean mantle as a legitimate augustus. He was identifying with his now-dead father, while at the same time declaring his father's executioner—Constantine, who had rejected his Herculian identity—to be a mortal enemy. It was a savvy political move, dripping with symbolism that the pagan aristocrats of Rome could hardly miss.

The lion squinted in the sunlight, apparently more confused by its surroundings than hungry for human flesh. Maxentius did not wait. He tripped the mechanism of the ballista in a point-blank shot. The thick dart smashed the cat in the rump and knocked it off its feet. It struggled up again, letting out a thunderous roar, but before it could get away Maxentius ran to the second ballista and put another easy shot into the lion's flank. The beast tumbled across the track, coming to rest on its side. It lay motionless, except for one huge paw that spasmodically raked the sand.

A hunter handed Maxentius a massive wooden club, just like the one used in Hercules's first labor when he slew the Nemean lion. Maxentius struggled with its weight, needing both hands to lift the huge olive-wood log above his head. Uttering a loud cry, he smashed the lion's skull, then jumped back. The beast heaved itself to its feet once more, its face a bloody mess. Hunters stepped in with whips, but they weren't needed, for the lion collapsed to the sand again. A second time, Maxentius crushed the animal's head, and this time it lay still. Then, in a final ceremonial act, the emperor straddled the beast from behind, reached under its bushy mane with gauntleted hands, and mimicked the death grip of Hercules. The lion never moved, and the fatal charade was complete.

Maxentius removed his helmet, the sweat of exertion running down his face. "I bind my soul to thee, O great Hercules Victorious!" he shouted to the heavens. "Let the statues of Constantine come tumbling down! On him I declare war—the usurper, the false augustus! O mighty Hercules, make war against Jesus! May you, O god, give me strength against my foe!"

Pompeianus could only smile at the clever stagecraft. The act was the perfect way to symbolize Maxentius's identification with the legitimate college that ruled the empire. Hercules Victorious was a long-standing patron of Rome, a god whose distinct round temple and Great Altar in the cattle market were landmarks as ancient as the city itself. Maxentius's adoption of his father's god would inevitably cast Constantine as the murderer of Rome's rightful ruler Maximian—a deed that must be avenged by his son. No one would want to associate with the upstart Constantine and his foreign deity drawn from Eastern, Jewish superstition.

As Pompeianus turned to leave the viewing box, his eyes happened to fall on Neratius. Surprisingly, the man's expression was distraught. Apparently, he had not liked what he had seen. Although Neratius thought he wasn't being observed, Pompeianus watched him surreptitiously make the sign of the cross on his forehead.

No! Can it be? Neratius is a Christian?

Pompeianus wagged his head in disbelief. And yet now that he thought about it, there had been certain hints of this strange development. Neratius sometimes spoke highly of the catholic church. And that arrogant daughter of his had defended the "Highest God" to Maxentius.

Even so, it hardly seemed possible that a senator with such high standing would follow such a ridiculous cult.

But if it was true . . . then what?

I will find a way to use it against him, Pompeianus decided with a self-satisfied chuckle. *His political aspirations will come to nothing. This man and his family are finished in Rome!*

Rex had learned long ago that his commanding centurion, Aratus, held a firm commitment to early departures. There was only one way to explain how a man who had grown up as a street urchin and common thief could have become so self-disciplined: the Roman military. The army was Aratus's salvation. It took a back-alley brawler and turned him into the efficient war-making machine he now was. He was a stern and unforgiving commander. All his men were a little afraid of him—though their fear was born out of respect.

"Saddle up, soldiers," the centurion said. "It's light enough now to depart. We need to be in Saravus Village by nightfall."

Rex and Geta mounted their horses, along with a thick-lipped Scythian speculator named Hierax. There was going to be some hard riding for the foursome in the weeks ahead, but the augustus had said speed was essential for this important mission. "Go to Rome," Constantine had ordered. "Spy it out, learn what you can about the people and the Praetorians. Find out the level of support Maxentius has. Sow discord if you can. Live there through the winter. Then be ready to give me a full report whenever I arrive."

Handpicked by Emperor Constantine for an undercover mission in the capital! Rex couldn't help but think that his father, King Chrocus of the Alemanni, would have been proud.

Outside the city walls, tombs lined the road on both sides. The four men had already gone a hundred paces from Augusta Treverorum when a guard at the massive northern gate hailed them from behind. The riders turned to see a chariot emerge from between the gate's round towers. A tall, commanding figure, his identity obscured by the morning twilight, stood next to the chariot driver. But as he drew nearer, Rex discerned it was Constantine himself.

The speculators saluted their lord when he reached them. "Long live the Divine Augustus!" Aratus said.

"Ah! You wish me to live long? Then listen closely, men. Maxentius has declared war on me, and powerful gods stand ready to help him. He is well-known as a practitioner of the magic arts. Therefore I have come to send you off with my personal blessing, that you might know how important this mission is to me. And also"—the emperor reached beneath his cloak—"that I might give you these."

Aratus extended his hand and received four items from Constantine. The centurion swiveled in his saddle and pitched one each to Rex, Geta, and Hierax. Rex caught the item and held it up by its leather thong: a small, round pendant that had been gilded and engraved. *An amulet!*

"Behold the sign," Constantine said.

Rex cupped the necklace in his palm and inspected it more closely. It was marked with the magical tau-rho—the special sign of the Christian deity. Such a powerful amulet would probably do some good, serving at least as a lucky charm or protective talisman. Grateful for the honorable gift, Rex tied the pendant around his neck and tucked it beneath his tunic.

"We will serve you faithfully unto death, Your Highness," Aratus vowed. "We go now to Rome, the first step in your glorious liberation of that city from tyranny!"

"Yes. You are sworn to me, and I know you will defend me with your lives. Together we will take Rome back from the usurper Maxentius."

"Bless us, my lord, as we depart." Aratus signaled to his men to align their horses side by side on the road, facing the destination. The centurion urged his mount into a brisk walk, then up to a canter. The other three horses kept perfect pace as the expedition set out.

Constantine raised his arms over the riders like a benevolent priest. "May the power of the cross guard you!" he called after them.

It wasn't long before the party rounded a bend and lost sight of the emperor and the city. Dew was still on the grass, but the morning fog had lifted, and a warm light bathed the road ahead. Rex withdrew the amulet from his collar and gripped it in his fist as he rode along.

"I'll ask for your help if I ever need it, Jesus," he whispered to the rising sun. "But for now, I think I've got this mission under control."

4

Pompeianus had always believed that Fausta, the homely sister of Emperor Maxentius, didn't deserve such a grand house atop a famous Roman hill like the Caelian. She was a traitor—a willing supporter of her husband, the devious and arrogant Constantine. *Far more fitting*, Pompeianus assured himself, *that a mansion like this should belong to me, the Praetorian prefect. And someday the city prefect?*

Only time would tell.

Pompeianus stood at a high window of the so-called House of Fausta, more properly known as the Lateran Palace after its original owners, the Laterani clan. The vista below formed a landscape of lazy opulence and vigorous power at the same time. The formidable city walls curved off into the distance, while in the foreground, the "New Camp" of the Emperor's Personal Cavalry bustled with activity. This famed unit of elite riders, founded by Trajan two centuries earlier, had now essentially become the cavalry counterpart to the infantry of the Praetorian Guard. Though the Praetorian footmen had a camp of their own farther around the walls, the imperial horse guard was based here, in a district of luxurious gardens and mansions, where there was a suitable residence for the commander of so great a unit as the Praetorians. Rome was not some frontier outpost with no home for the general but a hut in the middle of fortified barracks. The Praetorian prefect deserved to be housed in a palace like this, overlooking his splendid horsemen. Emperor Maxentius understood this truth—thank the gods—so he had converted the home of his traitorous sister to a much nobler use. *Never again would Fausta tarnish the reputation of this historic mansion!*

A chamber steward approached Pompeianus from behind as he gazed out the window. "Your visitors have arrived, my lord."

The prefect turned from the view and walked to a carved chair inlaid with ivory. "Bring them to me," he replied as he seated himself. "And bring me some wine."

The two arrivals made a remarkable pair. One was a bulky commoner with dirt under his fingernails and the coarse tunic of a laborer. The other was a wiry man with tight ringlets of hair and black skin as dark and shiny as obsidian. "Burnt face," they called slaves who were imported from south of Aegyptus. The Greek word for "burnt face" provided the name of their homeland: *Aethiopia.*

"I'm thirsty. Bring me the cup," Pompeianus said irritably. The steward brought a silver goblet filled with an excellent Falernian wine—golden, sweet, and satisfying. When his thirst was quenched, Pompeianus turned to his visitors. "What do you want with me?"

The big laborer stepped forward, evidently the spokesman. "Sir, we heard you're paying for information about crimes committed by Christians. We have some news for you."

"Go on," Pompeianus said, taking another sip from the goblet.

"My friend here"—the laborer pointed to the Aethiops—"has been following a girl who goes to the Christian temple in Trans Tiberim. Recently he found out where she lives. It's a mansion on the Aventine."

"So what? Christianity isn't illegal here in Rome. The only colleague who has the guts to eradicate those vermin is Daia. He's persecuting again in the East. But Emperor Maxentius received a divine message to hold steady on the Christian question. It's disgusting, but it's the law. For now, at least."

The Aethiops spoke for the first time. "The girl lives in the home of Senator Neratius Junius Flavianus," he offered in a shy voice.

Pompeianus sat up in his seat so quickly, he spilled wine on his white toga. Ignoring it, he leaned toward his visitors, who had backed away in case he was angry. "Come here to me, you two! I'm not going to hurt you!"

The men edged closer. "Tell me about the girl. Was she a dark-haired little thing with long eyelashes? Not yet twenty?"

"I . . . I think so. I believe she's the senator's daughter. Dresses like a rich girl. Goes about with the son of an equestrian merchant who has dealings in Sicilia."

Pompeianus stared at the floor as he considered the matter. *So . . . the father crosses his forehead and the daughter goes to church. That's two pieces of evidence the Junii are Christians. Even if it's not illegal—how could I use it?*

"There's something else," the big laborer said. An arched eyebrow from Pompeianus was enough to encourage the snitch to continue. "My boss is a groundskeeper for some cemeteries on the Appian Way," he went on. "I dig the grave niches in the tuff. About a year ago, this same girl came to a cemetery with her mother—"

"Lady Sabina Sophronia?"

"I don't know her name. It took us a long time to figure out who she might be, just by asking around when we had a chance. But, yes, the lady lives in the Aventine house. I think some Christians meet there too. Lots of people coming and going around sunrise."

"You were saying? About the cemetery?"

"Yes, sir. So this lady and her daughter bring a body into the cemetery. By themselves, mind you. No mourners. They go through a hole in the wall and go underground and lay the corpse in a grave. Then my boss catches them."

"Women burying bodies? It happens all the time. Someone has to do it. It's not a crime."

The two visitors exchanged triumphant glances. Excited now, the grave-digger continued his tale. "But, sir, this body belonged to Bishop Eusebius, brought back from Sicilia! I heard the girl tell it to my boss. How she planned it all, had him embalmed, brought him to Ostia, and shipped him up the Tiberis to Rome. She even paid for it with her own money."

Though Pompeianus had always believed it wasn't dignified to show emotion in front of commoners, he couldn't hold back the huge smile that spread across his face. "That's illegal!" he said triumphantly. "The Divine Augustus exiled that man!"

"Not only that, sir," the Aethiops added, "but the cemetery was the one called Callistus—a Christian property that was forbidden to them."

Now Pompeianus rose to his feet. "*What*? You mean that girl shipped an exile's body back to Rome and snuck it into a confiscated burial ground? There's no way that isn't injured majesty!" At the men's blank stare, Pompeianus explained the legal term. "*Injured majesty*—it means high treason against the glory of the emperor."

"Our information pleases you, then?" the gravedigger asked.

"Indeed, it does." Pompeianus waved the steward over. "See that these men each leave here with a month's wages. And go find Tertius right way. Tell him I have an urgent legal matter to discuss."

The steward escorted the two informants out the door, returning an hour later with the distinguished advocate Tertius, a freedman whose keen mind and polished eloquence had helped him rise through the lawyers' ranks. Pompeianus welcomed him warmly, for unlike the earlier visitors, this was a man of substance. The two reclined on couches, sipping the Falernian and pairing it with various cheeses.

"So what's this about injured majesty?" Tertius finally asked after sufficient pleasantries had been exchanged.

"I have a case I want to run by you, to see what you think the maximum penalty could be. It involves a couple of Christians, but I can't take that angle. Has to be purely legal—a violation of the existing laws of the state."

"We can't persecute, but we can always prosecute," Tertius said around a mouthful of alpine goat cheese.

Pompeianus explained the full case against Flavia and Sophronia. "So what do you say?" he asked when he was finished. "You think that would count as injured majesty?"

"Absolutely. The violation of an emperor's direct order is clearly treason."

"And it's provable?"

"Probably not for the mother, if she didn't conspire to move the body to Italy," the lawyer replied. "But for the girl—definitely."

"Excellent! For the humbler class, treason would carry the death penalty. But this girl is among the honorables. Do you think we can win more than a sentence of banishment against her? Can she be executed?"

"Banishment is for rich people whom the emperor wants to spare. If we press for capital punishment, I think we can get it. The rules aren't as strict as they used to be."

Pompeianus wiped his lips and leaned back on the couch. His mind was working feverishly now, leaping from one idea to the next. The city prefect position had come open again, and this time, everyone expected Neratius to get the job at last. Unfortunately, that outcome probably couldn't be stopped. But the execution of his daughter would shame him just as he assumed the prestigious new office. His Christianity would be exposed too—a foreign and superstitious cult unworthy of a senator. The emperor would surely toss Neratius aside.

Then who would get the job but me? But Maxentius mustn't suspect my motives. This has to be a case of neutral courtroom justice taking its normal course, or the augustus will think I'm persecuting Christians against his command. The problem is, neutral courtroom justice is boring. For this to shame Neratius, the execution has to become infamous throughout the city. I need this to be legal and sensational at the same time! How?

"Alright, listen," the prefect said, turning back to his guest. "Let's say we win a capital judgment against the girl. Honorables are usually decapitated. Quick and painless. But could we make the beheading noteworthy so as many people as possible would see it? Maybe schedule it on a busy day outside a major gate? Put up signs about it? Pass out anonymous flyers?"

"Ha! You forget what kind of advocate you're dealing with here," Tertius bragged. "I can do better than that. Even if Lady Junia wasn't involved in a violent plot, there's plenty of legal precedent for revoking honorable status for insults to the imperial majesty. Give me a month or two to line up all the bribes in the jury, and I can have the girl reduced to the rank of a humble. Then all her legal protections would be gone. I think you know what that means."

Excited, Pompeianus glanced over at the lawyer and was gratified to receive a confirmatory nod. The final piece of the plan had just fallen into place, for the humble class was subject to the most horrific execution of all. Snatching up his goblet, Pompeianus raised it high. "Fantastic work, my dear friend. I propose a toast."

Tertius also lifted his cup. "Yes, a toast! To whom?"

"To the wild beasts of the arena!" Pompeianus cried, then threw back his head and drained the last of his wine.

—⁓⁓—

OCTOBER 311

The dark day when the soldiers came was one Sophronia would never forget.

It was cold and wet outside, for it was October now and the constant summer sunshine had begun to give way to autumn's frequent squalls. Sophronia was resting in the tepidarium of her home's small bath, enjoying the pleasant warmth after a long soak in the hot water. The first sound to suggest any trouble was the jingle of armor and horse tack outside. Rude shouting quickly followed. Because the window was too high to see out, Sophronia didn't know what was happening in the street. Yet the commotion had an ominous ring to it.

"Bring my gown and stola," she said to the bath attendant. "Then go make sure the outer doors are barred. It's probably nothing to worry about, but let's be cautious just in case."

The servant girl scurried away after bringing the garments. Sophronia tried to convince herself the sounds meant nothing. However, by the time she had dressed, she could no longer deny something was terribly wrong. The shouting had moved inside the house, and all the servants were running about. Then a male voice let out an agonized groan, accompanied by a high-pitched female shriek.

Sophronia hurried to the atrium, not caring that her hair was wet and loose on her shoulders. She found the doorkeeper sprawled on the floor, clutching his upper arm in his bloody fingers. His wife, the ornatrix of the house, knelt beside him with a look of horror on her face. Eight Praetorians were assembled around the atrium's pool, their swords drawn. One of the blades glistened red.

Realizing this was no time for timidity, Sophronia marched boldly into the room. "I am Lady Sabina Sophronia, mistress of this house! My husband is a member of the ancient Senate! How dare you barge in here and injure my servants!"

"There is one power in Rome higher than the Senate, and that is the law itself," said the soldier with the bloody sword. His insignia revealed him to be the decanus, the squad's leader. "No man is above the law—and certainly no woman."

"If you have a legal matter, I am confident it can be handled without violence."

"That depends on whether you cooperate. See here." The decanus showed Sophronia a wax tablet in a folding case, which she snatched from his hand. As she began to read it, a twisting knot of fear gathered in her gut. Dizziness threatened to engulf her, so she put her hand on a column for support. The document was an arrest warrant signed by the Praetorian prefect himself. And the accused—

No!

"She's not here!" Sophronia exclaimed, glancing around at the soldiers. "She's out."

"We'll see about that." The decanus gestured toward the rest of the house with his sword. "You boys search the whole place. Check every room. Make sure anyone who gets in your way looks like this guy." He tossed his head toward the wounded doorkeeper on the floor. "Bring the girl to me if you find her—unharmed."

Sophronia started to ease away, but the decanus quickly moved to block the exit. He sheathed his sword and took back the tablet. "I'll just keep you company here, fancy lady," he said with a smirk.

The seven Praetorians scattered and began ransacking the house. Sharp yells and the crash of broken items echoed from the rear rooms and upper stories. It was all Sophronia could do to stand still and listen. *Oh God*, she prayed, *let Flavia slip out of a window! Let her find a hiding place! You are her shield and defender!*

A breathless servant burst into the atrium from outside. "The master is coming!" he announced. Then Neratius entered his home.

"Guardsman!" he barked to the decanus. "I am the new city prefect of Rome! Come here to me at once."

The soldier thrust out his chin and locked eyes with Neratius. "My commander is Ruricius Pompeianus, prefect of the Praetorian Cohorts. I answer to him alone." For several moments, the two strong-willed men engaged in a stare down. Finally, Neratius said, "What is that document?" The decanus handed the tablet to Sophronia without breaking eye contact with Neratius. "Here. Take that to your husband."

Neratius opened the tablet and glanced down at it. His eyes widened as he read it.

"It's an arrest warrant," he said softly.

"You must prevent this travesty!" Sophronia urged. "You're now the city prefect . . . *do something!*"

Neratius put his hand on his wife's arm. "It will all be worked out soon, dear," he soothed, then looked back at the Praetorian, who was still giving him the evil eye. "I will not forget your impudence," Neratius vowed.

The soldier shrugged indifferently but never averted his gaze.

"Found her, sir!" shouted one of the searchers from Neratius's adjacent office. He entered the atrium with Flavia's wrist in his grip.

Sophronia cringed. *Oh, Jesus Christ, help my precious girl!*

"Let go of me!" Flavia said, wrenching her arm away from her captor. "Father! Don't let these men take me!"

"They accuse you of trespassing the forbidden cemeteries."

"Those burial grounds aren't forbidden anymore, by order of the emperor!"

"But they were off-limits at the time," the decanus snapped. "Take her outside, men."

As the soldiers forced Flavia toward the vestibule, Neratius spoke into her ear. "You have to go with them now, daughter. But don't worry. I will take care of this."

"I'm not afraid," Flavia said. "I'm in God's hands."

In the street, Flavia mounted the horse that had been brought for her. She sat erect in the saddle, soaking wet in the rain, yet dignified and unwavering. The household servants, along with many onlookers in the doors and windows of nearby houses, stared in quiet awe at the spectacle. Neratius went up and squeezed Flavia's hand, but Sophronia could only watch from the vestibule, clinging to the doorpost to remain upright. Tears finally came to her eyes as she watched the squad of Praetorians ride away with Flavia.

"I will make a petition straightaway," Neratius said when the riders had disappeared.

So will I, Sophronia decided, *for it is God's intervention we need most.*

Two hours later, she was at the house of Bishop Miltiades. He lived in a small yet comfortable domus in the Trans Tiberim neighborhood near the Hall of the Church. The residence was well appointed and tastefully decorated, since it was important for outsiders to see that the leader of the catholic church was honored by his own people. Nevertheless, the home was unusual in many respects. All the household servants were male, and several deacons lived there, too, in a holy brotherhood. Many rooms that would have been devoted to luxuries were used instead as storerooms for charitable goods. And the bishop's residence certainly did not have the shrine to the household gods that most homes had. In the idol niche normally reserved for ancestor worship, Miltiades had placed a beautiful copy of the Greek Old Testament, along with a lamp by which to read the volumes.

The bishop observed right away that Sophronia was distraught. He escorted her to a comfortable couch next to a fountain, urging her to sit and explain what was on her mind. When he learned Flavia had been arrested, his brow furrowed, and a resolute expression came over his face. With his eyes closed, he began to stroke his whiskers—perhaps thinking of possible solutions or maybe even praying. Sophronia hoped he was doing both. Finally, he lifted his eyes to meet hers.

"Dear sister, I will go straight to Prefect Pompeianus about this," he promised. "Let us keep the matter away from Maxentius for the moment. Perhaps we can resolve it without the emperor learning of it."

"Do you think the prefect will respond to your petition?"

"I think all men respond when God moves their hearts. We must marshal the forces of righteousness on Flavia's behalf. Let us ask everyone in the church to pray."

"Holy Father, I . . ." Sophronia's words faltered, and she felt sweat break out on her brow. She started to squirm on the couch. "I'm so afraid for her! What are those men doing to her right now in that dungeon? Is she being—"

"Peace, Sophronia. Do not let fear rule you. Think instead on the power of God." The bishop rose and went to the book of the scriptures, flipping the pages until he found the text he sought. "Listen to these sacred words: 'The Lord is my light and my Savior; whom shall I fear? The Lord is the defender of my life; of whom shall I be afraid? When evildoers drew close against me to consume my flesh, my persecutors and my enemies, they fainted and fell down.'"

"Ah, the twenty-sixth psalm. Might I have a copy of it?"

"I will have a scribe make one before you leave. In the meantime, let us pray together. Come stand by me."

Sophronia rose from the couch and took a position next to her bishop.

The earlier rain shower had passed now, and a bright sunbeam from the skylight shone upon her. She lifted her palms and closed her eyes, feeling the warmth of the sun on her face.

"Apollo is not God," Miltiades declared. "Sol is not God. Nor Hercules, nor Mars, nor even Jupiter. There is but one God in the heavens. Do you remember the words of your baptismal catechesis?"

Without further prompting, the apostolic words came gushing from Sophronia's lips. "I believe in God the Father Almighty, and in Jesus Christ, his only Son our Lord, who was born from the Holy Spirit and the Virgin Mary, was crucified under Pontius Pilate, and was buried. On the third day he rose from the dead. He ascended into heaven, and sits at the right hand of the Father, from where he shall come to judge the living and the dead. I believe in the Holy Spirit, the holy church, the remission of sins, and the resurrection of the flesh."

After reciting the symbol, Sophronia opened her eyes. Miltiades was smiling broadly, and the sunlight made his oiled beard glisten. His tone with her was gentle yet firm. "Where do you put your trust, my sister?"

"I cast myself on Jesus," she said.

"And he will not let you fall," answered the godly bishop of Rome.

Rex was pleased to find his current ascent to Poeninus Pass quite a bit easier than the footrace Aratus had imposed on his cadets two years earlier. For one thing, the autumn sky today was sunny and clear. And another benefit was that the imperial post mules were doing the hard work of fighting their way up the incline. All Rex had to do was stay in the saddle and let his mount carry him to the summit.

The four speculators were making the trip in reverse this time, climbing not from the Italian side but from the Gallic lowlands to the inn at the crest. Somewhere up there was the imaginary line where Gaul stopped and Italy began. Aratus had started calling this "the true beginning of the mission."

"Not far now," the centurion said, tilting his head back as he scanned the high peaks that loomed ahead. "Less mountain, more sky with every step we take. This road can't keep ascending forever. Eventually it will top out."

The squad of soldiers—a typical Roman detachment of four tentmates—

had left Octodurus at Aratus's favorite time of dawn. With the hours of daylight short this time of year, combined with the need to take frequent rest breaks, their only goal for the day was to reach the crest of the pass. The journey was uphill the whole way: twenty-four miles along a steady 10 percent grade. A station at the halfway mark had allowed them to exchange their exhausted mules for fresh ones to finish the trip.

Two hours before dusk, the squad reached the snow line. The way ahead became more treacherous, and Rex could sense that even the sure-footed mules were struggling to keep their balance. Though the snow wasn't deep yet, daytime thawing had made it slick. More snow would fall on the road each night. It wouldn't be long before this pass would be closed for the season.

The Scythian speculator was in the lead now, his mule anxious to reach the stable. Rex could see he had swerved off the faint contours of the road, which curved sharply to the left. "Hierax!" he called. "That's a shepherd's trail! The road's over this way!"

Hierax had just started to turn back when a shaggy brown creature exploded from the nearby brush. Its resonant, low-pitched barking signaled it was some kind of mastiff. *A Molossian hound!* Rex knew the breed well. With its massive shoulders and huge jaws, it was a fearsome sight. The dogs were ill-tempered and fiercely protective.

Hierax's mule spooked as the hound barreled toward it. Slipping in the icy mess, the mule sent its rider sprawling. The Molossian looked like it was going to tear the helpless rider apart. Grabbing his javelin, Rex leapt from the saddle and sprinted to intercept the barking dog.

"Easy, boy! Easy!" he said in an authoritative voice, waving his spear above his head to offer some intimidation. Though the animal halted, the fangs bared in its droopy jowls announced it wasn't there to play. Rex had never seen such a thick, muscular neck on a dog.

"Kill it!" Hierax shouted from his sprawl on the ground.

"He's only protecting his home," Rex said, keeping his eyes on the Molossian. "These dogs are loyal to their master and their flock. They'll find you in the snow if you ever get lost. Great noses. Good working breed too. We have them in the forests of Germania."

"My leg's broke! That dog deserves to die!"

"You went off the road. It's your fault, not the dog's."

117

The injured soldier muttered a curse, but Rex ignored him. He began to back away, making no sudden movements. Though the Molossian was still growling, it did not advance, suggesting the standoff might end with a peaceful resolution. Rex risked a glance over his shoulder—and was shocked by what he saw.

Hierax stood braced against a boulder on one leg. His bow was in his outstretched hand, with an arrow nocked on the string. The man had seen action along the Euphrates River against the Persian bowmen. Like all Scythian legionaries, he was a skilled archer who rarely missed his mark.

"Hierax! No!"

Rex flipped his javelin around and grasped it near the head. Swatting the butt end at Hierax, he managed to jostle the man's forearm as he released his shot. The arrow went wide and plunged harmlessly into a snowdrift. The dog let out a series of deep-throated barks but held its ground.

"You raise a weapon against a fellow soldier?" Hierax roared, drawing his spatha from its sheath.

"Calm down and put your sword away. Your leg is broken and you're about to faint. I wasn't attacking you. I just didn't want you to kill the dog. Let's get you up into the saddle. It will be dark within an hour."

Aratus and Geta arrived then, dismounting to help the injured legionary climb astride his mule while the hound watched suspiciously. The men returned to the main highway, riding in silence until they reached the military hostel on the pass just as the sun's last rays were disappearing from the sky. A milestone stood outside the inn, inscribed with the letters *IMP CAES CONSTANTINUS*. Rex saluted the stone and offered a short prayer for the success of the emperor's mission.

That night after dinner, Rex, Geta, and Aratus gathered around the hearth fire with cups of hot mulled wine and a big bowl of nuts. Hierax was dozing fitfully in the next room, moaning occasionally.

"It will take a while to get a doctor up from the valley," Aratus said. "Hierax is going to need his fracture set and splinted. Then they'll transport him by wagon back to Octodurus."

"I hope they can do that before the really big snows arrive," Geta said, "or it's going to be a long winter for him." The other men nodded their agreement. They huddled into their blankets and stared at the flames.

"Looks like it's just us, then," Rex observed after a thoughtful silence.

Aratus shrugged, his demeanor steady and confident as befitted a Roman centurion. "Three is enough for the mission. We'll be fine."

"What's our cover?" Geta asked. "We're obviously not Italians." He gestured toward Rex with his cup. "Especially not this guy. With his yellow hair and those bulging muscles, the Romans are going to think Thor has descended from his thunderstorm straight into the Forum!"

"And with that golden princess braid running down your back, they'll think pretty Freyja has come with me!" Rex shot back. Geta pelted Rex with a chestnut, and the two men broke into boisterous laughter.

Aratus chuckled at his men's jests. "I would think you two hated each other if I only had your words to go on." He rubbed his palm across the flat, close-cropped stubble on his scalp. "But you're right. This Greek stuff will go unnoticed in the capital, but you fair-haired boys will stand out as Germani. I'm not worried, though. All kinds of people pass through Rome. We just need a good excuse to explain your presence there."

Geta raised his hand. "I volunteer to be the exotic barbarian lover of some rich lady."

"Rich *blind* lady," Rex added.

Aratus shook his head with another laugh. "Bad idea. You don't know that upper-class culture well enough. You'd stick out too much. What we really know is the army. So how about this? We're former mercenaries from along the Rhenus. Our unit was disbanded, and now we're hunting work. We're just some soldiers of fortune whose lifelong dream has been to serve in the emperor's bodyguard. Rome is our great hope and destiny."

"Do the Praetorians admit Germani?" Geta asked.

"The Praetorian prefect is a man named Ruricius Pompeianus. He's known to be cruel, vindictive, and utterly ruthless. He gets what he wants, and if that means using frontier boys alongside the Italians, he's not above it. Show him a little courage and a strong arm, and he'll enlist you among the Praetorians. Or you can try the imperial horse guard—it has always been composed of Germani. The times are gone when Rome can be snobby about who fights its wars. There are lots of barbarians in the army these days, and that number isn't going down anytime soon. Yes, you can get in."

"So we'll be enlisted into the famous Praetorian Guard, or maybe even the Emperor's Personal Cavalry," Rex said. "But that means we'll be fighting against our own side once Constantine shows up. We'll have to switch back if it comes to a battle."

"Right. I hope it'll be as simple as riding over to Constantine's battle line and exchanging your insignia. In the meantime, this mission will test your undercover skills. How well can you maintain your secret identity in the midst of your enemies? I guess we'll find out."

"You won't be disappointed, sir."

Aratus gave Rex a firm stare. "I'd better not be. I thought I was going to have to stop a civil war on the road today. Trouble seems to follow you wherever you go."

"It wasn't my fault! That dog came out of nowhere. Hierax was going to kill him."

"Better the hound than you."

"Sure! Like Hierax could manage that," Rex scoffed.

"You're not invincible, son." Aratus tipped back his head and finished his hot wine, then set down the cup. "Alright, men, this is where we go undercover. I guess we're now provincial mercenaries seeking work. We'll ditch our armor and military uniforms. Just the rough clothes of the Germani from now on. Start growing out your beards. Your hair's plenty long already. When we get to Rome, you should hide your combat skills. Fumble with your sword, ride a little awkward, perform just well enough to get enlisted. Act like farm boys from Germania trying to make a future for yourselves in the army. And whatever you do—don't make a scene! Always stay in the background. We're trying to keep a low profile and blend in."

"Stealth," Geta said. "The speculator's most basic art."

"Exactly." Aratus rose to his feet. "Now follow me outside. I want to show you something."

The three men went out to the cold, barren pass. The marble temple of Jupiter Poeninus glowed white in the pale moonlight—the very place where Rex had finished the race in triumph two years earlier. Aratus had ended his training that day, along with Geta. Now he commanded his two soldiers to stand next to the official milestone that marked the road's high point. "Whose name is written there?" he asked.

Geta had somehow acquired a decent education despite his humble background, so he read the letters—and since Rex's mother had taught him to read, he could follow along too. "It says, 'Emperor Constantine, the caesar,'" Geta declared. "At least that's what he was when the stone was made. Now he's claimed the higher title of augustus."

"Yes. And here at this spot, I want you to swear an oath of loyalty to him. Renew your vows to his genius. Pledge to give your lives to protect his divine personage."

The two speculators placed their hands on the milestone and swore the oaths demanded by their centurion. When they were finished, they looked up at him. He had moved a few steps away in the snow. Behind him, the mountains receded toward the southern horizon. Beyond that were only the stars.

"At attention!" Aratus ordered in a crisp military voice. Rex and Geta straightened their shoulders and stiffened their backs.

"Three steps forward, then halt!"

The men complied.

Slowly, Aratus approached his two young speculators, looking them both in the eyes. He put one hand on the shoulder of each. Rex felt his commander give his arm a squeeze.

"You just crossed into Italy, boys," Aratus said. "Your mission begins at dawn."

They will not break me, Flavia vowed. *I will not give them that satisfaction!*

She had made that promise more times than she could count since the soldiers brought her to the prison. But in truth, she wasn't so sure anymore. She could feel her resolve ebbing, along with her body heat, into the cold stones on which she lay.

Life in the infamous Carcer had been about as bad as Flavia could have imagined. Everyone knew the prison's reputation: it was the dank holding cell at the foot of the Capitoline Hill, where Rome's most notorious prisoners were kept until they were paraded to their executions. The place was almost completely dark, lit only by whatever light trickled between the stone blocks of the walls or beneath the ironbound door. The air reeked of excrement and body odor and moldy straw. Flavia's wrists were rubbed raw by her shackles, the cuffs now sticky with blood. A bribe from a Christian deacon had assured that bread crusts and lentils were provided daily, along with a jug of brackish water and a chamber pot that was exchanged when it was full. But these were Flavia's only comforts. She passed the time in darkness, fear, and boredom. Through two long days and nights, Flavia had languished in the Carcer with no visitors allowed. Now it was the third day—and Flavia was praying for a triumphant resurrection just like the Lord Jesus Christ's.

But it did not come. She dozed off and on, grateful for the snatched moments of sleep, since there was nothing else to do. Outside, a rainstorm developed, dropped its water, then passed. The sun came out again and the prison grew warmer—a welcome relief from the chill.

Suddenly the door burst open and bright sunlight flooded the gloomy chamber. Flavia squinted against the glare, trying to discern who had entered. From the jingling sound of armor, she realized the men were Praetorians.

"Get up, canicula!" one of them said. "It's judgment time."

Flavia was hauled to her feet. The nice woolen dress she had been wearing the day of her arrest was filthy now, and her expensive sandals had been confiscated as "payment" for the jail's "hospitality." With her hair tangled and her feet covered in slime, Flavia knew she looked more like a street orphan than a member of the senatorial class. *Surely Father will be waiting outside, ready to put an end to this travesty!* But the only people in the street were gawkers and guards.

The Praetorians escorted Flavia to the Senate House next door. She had been here on several prior occasions, though never while the congress was in session. Now a few important men sat in the rows of chairs, wearing elegant togas with purple stripes while servants and bureaucrats in less impressive garb scurried here and there on unknown errands. Flavia craned her neck, trying to spot her father among the other aristocrats, but it soon became obvious he wasn't present. The only face she recognized was that of Ruricius Pompeianus, the stocky Praetorian prefect with the nasty scar on his cheek. He stood next to the Altar of Winged Victory at the rear of the chamber. Another man stood next to him—handsome, fashionable, and self-assured. His satchel was made of expensive leather. He had the slick look of a lawyer.

The guards brought Flavia to the altar, where Pompeianus was waiting. He gazed at her with disapproving eyes, looking her up and down. "Dirty little thing," he muttered to the lawyer next to him, not even lowering himself to insult her to her face.

"What do you expect? I've been kept in the Carcer for three days," Flavia said, trying to be bold.

Pompeianus didn't answer but only waved at some senators who had congregated in a corner of the hall. They began to shuffle over, their expressions cold and aloof. Dread clawed at Flavia's heart. *Surely these men aren't my jury? Can this be my trial? Where is my advocate? My witnesses? My impartial judge?*

And great God, where is my father?

When twenty or so senators had seated themselves around the Altar of Victory, Pompeianus signaled for their attention. "Esteemed colleagues," he began, "I thank you for your service on behalf of the great Maxentius. The wise and ever-busy augustus cannot grace us with the scintillating illumination of his glorious presence today. In fact, his placid mind does not even need to be disturbed with news of trifles like this! Therefore we shall protect his sensibilities and leave it to you, O illustrious senators, to render a verdict in the case of"—he swept his hand at Flavia—"this *infection* upon the face of Rome."

The senators mumbled at the prefect's effective preamble. Flavia glanced from face to face, pleading with her eyes, but no one offered any support.

"Lest it seem that this case is one-sided and justice has been miscarried," Pompeianus went on, "Lady Junia Flavia has been provided with legal counsel today."

A skinny man with an unruly shock of white hair and a beak-shaped nose was introduced as the lawyer Gracchus. He would speak on behalf of Flavia, while the distinguished lawyer standing next to Pompeianus—Tertius, his name was—would prosecute on behalf of the Senate and People of Rome.

With a gravity and solemnity more suited to an assassin caught in the act of regicide than a seventeen-year-old who had buried a priest, Tertius paced before the circle of senators and spun a tale of Flavia's devious misdeeds.

Though she was forbidden to speak, she wanted to correct nearly every sentence that oozed from the lawyer's mouth. His exaggerations and insinuations put her in the worst possible light. Several senators were nodding vigorously, while others were daydreaming or taking a few desultory notes on wax tablets. Flavia could see that, unless Gracchus was the best rhetorician since Cicero, this wasn't a case she could win. In fact, even Rome's greatest orator himself couldn't have won this case after all the lies Tertius was spewing.

The oily lawyer was building to a climax now. "Not only did this rebellious woman have the audacity to bury a despicable Christian bishop," he declared, "it seems she is one of those fanatics herself—"

"Wait! Stop!" Pompeianus held up his hand and called for the stenographer's attention. "Scribe, strike that statement from your report. The religious status of the defendant is of no concern to us today. We are only considering her crimes against the emperor's majesty under time-honored Roman law."

With the correction made, Tertius finished his case with a flourish, indulging in a stream of vituperation against the frivolity of upper-class girls in Roman society. Satisfied, he took his seat and ceded his place to Gracchus.

The beak-nosed advocate was, as Flavia expected, no Ciceronian orator. He defended his client with such amateurish rhetoric that half the senators in the jury turned up their noses at his infelicitous wording while the other half dozed off. His actual rebuttals were few, and the many accusations he left unrefuted were damning. Tears gathered in Flavia's eyes as she realized the verdict was now certain to go against her. After a brief consultation, the most powerful men in Rome returned their decision: guilty of treason and degraded in rank to "more humble" status.

"I am the daughter of the sitting city prefect," Flavia said firmly, trying to mask her hurt and frustration at the injustice. "Senators of Rome, I respectfully ask why he is not here today."

Pompeianus flicked his hand dismissively. "A messenger was sent to summon him. But how can we help it if those lazy messengers get distracted and stop at a tavern along the way? The work of the law must go on, despite any human shortcomings." He bowed toward the jury. "Gentlemen, your work today is done. Rome thanks you."

As the senators dispersed, Pompeianus turned to Flavia. "And now, Lady Junia, it seems it is my prerogative to hand down your sentence. I have mulled it over carefully, and I have even prayed to holy Jupiter for wisdom. The highest and best god has made it clear to me what the penalty must be." Though the prefect's thin smile attempted to feign civility, the scar on his cheek only made his grin look maniacal. "I am very sorry to say you will have to be damned to the wild beasts."

No more terrifying words had ever been uttered in Flavia's presence. The prospect of being mauled by animals and devoured alive as entertainment for the masses was a fate too horrific to comprehend. Her mind reeled at the idea, rejecting it as unreal. *What's going on here? This can't be happening! When will this nightmare end?*

Two guards approached at Pompeianus's signal. "Praetorians, escort the lady straight to her accommodations. The games begin tomorrow morning. We'd like her to be well rested so she can give the lions some strenuous exercise before they dine."

"You can't throw me into the amphitheater!" Flavia exclaimed. "I'm of the honorable class—free from corporal punishments!"

"Not anymore, little one. You've been degraded as part of your sentence. No more legal immunity. The beasts it is." Pompeianus waved away the guards with the back of his hand. "Go on, now. Take her back to the prison. In fact—drop her into the Tullianum this time."

No! Not the dungeon!

The Praetorians hauled Flavia to the Carcer, dragging her whenever she dug in her heels. She quickly realized there was no point in resisting, for the men were far too strong. Back at the prison, the soldiers forced her toward a hole in the floor. When the trapdoor was opened, the gush of putrid air made Flavia retch. That wasn't just the stink of human waste—it was decomposed human flesh.

Oh God, please . . . not that!

The men paid no attention to Flavia's squirming and frantic begging. They lifted the hem of her dress and forced a board between her thighs, making crude remarks the whole time. The board had been fastened to a rope by which to lower her into the pit. Flavia was forced to sit on the edge of the hole, her legs dangling into the blackness.

"No! Stop! Don't make me—"

Cruel hands gave her a hard shove in the back. Flavia screamed.

She landed in a puddle of vomitus that could only have trickled from the mouth of Satan himself. The thick paste reeked of death and decay. A sudden yank on the rope snatched the board from between her legs, scraping her skin and overturning her into the cesspool on the floor of the Tullianum. Flavia gagged as the stench filled her nostrils.

"Next time, be a good girl and obey your betters," one of the Praetorians said from the circle of light above. He guffawed and began to close the trapdoor.

Flavia reached her hand to the ceiling. "Wait! Wait!" she cried weakly.

The world went utterly black. No way out.

Deafening silence.

Ocean waves of fear washed over Flavia. The subterranean walls seemed ready to collapse, to press in, to suffocate and extinguish all semblance of life and breath and hope. The earth had swallowed her whole. She couldn't move. She forgot to exhale. All she could do was clutch her skirt in her fists, fighting to keep from going insane.

And then a blood-chilling voice spoke from the darkness. "Hello, my lovely," it croaked. "Come over here and see me. We're going to have some fun."

Oh no . . . I'm not alone.

❦

The big gate at the suburban villa of Maxentius on the Appian Way was ominous and overbearing. Sophronia hated the very sight of it. Only one impetus was strong enough to bring her to the emperor's residence: the love of a mother for her child.

Bishop Miltiades had visited Pompeianus a few days earlier, but his petition about Flavia had been rebuffed with cruel disdain. The godly priest had practically been tossed from the House of Fausta by force. Neratius was likewise thwarted by the politics of the matter, for Pompeianus deeply resented being passed over as city prefect, and he was powerful enough to keep the case tied up in legal wrangling for the time being. *And while the men bickered, maneuvered, and hashed things out, poor Flavia was languish-*

ing in a filthy dungeon! It was more than Sophronia could bear. *Surely the emperor will have regard for an anguished mother*, she told herself as she stared at the foreboding gate. *Perhaps he will receive a petition from an old acquaintance begging at his door?* It was worth a try, at least.

And so she rang the bell.

The gatekeeper emerged from his booth with an irritated frown. He scratched himself and yawned. "Who are you?"

"Sabina Sophronia, a senator's wife. I have a petition for your master, the augustus of Rome."

"Does he expect you?"

"No. But he knows me. We attended parties together in our youth." The statement was not a lie. Sophronia and Maxentius were approximately the same age, and when both were in their teens, they had known each other casually in aristocratic circles. She had been under her father's authority then: a daughter of the Sabinus clan whose roots went all the way back to the Republic. In her teenage years, she had been known as Sabina, and she had acquired her identifying name of Sophronia, which meant "chastity," in part because of the moral restraint she had displayed as a Christian in those decadent circles. Upon marrying Neratius, she had not been given formally into his hand but remained instead under the legal jurisdiction of her family of origin and retained the clan name. Either way, the Junii and Sabini were families of high esteem, so an audience with the emperor did not seem out of the question.

Unfortunately, the gate attendant was unimpressed by Sophronia's credentials. "If you have something to pass along, I will give it to the chamberlain. Otherwise you can sit right here, because the Divine Augustus is headed into the city at noon."

He's coming out? Thank you, gracious Lord!

"I will remain here and wait," Sophronia said, then retired to the shade of her carriage.

The sun had dropped passed its zenith when the gate finally swung open and an imperial procession emerged. The emperor's carriage was obvious, for its every surface was gilded. Sophronia knew that when the procession reached the city walls, Maxentius would transfer into a litter, because the noise of vehicles was forbidden on urban streets. For now, though, he rode along in golden splendor behind four white stallions. This quiet spot in the countryside was the perfect place to catch his attention.

When the ornate carriage drew near, Sophronia stepped onto the ancient cobblestones of the Appian Way. "Great Augustus," she cried. "I am an old friend of yours! I seek a word!"

The vehicle kept rolling. Sophronia watched it go, unsure if her chances would be helped or hurt by running after it. Abruptly, the carriage came to a stop. A man emerged from the cab, clearly some kind of palace functionary. He signaled to Sophronia that she may approach.

Although Sophronia kept her eyes down, a quick glance from beneath her brows allowed her to spot the emperor in the depths of the carriage. He had a thin beard now but otherwise looked much the same: sallow, morose, and haughty.

"Lady Sabina Sophronia," came his smooth, regal voice from the cab. "Let me have a look at you." The emperor paused for a moment, then remarked, "You still have all the womanly charms of your youth. I only pray you have not retained so much *sophrosune*." His use of the Greek word for chastity was both a pun and a proof of his high culture. A little titter of laughter emanated from the carriage.

Sophronia switched into Greek. "I greet you, Augustus, with all the modesty and chastity suitable to a noble Roman matron like myself. Though I hesitate to stop you on the highway like a common brigand, nonetheless, my business demands it. I wish to give you a petition regarding a grievous matter that must come to your attention."

"Very well," Maxentius replied in equally fluid Greek. "Hand it to my servant, madam, and I shall read it. But I cannot delay for long."

After handing over the scroll, Sophronia waited anxiously for a reply. One simple prayer tumbled through her mind, prompted perhaps by just having spoken in Greek. *Kyrie eleison*, she prayed again and again. *Lord, have mercy!* Though it wasn't the most eloquent prayer she had ever offered to the heavens, it was all she could manage right now. She thought God wouldn't mind.

The crumpled parchment flew from the carriage and fell to the cobblestones. "Lady Sabina, you disappoint me," Maxentius said. "Treason against your emperor is never excusable. Perhaps I should have you come visit me sometime so I can make sure your love for your lord is as fervent as ever."

"Your Highness, I—"

"Onward!" Maxentius shouted, and the driver immediately snapped the reins. Sophronia could only watch from the middle of the highway as the gilded carriage rolled away toward the city.

Disconsolate, Sophronia returned to her own vehicle and climbed in. Now she knew where she needed to go. All of her supporters and allies had failed. No politician, no powerful husband, not even a bishop had been able to avert the disaster that awaited Flavia. There was only one group of patrons who could help now—one group of friends who would rally in fervent prayer to turn aside the terrible course of events. God alone would be Flavia's protector! Sophronia intended to usher a prayerful host of her fellow Christians into the throne room of the Almighty. It was exactly the privilege the Risen Christ had made available to true believers. Now, in her moment of greatest need, Sophronia decided to avail herself of that privilege.

The carriage stopped a short distance up the road. Sophronia stepped down and passed through an archway whose gate stood wide open. Another door took her deep underground. By the light of a single lamp she located the grave of Eusebius. After setting the oil lamp on the marble lid of his tomb, she knelt before it.

A deep silence descended, surrounding Sophronia in its holy embrace. And there, in the gloomy darkness that mimicked Flavia's dungeon, the terrified mother asked the saints of all the ages to add their voices to the groanings of her soul.

<hr />

The Milvian Bridge marked, so it seemed to Rex, the outer limits of Rome. It was an old bridge that carried the Flaminian Way across the Tiberis. *The ancient and famous Tiberis!* There it was beneath the arches—a muddier and more turgid river than one would normally imagine for such a great city, but historic, nonetheless. Rex felt that having crossed the Tiberis, he had now officially arrived at the capital. From the bridge he could see the city walls only two miles to the south, stretching west and east with no visible end in either direction. The circumference of those walls was beyond comprehension. Rome was more vast than Rex had ever imagined.

Aratus reined up next to Rex on the road. "First look at the Eternal City, eh? I remember being stunned the first time I saw her too. I had thought Athenae was magnificent. And Antiochia impressed me even more. But Rome? It's no wonder this city rules the world. So many people gathered in one place can't be stopped."

"Let's see if Rome's women are as impressive as its walls," Geta said. A little kick of his heels goaded his horse into movement, and the others followed him.

Two miles down the highway, at the Flaminian Gate in the Aurelian Walls, the road became an urban street called Broadway. The three speculators left their mounts with the hostlers at the imperial post station and traveled by foot into the city. Rex thought the smells and sounds were much like he had experienced elsewhere, but the sheer scale of them was dizzying. The buildings themselves seemed to hum and throb with frenetic energy.

Broadway offered a straight shot from the outer gate to the original defensive ring of the city, the ancient but now defunct Servian Wall. Here the street terminated at the foot of the Capitoline Hill. Rex couldn't help but stare at the temple looming above him on Rome's highest peak. Its polished marble columns and golden roof gleamed in the morning sunlight like celestial beacons. Surely a god who occupied such a powerful and commanding site must be worthy of his name: Jupiter, the Best and Greatest.

"Let's go up and take in the view," Aratus said. "Remember to act like provincials. Wide-eyed and amazed. Frontier yokels coming to the big city."

Geta chuckled. "That won't be hard. That's pretty much what we are."

"Hoods up, men, and don't make eye contact." Aratus pulled his own cloak over his head and started up the Capitoline.

The view from the top was worth the ascent. Rex could see the vastness of the city spread in every direction, reaching almost to the horizon. "See there? That's the Palatine," Aratus said, pointing to the next hill over. It was surmounted by one glorious building after another. "The emperors live there. Down below is the Forum, the beating heart of Rome. Senators speak to the masses from that platform, the Rostra. The Senate House is beside it, to the left."

"What's that building at the far end of the square?" Rex asked.

"The Temple of the Divine Julius Caesar. It marks the spot where his body was cremated after his assassination on the Ides of March. His soul ascended into heaven as a comet."

Rex turned to his centurion. "You really know a lot about Rome, sir. I'm impressed."

"Every good Roman knows this stuff. Get used to it—this is your new home."

In the distance, a roar arose from the Flavian Amphitheater. Rex turned to a slave passing by with a handcart. "Games happening today?" he asked in a friendly voice.

"Just some mimes and clowns for the early arrivals right now," the slave said as he hurried on. "The beast hunt starts in three hours. People are saying fifty fierce lions have been brought in from Africa."

"Fifty lions!" Geta exclaimed. "I've always wanted to see a lion." He turned to Aratus. "We should go. What do you think?"

"I think frivolous entertainments might deter you boys from your mission."

Rex shook his head at this. "Sir, nothing on this wide earth could deter me from my mission."

After a moment of contemplation, a slow smile spread across the centurion's face. "Alright, boys, I guess it won't hurt. We should go see the spectacles. After all, we're Romans now."

Romans now, Rex mused. *I could get used to that.*

Day and night were irrelevant. There was only the cruel darkness of the Tullianum—oppressive, indifferent, and unrelenting.

Flavia couldn't remember the outside world anymore. Her will to live was gone. She sat silent and numb, leaning against a wall so she could at least have a sense of space in the total blackness. A warped and twisted man was down here too, or maybe he was some kind of demon from the underworld. From time to time he spoke, and he had even grabbed her leg at one point. A hard kick had silenced him. The rattling of metal indicated he was chained. He seemed too weakened by hunger to move around much. Most of his incoherent babbling had to do with food—although sexual lust was mixed into his rants too, which made Flavia very glad for the chain.

Hours passed—or maybe they were days? When a circle of light suddenly pooled on the floor, Flavia had a hard time recognizing what it was. "Woman!" a voice shouted from above. "Seat yourself on the board if you want up!"

Though her mind was fogged and disoriented, Flavia still had enough sense to realize she was being offered release from the dungeon. She straddled the board and was hauled through the hole into the upper chamber of the Carcer. Compared to the pit, it seemed like a palace.

"Don't get too happy," one of the soldiers said roughly. "By noon you'll be in another dark hole—only in bite-size pieces!" The joke made the other Praetorians burst into laughter.

A spark of defiance rose up within Flavia—a renewed burst of strength that she could only attribute to the Holy Spirit. "My father will be intervening soon," she declared, "but if not, I will be received into the arms of my Savior. I am not afraid of death. Many will see my faith and believe. The blood of Christians is seed."

"The blood of Christians is great entertainment," the guardsman replied. "People love to watch it gush into the sand. Now get going."

The man gave Flavia a hard shove toward the door of the Carcer. She was led out into the Forum by the soldiers. Though she had to squint and shade her eyes in the early morning glare, she could still see the looks of horror on the bystanders' faces. Some covered their mouths and retched as they backed away. Others gawked and pointed. Flavia knew she must have looked like a corpse dredged up from the Great Sewer by the watermen.

"Take her to the House of the Vestals," the jailer ordered. "Prefect Pompeianus said to make her look recognizable as a senator's daughter. Pay the virgins to fix her up, then escort her to the amphitheater."

Flavia was marched across the Forum to the mansion where the priestesses of the goddess Vesta lived. Supposedly they were the pure, virgin daughters of Rome who tended the sacred hearth fire for the entire city. In reality, they were privileged elitists who wielded a lot of power and would lead comfortable lives when their thirty-year term of service was over.

The House of the Vestals stood next to the round temple that mimicked the huts built by Rome's original settlers. A lone guard took Flavia into an oblong courtyard centered on a lovely pool. Though the priestesses themselves were nowhere to be seen, a few female servants were busy with their work. One of them, obviously high-ranking, stopped the Praetorian in his tracks. "Don't take another step, guardsman!" she barked. "No vile man should ever peer into this sacred house, much less enter it!"

The soldier swallowed and shifted his feet. "Pardon, lady," he said. "The Praetorian prefect wants this girl cleaned up. He asks that you wash her off and put her in a decent robe, then bring her back to me. He will compensate you generously."

The servant frowned but nodded her agreement. Two girls came forward and escorted Flavia to a small bath facility. Hurriedly, yet without apparent revulsion, the girls scrubbed her body with sponges, oiled her skin, and scraped away the filth with a strigil. A rose-colored tunic of good wool was brought, which Flavia gladly slipped over her head. She found herself alone in the bathroom with a stout, olive-skinned girl whose expression was crafty.

"Where are they taking you?" the servant whispered as she tied on Flavia's sandal.

"The games. Wild beasts."

The girl glanced over her shoulder and looked about. "I unlocked the door on the far side of the courtyard. It leads up the Palatine. The alleys are like a maze up there. You could disappear."

"You would do that for me? Why?"

"People like us have to stick together. We can't let the arrogant win."

Flavia's heart began to beat rapidly. *This is my deliverance!*

"Wh-when should I go?" she asked.

"I'll make a disturbance. Be ready."

Flavia nodded, and the girl disappeared out the door. A few moments later, there was a loud crash and a shout, accompanied by the barking of a dog. "Catch that stray mutt!" a female voice bellowed.

God help me, Flavia prayed, and bolted from the room.

———⌘———

Strolling through the Forum, Rex imagined himself a senator in a purple-striped toga, having just delivered a great speech that won him an elected office. Though he knew it was a silly fantasy, it was fun to pretend, nonetheless.

Rome's glory was too bright and splendid not to indulge in a little wishful thinking.

The three speculators jostled their way through the crowds along Sacred Street, taking in all the eye-popping sights at every turn. Just like Aratus had suggested, so many kinds of people clogged this city that a blond, long-haired barbarian drew no special attention. Rex sensed he and Geta were going entirely unnoticed. After passing the Temple of Julius Caesar, they stopped in front of a huge government hall that was currently under construction.

"That's the New Basilica of Maxentius," Aratus announced. "There's going to be a colossal statue of him seated in the apse."

"Look at the size of that place! The statue will be huge once they put it in. I hope I'll still be here to see it," Geta said.

"No you don't," Rex countered. "We hope the statue will be of Const—"

"Quiet, soldier," Aratus said sternly.

Rex nodded dutifully to his commanding officer. "Sorry, sir. Forgot."

A little farther on, Sacred Street ran under the Arch of Titus. Rex walked beneath its high, curved vault. A frieze on the right side depicted downcast captives being led away with their treasures—among which was a seven-branched candlestick.

"Jews?" Rex asked, having seen the same image on a synagogue wall.

"Aye. Conquered by Emperor Titus in Hierusalem. They were brought here as slaves to build the Flavian Amphitheater."

"Let's get there quick," Geta said. "I'm starving. I want to find a seat and get something hot to eat."

The three men turned to go when a commotion arose behind them. Shouts could be heard above the general din, and people were being shoved out of the way. Soldiers were running after a fugitive—a woman in a pale pink tunic. She was dark-haired and slim yet curvaceous. As she drew near, Rex could see she was young, probably still in her teens. The cruel soldiers were gaining on her. Rex found his gaze transfixed by the young woman and her desperate plight.

Aratus pulled his men back into the crowd. "Stay quiet," he said. "Keep a low profile."

The woman had just reached the arch when one of the Praetorians finally tripped her from behind. She went sprawling, coming to rest near Rex's feet.

"Thought you could get away, did ya?" The guardsman put his boot on his captive's back and pressed her down while he clamped a manacle on her raw, red wrist.

"Who is she?" Rex whispered to a bystander.

"Senator's daughter, Lady Junia Flavia," the man said. "She's been convicted of treason. It'll be the wild beasts for her!"

The soldier raised Flavia to her knees and started fiddling with her second handcuff. She held her head high, still noble and defiant despite the harsh mistreatment. At the same time, Rex could sense her desperation too.

"She's gorgeous," Geta murmured.

Flavia's determined gaze scanned the faces in the crowd. Each person looked away as she sought an ally or friend. But when her attention came to rest on Rex, they locked eyes for what seemed like a very long moment. At last she said simply, "I am an innocent woman. Help me!"

"Shut up, wench!" snapped one of the soldiers—and then he did something Rex would never forget.

Raising his hand above his head, the huge man brought it around in a swift arc that caught Flavia square on the cheek. The sound of the slap was noticeable even above the hubbub of the crowd. A cry burst from Flavia's lips, and she tumbled to the pavement, her hands fastened behind her back. The other soldiers cheered.

As Rex started to move forward, Aratus grabbed his forearm. "Stand down, Rex," he muttered. "That's an order."

"But the girl needs my help—"

"So what? You're on a *mission*."

"I want to help her. Someone has to. There's no one else!"

"What are you talking about, soldier?" Aratus hissed. "You said nothing on this wide earth could ever deter you from your mission!"

Rex paused, gathering his resolve.

He wrenched his arm from his commanding officer's grip. The woman's crisis had touched something inside of Rex, something primal within the soul of every man. *I am one of the most proficient warriors in the empire! I can stop this travesty if I wish. And right here . . . right now . . . for this woman . . .*

I wish.

At last he looked straight at Aratus. "I just found the one thing that can," he declared.

He bent down to Lady Junia Flavia and helped her to her knees. Her brown hair dangled in her eyes, but a flick of her head revealed her delicate face. One cheek was red where she had been slapped. Rex stared at her, and the woman looking back at him with hazel eyes was undoubtedly the loveliest creature he had ever seen. Though she was frightened, she was tranquil too—somehow peaceful even in the midst of adversity. "I am Brandulf Rex," he told her quietly as the soldiers began to yank her away, "and I'm going to get you out of this."

"I know," the woman called over her shoulder. Then she was swallowed by the crowd.

ACT 2

RESISTANCE

5

OCTOBER 311

The Flavian Amphitheater was Rome's greatest temple, a place to worship what the empire admired most: the conquest and destruction of the weak by the strong. Here, mighty gladiators fought to the death, hunters confronted fearsome animals, and the noxious elements of human society were reduced to fodder for wild beasts. Before an eager audience, the sandy floor of the arena combined bloodshed, sport, voyeurism, drama, and death. When filled to its brim with thousands of spectators, the oval building would shiver and roar and gasp like a living creature. Even as Flavia approached it now, pushed along in her chains by the cruel Praetorians, she could hear the growl of its bestial stomach as it hungered for fresh meat. The great amphitheater of Rome always clamored to be fed.

That building won't devour me today! Flavia vowed.

Yet what could she do to stop the insane course of events that had brought her to this place? It seemed unreal, like it wasn't actually happening. *Is this really the last day of my life? Has it all come down to this?* Ducking her head as she was forced through a small door that led into an underground tunnel, Flavia found herself wavering between faith in God's deliverance and the awful realization that his martyrs were manifold. There was no reason she couldn't join them today.

The dimly lit tunnel ran a short distance from the gladiator barracks to the subterranean chambers beneath the amphitheater's floor. Down here, the air was stuffy and hot. The narrow passageways stank of sulfurous torches and animal dung. Flavia was led to a holding cell, where her handcuffs were removed. She could feel the thrum of the crowd above her now, pulsing through the stone walls, pulsing into her very bones. It was the cumulative vibration of fifty thousand people, all of them calling for her blood.

"Enjoy the last hour of your life, *canicula!*" one of the Praetorians sneered. Flavia recognized him as the cruel man who had slapped her. Though his term *canicula* was designed to degrade her to the status of a dirty female dog wandering the streets, Flavia refused to let the man's words rule her.

"I am a daughter of God," she said plainly, "no matter what you say. And you could be his child too, if you would leave your life of violence and turn to him."

The Praetorian's face scrunched into an angry grimace. He stomped over to Flavia, staring her down. "Listen to me, you piece of dung," he said with a vicious snarl, "I'm going out now to get a cup of wine. Within an hour, I will be sipping it in my seat, laughing as I watch the lions feast on your steaming guts while you're gasping your final breaths." The hulking soldier hawked up a wad of mucus and spat it on the ground. "That's what I think of you and your jackass of a god."

Flavia could only stand wide-eyed and speechless in the face of such savage hatred. Though cruelty from the Praetorians was nothing new, the utter lack of compassion in these words hit her like a physical blow. When the soldier slammed the door to the cell and locked it behind him, leaving her alone, she crumpled to the hard stone floor.

The last remnants of Flavia's resolve drained away. Sweat broke out all over her body, and she began to shake uncontrollably. There had been so many chances for deliverance, but they had all failed. What hope was left? Her powerful father had been exposed as impotent. Her dash from the House of the Vestals had been intercepted by her captors. Even the muscular barbarian in the street—a man who looked strong enough to help if anyone could—had vanished into the crowd and was gone. Would he come and save her? Flavia had believed his words of intent, knowing them to be true on some instinctive level. Yet with so much hatred directed against her, even that firm assurance now evaporated. All rescue had fallen short, and that could mean only one thing.

I am indeed going to die today—in great pain, hated for my faith, and scorned by a bloodthirsty mob.

"Make me worthy," Flavia whispered. It was all she could say. Though the martyrs in the stories were always tranquil at this point, Flavia could feel nothing but the icy grip of horror at what awaited her. She closed her eyes. A numbness settled on her, perhaps even a kind of fitful sleep.

The loud bang of the door slamming against the wall awakened Flavia with a startled yelp. Two burly slaves barged into the cell and hauled her to her feet. "It's a good day to die," one of them said, laughing as he shoved her out the door. He led her to a wooden contraption in the dim underground chambers. It was a sort of cage that could be raised by ropes and wheels. She was about to be forced inside when a high-pitched voice called for a halt. "Wait! Bring her to me," the effeminate speaker said.

Flavia was taken to an extravagantly dressed stage actor holding a tray of face paints. He gripped her chin and inspected her face for a moment, then slathered some rouge on her cheeks and colored her eyelids blue. After applying garish lip paint and tying a pink ribbon in her hair, he stepped back and smiled as if he had accomplished something great. "Remember, little pretty, this isn't just an execution," the mime said with a girlish tit-ter. "It's a *spectacle*. You're part of a bigger story. Let's give the people the drama they deserve." He beckoned to Flavia's two handlers. "She's ready to go. You can take her away."

Now Flavia was enclosed in the cage. A moment later she felt herself being hauled upward; the higher she went, the louder the roar of the crowd grew. It swelled from a sonorous rumble to a throbbing resonance, then finally to a fierce and restless roar. The cage stopped beneath a wooden ceiling the slats of which, glowing bright with sunlight, indicated the arena floor was just above.

Flavia's heart was beating wildly now. Her skin was sweat-slick beneath her dress. A crazy cacophony assaulted her ears: drumming hoofbeats, wild battle cries, animal bleatings, groans of collective pleasure from the crowd. Desperate to escape, Flavia kicked the bars of her cage, but they held firm. "Let me out! Let me out!" she cried, though to whom she was pleading, she no longer knew. And then the cage began to rise once more.

The ceiling folded back as Flavia's elevator emerged into the blinding glare. A cheer erupted from the crowd, its force so powerful Flavia had to cover her ears. In every direction, a turbulent sea of spectators churned and roiled in the stands, shaking their upraised fists and yelling with all their strength. The sound of their madness reverberated around the amphitheater's bowl and crashed onto the arena floor in a frothing cascade of malice. As the full brunt of the crowd's bloodlust bore down on Flavia, she found she couldn't bear its weight. Her legs buckled, and she collapsed to a kneeling position. Sweat stung her eyes, and her vision dimmed. Colors and objects swirled around her on the sandy field—demons of Satan whose identity she could not discern.

A huntsman wearing nothing but a leather helmet and loincloth dashed close and heaved a fishing net over Flavia. She writhed in its tangles, trying to throw it off, yet she only grew more enmeshed as she struggled.

"Get moving!" the man yelled. A snap of his whip sent a fierce sting across Flavia's back. She shrieked and lurched to her feet, drawing a great cheer from the crowd.

Stumbling across the sand, Flavia spotted a gate and decided to make a break for it. But no sooner had she started than a shaggy cow stepped into view. She pulled up. The beast wagged its head and shook its horns in warning. It was no docile milk giver but one of the wild aurochs of the northern wastes. Three javelins protruded from the cow's shoulder, the wounds oozing blood down its leg. The injured animal swayed uneasily and pawed the earth, confused by its surroundings.

"Easy, girl . . . easy . . ." Flavia soothed as she backed away. But the cow kept staring at her, huffing and grunting as if blaming Flavia for all its pain. With an irritable snort, it lowered its deadly horns and began to trot toward her. She tried to retreat but caught her legs in the net and collapsed. Though she thrashed about, she couldn't regain her footing. The world shrank to this one deadly moment. Everything seemed to close tight. Flavia's vision constricted. Her breath was coming in ragged pants, yet air refused to pass through her dry, dusty throat.

The cow paused a few steps away, rolling its eyes, unsure whether it should attack or withdraw. Then one of the huntsmen ran up behind it and cracked a whip against its rump. The tormented beast squealed and broke into a charge.

"God help me!" Flavia screamed.

Though she curled into a ball and closed her eyes, the pounding thunder of the oncoming hooves didn't stop. A peace settled on Flavia as she realized the ordeal would soon be over. It couldn't be much longer now.

Jesus, I'm coming to you!

A deafening bellow exploded in Flavia's ears, followed by a massive impact that shook the earth. The crowd shuddered in a spasm of satisfaction, then burst into spontaneous applause.

Flavia opened her eyes.

The cow lay dead on the ground with a gladiator's trident protruding from its skull. A lone huntsman stood over the carcass, his helmet glinting in the sun, his muscles as glossy and feral as any other beast in this arena of death.

The huntsman ran to Flavia. Standing over her, he extended his hand. "You're coming with me," he declared.

———❧———

Rex grabbed the girl's hand and helped her stand. With rapid motions, he sorted the net's tangles until he could snatch it off her. "This way to the trapdoor! Hurry!"

He turned to run but immediately stopped short as a male lion bounded up to the pair, its heavy mane matted with blood. The creature halted a short distance away, growling deep in its throat, trying to assess the vulnerability of its prey. Though Rex pulled a dagger from the belt that cinched his loincloth, what he really wanted was the trident stuck in the head of the aurochs. Most of the good weapons in the gladiators' arming room had already been taken by the time Rex snuck in, so he had grabbed whatever was available to disguise himself and get onto the arena floor. But now that he was face-to-face with the wild beasts, he longed for a stout shield and a spear instead of a cheap bronze knife.

Rex saw the lion flatten its ears and bunch its muscles for a pounce. He grabbed Flavia's wrist and pulled her around behind him. "Stay back until the beast charges," he said, "then run straight for that hole!"

"What about you?"

"I'll come after. It's just a cat. It'll back down when it feels the edge of my knife. Now get ready!"

Rex locked eyes with the lion and assumed a low stance. The enemies stared at each other, preparing for battle while the spectators went wild. To them, it was all part of the entertainment—another bit of mortal combat to heighten the elegance of the narrative. Didn't every great saga end with tragic deaths? The pleasure came from learning whose they would be.

The lion bared its fangs and tossed its mane. Rex focused his attention on the cat's nose, the sensitive and vulnerable place he hoped to injure quickly enough to force a retreat. He knew the fierce behavior of many beasts in the amphitheater came from fear more than natural aggression. *Maybe if I attack first, I can drive it off.* He feinted toward the lion, waving his knife like a madman. Unfortunately, instead of retreating, the cat leapt forward—until a brown blur smashed into it from the side.

The attack from a large female lion caught the male by surprise and knocked it to the sand. The screeching female was clearly maddened by pain, for her whole body bristled with darts, and her tail had been burnt to a blackened stub. When the snarling, biting, clawing fur ball started to roll across the sand, Rex saw his chance. "Now!" he yelled. "Get to the hole!"

The pair made a break for it, reaching the trapdoor and sliding down a ramp just ahead of several other huntsmen. As Rex was pulling down the hatch, one of the men grabbed the door and tried to prevent it from closing. A slash of Rex's knife made the hand disappear, leaving behind a single chubby thumb that fell to the floor. Rex slammed the trapdoor and latched it. Up above, the crowd began to boo.

"Who are you?" Flavia gasped into the sudden quiet and gloom.

Rex pulled off his bronze helmet. It was the crested type worn by the murmillo gladiators, with a wide protective grate that obscured his face.

"It's me—Rex," he said, shaking loose his long hair that had been stuffed into the helmet. "Remember? I met you beneath the Arch of Titus."

"I remember. I knew you would come. Somehow . . . I just knew it."

"You never doubted?"

"I admit, I started to. I wondered if you might have given up."

Rex frowned. "Lady Junia, learn this about me today—I *never* give up. I was coming for you even when you couldn't see me." He glanced over his shoulder at the passageway beneath the amphitheater. "Come on, we've got to get moving. There's still a lot to do to make you safe."

The labyrinth was dark and oppressively hot. Countless torches—each burning an oily mixture of sulfur and lime—were stationed a few paces apart, adding their fumes to the stench of moldy straw and manure. Strange animal sounds echoed down the halls, while a few nearly naked slaves scurried in the shadows like ghosts of the netherworld. Rex ignored them, for they were just lackeys who did whatever job they were assigned and paid no attention to anything else. At one point he even demanded a tunic from one of them, and the man dutifully handed his over. Shrugging, the fellow walked away in his loincloth, and the two fugitives resumed their wandering.

"You know the way out?" Flavia asked.

"I did, but now I'm lost."

"What should we do, then?"

"Keep wandering until we find the exit, I guess. I came in through the arming room, but any exit will do."

"What if somebody tries to stop us?"

Rex turned around and looked Flavia in the eye. "Lady Junia, there isn't a single person in this arena right now who can stop me. I'm a highly trained—" Rex broke off, reconsidering his words. "I can fight if I need to," he finished.

"But you . . . you just seem so young! I mean, I can see you're strong. And, clearly, you're brave. But maybe we should hide for a while?"

Rex snorted. "No! Going to ground isn't the right tactic here. You have to clear the area as quickly as possible. Then you disappear into the mob. Just stick with me and you'll be fine."

A flash of movement over Flavia's shoulder caught Rex's eye. "Uh-oh," he muttered. "Soldiers down the hall. We've been spotted."

Flavia inhaled sharply and ducked behind Rex as four guardsmen pointed toward the fugitives with angry shouts. They began to charge down the long, narrow passageway, their battle cries echoing off the stone walls. They were armed with swords, and Rex knew he'd have a harder time disarming them in the tight confines of the hall than if he were operating in open space.

"In here!" he shouted to Flavia, yanking her into a side room. What he found inside brought him up short.

"An *elefantus*!" Flavia shrieked, stepping back from the humongous creature. It shifted nervously on its giant legs, each as sturdy as an oaken post. Fortunately, a chain was secured around one of them. The animal's strange face, with its long serpentine nose and white tusks, was pointed toward the wall, so it couldn't see exactly what was happening in the holding pen.

Rex dashed behind the elefantus to a large wooden gate on the far side of the room. "If that thing got in here, this has to be the way out," he said, beckoning to Flavia. "Quick! You go on ahead."

She hurried through the gate and started down the wide passage that led away from it.

"Stop where you are!" shouted a guardsman who had just appeared in the human-sized door through which Rex and Flavia had entered. Although he was only a youngster with skinny arms and an ill-fitting helmet, he was defiantly threatening to hurl his javelin. His three comrades behind him were egging him on.

"You gonna throw that spear, boy?" Rex challenged.

The soldier—surely a brand-new recruit—scowled at Rex and launched his javelin across the room. Rex almost had enough time to laugh as the spear sailed toward him. What most throwers didn't know was that the motion used in cocking the arm would predict the spear's trajectory once it left the hand. Anyone who knew what to look for could anticipate the flight path of the spear—and get out of its way. Many times, Rex had even used the trick to catch a poorly thrown spear in midair. When it came off the boy's fingertips, Rex knew exactly where it would end up. Ducking low, he snatched the javelin above his head and spun it around. The soldier's eyes went wide, and he stepped back.

"Sorry, old fella," Rex said. "I hate to do this to you."

Gripping the javelin in two hands, he gave the elefantus a hard jab under its tail. The beast exploded into a rampage in the cramped room, causing the four soldiers to shrink back from the maelstrom. While the elefantus trumpeted its pain and anger, Rex dashed through the gate and caught up to Flavia in the wide passageway.

The clamor of the elefantus's rage didn't fade until the fugitives emerged into the exterior animal pens at ground level. Shading their eyes against the bright sunlight, they crossed a courtyard and found the nearest door.

After calming themselves and straightening their clothes a little, Rex and Flavia casually strolled into the streets of Rome.

—⟨∿∿⟩—

No great feast had ever tasted as good to Flavia as the cheese-smothered sausage served by the potbellied Greek at the cheap corner restaurant. Flavia laid into the food, not like the well-bred aristocrat she was but like a farmhand coming home after a long day in the field. At first she wondered if Rex would consider her unladylike, but she quickly dismissed the thought. The sausage tasted too good to waste time reflecting on her bad manners.

"Looks like you were hungry," Rex observed, chewing his bread nonchalantly. He seemed amused by Flavia's gusto.

Flavia put her clay bowl to her mouth and guzzled the hot, runny cheese, then wiped her lips with the back of her hand. "Well, don't forget," she replied with a smile, "the hospitality in the Carcer is rather poor." The remark elicited a nod of sympathy from her companion.

At Rex's insistence, the pair had put some immediate distance between themselves and the Flavian Amphitheater. After a brisk walk, including several twists and turns, the tall Germanic warrior had finally allowed a stop. He had even been gallant enough to pay for Flavia's meal at the hot food bar—an unexpected courtesy that suggested not all the barbarians were as barbaric as the history books claimed.

With her stomach full and her safety assured for the moment, Flavia took the opportunity to consider her next steps. Fortunately, they had meandered south from the amphitheater toward the Circus Maximus. Her family's mansion on the Aventine Hill was only a little farther on. Flavia could be there within half an hour's walk. Then she could regroup and make a plan. Her father would surely compensate Rex well for his bravery.

Flavia turned toward her unexpected rescuer as they sat on a bench outside the restaurant. "How do you plan to spend the money?" she asked. "Any grand ideas?"

Rex arched his eyebrows as he returned Flavia's glance. "Money?"

"You know—your reward. I just wondered what you dream of doing with it. I mean, I don't really know you. Actually, you're the first German I've ever met! I'm curious. What will you do with the extra spending money?"

"I don't know what you're talking about, Lady Junia."

Flavia took a closer look at Rex. He was no doubt a handsome man—in fact, one would have to say "beautiful" to properly describe the chiseled perfection that so often characterized the Germani. Though Rex's beard was scruffier than Flavia would have preferred, there was no hiding his manly good looks. The jut of his chin was strong, and he had the lean cheeks of a fit, athletic man. His exotic blue eyes and long blond hair only added to his mystique. Yet right now, the brash self-assurance that so often marked attractive men had been replaced by what seemed to be genuine confusion. A realization dawned on Flavia: perhaps Rex's daring rescue was in no way motivated by monetary compensation.

The thought was disconcerting.

What else could it be, then? What does he really want from me? In fact, who is this man? And why am I sitting beside him eating sausages like we're old friends?

Flavia shifted her position on the bench, unconsciously pulling back a little from Rex. "I . . . well, I guess I just assumed you were helping me in hope of a reward," she said sheepishly.

"That thought never crossed my mind."

"So then—why?"

"Because you had a need," Rex answered simply, "and I knew I could meet it." The barbarian's cockiness came flooding back as he flashed Flavia a broad grin. His teeth were even and white, and she found his smile endearing. He leaned closer, a lock of his long hair dangling across his face. "Of course, it didn't hurt that I was immediately attracted to you," he added.

Though Flavia had always considered herself adept at bantering with the boys, she now found herself fumbling for a witty reply. As her mouth hung open in awkward silence, she felt a rush of warmth rise to her cheeks. *I'm blushing!* she realized. *And even with all this makeup, I know he can see it!* The horrifying realization only made Flavia's face grow hotter.

Chuckling to himself, Rex stood up. "Come on, pink cheeks. We've waited here long enough. It's time to move. We've got to figure out your next destination."

Though Flavia was glad for the change of topic, Rex's announcement seemed strange. "Next destination?" she asked. "What do you mean? Where else would I go but home?"

"*Home*? Lady Junia, you can't go home! That's the first place anyone would look! They'll have you back in the amphitheater before you can settle down to your next sausage. You're going to have to disappear for a long time while your father gets your legal situation under control. If you show up in any familiar setting, you're as good as dead."

"Oh my! I guess I hadn't thought of it like that."

The burden of dread that Flavia had been carrying since her arrest—which Rex's rescue had alleviated—settled on her again. She put her hand to her forehead, feeling unsteady. *Where can I go if not home? Who can help me?*

"Maybe I could go to my bishop?" she suggested.

"You're a Christian?"

"Mm-hmm. All my life."

"It might work. I hear they're charitable toward their people. Are there any temples near here?"

"There's a house of worship up that street, the Scaurus Rise. It's called the House of Byzans. I don't know any of the brethren there, but you're right—we Christians do take care of our own, whoever they may be."

"Hey! Look at this!" Rex grinned as he reached to his collar and pulled out a necklace. "Maybe I can pass for a Christian too!" The pendant was marked with a superimposed tau and rho, the powerful sign of Jesus.

"Where did you get that?" Flavia asked, intrigued by the discovery. *Evidently, there's more to this barbarian than I thought!*

"I'll tell you the story sometime. For now, let's go see if we can find you some shelter at your temple."

It's a house of worship, not a temple, Flavia thought, but she realized now wasn't the time to discuss the finer points of theology with the pagan who was being so kind to help her.

The House of Byzans was actually much more than a simple house church. Over time, the Christians of this neighborhood had come to possess an entire city block. Though the ground floor consisted of rented shops under a covered portico, the upper two floors had been converted into a spacious assembly hall accessed by a monumental staircase. Beautiful Christian frescoes decorated the walls. Flavia had seen this place once when she was a little girl, but she hadn't been back since.

As she started to cross the street toward the building, Rex grabbed her arm. "Turn around and walk this way," he whispered.

She pointed to the apartment block. "But the church—"

"Just do it!"

Rex was walking double time in the opposite direction. Suddenly he darted down a side alley.

"What's the matter?" Flavia asked, hurrying to keep up.

"There are spies outside the temple."

"How do you know?"

"Trust me, I know them when I see them."

"Why would there be spies?"

Rex turned and looked intently at Flavia. "Who knows you're a Christian? Is it common knowledge?"

"Nobody makes a big show of it these days. Not when we just had a terrible persecution that only ended recently."

"Do your political enemies know?"

"Yes."

Rex nodded gravely. "That's why the churches are being watched."

"So what do we do next?" Flavia's heartbeat had accelerated now, and her legs felt shaky. She tried to swallow, but her throat was too dry.

"You there!" a gruff voice shouted from behind. "Stop in the name of Maxentius!"

Rex grabbed Flavia's hand. "We run," he said, and yanked her into action.

Though Rome possessed several long, straight avenues, most of its streets hadn't arisen from the kind of careful urban planning that the empire now imposed on its new colonies. The tangled streets of Rome were instead the product of a thousand years of organic growth. Rex didn't know his way through this maze, but that didn't matter. The only place he was trying to reach was anywhere else than where he was. He felt confident he could lose the Praetorians in such a cramped and crowded labyrinth.

Lady Junia Flavia, though an aristocratic girl, was turning out to be more athletic than Rex would have guessed. As the pair dashed through the streets, dodging pedestrians and making quick direction changes, she stayed right by his side. "This way!" he called, switching into a narrow lane with an entrance that was hard to see. It would take only one such disappearance, unnoticed by the pursuers, to bring the chase to an end. So far, though, it hadn't happened. In fact, more guardsmen seemed to be arriving every moment to tighten the noose.

Rex and Flavia continued to sprint through the maze of apartment blocks and market stalls, constantly eluding the opportunists who made grabs for them. The soldiers were shouting for help from the bystanders, offering a reward, so numerous people found it worth their while to try to apprehend the fleeing outlaws. Most of them lunged for Flavia, but whenever her feisty squirming didn't break her loose from their grasping hands, Rex's approach quickly persuaded them to let go. At one point he overturned a wagonload of terracotta jars, spilling olive oil across the cobblestones. Although the trio of soldiers in pursuit slipped and fell in the mess, Rex knew other potential captors lurked around every corner.

"We've got to get out of these crowds," he said, scanning the way forward, alert for one of the many gardens and parks in this part of Rome. He thought a secluded patch of greenery would make a better place to hide than the busy streets—so long as they could get there unseen.

Flavia let out a sudden gasp. "Praetorians up ahead!" she cried, ducking into the shadow of an awning. Rex joined her, panting. Though the guardsmen moved on, more would soon be coming. Rex knew they couldn't afford to stand still.

A giant man who reeked of body odor rose up in front of the two fugitives. He seemed as bulky as some ogre out of the ancient myths. "Got you!" he growled, grabbing Rex's forearm. Flavia squealed and jumped back, but Rex's instinct was honed by years of hard training. As every speculator knew, sheer size meant little in hand-to-hand combat. What mattered was how you used your body—where you exerted force, which contact points you made, what angles you took. The swarthy brute holding Rex's arm knew none of that, so he was actually as harmless as a cow chewing its cud in the pasture. And he was about to learn it the hard way.

Rex gripped the man's tunic and twisted him until all his weight rested on one leg. Hooking his opponent's ankle, Rex then took out his only support, which hurled him to the pavement like a heavy sack dropped at the end of a journey. The man's breath burst from him as he hit the ground. To add to his confusion, Rex delivered a hard kidney punch and three head shots in quick succession. The man gurgled and moaned as Rex stood over him. His eyes were closed, and his nose was a bloody mess.

"How did you do that?" Flavia exclaimed. "I thought that monster was going to kill you!"

Rex shook his head. "There's no man around here who can kill me." He glanced over Flavia's shoulder, then pointed down a long, dim alley between two high-rise tenements. "See that green up ahead? That's a garden. Let's make a break for it. I think we'll be safer there. Ready?"

"I'll follow you, Rex. Lead the way."

He started to move, then paused. A playful smile came to his face. "That's the first time you've called me by my name," he observed.

"I guess that makes us friends," Flavia replied saucily.

The senator's daughter looked up at Rex with her wide, bright eyes. She had garish blue liner on her eyelids and streaks of rouge on her cheeks, now smeared and overlaid with grime. A lone shred of pink ribbon dangled in her dark, tousled hair. Her rose-colored tunic was a filthy mess. But none of that mattered. Rex stared at Flavia for a long moment, unable to tear his eyes away. *By the gods, she's a pretty one*, he marveled, then shook away the thought and tossed his head toward the alley. "Come on, let's go," he said as he broke into a run. Flavia followed right behind.

The alley opened into one of the neighborhood plazas around which so much of Roman life was centered. Just beyond it was the large, green park. But as the pair was about to make a final dash for it, five Praetorians appeared from a street on the left. The men were well armored, and their swords were drawn. They spotted the fugitives and started forward. Rex's only choice was to cut right. He rounded a corner, then skidded to a halt.

"Dead end!" Flavia cried, whirling. "Go back! Quick!"

But it was too late. The five Praetorians had them trapped. They fanned out and began to creep closer, holding their swords low. Their expressions were wary yet confident. Rex drew his pitiful bronze dagger and began to plan his first steps.

"Same reward for the German, dead or alive," one of the men remarked to his buddies.

"I prefer dead," another said, his eyes not leaving Rex's face.

"How about alive but dismembered?" a third quipped. The joke brought cruel laughter from the others.

Rex bent to the ground and picked up a heavy brick, handing it to Flavia. "When I put a man down, you have to smash him hard in the throat. Strike to kill."

"I can't do that!"

"You have to," Rex said firmly, "because they'll do the same to us."

"I thought you said no man can kill you!"

"I said no *man*. These are five *men*. And they all have swords." Mentally, Rex steeled himself for what was about to come. He knew he was going to get cut. The only question was whether he could subdue five fully armored Praetorians before he took a fatal wound himself.

The soldiers drew close. One of them, more eager than the others, made a lunge toward Rex. And so it began.

Sidestepping, Rex seized the soldier's outstretched wrist and yanked his overextended opponent forward, while at the same time twisting the sword from his hand. The man fell face-first into the gravel. It took nothing more than a thrust of Rex's newly acquired sword into the base of the man's spine to keep him there. Though the soldier started screaming and flailing his arms, nothing below his waist was moving anymore.

Armed now with a sword as well as his dagger, Rex eyed his remaining opponents. They fell back at the unexpected display of skill.

"How much is your life worth?" Rex taunted. "A couple of extra coins? Some of you are going to die today even if you take me down. What's the chance it won't be you? Are you willing to play games with your life for such a small reward?"

"He can't defeat four of us at once!" the tallest soldier said. "Rush him!"

Rex had been hoping no one would say that—because it was true. *Help me, Hercules*, he prayed, then added for good measure, *Jesus, help me too!*

The four men converged, but Rex maneuvered into open space, creating maximum mobility and forcing his opponents to spread out again. A flurry of parries and counterthrusts kept the attackers at bay, and Rex even managed to draw blood from two of them. He dodged around chunks of debris and kept moving his feet so the men couldn't attack him simultaneously. Yet the constant effort of eluding four assailants required an exertion Rex knew he couldn't keep up.

"Press the attack!" the tall soldier cried, glancing at his comrades to encourage them. The error was fatal, for no sooner had he looked away than a lightning-quick stab from Rex's sword caught him in the low belly beneath the hem of his chainmail shirt. The man collapsed to his knees, clutching his gut. Blood oozed between his fingers. Visceral wounds always festered, and this one would be no exception.

With two comrades down, the three remaining soldiers mustered a new level of determination. Their fury quickly forced Rex into a corner. Though he tried to persevere through the wearying effect of the mismatch, he could feel his strength ebbing away. Dread seized him as he realized the battle had just taken a deadly turn. "Run!" he managed to shout from the cloud of sweat and dust that surrounded him.

Yet behind the attackers, he saw Flavia do just the opposite. The slender waif picked up a bloody sword, grasped it in two fists, and prepared to make a rear assault on three elite soldiers of the Roman army. Rex was certain she would have followed through, had not a second warrior burst into the fray at that very moment—a colossus whose long braid flew about his head like a proud war banner catching the wind.

Geta was a true brother-in-arms, a man to fight beside when the battle took a deadly turn. Like so many times before, Geta had once again located his comrade in a moment of desperate need. The man was a savage beast amid defenseless lambs, dealing out destruction to his prey before they knew what hit them. Now that the Praetorians had to divide their attention, they were no match for the highly trained speculators. In a flash, the three remaining soldiers went down with grievous wounds. The battle was over before Geta had even winded himself.

A sudden quiet descended on the dead-end alley. Panting heavily, Rex surveyed the scattered bodies that lay on the ground before him. Three of the groaning men would eventually heal; the fourth would live but never walk again; and the fifth would die in a few days from a gut infection. But Rex was alive, and—thank Hercules—his own wounds were superficial.

That certainly wouldn't have been the case had his friend not arrived to bail him out.

Rex turned toward Flavia, who was standing off to one side, covering her mouth and staring at the carnage. Her face was pale, and she was trembling badly, sword still in hand. He approached her and rested a hand on her shoulder.

"Jesus said to turn the other cheek," she whispered.

"Aristotle said we make war so we can live in peace." Rex waited for a moment, then took the weapon from her fingers and spoke gently once more. "Come on, Lady Junia. Let's get you out of here."

———⟨ଓୄଓ⟩———

"Allow me to get that for you," Geta said, reaching up to a tree limb. "Duck your head, my lady."

He politely held aside the branch to let Flavia pass into an artificial grotto surrounding a trickling fountain adorned with sculptures of frolicking fauns and nymphs. The air inside the shady nook was cooler than the rest of the park, and Flavia was grateful for the relief, for she was hot and sweaty. Rex and his friend Geta had decided that this little nymphaeum in the Gardens of Pallas was the perfect place to hide until they developed a plan. The shrubbery had grown thick around the moist grotto, providing good cover, yet a secret path curved behind the fountain and ran through a tall hedge should a quick escape become necessary.

Flavia immediately approached the fountain with Rex at her side, for both were eager to slake their thirst. They cupped their hands beneath a stream of water dribbling from the jar of a dancing maiden while Geta kept watch through the shrubbery.

"I think we've lost our pursuers," the braided warrior said at last, letting the screen of leaves slip back into place as he turned to face his companions. "I have to admit, Rex, I didn't think you could snatch the girl out of the amphitheater. Nice work! Occasionally you surprise me. Someday you might make a good soldier after all."

Rex shook his head and suppressed a smile—unwilling, apparently, to tease his friend in return. Flavia watched as the two men locked eyes. Neither said anything to the other, yet something profound was being communicated between the two warriors. Rex put a fist to his chest, and Geta gave him a little nod in return. Flavia could only look in from the outside. This was a bond she couldn't fully understand.

"So what now?" Flavia asked when the moment had passed. "I can't get help from my home or my church. Both are being watched. I seem to be running out of options."

Geta frowned and nodded his understanding. "My lady, if I may say so, I think you need to leave the city for a while."

Flavia glanced over at Rex for confirmation. His nod signaled that he agreed.

"Where should I go, then? Any ideas?"

"That's probably a question only you can answer," Rex replied. "Do you have any properties in the countryside?"

"No, my father's lands are across the sea in Sardinia. He has massive holdings there. But he never wanted to invest in local real estate."

"That's strange," Geta mused. "Most senators keep at least one villa nearby to get out of the city once in a while."

Flavia's mouth fell open. "Tibur!"

"Who's that?" Rex asked.

"It's not a who, it's a where! About twenty miles east of the city, up in the mountains. My uncle has a villa there!"

"Would he hide you?"

"Well, he and my father had a falling out, so I haven't seen him in a few years. But he's a Christian. I think that's why he always doted on me when I was little. So, yes, I'm pretty sure he'd help me now."

"We're already near the eastern gates," Geta said, "but there's bound to be watchers at every one. We can't just stroll into the suburbs like we're going to a picnic." He faced Flavia and made a solemn vow. "Do not worry, my lady. Whatever it takes, we're going to get you out of here."

"Thank you, Geta," Flavia replied, inclining her head to him. "You've been so kind to me." She turned to Rex and gave him a nod as well. "Both of you have."

"Somebody is paying for all this surveillance," Rex observed. "You must have made some very powerful enemies."

Flavia sighed deeply. "Yes. The Praetorian prefect hates me. Actually, he hates my father because he's a political rival. Convicting me of treason and throwing me to the beasts was his strategy to shame my family. Then Emperor Maxentius would cast my father aside and Pompeianus would swoop in like a hawk."

"Ruricius Pompeianus is your enemy?" Geta shot Rex a quick glance. "We were actually hoping—"

"—to steer clear of him," Rex continued without missing a beat. "Brutal man. But a very fine tactician. Ruthless in war."

"And in politics," Flavia replied glumly.

Geta abruptly crossed to his peephole in the shrubbery. "Shh!" he hissed. "Someone's coming."

The three companions fell silent as the crunch of footsteps on gravel drew closer to the grotto. From the sound of the walker's shuffling gait and his absentminded mumbling, he seemed to be an old man. The boughs around the nymphaeum parted and a bald-headed laborer stepped into the grotto with a bucket and a scrub brush.

Nobody said anything for a long moment. At last the man dropped his bucket with a bang. "You're those—"

"Silence, my friend," Rex said. "We're just some visitors who happened to find this cool and shady place. You've never seen us before."

"But—"

"Silence, I said."

"So . . . can I leave?"

"Walk away and disappear," Geta ordered firmly. "Talk to no one until you're long gone."

Rex shook his head. "That's not a good idea. We should tie him up."

"He's just an old gardener. What harm can he do?" Geta grabbed the man by the elbow and escorted him to the grotto's entrance. "Be off with you. Not a word to anyone."

The bald gardener shuffled back the way he had come. Tensely, the three fugitives watched him go. Reaching the far end of the park, the man paused, then began to yell and wave toward someone across the street.

Rex scrunched his nose and spat out a curse. "I knew it!" he said through gritted teeth.

"It won't matter. I can handle this." Geta hurried over to Flavia and looked at her intently. "Lady Junia, I know I've only just met you, but even in that short time I've found you to be noble and worthy of honor. I'm willing to do anything to help you gain your freedom. Therefore"—he switched his gaze to Rex—"I will hold the gate in the hedge and buy you time. You take the lady out of the city and get her safely to Tibur."

Rex nodded. "I will."

Reaching out to his friend, Geta clasped hands with him. "Brothers, always!" he declared.

"To the death!" Rex replied.

The secret path led from the grotto to the gate in the hedge. A commotion had started up in the area where the gardener had cried for help, and angry shouts were now coming from that direction. Geta drew his sword. "No one will get through," he promised.

Rex and Flavia had just passed through the opening and were about to depart when Geta reached out and caught Flavia's sleeve. Taking her hand in his, he pressed it to his lips.

"Christ be with you," he said.

"And with thy spirit," she answered instinctively, then took her place at Rex's side and moved into the city streets again.

The Tiburtina Gate was crawling with workers when Rex and Flavia arrived. A full crew of imperial masons swarmed the massive structure like ants on a dropped morsel, scaling every surface, sealing every crack. Although city gates always had a way of concentrating people's attention in one place, the current strengthening of the walls ordered by Emperor Maxentius had made the portals an even greater point of focus.

"That is a huge project they're undertaking," Rex remarked, more to himself than to Flavia. "Maxentius is clearly anticipating a siege."

"Any of those men could be a paid watcher. I'm nervous, Rex! I don't want to approach any closer. Can we get out of here?"

The shady portico where Rex had stationed himself wasn't visible to anyone at the gate. Still, Flavia's instinct was right. To exit that gate into the countryside would be to invite a squadron of soldiers to follow. Even random pedestrians presented a threat if they happened to recognize Flavia as the girl snatched from the amphitheater a few hours earlier. Though Rex's face had been covered by a helmet, fifty thousand people had seen hers, and word of such dramatic events always spread quickly. Many people across the city were probably gossiping about it even now. Though Rex was tempted to make a dash for it, the stakes were just too high. It would take only one person creating a disturbance for Flavia to be back in the hands of the Praetorian Guard.

"I agree, it's too risky," he said, turning away from the gate and withdrawing into the shadows. "I don't even like walking the alleys with you wearing that same pink dress you had on in the arena."

She shrugged. "What else can I do? I'd buy a new one if I had any money."

Rex reached through a slit in his tunic and pulled out a leather pouch. "First I abandon my job and make my boss furious. Then I almost die several times while snatching you from danger. After that, I buy you a sausage. And now I'm buying you clothes?"

"Oh, Rex! No, I wasn't saying . . . I mean, it was just an offhand comment—"

"I'm just teasing you." Chuckling and shaking his head, Rex handed Flavia a silver argenteus. "Please, take the money."

"I couldn't."

Rex pressed the coin into Flavia's palm. "Truly, I want you to. It's yours."

"It's just a loan, I promise! I'll pay you back as soon as I can!"

"Lady Junia, that's not necessary. Go find a plain tunic to disguise yourself while I consider our options."

She nodded gratefully and disappeared. Seating himself on the doorstep of an abandoned shop, Rex stroked his beard and tried to think of a way to get out of the city. Only two options seemed possible: hide in a cart passing through a gate or go over the wall under cover of darkness. The second idea seemed less viable. Rex knew that with a rope and hook, he could get himself over the fortifications, but what about Flavia? She had proven herself sufficiently athletic to dash through the streets, but could she really surmount the Aurelian Walls? Emperor Aurelian hadn't put up those walls for decoration forty years ago. That was a time of great chaos. The walls were there to prevent people from crossing them—and they worked just as well in either direction.

The sound of shouting snapped Rex's attention back to his surroundings. He rose quickly and went around the corner to investigate. As he had feared, Flavia was the cause of the scuffle—but not because she had been recognized from the amphitheater. Instead, a stocky, middle-aged blacksmith had interpreted her garish makeup to mean she was a prostitute.

"I said *no!*" Flavia cried, trying to squirm away from her would-be lover's grasp. But the man kept a firm hold on her wrist. Rex could see right away that he was one of those egotistical brawlers who thought more of his fighting skills than his actual prowess warranted. Although it wouldn't be hard to put the man on the ground, Rex knew that sometimes a lighter touch was needed to prevent an escalation.

The blacksmith snickered at Flavia's attempt to break free. "You can play games all you want, honey, but the end's going to be the same," he said.

Rex approached the pair, keeping his demeanor unthreatening. "Hail, friend! Where'd you find this woman? I like the look of her too."

The blacksmith frowned and jutted his chin at Rex, sizing him up, though without releasing his grip on Flavia. "She's mine, you dirty German. Beat it."

"How much is she asking?"

"We're still negotiating. She's about to learn I drive a hard bargain."

Rex took a step closer. It was all he could do not to deliver a forearm to the man's voice box and leave him choking in the gutter. Instead, he smiled agreeably and gave a little shake of his head. "Ha! From the look of you, I wouldn't want to be her! But listen, friend—I've been traveling for weeks and just sold my horse. I got money to spend, and I need a woman bad. What if I buy this one off you, and buy you another as well? There's plenty more where she came from. The brothel is right up the street. You'd come out ahead, and we'd both be happy."

By now a crowd had gathered around the trio, eager to be entertained by any sidewalk drama, especially one that might end in a fight. "Don't do it, man!" someone called. "There ain't other harlots what look as good as her!"

"He's right," Rex said to the blacksmith. "So I'll tell you what. You let me go first with her. Then when it's your turn, I'll pay for both of us. And I'll even buy you a jug of wine."

"Don't pass that up, Cassius!" a voice shouted. "What have you got to lose?"

A slow grin broke out across the blacksmith's face. He put his fist to his chest. "Deal," he said. The crowd broke into a cheer.

Rex offered the same gesture, then made a big show of handing Flavia a pair of coins for her "services." As he began to lead her away on his arm, he bent down until he could speak in her ear. "We enter the brothel and go straight out the back. Stay beside me."

"Hey!" somebody shouted. "That's the pink girl who faced the cow in the amphitheater!"

Rex's stomach clenched. *Gods! Not now! Keep quiet, whoever you are!* Though he kept walking beside Flavia, he casually reached through a slit in his tunic and grasped the hilt of his hidden knife.

"Don't you remember?" the speaker continued. He stepped out of the crowd now, a remarkably handsome boy with a fashionable tunic and long hair pulled back in a ponytail. "I was there in the stands. A gladiator saved her from a cow and a lion! Then she went down a hole. What's she doing here?"

"It's not the same girl, you little sissy!" someone else said.

"I think it is," chimed in a third. "She's wearing the same color. And look! There's a bit of ribbon in her hair."

"Rex!" Flavia hissed as she clung to his elbow. "We've got to get out of here—quick!"

"I know! I'll think of something. Just don't run."

"Somebody find a Praetorian," the long-haired boy demanded. "They'll know for sure."

"Do we run yet?" Flavia whispered, picking up her gait.

"Steady. Keep walking. Just go into the brothel, like we said."

"Psst!"

Rex shot his glance to the left. A street urchin beckoned from the supporting arches of an aqueduct. "I can make you disappear, mister!"

Flavia's grip on Rex's elbow tightened, and she let out a little moan. "There are two soldiers back there," she said urgently. "They're starting to come this way."

"Your choice," the urchin said. "Face the Praetorians or let me help you disappear."

Rex veered left and darted under the aqueduct, tugging Flavia with him into an obscure alley. The boy smiled and spun toward a dilapidated apartment building with a pile of brushwood stacked against it. Ducking behind the sticks and branches, he opened a small door and crawled inside. "Welcome to my home," he said, then vanished into the gloom.

Out in the main street, the sound of hobnailed boots drew nearer. Rex bent his head and ducked through the little portal. Instantly he stepped to one side and scanned the room, ready for any attack that might come, but only the boy was there. Rex reached back through the low door, grabbed Flavia's hand, and helped her inside. The boy quietly latched the door behind them. After a few moments, the hobnailed boots moved on, and everything became still.

Though debris was strewn everywhere and the windows were boarded, Rex could see he was in the back room of what had once been a shop for rent. He stood up to his full height and looked at the scrawny, shaggy-haired boy wearing a loincloth and cheap sandals. "Why are you helping us?" he asked.

The urchin pointed to the slight bulge on Rex's hip. "Why else, Mister Moneypouch? I ain't no Christian, feedin' the sick for free. We can do a deal if you want."

Amused, Rex smiled at the boy. "What's your name?"

"My name's Businessman. That's all you need to know, Moneypouch."

Rex bowed. "Nice to meet you, Businessman. I'll go by Moneypouch, if that's what you want. This here is Curvy Hips. What line of work are you in?"

"My boss calls it transmural freight. Taxes and customs are really low in that business." A sly smirk came to the boy's face. "Like zero."

"You're a smuggler," Flavia said. "You move stuff past the walls."

"Aye. Usually into the city. But sometimes we're willing to go against the flow." The remark brought a little giggle from the boy.

"What does that mean?"

"You'll learn soon enough, lady. We go against the flow whenever somebody has an export."

"What makes you think we have a product to export?" Rex asked.

"Who else snoops around a gate for a long time, staring at it from every angle but never going through?"

Rex cursed under his breath. *I'm supposed to be an expert speculator, fully trained in stealthy surveillance—and this child spotted me!*

"Good eyes," he told the boy.

"I'm the Businessman. I know my business," came the simple reply.

"Alright. So let's say we had two products for export. One about my size, one hers. Could you get them both out?"

"Of course. But you'd have to wait until dusk. We don't want anybody spotting anything on the receiving end."

"It's late already," Rex said. "We can wait. How much for the job?"

The Businessman eyed his client. "Five hundred denarii," he said flatly. "This is extremely risky for us."

"Five hundred!" Flavia exclaimed. "That's outrageous!"

Rex flashed Flavia a playful grin. "Hey now, Curvy Hips! Hold your tongue and let us men do our deal."

Flavia rolled her eyes and pursed her lips. She folded her arms across her chest and remained silent.

Having fun now, Rex took a step closer to her. "From what I can tell, there's a rich man who cares a *lot* about this export. Am I right? Let's call him the Big Papa. I imagine he'd be willing to pay just about any price to get his product back safe and sound."

After a long pause, an unwilling smile began to turn up the corners of Flavia's lips. At last her resistance broke. "Yes," she admitted, "the Big Papa would pay whatever it takes."

Rex turned to the urchin. "I'll give you a new solidus for this double export. But I also want a good horse at the other end."

Now it was the Businessman's turn to be surprised. "A solidus! That's pure gold. Folks like me don't ever see the yellow stuff. For that coin, I'd include Pegasus himself!" He thrust out his hand. "You have yourself a contract, Moneypouch."

The boy left the abandoned shop, returning an hour later with his boss. Rex eyed him warily, but the newcomer was a small, wiry man and seemed harmless. He led the party up a flight of rickety stairs to the third floor. Apparently, the whole apartment building had been condemned, for it was in serious disrepair and looked as if it hadn't been inhabited for many years.

"So what's the plan?" Rex asked.

The boss pointed to the rear wall of an apartment. It had once been decorated with a series of painted panels, but now the remaining flecks of the pictures were indecipherable. "Put your ear here," he said.

Rex leaned against the wall for a moment, then pulled back and gave Flavia an approving nod. "I know what they're doing. This is going to work. Watch this."

The boss knelt before a wooden panel and removed it. A blast of cool, moist air whooshed into the room, along with the sound of gurgling water.

"Against the flow!" the street urchin said gleefully.

"What is it?" Flavia asked.

"My boss is a repairman for the Curator of Waters," said the boy, obviously proud of the setup. "One day when we were cleaning the duct in the Aqua Marcia, we discovered that this old building is one of the few that rests up against it. Nobody bothered to tear it down when they built the new line. They just ran the aqueduct right past it. So we cut this hole into the pipe. We never divert any water, so the other watermen don't notice a leak or reduction of volume. All we do is bring our imports into the city on float-boards. Or if we have a good reason"—the triumphant smuggler swept his hand toward the hole—"we send exports out."

Flavia recoiled from the cold, black opening. "I'm not getting in there! It's too dangerous! And dark! And confining!"

Rex put his hand on her shoulder. "Aqueducts have access shafts along their length, Lady Junia. If we go now, there should be enough daylight coming through each hole to see our way to the next."

"It's not like you can get lost," the boy said. "Just keep pushing against the water coming down from the mountains. When you look up and see no bars, that's the exit hole we use. It's in a lonely forest outside the city. We'll be there with your horse."

The boss pointed into the gaping maw of the Aqua Marcia. "You'd better leave now if you want any sunlight along the way. If you wait any longer, the light will belong to Luna, not Sol."

Flavia grasped Rex's tunic and drew close to him. "This scares me so much."

"I'll go first, and I won't leave you," he promised. "We'll go vent to vent, manhole to manhole, one by one. Eventually we'll get there. It's the only way out of the city."

Closing her eyes and nodding, Flavia released her grip on Rex. He poked his head into the opening and looked upstream. After his eyes had adjusted a bit, he could see a shaft of light far down the tunnel. He clambered into the murky constriction—a space not much wider than his shoulders and just high enough to allow him to crawl on his hands and knees. The water filled the duct about halfway, reaching up to his elbows as he inched forward in his crawling stance. The stream was icy cold.

Flavia followed behind, groaning a little in her reluctance. Upon hitting the frigid water, she sucked in her breath and let out a shivery whimper. Unexpectedly, Rex found himself feeling a sense of admiration for her courage. *Being trapped in this snake belly scares her even more than it does me,* he marveled, *and yet there she is, right behind me. She got in, and she's determined to see it through to the other side. This rich girl is braver than I would have guessed!*

"Rex, don't leave me!" she cried, grasping his ankle.

"I'm right here, my lady. Let's get this over with. We'll stop at the light up ahead."

And so began the long, dark crawl that Rex, for all his bravado, would recall with a shudder for the rest of his life. Soon there was no sound but the swish of water and his own grunting exhalations. The first cleanout shaft let in only enough light to remind the two underworld voyagers that they were completely encased in a rock-hard tube of death. Flavia rose up and pressed against the iron grid of the locked manhole above. "I need to get out!" she screamed, pounding on the bars. But the iron remained cruel and unyielding despite her urgent pleas. There was nothing to do but push on.

The next two beams of light seemed dimmer, and the third one had a definite redness to it. Rex knew the sun was setting outside. He hated the thought of the utter blackness that nightfall would create inside the duct. By an act of his will, he forced the terrifying idea from his mind and resumed his crawling.

The pair forged ahead as the inky blackness deepened. Rex's arms and legs were numb now, and his mind seemed hazy too. A cry from Flavia was cut off by a splash and a desperate thrashing behind him. "Lady Junia!" he shouted. "Are you alright?"

There was no answer.

Terror seized Rex as he imagined that a heavy pulse of water must have engulfed her—immersing her in the tunnel, pouring into her lungs, swirling her through the pipe like a bug washed down a putrid sewer.

"I'm here! Grab hold of me!" he cried, thrusting his leg backward in a futile attempt to find his courageous companion. But despite his urgent probing, he felt no clutching fingers on his ankle, nor perceived any sound but the constant drone of gurgling water.

At last a choking gasp burst from the darkness, followed by a long fit of desperate sputters and coughs. When Flavia finally had her wind back, she broke into a forlorn cry. The heart-wrenching tones echoed around the stone conduit.

"What happened? What hit you?" Rex asked, still feeling a little frantic. His rational mind knew there were no pulses of water in Rome's aqueducts, only perfectly engineered grades along a gradual slope. Still, a whispering voice told him it must have happened just this once—and probably would again.

"My arms slipped, and I couldn't push myself up," Flavia sobbed. "I want out of here! Please, God, help me! Christ, my Lord, get me out of here!"

"I told you, I ain't no Christian!" came the unexpected voice of the feisty street urchin. Rex looked up to see his grinning face at the final manhole—one with no bars in the way. "But I'll be your savior anyway, Curvy Hips," the boy added. "Now reach up here, and I'll help you out. Looks like this pipe ain't gonna be your tomb after all."

6

OCTOBER 311

As Flavia climbed behind Rex in the saddle, she found herself unsure where to put her hands. *Around his chest? Or is that too personal? But wouldn't that be better than his stomach? Surely not his hips! Do I grip the folds of his tunic? Or maybe I should just do what I really want and pull him tight against me like my barbarian lover come down from the wild forests?*

I'm only seventeen! Nothing in my life has prepared me for this!

The lurch of the horse breaking into a fast walk solved Flavia's dilemma. Rather than tumble backward over the gray mare's rump as it stepped out, she tightened her grip around Rex's torso, interlocked her fingers, and settled in for the ride.

It was completely dark now. The moon hung low in the sky, its fat, tawny orb crisscrossed by the bare branches of the trees. No sound broke the nighttime stillness except the quiet crunch of the horse's hooves on fallen leaves. Flavia inhaled deeply, reveling in the sheer pleasure of fresh air and open space around her. When the youthful smuggler had helped her clamber from the aqueduct's maintenance shaft, the feeling of relief had been more intense than when she had escaped the Carcer. Flavia wasn't sure how much longer she could have held on to her sanity in the tight confines of that water pipe.

The gray mare had been waiting at the bottom of the ladder when she climbed down from the duct, which was running on arches above the ground at that point. Rex had followed behind her, and after the money was exchanged, the two escapees had been turned loose with a simple farewell. Perhaps due to the honor code that criminals are said to share, the smugglers had thrown in a pair of woolen cloaks that could double as blankets, plus a small bundle of food. Though it felt strange to share a bond with these dealers in illegal contraband, Flavia realized she wasn't in much of a position to be picky about where her next meal came from. *I had better get used to being an outlaw*, she thought, *because that's what I am now.*

As the night wore on and the air grew colder, Flavia found herself trembling from time to time. At a little clearing under the pinpoint stars, Rex halted and dismounted. "It's gotten chilly," he said. "Are you uncomfortable?"

"Yes. I think mostly because my dress is still damp."

Rex dug into the saddlebag and produced one of the cloaks. "Sorry I didn't notice it earlier. I'm one of those people who's always too warm. I guess my body makes a lot of heat. You'll feel better with this around you."

"Are we going to ride all the way to Tibur?"

"No, I think we've endured enough hardship for one day. You started this morning in a Roman dungeon, and things haven't gotten easier since. I'm looking for water, and when I find it, we'll camp."

After climbing back into the saddle, Rex flung the cloak around Flavia, then fastened it at his own neck to contain and share their body heat. The move forced her into an even closer embrace than before. As she leaned against the hard muscles of his back, she was surprised to feel a little warmth rising to her face and neck. *He's right*, she thought, smiling in the secret depths of the cloak. *He does make a lot of heat!*

After what Flavia imagined was about an hour of riding, they arrived at a tumbling brook in the bottom of a wide, sandy ravine. The moon was higher now, bathing the forest in a white glow. Rex reined up at a clump of boulders beside the stream. The rocks made a kind of enclosure with a flat space in the midst of it.

"This is a good spot," he said. "Soft ground for sleeping, and that circle of rocks will hide our campfire. Let me help you down."

Flavia took Rex's hand and let him assist her. "I used to ride often on my father's estates in Sardinia. But as tired as I am now, I'm glad for the help. Thank you."

The packet of food provided by the smugglers was wrapped inside a clay cookpot. It contained barley, oil, beans, salt, a loaf of bread, and a flint. While Rex cared for the horse, Flavia got a fire going and prepared a porridge, adding some wild onions that she had found nearby. Though it was chestnut season now, Flavia knew she would have to climb a little higher into the Apennines to find those sweet, nutritious nuts. Her uncle's estate included several hillsides covered with the splendid old trees. Yet tonight, even a hot barley porridge sounded like a meal fit for an emperor.

When the food was ready, the hungry travelers huddled around the campfire and passed the plain wooden spoon back and forth. After the first bite, Rex offered a nod of approval. "How did a rich girl learn to cook like that? I thought the kitchen was the slaves' domain."

"Oh, I love the kitchen!" Flavia said. "Our cook is the sweetest old man you could ever meet. The scullery maids always show me how the ingredients go together. It's fascinating."

"The master's daughter socializes with the slaves?"

"Of course. It's not a problem. In my house, we don't treat our servants like they're beasts. We love them like family."

"But they're still slaves."

"Actually, my father offered every one of them their freedom if they wanted it. Each servant in the home chose to stay rather than take their chances on the streets. That mansion on the Aventine is a shelter for them. Unlike most slaves, they know they'll never be whipped. They are treated with respect and are free to marry. And they receive plenty of food. They have security for life."

"I suppose that's better than what most people face in this world," Rex acknowledged. "But doesn't that sort of leniency make them rebellious?"

"Not at all. Almost the whole household is Christian. While we have different ranks in the house, we're all held together by love. Our scriptures say, 'There is neither slave nor free, but all are one in Christ Jesus.'"

"What does that mean? I thought Christ was a war god."

Flavia burst into laughter. "A war god! He's not a war god with a hammer in his hand like your Germanic Hercules! What's his name again?"

"I think you mean Thor."

"Yes, Thor. Whatever you call them, those gods aren't like ours. He is the only true God, and his message is one of love."

"Apparently, I don't understand Christianity, then," Rex said around a mouthful of porridge. "You tell me it's about loving your slaves like family, but all the Christians I've ever met think Christ is a mighty warrior."

"And what do you think, Rex?"

"I think he's another form of Hercules. I've also heard him equated with Apollo, and Mithras, and the Invincible Sun. All of them have something in common: they're victory gods. They slay evil beasts or the forces of chaos. They defeat the darkness every night. They rise up from death, bright and triumphant like a sunrise. Isn't that what you believe about your Jesus?"

"Mmm . . . not quite. Christ did rise from the dead, and he did attain victory—but not so he could give help in a soldier's battles. His victory was over the evil Serpent and sin and eternal death. Christ helps the soul in its battle for virtue. That's what my bishop says, anyway."

"I think the God of the Jews helped them win earthly battles," Rex countered. "I used to stand outside a synagogue and listen to a rabbi explain their scriptures. The king in their songs was always praying for help against his enemies. And I mean real enemies—people who wanted to kill him."

"King David was the ruler of Israel. He wrote psalms asking that God would strengthen his hand in war."

"Right. And aren't the Christians a type of Jew?"

Flavia pursed her lips and nodded thoughtfully. "Well, we do come from the Jews. We definitely have the same God. And King David was a mighty hero who fought the Lord's battles. So, yes, I guess in that sense, our God is a warrior God."

"Did Jesus reject the Jewish message?"

"No!" Flavia said adamantly. "That's the heresy of Marcion, who was condemned by the bishop of Rome long ago. The God of Israel is the Father of Jesus."

Rex broke into a triumphant grin. "Ha! What do you know? It looks like I just taught a Christian girl something new about her deity. Jesus is a war god after all! He comes from a God who fights battles, and he preaches that God's same message. You can't argue with my logic. That's why"—Rex reached to his collar and removed his amulet with the tau-rho on it—"I'm keeping this around my neck. It's powerful."

"Yes, it is, brave warrior," Flavia said with a gentle smile. "I think you should keep it there and see where it might take you."

Rex inspected the bottom of the cookpot, then handed it across the campfire. "Here, Lady Junia, finish up the rest of the porridge. You need to keep your strength up."

Flavia took the pot, still warm, from Rex's hand. *This man isn't at all what I thought the barbarians were like*, she thought as she received the gift. *He's kind, and generous, and he's even interested in theology!*

And he's an unbeliever, she reminded herself. *But for how long?*

Flavia handed the pot back to her new barbarian friend. "You eat it," she said. "I think you need your strength more than I do. Anyway, I'm full."

Rex shrugged and finished the porridge, then rose to rinse the pot in the stream. When he returned to the fire, Flavia sensed the mood had shifted from any further discussion of weighty spiritual topics, so she asked, "How did you break into the amphitheater, Rex? I would have guessed it was impossible."

"No, just the opposite. It's actually easy, because no one is guarding it. Only the fear of punishment keeps people out. If you're not afraid, you can go right in. I just followed the animal handlers into the tunnels, then found the gladiators' arming room and took what I could. When I saw them haul you up in that cage, I went to the next hatch and crawled up. As soon as I came out into the sunshine, that crazy cow was about to charge. I stuck a trident in its head just before it gored you. You know the rest."

"No one tried to stop you?"

"One guy did, but I threw him down hard. He didn't argue after that."

Flavia hunched her shoulders and held up her hands in amazement. "How do you do that?"

"Do what?"

"Toss grown men around as if they're dolls! Like that monster who grabbed you in the street—he was huge! But before I could blink my eyes, you had him on his back like he was a little child."

"It's all about technique. Stand up. I'll show you."

Flavia obliged, and Rex came around the fire to stand facing her. "Hurl me to the ground," he said. "I won't resist. Just throw me."

She grabbed his tunic and tried to move him, but he was like a statue of marble—firm and unyielding. Suddenly his arm curled around her waist and his stance changed. Before Flavia knew what was happening, she was upended with her feet in the air. She would have crashed to the earth had Rex not laid her down gently on her back. She gazed up at him, towering overhead in the moonlight.

"That's impressive," she admitted.

"Not really. You could do it too." He offered a hand and helped her up. "Try it. Just follow my lead."

Rex and Flavia clinched like a pair of wrestlers. "Step here," he ordered, and she complied. "Good. Now turn all the way around and throw your hips into me."

Flavia tried the move but felt tentative and cautious. Rex told her to put full effort into her attack. Clasping Rex's wrist in her left hand, she turned until he was behind her, then lowered her stance and used her hips as a pivot. Surprisingly, with her other arm around his body, she found she was able to lift him off his feet. As Flavia followed through, Rex came rolling over her hip and landed on his back. Playfully, he tugged her wrist, knocking her off balance.

"Eek!" she squealed as she fell on top of him, her elbows resting on his chest.

Both of them were laughing at their ridiculous mock combat.

"Look at me! I claim victory! I have slain the mighty barbarian!" Flavia bragged.

"Maybe you have, Lady Junia."

There was a certain tone in Rex's voice that made her give him a second look. Though his demeanor was friendly and nonthreatening, Flavia was suddenly aware that she was alone in the woods at night with someone she hardly knew. Nothing in Rex's behavior suggested he would take advantage of that. He was only letting her know that he was a virile young man, and she was a beautiful woman, and that potent combination was having its effect on him. Flavia found the realization scary and exhilarating at the same time. The sudden swirl of emotions made her push away and sit up.

Still wearing a mischievous smile, Rex rose to his feet. He stretched his long arms and yawned. "It's gotten late," he said, glancing up at the moon. "I want to get moving at first light tomorrow. We'd better get some sleep." He bent to the ground and pitched one of the woolen cloaks to Flavia. "Our cozy campsite has warmed up now, but you're going to want that when the coals die down."

Flavia wrapped herself in the cloak and curled up in the sand beside the campfire. The boulders at her back reflected some of its heat; but more importantly, the rocks gave her a sense of shelter from whatever might be lurking in the woods. She stared at the flames for a long time, glancing across them occasionally at Rex, who had rolled the other way. Bundled there in his gray cloak, he looked like one of the boulders that made up the circle—except this boulder was breathing steadily and even snoring a little. Flavia stared at Rex's broad shoulders as they rose and fell. *Who is this protector of mine?* she wondered. *And why did he risk his life to save me?*

The campfire popped, sending up a pair of swirling sparks.

Maybe he really is my barbarian lover come down from the wild north.

The fleeting speculation was, Flavia had to admit, an exciting thought. She was still imagining its possibilities when sleep claimed her beneath a Roman moon.

Frost was on Rex's shoulders when he awoke in the gray light of dawn. A heavy overcast had rolled in, the kind of October sky that might spit rain all day or could just as easily give way to sunshine. Regardless, the air was noticeably chillier than yesterday, and Rex silently thanked the honorable smugglers for the hooded cloaks.

After stirring and blowing on the embers, he was able to rouse the campfire without waking Flavia. He pushed the little vial of olive oil into the coals, then cut the loaf of bread and began broiling the pieces on a stick. By the time Flavia awoke, he had prepared enough toast slathered in hot oil to make a suitable breakfast, which the pair washed down with cold, clear water from the stream.

"Do we have a full day's ride?" Flavia asked as they mounted the horse, one behind the other, both clad in their cloaks to ward off the chill.

Rex kicked his heels against his mount's flanks and moved out. "If we could go straight to Tibur, it wouldn't take all day. But we're outlaws. We have some complications. Last night we rode north from the Aqua Marcia to intercept the Tiburtinian Way. I think it's just ahead of us now. We could turn right when we hit it and be in Tibur by noon, even with two of us in the saddle."

"I don't like the idea of being seen on a busy road."

"Yes, that's the complication I was talking about. We're not actually very far from the Tiburtina Gate where we were running around yesterday, evading soldiers and making a big scene. Some of the people who saw us could be on the road. The Praetorians will certainly be on the lookout. We're pretty conspicuous—a long-haired barbarian and an Italian girl riding double on a horse. So our real problem is avoiding recognition. Underneath our cloaks, we're still wearing the same garments we had on yesterday."

"I never had time to buy that tunic," Flavia said sheepishly. "I was too busy staying out of the brothel! But at least I didn't spend your argenteus. Remind me to give it back to you when we dismount. It's hidden in the hem of my dress."

"Good. That silver coin is all we have left. I spent a month's salary when I put that solidus in the greedy hand of the Businessman."

There was a pause, then Rex felt Flavia's arms tighten around his chest as she gave him an affectionate squeeze from behind. "Thank you for doing that, Rex. When something needs doing, you just do it without hesitation. My father will certainly pay you back for that noble deed."

"I hope he does. It was a lot of money. But even if not, I still would have done it."

"I know. Thank you."

Rex chuckled and glanced over his shoulder. "Don't be too impressed. A month's salary is a small price to pay for saving my neck and escaping those Praetorians."

"Hey! *Your* neck? What about mine? How much is my life worth?" Flavia teased.

"At least a nummus or two," Rex replied good-naturedly.

Flavia tsked at the mention of the common bronze coin and gave Rex a swat on the shoulder. He laughed along with her playful rebuke.

The pair lapsed into silence as they followed a muddy trail, its footing made even sloppier by the hooves of some wild boar that had been foraging in the night. After rounding a bend, Rex spotted a cottage off to one side in the forest. "This could be an opportunity," he said.

"Or trouble."

"That's true. Let's go find out which it is."

The travelers dismounted and approached the home through the dense shrubbery. Rex left Flavia in a thicket and snuck to the henhouse. After opening the door, he went around back and gave the flimsy structure a hard shake. The chickens burst from their roosts and began to flutter and cluck around the cottage's yard. Rex and Flavia hunched low in the bushes as they heard cursing from inside the home.

A man came out, and Rex could see immediately that he was harmless. He was an older fellow, gaunt and wiry like so many peasants who work hard but still manage to eat only a little. Though he hurried around as best he could, trying to corral his chickens and get them back into the coop, the birds weren't having any of it.

"Call out to him," Rex whispered. "A woman will be less threatening than a tall stranger appearing out of the forest."

Flavia hailed the man, who immediately straightened from his chicken chase and scanned the underbrush. "Show yourself," he ordered.

After stepping forward, Flavia approached slowly. "My friend and I need help," she said. "We could use a little food, and maybe some clothing. We can pay."

"Who's your friend?" the old man asked warily.

"A German from the north, come to Rome to seek his fortune in the army. He's gentle with friends and doesn't want any trouble."

The man sighed. "I'll never have it be said that I didn't feed a guest who showed up at my doorstep. Come in, and I'll pour some hot wine. As for clothes, my wife died a year ago, and I sold whatever she had. But maybe I can find something for your friend."

However, when Rex emerged from the trees, the man burst into laughter. "I'm not going to have any clothes that size," he exclaimed, casting down his eyes at his own average frame, then gesturing toward Rex. "He's twice my height!"

Inside the cottage, the man introduced himself as Uranio, a former shoemaker who now lived a solitary life of retirement. Rex returned his host's introduction without using his full name, and he also made sure to use the simple cognomen "Flavia" instead of "Lady Junia," which would have indicated her noble status. *It helps that she doesn't look like a rich girl right now,* he thought, studying Flavia as she chatted with Uranio. A strange question suddenly occurred to him: *I wonder if makeup and perfumes and aristocratic finery would make her prettier?* Rex had never seen Flavia dressed up, yet he didn't think it would matter too much. Though she was as unkempt as any commoner right now, she possessed such natural beauty that even when she was grubby, she wasn't unattractive. It only gave her a different sort of allure—wilder and more primal. She even had a certain smell that he found enthralling. Rex decided he liked her just fine the way she was.

Uranio turned to the big stone hearth and swung an iron kettle from the flames. Holding it in a cloth, he poured three cups of spiced wine. "That should stoke your inner fires," he said with a wink.

Rex reached for one of the cups and raised it. "Health to you," he said. The others returned the toast, then the three drinkers carefully put their hot cups to their lips. As Rex sipped his wine, a plan began to form in his mind. He decided to tell Uranio he was on his way to Rome with his "girlfriend" from Verona, but they were low on funds. That last part was true enough. The main thing they needed now was money—enough cash to buy food for a few days—and some new clothes, and lodging in Tibur until the situation at Flavia's family estate could be determined. Once she was safely hidden there and her father was notified, Rex would take his leave and make his way back to Rome. Of course, that would mean facing his centurion's wrath; but since that was a dilemma for another day, he pushed it from his mind. Rex's main problem now was how to get some spendable funds without revealing the real situation.

It was Uranio who suggested the deal that Rex had already been considering. "That's a mighty nice mare you got out there," the old man said, tossing his head toward the cottage door. "She's good for riding and could pull a cart too. Where'd you get her?"

Rex waved his hand nonchalantly. "You interested in buying?" he asked, deflecting the delicate question of ownership with a question of his own.

"Could be, if the price was right."

"I might make you a good deal. We need some coins for buying clothes, since you have nothing like that to sell."

"Ha! I truly don't. My tunic would be much too short on you, German. You'd be revealing more than you should to your cute little girlfriend!" Uranio punctuated his bawdy assertion with a booming laugh.

"Oh my," Flavia murmured. She glanced away and raised her hand to cover the embarrassed smile that turned up the corners of her lips.

Rex ignored the joke and stroked his beard as if he were mulling a sale, though in truth he had already decided to go through with it. "Well," he reasoned, "the price of a horse would certainly buy us all the clothing we need, with plenty left over for other necessities."

"Such as a bath," Uranio added forcefully. "You two are a mess."

Rex turned to Flavia and subtly winked at her so she would know to play along. "The man thinks we're dirty, sweetheart. It looks like we're in for a good scraping, a haircut, and some new clothes. It sounds like a refreshing kind of day."

"That's very nice, my turtledove," Flavia replied, assuming her role. "But we'd be on foot from now on."

"Not a problem, dear. It's a nice day for a walk."

Flavia shrugged and nodded to indicate her agreement. Turning back to Uranio, Rex offered him a broad grin. "Give us a hundred large silver pieces and you've got yourself a deal, my friend."

"Agreed! I'll get my moneybag while you put the horse in my barn."

"How far of a walk is it to Tibur?" Flavia asked.

Rex spoke up before Uranio could answer. "Remember, sweet honeybee, we changed our plans. We're headed into the city for our bath and shopping."

"Oh, that's right, lovebird," Flavia said, shaking her head. "I don't know what I was thinking. Sorry."

"How far is it to the Tiburtina Gate?" Rex inquired of his host, though he knew it was about five miles away, and it was the last place he wanted to go.

"Five miles," Uranio said. "Turn left when you hit the road. You'll be in the caldarium before the sun has reached the top of the sky."

Flavia sighed deeply. "That sounds lovely! I've always wanted to visit Rome. I can't wait to see it."

Uranio gave the couple a look of stern, fatherly wisdom. "Listen, you kids should watch your step there. You're inexperienced. Rome can be a rough place."

The remark caused Rex and Flavia to exchange another quick glance, each suppressing a smile as they communicated solely with their eyes. Flavia reached across the table and grasped Rex's hand, interlocking her fingers with his. "My boyfriend is a strong protector," she said in a shy voice. "We'll be fine in the big city."

"Above all, make sure you steer clear of the Praetorians," Uranio advised. "Maxentius is turning into a real dictator, and those soldiers of his are running loose in the streets."

Rex grimaced and nodded. "So we've heard. Something definitely needs to be done about that."

"Don't count on it, young fellow. Nothing ever changes in Rome."

"Sometimes it does," Rex said. "Just wait and see."

The home of Bishop Miltiades was a refuge that Sophronia had been seeking often in the days since Flavia had been taken away to prison. At first it was desperate worry that had driven her to the comforting words of the godliest man she knew. Sophronia had prayed with him not only on the day of the arrest but many times subsequently, right here in the atrium that served as his reception room. The skylight let in the sunshine of the Creator, a bubbling fountain added a tranquil reminder of the Spirit's outpouring, and a niche in the wall held the books of the Old Testament, beautifully written on fine vellum. The atrium was the perfect place to lift holy hands in prayer.

And prayer is what I need most, Sophronia reminded herself as she awaited the bishop's arrival.

Strange rumors about Flavia's whereabouts were flying among the Christians, rumors that ran from morbid despair to euphoric hope of a miraculous escape. What seemed certain was that some kind of trial had been conducted. A highly placed witness had seen her hauled into the Senate House for a bogus inquisition. From there, the reports conflicted. Some people spoke in hushed tones of prolonged tortures in the dungeon, followed by the relief of strangulation. A more hopeful group was saying Flavia had been spirited out of prison like Saint Peter in the *Acts of the Apostles*. Still others believed she had escaped into the House of the Vestals, where the virgins were hiding her because they respected her Christian devotion to chastity. There was even a rumor that Flavia had been thrown to the wild animals in the amphitheater, and as a fierce dragon was about to devour her, a golden angel of God had descended to whisk her away. Many were calling Flavia a new Saint Thecla—a beautiful virgin rescued from the jaws of the beasts just when her doom seemed certain. It all made for exciting gossip and thrilling stories. But what the protagonist's mother wanted most were some cold, hard facts.

When the bishop finally entered the atrium, he immediately came to Sophronia and greeted her with the holy kiss. The pair took seats next to the fountain, where she began to press him for any new information that the Roman Christians might have heard about Flavia. Unfortunately, Pope Miltiades had nothing substantial to disclose. A certain believer at the House of Byzans on the Scaurus Rise had reported a commotion yesterday that some were saying involved Flavia, but the report was doubtful because it also involved a strange Germanic warrior with flaxen hair and shoulders like an ox. Separating fact from fiction was proving extremely difficult.

"I know your fears for your daughter's safety are taking a great toll on you," Miltiades said, his deep voice resonant and soothing. "In many ways, the burden is greater on parents who have to watch their children suffer than on the children themselves. How is our brother Neratius holding up?"

Neratius. Lord God . . . where do I begin?

Sophronia took a deep breath and collected her thoughts before speaking. "My husband is—well, how should I say it? He is extremely preoccupied with the politics of all this. He knows the Praetorian prefect is behind the arrest, and he believes that man is somehow making a direct assault on him. Neratius feels that if he does not defend himself against Pompeianus at all times, his enemy will sweep him away like a wave of the sea. And now is no time to get on Maxentius's bad side! People are saying the emperor is starting to descend into madness. One wrong move, and Neratius will find himself cast from office, maybe even executed. Needless to say, my husband has been so busy fighting for his career, he has had little time to mourn his daughter's absence."

"Yet surely he cares for Lady Junia—his only child?"

"Oh, yes, he does care," Sophronia agreed with a sigh. "But you know how senators can be about their daughters. Sometimes girls are a hindrance to a wealthy family. Their big dowries dilute the estate, and they don't go on to form prestigious careers that enhance the clan's name. Daughters are useful for making alliances through marriage, but not much else. At least that's how many upper-class fathers see things."

Miltiades stared at the ground, shaking his head as he tried to comprehend the strange family dynamics. At last he said, "I've heard that sort of thing, but as a Christian, I would imagine Neratius's outlook would differ from unbelievers. Have you found him to be lax in his duty to protect his daughter from harm?"

The bishop's simple question, intended only to clarify matters, hit Sophronia like a wagonload of bricks.

Yes, she realized with a wrenching pain in her gut. *Yes, that is exactly right! I've been trying to deny it—but it's true. My husband is standing by idly as he lets our daughter die!*

Now that the awful truth had become apparent, Sophronia found she could no longer hold back the deep waters of her sorrow. Like a dam finally breaking, the hidden ache of her heart came spilling out, and she burst into tears.

The kindly bishop signaled for a deacon to fetch a kerchief. The man returned quickly and gave it to Miltiades, who handed it to Sophronia. She took it gratefully, embarrassed that her tears had grown so abundant. She could feel them trickle down her cheeks, each one a bitter reminder that Flavia was gone—*who knew where?*—and the one man who should be defending her was more concerned about his political aspirations than fighting for his family. It was too much to bear. Sophronia's shoulders began to shake as she finally acknowledged her grief. For a long time she wept in the quiet atrium, a woman vulnerable and unprotected in a world full of malice.

The bishop did not attempt to intervene, nor did he admonish Sophronia for crying. He simply waited until she had collected herself and was ready to speak again. She started to apologize for the outburst, but when she looked into her pastor's face, she realized it would be wrong to express such remorse. Miltiades's eyes were glistening too, for he was grieving along with her. Clearly, he didn't consider Sophronia's sorrow a thing for which she must beg pardon. It was what people did in moments of great pain. This long-time shepherd of souls knew it well and accepted it as deeply human.

"My husband is a weak man," Sophronia said at last, gaining strength as she voiced what she had been afraid to reveal until now. "He wants to do right, but whenever he's pressed, he chooses poorly. Now he has abandoned Flavia, just like he already aban—" Sophronia stopped, feeling that perhaps she was speaking too personally in front of a holy man.

"You should speak your mind, dear sister. Say it aloud, for words spoken into the light of day have great power."

"He has abandoned me too," Sophronia said flatly. "And since that withdrawal began, I am not certain he has kept the marriage bed undefiled. It is common for a wealthy man to have mistresses. And certainly to have the slaves, if he wishes."

"Indeed."

"I feel so alone," Sophronia continued. "At least when Flavia was around, I had one family member whose faith was strong. Together we would encourage Neratius to walk in the ways of God. But now—where is my daughter? Where is she, Holy Father? Should I keep hoping she will return? Should I have faith like a mustard seed and just press on? Or is it time to start mourning? When should I begin to rejoice that her earthly sufferings are over?"

Miltiades took Sophronia's hands in his own. "These questions cannot be answered today, can they?"

"No," she admitted.

"Nevertheless, I will stay with you, each and every day. I will walk alongside you until we learn where this difficult road will lead. In fact, all the brethren are laboring with you in fervent prayer. Even the apostles pray for you! Are they not alive in God's presence? It is a marvelous thing to Realize the body of Christ has no dead members within it. Did the Resurrected One have gangrenous limbs? Of course not! No spot of death mars his holy body. The living head of the church nourishes every organ and part. The Spirit gives breath to all who are in Christ, even those departed from us to the other side. Yes, my sister, the communion of the saints is a living, breathing thing."

The words of Rome's bishop surrounded Sophronia and gathered her into the warm embrace of the catholic church. She could feel strength returning to her battered soul as the pain of her loneliness receded. Raising her eyes, she looked into Miltiades's face and addressed him with new resolve: "In the scriptures, King Solomon wrote, 'There is a time for mourning,' but I do not believe that day has yet arrived. Until I know for sure what has become of Flavia, I shall feast before the Lord, living in hope and not in despair."

Sophronia turned and beckoned to her doorkeeper, who stood a few paces away. Onesimus was his name, a faithful household servant who had insisted on accompanying her through the streets of Rome today. Though his shoulder had been slashed a few days ago when the Praetorians stormed the house, a doctor had sewn up the wound, and now Onesimus could move around with his arm in a sling. In his free hand, he held a coin purse, which he brought to his mistress and laid in her lap. Bowing, he backed away.

"What do you have there?" Miltiades asked.

"Do you recall the day last summer when Flavia asked to schedule a refreshment feast for the needy?"

"Ah, yes, I do. She wished to have it at the Apostolic Monument in the presence of Peter and Paul."

"I am glad you remember. Here now is the money taken from her dowry that she set aside for the banquet. Let us call together the one body of Christ, whose beautiful harmony you just described. Rich and poor alike shall feast and pray together. We will ask the blessed apostles to join us in our petitions for Flavia's safe return. Do you believe this to be a godly desire, my bishop?"

"Splendid! Indeed, it shall be done."

"When do you advise?"

Miltiades smoothed his whiskers as he thought it over. At last his eyes lit up. "The ninth day before the Kalends of December shall be the day! It is the feast day of Bishop Clement, the second pastor of Rome, who was ordained by Peter himself. Such a day will be most fitting to celebrate a banquet in the presence of the apostolic relics."

Sophronia held the coin purse for a moment, then passed it to Miltiades. "So it is decided! We shall have the refreshment banquet at the Apostolic Monument, just as Flavia wanted. Until then, let us pray that she still lives."

"My precious sister," Miltiades said, "Flavia belongs to the Lord Jesus Christ. There is no question but that she lives."

—⁂—

The town of Tibur sat on a ridge of the Apennines at the spot where the Anio River tumbled over a cliff, splashed into the valley, and began its final run across the flatlands around Rome. Flavia could see the settlement ahead on the Tiburtinian Way—not far now, though much higher than she wished. The road had grown steep over the past few miles.

"Why did we sell that mare, again?" she asked Rex as she trudged beside him under the hot sun.

Laughing, he put his hand to his hip and shook the moneybag beneath his tunic, which made a jingling sound. "You want to eat tonight, don't you?"

"I'd skip the meal as long as I can have a hot bath."

"With what we've got here, you can have both. And a bed. And fresh clothes. By tomorrow, you'll be a new woman."

Another hour of uphill walking brought the travelers into Tibur, the famous resort town celebrated for its stunning views, healthy air, and picturesque waterfalls. Rich aristocrats had long considered Tibur their favorite country escape, including the great emperor Hadrian, whose ancient villa here was renowned for its luxury. Tibur was a very old settlement, dating back to the mythical times when the Greeks still had a foothold in Italy. That Greek heritage accounted for the prominence of the god Hercules Victorious, whose opulent sanctuary was the most eminent building in town.

A few inquiries pointed the way to the public thermae. Across the empire, the bathhouses were a focal point of everyone's afternoons—though less so for Flavia, whose home had its own private facilities. Still, even the richest senators, men who had deluxe baths in their mansions, would often visit the public bathing complexes of Rome. In contrast to those palatial establishments, the one here at Tibur was much more modest. Even so, like all thermae, it was a beautiful and impressive centerpiece of civic life.

Flavia stared up at the ornate facade of the bathhouse. "Rex, if we ever make it safely back to Rome, you'll have to see the Baths of Diocletian. Absolutely amazing! They're brand-new, commissioned by Augustus Maximian only a few years ago."

"The former augustus, you mean. He's dead now. Has been for more than a year."

"So they say. But maybe not."

"No, I'm very certain he's dead."

"Really? How do you know?"

Rex paused, then glanced over at Flavia. "Because I hung him by the neck

183

from the rafters of his daughter's bedroom. His face turned bluer than I've ever seen on a man."

Now it was Flavia's turn to shift her eyes toward Rex. "What are you talking about? You shouldn't even say a thing like that!"

Rex shrugged. "You're right. Sorry about that. It was a bad joke. Come on, let's go inside." He went through the door, and Flavia followed—but only after shaking her head to clear her mind of Rex's disturbing attempt at humor.

The interior of the bathhouse had a high dome over its central hall and beautiful marble floors. Here and there, carved nymphs and satyrs frolicked in fountains with tumbling waters that created a gentle, soothing sound. A courtyard surrounded by arcades gave access to a swimming pool that sparkled in the bright sunshine. Inside the bathhouse, beneath the shade of the lofty dome, a second pool—heated to a pleasant, tepid warmth—offered refuge to swimmers who had reached their limit of basking in the sun. The steam room was located to the left of the dome, and the cold plunge to the right. Although the sexes were free to intermingle in the main areas, Flavia was relieved to learn that separate changing rooms were provided for men and women. And for those who desired it, single-sex bathing in smaller facilities could be purchased for a few copper coins.

"This is going to feel great after all we've been through," Rex said. "Meet you back at the tepidarium after we undress?"

Flavia held up her two palms. "Uh, no. I don't think so."

"Why not?"

"Because it isn't like that between us! Just to be clear, Rex, you do understand all that talk about lovebirds and turtledoves was a pretense, right?"

The recollection of the mischievous banter with Uranio made Rex chuckle. "Of course, yes, I knew that," he said soothingly. "I was playing along too. I don't normally call my lovers sweet honeybee. I might be a barbarian, but I can do better than that."

"I did think it was rather awkward," Flavia agreed.

"So are you saying you don't want to bathe together because of the nakedness?"

"Exactly! I'm not letting you see me naked! I know it's considered normal in bathhouses, but not for us Christians. I believe that's something for only a husband to see. I'll pay the extra fee and bathe with the women."

"Suit yourself," Rex said. "I'm so dirty, I'm going straight to the scraper. Although what I'd really like is some good Germanic soap."

"Soap? What's that?"

"It's made with animal fat and ashes. It smells bad, but it gets you clean. Better than oil and scraping. All the Germani and Gauls use it."

"That sounds disgusting. We Romans are too civilized to ever use soap."

"Trust me, soap works. But people down here don't like it. That's why I have to settle for scraping. As the rabbi once said, 'When you enter a town, follow its customs.'"

"Who said that?"

"It was an old rabbi from long ago. I forget his name—Meir, maybe? My mother taught me that. She was a great lover of books. We used to stay up at night and read for hours."

Flavia couldn't help but stare at the tall, blond mercenary—this killing machine who once read Jewish books with his mama. For a long moment, she was speechless. At last she said, "You confound me, Rex."

He gave her a cocky wink. "I tend to have that effect on women." He started toward the men's changing rooms, then called over his shoulder, "Meet you back here in two hours. Clean and fresh."

Flavia proceeded to the female area, where she left her tunic, breast band, and loincloth in a cubbyhole. Although thieves were known to frequent such places, she didn't think anyone would be tempted to steal the clothes she had gotten so dirty in her recent escapades. And even if she had reason to worry, she didn't have the necessary coin to pay an attendant to keep watch. Rex had the moneybag with him.

Oh! The coin in my hem . . .

The silver argenteus was far too valuable a coin to be left in an open locker. Muttering to herself, Flavia redressed so she could go back into the public space and give it to Rex for safekeeping. She could also obtain the copper coins for private bathing that she had meant to get from the money-pouch. Flavia smiled as she walked across the hall. *What is it about Rex that always makes me forget what I'm doing? That man has a way of flustering me, even when he doesn't intend it!*

The bathhouse scrapers typically plied their trade in a designated part of the tepidarium, an area marked off by a waist-high divider of dark-red marble. Rich patrons of the thermae brought their own slaves to do the job, but for those visitors who had no assistants, a scraper could be hired to apply the curved tool called a strigil to a well-oiled body. If the olive oil had been worked deep into the muscles, the scraping action of the bronze instrument would take off the top layer of grime, sweat, and dead skin. With a couple of good soaks, a hard scraping, and a massage, followed by a cold plunge and the application of scented lotions, a Roman bather would come out much cleaner than anyone using that ridiculous soap Rex had mentioned.

As Flavia approached the red divider, she was suddenly reminded of the difference between her typical bath experience and that of the common masses. In contrast to the privacy of her home, the people here were in varying stages of undress. A few bathers of both genders wore loincloths, and several women wore breast bands, but many others were completely nude. Though the light was dim and the mood was practical rather than erotic, Flavia, nonetheless, began to second-guess her decision to look for Rex. And then she saw him.

He was standing in a shaft of light from a high window, as if the sun were trying to spotlight this perfect icon of masculinity. Rex's long hair hung loose over his shoulders, giving him a wild and rugged appearance. One of his arms was raised to cradle his head—a gesture Flavia found strangely exciting, though she knew he was only giving access to the attendant who knelt at his side to scrape his ribs. The oil had slicked the muscles of Rex's torso, defining his physique in exquisite detail: the square cut of his chest, the ripples of his shoulders, the gridiron of his stomach. Veins traced their lines down the rock-hard contours of his arms. The bulges of his biceps were rounded like pomegranates, and to Flavia they seemed sweeter than any fruit could be. This was a young man in his prime—as lean and fierce as any savage beast. She stared at him for longer than she intended, then finally looked away.

Then she turned back and stared some more.

Although the divider Rex stood next to obscured his lower body, Flavia knew if she walked forward, he would come into full view. Suddenly her right foot took on a life of its own—lifting, extending, and finishing the step despite the warning voices in her head. The rapid flutter of her heart made her dizzy, though not enough to stop her progress. Aghast at what was happening, yet also thrilled, Flavia felt her disobedient left foot take another stride toward the oblivious bather glistening in the sunlight.

Just a few more steps, and then— No!

Flavia finally halted, unable to retreat, yet prevented from advancing further by her long-cultivated habit of holiness. A war raged in her soul, the ancient battle between lust and self-control.

You have to drop off the valuable silver, she told herself. *And you need this bath. He has the money for the fee. Go get it. Just ask him. It won't take long. Nudity is considered normal here. No harm done.*

Flavia, don't be crazy! You can't have a conversation with a naked, oily man!

But the money is actually for modesty—it's for the women's area. This is just a brief conversation so you can bathe in private. It's all for the right reason.

No! Your mind will never forget what you see!

"Choose wisely, daughter," said a voice.

Who said that? Mother? Bishop Miltiades? God? Was it even real?

"Lady Junia! I'm over here!"

It was Rex. He was waving at her, his expression uncertain. "Do you need something?" he asked.

Oh no. He's coming toward me!

Flavia started toward Rex in return, hoping to meet him at the dividing wall before he left the partitioned area. *Eyes up,* she reminded herself. Yet she knew he would step into the open before she reached the wall. That meant his approach was going to be . . . what? *All there.* Her heart was racing wildly now.

The tinkle of metal against stone sounded at her feet. Flavia glanced down to find that the silver argenteus had slipped from her hem where she had hidden it. The coin had landed on its edge and was rolling away. A man passing in the opposite direction noticed it too. He started to pick it up.

"That's mine!" Flavia exclaimed, darting to the coin and snatching it from the ground. She stared at it in her palm—the price of at least a hundred private baths at a facility like this. Rex's money really wasn't necessary. She had known it all along. With that coin, she could buy an individual bath and hold the change in her hand the whole time. Whirling, she hurried to the women's dressing room and closed the door behind her. No one else was there.

A travertine bench lined one side of the room. Flavia sat down and put her head in her hands, exhaling a long breath as she gazed at the marble floor. Even now, seated on the bench, her legs were trembling. *Why? Out of fear?*

Yes, fear.

And also desire. No one had ever made her feel like this before.

"You confound me, Rex," she whispered into the empty room. The honest admission was terrifying to Flavia. Yet one vital truth had now become clear. Rex represented not just rescue but peril too.

⎯⎯⎯⎯⎯⎯ ⁌⁆ ⎯⎯⎯⎯⎯⎯

It was the sound of the chickens that first alerted Uranio to the arrival of more visitors. He still hadn't managed to get all the birds back in the henhouse after the two young lovers left earlier that day. With the new mare to care for, he simply hadn't found the time to round up the last of the scrawny hens. Now their squawking signaled that more guests had shown up. It was turning into a busy day at the cottage.

Uranio set down the currycomb with which he was brushing the mare's coat and walked to the barn door. As soon as his eyes fell on the arrivals, he sucked in his breath and retreated into the shadows. But it was too late. The four Praetorians had seen him.

"Come over here," one of the men barked. "We'd like a word with you." Uranio obediently shuffled into the cottage yard. The soldiers remained astride their horses, their expressions stern and unreadable. Each man rested a hand casually on the pommel of his sword. Uranio decided to say no more than necessary, giving the visitors reason to leave quickly.

"We're patrolling the area looking for a couple of fugitives," the squad leader said. "We believe they might be in the countryside east of the city, so we're checking every cottage and farm."

"The Tiburtinian Way is only a short distance from here," Uranio observed. "Many people are coming and going all the time. Occasionally they stop at my place to buy a meal. I am glad to feed them for a coin or two. But I don't deal with outlaws, sir."

"These two wouldn't have looked like outlaws. We're searching for a tall German with long yellow hair and a pretty little Roman girl."

A chill ran through Uranio as he realized the soldiers were looking for Rex and Flavia. *The mare must have been stolen! Do I conceal it or confess? Can they see the fear on my face? Venus Victrix, help me!*

"Have you seen them?" the Praetorian asked.

188

"No, sir."

The leader stared at Uranio. "Are you sure? You'd better not be lying to me."

"I'm . . . not," Uranio managed to say.

Another one of the soldiers dismounted and began wandering back and forth, inspecting the cottage yard. After examining some tracks in the dirt, he turned to his commander. "He is lying, sir. Two other people have been here today. A tall man and a woman. They led a horse."

The commander leapt from his saddle and grabbed two fistfuls of Uranio's tunic, nearly lifting him off his feet. Fury scrunched the soldier's face into a grimace and turned his cheeks bright red. "How dare you lie to the emperor's troops!" he screamed, shaking his terrified captive. "Tell me what you know about those outlaws!"

"I didn't know they were outlaws!" Uranio bawled. "How was I supposed to know the horse was stolen? I thought it was bought honestly! Take it back! Return it to the owner! I'm sorry!"

A third Praetorian came over now and soothed his furious commander. Somehow his tactics worked on his boss. The leader cooled enough to step aside, though he didn't lose the scowl on his face. The new man put his hand on Uranio's shoulder. "Listen, my friend, you have one chance to get it right here. You tell us about those outlaws, and we'll leave you and your horse forever. But if you lie to us, you won't like what happens."

"They . . . they called themselves Rex and Flavia," Uranio said tentatively. When this report drew approving nods from the soldiers, his resistance broke, and he decided to tell the whole story. "They said they're young lovers just arrived in the area from Verona," he went on. "She met him when he was coming down from Germania in hopes of joining a legion. She ran away with him. They're headed into the city for shopping and baths. Yes! Check the big bath complexes in Rome. You'll surely find them!"

Although Uranio didn't know why, his words infuriated the volatile commander again. He stormed back into the fray and seized the trembling cottager by the wrist. "No!" Uranio cried, but he was helpless in the soldier's fierce grip. The man slammed Uranio's hand onto a flat tree stump and wrenched the hatchet from the pile of firewood.

"You lie!" the Praetorian accused. "Every foot of the road between here and the city is crawling with soldiers! The eastern gates are being watched!

Those two outlaws didn't get back into Rome since the time you saw them this morning."

"I'm just telling you what they told me!"

The commander beckoned to one of his men, who came over and held Uranio's outstretched arm against the tree stump. "Evidently, your two friends are worth losing a hand for," he said as he raised the ax above his head.

Uranio wriggled and squirmed against the rock-solid hold of his captor, but to no avail. "Stop! Please! I'm not lying!"

"Yes, you are."

The hatchet started down. "Tibur!" Uranio wailed.

At the last moment, the squad leader arrested the fall of his arm. "What did you say?"

"Tibur!" Uranio repeated. "The girl said they were going to Tibur, but the man corrected her. I thought she was confused. But maybe he was covering for her!"

The four Praetorians glanced at each other. "Are you making this up?" the leader demanded.

"No! I swear it on the right breast of Venus Victrix!"

"You two, mount up," the commander said to the pair of soldiers watching the drama at the tree stump. He turned back to Uranio, whose forearm was still in the third Praetorian's grip. "If we find out you've been lying to us, peasant, we'll be back for that hand."

"I'm not lying! It's the whole truth, sir."

"It had better be."

The hatchet slammed into the stump with a solid *thwack*, cleaving off the end of Uranio's pinky finger. A streak of pain shot up his arm, and a squeal burst from him as he snatched his bloody hand to his chest.

Bending to the dirt, the cruel squad leader picked up the severed fingertip. He held it out for Uranio to see. "Emperor Maxentius warns you to be faithful to his purposes," he said, then flicked the chunk of flesh at the weeping man. "Let that be a reminder to serve your lord well."

———❧———

I knew this day was coming sooner or later, Rex told himself. *If this must be the day, so be it. I must have courage and face my destiny.*

He grasped the mirror in his fist, raised it up, and gazed into it. "I look terrible!" he exclaimed.

"No, you look civilized," the barber replied as he used a bristle-broom to sweep the locks of Rex's shorn hair into a pile. "Now you look like someone who belongs here in the empire."

Rex rubbed his bare chin and inspected himself in the bronze mirror. The face staring back at him had his own familiar blue eyes and square jawline. Even so, the absence of whiskers and the long strands that used to tumble onto his shoulders made him feel effeminate. He ran his palm across the fuzz on the back of his head, then smoothed a stray wisp on his forehead, grateful that at least he still had some length on top. *When this mission is over*, he vowed, *I will become a man again.* Until then, he would adapt to the local customs and blend in: short hair, shaved chin, and a Roman style of dress. Too many people were on the lookout for a "long-haired German outlaw" east of Rome, so the new appearance would serve as an excellent disguise. Besides, once he won a spot in the Emperor's Personal Cavalry, the haircut of a recruit would be required of him anyway. *Might as well get used to it now*, Rex reasoned.

After paying for the haircut and shave, he adjusted the wine-colored scarf at his neck one last time, then went out into the street. He crossed to the other side, dodging a deep puddle lest he dirty his new leather boots or splash mud on his expensive tunic. It was a fine woolen garment, expertly bleached to the color of ivory and trimmed with embroidery that matched his scarf and maroon trousers. Having invested in such nice clothes, Rex intended to keep them in good condition for his dinner with Flavia.

The inn across from the barbershop, a charming little establishment with stucco walls and a red-tiled roof, had seemed like the perfect place to reserve two rooms for the night. As a more upscale kind of lodging, it was suitable for respectable ladies. Its rear terrace, enclosed by an arbor of ivy and grapevines, sat on the edge of one of Tibur's many cliffs. The terrace had been arranged as a dining room—not the kind with a U-shaped couch like a banquet hall for the upper classes, but with separate tables for guests who wanted to share a more intimate meal together. It possessed a stunning view of the waterfall that gushed past the Sanctuary of Hercules and went tumbling down a deep gorge. In the distance, the flat plains around Rome receded toward the endless western sea. The sun was perched on the horizon now, bright red like a cherry, and swathed in feathery clouds as it made its way to the end of its daily journey.

Since no other diners had yet arrived, Rex chose the table closest to the edge of the cliff. He lit the oil lamp from a nearby brazier. Autumn wildflowers were bunched in vases on each table, but what made Rex even happier was the loaf of warm bread wrapped in a cloth. He hoped Flavia would arrive soon so they could begin that age-old Italian practice of satisfying their appetites with one delectable course after another.

It wasn't long before he heard Flavia's aristocratic voice behind him. She hailed him as she arrived at the terrace, and he politely rose to greet her. Turning around, Rex was stunned as he caught sight of the woman walking toward him. His mouth fell open, and he had to look twice to make sure it was actually Flavia. She had bought new clothes as well and had obviously visited a professional ornatrix. Instead of her dirty pink tunic, she now wore a long, white gown beneath a mantle of light blue silk. The ornatrix had put on the right kind of makeup for a lady and had woven tiny white flowers into her hair, which was bound up in a fashionable style while leaving a few chestnut ringlets to dangle against her cheeks. Flavia's eyelids and lashes were outlined with a dark paint that gave her a mature appeal. Truly this was no mere girl gliding across the terrace, but a beautiful woman of mature elegance. With her bright eyes and excited expression, she seemed open to whatever opportunities the evening might hold. Rex decided he wanted to discover them all.

"Oh my!" Flavia exclaimed when she arrived at the table. "Rex, you look so different with your hair cut off!"

"And my beard shaved," he answered, rubbing his chin with a rueful grin. He gestured to Flavia's chair, then noticed that a passing rain shower had left drops on it. He wiped the seat with his sleeve and offered it to her.

"Well, isn't that polite," she said as she sat down and smoothed the folds of her wrap. She flashed him a shy smile, and Rex decided he liked the dark red color of her lips. Though it wasn't sultry or brazen, it was exotic enough to catch the eye—and sensual enough to make a man think of more.

"You look nice," he remarked, then added, "Dazzling, in fact, if I may say so."

The compliment seemed to please Flavia. She opened her mouth to answer but held back from speaking. At last she said, "And you . . . I just can't believe how different you look."

"Hmm. I don't quite know how to take that. Is it really that bad?"

"No! Not at all! You look—" Again she seemed to search for the right words. "You look like an equestrian's son," she finally said. "There are a lot of Germani among the knightly class these days. You could easily pass for a young nobleman." She paused, studying his face. "How old are you, anyway?"

"Eighteen. What about you?"

"Seventeen."

"Marriageable age," Rex observed. *Idiot! What does that mean?*

"Yeah. I guess so," Flavia agreed, then fell silent.

The arrival of the innkeeper broke the awkward lull in the conversation. "Good evening, friends! Did you find your rooms clean? I told the houseboy to sweep them well for you."

"Everything was fine, thank you," Rex said casually. He hoped to say enough to be polite, yet not engage in such animated conversation as to leave a distinct impression on the man.

"You are my first diners this evening," the host went on, "early enough to catch the sunset before Lady Luna makes her appearance over Rome a little later. Enjoy yourselves! I will be back shortly with the gustatio and some wine."

The host left the table, but his remark about the sunset drew the couple's eyes toward the west, where a hazy smudge on the plains marked the presence of the capital city. Beyond it, the rays of the setting sun had ignited the tattered clouds into a celestial bonfire of red-gold flame. The vibrant colors along the horizon faded to orange, then copper, then a delicate pink before disappearing into the deep blue heavens.

"Look at that vista," Flavia breathed. "It's gorgeous."

"Indeed. And yet it's nothing compared to the view closer in."

Flavia shot Rex a quick glance, then locked eyes with him for a moment. Slowly, the faintest hint of a smile turned up the corners of her lips. Although she broke the gaze and stared down at her lap, trying to hide her obvious pleasure, Rex could see a blush rise to her cheeks. She peeked up again from beneath her lashes, and when their eyes met once more, neither could help but break into a little embarrassed laughter.

The innkeeper returned with his amphora and poured up a new wine: a dusky red vintage, fresh from the press and still very sweet. After scurrying back to the kitchen to get the appetizer, he returned with a plate of olives, salted anchovies, figs, and artichoke hearts. After that came a course of whitefish with fennel. The main course was wild boar in plum sauce, served with roasted chestnuts. By the time Rex had finished the pork and sopped up the sauce with his bread, he thought he couldn't eat another bite.

"I hope they bring out something sweet," Flavia said, licking a little sauce off her thumb.

Rex chuckled. "Really? You're not full yet?"

"Don't you remember how I devoured that sausage? Running from soldiers gives me a big appetite! I could use a little cake or two to finish the meal."

"Here it comes now," Rex said.

The innkeeper emerged from the kitchen with a tray of honeyed pastries, melon slices soaked in grape must, and a bowl of dark, juicy cherries. Cubes of soft, mild cheese made a nice pairing with the final course. It didn't take long for the two diners to empty the platter.

"Now I'm full," Flavia admitted as she covered her mouth and let out a tiny burp.

Around the inn's terrace, more patrons had arrived with the deepening darkness. Each table was lit by the flickering glow of a lamp. Just as the innkeeper had predicted, the moon had made its appearance in the sky, looming round and full over the plains of Latium. Two slave girls stood off to the side of the dining room, one playing a double flute, the other a cithara. Their sweet music and the gentle murmur of the diners' conversations created the perfect ambience for such a mild and pleasant night.

Rex unstopped a crockpot of tawny wine that the host had warmed in the oven. He ladled out a small cup for Flavia and himself, then filled a third and poured it over the edge of the cliff next to the table. "For Jesus and Hercules," he said, mentioning Flavia's god first out of respect for her beliefs. Surprisingly, though, she grimaced.

"What's wrong?" he asked. "I thought you'd be happy that I included Jesus in the libation. I even put his name before my own version of the god."

"I know what you meant, Rex, and I appreciate it. Thank you. But it's important for Christians that we don't make associations like that."

"Why not? The gods always appear in various forms. They show up in different nations under different names. Maybe I could worship my god as Hercules, and you would just call him Jesus? Then we'd agree about religion."

"No," Flavia said, shaking her head. "The essence of Christianity is that Jesus alone is Lord. He casts aside all other gods as false."

"That's arrogant."

"Not necessarily. Not if it's true." Flavia reached for a bottle of vinegar on the table and held it up. "See this? When you say Jesus is equivalent to Hercules, it's like insisting that all wines are the same. But the other gods are like a thousand bottles of sour vinegar. If you set a Falernian among them, it's not wrong to say, 'Now, this is real wine! Taste it. It's better than every one of the cheap pretenders.' Do you see what I mean? That's not arrogance. It's just a statement of fact."

"Well, I'm a soldier, so I need victory gods like Hercules or Sol or Mars. If Jesus isn't actually one of those, what good is he to me?"

"Jesus is Lord of all things, including the wars waged by men. The one true God isn't limited to a particular area like the evil spirits that people call gods. You were right when you said God sometimes strengthens warriors for his purposes. But you have to remember that at its heart, Christianity is about love. That is the message of Jesus. Murder and bloodshed have no part in that."

"Not all bloodshed is murder, Lady Junia."

The remark seemed to startle Flavia. "What do you mean?"

"When I kill, it's not for personal gain but to advance the good of the Roman Empire. That's not the same as what a thief does in a back alley when he robs a rich man and leaves him dead. The thief commits murder. I wage war. Those are two different things entirely."

Flavia started to reach across the table for Rex's hand, then curled her fingers and returned her arm to her side. Even so, she looked into his eyes and spoke with great earnestness. "I do understand that, Rex. I know you shed blood for good purposes—for the defense of the helpless and innocent and weak. I have seen that done by you. In fact, I am only sitting here today because of it."

"Does Christianity allow that sort of killing?"

"I don't know," Flavia admitted. "I have only ever known it as a religion of love."

"What is love?" Rex scoffed. "Who can define it?"

"Greater love has no one than this: that he should lay down his life for a friend."

Rex glanced at the innocent Christian girl across the table. "Did Jesus say that?"

"Yes. It's in our scriptures."

For a long moment, Rex didn't speak but only stared across the moonlit landscape. Finally, he brought his attention back to Flavia. "Jesus laid down his life on his cross. That's what it means, right?"

Flavia nodded, and when Rex looked at her face, he could see tears glistening in her eyes as she begged him to understand what was, for her, the most profound truth that humanity had ever encountered.

"And then what happened to Jesus?" he asked.

"He rose from the grave."

"Like no one else ever has?"

"Yes, my friend," Flavia whispered. She seemed to be frozen in her seat, unable to reach out and touch Rex physically, yet trying to do so spiritually with the intensity of her desire. "Yes, Rex," she said again. "Jesus rose from the dead like no one else ever has. Just believe."

"I do believe," Rex replied. "It's not impossible. I accept it."

Flavia's mouth fell open, and her eyes widened in what appeared to be a rush of joy. But Rex shook his head and reached to his belt. He withdrew the cheap bronze dagger he had been carrying since the amphitheater and held it up for Flavia to see. Its hilt was in his fist, and its point dangled above the table like the fang of some hideous beast. "I'm a fighter, Lady Junia," he declared. "If Jesus rose from the dead, fine. I can believe it happened. But until I learn how to do it too, I need to worship a victory god."

Without warning, Rex slammed the dagger's point into the tabletop. Flavia sucked in her breath and jumped back. The dagger stood on its end, quivering, its golden blade gleaming in the light of the oil lamp.

Rex looked up and raised his palm toward the temple atop the waterfall. "Hail, Hercules Victorious," he said.

"He will not be," Flavia replied, and dropped her eyes to her lap.

7

October 311

Three days had passed since the sentence of execution had come down, and still the criminal wasn't dead. *She's just a pathetic little girl!* Pompeianus fumed. *Why is she so hard to kill?* Despite his frustration, though, he knew the answer. Lady Junia Flavia couldn't be strangled in the depths of the Carcer nor stabbed in a dark alley and left to bleed out. A citywide scandal was needed if Neratius was to lose the public's—and thus the emperor's—confidence. Flavia's death had to be visible and theatrical—and that was proving more difficult than Pompeianus had first imagined.

The prefect raised his eyes to the idol of Mars in the camp shrine. Firm and resolute, Mars gazed back with the placid expression that all gods should have as they considered the petitions of mortal men. The nude statue stood in the apse of a little hall at the center of camp, spear in one hand, shield in the other. On either side of the idol were the standards of the illustrious Praetorian Guard, emblazoned with eagles' wings and jagged thunderbolts. The spiritual power of Mars inhabited the very fabric of those flags. Worship of military standards was as old and venerable as the legions themselves.

"O great and holy Mars," Pompeianus prayed as he sprinkled incense into a smoking brazier, "hear my request and lead us to my enemy's daughter. I worship you with fragrant myrrh and frankincense, that you might give me success."

Would it be enough? One never knew with the gods. They could be capricious. But at least they could be coerced with gifts. It gave humans a certain measure of control.

Pompeianus walked outside into the cold October drizzle, hunched into his cloak, and crossed the cardinal street to the headquarters building. For a fortress as important as the Praetorian Camp in the capital city, the headquarters wasn't much of an edifice—less impressive, really, than you'd find at a good-sized frontier outpost. Yet that was the nature of the Praetorian Camp. Because it was attached to the defensive wall of Rome, its internal gate emptied into the city streets, where plenty of nearby buildings could be rented for administrative functions that normally would be housed inside a fort. Thus the Praetorian Camp was used almost exclusively as a tight-packed barracks. Four thousand footmen were billeted here, the infantry's counterpart to the New Camp of the emperor's horsemen. Together the foot soldiers and cavalry made an impressive fighting force for the city of Rome.

Though Pompeianus lived in the luxurious Lateran Palace and ran the army from there, he felt he needed to show up occasionally at the Praetorian Camp and mingle among the rank and file like a good commander. If the headquarters building was a little spartan, well, that would only make him seem more like a hardy field general than a rear-lines military bureaucrat. Pompeianus believed his reputation among the men was an important means of controlling them.

"Have the guards arrived yet?" he asked the junior tribune as he entered the command center and flung off his wet cloak. He handed it to a servant who had just delivered a tray of food. The slave shook the droplets from the cloak and hung it on a peg, then scurried out.

"Not yet, sir," said the tribune. "But they're on the way. I expect them shortly."

Pompeianus eyed his camp administrator, an up-and-coming officer in his late twenties. Efficient and clever, he was one of those military functionaries who had managed to climb through the ranks without a lot of duty in dangerous combat situations. Lacking that wartime résumé, the man knew his advancement depended on currying favor and delivering results. It was a great skill set in a fortress administrator—as long as a horde of barbarians wasn't clamoring outside the walls. Fortunately, no barbarian army had attacked the city of Rome for seven hundred years.

"Son, let me give you a lesson in leadership," Pompeianus said to the eager young man. When he had the tribune's attention, he clasped his hands behind his back and assumed the air of wise mentor. "Our problem is that when we lost the girl, we lost prestige. We declared her to be outcast from society—fit only to be food for the beasts. She needed to die a horrible death. We publicly committed ourselves to that outcome. All our plans were unfolding just as we had decreed. That makes us seem invincible, you see? Then some gladiator pops up from below the arena and whisks her underground. Now we have no idea where she is. But wherever she may be, she isn't lion's caca right now. Her powerful father and his supporters will surely view that as weakness. The ability to impose your will is the essence of leadership. Don't forget it, son! When you declare what shall be, you had better be prepared to *make* it so. Otherwise people will treat your words like morning fog—a harmless vapor that can be ignored at will."

"A good lesson, sir. I certainly won't forget it."

"See that you don't. Aha! I think I hear our guests."

The tribune went to the oaken door of the headquarters and ushered in three common soldiers of low rank. They had arrived under armed escort, their wrists cuffed. Pompeianus signaled that the guard should remove the men's shackles. After doing so, the guard saluted and left the three soldiers alone with Pompeianus and the tribune.

"You had one simple job," Pompeianus said flatly, "and yet you failed. What happened?"

The guardsmen exchanged nervous glances, each remaining silent lest he draw the prefect's attention. Finally, one of the men spoke up, a big dullard with an obvious mean streak. "We delivered that little canicula to the amphitheater just like you said. She was right there in front of the beasts! What more could we do? How could we know one of the gladiators would decide to run away with her?"

"Who was he?"

"No one knows. None of the gladiator companies will admit they're missing a man. He might have been a new guy from the northern frontiers, still unregistered. He looked pale-skinned like the Germani."

Pompeianus frowned. "That girl was condemned to die by the decree of the all-powerful Senate. Now she's running free somewhere in our empire. How did that tiny waif trick the soldiers of the greatest army in the world?"

"She didn't trick us, sir!" The big man held up his palm. "Look here. I beat her into submission with this hand. Chained her up like a dog! When I left that girl, she was locked in a cell under the amphitheater. It was them show planners that let her get away! The people who turn the cranks and hoist up the beasts in cages. Not us!" The emphatic statement elicited vigorous nods from the two soldiers on either side of the spokesman.

"Your job was to guard Lady Junia until she was dead. Not until she was in the House of the Vestals. Not until she was delivered to the amphitheater. Not until she was standing on the arena floor. Until she was *dead*."

The three guardsmen could only stare at the ground. "We'll find her, sir," the big man muttered at last.

"I am confident of it. Even so"—Pompeianus paused dramatically—"I feel compelled to hold one of you responsible for the disappearance." The assertion sparked a forceful barrage of accusations and recriminations. Pompeianus let the men fight it out. Finally, two of them ganged up on the third and assigned sole blame to him. The wide-eyed man was defending himself when Pompeianus cut off the arguments by drawing his sword. "Kill him," he said, handing the hilt to the hulking leader.

"No! It's not my fault!" screamed the third man, but his cry was futile. The second held him still while the leader ran him through. When the bloody blade was withdrawn, the scapegoat collapsed to his knees, then toppled onto his face. Beneath his belly, a dark red stain began to ooze across the tiled floor.

Pompeianus nodded crisply as he took back his ornate officer's sword. He wiped it on a towel. "Well done, soldiers of Rome. You are dismissed."

The two survivors saluted, trying to be brave, though the prefect could see the tremble in their hands as they put their fists to their chests. Chastened, they headed for the door. They were about to exit the headquarters when Pompeianus called out to them.

"Soldiers!" he barked.

The pair held still for a moment, then slowly turned back around.

"I blame one more of you. Since we cannot get the testimony of two witnesses in this instance, we will let the gods decide who has sinned."

Pompeianus walked over to a wooden trunk and rammed the sword's point into its lid. He watched it quiver there for a moment, then looked up at the guardsmen. They, too, were staring at it, trying to comprehend their commander's intent. He gestured at the blade with an open palm. "May the gods aid the innocent."

The soldiers' eyes grew large and round, and their jaws dropped. Suddenly they burst into a mad scramble for the weapon.

The battle was brief. One tackled the other and they both hit the ground. The adversaries clawed their way across the room, kicking and dragging each other as they extended their arms toward the trunk. The bigger man finally smashed his heel into his opponent's face, which gave him the advantage he needed to spin around and reach the sword first. He wrenched it from the trunk and plunged it into the top of the second man's shoulder as he lurched along the floor in a last, desperate dive. The blade slid all the way in without meeting resistance. The big man let go of the sword as his opponent went limp, the ivory hilt protruding from his collarbone.

Pompeianus came and stood over the winner, who was breathing heavily. "The gods have decided the matter," he said. "Now stand up."

The big guardsman got to his feet. Though sweat glistened on his brow, and four claw marks ran down his cheek, the wild exhilaration of victory lit up his face. He had been tested by the gods and found innocent.

"Retrieve my sword, soldier, and bring it to me."

Immediately the victor bent to the second man's corpse and extracted the blade from the length of his torso. He bowed to Pompeianus, offering the hilt to his lord.

"Keep it for yourself. Clean that fine blade and strap it to your side as a reminder to do your duty in the future."

"Yes, my lord," the big man said, visibly relieved though still shaken. "I will do my duty forevermore." After offering another tenuous salute, he hurried to the door and took the latch in his hand.

"One more thing, Praetorian!"

At the sound of his commander's voice, the big man instinctively spun around. With the practiced arm of many years on distant battlefields,

Pompeianus hurled a weighted javelin through the soldier's chest. The force of it pinned him to the oaken door. He grunted and began to wriggle, his arms dangling at his sides. The fine officer's sword clattered to the ground.

The prefect approached the delinquent soldier and stared into his eyes as they fluttered erratically. Blood welled up in his mouth and trickled down his coarse military tunic.

"Today it is your duty to die for your failure," Pompeianus declared. The man's eyes fell shut and his whole body sagged. Pompeianus yanked the spear from the door and allowed the corpse to tumble to the floor. He whirled away and shot a firm glance to the white-faced tribune. "That, my son, is how you rule men. Now go find someone to clean up this mess."

Rex examined the cut on his forearm, the worst of several nicks he had taken in the battle against the five Praetorians in the dead-end alley. He had treated it with a poultice made from wild garlic that he had found growing on the side of the road. Thanks to that herbal remedy, the wound was healing nicely. It was hard to believe he had come out of the fight with only a few minor injuries. In truth, he should be dead—and probably would be, if not for two things. One was the intervention of his friend Geta, always a rival yet faithful when it counted. The second intervention, the one behind Geta's fortuitous arrival, could only have been divine. Hercules had smiled on Rex that day—leading Geta through the streets, helping him catch up at just the right time, giving victory in battle. Now Rex intended to thank the god for his heavenly favor.

The conversation with Flavia over dinner had solidified Rex's desire to offer a sacrifice of thanksgiving for the god's protection. Though the experience of worshiping at a temple was new to Rex—at least, temples on such a grand scale like they had in Italy—he was determined to give it a try now that he had come to the heart of the empire. Flavia could observe her Christian religion of peace and charity, an entirely appropriate form of devotion for a wealthy girl living a comfortable life on the Aventine Hill. But soldiers needed a different kind of patron. Despite the current diversion from his mission, Rex hadn't forgotten that Emperor Constantine was on his way to Rome, and he wasn't coming to pick poppies in a meadow with

Maxentius. He was coming to make war, a war in which Rex expected to fight mortal enemies with swords in their hands and bloodlust in their eyes. Therefore Rex needed a victory god. And who could be more victorious than a hero who had attempted twelve impossible labors and achieved them all?

The famous Sanctuary of Hercules Victorious sat on the brow of a ridge at Tibur, keeping watch over the plains around Rome. Several cataracts poured over the ridge at the temple's base and tumbled into the valley, just one of the many places in Tibur where waterfalls could be seen. The temple had been laid out on an artificial terrace that gleamed white in the midday sun like the summit of Mount Olympus itself.

Yet as Rex followed the road that led him to the foot of the temple, he quickly realized the place was not only a religious hub but also a commercial one. The Tiburtinian Way served as a major highway that passed through the rustic mountains around Rome, where shepherding was a way of life. As the herders approached Tibur with their sheep, goats, and cattle, they were channeled into a tunnel that ran beneath the temple's terrace. There, in that narrow chute known as the Covered Way, the animals were counted one by one and taxed. This meant the road was, essentially, a kind of money pipeline—and the priests at the Temple of Hercules were raking in an enormous income.

Rex stepped inside the Covered Way, immediately grateful for its cool shade, though not its stench of fresh manure and wet wool. While a few cows and goats were in the stream of livestock today, for the most part sheep were moving through the chute right now. The sound of their bleating, combined with the cries of the shepherds and the haggling between tax collectors and overseers, created a bizarre cacophony in the barrel-vaulted passageway. At intervals, the roof's length was penetrated by skylights that let in not only light and air but also hooks suspended from the booms of cranes. The sheep selected as taxation were being hauled up by belly straps into the market, their black legs dangling and their tongues lolling out of their mouths as they were separated from the flock. Men with tally books counted each animal snatched away from the peasant farmers. It was a stark reminder of what Rex knew all too well: *the empire always takes its cut.*

Rex approached one of the shepherds and asked about buying a lamb. The man beckoned to his overseer, who came over and offered a steep price. Rex worked him down a little and finally struck a more reasonable bargain. The shepherd reached into the steady flow and hauled out a fluffy lamb with no obvious defects. Rex paid the overseer, then cradled the animal under his arm and left the Covered Way. He ascended a staircase to the market above.

The spacious plaza around the temple of Hercules was surrounded on three sides by a colonnade. Most of the shady walkway, which might have been designed by its architect for a leisurely stroll, was instead being used as a public market. Vendors in their stalls offered all manner of products, from leather goods to woolen fabric to roasted chestnuts. Other vendors had set up awnings in the plaza for selling cuts of meat from the newly slaughtered livestock. And, of course, the money changers had their booths as well. The volume of commerce pouring through the holy sanctuary required a team of bankers to maintain the pipeline's constant flow.

Rex stopped at a stall dealing in local honey. "Where can I find a priest?" he asked.

The beekeeper pointed to a doorway a short distance along the colonnade. "That's the hall where they feast. But they're all senators from the city or the top local magistrates. They probably won't admit the likes of you."

"We'll see," Rex said, and headed for the banquet hall.

The priests of Hercules, known as the Salii, were identifiable by their special caps crowned by a spike of olive wood. Rex peeked into the dining room and was greeted with a scene of extravagant decadence. Nine fat noblemen in their spiked hats reclined on three couches around a table overflowing with meats and other delicacies. Busty girls in gauzy linen shifts scurried back and forth, filling the priests' goblets with wine.

The walls were adorned with gold mosaics, and the floor was paved with expensive Tuscan marble. At the rear of the room, an idol of Hercules rested on a padded couch with a tray of food in front of him so he could join the feast. Apparently, the god wasn't hungry, for he hadn't yet touched his food.

One of the serving girls approached Rex at the doorway. "The priests can't see you now," she said in a breathy voice, "but I'd be glad to meet you later to receive an offering in private." A little wink signaled the wench had nighttime duties around the temple in addition to her day job.

"I wish only to make a blood sacrifice," Rex said, dipping his chin toward the lamb squirming in his arms. "Can you direct me to a priest who can help?"

"One of the acolytes at the altar can do it, but you'll have to pay."

"I have to pay? I already had to pay for this lamb."

The girl shrugged. "You have to buy a token. Only then will the acolyte make the sacrifice. It's the rule. I can sell you one."

"How much?"

"Twenty-five common denarii."

Rex tsked and shook his head. "A day's wage just to make the sacrifice?"

"Usually I charge fifty and keep half for myself. But I have a weakness for handsome men."

Frowning, Rex fished the amount from his moneypouch and paid the girl, who gave him a token stamped with the image of muscular Hercules holding his club. As she handed over the little clay disc, a sly smile came to her face.

"Come to the theater tonight," she invited, leaning close. "I have a small part in the play. I'd be happy to serve you afterward."

"I have other business tonight," Rex said, then turned and left the girl pouting in the doorway of the banquet hall.

The actual temple of Hercules sat on a high platform in the middle of the sanctuary's plaza. Because the whole edifice was faced with white marble, it gleamed so brightly that it hurt Rex's eyes. Isolated above its surroundings in lonely splendor, the temple could be approached only by a travertine staircase flanked by fountains for ritual washing. Its porch was supported by a double row of eight columns, in front of which the acolytes were gathered around a portable altar. Each man held a knife. After rinsing his fingers, Rex mounted the stairs with his clay token and his lamb. "I wish to commune with the god," Rex said to a young man at the altar.

"You have the proof of payment?"

Rex handed over the token. The man inspected its front and back, then nodded and extended his palm. "Very good. That will be twenty-five common denarii."

"I already paid the girl at the feasting hall."

"I know. That was the sacrifice fee. This payment is for the knife rental." The acolyte waved the blade in his hand.

"The knife rental?" Rex pursed his lips and held back the curse he wanted to utter. "How is that different from the sacrifice fee? Shouldn't the knife be included?"

"The sacrifice fee pays for the blood that is shed," the young priest explained, "but the knife fee pays for the instrument that sheds it. As you can see, those are two very different things."

"No, they're not."

The acolyte offered only a blank stare. Shaking his head in disgust, Rex paid the man a second amount, then gave him the lamb.

"Don't make the sacrifice right away," he ordered. "I want to pray to Hercules first. I'll let you know when I'm ready."

Rex had crossed the portico and was about to enter the temple when a pair of armed guards stopped him. "Hey, stranger, stop right there!" one said. "You aren't allowed inside."

"Why not? I'm a devout man, here to worship. I even brought an offering."

The acolyte who had received the token intervened. After waving the guards away, he came and stood between Rex and the main door. "The temple is the god's house. His idol is protected inside the cell. We priests are the mediators between you and him. If you have a request to make, tell it to me, and I will relay it."

"I can't go inside? Out in the provinces, free citizens can stand in the doorway of many temples. And there are shrines for the soldiers in army camps. People want to see the idol they're praying to."

"My friend, this isn't some rustic temple for country yokels and barbarian legionaries. It is the holy and most splendid Sanctuary of Hercules Victorious, patron of commerce at Tibur, and divine protector of all Latium. Entrance is forbidden to the common people."

"So what did my coins and that lamb buy me?"

The acolyte rolled his eyes and tsked, then gave Rex a patient smile, as if explaining basic truths to a child. "The god's awareness of you, obviously. Why else should mighty Hercules pay attention to a mere mortal? You need to draw his notice with a gift. Come now! Step over here and watch your sacrifice. You have brought a good one. Even more than grain or wine, a blood sacrifice will surely earn the god's favor."

Rex followed the acolyte to the altar, from which a thin column of smoke rose to the sky. After sprinkling wine and salted flour on the lamb's head, the man slit its throat with a practiced hand and deftly caught the blood in a bowl. When the dribble finally stopped, the priest skinned and butchered the animal. He dumped the entrails and scraps into the bowl of blood but left the choicest cuts of meat on a silver tray.

"You have a petition for glorious Hercules?" he asked, gesturing toward the temple with his bloody hand.

"A thanksgiving for his past protection. And a request for his continued watchcare. He knows the details of what happened."

"Perhaps you might want to remind him. Hercules is a popular god. He receives many requests."

"It was a fight with five evildoers. I thank him that I got only this cut on my arm. I ask for no further injuries."

"Hmm. Alright, that should probably be enough to jog his memory." The priest pulled a veil over his head and began to intone the words of an ancient ritual. A flutist joined him at the altar, so the words themselves could not be discerned. When the priest's liturgy was finished, he dumped the lamb's bloody guts onto the hot coals. A cloud of dark, pungent smoke immediately billowed up. Rex watched the smoke rise toward the sky and dissipate into the heavens.

"Is that all?" he asked the young priest.

"I just sent up a good smell to Hercules. I also sent him your prayer in exactly the right words. What more do you want?"

"Nothing, I suppose."

The acolyte turned and beckoned toward a slave standing in the shade of the temple's porch. "Take that tray of meat to the kitchen and be quick about it," he instructed. The slave bowed, then grabbed the silver tray by its handles and carried it away.

"Don't forget the mint sauce!" the acolyte called after the slave.

"Mint sauce?" Rex asked. "What's that for?"

"My dinner, of course." The priest smiled broadly at Rex and bid him good day. Then, glancing over Rex's shoulder, he signaled for the next worshiper to step forward.

—⁂—

The Palace Hall at Augusta Treverorum wasn't decked out in imperial splendor today, but Constantine still preferred to meet his guests here whenever possible. It was a beautiful and spacious basilica, obviously worthy of an emperor even though it was located in a frontier city. And best of all, it was heated. Although autumn days in northern Gaul could be cold, the hot air flowing beneath the floor of the Palace Hall was always up to the challenge.

The mood in the hall was suitably casual, with the fine banners having been removed and the floor runners stored for more ceremonious occasions. An ample meal had been set out for Constantine, and though he nibbled at it, in the end he decided he wasn't hungry. Squatting on his heels, he whistled at his two favorite hunting dogs asleep on the warm floor. The hounds lifted their heads and pricked their ears. When they scented the hunk of swine flesh in the emperor's hand, they sauntered over and gulped down the pieces that Constantine tore off for them. He ruffled the dogs' ears and let them lick his hand clean.

Standing again, he returned to the table, preferring it over his imperial throne for this meeting. His general Vitruvius was bringing documents and maps today, so a table seemed like a better choice since the meal was likely to turn into a strategy session. A military man himself, Constantine liked to foster a more informal and intimate relationship with his generals. They deserved his personal friendship. It was only right that there be mutual respect among those engaged in the noble art of war. Sharing an afternoon meal was a way to demonstrate that high regard.

Vitruvius arrived a short while later and was escorted to the table. A finely tooled calfskin satchel was draped over his shoulder. He reclined on the couch opposite Constantine, and plates and silverware were set before him. The emperor knew that refraining from eating would be impolite, so he picked at his food and ate enough to make his guest feel welcome. When the dishes were cleared and the goblets refilled, the two battle-tested warriors got down to business.

"My servants tell me a courier arrived late last night from Pannonia," Constantine said. "I'm anxious to hear the news."

Vitruvius couldn't suppress a smile. "You're not going to believe what you hear."

"Go on."

The general reached into his satchel and removed a large book written on expensive parchment and bound in wood and fine leather. "It is a gift from a friend," Vitruvius said, sliding the book across the table. "He had it made specially for you. I'll let you read it."

Constantine opened the codex and immediately recognized it as a selection of the Christian scriptures. The dedication page, which was in Latin, read: *To Flavius Valerius Aurelius Constantine, Augustus of Gaul. May you live, flourish, and rejoice in God. I, Gaius Valerius Licinius Augustus, have dedicated to you in friendship this Book of the Fourfold Gospel, whose most holy words about the Savior are written here, copied by expert scribes from ancient versions.* On the first page, *The Gospel according to Matthew* began in Greek, followed by that of Mark, Luke, and John.

"Since when is Licinius a Christian?" Constantine asked, setting the book back on the table.

"Probably since he heard you had adopted Jesus as your patron. After you saw the heavenly cross in the sky, he decided to get in on the god's power as well." Vitruvius paused, considering his words, then arched his eyebrows at the emperor. "May I assume you see the significance of this gift?"

"Yes, of course. It's a bid for an alliance. Two Christians working together."

"That's right. And we should probably accept it. Better to have friends than enemies."

"I could marry my sister to him. Then the alliance would be much more lasting. And Constantia would surely enjoy the prestige of being an augusta." Constantine drummed his fingers on the couch, reflecting on this interesting development. "So why do you imagine Licinius is making this move?"

"Licinius is ruthless, entirely focused on his own interests. There can be only one reason he would seek to join with you. Let me show you what we know."

Vitruvius reached again to his satchel and unrolled a large map across the table, weighting the corners with lead pellets. "Here is your territory," he said, tracing his finger around Hispania, Britannia, and Gaul. "Down in Rome we have Maxentius. He might be a nobody in the Imperial College, but in his mind, he's an augustus, and his army holds Italy and Africa whether we like it or not. So he's functionally the ruler there, no matter what the college says." Vitruvius next circled the lands along the Danubius River to the east of Italy. "Here is what Licinius controls. It's not much, just a few poor provinces. And then the rest of the East, as far as the Euphrates and all the way around to Aegyptus, belongs to Daia. That is a great holding, but Daia isn't satisfied with it. He wants the whole empire for himself. To get it, he's making overtures from here"—Vitruvius slid his finger from Asia to the peninsula of Italy—"to here."

"Daia wants to join forces with Maxentius?"

Vitruvius grimaced and nodded. "I'm afraid so. That's what we're hearing from our spies. You can see, then, why Licinius would be looking for an ally. He's pinched between you on one side and two enemies on the other who are uniting against him. Predicaments like that often lead men to make new political alliances—or religious conversions, if that's what it takes."

"Crafty little fox, isn't he?"

"More than you know. Look here." Vitruvius indicated the broad arc of the Alps that curved above the Italian peninsula. His finger came to rest on the mountainous province of Noricum, just north of Italy itself. "Licinius has armies here. But see? You take some troops across one of the alpine passes, and just like that, you're at the gates of Aquileia, then Ravenna, then—"

"I see it, General. Our friend Licinius is poised at the gateway of Italy. And there's only one thing stopping him from claiming the prize of Rome: my dear brother-in-law, Maxentius."

"Right. So let's say Licinius is successful in making an alliance with you against Maxentius and Daia. That means you and he are Christians, and you're united against two pagans. It's perfectly reasonable for one or the other of you to march down to Rome and take out your challenger. All the reports say Maxentius is becoming a tyrant. The people are turning against him. Whoever goes down first and conquers Rome will be hailed as a liberator—and he'll have complete control of Italy and Africa. The man who holds those lands will be hard to stop."

"What do we know about Maxentius's strength?"

"Nothing yet. Centurion Aratus and his team of speculators are there now, collecting intelligence."

Constantine chuckled as he recalled the long-haired youth who had confronted him in this very hall. "That Germanic kid of his was impudent, but I like him. I think he'll get the job done."

"Young Rex is indeed impressive. The centurion tells me he's never seen such a strong fighter at his age."

"Remember how he grabbed the battle standard and handed it to me? He said, 'In this sign, you shall conquer!' That's essentially the same message God gave me in the sky. It was written in the heavens that the cross will bring me victory."

"It was a bold prediction indeed."

"From a bold young man. Let's hope he was right." Constantine paused, tilting his head and staring into space. "You know what we should do?"

"What, sire?"

"We should make a special battle standard like the one Rex handed me—something impressive to go before the troops. It should be marked with the Christian cross. Maybe we could gild the pole and put some gems on it. That would surely give the men confidence."

"It can be done. There's a jeweler's shop across the street from the palace. I've seen the man's work. He's quite skilled."

"Excellent! See that it gets done. But Vitruvius—run it past the bishops first to make sure it would be pleasing to the Highest Divinity. I don't know this God very well, and I don't want to upset him." The emperor returned his attention to the map. "So then, we'll march for Italy as soon as the alpine passes open up next spring. Which one would you take? Poeninus?"

Vitruvius shook his head. "That one is more northerly, so it stays closed longer. I think we should try this one." The general traced his finger from Poeninus Pass around the western curve of the Alps to the town of Brigantium in southern Gaul. "This area is warm and sunny. The pass here isn't much higher than the city, and it faces south, so it thaws early. If we get a quick jump, we can vault over the mountains before the first flowers are pushing through the turf at Segusio."

"That sounds good. What's it called?"

"It has different names, but the oldest is Mons Matrona."

"Mons Matrona?" A little laugh escaped Constantine's lips. "When I was a boy, my tutor taught me that was the pass Hannibal crossed with his war elefanti!"

"It's true. And Your Majesty, while I can't provide any of those great beasts, I promise to be a general worthy of our ancient Carthaginian foe."

"I know you will, Vitruvius." Constantine stretched across the table and clasped the old warrior's shoulder. "I believe in you. And we will also have the new battle standard going ahead of us."

Vitruvius said nothing for a moment, only nodding as he gazed at the heavy platter of pork on the table. Finally, he raised his eyes and gave Constantine a pointed stare. "There is one thing I must emphasize to you, my lord."

"Yes?"

The general picked up a hunk of meat, then rolled over on his couch and tossed the tidbit in a high arc. It landed in a splatter of sauce on the smooth marble floor.

"Your manners are somewhat lacking," Constantine said, feigning disapproval. Yet he knew his friend was trying to make some kind of point.

The heads of the two hounds dozing by the wall suddenly lifted. They scrambled up and raced toward the juicy morsel. One dog managed to outdistance the other. It snatched the meat and gulped it down before its competitor could grab a share. The winner licked its muzzle, smug in its victory, while the other hound wandered back to its place and resumed its nap.

"The prize will go to the first to claim it," Constantine said.

"Yes, Your Majesty. Let's make sure it isn't Licinius."

———— ✤ ————

The tall man in the distance obviously wasn't a shepherd or a local Italian. Though he had lost the long-haired look of a Germanic barbarian, Flavia still knew it was Rex walking back toward the walls of Tibur from the Sanctuary of Hercules. She found herself a little excited at his return, then immediately chastised herself for it. *He's coming from the worship of demons*, she recalled. *You mustn't let your heart be drawn to a pagan.* According to the scriptures, it wasn't proper for a Christian to be unequally yoked with an unbeliever. Even so, Flavia couldn't help but feel safer when Rex was around.

She left the gate and followed the Tiburtinian Way to meet Rex halfway between the town and the temple. The plan today was to approach her uncle's villa under cover of darkness, where—God willing—she could find refuge until further arrangements could be made. All the running and hiding was beginning to take its toll on Flavia. She was ready to get somewhere safe for a while and rest.

The pair greeted each other when they met on the road. "What did you think of the temple?" Flavia asked as they walked side by side. "From a distance, it certainly looks like an impressive building." Flavia thought she could acknowledge that much, at least, about the huge religious complex.

Rex shrugged. "Not what I expected."

"Really? Why not?"

"It's as much a cattle market and toll station as a temple. Hercules is doing alright for himself there. Or at least his priests are."

"Were you able to make your sacrifice?"

"Yes, if you can call it that. More like a bribe." Rex glanced sideways at Flavia as they walked back to Tibur. "How does Christianity make its sacrifices? I know you don't have idols, so where do you leave your offerings?"

Lord, help me explain your truth rightly, Flavia prayed as she considered her friend's honest question. "The Jews used to do it at the temple," she said, "but it's not like that anymore in the Christian religion. We do make a sacrifice, but it's only bread and wine, not animals. We consider Christ's body and blood a sufficient sacrifice already. So it's a remembrance that we offer in church—a sacrifice that looks back to what the Savior did. My bishop says the Eucharist makes Christ present in our midst. He is truly there with us, to nourish us. We like to say we feed on him. Not literally, of course, but spiritually. The Spirit of God is in that consecrated bread and wine. Grace comes to us in this holy meal."

"So there's no need to buy anything? I had to buy the lamb and pay a bunch of fees. 'Votive offerings,' they call it. When you bring a request, or when your vow is fulfilled, you have to give something valuable."

"I know how it works. The standard prayer made to your gods is, 'I give so that you might give.' But our scriptures say, 'God demonstrates his love to us in this, that while we were still sinners, Christ died for us.' See the difference? The giving goes the other way in Christianity: from God to us. You don't have to bribe him first."

"Then how do your priests pay for everything if you don't have to buy your way in?"

"Oh, Christians definitely pay money! But it's not a required fee. It's a freewill offering. We come up and leave it on the table, and the deacons use it to buy food and clothes for the poor. One of the main purposes of our meetings is to gather money to be distributed to the needy. That is the essence of love."

"Love?" Rex waved his hand. "Love is just a feeling. It isn't something real."

"Yes, it is. Love becomes real when the feeling becomes an action."

Rex didn't reply. He seemed lost in thought as the pair walked toward the gate of Tibur. Suddenly he gripped Flavia's arm. "Hold up. There's some kind of commotion on the road ahead. Let's not get involved."

"Can we hide in the bushes?"

"That would be even more suspicious. Let's just pass by quickly with our eyes down. The gate isn't far ahead. Stay close by me."

Flavia took Rex's arm, feeling a little guilty for enjoying it yet considering the gesture necessary in this case. As they approached the troublemakers, she was surprised to discern the wail of an infant amid the shouts and raucous laughter. Three husky ruffians were harassing a much smaller, thinner man. One of the thugs held a wailing baby upside down by the ankle, as if it were a toy doll.

"I will gladly pay you double the cost of a new slave if you'll just hand me that infant," the slender man said to his harassers. "Name your price and it's yours."

A tall fellow with long strings of greasy hair stomped over to the man who had made the offer and shoved him hard in the shoulder. "Shut up, runt!" he roared. The tiny, naked baby dangled from his fist as he held it up. "You don't have enough money to buy this little sweetheart from me."

"I can obtain your asking price. Name it."

"You don't understand nothin'!" another man cried. "It's not just about a sale right now. It's a lifetime of income! She'll work every day until she's forty and bring in good silver the whole time. Why would we give that up for a few coins now?"

"C'mon, boss, I'm thirsty," said the third man. "Forget this guy and let's get back to town. I don't know why people have to leave their babies so far outside the gate! Just drop it close and run along, why don't ya? It's so annoying."

Instinctively, Flavia tightened her grip on Rex's arm as she discerned the meaning of the rough banter. A female baby had been abandoned on the roadside by a desperate mother. Three pimps had come out to claim it, and a brave passerby was daring to contest their horrific plans. However, he was too small to do anything.

"Just keep your head down and walk on by," Rex said, edging to the far side of the road. "Brisk pace, but don't act scared."

The shouting continued as Flavia and Rex hurried past the conflict. A burst of guffaws made Flavia glance over her shoulder. The three bullies were arranged in a triangle around the would-be rescuer, and now they were tossing the baby back and forth in a twisted game of keep-away. Tears sprang to Flavia's eyes, and she bit her knuckle to stifle a cry at the cruel spectacle unfolding on the road. *Lord God in heaven, do something!*

Rex halted midstride, though he did not turn around. "We shouldn't get involved," he said in a flat voice.

"I know, Rex. We really shouldn't."

Flavia put her hand to her mouth again—this time not to stifle a cry but to hide the smile she could not contain. She knew everything had just changed. The uncivilized barbarian whose arm she clutched was about to unleash some serious justice.

"Go, warrior," she whispered. And so he went.

"You there!" Rex shouted to the pimps. "Hand me that child right now, and I won't break any of your bones."

Flavia took a few steps back, realizing that Rex was headed into this thing at full speed. Clearly, this altercation wasn't going to be ended by a few coins and a mutual parting of the ways. The stakes were too high.

The greasy-haired man whirled toward Rex, his scowl nasty, his fists raised. "Who do you think you are, telling me what to do?" he snarled.

Rex moved so fast, it seemed he wasn't a man at all but some kind of wild creature—like a ferret darting toward its prey. He spun Greasy around and bent him at the waist. His oily locks dangled beside his cheeks as he stared at the pavement. The man's arm was pinned against Rex's chest, held there so tightly that even the tiniest pivot on Rex's part could wrench the limb out of socket. Greasy screamed for help, but before the other two could assist, Rex barked, "Give the man that baby!" When no one moved, he put a twist in his captive's arm that drew an even louder screech. "I said hand over that baby! Now!"

"Do it!" Greasy bellowed. "Hurry! It hurts!"

When the slender man had taken possession of the infant, he retreated toward Flavia and left Rex to face the three pimps. Rex swept Greasy's feet from under him and dropped him prone on the road with a knee pressed into his back. At no time did Rex relinquish his grip on his opponent's arm. "You two start walking that way," he ordered, nodding toward the distant temple. "Once you're out of sight, your friend can get up with his arm still attached."

"Maybe we might come at you," one of the pimps threatened, taking a step forward with his fists clenched.

Rex gave Greasy's arm a hard twist. There was an audible pop as his shoulder was dislocated. "Argh! Get moving!" he wailed through gritted teeth, and his men quickly retreated. Only when they were long gone did Rex finally stand up. His enemy remained facedown on the ground, moaning a little, all the fight wrung out of him. Rex backed away and left the man writhing on the pavestones.

"That was scary," Flavia said as she came to Rex's side.

"Not really. Those lowlifes don't know how to fight. Let's get into Tibur now and disappear." Rex gently took Flavia's arm and began to lead her away from the scene of the conflict.

"Where to? The inn?"

"No, it's too public."

"Where else, then?"

A voice broke in before Rex could answer. "I can give you shelter."

Flavia and Rex turned to face the man who had rescued the baby. He cradled the infant in his arms. The little girl was asleep now, exhausted from her ordeal.

"You should know, my friend, that to shelter us could get you in trouble," Rex said.

"Nevertheless, I am willing to help you, if you are in need."

Rex started to reply, then fell silent. The afternoon sun beat down on the empty road as the three travelers considered their next move.

"Why did you do what you did back there?" Flavia asked the stranger.

"Should this little child, created in the image of God, face a life of prostitution just because she was found by those sinful pimps?"

"No, she shouldn't. Your deed was brave. And if I judge you correctly, worthy of Christ."

The man's eyes darted to Flavia's. "You are a believer too?"

"Yes, brother, I am," she said, then turned to look at Rex. "I think we should go to his house."

Rex was motionless for a long moment. Flavia watched his face, trying to read his expression. She thought he might consider the home of a Christian an unwise refuge in these tumultuous times. Instead, Rex surprised her and agreed.

"Follow me, then," the man said.

"What made you say yes to him?" Flavia whispered to Rex as the threesome began to walk back into town.

"I think it was his love," Rex said simply.

Flavia's mouth fell open. "I thought you didn't believe in love! You said it was just a feeling!"

"Lady Junia, don't you know anything?" Rex shot back with a grin. "Love becomes real when the feeling becomes an action."

—⁓—

Senator Neratius Junius Flavianus was a man with needs like any other. At least that is what he told himself as he grabbed the chambermaid by the wrist and pulled her into an amorous embrace.

"What's the matter, Daphne?" he breathed in her ear as she squirmed in his arms. "Don't you love your master?"

"My lord, please, no!" the girl cried, turning her face aside as Neratius nuzzled her. "It isn't right!"

"Of course it is. All men do it."

"Not those of our faith!" Daphne countered, breaking free from Neratius's grip. She stared at him, wide-eyed and breathing hard. Clearly, she was scared. Even so, her face was defiant. For a girl of only thirteen, Daphne had a lot of spirit.

Neratius started toward her again, but Daphne whirled and snatched up the chamber pot. She clutched it against her chest. "My lord, I'm afraid I'll spill it if you come closer!"

"Put it down, child, and come here to me."

"But the mistress! She will be angry!"

"Never mind her," Neratius said as he lunged at Daphne.

Uttering a little squeak, the chambermaid jumped backward. Some of the pot's foul contents dribbled down the front of her dress—whether by accident or intention, Neratius wasn't sure. Either way, it was repulsive. He wrinkled his nose and turned away.

"I'm soiled now, lord. I must be gone." Daphne bowed, then hurried out of the bedroom.

Neratius crossed to a wheeled cart and unstopped a glass bottle. Pouring himself a cup of white wine sweetened with lead, he gulped it down and poured another. Absently, he used a poker to stir the embers in a charcoal brazier on a stand, warming his hands in the heat. *Maybe I shouldn't harass Daphne*, he thought as he sipped his wine. *God might punish me. But she's such a pretty little thing!*

Sharp words from outside drew Neratius to the doorway. He cracked the door and gazed down into the rear garden of the home, which was centered on a deep cistern and enclosed all around by a lovely peristyle. Sophronia was there, speaking sharply to Daphne, who hung her head in shame. Yet even as Neratius watched, it became apparent that his wife was growing less angry at the chambermaid and more angry at him. He withdrew just in time to avoid being seen by Sophronia, whose disgusted gaze flicked up toward the second-story bedroom. Daphne was urgently protesting her innocence: gesturing to her stained dress and mimicking how she had wrestled with her master. At last Sophronia put her hand on the servant's shoulder and dismissed her with a gentle nod. The girl gratefully fled to some other corner of the mansion. It was an annoying scene, and Neratius turned away from it in disdain.

He was seated at his desk two hours later when the doorkeeper, Onesimus, returned from the errand on which he had been sent. The slave stood at the door of the study with a parcel in his hand, a small box tied with strings. A droplet of wax, impressed with a signet, sealed the knots.

"You may enter," the senator said.

"I found something lovely for the mistress of the house. I think you will be pleased." Onesimus set the package on the desk, along with a bill of sale. Neratius untied the strings and opened the box to reveal a gold necklace decorated with what looked like green gemstones. Fortunately, the glass blowers at the foot of the Aventine were so skilled, they could make bits of colored glass look enough like gems that no one could tell the difference. Neratius checked the receipt and verified that he had indeed been charged only for glass and not emeralds.

"Very good, Onesimus," he said. "Now go summon the mistress and tell her I would like to see her immediately."

A short time later, Sophronia appeared at the doorway. Although the ornatrix had tried to hide it with makeup, Neratius could tell his wife had been crying.

She's sad now, but not for long, he thought as he reached for the jewelry box. He held it up, beaming with pride. "I have purchased something expensive for you," he declared.

Sophronia inclined her head respectfully as she entered the study. She opened the box, but upon seeing what was inside, she seemed far less pleased than Neratius had expected. He wondered if she could tell the gems were actually glass.

"You don't like it?"

"I like gifts from the heart. I do not like to be placated with trinkets."

"Gods, woman! Most wives would be overjoyed to receive something like that."

"All I have ever wanted from you is your love and fidelity, my lord."

"You have all that, plus great riches."

"Do I?"

"Look around! Is this magnificent house not rich enough for you?"

"It is sumptuous indeed. But do I also have your fidelity?"

Neratius wasn't in the mood to play games. "I suppose you are referring to the servant girl?"

"Yes. Daphne says you have been pressing her. Today she only barely escaped."

"It happens in every mansion in Rome. The slaves are there for the taking."

"But this is a Christian home, Neratius. It should be different."

"It is different! Do I whip them? Starve them? Sell them off and break up families? No! What harm is done if one of the girls takes a fancy to me and I bed her?"

219

"The harm is done to your wife, and to an innocent virgin, and to your own soul. What do you see in a mere child that you do not see in me?"

Neratius sighed, exasperated by his wife's inability to comprehend the desires of a man. She had mirrors in her bedroom. Could she not see that she had grown old? Daphne, however, was so *cute*. She was fresh and nubile in a way Sophronia was not. It was hard to imagine that his wife could not understand this. Yet perhaps she truly did not know how much of a toll the years had taken on her.

"The truth is, Lady Sabina," said Neratius, addressing his wife formally, "you have aged. It is inevitable. Just accept it—that is my counsel. It happens to all women. You cannot expect a man's interest to be held in one place for so long."

"My lord, I am only thirty-five. That is *not* old. I am just now coming into my best years."

"It is very old," Neratius replied, then snapped the jewelry box shut as if to emphasize his point.

Sophronia came around Neratius's desk and leaned against it while he sat in his chair. She looked down at him for a long while. Unexpectedly, she reached out and caressed the gray locks that ringed the back of his head, smoothing them with her hand. "My husband, we should not live like this," she said softly.

"Like what?"

"As two strangers cooperating in the maintenance of a household. I want to be more to you. And you to me."

"What do you lack, Lady Sabina? We are one of the richest families in the empire. You have everything you could dream of."

"Everything but what I really want."

"And what is that? Name it, and it shall be yours."

"A husband."

Neratius rolled his eyes and threw up his hands. "Is that not what I am?"

"Perhaps legally," Sophronia said. "But emotionally? Spiritually? I think not."

"What do you mean? Do I not attend the church that meets in our house? I give a sack of coins each week for the care of the poor! Is it baptism you desire of me? If it can be arranged in private with the bishop, I might consider it."

"Baptism is an outward washing that signifies a cleansed heart. So, Neratius, I ask you: is your heart clean in the Lord Christ?"

"Yes, of course."

"Then will you do something for me?"

Though Neratius said nothing, his arched eyebrows indicated that his wife could make her request.

"Stay away from little Daphne."

"Fine!" Neratius spat, flicking away the request with the back of his hand. "She means nothing to me!"

"But do I?"

"I married you, didn't I? It was a fine union, a Sabinus and a Junius, two great clans merged in a single household."

Sophronia took Neratius's hand in hers, clutching it tightly. "Two hearts merged as well?"

"Yes! Two hearts merged."

"And not so long ago—two bodies."

Removing his hand from his wife's grasp, Neratius stood up from his desk chair. He looked her in the eyes and spoke firmly. "There is no need for that. We have one daughter already. I do not wish to divide my estate further. Nor is it likely that you are fruitful enough any longer to produce a son. It seems we must be content with what Juno has already given us. And Jesus too. Juno and Jesus together. Or only Jesus, I suppose. Yes, what Jesus has given us—a daughter."

Though Sophronia's face was crestfallen, fortunately, she did not start to cry. All she said was, "So be it, my lord." She turned to go.

At the door to the study, Neratius called to her. "Sophronia?"

Slowly, she turned.

"Could you send Onesimus back in? This necklace was costly, and I believe I can still return it to the jeweler."

For some strange reason, the simple request caused Sophronia to burst into tears and flee the room.

Who can really understand the ways of women? Neratius wondered. He smiled to himself and shook his head at the craziness of female antics.

Then, with a little sigh, he turned his attention to the stack of contracts that awaited his signature.

⤝✴⤞

The small Greek man with black curly hair who had rescued the baby on the road—his name, Rex had learned, was Alexamenos—handed the baby to her new parents, a hardworking shepherd and his seamstress wife. By combining their skills, the couple had established a nice little business in Tibur selling woolen garments. Together they could provide for their six children—or seven, now that the family included Charis, the latest addition picked up from the side of the road. Three of the couple's children were naturally born, while four had been rescued from life in the brothels. The family received a weekly stipend out of the Christian coffers to aid in their upkeep. A deacon came with money every Moon Day after the church had met on the day of the Sun. In this way, the whole Christian community contributed to the raising of orphans. The same thing also happened for their widows. It was a financial distribution system unlike anything Rex had ever seen.

Alexamenos had brought his new friends to his modest villa outside the walls of Tibur. Though he normally lived in Rome, Alexamenos had saved up enough money to buy a few acres of arable land and some apple orchards in the countryside. A handful of resident servants ran the farm, generating sufficient profits to fund—what else?—the church that met in the farmhouse. And to Rex's delight, there was going to be a church meeting at sundown, once the worshipers were freed from their daily labors. Rex had heard so much about Christianity in recent days, yet he had never seen it up close. He was intrigued to learn what had drawn Flavia to this religion, along with so many other believers across the empire. When these people committed themselves to the god Jesus, they weren't afraid to die. The rituals of the Christian faith must be extraordinary indeed. It would be an interesting spectacle, if nothing else.

Though the shepherd and seamstress had been the first worshipers to arrive, more began to trickle in as soon as the sun went down. They came in small numbers so as not to attract attention; for while the persecution had ended in Italy, the habit of keeping a low profile was ingrained in the Christians, giving the meeting an aura of clandestine activity.

Alexamenos welcomed each new arrival, making sure to introduce Rex as an honored guest and Flavia as a catechumen. Rex asked her about the term. "It means I believe in Jesus but have not been baptized," she explained. Apparently, baptism was a big event for a Christian. The catechumens had to study the teachings and moral precepts of the religion before undergoing the rite of washing. It was an immense responsibility to live according to the ways of God. The Christians insisted that their people must know what they were getting into, so a long period of instruction was needed.

Rex took a seat at the rear of a pleasant patio behind the villa. A vine-covered trellis overhung the area. Although the moon shone through the leaves, its meager light was augmented by the warm glow of oil lamps on high stands. Strangely, Alexamenos did not seem aware that some of the guests were respected businessmen, while others were slaves in ragged tunics. In many places, the slaves sat closer to the front than the free men. On one bench not far from Rex, a barefoot herdsman even sat beside a distinguished aristocrat wearing a town councilor's toga—as if the two men were actually equals. Clearly, the Christians didn't have much understanding of proper social distinctions.

The priest of the community was not Alexamenos but a former imperial scribe who now lived in the farmhouse. Since the man was literate, he was able to read from the group's sacred writings. The holy scriptures of the church were kept in a locked cabinet, which held several texts in codex format instead of scrolls like the Jews used. Today the priest read the story of a patriarch named Noe who saved his family from a worldwide flood by enclosing them, along with all the animals of the world, in a giant box that could survive the waves. The priest went on to explain the allegorical meaning of the narrative: only the sturdy wooden chest of the church could save its inhabitants from the demon-infested waters of the world.

When the speech reached its end, the whole community offered prayers in response to the priest's exhortations. They stood and faced east for this part of the service. Although Flavia had remarked that the urban congregations were more ritualized than this country church, even so, the people seemed to know when to make certain acclamations, such as "Amen!" "Lord, have mercy!" "Hosanna!" and "Thanks be to God!" At one point, they sang a hymn with the words *Holy, holy, holy is the Lord God of armies*. They also kissed each other in a chaste expression of affection. Since the kiss was exchanged even between men and women, Rex was glad he wasn't sitting by Flavia, because the awkwardness of that surely would have been noticeable.

At last it was time for the most holy ritual of the Christians, the so-called Eucharist of bread and wine. Rex was uncertain what to think about this, and he even found himself feeling a little nervous. He knew the magic involved here was especially profound, so he could only imagine what kind of heavenly incantations the priest would use to bring the savior god into the food, as the Christians always claimed.

However, as the community began to proceed inside the farmhouse to gather in a private room, one of the householders stopped Rex as he crossed the threshold. "I'm sorry, my friend," he said gently, "but you cannot witness the holy mysteries."

"Really? Why not?"

"It is only for the baptized," Flavia explained. "Even I cannot go. We maintain the discipline of secrecy in our faith. I myself have never partaken of the Eucharist. The Lord Jesus becomes present in that bread and wine. Such a holy thing is to be received only by the fully initiated."

Though disappointed to miss a ceremony that surely would have been remarkable, Rex accepted the limitation since it was common for mystery religions to bar the followers of other deities from their most arcane rituals. He and Flavia waited politely on the moonlit patio for the service to end. When at last it had finished and the people had been dismissed, Alexamenos joined the pair beneath the trellis. A deacon brought a tray of olives, cheese, bread, and the salty fish sauce called garum. Cups of vinegar, flavored with herbs, made a tangy complement to the foods on the tray.

"So what did you think of the Christian gathering?" Alexamenos asked. He popped an olive into his mouth and waited for an answer.

"Very different from what I've experienced before. It's upright and respectable. I can see why people are drawn to it." Rex though for a moment, then added, "Probably not the religion for me, though."

"Why not?"

"Like I've told Lady Junia, it's too peaceful and kind."

Flavia cocked her head and looked at Rex. "Didn't you say you admired the love you saw in Alexamenos on the road?"

"Absolutely. There are few men who would have done what he did out there. And the people tonight showed love like no one I've ever seen."

"Yet that's not a religion for you?" Flavia pressed. "Not ever?"

Rex could sense she earnestly wanted him to believe, though he wasn't sure why. "I think Christianity is something for me to appreciate in others," he said honestly. "But how can I kill men in battles and show love at the same time? I have to choose one or the other. Which will it be? The way of love, or war? Clearly, I am a man of war. So while I can be grateful for all the loving people in our society like you Christians, I must fight under the patronage of mighty Hercules."

"I notice your amulet is not Herculean," Alexamenos remarked, extending his finger.

Rex glanced down to his neck, where the cross pendant given him by Constantine had worked its way outside his tunic's open collar. He held it in his palm for a moment, staring at the tau-rho, then glanced up at Alexamenos. "You are a longtime Christian, sir. Maybe you can explain this to me. Is the cross a talisman of victory? Or a mark of shame and defeat?"

"It testifies to shame and defeat, but the defeat was followed by victory three days later."

"What kind of victory? That word can mean many things. Are we talking about staying true to your convictions all the way to the point of death? Merely a moral victory? Or is it the kind of victory I need most—my enemy flat on his back with my blade in his chest?"

Alexamenos sighed and did not answer right away. "I work in the imperial palace, you know," he said at last. "I train the page boys who serve on the Palatine Hill. So in that way, I am part of the apparatus that runs this empire. Even if it's a small role, my job contributes directly to the conquest and subjugation of foreigners for the glory of Rome."

"And yet you are a disciple of Jesus. Aren't those two things at odds with each other?"

"Did you hear our hymn tonight?" Alexamenos asked. "What was God called in it?"

"I noticed it. You sang, 'Holy, holy, holy is the Lord God of armies.' I've discussed this with Lady Junia as well. The God of the Jews was a fighter of wars. That same God is worshiped by Christians. Yet Jesus was a peaceful man. So there seems to be a conflict in your religion."

"Is it really a conflict? Maybe not. It's true that while on earth, Jesus wasn't a warrior. Yet he interacted with soldiers and did not tell them to give up their profession. He even said to render to Caesar what Caesar is owed. And listen to this." Alexamenos rose and went to the church's book cabinet. He returned with a volume that he called the *Book of the Revelation of John*. Holding it beneath the lamplight, he selected a passage and read it aloud: "And out of his mouth goes forth a sharp sword, that with it he might strike down the nations. And he will shepherd them with a rod of iron. And he treads the winepress of the fury of the wrath of God Almighty."

"Is that talking about Jesus?" Flavia asked.

Alexamenos nodded and closed the book. "Indeed, it is. Remember, my friends, Jesus is the son of King David. And David was nothing if not a great man of war. It might sound strange to you both, but in a world full of sin and violence, warriors are needed to protect good citizens until the true Judge of the nations returns. What if some barbarians cross the Rhenus to pillage Roman lands? Should we not defend our people? If the legions stopped fighting, the whole empire would soon fall."

"But wait, Alexamenos," Flavia objected. "It might be necessary for pagans to fight. But surely it cannot be right for a Christian to shed another man's blood?"

"It is a difficult matter. There are many church leaders who agree with you. But many Christians serve in the army. The catholic church does not have a unified position on this."

"And what is your position, sir?" Rex asked, intrigued by the debate.

"I believe sometimes the most loving thing a man can do is to draw blood from evildoers for the achievement of justice and peace. If no one stops unjust aggression, the innocent will perish. It is therefore proper to defend them. What is wrong, however, is to exert power for your own selfish gain. Yet warfare for good purposes could be holy—or at the very least, it might be the lesser of two evils. That is why the blessed Paul says in his letter to the Romans that he who bears the sword is an instrument of God."

Rex was considering those words when the theoretical discussion suddenly took on real-world significance. The deacon who had brought the food hurried across the patio. "Sir! Riders are approaching! And from the sound of them, they wear mail!"

Rex leaped to his feet. "Soldiers coming at night? That can't be good!"

"Follow me to the stable," Alexamenos said. "You can hide there until the men are gone. Lady Junia, stay close to Rex at all times. Hurry!"

The threesome crossed the farmyard to a stable near an apple orchard. They had just slipped inside when eight torches appeared on the lane that led to the villa's front gate. Moments later, the soldiers were hailing the house, demanding entry. The deacon came out, remaining calm even as the eight Praetorians badgered him for information and rattled their swords. A ninth man remained in the saddle, keeping back from the fray.

"Rex, look at that!" Flavia whispered through gritted teeth. "It's that stringy-haired pimp from the road. He led them here!"

"I saw him," Rex said as he tightened the girth strap on the horse he was saddling. "We've got to get out of here right away. Get ready to ride." The soldiers had hold of the deacon now, threatening him with their torches. Though he squirmed in their grasp, one of the Praetorians stretched out the deacon's arm. Another man got in his face. "Where are those fugitives? Tell me!" he demanded.

"I have no idea!" cried the deacon.

"Maybe fire will help you recall."

A blood-chilling cry pierced the night as a torch was thrust beneath the deacon's forearm. "Stable! The stable!" he screamed.

"Oh no," Flavia muttered.

"Come on! Let me help you up! It's time to go!" Rex grasped Flavia's waist in two hands and vaulted her into the saddle, then swung up in front of her. "Hold on tight!" he said. She slipped her arms around his chest and interlocked her fingers.

Alexamenos opened the stable's rear gate. "Take the path across the meadow into the deep woods. And whatever you do, go left at the fork in the trail!"

"You there!" shouted one of the Praetorians. "Stop where you are!"

"The God of armies be with you," Alexamenos said, then slapped the horse hard on the rump. It bolted from the stable and began to run.

"There they go! Catch them!"

Rex and Flavia raced across the moonlit meadow with eight soldiers galloping behind. One of the pursuers was an archer, and he loosed a few arrows, though they didn't come close. At the tree line, Rex guided his horse onto the trail. He hoped his superior horsemanship in the dim light of the tangled forest would help him outdistance his enemies.

The Praetorians, however, began to gain on their quarry, for they were riding singly instead of carrying a double burden. One rider, clearly a skilled cavalryman, drew near on Rex's left flank. Rex leaned out and grabbed a branch, which snapped off in his hand. The pursuing soldier had pulled close enough to use his sword. He slashed Rex's horse across the hindquarters. The terrified beast let out a squeal as it charged down the trail.

"I'll cut you, girl!" the man growled, swiping at Flavia.

She twisted in the saddle, hanging off the right side. "Get away from me!"

Rex swung the branch around in a wide arc and smashed the attacker in the face. He bellowed and immediately fell back. Rex kicked his heels and urged more speed from his injured mount.

"That was the left fork!" Flavia cried. "We just passed it!"

"I couldn't make the turn! We'll have to see where this path leads!"

The thunder of many hooves pounded behind Rex and Flavia as they broke into an open field under the pinpoint stars. The mountain meadow offered a broad view of the Roman lowlands in the distance. Up ahead and to the left stood the mighty temple of Hercules Victorious, perched on its rocky crag. The meadow's far edge was undefined, merging with the distant horizon. A feeling of dread gathered in Rex's mind as he began to discern the lay of the land.

The Praetorians fanned out now, like a predator trying to snap its jaws on its prey. Rex could only keep churning ahead at full speed. Even so, the enemy was closing the gap.

"What's that sound?" Flavia asked, her voice tinged with fear.

Raw terror seized Rex. He could no longer deny where this branch of the trail was headed: to the top of the roaring waterfall that tumbled over the sheer bluffs of Tibur. He muttered a curse as his predicament became clear. Nothing lay ahead of the fugitives but the edge of a cliff for several miles in either direction.

An arrow whizzed past Rex's ear. Out in the open, the archer's aim was much better. He wouldn't keep missing for long. Rex slapped his horse's neck, demanding every last bit of effort from the exhausted animal.

"Do you pray, Lady Junia?" he shouted as the drop-off came into view.

"Of course I pray!"

"Then now is the time! We're going over the edge!"

"Rex, no! We'll be smashed on the rocks!"

"We're dead either way!"

The rim of the cliff lay just ahead. The horse strained toward it, snorting and tossing its mane, driven mad by pain and fear. Nothing could stop it now.

Flavia let out a long, terrified shriek. "Aaaaah! Rex! Don't do it!"

"Hang on to me! Here we go!"

"Jesus!" Flavia screamed as the horse leapt over the precipice and into nothing but moonlight.

Do I tell her I love her before I die? Rex wondered. And then the plunge began.

8

Now that her death had arrived, Flavia embraced it willingly. Yet who could have guessed it would be such a slow and peaceful event? As the horse leapt over the cliff and the ground plunged away beneath its hooves, Flavia's terror was replaced by an unexpected calm. Time slowed to a crawl. She seemed to watch her demise from an outsider's perspective.

Gliding gently downward, she found herself afraid only for Rex. He would descend into the gloomy underworld and be lost forever, while she would be with God. In the final moments of her life, Flavia mourned the end of a brief friendship that had so much potential. *How sad that the friendship will go no further than this!*

She could hear the horse squealing, though its panicked cry was muffled and faint, as if from far away. Moonlight cast a soft glow across the tree-tops that surrounded the base of the cliff. The vista was beautiful, indeed captivating. Flavia was admiring the scenery when she felt strong arms wrap her in a tight grip. Were they the arms of an angel? Or maybe Christ himself? It was hard to say. Yet Flavia knew she was in the care of someone who loved her.

The protective arms pulled her from the horse's back and tugged her onto a new trajectory. She felt two legs encircle her as well, pinning her tight. Immobilized now, she relaxed and accepted the embrace, for what else could she do? The angel was taking her to the city of God.

Strangely, her guardian's body, pressed against her own, felt much harder than she would have imagined for a celestial being. The angel rolled in midair to give her the top position. Flavia could see the pale moon and the churning waterfall and the pagan temple on the clifftop. All was as it should be.

And then the fist of Satan punched her in the face.

In an instant, everything went cold and wet and terribly black. The devil's hard blow knocked the air from her lungs, and no sooner had it escaped than an icy poison rushed in to take its place. Frigid water flooded her nose and mouth, causing her throat to clamp tight in defense. Confused and distressed, Flavia sank deeper into the hellish world that was now her eternal home. *How can this be? Jesus has sentenced me to the torment of Hades!*

Yet Flavia did not give in. Though her urge to inhale was intense, she refused to open her mouth. Her brain screamed for relief and her lungs demanded air, yet she knew in some instinctive way that to allow herself even one gasp would increase her agony a millionfold. She could only purse her lips and tumble deeper into the watery gloom, abandoned to the abyss like a pebble dropped in the sea.

Perhaps her strong protector might have rescued her, but apparently, that angel had fled. Now Flavia found herself locked in an inescapable torture chamber. The intensity of her need to breathe was unbearable, and it only kept getting worse. Her soul's pitiful cries—*Help me! Save me! Get me out of here!*—went unheard by any who could give relief. Nothing could stop Flavia's free fall into the netherworld.

At last she came to rest on solid rock. Her eyes were blind now. The cold had taken over. Mercifully, her abject terror eased up, and a quiet peace began to take over. Yes . . . a quiet peace. It would feel so much better to embrace it. Just let it come. Accept what must be. Flavia felt her body go limp.

It is time to give up, my sssssweet one, said a voice in her head. *Open those pretty lips and give me a kisssss . . .*

Yes, I will, Flavia decided.

Her lips parted. Water gushed into her mouth. Her chest heaved. And then the deep darkness took her away.

The impact against the pool at the base of the waterfall felt more like pavement than water. Rex took the full force of it on his back, cradling Flavia above him to protect her as best he could. Despite his encircling grip, the devastating blow knocked her body loose and sent Rex tumbling alone into the inky blackness. His head spun, and he fought to right himself in the turbulent abyss. Dizziness threatened to overwhelm his brain. Only with great effort was he able to keep his grip on consciousness and claw his way out of the depths.

"Lady Junia!" he cried as he burst from the water. He scanned the ruffled surface of the plunge pool but saw no one, nor heard any voice above the roar of the cataract. "Lady Junia!" he called again, this time with more urgency.

"There he is!" someone shouted from above. "Right there, near that log! Put a shaft in him!"

A moment later, the whiz of an arrow was followed by a small splash only an arm's length away.

Rex heard the words, "You missed him! Try another!" but he was back underwater before the second arrow could be loosed. He kicked down into the darkness until he felt rock, then groped along the bottom but found nothing. Despair gripped him, for he knew Flavia could be anywhere. *Mighty Hercules*, he prayed, *give me your favor right now!* No sooner had Rex prayed than his hand closed on what he recognized as Flavia's cold wrist. He scooped her into his arms and bunched his legs in a squatting position against a flat stone. With all the impetus his legs could impart, he shot to the surface and burst into the open, sucking great gulps of the cool night air. Flavia, however, never moved.

Although more shouts sounded from above, none of the eight Praetorians seemed inclined to jump from the cliff to continue their pursuit. Rex thrashed his way to a pebbly beach and stumbled onto solid ground with Flavia still limp in his arms. He whirled to face the riders, their dark forms outlined against the night sky as their horses paced among the crags.

"Curse you!" Rex shouted. "Look what you've done! You killed an innocent woman! The Furies take you all!"

"She had it coming!" a cruel voice replied. "You lose, gladiator!"

"Dirty little canicula!" someone else taunted.

"Eat this!" shouted a third man, then backed up his threat with an arrow that slammed into a tree trunk near Rex's elbow. He backed farther into the shadows.

"I'll kill you all!" Rex screamed, but his words only drew rough laughter. When another arrow swished past his cheek, he turned and ducked into the forest.

The foliage was dense and would offer good cover. Kneeling, he laid Flavia on a bed of moist leaves. "Come back to me, my friend!" he urged. "Please! Wake up!"

Rex's heart was beating wildly, and he found himself experiencing a level of terror he had never encountered before. No daring stunt from his training had ever made him feel so afraid. Even the first charge of battle was nothing compared to the dread he felt now. This new fear was slashing across Rex's soul, hurting him in places he didn't know existed. He pressed Flavia's hand to his chest and shook her by the shoulder, calling her name, begging her to awaken. But her body remained lifeless and cold.

"Rex!" someone whispered.

He spun, ready to fight, but the intruder identified himself as Alexamenos. The little Greek sidled up to Rex and knelt beside their inert friend. "Quick, man!" he said. "Help me roll her over!"

"I can't!" Rex cried as he collapsed backward, gripping his forehead in his palm. "It's no use! She's dead!" The unexpected pain of those words took his breath away. He put his fingers to his throat, fighting for air, trying to beat back the panic that threatened to undo him.

"No, I've seen this before. When it's really cold, you can sometimes bring people back."

"Impossible! By now she's full of water!"

Alexamenos shook his head. "After you take in a little bit, your throat shuts. You pass out and turn blue, then the body goes to sleep. A person can stay alive like that for quite a while."

Rex wanted to believe it, but the weight of his dismay crushed all hope. Never had he felt so unsure of what to do next. He couldn't speak, couldn't act, couldn't even string two coherent thoughts together.

Alexamenos had turned Flavia on her side now. Though a trickle of water dribbled from her lips, still she did not move. Tugging her shoulder, he rolled her face-up again, then pinched her nose. "There was a doctor in my village who used to blow air into a patient's mouth to restart their breathing," he said. "He believed the feel of new air in the lungs would wake them up."

"Do it!" Rex gasped through gritted teeth.

Alexamenos bent down and covered Flavia's mouth with his own. Five times he blew into her lungs. With each breath, her bosom rose and fell. Then Alexamenos straightened and waited. For a long moment, nothing happened.

Suddenly Flavia coughed, and her body spasmed. She gagged and spit out water.

Alexamenos bowed his head with his palm raised to heaven.

Rex burst into tears.

It was the uncontrollable shivering that brought Flavia back to full alertness. The more the fog cleared from her mind, the more she became aware of how cold she really was. The chill went deep into her body—so deep it was scary.

"R-r-r-ex," she said, extending a shaky hand toward his cheek. "H-h-h-help m-me . . ."

"I'm right here, Lady Junia." He raised her to a sitting position and enfolded her in a tight embrace. She trembled against him. Strangely, she perceived he was shaking too. He even made little whimpering noises.

"Y-y-you're c-crying," she managed to say, unsure what was happening. Her memory of recent events was fuzzy.

Rex pulled away from Flavia and gripped her by both shoulders. As he stared at her face, she could see her assertion was true. Rex's eyes brimmed with tears, and his voice carried powerful emotions when he spoke. "I thought I had lost you at the bottom of the pool," he gasped. "It was awful."

She nodded. "But you f-f-found me."

"Yes! I couldn't stop searching! Somehow I had to bring you up."

"Th-thank you. It was d-d-dangerous."

"Doesn't matter. I'd do anything for you!"

The spontaneous intensity of Rex's words caught Flavia's attention. This wild, violent man wasn't the aloof loner she had assumed him to be. The tears in his eyes proved it. Flavia could only stare back at him. *How many times will you confound me, Rex?*

A very long time, I hope.

Alexamenos intervened, breaking the moment. "My lady, you're dangerously cold," he said, "and there's no telling whether those Praetorians will find their way here. We need to get moving."

The words seemed to snap Rex back to his normal, assertive self. He stood up and looked around. "That's right. We have to find shelter immediately. Lady Junia needs to get near a fire and out of harm's way. Did you bring a horse, Alexamenos?"

The Greek shook his head. "I ran down the trail after you left the stable and saw you missed the left fork. The path down the bluffs is hard to find in the dark, but I know where it is, so I came straight here."

"Alright, then here's the plan. I saw our horse get out of the water near the falls. I'm going to go find that poor beast and get us out of here. Fast."

While Rex went to collect the mare, Alexamenos unfastened his cloak and removed it from his shoulders. "I hope you'll pardon me, my lady, but I learned a few things about medicine back in Graecia. A drowning isn't solved only by getting out of the water. That wet clothing is still a danger on a chilly night like this. You need dry fabric against your skin."

"Our d-d-octor is Greek t-too," Flavia said. "I under-s-s-stand."

By the time Rex returned, Flavia was standing upright, swathed in the woolen cloak like a butterfly in its cocoon. Alexamenos had made sure to tighten the hood around her neck to preserve as much body heat as possible. Only her bare feet protruded from her wrapping.

"Let's cover those too," Rex said. He bent low and whisked Flavia into his arms. She squeaked a little at the sudden move yet didn't mind letting Rex turn her so Alexamenos could wind his scarf around her ankles until all her skin was covered. Effortlessly, as if Flavia were no more to him than a sack of wheat, Rex stepped onto a flat boulder next to which he had led the mare. After setting Flavia in the saddle, he slid behind her.

Mounted on the horse once more, though sidesaddle this time, Flavia had no qualms about nestling against Rex's chest. She actually was feeling warmer now that she was out of the soggy linen gown, and the sensation of being in Rex's embrace heightened that feeling. As Alexamenos gathered the reins and led the mare away, Flavia tried not to dwell on the fact that she was wearing hardly any clothing beneath the cloak.

The party of three traveled for what seemed like an hour, meeting no one at this late watch of the night. Though the horse's rump had been cut and it had been pushed to its limits, the creature's survival instinct kicked in, and it found the will to press on. At last the bedraggled party came to the gate of the villa belonging to Flavia's uncle. The sight of it flooded her with a rush of childhood memories: playing chase in the meadow, picking sweet apples in the fall, feasting around the farmhouse's huge fireplace.

The sound of a barking dog broke the fragile stillness. As the hound bolted across the grassy expanse, a lantern flickered to life inside a nearby gatehouse. A huge man appeared in the doorway at the same time the dog reached the gate, still barking its deep-throated warning. A bow was in the watchman's hand, and an arrow was on the string. "I did twenty years as a sagittarius in the legions," he said gruffly, "and I never learned to like night visitors. Be off with you before I put a point in your eye. I've killed many men in less moonlight than this."

Rex held up both hands. "Just hear us out, friend. We're unarmed and escorting a relative of your master. She's sitting on the horse with me, and she needs help. We're seeking shelter in this house."

"You know his name?"

"Titus Junius Ignatius," Flavia called.

Despite the accurate statement, the gatekeeper's suspicions didn't seem alleviated. He stared uncertainly at the visitors, his arrow still nocked. Flavia turned in the saddle and spoke in Rex's ear. "Help me down," she whispered. "I'll prove it."

Rex dismounted, then removed the scarf from Flavia's feet and set her on the ground. The grass was damp beneath her toes. Holding the cloak tightly around her, she walked to the gate and bent toward the fierce mastiff on the other side. It laid back its ears and growled, but Flavia spoke soothingly to the beast and extended her hand through the slats. Abruptly, the dog's ears perked and its docked tail began to wag. It approached cautiously, sniffed Flavia's hand, and uttered a series of excited yips.

"Go tell your master that his niece who loves Alpha has come to him in trouble and needs his help," she said.

The gatekeeper turned his head into his cottage and called for a boy to run to the main farmhouse. When the youth returned with a response, the gatekeeper's demeanor instantly changed. He unlatched the gate and ushered the nighttime visitors to the villa after promising to take good care of their horse. A well-dressed slave met them on the veranda.

"Lady Junia, it truly is you!" he exclaimed.

"Septimus! It has been so long!"

The servant bowed to Flavia, and she inclined her head in return. "I can hardly believe it's you, my lady," Septimus said. "How you've grown! You've become such a lovely young woman."

"I'm seventeen now," Flavia said. "That's quite a difference from the little child you once knew."

"Indeed, it is. What a delight to see you!" Septimus beckoned to the party of visitors. "Come, all of you. I see you have been in distress. We have rooms to refresh yourselves and get some rest. In the morning, Master Ignatius will meet with you and give you the aid you need."

Since Alexamenos wanted to check on the deacon who had suffered burns, he declined the offer but promised to return the next day, making sure he wouldn't be followed. After he took his leave, the servant led Rex and Flavia to a pair of upstairs bedrooms. An oil lamp in a wall niche was the only illumination in this dark wing of the house. After lighting charcoal braziers and setting a pitcher of water in each room, Septimus said good night. Flavia went to her bedchamber, then paused at its entrance and glanced over at Rex.

"Sleep well, Lady Junia," Rex said as he also stood at the entrance to his room.

"After a day like this, I surely will."

Rex nodded his agreement and cracked his door. He was about to enter when Flavia stopped him.

"Tell me one thing," she said. When Rex indicated for her to go on, she asked, "How did you know we would hit the water and not get smashed on the rocks?"

"Maybe I didn't."

Flavia sucked in her breath. "You took a chance with our lives like that?"

"A calculated risk," Rex admitted with a grin. "I was staring at the falls while I waited for you at dinner. I knew there was a pool at the bottom. I thought we'd hit it."

"So you weren't scared?"

Rex examined Flavia's face for a moment, then began to approach. His sudden move reminded her that she was wearing little but a cloak in a remote part of a dark villa. Only one small lamp cast its glow in this secret, quiet place. Casually, she eased closer to the bedroom door and hoped Rex's advance would stop.

He halted in front of her, not far away, though not close enough to be menacing either. "What's wrong with being scared?" he asked.

"Nothing, I guess."

Rex took a step closer, and this time Flavia could sense the energy between them. The feral undercurrent in Rex's personality unnerved her. Even with a shave and a haircut, the man was an untamed barbarian.

"Are you scared right now, Lady Junia?"

"A little," Flavia admitted. Her words came out breathier than she intended.

"It helps to be afraid, doesn't it? It makes you ready for action. Or sometimes it prepares you to run."

Flavia swallowed hard, trying to moisten her suddenly dry mouth. "Do I . . . need to?"

"Run?"

"Mm-hmm."

Instead of answering, Rex closed the final distance between them. Though he did not touch her, he came very near, gazing down with intense desire in his eyes. The flickering light of the lamp danced on his cheeks. *This man is too handsome for me to resist*, Flavia realized.

"You don't need to run from me, my friend," he said.

"I think I do," Flavia whispered. She felt shaky and weak.

For a long time Rex did not speak. A hint of a smile lurked at the corners of his lips as he regarded her with a playful stare. At last he raised his hand and caressed Flavia's cheek with his finger. The feel of it was as light as a feather, yet its impact was like an ocean of sweet wine. Her legs sagged, and she had to steady herself against the wall.

"Run toward me," he offered. "Come all the way."

"I . . . I can't . . ."

Rex remained motionless and silent. He didn't need to say more. His eyes were doing all the talking. The invitation was there. The invitation to *everything.*

"Oh, Rex . . ." The words were more of a moan than an act of speech.

"I see you aren't running away," he observed. "Yet neither are you advancing."

"I don't know what to do," Flavia replied. *Actually, I'm completely helpless.*

Rex eased forward and inclined his head. His body touched her cloak now, and his cheek was next to hers. For a long moment he did nothing. Flavia's heart fluttered out of control.

Ever so gently, Rex turned and kissed Flavia's cheek. Then he backed away.

"W-w-why?" she asked, barely able to speak.

"Because you're not like other women. Let's walk side by side for now. If you're ever ready to run to me, you'll know."

"Are you sure?"

"I'm sure. You have a hold on me. Never forget this, Flavia—I'm *for* you. For you in every way."

She nodded gratefully. Rex smiled and turned toward the wall niche. After blowing out the lamp, he retired to his room, leaving Flavia alone in the silent hallway.

Titus Junius Ignatius was one of those men accustomed to privilege from birth, so he wielded his power naturally and didn't come across as arrogant. Rex had known a few men like him in the army. They believed the world was the way it was for a reason; and in that world, they had been placed on top. Such self-confidence meant that men like Ignatius didn't go around trying to show off their power and wealth. In fact, they could often be quite generous. Men of this station felt it was their duty to display beneficence, especially toward needy relatives like a favorite niece. And that meant Flavia was—at least for now—in good hands.

The servant Septimus had laid out a light breakfast for the master's guests in one of the villa's smaller, more intimate dining rooms. Alexamenos had arrived not long after dawn, and now the three friends were gathered around the divan of Senator Ignatius, breaking their nighttime fast with honeyed pears and warm, wheaty bread. The senator was a tall man with long, spindly limbs. His angular frame made him look a little ridiculous as he leaned on his elbow and picked at his food. Alexamenos and Rex sat on wicker chairs to one side of the room, while Flavia was stationed across from them on her own couch. The privilege of letting her, a woman, dine with the men displayed the high regard in which the senator held his niece.

For a while, no one spoke, as each enjoyed the quiet morning and the tasty food. Birds chirped from the patio outside the little room. At last the master signaled for the plates to be taken away, leaving behind only cups of spiced cider. The meal had made Ignatius chatty. Like the excellent conversationalist that men of his class always are, he indulged in congenial small talk, mostly with Flavia. Their exchange was marked by the formal tone so often used by aristocrats.

Finally, the master turned his attention to Flavia's plight. "I hear you have come back to me under difficult circumstances, dear one," he said. "Although I would have preferred to see you under happier conditions, I must say, it is delightful to hear your footsteps again in my home, no matter what brought you here. Tell me a little about your dilemma, my dear, and let us consider what needs to be done."

"Thank you, Uncle! I have such fond memories of this place. It was a wonderful retreat for me as a girl, and now I hope it will serve as a sanctuary once again." After collecting her thoughts, Flavia proceeded to explain that her father had run afoul of Ruricius Pompeianus, the powerful Praetorian prefect. Seeking to destroy Neratius's reputation, the prefect had trumped up charges against Flavia and condemned her to the beasts. Fortunately, Rex had come to the capital from the frontier farmlands to seek his fortune. Motivated by nothing but compassion for an innocent woman, he had intervened on her behalf, and because he had briefly served as a mercenary before coming to Rome, he was able to defeat Flavia's captors and help her escape.

"That's quite a feat for an untrained soldier of fortune," Ignatius said to Rex. "I wouldn't have imagined you could get the best of so many crack troops from the army's most prestigious division."

"The gods favored me, I guess," Rex said with a shrug.

"Either that, or you are not what you seem."

The men exchanged a long look before Rex said, "You honor me, sir.

But I'm just a humble farmer's son from Germania with a strong arm and a big dream."

"And what do you dream of?"

"To serve Rome, of course."

"Serve it or conquer it?"

"To conquer Rome seems impossible for anyone, sir."

"So it would seem. Yet some are saying Constantine could do it."

"Not if I can help it," Rex said smoothly. "I hope to win a place in Maxentius's army. I would gladly shed my blood for Rome's defense."

Ignatius sipped his cider, seeming to savor the mouthful before swallowing it. "I fear, young man, that you'd only be shedding your blood to perpetuate tyranny. Maxentius has become hostile to his own people. In light of that, one could consider Constantine a liberator, not a conqueror."

The bold remark, bordering on seditious, startled Rex. *What does this man know? And why is he probing me?*

"I don't claim to understand the politics of great men," Rex lied. "I only want to serve in the famous horse guard of Rome. Although I had to oppose some local soldiers to help your niece, I'm sure I've gone unrecognized by them. Once things have stabilized for her, I hope to leave Lady Junia in your care so I can resume my dream of enlistment."

"Hmm. Is that so?" Ignatius raised his finger and pointed at Rex. "I don't think you're telling the truth, young man."

The comment burst from the master's mouth like a slingstone, its challenge unmistakable. Yet Rex wasn't fazed; speculators, who often worked as covert operatives behind enemy lines, were trained in the art of misdirection and disguise. Rex wasn't about to let a little clever banter from a rich aristocrat blow his cover. Setting down his cup on a side table, he looked directly at his host. "Master Ignatius, this is your home, and I will dishonor neither it nor you by arguing at a meal. But you should know that in the frontier lands where I am from, my people value truth above all else. I can assure you I would never lie to someone who has extended such gracious hospitality to me. What I have told you is the truth, nothing more."

The room was silent for a long, tense moment. Flavia shifted uncomfortably, while Alexamenos watched with wide eyes. Suddenly Master Ignatius broke into a kindly grin. "Ah, young Rex, forgive my forceful words," he said.

"I intended no offense. I only meant to imply that our hearts are sometimes hard to read. How often do we say one thing, unaware that the truth lies somewhere else? This is what I sensed when you said you intend to leave my niece behind. From what I have observed, I think that will be difficult for you."

"Perhaps. But a courageous soldier must learn to do difficult things."

"And that is exactly why you will remain to help me save the young lady whom we both admire so much."

Before Rex could reply to the strange assertion, Flavia rejoined the conversation. "Uncle, would you show me the grace of explaining your words? I think all of us are a little confused right now."

"Yes, I am completely confused," Alexamenos admitted.

Ignatius rose from the couch and assumed a more authoritative air, like a politician about to deliver an important speech. He made eye contact with Flavia as he paced about. "Prefect Pompeianus seeks your life, is that correct?"

"With all the hatred a man can muster."

"Do you think he will stop at anything until he claims it?"

"Unfortunately, no."

"Surely there must be *something* that would make him give up?"

"I don't think so, Uncle."

Ignatius's face turned grave. "Then that is a serious problem, isn't it? He wants your life above all else. He will stop at nothing. It leaves us only one solution."

"What?" Flavia asked.

Before anyone could answer, Rex grimaced and nodded, for he now understood what Senator Ignatius intended.

"We must give it to him," Rex said.

—◦∾◦—

Senator Ignatius peeked around the corner in one of Tibur's many ancient alleys. The blond German who called himself Rex was standing not far away, about to make his move and set the plan in motion. Ignatius watched the youth from behind as he crept down the narrow alley to approach Tibur's main street.

Who are you, young man?

Was this newcomer to Italy really a farm boy from the frontier villages along the Rhenus? Just a strapping lad with a strong arm and a sword for hire, dreaming about the glories of war? So he had declared, but it hardly seemed likely. Not many farmers' sons—even among the chiseled barbarians—had a physique like his. Rex's body had been honed for one purpose: battle. And not just the battles of an ordinary legionary but combat of a more elite type. Ignatius had seen many men like Rex during his military days. For two years, he had supervised a cohort of secret operatives who infiltrated enemy territory for months at a time. They were all the same, these men, with their swaggering self-assurance; their sharp, attentive eyes; their fluid way of moving that wasted no motion. In truth, young Rex could be only one thing: a speculator sent to Rome on a secret mission. And Senator Titus Junius Ignatius intended to find out what it was.

But until then, this man's skills will be useful in helping my niece . . .

Rex stepped into the bright light of the main street and turned left—just the way the two of them had planned it after the strategic breakfast yesterday. By the time Ignatius reached the street and ventured a glance around the corner, a commotion had already begun to develop. Rex had been recognized as the fugitive the soldiers were after. Things were going exactly according to plan.

"Stop right there!" a man shouted. Then Rex dashed past the alley. Ignatius drew back into the shadows as three Praetorian guardsmen followed Rex at a full run, yelling for him to halt. But, of course, he didn't.

Ignatius retreated down the alley and turned into a side street. He hurried to Tibur's southern gate, a rarely used one, and went out along the road until he came to a necropolis. The cemetery was heavily forested, and many of its tombs were overgrown with vines. Ignatius took up a position in a copse of trees and waited. It wasn't long before Rex arrived, running well ahead of his three pursuers.

The young German ducked into a dense oak thicket. When the soldier in the lead reached the trees and paused to search for his quarry, Rex burst from the foliage and threw his arm around the man's neck, clasping his forearm with his other hand. The blood choke—a classic speculator's technique—quickly did its work. After a little thrashing, the soldier went limp and sank to the ground. Rex threw a hank of rope around his wrists and bound them to his ankles.

Once he had dragged the groggy man into the thicket, Rex emerged into plain view again and caught the attention of the second pursuer, who had become separated from the third. Rex lured him close to the dense woods and disappeared. No sooner had the bewildered soldier lost sight of his quarry than he was subdued from behind, bound hand and foot, and dragged into the underbrush.

With the first and second men gone, the third Praetorian searching the cemetery began to grow wary. This time Rex charged straight at him.

Though the Praetorian tried to escape, Rex caught him and forced him to black out by once again cutting off the blood to his brain. After the tight squeeze of such a choke was released, the victims always recovered quickly, but by then it was too late. The third man was down on his belly like the other two, his wrists tied to his ankles.

Rex dragged the third soldier, wriggling and spitting curses, into a nearby crematorium. He returned and dragged the other two Praetorians into the squat little building as well. When all the men were inside, Ignatius rose from his hiding place and moved toward the brick structure with its large central chimney. The place was windowless, and Ignatius knew its interior would be dark. He approached quietly and peered into the open doorway.

A pile of crisscrossed logs the height of a man's chest stood beneath the chimney's flue in the ceiling. The three bound captives lay on the floor, quieter and more subdued by their ominous surroundings, with no hint of their former belligerence. Rex stood above them. He held a woman's limp body wrapped in a white funeral shroud. Only Flavia's head was exposed. Her neck was arched backward, and her mouth was slightly agape. The unbound locks of her long, brown hair dangled over Rex's forearm as he lifted her body into the ray of light from the door.

"Behold what you have done!" he accused the Praetorians. "You have slain an innocent woman! The Furies will snatch your souls to hell today for this deed!"

"No, stop! We're good soldiers! Let us go!" cried one of the captives. "We were only doing our duty!" whined another.

"No excuses! Your lives shall be required this day," Rex said in a firm voice, unmoved by the men's desperate pleas. "By the fires of divine vengeance you shall be consumed!"

Ignatius pulled his dark cloak tight around his shoulders and drew the hood over his head. The oversized cowl obscured his face in shadow. He stepped inside the crematorium and closed the door, plunging the space into blackness. The men on the floor whimpered and moaned. A quiet rustling could be heard around the logs, then all fell silent. Groping in the dark, Ignatius found an upside-down jug on the pyre. He lifted it to uncover a small oil lamp. The dim glow revealed that Rex had now departed, and Flavia's body had been laid on the pile of wood. Her facecloth had been cinched tight, enclosing the entire corpse in a white mantle of death.

"Set us free," a Praetorian threatened, "or the Furies will take you too!"

"The Furies only take revenge for the shedding of innocent blood," Ignatius replied, "but yours is the blood of the guilty."

The third soldier squirmed on the floor and tried to lift his head to look his executioner in the face. "Please! Have mercy!" he begged, but Ignatius's only answer was to pick up a torch. The stick was tipped with rags soaked in sulfur and lime, and it quickly took the flame from the lamp. By its flickering glow, Ignatius could see the pyre was drenched with glossy oil. Shadows danced on the ceiling vault, made all the more eerie by the echoes from the men writhing on the floor and pleading for their lives. Ignatius emptied the oil from the lamp onto Flavia's shroud so the body would be sure to burn. Then he stepped back.

"Murderers!" he accused. "The time has come for your judgment." Ignatius touched the torch to the pyre. A bright flame erupted from the slick wood.

Now the men on the floor began to roll furiously toward the door. Ignatius sidestepped them and reached the exit first. "My vengeance is complete," he said as he left the crematorium and stepped into the evening light. He dropped a bar across the door and retreated into the thickening shadows under the tangled oaks.

Smoke began to rise from the crematorium's chimney. By now the logs must be burning hot, and the body was surely aflame. Any moment now . . .

Yes! There he is!

A gardener rushed toward the crematorium with a knife in his hand. He threw aside the bar and yanked open the door. Smoke billowed from the upper half of the opening. Ducking low, the gardener entered the little building and remained inside for several moments. Suddenly one of the Praetorians burst from the crematorium, stumbling across the grass like a madman. He was followed by the second and third soldiers, then the gardener came out as well. The three rescued guardsmen fell to their knees, gasping and coughing as they sought to fill their lungs with fresh air. Once they could catch sufficient breath, they shouted prayers of gratitude to Mars and Mithras.

"Thank you, sir!" one of the soldiers sputtered, clasping the gardener's hand.

"I saw the smoke and heard you yelling. I couldn't let you burn!"

"Vile treachery!" another soldier declared.

"Powerful people are arrayed against you," the gardener said. "I think you had better leave right away."

The three soldiers needed no further encouragement to escape the site of their close brush with death. They hastened from the necropolis, leaving the gardener alone in the dusk.

Ignatius picked his way through the trees and went out to meet him. The gardener remained silent as the senator approached. Ignatius did not remove his hood.

"You did well," he told the waiting man.

"I did just as you told me, sir."

"Indeed, you did. Here is your reward." Ignatius put a sack of small silver coins in the gardener's outstretched hand, then added a gold aureus. "That is for the family of the boy who died yesterday. I will check to make sure you have delivered it to the father. Be sure also to take them the boy's ashes in an urn."

"I'm an honest man, sir. I will pass along the coin when I bring the remains. And the family needs the money. They are poor and were very frightened when their son took ill. The boy was just coming into his manhood. He was to be their means of support. Now he's gone. His death was a grievous blow to their futures."

"May the power in heaven be propitious to them," Ignatius said, not wanting to offer any specific religious details. "Be gone now, and speak not a word of this."

The gardener bowed and withdrew. When all was quiet, Ignatius returned to the copse of trees. Two figures emerged from the underbrush.

"Do you think they fell for it?" Rex asked.

Ignatius nodded. "No question."

"Uncle, that was risky!" Flavia said. "A little longer and those soldiers would have died!"

"I think not. The flue was open and the smoke was rising. The air near the floor would have been breathable for some time."

"Perhaps. But I still wouldn't have wanted to be them!"

Rex turned to Flavia. "Nice work," he said. "You held perfectly still in my arms. Lifeless as a doll. Those Praetorians were convinced it was your dead body I put on that pyre. They never saw us slip out in the dark."

"And now they think your body has been consumed by fire," Ignatius added. "As far as those men are concerned, you are in the underworld now. Gone from this earth forever."

Flavia stretched out her right hand, palm up. "Clasp it."

Ignatius took his niece's hand in his own.

"You too, Rex," Flavia said, extending her left. After Rex complied with her wish, she lifted both men's hands. Ignatius felt Flavia give his fingers a squeeze.

"As you can feel, gentlemen, I am still quite alive on this earth. I am a woman made of flesh and blood despite our little ruse. And so I shall remain, until the Father God calls me to his heavenly city. When that day comes, I will be ready. Until then, I believe he has important work for me to do in the city of man."

"Yes! I believe he does too, my precious niece," Ignatius said. "May the God of heaven bless your journey."

Flavia gave one last squeeze, then released the men's hands. Silence hung between the threesome for a long moment.

"It's dark now," Rex observed at last. "We should probably go. Those soldiers might come back."

"I doubt it! You were much more than they could handle!" Flavia said admiringly.

Rex waved off the remark. "Caught them by surprise," he said with a little laugh. "I was lucky."

No, Ignatius thought. *You were trained.*

The so-called House of Fausta—or the Lateran Palace, as Pompeianus preferred to call it—was unusually quiet this morning. For one brief moment, no pressing matters demanded the prefect's time, no momentous rumors swirled in the halls, no deadly crisis seemed imminent.

Then the three Praetorians arrived.

Pompeianus met them in the palace's reception hall, irritated by the disturbance and ready to dish out punishment if the news that the soldiers brought was anything but the most urgent. The guardsmen had made sure to look their best to meet the prefect—their chainmail sanded to a shine, their neck scarves clean, their metal trim polished, their helmets plumed with bright red horsetails.

"What brings you here today?" Pompeianus demanded, dispensing with the usual formalities.

The leader stepped forward, saluted with his fist to his chest, and proffered a small urn.

"Bring it to me," the prefect said to his slave.

Pompeianus received the clay jar and peered inside. A fine gray powder was there. "What is this?"

"Human ashes, sir."

Grimacing and turning away, the prefect motioned for the slave to come get the jar. "Whose?"

"Lady Junia Flavia, sir."

Pompeianus froze. His jaw clenched, and his grip on the urn grew tighter. The hall was silent as he sought to control his anger. Finally, he burst from his chair and hurled the urn to the floor. It shattered in an explosion of pottery shards and pale dust. The three Praetorians took several steps backward.

"Tell me everything!" Pompeianus screamed.

The spokesman for the three soldiers gathered his courage and returned to his place. The two others joined him, one on each side. After a quick glance at his comrades, the leader in the middle said, "We chased the fugitives on horseback and trapped them at one of Tibur's cliffs. Foolishly, they leapt over the edge, and the woman was killed on rocks at the foot of a waterfall. To confirm this we"—the man shifted his feet and licked his lips—"inquired around and found where the funeral was to be held. The mourners were about to burn the body when we arrived. We saw the barbarian there—a German gladiator, we think, escaped from one of the schools. He held the woman's corpse in his arms."

"Did you get a good look at her? Were you sure it was her?"

"No question," the leader said, and his comrades signaled their agreement with nods. "Her face was visible to us. We couldn't stop the funeral because the mourners locked the gate. But we saw the body burn. Up close, actually. And later we got her ashes by bribing some relatives. They were surprisingly happy to cooperate." The soldier gestured to the gray dust on the floor. "That's all that's left of Lady Junia Flavia. We thought you'd want to know, sir, so we came right away."

Pompeianus felt the claws of anger gripping his gut, but he restrained his urge to lash out at the men who had brought the news.

Jupiter's beard, this is so annoying!

The purpose of putting the girl to death was to shame her—and thereby her father, Neratius—in front of the whole population of Rome. Instead, she became the talk of the town when she escaped the floor of the Flavian Amphitheater. And now she had just been privately cremated in some obscure village necropolis! The plan had failed.

After dismissing the men with more courtesy than he actually felt, Pompeianus retired to a private garden and called for wine. He paced back and forth under the shade of a tall pine with an umbrella canopy, considering his dilemma. Senator Neratius Junius Flavianus was growing in power, newly appointed as the city prefect and enjoying Emperor Maxentius's favor. A successful term in that prestigious office could ruin Pompeianus's aspirations for political advancement. Since Maxentius—unlike the other members of the Imperial College—spent all his time in Rome, the accomplishments of a capable urban prefect would quickly come to his attention and call for rewards or promotion. The situation was getting out of hand. Neratius had to be brought down.

It was Pompeianus's wife who provided the inspiration for a solution. Livia glided into the garden at just the right moment, fashionably coifed and bedecked with jewels like always. She was a beautiful woman. And unlike most aristocratic wives, Livia knew what it meant to be seductive. Modesty was a meaningless word to her, and that was just how Pompeianus liked it. *So unlike Neratius's prissy wife. Hmm. I wonder if . . .*

The thought of virtuous Sabina Sophronia raised some immediate questions in the prefect's mind. A devious plan began to come together.

Yes, this could work, he realized. Everyone knew about Emperor Maxentius's taste for adultery. He enjoyed bedding the lawful wives of Rome's elite much more than the professional courtesans so readily available to him. Until now, the ancient rules of aristocratic propriety—going back to the times of Caesar Augustus himself—had prevented most liaisons with senators' wives. Only the most unchaste and lascivious matrons had found their way to Maxentius's private chambers. But lately the emperor had shown all the makings of a tyrant. If he could be persuaded that the Senate was turning against him and that they might support a coup led by Licinius or Constantine . . . *What would he do?*

Everything in Maxentius's history suggested he would respond to feelings of insecurity with violent retaliation and paranoid domination of his perceived enemies. Those who bent the knee would regain the emperor's favor. But those who seemed reluctant to obey his commands would become instant villains in Maxentius's suspicious mind. *Perfect.*

"Your brow is furrowed, my love," Livia said. "Does that fine Falernian not soothe you? Shall I call for medicinal herbs or a tincture from the physician?"

Pompeianus approached his wife. "No. The medicine I need is one only you can give."

"In that case, I shall grind the pestle myself."

A little laugh escaped Pompeianus's lips. "Ah, my dear, you are quite adept at that. Perhaps a little mandrake root later?" When Livia gave him a quizzical look, he waved it off and continued. "You know that I have been pursuing a case against the daughter of Neratius Junius?"

"Yes. It is said the girl escaped the amphitheater."

"That is true. But my men chased her down in Tibur. She's dead now."

"So your problem is solved. Why the anxious face?"

"My problem remains, for the city prefect wasn't shamed in the eyes of Maxentius. In fact, he enjoys greater favor by the day. I must find a way to make Maxentius hate Neratius. That man is the biggest obstacle to my career."

"How can I help, my love?"

Pompeianus directed a stern gaze toward his wife. "I intend to whore you out to the emperor."

The statement, shocking though it was, did not make Livia flinch. She returned her husband's stare. "Whatever it takes, lord," she said with fire in her eyes.

"Excellent!" Pompeianus spun away and poured a second glass of Falernian wine from a decanter on a cart. "I feared you might protest. At least a little." He handed his wife the glass.

"Why should I? Power always has its price."

"Ah, yes. I can see we understand each other perfectly."

"What will my seduction accomplish? Do you wish me to uncover a secret from the emperor?"

"All you have to do is plant an idea in his mind. I am going to meet with Maxentius as soon as possible. I'll tell him my spies are saying Licinius and Constantine are moving against Rome. And I'm going to say the whole Senate is ready to go over to the invaders. That will terrify the little coward, and he'll want to lash out. He'll feel the need to prove his dominance, especially over the upper classes. I'm certain I can convince him to send out some Praetorians as pimps. He's done that often with peasant girls. He has his soldiers procure the local daughters wherever he goes. Now it's time for the next level: senators' wives. You must convince Maxentius to put Neratius to the ultimate test."

Livia giggled. "Getting Maxentius to commit adultery is like getting water to run downhill. It comes naturally to him."

"Exactly! But what is the biggest faction in our empire that avoids adultery? Speaks out against it? Calls it wrong and immoral?"

"The Christians."

"And did you know Senator Neratius Junius is one of those scum?"

"Ugh. I didn't know that, but it doesn't surprise me. What is Rome coming to when the city prefect worships a crucified criminal as a god?"

"It's disgusting, I know. But it works in our favor. If Neratius is a Christian, he certainly won't send his wife to the emperor's bed."

"And Sabina Sophronia wouldn't go even if she were ordered to by her husband. Ha! 'Sophronia,' she's called. What a name! Everyone, please notice the lady's *sophrosune*!" Livia put her hand to her bosom and fluttered her eyelids. "Oh! I must remain faithful to my husband!" she said in a high-pitched, mocking tone. "I must wear dowdy dresses! I must keep my legs together! I must follow ancient Jewish morals!"

"The Christians disgust me."

"Me too, my love."

"So you'll go to the emperor's bed when called?"

Livia gulped down the last of her wine and set aside her glass. She turned toward Pompeianus and grasped him around the waist, pulling him tight and gazing up at him with delightfully painted eyes. Her expression was sultry. "For you, my love, I will do anything."

"Good. In this way, we shall gain ultimate power."

"I can see we understand each other perfectly," Livia replied, then drew her husband into a passionate kiss.

——◦◦◦——

The time had come to part ways. Though Rex had often tried to deny it, in the back of his mind, he had always known this time would come. He just hadn't thought it would be so complicated. And he certainly hadn't anticipated that Flavia would cry.

She stood facing him outside the stable at her uncle's villa. Even in the faint light of dusk, he could see her eyes were moist. *Does she care that much about me?* he wondered. *Or is it just the safety I've been providing her? Or maybe it's the bond we share from facing danger together? And what does she think of me, really? Am I her friend? Her peasant bodyguard? Or something more?*

Rex had considered pulling Flavia aside and asking her about it, but he knew that would only make things worse. The emotions would be complex and awkward. In any case, it didn't matter. The plan was to send her to her father's estate across the sea in Sardinia, so it was unlikely Rex would see her again soon. And it was time, he told himself, to refocus on the mission for which he had come to Italy. Rex hadn't been sent to start friendships, and certainly not romances. He was here on the direct orders of Emperor Constantine, the rightful Augustus of the West and true ruler of Rome. Rex felt he had already spent too much time away. Once he got back to the city, Centurion Aratus was going to bawl him out like a drill instructor breaking down a new recruit. Any regular soldier would be facing a severe beating for an escapade like this, though Rex thought Aratus would refrain because a two-week recovery period would compromise the mission. Even so, the reunion was going to be nasty.

And so it was time to say goodbye to Lady Junia Flavia.

Rex took a step closer to the beautiful girl with tears in her eyes. "We certainly had some exciting adventures out there, didn't we?" he remarked with a little laugh and a shake of his head. "I never thought I'd crawl through an aqueduct with a senator's daughter," he added lamely.

"You were brave, Rex. Always brave and protective. It meant a lot to me, even if I didn't say so at the time."

Rex shrugged. "It was nothing."

"It was everything," Flavia insisted. "You saved me from certain death. I am deeply grateful."

"Well, I was happy to do it for you. So, then . . . goodbye, I guess."

Rex had started to dip his head in a polite bow when Flavia took a step forward. Rex's mind immediately began to assess the proper social move. *She's a noblewoman. I'm a commoner. What do I do? Surely we shouldn't embrace like lovers, right here in front of her uncle?*

Fortunately, instead of moving toward an embrace, Flavia held out her hand. Rex wondered if he should kiss her ring, but he stopped when he realized how stupid that would be. Instead, he grasped her fingers and squeezed. *Ach! What is this weird handshake? She must think I am so strange!*

"Maybe you can write to me?" Flavia suggested, staring up at Rex with those wide, wet eyes.

"Uh, yes. Maybe I could. I think so." Rex released Flavia's fingers and turned over a pebble with his toe. "I learned it from my mother. I'm a pretty good writer, actually." No sooner had he spoken than he kicked himself for saying something that no well-educated aristocrat would ever think to say.

Ignatius cleared his throat. "I believe your friend must be on his way now, Flavia," he said gently. He turned toward Rex. "I have something for you, young man." The senator held out a gold solidus, pressing it into Rex's hand when he tried to refuse. "I intend to pay my niece's debts," Ignatius said. "My honor requires it."

Rex thanked the senator and tucked the coin into his moneypouch, then he mounted the sturdy cavalry pony Ignatius had given him. Up in the saddle, Rex felt a little more at ease, like he was back in a world whose rules he knew.

"Could you perhaps meet me at Ostia before I sail?" Flavia asked.

"I think . . . I think that wouldn't be possible, my lady. I'm afraid this is goodbye."

The statement elicited a nod and a little whimper from Flavia. She dabbed at the tears in her eyes with a silk kerchief. "You're right," she admitted, staring at her feet.

Rex gathered the reins and called for a trot from his mount. At the gate, he turned one last time and raised his hand. Ignatius had already begun to return to the villa, but Flavia was still there, alone.

"God be with you, Rex!" she called.

In response, he patted the tau-rho amulet at his neck, then reined around and passed through the gate. A heavy overcast had rolled in, making the evening darker than normal. From over his shoulder in the distance, he heard Flavia cry, "I love you!" *Probably some kind of Christian expression of sisterly affection,* he decided. *Something they often say.*

The lane from the villa eventually joined the main highway to Rome. Rex had been riding only a short time when rain began to fall. It started as a sprinkle but quickly became steadier. He pulled his hood over his head and eased up on the reins, letting his horse find its own natural pace on the slippery road.

Soon after Rex had turned onto the Tiburtinian Way, he heard hoofbeats from behind, approaching at a canter. *Not good,* he thought. The purpose of traveling after dark was to avoid being seen, at least by anyone who might be hostile. It seemed unlikely that any respectable citizen would be out here on such a cold, rainy night. Rex pulled up and waited for the rider to draw near, his hand resting on the pommel of his sword. The downpour intensified, but even the sound of the droplets pattering against the pavestones could not obscure the hoofbeats of the oncoming rider. He was clearly in a hurry.

A tall horseman emerged from the gloom, swathed in a heavy cloak. He slowed to a walk as soon as he spotted Rex, then stopped a few paces away.

"I know who you are," the nameless voice declared.

In the far distance, thunder rumbled. Rex loosened his sword in its scabbard but did not draw it. "State your business," he replied.

———⟨∾⟩———

A light mist began to fall as Flavia walked back to her uncle's villa. The sky was heavy and cold, as if the weather could somehow sense the melancholy state of Flavia's heart. Her trunk of new clothes and necessities was packed and waiting in her room. Tomorrow she would depart for the port of Ostia, and from there she would sail for the island of Sardinia. After that, what? Only the Lord God knew.

But whatever my future, it won't include Rex.

Alexamenos met Flavia on the path that led back to the villa from the stable. "It's wet out, Lady Junia," he said, stretching his cloak to shield her head. He escorted her to a courtyard with a lively fire burning in the fireplace. Raindrops fell on a pool at the center of the patio, but the chairs by the fire were dry under the surrounding porch. The two friends sat down by the hearth, its radiant warmth a welcome relief.

"I know it was hard to leave him," the kindly schoolteacher said. "Young Rex has been a comfort to you the past few days. For what it's worth, I would be willing to escort you to Ostia tomorrow. Then it's back to Rome for me."

"Thank you, Alexamenos. That is most kind of you. I'd be very glad for your company. And you're right about Rex. I didn't think saying goodbye would be so hard."

"It is easy for a woman's heart to get bound to a man's, especially someone as vigorous and handsome as Rex. But it is probably better that he left. After all, he is . . . well, he is perhaps not the man for a believer like you."

Flavia glanced at her new friend. He was about thirty, a common age for men to take a wife, which would usually be a girl of about seventeen, like Flavia. Even so, she did not sense Alexamenos had any such interest in her. He spoke instead like a Christian brother, with charity and genuine concern in his voice.

"You know, it's funny," Flavia said carefully. "I do feel drawn to Rex. I even feel that I love him. Yet in my heart, I wouldn't want him to be my husband."

"Because he worships demons?"

"Yes, primarily that. I couldn't live with a man who isn't within the catholic faith."

"And so you shouldn't. It is most unwise. All the best theologians counsel against it. For example, the African Tertullian."

"I have read his essays on marriage, and I agree. But beyond that, Rex and I have entirely different futures. He's going to join the imperial army, and I'm going into exile across the sea."

The statement was too bleak to discuss any further, and Alexamenos was wise enough to recognize Flavia's mood. Instead of offering inept words, he sat in companionable silence with Flavia and shared her sorrow. The steady rain pattered onto the courtyard pool. Every so often, the logs in the fireplace popped, but otherwise all was quiet.

At last Alexamenos rose from his chair. "I shall retire now, sister," he said, giving her shoulder a gentle squeeze. "You should follow soon. We have a long day of travel tomorrow."

"I'll come shortly. I just need some time to pray."

"Good night, then, Lady Junia."

Alone in the courtyard, Flavia raised her eyes to the dark sky and watched the drops fall like glittering flecks of moonlight. She tried to invite God into her looming Sardinian exile, yet her mind was distracted and unsettled, and the words of a coherent prayer would not come. The dancing flames in the fireplace lulled her into a melancholy silence.

Outside on the lawn, a stick snapped.

Is someone out there? Or is it just an animal?

Flavia rose from her cushioned seat and crossed the courtyard to one of the doorways that led outside. Though she tried to peer into the darkness, she had been staring too long at the fire, so her eyes couldn't discern anything. A brilliant flash of lightning illuminated the villa's rear yard. It was entirely empty.

Relieved, Flavia was about to return to her chair when a booming thunderclap made her jump. She sucked in her breath and spun away from the door—and bumped into a man.

Flavia screamed as two hands gripped her shoulders. "Let me go!" she cried, thrashing in her enemy's grip.

"Flavia! It's okay! It's me!"

Rex?

Yes! It's him! He came back!

One hand remained on her shoulder, and with his other, Rex flipped back his hood. Standing so close to him, Flavia found she had to arch her neck to look at his face. He gazed down at her with genuine affection in his blue eyes. Water dribbled down his cheeks and ran into his chin stubble. Droplets clung to the locks of hair on his forehead that he hadn't let the barber cut when he assumed his Roman disguise. A slow smile crept across his face as he stared back at Flavia.

"What are you doing here?" she gasped.

"I'll explain it, but . . ." Rex broke off his words as if considering what to say. The emotion on his face grew intense, almost fierce. He released his grip on her shoulder and threw both arms around her, drawing her into a soggy embrace. Rex held her against his body for a long moment. Just as Flavia was beginning to think the hug might turn into something more amorous, he let her go.

Senator Ignatius stood by the fireplace, warming his hands. Steam rose from his wet woolen cloak. Turning toward the pair, he nodded gently and offered a knowing smile. After unfastening his cloak, he removed it in a shower of little drops and hung it on a wall peg. Rex did the same, then took a seat before the fire. Flavia came and sat beside him on the divan.

"Did something happen out on the road, Uncle?" she asked.

"Indeed, it did. Your friend finally acknowledged his true identity."

Flavia glanced at Rex, who only shrugged and said, "Let your uncle explain it."

Senator Ignatius stirred the fire with a poker, then set it on the hearth and faced his niece. "There is something I need to tell you, Flavia. It might surprise you. Yet I believe God has an important role for you to play in what I am about to disclose."

"I'm listening."

With the eloquent command of Latin common to all aristocrats, Ignatius began to tell a story that Flavia could never have imagined. He explained that for several years now, he had belonged to a clandestine alliance of senators seeking to overthrow Maxentius and pave the way for Constantine. The secret conspiracy was very hush-hush, for it included members of Rome's most noble families. All of them had sworn an oath to do everything in their power to bring down the wicked emperor.

Though the news of the conspiracy surprised Flavia, she found what her uncle said next to be even more astounding. He declared that the coming of Rex had been a strange and intriguing development. From the moment Rex arrived, Ignatius had recognized him as a speculator. Flavia was unfamiliar with that term, but Ignatius said it referred to the empire's most elite warriors—secret operatives trained in hand-to-hand combat, disguises, and stealthy maneuvers behind enemy lines. If Rex was here on a spying mission, that would be something the conspirators would want to support. Ignatius had been torn about whether to reveal the secret alliance to him; but when Rex rode away, the senator finally realized he couldn't let the opportunity pass. He decided to take a risk and confront the newly arrived spy.

"Your uncle challenged me on the road," Rex said. "He insisted he knew who I was because he used to be a tribune in charge of a cohort of speculators. I played dumb until he told me about the resistance movement among the senators. Then I knew I had met an important ally. My mission's objectives would require me to explore the possibilities. So I admitted my identity to him."

"Rex! This is astounding! I mean, I knew you were a good fighter and everything, but I had no idea you were sent here by Constantine himself! Have you actually met him?"

"Of course. I was his personal bodyguard for a time."

"Unbelievable! You know the emperor personally! They say he is a Christian. Is that true?"

"Well, he seems drawn to the god Jesus, though I don't think his beliefs are exactly like yours. Yet it was he who gave me this Christian amulet." Rex withdrew it from his neckline and cupped it in his palm.

Knuckles rapped on the door that led from the patio to the house. It hung ajar, and Alexamenos was standing in the doorway. "Master Ignatius? Your servant said you asked for me."

"Yes, come in, my friend! Join us at the fire. I have just informed my niece and young Rex here about the secret conspiracy of which we are a part."

"Excellent, sir. Then our futures are now bound together, and our lives are permanently intertwined."

"You two already knew each other?" Flavia asked her uncle. "Before we arrived?" The surprises just kept coming.

"Yes, we ran in the same circles here in Tibur," Ignatius replied. "By that I mean spiritual circles, as fellow Christians—and as we came to realize later, we had political affinities as well. We found we were both supporters of Constantine. So I asked Alexamenos to join our society. He has some good connections back in Rome."

After Alexamenos took a seat, Ignatius continued to explain his plan. From his stance next to the fireplace, he leaned forward and looked intently at Flavia. "As I stated before—you, dear one, have an important role to play. We have long been trying to plant someone deep in Maxentius's palace, but so far we have found no one we could trust. Or at least no one we could trust who was also clever enough to spy on the emperor. But now, Flavia, you would be the perfect candidate."

"Me? What do I know about spying?"

"Nothing. But you don't have to. You only need to be clever enough to maintain your secret persona. Then just work hard, stay sharp, and keep your ears open. Information will find its way to you."

"But you're talking about the imperial palace! Won't that get the authorities on my trail again?"

"No! That's the beauty of our little charade at the crematorium. We did it to set you free so you could live far away, but it opened up some unexpected possibilities. Think about it. You're dead now, Flavia. Dead and forgotten. The only thing you can't do is show up in your mansion on the Aventine and try to resume your normal life. So what else? Sure, you could flee to Sardinia. You would definitely disappear. But you could just as easily disappear into Maxentius's vast palace as a common worker. It's the last thing anyone would suspect of a fugitive. And there you might actually contribute to the important events rising in our empire."

"I'm open to it," Flavia said cautiously, "but the idea seems scary. I'd live in the emperor's palace? What would I do there?"

Alexamenos put a gentle hand on Flavia's arm. "Remember, I train the imperial page boys. I have many connections at the palace, so I can easily get you a job up there. You'd fit in with the young girls who work in the emperor's kitchen. No one at the palace knows you, so they wouldn't suspect a thing. And I can provide you a spare room at the Gelotiana House where I live. All you'd have to do is go to work every day and listen for whatever you could pick up."

Flavia glanced at Rex. "Do you think I should do it?"

Rex nodded, though he grimaced as he did so. "It certainly would help my mission to have an insider deep in the palace," he acknowledged. "But you'd have to . . ." He made a snipping motion below his ear with two fingers. "And also, no more of this." Rex rubbed his cheeks with the fingertips of his two hands, then traced his index fingers across his eyelids.

"I don't need all that," Flavia said. "I can give it up if I need to."

"Good. You couldn't look bad even if you tried, so don't worry."

Though Flavia's mind registered the compliment, her thoughts were racing too quickly to linger over the sweet words. "What about you?" she asked. "What will you do, Rex?"

"Exactly what I've been planning all along: enlist in Maxentius's army and gather intelligence for my lord when he arrives. And also kill that snake Pompeianus if I get a chance."

Ignatius frowned. "No, Rex. That is not part of our plan."

"It might be part of my plan," Rex muttered, then let the matter drop.

Senator Ignatius spread his arms as if to gather everyone together. "My friends, we have all revealed some deadly information to each other tonight. A sacred trust now binds us. I propose we formalize it with a holy promise."

"Great idea!" Rex said. "Let's swear an oath."

"Only a promise before God," Ignatius countered. "No need to swear upon his name or risk punishments for oath breaking. Just let our yes be yes and our no be no, as the Lord has said."

Alexamenos jumped up and faced Ignatius. "I promise to serve the Christian emperor and help him succeed."

"Me too," Flavia said, rising to join the other men. "It is clear I have been called to this task. Therefore I will do my part."

Now Rex was the only person still seated. Slowly and with thoughtful deliberation, he glanced at the three others. Finally, he stood up. He reached to the back of his neck, unfastened the thong of his amulet, and held it out in his palm. The incised tau and rho stood out clearly on the medallion's metal face. Curling his fingers, he enclosed it in his fist.

"If the Christian God really is the creator of all," Rex said, "let him behold me now. I promise before this God of yours to return to Rome and do whatever I can to prepare the way for Constantine."

Flavia felt a strong emotion sweep over her as she gazed at Rex. He was so strong, so resolute, so courageous—and also, she had to admit, so handsome as he stood there in the hearth's soft glow. Firelight danced on his face, highlighting his stark cheekbones and strong jaw. With his wide shoulders and impressive height, Rex seemed capable of achieving anything. Drawn to him by a potent and primordial force, Flavia took up her place at his side, then reached out and clasped his fist in her palm.

"I promise to serve God alongside you," she said, "no matter what it may require."

Alexamenos added his hand to the pledge. "And I as well."

After a moment of prayerful meditation, Ignatius stepped close and covered the hands of the others with his own. "It is indeed a solemn promise we are making here tonight, my friends. I join you freely, for God has called us to a great task. Let us continually ask him to help us see it through. For I have the feeling—"

The senator's brow wrinkled, and he sighed deeply as he caught Flavia's eye. She looked back at him, waiting for him to finish his words.

"I have the feeling," Ignatius continued at last, "that we shall need the full measure of God's strength before our work is done."

9

NOVEMBER 311

The pleasant days of early autumn had begun to lapse into a dreary Roman winter. It was November now, and like every year, Flavia was trying to adapt to more chilly drizzle and less beautiful sunshine. Today was yet another one of the rainy days. As she gazed out her window at the Gelotiana House, she could tell it was going to be like that all day.

"Enjoying the view?" Alexamenos asked as he entered the room behind her, obviously joking. The only thing Flavia could see was the rain-drenched wall of an apartment block a short distance away.

She glanced over her shoulder and rolled her eyes. "Of course! I always love to stare at wet bricks."

Alexamenos laughed at the reply, then came closer and pointed at the plain-looking building. "See those windows right there? Four in a row on the second floor? Guess what it is."

"Somebody's residence, I suppose," Flavia said with a shrug.

"Used to be. But now it's been turned into a church."

"Really?" Flavia looked over at her friend, mouth agape, eyebrows arched. "A church right here at the foot of the Palatine? That building touches the Circus Maximus! The emperor passes it every time he comes down to his box to watch the races!"

"I know. Hard to believe. Little does he know what's happening right under his nose. Quite a few high-level officials attend the church. It's named

262

for the lady who owns the apartments. She took some rooms off her rental roll and devoted them to sacred use. Her name is Anastasia. Quite an energetic woman. And very devoted to the faith."

"I wish I could visit," Flavia said wistfully.

Alexamenos shook his head. "Just keep your head down and do your job. No need to raise suspicions. There will be time in the future to start going to church again."

"I know. But I miss meeting with the brethren."

"Maybe you could go out to the Catacombs? There's a feast coming soon at the Apostolic Monument. The place is less visible to watching eyes."

Flavia was considering her friend's remark when, out in the main courtyard, the normal ruckus of the rowdy boys who lived in the house grew louder. Tensions had been running a little high today because everyone was cooped up by the rain. Now a fight seemed to be breaking out.

Alexamenos went to the portico to intervene, and Flavia followed. "Bassus! Zoticus! Break it up!" the teacher barked. "You want to mar those pretty faces with a black eye? You've got a banquet tomorrow!"

The mention of disfigurement was more than enough to make the handsome youths back down from whatever had aroused their fighting spirit. When Flavia had arrived a few days earlier at Gelotiana House, she immediately noticed that the boys—from slight youths with still-smooth cheeks to young men who were seventeen like herself—were all extremely good-looking. Their faces were beautiful, their clothes were elegant, and all of them were tall for their age. Yet what Flavia noticed most was their hair. Every single boy had long, thick locks that draped down upon his shoulders. Normally it hung free, but on formal occasions it was braided into plaits. These youths were being trained in the Paedagogium, the school for imperial pages who performed various ceremonial duties in the palace. Apparently, the officials from the government complex on the Palatine Hill needed handsome boys at their constant beck and call. The Roman Empire might be run by a bunch of fat old men, but the slaves who served them were angelic.

"Everybody, back to your duties!" Alexamenos said. "No fighting in the house!"

"He started it, Magister," the boy named Bassus whined.

"And I'd finish it, too, if we didn't have a banquet." Zoticus gave his enemy one last glare, then spun away in disgust. Flavia had met the youth already. He was cocky and arrogant, yet a likeable rascal. At age thirteen, his boyish cuteness was just starting to be tinged with the more rugged edge of a man.

"Let's talk for a bit, Zoticus. Step into your room." Alexamenos slipped his arm around his pupil's shoulder and steered him to the third bedroom from the entrance. The teacher looked over his shoulder and tossed his head at Flavia, indicating she could follow. Alexamenos had been intentional about making her feel welcome among the horde of boys. He included her in everything. As for the boys, they had long ago accepted the presence of a few females in their midst. In fact, several of the youths seemed a little too glad about it. Flavia had endured numerous crass comments already, not to mention a couple of advances from the older boys. Her roommate, Chloe, was pregnant by one of the pages, though she didn't know which one.

Zoticus shared his room with three other pages. Their sleeping couches lined two of the walls, while the third held wooden cabinets for their belongings. The fourth wall was a mass of graffiti scratched into the plaster by the many boys who had passed through the school over the years. One drawing caught Flavia's eye: a donkey was turning a grinding mill next to the words *Toil on, little ass, just as I have toiled, and it will profit you.* Evidently, the labors of the schoolboys could feel like drudgery at times, but in the end, the rewards were worth it.

"It's difficult to go through life so angry all the time," Alexamenos was telling Zoticus, who was pouting on his bed. "You always seem ready to explode like a volcano. A wise man learns to control his passions."

"Don't quote your Christian scriptures at me, Magister. I don't care what they have to say."

"The scriptures of my God do counsel against anger, but so do the philosophers. You need look no further than Seneca or Cicero to discover that turbulent passions disrupt the soul. This is wisdom you would do well to heed."

Zoticus folded his arms across his chest and would say no more, despite Alexamenos's best efforts. Finally, the teacher gave up and left the boy alone. Flavia was about to depart, too, when she paused and turned to the petulant boy. "You know, girls don't like angry men," she advised. "Maybe you should change your ways if you want to catch someone's eye."

"What makes you think I don't already have a girl?" Zoticus snapped. "I'm a grown man now. Look here"—he thrust out his chin—"I have whiskers."

"I see them, Zoticus. But there's more to being a man than having to pluck a beard."

"What do you know about men, kitchen girl? The only men you know are cooks and pastry chefs."

Refusing to take Zoticus's bait and argue with him, Flavia offered a warm smile instead. "All girls feel the same way about angry men," she said. "Trust me."

"Bah!" Zoticus scoffed, swatting at the air with his hand.

Flavia sighed and turned away. The wall in front of her was covered in scribbles. "Comicus is leaving the school," one grateful boy had written. There were several pictures of gladiators and racehorses, as one would expect in a school that adjoined the Circus Maximus. Flavia was considering what to say to Zoticus when her eyes fell on a much more shocking graffito. She sucked in her breath as she read the inscription, scrawled in crudely executed Greek. "Alexamenos worships God," it said. A man clad in a simple tunic was depicted raising his hand in prayer. Above him was a man nailed to a cross—except he had the ludicrous head of a donkey.

Flavia whirled to face Zoticus. "What is this?" she demanded, trying to keep her voice calm despite the outrage she felt at the blasphemy.

"How should I know? I didn't write it."

"Who did?"

Zoticus only shrugged, but the fact that he was blushing and avoiding eye contact made Flavia doubt his sincerity.

"Jesus Christ doesn't have a donkey's head! He's not some disgusting monster like the Aegyptian gods."

"Of course not," Zoticus said impudently. "Jesus was a stupid Jew who got himself crucified for challenging the authority of almighty Rome."

It was all Flavia could do to hold her tongue. *Lord, give me wise words,* she prayed, *and help me not to slap this smug kid!*

"So you disagree with your teacher's Christian faith, Zoticus?" she asked, keeping her voice level and her tone sweet.

"It's a stupid religion." The boy shook his long hair out of his face in a way Flavia found prissy. "Anybody who would follow that faith is a jackass, just like the drawing shows."

"Alexamenos follows it. You don't respect him?"

Zoticus sneered but said nothing.

"How much do you know about Christianity? Have you ever visited a church? Read the scriptures? Talked to a priest?"

"I wouldn't waste my time doing any of that, kitchen girl."

"Yet you're convinced Christianity is stupid. Why? On what facts is your opinion based?"

"I just know it's a dumb religion. And don't try to convince me otherwise. I'm not going to change my mind."

"Well, Zoticus, it seems you're the one acting like a donkey here. You're being stubborn, ignorant, irritable, and unpleasant."

The remark visibly angered Zoticus, but Flavia didn't mind. She had intended her words as a challenge. Over the years she had found that younger boys actually cared a lot about what an older, pretty girl might think, even if they wouldn't admit it. Now Flavia hoped to leverage that influence and break through the youth's hard shell.

But Zoticus's veneer of arrogance held firm. No matter what Flavia said about Christianity, no matter how many mistaken notions she corrected, Zoticus refused to have an open mind. He apparently enjoyed arguing and hurling insults. At last Flavia asked, "Are there any gods you do like? Any you think aren't a waste of time?"

The boy's face clouded. "I'm saving money for an offering to Aesculapius," he declared.

Aesculapius? The god of healing?

Flavia crossed the room and came over to Zoticus, who was sitting on the edge of his bed. She knelt on the floor beside him. "Is someone in your life suffering?"

Zoticus shook his head and stared at his feet. Only when Flavia gave him a soft pat on the hand did he finally mumble, "My mother's sick. She might die."

"I'm sorry to hear that, Zoticus. Does she live in Rome?" A nod from the boy was his only reply. "Does your mother pray to the gods?" Flavia asked.

Again Zoticus shook his head, his lip curled in a frown. "She follows the

Christian God. A lot of good that's doing. She's been bedridden for nearly a year, and still no change despite all that wasted breath sent up to heaven."

"No prayer is wasted when it's sent to the one true God. You can be sure he hears our prayers, even if his answer doesn't come right away."

Zoticus finally lifted his head and looked at Flavia's face. "Who are you, anyway?"

"What?"

"I said, who are you, Flavia? You arrive at this house out of nowhere to live with us while you work up in the palace kitchens. And you don't act like the other girls. They just want to steal wine from the cellars and have sex. You want to debate religion and philosophy."

"I'm not . . . I mean, it's okay to be different . . ."

"You're different, alright! You sound like a Christian! And you also seem like a rich girl, with your smooth skin and all your smart talk. You were reading the graffiti. How did a scullery maid learn to read Greek?"

Flavia rose to her feet, unnerved by the boy's probing questions. "I'm just a girl from the countryside who's trying to be your friend, Zoticus," she said. "Just because I had a good tutor before my father fell into debt isn't a reason to suspect me. People from all walks of life find themselves in slavery. Misfortune can strike anyone."

"Yeah. I guess you're right."

Flavia sensed it was time to leave before the boy's questions became even more pointed. Enough had been said already, and Flavia wanted to leave while Zoticus had accepted her story. She bid him a good day and retired to her room.

The rain outside had not let up. Flavia returned to her window and stared at the plain apartment block, which, she now knew, contained a church. Some of the rainwater ran down the roof tiles and dribbled onto the pavement, but Flavia knew most of the water was being channeled into the building's central impluvium. *Baptisms of converts to the true faith probably happen there*, she mused.

Though Flavia kept trying to clear her mind, Zoticus's suspicious accusations refused to leave her thoughts. The boy's bitter anger was clearly a cloak for his pain. Even so, he seemed dangerous. Everyone knew a wounded animal was the most apt to bite.

Perhaps I ought to leave it to Alexamenos to deal with him.

Flavia left the window and sat down on the edge of her bed. The only other couch in the room belonged to Chloe, her cheerful, heavyset roommate who now carried the baby of an unknown imperial page. Burdened by the many needs around her yet grateful for Alexamenos's steady presence, Flavia stood up and faced the window again. She lifted her palms. After offering some prayers toward the sky for her new friends, she finally felt a sense of peace return.

At last the rain slowed. The reduced patter of raindrops caused a quiet hush to descend on the house. It was afternoon now, and most of the boys were probably napping. Flavia let out a heavy sigh as she examined her surroundings. Like Zoticus's room, the plaster walls here were etched with graffiti. *I might as well leave my own mark,* she decided.

She snatched one of Chloe's hairpins and approached the wall. Still bothered by the graffito she had seen earlier, she scrawled a reply to the accusation that her friend worshiped a ridiculous, donkey-headed god. In reality, the Greek schoolteacher was a good Christian man doing a difficult job. He didn't deserve to be mocked. "Alexamenos is faithful," she wrote in Latin. Setting down the pin, Flavia vowed to be equally faithful in this strange little house at the foot of the Palatine Hill.

―⟡―

Livia winced as the ornatrix plucked yet another hair from her eyebrow. "Careful!" she cried, though there wasn't anything else the slave could do.

"Sorry, my lady. Only a few more."

The bony waif with the too-big eyes continued her work with the tweezer. Despite her personal ugliness, the girl was actually a good ornatrix. She knew the art of feminine beauty well. She just didn't have the looks to pull it off herself.

Once Livia's eyebrows were tweezed into two slender arcs, the ornatrix went to work on her face. She applied rouge to her mistress's cheeks, pink paint to her lips, and gold-flecked liner to her eyelids. An array of brushes, powders, oils, and perfumes smoothed and perfected the look. The whole process of painting Livia's face took about an hour. Yet there was no question it was time well spent. Livia needed to look her best. She was about to make love to the most powerful man in the world.

The fact that her husband, Pompeianus, was prostituting her to the emperor didn't bother Livia. She had learned long ago that sex with powerful men was a useful tool, nothing more. If any pleasure was to be had from intercourse, it was to be obtained from slaves. But the point of sexual relations with a husband—or with an influential politician—was to achieve an objective, not enjoy the moment. And no objective was more important than causing Senator Neratius Junius Flavianus to fall out of favor with Maxentius.

"I think, my lady, that you are ready to go," the skinny ornatrix said. She held up a silver mirror for her mistress.

Livia inspected her face and found that, indeed, it was appealing. The slave had done an excellent job once again. *By the gods, I look pretty good for a twenty-nine-year-old*, Livia thought. Setting the mirror on the dresser, she rose from her cushioned chair and went to find her husband.

Pompeianus was in his study, waiting for the emperor's guards to arrive. He wouldn't invite them into that formal room, of course. Only men of equal rank could join him there. Yet the study adjoined the atrium, a suitable place to meet the visitors and hand over his gift to the great Emperor Maxentius. Along with his wife, he would probably send a flattering note and an amphora of good wine. That was the thing about Pompeianus. He always knew exactly how things should be done.

"You look suitable," he said to Livia as she entered. He set down his stylus and wax tablet and leaned back in his seat. "The emperor will have no complaints."

"I shall leave him breathless."

Pompeianus broke into a smile and gave a little shake of his head. "I'm sure you will. That is exactly the sort of thing you were made for." He rose and traced a finger along Livia's jawline. "You're a good woman," he said appreciatively. "Be sure to leave a positive impression of me."

The tinkle of a silver bell signaled that the majordomo had come to the doorway with news. "The emperor's representatives are here, my lord," he said.

"Admit them to the atrium and offer them refreshments. The soldiers of the empire are always welcome in the Lateran Palace."

The majordomo looked hesitant. "If I may say, sir, these men aren't Praetorians. In fact, I find them to be rather—"

"What?" Livia asked.

"Common."

"What do you mean, common?" she pressed.

"Like . . . street thugs. Professional procurers."

"You mean pimps."

The majordomo nodded.

"Admit them anyway," Pompeianus ordered. "Keep them at a distance from me, and offer them no drinks. But be cordial."

The majordomo disappeared. Soon the sound of voices at the main entrance of the residence indicated the men had been let inside. Pompeianus rose from his desk. Sweeping aside the drapery that separated his study from the atrium, he strode out to meet the visitors. Livia followed her husband with a stately and dignified gait.

The men truly were common pimps from the streets—expensively dressed, suggesting they were good at their trade, but part of the rabble, nonetheless. *That must be Maxentius's strategy*, Livia thought. *Push the senators to the limits of their shame, then see who's truly willing to submit.*

A few brief pleasantries were exchanged, but a lot of talking wasn't necessary. Everyone knew what was happening here. The pimps returned to the street, while eight of Livia's slaves arrived with the house's most fancy litter. They set it down and returned to the vestibule until their mistress would signal she was ready to go. Livia was about to climb into the plush, upholstered box when a shout rang out in the atrium.

"No! This is wrong! You should not let it happen!"

Though the statement was bold, the voice itself was notably high-pitched. Livia whirled to confront the speaker but was taken aback when she realized who it was.

Agrippa!

Her chubby son stood at the entrance to the atrium. Though he was only ten years old, Livia could already see that he would never be his father's equal in terms of confidence, ambition, or sheer ferocity. The boy might make a good philosopher someday. Perhaps even an orator, if he were given enough training. But he would never run a military machine like the Praetorian Guard.

Pompeianus's face turned dark as he strode across the room to chastise his son. To the boy's credit, he did not flee but instead hurried to stand between Livia and the waiting litter.

"How dare you challenge me in my own home!" Pompeianus roared.

Agrippa cringed but stood his ground. "My duty—"

"Your what?"

"My duty," the boy continued bravely, "requires me to protest this action."

"Get out of my sight, Agrippa, or I'll have you whipped like a houseboy!"

"I know I can't stop you, Father. You might even cast me out of your home. Even so, I have to speak against this violation of ancient Roman laws."

The words rendered Pompeianus speechless for a long moment. He just stood there, seething, his face contorted in a grimace, his fists clenched like eagle's talons. The scar on his cheek made him seem all the more monstrous. Yet as terrible as he looked, his quivering silence seemed preferable to the storm that was surely gathering within him.

When the thunder and lightning finally burst forth, Livia feared that real violence was about to be done to her son. Pompeianus cursed him like a cur on the street. He screamed that the boy's high-paid tutors had filled his head full of lofty ideals that sounded noble in books but were far removed from the real exercise of power in a blood-soaked world. Bending low, Pompeianus delivered a vicious tongue-lashing to Agrippa, who—again to his credit—scrunched his eyes and weathered the storm with his feet planted firmly in place.

"I married that woman for the sake of my career!" Pompeianus shouted, jabbing his finger toward Livia. "Now I'm sending her to the emperor for my career! Listen to me, boy, and listen well. Learn this lesson early if you want to have any hope of success in your pitiful life! Love is a luxury reserved for the commoners. Patricians like us deal only in power!"

Agrippa thrust out his chin. "Patricians like us do not pimp out our wives."

The room fell silent. The majordomo, who had been watching the tirade from the corner of the atrium, edged toward the door. Even Livia was afraid now.

Pompeianus's hand shot from his side. He grabbed his son by the throat and lifted poor Agrippa onto his tiptoes as the boy clawed at the fingers that choked off his breath. Pompeianus dragged him to the pool in the center of the atrium and threw him into the water, then splashed in after him and thrust the boy's head underwater. He held Agrippa down for a long time despite his furious thrashing.

Livia willed herself to stand still. *Holy Isis, Great Mother in Heaven, don't let him kill that boy!*

After what seemed like an age, Pompeianus yanked Agrippa's head from the water and left him gasping on his hands and knees in the pool. With unnatural calmness, Pompeianus removed his outer mantle, the hem of which was now soaked. He used a dry fold of it to wipe the moisture from his shaved head, then summoned the majordomo with a flick of his fingers and handed him the garment.

"Take that robe and have it washed," he said.

"As you wish, my lord." The majordomo bowed and turned to go, but Pompeianus stopped him.

"Also take the boy and have a slave administer a beating with rods until he passes out. Then send him to his room and have the physician attend him."

"Y-yes, lord," the majordomo said with another bow. At these words, Agrippa scrambled out of the pool and fled the room. The servant exited behind him.

Pompeianus let out a heavy sigh and crossed the atrium to Livia. She stood rooted in the same spot from which she had watched the conflict unfold.

"You fault me?" he asked.

She shook her head. "No, lord."

"Why not?"

"Power always has its price."

Pompeianus nodded thoughtfully. "Indeed it does," he said at last. After patting Livia gently on the shoulder, he turned and walked toward the door that led to his study. Just before leaving the atrium, he glanced over his shoulder. "Give Maxentius my warmest greetings, Livia," he said, then parted the curtains and disappeared.

⸻ ∿ ⸻

"So you think you can ride, eh, German?"

Rex kept his expression pleasant. "I grew up in the saddle, my friend. The

272

Alemanni love the horse. My father was the manager of the king's stables, so I've been around riding my whole life."

My father was actually the king, Rex thought, *but you don't need to know that.*

The riding instructor at the New Camp of the Emperor's Personal Cavalry—a man known as an exerciser—looked skeptical despite Rex's claim of good equestrian credentials. "It's one thing to dodge falling chestnuts in a barbarian forest," he said, "and quite another to hold a full gallop while enemy javelins are coming at you."

"I know a little about war. I was a mercenary for a while, so I've got some training. And like I said, I've been riding since I was a child. If you let me join the cavalry, I will serve the great Maxentius well."

"Can you throw while wheeling?"

"Yes, sir. Either right or left."

"You can wheel left? Only our better riders can do that."

"Up in Germania, we learn all the arts of horsemanship. I can wheel left, shift my shield, and make a throw across my body."

"Hmm. So you claim. We'll see whether you can back up your words on the field." The exerciser turned and beckoned to some seasoned cavalrymen. They sat light in the saddle as they approached, their leathery faces etched with the lines of men who had spent much time in the sun. "This recruit thinks he can ride and throw," the exerciser told the horsemen. "Push him hard, and let's see what he's made of."

Rex leapt smoothly onto the back of his cavalry pony, gripping the saddle and swinging his leg over the animal's back to gain the seat instead of stepping on a mounting block. One of the cavalrymen guffawed. "Fine, boy. We see you can mount a horse. Getting up is one thing. *Staying* up is the business of real men."

Reining around, Rex approached the trooper who had spoken to him. He seemed a decade older than Rex, maybe even in his early thirties. His red shield was marked with a scorpion insignia, and his helmet sported a yellow plume. Though Rex knew he was this man's equal as a rider and fighter, he wasn't about to reveal the full extent of his training. At the same time, to show himself weak right now would hamper his ability to integrate into the unit. These men were warriors; they respected strength above all else. Rex decided bold confidence was called for here—though not enough to blow his cover. He looked the yellow-plumed cavalryman in the eyes. "I wager I'll put you flat on your back in the dirt before we're done today," he said.

The challenge drew brusque laughter from the other soldiers, and even some taunts. The yellow-plumed rider leaned from his position in the saddle until he was almost nose to nose with Rex. "You talk big for a frontier boy! So you want to wager? Then let's do it! What've you got?"

Rex drew the gold solidus from his pouch and held it up. "I offer this coin if you knock me to the ground. It's all I have to my name."

The gold glinting in the sun drew murmurs from the men. "That's a whole lot of money there," the trooper said, "and I'll be happy to take it from you! You'd better tighten that chin strap, boy, because I'll be aiming for your head." The man glanced around at his comrades, who urged him on with cheers and acclamations. After receiving their praise, he turned his attention back to Rex. "Just for the sake of argument, what do you want from me if you should win the bet?"

"What I seek isn't yours to give." Turning away from his adversary, Rex stepped his horse close to the exerciser who was in charge of field instruction. "All I want is to be enlisted as a cavalryman in the service of Emperor Maxentius."

The exerciser stood on the soft earth of the parade ground, resting his hands on his hips. He stared up at Rex with an appraising look. "Kid, if you can knock a trooper like Decimus out of the saddle, I don't see why we wouldn't sign you into the unit on the spot. We can never find enough good riders these days. But you won't be able to do it. He's one of the best horsemen we have. That man hasn't felt the ground against his back since his first day in training camp."

"Until today," Rex said, then prompted his mount toward the new recruits who were forming up for the competition.

The maneuver in which the recruits were being tested today was known as the Cantabrian Circle. Used by the Spanish Celts in wars from the earliest days of the empire, the maneuver had been adopted by the Romans after they learned from hard experience how effective it could be. Now it was a standard part of a horse trooper's training. Two sets of riders would gallop single file in a ring formation, making a pair of contiguous circles. Both circles moved in the same direction, which meant that at the place where the two circles touched, each rider would find himself constantly coming around to face an opponent head on. In war, this circular barrage was a devastating tactic, for a stationary enemy would find himself subjected to a steady stream of missiles; yet the throwers were always veering away, so return shots were difficult. On the parade ground, the Cantabrian Circle made for great show—a swirling maelstrom of soldiers and spears that left no doubts about the incredible horsemanship of the Roman cavalry. And since contact between opposing riders was always happening at the same point, it was easy for observers to focus their attention there and analyze the strengths of each trooper.

Rex lined up with a motley group of provincials who were much like what he was claiming to be: idealistic youths with strong arms and a willingness to work hard to learn the art of war. Half of these men would make it into the army, and half of those would die before the age of forty. But the one-quarter who pursued a successful military career and were discharged with honors could look forward to all the prestige, camaraderie, adventures, health care, good pay, and comfortable retirement that came with being a Roman soldier. Certainly it was beyond anything they could have achieved in the villages of their birth. And that was exactly why they had come to Rome.

"Here you go, German," the exerciser said, handing Rex a small round shield and a quiver of three javelins. Instead of iron points, the wooden shafts were tipped with stiff leather—not enough to pierce armor or kill a man, but certainly enough to break a rib or crush a nose. "Keep that shield up," the exerciser advised. "Decimus is out for your gold."

Rex gave the centurion a brash smile. "Keep a stylus handy, sir. You'll need it to sign my enlistment contract." The centurion only rolled his eyes at the cocky remark and moved on to the next horseman.

The two teams were furnished with scarves of either red or blue. Rex found himself on the blue squad, joined by recruits who were mostly from the far northern provinces. The red team consisted of hopefuls from the territories along the lower Danubius. A few seasoned veterans were in the mix too, just to make things interesting.

At the exerciser's command, the first riders led out at a canter to get the feel of the Cantabrian Circle. Each time the opponents passed each other, they made hurling motions with their spears but didn't actually release. As Rex entered the fray, he feigned a level of awkwardness he did not actually feel. During his three years of intense training as a speculator, Aratus had run him through exactly this drill more times than he could count. Rex had been particularly good at it. Now he felt he could do it with his eyes closed. But he didn't want the watchers to know that.

The exerciser ordered the competitors to move up to a gallop. The increased speed heightened the intensity of the competition, and even Rex began to feel a rush of battle excitement. As he watched the circle of the opposing team go round, he noticed Decimus enter the flow, unmistakable with his yellow plume and blood-red shield. Rex could see immediately that he was indeed a superb horseman.

A trumpet sounded, signaling the onset of full-combat maneuvers. As the first pair of riders came around their circles and met head-on, each threw his leather-tipped javelin. One man missed completely, while the other's spear made a loud clatter as it ricocheted off his opponent's shield.

Rex rounded the circle at a full gallop and fixed his eyes on Decimus coming toward him. His yellow plume streamed behind him, and his oblong shield covered more of his body than Rex's little round one. Taut muscles, slick with sweat, stood out on the man's upraised spear arm. Rex knew it was going to take all his skill to defend himself against such a worthy adversary.

The impact of Decimus's javelin on Rex's shield sent a tremor up his left arm. A hit like that against his head surely would have unhorsed him. Just before Rex felt the tremendous blow, he sent his own spear flying, but his rival successfully deflected it. The two men swept past each other in dual arcs and began the revolution toward their next encounter.

The second time they met, Rex decided to set up his final shot by luring his opponent into overconfidence. As every cavalryman knew, his shield wasn't his only defense; his javelin served that purpose too. The act of throwing it required an oncoming rider to watch it closely and adjust to its trajectory, greatly affecting his own aim. Any competitor who held his spear too long was asking to get hit because his enemy could focus on his throw instead of defending against a counterattack. For this reason, the paired opponents in the Cantabrian Circle usually released their spears at exactly the same moment, the brief instant when they were close enough to score a hit yet not so close as to give the enemy an easy shot.

But as Rex sped around for the second time, he deliberately waited until his opponent had thrown first. Rex took the impact on his shield, then hurled his own spear wide of the mark. "Too late!" Decimus cried as he galloped past. Such a late throw was exactly what an inaccurate spearman would try to do: draw closer before releasing his weapon to achieve better aim. It felt instinctive to an untrained rider. However, it was actually a foolish, even deadly, strategy.

On the third pass, Rex waited again to make his throw. Decimus, now aware of his opponent's tendency to delay, also waited for a can't-miss shot. Rex knew he would be aiming for the helmet, since cavalrymen couldn't resist the glory that came from making a successful head strike, driving a spear through the enemy's face and hurling him to the ground. Brazenly, Rex lowered his shield and left his head unprotected. Yet he kept his focus on Decimus's arm.

The two riders churned toward each other, each wheeling right as they approached the junction of their circles. A battle cry escaped Decimus's lips, and Rex roared in return. The enemy's arm started forward. The spear shaft moved. And with a tiny flex of his thighs, Rex turned his horse onto a slightly different trajectory—a collision course with Decimus.

The javelin flew past Rex's head with the hissing sound of a snake. Ignoring it, he barreled directly at his enemy. Wide-eyed, the red-and-yellow rider tried to turn aside from the deadly impact, but Rex urged his horse to keep galloping toward his opponent's mount. Both men were screaming now, venting their battle lust even though they were only on a parade ground. Rex knew the time for a throw had passed. Decimus held his oblong shield high, covering his entire body. The defensive posture would prevent the javelin from getting through.

At the moment before impact, Rex squeezed his thighs and turned his mount aside. Only an equestrian with complete control of his steed would have tried it, for it required a level of mastery that few riders could achieve. The cavalry pony that Flavia's uncle had given him was a good one, battle tested and responsive, and Rex felt confident in the saddle. The two horses brushed past each other, screeching their protest at the near collision. In the instant that Decimus was alongside him, Rex leaned out and smashed his opponent with his shield.

The blow wouldn't have knocked a man down in foot combat, but with the force of a galloping horse behind it, the shove was plenty hard enough to destabilize Decimus. Unprepared for the sudden shock, he lurched backward in the saddle, flailing his arms, then tumbled over the rump of his horse. Rex glimpsed him hit the ground as he flew past in the Cantabrian Circle.

The final time that Rex rounded the arc, he left the swirl of riders and reined up in front of his opponent's body. Decimus's helmet had come off, and the grimace on his face left no doubt about the pain he was in. He writhed on the ground, not mortally wounded, though perhaps seriously injured, and certainly stunned. Yet Rex felt no pity for his defeated foe. This was what he had asked for—and the man had been trying to do the exact same thing to him.

Rex raised his javelin above his head. "Feel the ground at your back once again, Decimus." He hurled the spear into the earth near his opponent's head. With its shaft still quivering, he turned his horse and rode in a direct line toward the supervisor of the parade ground. The centurion eyed Rex as he approached.

"Impressive work, German."

"Thank you, sir," Rex replied with a grin.

"I've got forty riders still out there on the field. What do you want?"

"I think you know what I'm here for."

The exerciser nodded thoughtfully, then turned to the junior aide at his side. "Go get me a stylus and tablet," he said. "The Emperor's Personal Cavalry has its newest recruit."

—◦◦◦—

The Roman Forum was the original town square of the capital city. Although Flavia had always enjoyed the vibrancy of the place, she now viewed it with significant trepidation. Of course, everything looked the same as it did two weeks earlier when she was thrown into the fearsome Carcer, dragged into the Senate House for a fake trial, and slapped by a cruel soldier at the foot of Titus's arch. Back then, she had been the privileged daughter of one of Rome's ancient families, a member of the more honorable class.

But who am I now?

In everyone's eyes, she was just a nondescript scullery maid with a plain tunic, shoulder-length hair, and no makeup to grace her cheeks. Though Flavia tried not to let the social demotion bother her, she couldn't help but feel its sting. She had lost her sense of belonging. Rome's central plaza had morphed from a friendly place where she was once welcome to an alien and hostile land. Though no one in the crowds recognized her as an aristocrat—or even paid her much notice at all—Flavia sensed the very stones of the Forum were now arrayed against her. Perhaps she would never again feel at home here.

"Flavia!" Chloe called. "Wait for me!"

Flavia paused next to a street vendor's stand to let her new friend catch up. Chloe was several months pregnant, and though she had a stout frame and her stomach hadn't noticeably expanded, she certainly looked more buxom as she bounced along the Forum's cracked travertine paving. Several times Flavia had noticed the girl wincing and rubbing her lower back as she carried out her kitchen duties. *It's hard enough to do the daily work of a slave. How much harder must it be with a baby in your belly?*

"Raisin cakes for the pretty ladies?" the street vendor asked. "Buy two and I'll throw in a third for free."

Flavia nodded to the man. "Sounds like an excellent deal." The vendor wrapped the treats in a cloth and tied up the bundle, then handed it to Flavia in exchange for two bronze pennies. She thanked him and turned to her friend.

"Look! I got us a little something," she said as Chloe approached.

"Ooh, lovely! Let's find a good place to sit and enjoy it."

The two girls meandered through the Forum under a bright, sunny sky. Yesterday's rain had passed, leaving Rome with a newly washed feel. After passing the Temple of the Divine Julius—the very spot where Julius Caesar's body had been cremated after his assassination—they exited the Forum onto Sacred Street. Flavia briefly recalled passing this way as she was dragged in chains to the beasts, but that memory was scary, and she dismissed it from her mind.

"I'm not sure I can go much farther without a break," Chloe said at last. "Can we rest in the shade of the basilica and eat the cakes?"

"Of course. Whatever you need."

The friends climbed a set of stairs and ducked into the massive New Ba-silica, begun by Emperor Maxentius a few years earlier and now in its final stages of construction. The place was reported to be the largest covered hall in the whole empire. Its lofty roof encompassed a vast space that remained cool and shady at all times. The floor was made of the most beautiful marble, and the ceilings above the vaulted aisles were adorned with dimple-like cof-fers inlaid with gold. But most impressive of all was the semicircular apse at the far end of the hall. Here a giant statue had been placed: a mighty man seated on a throne, holding a spear in his hand. Yet one thing remained to complete the statue—its giant marble head was still being carved. Although Maxentius believed his own likeness was going to be erected there, Flavia offered a silent prayer that the Christian emperor Constantine might come to power instead. If God willed it, perhaps Constantine's face would soon loom over the grand basilica.

Wooden benches lined several of the walls. Flavia found an empty one in a private nook. She opened her bundle and gave one of the cakes to Chloe, who brushed a strand of her reddish-blonde hair from her sweaty forehead and accepted it gratefully.

"Who's the third for?" Chloe asked as she took a big bite.

"I thought I'd take it to Zoticus."

"You sure are nice to that little brat. Even though he despises you."

"I don't think he actually despises me. He just . . . he has some problems."

Chloe wiped a sticky crumb from her lip. "What kind of problems?"

Flavia considered her answer. In her role as an undercover spy in the imperial palace, she had been told to trust no one and give out as little in-formation as possible. Though being a Christian wasn't illegal in Rome, it was unpopular. Flavia's current mission required fitting in, not alienating people. For this reason, she had been planning to keep her faith to herself in the weeks ahead. Yet somehow it didn't seem right to hide the Savior from someone as obviously needy as Chloe. Maybe there would come a time to point her to Christ—but not now.

"We have different views of religion," Flavia said, smoothing the hem of her tunic. "Zoticus reveres Aesculapius. I prefer . . . another."

"Which one?"

I knew she was going to ask me that.

"The Highest God. The one who reigns over everything."

"You mean the sun god? Sol?"

"Some people would make that connection," Flavia replied evasively. "The sun is the highest light in the sky, so I suppose it could stand for the Highest God." She looked down at the raisin cake in her hand. "Do you want this one too? I'm not really that hungry."

"Yes!" Chloe exclaimed, reaching out for the treat.

The distraction was successful, and the conversation turned to other matters. Eventually the two girls sensed it was time to get back to the palace on the Palatine Hill. A lavish feast was planned for tonight, and all the kitchen maids had work to do. The boys at Gelotiana House had been talking about the banquet for weeks. It was going to be a grand affair.

After a long afternoon of cleaning dishes, scrubbing floors, running errands, and polishing silver, the banquet hall was deemed ready to receive its guests. The great feast was being held in the Domitianic wing of the palace. Unlike the private residence, this wing served as the public area of the imperial complex. It consisted of three main parts: an enormous throne room for formal receptions; a lovely courtyard that centered on a pool with a magnificent octagonal fountain; and the Jupiter Dining Room, where the feasting would take place.

Even Flavia, who was used to beautiful buildings, had to admire the grandeur of this hall. Coming in from the courtyard, visitors' eyes were immediately lifted to the high ceiling. Columns of pink granite and milky marble supported its great height in three distinct stories. To the right and left, the hall was open to more courtyards, each adorned with a stately oval fountain, so that the sound of trickling water and natural light filled the entire space. The walls were painted with bright colors and designs, rivaled only by the intricate pattern on the marble floor. Tables and couches had been set up everywhere, arranged according to the social rank of their intended occupants. And if this vast hall were not enough, more guests could be accommodated in the many dining rooms that surrounded the octagonal fountain. Probably a thousand people would be in attendance tonight, all from Rome's upper crust. The one noteworthy guest who would be absent was Maxentius himself. He was said to be out in his suburban mansion on the Appian Way, fretting about rumors of war.

Once the banquet had commenced, the scullery maids retired to the downstairs kitchens, leaving the table service to the page boys. Flavia, however, realized the event would present a unique opportunity to gain intelligence, so she found an excuse to linger on the periphery of the hall. The guests did not stay on their couches the whole time, gulping wine and scarfing plump dormice. Little groups formed here and there, often wandering out to the fresh air of the courtyards. As Flavia lurked in the dim peristyle with an ornate amphora of wine in her hands, she was no more noticed by the banquet guests than a piece of furniture. She knew the whispered conversations among the senators, generals, bureaucrats, and courtiers might only reveal who was conducting an illicit affair—but they might also reveal a battle strategy or rebellion plot that would be important to Constantine's cause.

Flavia listened for tidbits of information for almost an hour, but unfortunately, she heard nothing of value. Glancing at the main hall, she didn't see Zoticus, though she did recognize several other young pages. All of them were looking smart with their plaited hair and tailored uniforms. The guests ate and drank their fill, laughing and chatting the whole time. Seated in the exedra, a band of pipers and harpists added their musical contributions to the convivial atmosphere. Wine flowed freely as the waiters filled cup after cup. Because it was November, the hall grew dark rather early, but the pages lit oil lamps on high stands. With the Jupiter Dining Room suffused by a soft evening glow, the tipsy revelers began to turn their attention to after-dinner activities.

A horde of dancing girls was ushered into the hall amid masculine shouts of appreciation. Many of the matrons now left the feast, though a few wives and courtesans stayed to enjoy the show. The scantily clad performers pranced and undulated around the room in the way that always transfixes the eyes of men. One dance in particular caught Flavia's attention. The girls rolled in an ornate box on wheels, then swirled around it with gauzy kerchiefs as they went through their routine. At the climax of the dance, all the girls fell prostrate before the box—and with a trumpet fanfare, out of it popped Maxentius himself.

A gasp went up from the crowd as the emperor strode down the center of the feasting hall in his purple robe and pearl diadem. His hair was waxed close to his head, and his cheeks were slathered with a pink rouge that stood in weird contrast to his stubbly beard. Though traditionally he had been regarded as a charming young man, the strange glint in his eye gave Flavia a squeamish sensation. Gone now was the capable politician who had been running Italy and Africa. This man who was waving to the onlookers and soaking up their acclaim was nothing but a decadent carouser with a colossal ego. In fact, Maxentius's mind seemed touched with insanity.

A whisper at Flavia's side made her turn her head.

"There you are! I've been looking all over for you!" It was Chloe, up from the kitchens below. She looked pretty with her red-gold hair tied at the nape of her neck. "Where have you been?"

"Just observing the banquet. Look there! The augustus has come."

Maxentius had taken up a position not far from the two watching girls. A retinue of sensual dancers and pretty boys trailed behind him like the sparkling stardust of a god. He gestured to a group of aristocrats reclining on a couch, all of them holding goblets made of expensive blown glass. "What is this?" he demanded in mock outrage. "Senators drinking wine but no cup for their lord? Some would call that treason!"

Aghast, the senators waved frantically to the page boy stationed behind their table. The waiter's face contorted into a terrified grimace as he signaled that his jug was empty. Now the tension in the room was palpable as the incompetent servants tried to find a cup of wine for the waiting Maxentius.

The page boy Bassus glanced into the shadowy peristyle and noticed the amphora in Flavia's hands. "Bring it to me!" he hissed.

"Go on!" Chloe urged.

Flavia shrank back. "I can't! He'll see me!"

"You have to! Everyone's waiting!"

"But—"

Chloe snatched the amphora and marched into the brightly lit feasting hall. Bassus had found a goblet at his station and was about to take the jug from Chloe when the emperor's voice stopped them.

"Now there's a faithful Roman girl!" he declared. "At least somebody here is ready to give her lord some wine. And look! She has quite the curves as well. See what fine women we Romans produce?"

Bassus and Chloe bowed their heads as Maxentius approached. Horrified, Flavia watched the exchange from behind a column. The emperor took the goblet from Bassus. "Fill my cup, pretty lass," he said to Chloe.

She held the ceramic jug in two hands and tipped its mouth into the cup. When it was full, Maxentius threw back his head and drained the wine in one long gulp. Tossing the cup aside, he exclaimed, "A fine vintage! Now give your lord a kiss."

The emperor drew Chloe into a lusty embrace, pinching her rear and smothering her face in wet kisses while she awkwardly cradled the jug. The crowd in the feasting hall cheered him on, relieved at this happy turn of events. The dancing girls clapped and shouted their encouragement. Only Chloe seemed uncomfortable as she squirmed in Maxentius's grip.

"What is this?" he demanded as he pulled back from her. "No love for your master?"

"No, sir . . . I mean yes, sir . . . I love you, my lord . . ."

Maxentius glanced around the room. "What do you think? Should I have her whipped for disrespect?"

A mixed shout went up. Some cried yes, others no.

"I can't hear you," the emperor said, "but I think you called for a hard beating with the scourge, eh?"

Chloe fell to her knees and clutched her stomach with one hand. "Please, sir, have mercy! I have a baby."

Maxentius put his hands on his hips as he loomed over Chloe. "Oh, so you're pregnant, are you? You invite common slaves to your bed, but when a god on earth grants you a kiss, you writhe about like an eel?"

"I'm sorry, Augustus . . . I didn't mean . . ."

In the shadows, Flavia could stay still no longer. While everyone's eyes were fixed on the drama unfolding in the hall, she sneaked to one of the lampposts and tipped it over, withdrawing before the heavy bronze lamp struck the ground. The loud crash made everyone turn. Flaming oil cascaded across the floor and began to lick the edge of a tapestry. The guests at the nearest tables scrambled away.

"You there! Boy! Put it out!" Maxentius shouted to the nearest page. The youth stomped on the fire to no effect. A commotion consumed the feasting hall as everyone stared and pointed at the uncontrolled blaze.

"I'll fetch water, lord," Chloe said at the emperor's feet. He scowled and waved her away with the back of his hand. She dashed out of the room.

Flavia realized it was time to make her escape as well. The fire would soon be put out, and then people might start asking questions. It was a close call, but she and Chloe had managed to dodge the emperor's cruel intent.

May that be the end of it, Lord, she prayed as she hurried down the staircase to the kitchens.

―❦―

The long, boring wait in Maxentius's private chambers wasn't the hard part for Livia. It was knowing she was missing the lavish banquet in the Jupiter Dining Room next door that really bothered her. All her friends were over there, dressed in their best gowns and draped in fabulous jewels. Livia loved fancy parties like that. She hated to skip the festivities.

But power always has its price.

She glanced at the water clock. The dial indicated it was already the sixth hour of the night, and still the banquet had not ended. Perhaps Maxentius would come back so drunk he wouldn't want to make love? Livia hoped that wouldn't happen. Sex was her most effective tool for achieving her goal. Without a romp in bed, this visit would be wasted.

The pointer on the clock had moved halfway into the seventh hour when the doorkeeper finally announced the emperor was on his way. Livia inspected her face in a mirror, touching up her lip paint and dabbing her neck with perfume before settling into a plush divan in the antechamber of Maxentius's bedroom. He rarely used this residence because he preferred to stay in his suburban villa, away from the bustle of Rome. However, the threat of possible invasion had forced him to spend more time in the traditional residence of the emperors up here on the Palatine. This was no time for a life of country retirement, even if that's what the timid Maxentius would have preferred.

A few moments later, he arrived. The emperor was indeed drunk, but not so much that he wouldn't—or couldn't—do what was expected. Livia thought he greeted her rather stiffly. Something was clearly bothering him, weighing down his mind. She vowed to use whatever it was against him.

"I hated to miss the banquet, Divine Augustus," she purred, "but a night with you makes a sumptuous feast seem like a bowl of lentils in comparison."

"Eh, well, you didn't miss much. Standard fare. The only excitement was when the dining room caught fire."

Livia put her hand to her breast and inhaled sharply. "How dangerous and thrilling!"

"It was no great matter. The servants put it out with wet sand."

"How did it start?"

Maxentius frowned. "I had just surprised the guests with my dramatic entrance. Everyone adored me! I was starting to seduce a kitchen wench, but she was less than amorous. I rebuked her, and the crowd loved it. Then a lamppost toppled and the whole place burst into a frenzy. I lost their attention after that. Stupid girl! She was curvy, though. I like them like that."

"A man like you appreciates women of every shape and size."

Maxentius's gaze flicked over to Livia. "I appreciate your shape and size."

She smiled coyly and narrowed her eyes but said nothing.

"I need a tonic," Maxentius declared, crossing to a medicine cabinet. "I have a pounding headache."

"Let me do it for you, my lord. Just sit and rest."

Maxentius took a seat while Livia prepared a concoction of vinegar and willow bark. It wouldn't taste good, but it was known to be very effective. She gave the drink to the emperor, who gulped it down and winced.

Now is the time, she decided. *Hit him while he's weak.*

"My husband tells me Rome is about to be invaded, Augustus. I must admit, it worries me. People are saying both Licinius and Constantine are strong. That is the real reason I have come here tonight: to remind myself of the vigor and fortitude of our great protector. Only in your arms shall I feel safe."

Maxentius uttered an expletive and pitched his empty vial of medicine across the room. "Curse them both! They won't claim the prize of Rome. I won't let them!"

"Of course not! Let it be known that my husband, the esteemed Ruricius Pompeianus, feels as I do. We are behind you without fail, Your Highness. And that can't be said for the whole Senate."

The comment made Maxentius's head swing around. "The Senate is disloyal, you say?"

"Some of the senators are. You will know who is obedient when you summon their wives. Only when a man is tested with a heavy burden can you learn his true level of devotion. If he values his mere wife more than the command of his divine lord and king, would he not just as likely change sides and go over to any invader who shows up at our gates with an army?"

Livia could see the lines of fear and exhaustion etched on Maxentius's face. Everything about him was disheveled. His hair was askew, his rouge was smeared into his whiskers, and dark circles underlined his eyes. The man was a mess. *Good . . .*

"Surely there are not many senators who would stab their emperor in the back!" he cried, leaping up from his chair. "I am the father of the fatherland! The beneficent provider for my people! The preserver of my city! Like the first augustus, I found Rome a city of brick and made it a city of marble!"

"Calm your nerves, my lord," Flavia soothed. She stroked Maxentius's shoulder and gently pressed him back into his seat. "I know of only a few men with traitorous intent."

"Like who?"

"Senator Neratius Junius Flavianus, for one."

There. It is done.

The emperor's face paled. "You know this?"

"I suspect it. You would have to inquire. Test his loyalty like the rest of the Senate. I feel certain that he loves his modest wife more than his caesar."

"I don't believe he's a traitor," Maxentius insisted. "We have been friends since childhood. Neratius would not betray me."

Livia fiddled with her bracelet and considered her next move. She had not expected Maxentius to be so trusting of Neratius. *How can I convince him otherwise?*

"Enough of all this," Maxentius said, rising again to his feet. "I'm finished with conspiracies for the day. My headache has abated. Come, let us retire."

"Indeed we shall, my lord. But may I say . . . ?" She paused.

"Go on, Livia."

"May I suggest you truly should inquire about Senator Junius? I believe he may be more of a threat than you think."

Maxentius shrugged. "How could I possibly find out the truth? He would deny it if I asked. And I cannot torture him. He is a noble."

"There are . . . there are those who can uncover truths hidden from all other eyes."

"Who? Speculators behind enemy lines? Household slaves who eavesdrop on their masters? They just lie whenever you turn the wheel of the rack. Some things are impossible to know."

"The soothsayers could tell you."

Maxentius fell silent for a long time. At last he turned and eyed Livia warily. "The haruspices? I had not thought of that. I have used them on occasion to read certain omens. But not to discern my enemies."

"The entrails of living things do not lie. It is only a matter of obtaining a proper reading."

"Ah, but that is the thing. Divination is always tricky. The spirits hide the truth as often as they reveal it. They part with their wisdom only reluctantly."

"I know. But for the most important questions, you can assure yourself of a truthful answer by giving the spirits what they want."

"And what is that?"

"The most innocent blood."

Maxentius approached Livia slowly. She waited for him, then moved to meet him when he drew near. He caressed her cheek, his finger toying with the jewel that dangled from her ear. She closed her eyes and allowed a little smile to come to her painted lips.

"You are a dark woman, Lady Cornelia Livia."

"Yes, I am. But we live in dark times, my augustus."

The remark caused Maxentius to chuckle and shake his head, yet it clearly pleased him. He reached down and took Livia's hand.

"I think I'm going to enjoy getting to know you," he said.

———❦———

This isn't going to be fun, Rex thought.

But it had to be done.

He knocked on the door of an apartment in a block not far from the New Camp of the imperial horse guard. At first there was no response. Then Rex heard a rustling inside.

"Who is it?" came the muffled voice.

Might as well get this over with. "Brandulf Rex, sir."

For a long moment, there was total silence. Rex steeled himself, waiting for the door to explode from the frame and bang into the wall. But when it finally opened, it wasn't hurled with the force he had anticipated. It simply creaked on its hinges until it was ajar. A man stood there. Centurion Aratus.

"Come in, soldier," he said.

Rex followed his commanding officer into the little apartment he had rented. The room had no furniture, only a straw mattress on the floor. A chamber pot and water jug sat on one side of the bed, and a military ruck-sack had been dropped on the other. No other people were in the room.

"Sir, you are probably wondering—"

Aratus hit him.

The blow was like iron, and the centurion took nothing off it. If Rex were facing an adversary, he probably could have deflected the punch, but he hadn't anticipated the attack, and his guard was down. Aratus's fist struck Rex on the point of the chin and sent him reeling. He hit the wall hard and caught himself just before he fell to the floor. Dizziness engulfed him for a moment until his head finally cleared.

"I . . . I guess I deserved that, sir."

Aratus, his teeth set on edge, glared at Rex. "I ought to have you flogged, soldier! If I had my vine with me, I'd do it myself! Then I'd discharge you for desertion."

"Yes, sir," Rex said, rubbing his chin. "But I can explain."

"You sorry bag of filth! There's nothing you can do but pack up and go back to the mud hut where your mother spawned you!" Aratus growled like a wild beast and shook his head. "I trusted you, Rex! I brought you here for a mission, but instead you catch sight of a pretty girl and go off for a fling. You disappear for more than two weeks! Curse you, boy! By Jupiter, Juno, and Jesus, you're not worthy to be called a . . ." The walls were thin, so Aratus stopped short and did not utter the word *speculator*.

Rex rose to his full height and straightened his shoulders. The harsh words hurt. Aratus was more than just his commanding officer. He was a mentor, even a kind of father figure. Rex felt the pain of his criticism more acutely than the punch to his jaw.

"Centurion, may I speak?"

Aratus huffed and swatted at the air, then turned away.

"Since we arrived in Rome," Rex continued in a quiet voice, "have you joined the army like we planned?"

"Of course not! I've been too busy looking for my missing soldier!"

"Have you infiltrated the imperial palace?"

"Don't be stupid. You can't just walk into the emperor's war room and ask for details."

"Have you met any influential conspirators seeking to bring Maxentius down and install Constantine in his place?"

Aratus stared at Rex as if he were crazy.

"What if I told you, sir, that since the day I disappeared, not only have I been enlisted into our enemy's cavalry unit, but I have also cultivated two high-value informants and have furthermore connected with a group of senators plotting the emperor's downfall? One of my sources has been embedded in the imperial bureaucracy for many years, while the other I have managed to install directly in Maxentius's personal kitchens on the Palatine Hill. In addition, I have joined forces with powerful insurgents whose members include some of the oldest aristocrats of Rome. Knowing this, would you still continue to believe I'm a deserter?"

Aratus's jaw dropped. He started to speak, clamped his mouth shut, started to speak again, then fell silent.

"It's true," Rex said, still keeping his voice near a whisper. "I've done all those things. I can give you details if you want."

"But why did you go chasing after that girl?"

"Sir! Do you really think I'm some foolish youth, led along by my member instead of my mind? You always taught us: 'The good speculator *finds* a way to the goal; the great speculator *creates* one.' When opportunities come, you have to seize them without hesitation. Fortune brought Lady Junia Flavia across my path. I saw an opening toward the goal, so I jumped in with both feet and followed the path where it led. And by the gods, it led to some good results."

Aratus stared at the floor a long time. With one hand, he rubbed the flat top of his close-shorn hair. Finally, he looked up at Rex.

"You should have reported in," he said.

"I know."

"You should have gotten my permission first."

"Yes, sir."

"You should execute the approved plan, not just follow your instincts."

"I should do that, you're right."

"And you should work with your partners, not on your own whims."

"Right again, sir."

Aratus sighed, wrestling with his thoughts. "Rex?" he said quietly. "One more thing."

"I'm listening."

"I take back what I said. You're a great speculator."

Rex broke into a wide grin. "Correct once more, Centurion." He saluted his commanding officer, clasping his fist to his chest with a bow of his head. "And thank you."

———•✦•———

It was the ninth day before the Kalends of December, the feast day of Saint Clement. To Sophronia's way of thinking, this great saint was the perfect person to honor at the suburban shrine of Peter and Paul on the Appian Way. Long ago, in the days of Jesus's apostles, Clement had helped to establish the church at Rome. Hadn't Paul called Clement his beloved coworker at the end of his letter to the Philippians? Hadn't the African theologian Tertullian proved Clement was the second bishop of Rome after Peter? As Sophronia took her seat in the dining room at the suburban shrine, she thanked God that men like Clement had laid such a solid foundation for the catholic faith.

Bishop Miltiades reclined at the dining room's head couch, with Neratius on his right and the young priest of the Aventine house church, whose name was Felix, on his left. Sophronia sat behind the bishop on a chair near his feet. A few other leaders of the house church, along with some high-ranking servants from Neratius's household, had joined the others on the cushioned benches—about twenty diners in all. Beyond these, out in the flagstone courtyard, a hundred or so of the Christian poor from the Aventine Hill had been invited to the feast. Several pots of stew bubbled over charcoal braziers, while a long table had been spread with more fruits, cheese, fish, and wheat bread than these needy folks had ever seen in one place. The wine being served wasn't the cheap vinegar of the masses, but a good, white vintage that only the wealthy could afford. This feast had been Flavia's personal request of Bishop Miltiades, paid for out of her own dowry.

Now, in honor of her missing daughter, Sophronia intended to carry out every detail of the request just as Flavia had wanted it.

The bishop had begun the festivities with a fine sermon about Clement's adventures as Peter's traveling companion. All the poor had listened with rapt attention, along with some sanctified virgin sisters who were attending the feast in their veils. Now it was time to eat, so the kitchen staff of Sophronia's mansion were ladling out the stew as fast as the hungry Christians could extend their bowls. The clergy and household members in the dining room would wait until all the brethren had been served before beginning their own meal.

"There is some debate about the authenticity of the Clementine texts," Bishop Miltiades told the waiting diners as they reclined at a table. "A new history from the pen of a certain Eusebius, bishop of Caesarea by the Sea, discounts them. Yet many of our local scholars accept them as genuine."

"And what is your opinion, Father?" Neratius asked.

As distinguished and stately as Miltiades was, his words always carried great weight. "I am inclined to accept the historical essence of the tale," he said, "though as always with popular literature, fantastic legends get added over the years."

"We know at least that Clement was a real historical figure, for the holy scriptures mention him," Sophronia said. "The stories just give us more detail." Miltiades stroked his oiled beard and nodded sagely at this.

In due time, after the other guests at the charity feast—or the *agape*, as the Greek Christians called it—had been served their food and had lapsed into pleasant conversation, the servants brought a meal for those waiting in the dining room. Sophronia munched on a sardine and gazed out at the contented picnickers relaxing in the warm sun or under the shady porch. *Blessed are you poor*, she thought, *for yours is the kingdom of God.*

Although the dining room was enclosed on three sides, its fourth wall was open to the courtyard, forming a pleasant loggia with a light and airy feel. The structure was fifty years old, and over that time, many prayers to Peter and Paul had been scratched into the red plastered walls, for the mortal remains of the two apostles had been transferred to this secret place for safekeeping during an outbreak of persecution. "Please hear my petition" or "Keep me in mind" the scribblers had asked the saints, often providing their own names as a reminder. Many Christians had also recorded the banquets they had sponsored. Observing that same tradition, Sophronia's faithful doorkeeper Onesimus had just used the sharp tip of his spoon to write, "Flavia gave a refreshment on IX Kal Dec. Protect her, Peter and Paul, in God." Touched by this affectionate gesture, Sophronia whispered her own prayer: *Yes, holy apostles of the Lord! Protect her and bring her back safely!*

When the meal was finished, a general merriment broke out in the courtyard and spilled into the surrounding cemetery. Children ran around playing games, some of the young people danced, and more than a few guests seemed to have had too much to drink.

Bishop Miltiades, however, had more serious matters on his mind. "Do you know the history of this place?" he asked those around the dining table. When everyone shook their heads, he continued. "It was originally an open quarry pit for making cement. The Greek word for a scooped-out bowl is *kymbe*. The phrase *kata kymbas* means 'down in the bowls.' As you can see, we are in a natural valley here, and there were once many other mining pits in the vicinity. Therefore we call this place the Cemetery at the Catacombs, because it's the cemetery down in the bowls."

"I see no pit here," Neratius observed.

"No indeed, Senator! But trust me, that staircase in the courtyard goes down to a spring next to ancient graves. The pit was abandoned as a quarry long ago, but then several mausoleums were built into it, including some Christian ones. Eventually the catholic church bought this place for burying its own people. One of my predecessors filled in the pit and erected this little dining room so we could give charity to the poor and feast in memory of the apostles in the presence of their holy bones."

"But not like the pagans do when they commune with the departed shades," Sophronia added, making sure her husband understood the practice. "Saint Paul clearly said, 'You cannot partake of the Lord's table and the table of demons.' So we remember the saints and share our food with them as friends who are alive in Christ's presence. Certainly we ask them to pray for us, because in heaven, all is prayer. Yet we don't conjure up their spirits or feed them meals like dead ancestors."

Neratius arched his eyebrows and gave a shrug of indifference, then reached for a honeyed date and popped it in his mouth.

293

As the sun went down and the crowds began to disperse, the servants from the Aventine mansion drew water from the well and started washing the many dishes. Sophronia lingered near the Apostolic Monument, the marble edifice that held the sacred relics. She marveled that the bones of Peter and Paul were in her presence. The tangible reminder of such holy men was a comfort to her.

"Psst! Lady!"

Sophronia turned. One of the consecrated virgins, her face veiled, was beckoning from behind a nearby mausoleum.

"Lady!" the girl repeated. "I beg you, come join me for a moment."

The holy sisters were held in high esteem by the church, so Sophronia was happy to comply. Yet strangely, when she reached the quiet place behind the tomb, the girl was gently weeping with her head bowed low.

"The peace of Christ be with you, sister," Sophronia said.

"And with your spirit, Mother," came the reply. The girl did not lift her head, so her face remained hidden. Instead, she pressed a note into Sophronia's hand, stifled a little cry, and hurried away without another word.

Sophronia watched her go, not troubled by the encounter, yet somewhat confused. She looked down at the scrap of parchment. Unfolding it, she read its words. No sooner had she finished than she dropped the note and staggered backward, leaning on the brick wall of the tomb for support. A cry of joy escaped her lips.

O Jesus, my Lord, and all your saints, thank you! Thank you! She's alive!
Praise God, my daughter is alive!

10

"Look at you!" Rex exclaimed. "Geta with short hair? I guess only the Roman army could make you lose that golden princess braid!"

The teasing remark caused boisterous laughter to rise above the other sounds along the crowded, narrow street. Rex stood up from the edge of the curb where he had been waiting for his best friend. The two soldiers clasped hands and gripped each other's shoulders in a gesture of warm affection.

"It took me all my life to grow that braid down to my arse," Geta said, "and then with one snip of the scissors, it's on the floor of a tonsor's shop. But if Mars wants his boys short-haired and clean-shaven, I guess that's the sacrifice I'll have to make for the glory of serving with the emperor's horsemen."

Rex rubbed the fuzz on the back of his own head. "That's right. We're true Romans now. Wild barbarians no more."

Geta pointed to the hot-food restaurant behind them. "Come on. I want to hear about your enlistment. I heard you knocked one of their best riders out of the saddle! The guys at the camp were talking about it yesterday. And my own go-round had a few tales worth telling too. Let's order some lunch and swap stories."

The friends stepped up to a bar under an awning. For a few coins they were served thick, steaming mussel stew from a clay pot recessed into the counter—a welcome dish on this chilly winter day. Crusty bread was also set before them in a basket, along with a savory dipping sauce made of fermented fish guts called garum. Two cups of diluted vinegar rounded out the meal. The men leaned on their elbows as they ate their food, each recounting his experience at the parade ground of the New Camp. Rex told how he had unhorsed his opponent Decimus, while Geta regaled Rex with his own exploits in the Cantabrian Circle.

The bar was not crowded, so Rex took the opportunity to lean close and confer with Geta about the status of their mission. Following standard espionage protocol, the two spies had been operating independently over the past few months, establishing contacts in the army and integrating into Roman military subculture. Though their tryouts had been separated by several weeks, the outcome had been the same for both warriors: they were immediately offered enlistment in the Emperor's Personal Cavalry as cadets in training. Since they were tall, blond provincials with handsome looks and well-built physiques, they were exactly what the imperial horse guard had always wanted, ever since Caesar Augustus, the first emperor, established his private Germanic bodyguard. Every emperor since then had used the guard not just to protect his welfare but to awe the populace with impressive specimens of beautiful, robust manhood. Of course, as newcomers, Rex and Geta still had to win the trust of their comrades. Yet they were true soldiers of Rome now—not frontier legionaries but elite guardsmen of the capital city. Aratus had commended them for the achievement, announcing that the first phase of their secret mission was complete.

Satisfied by the food in their bellies, Rex and Geta decided to take a bath. The warm water sounded good to both men, to take the edge off the January chill. Though a big imperial bathing establishment wasn't close by, a neighborhood balneum was around the corner. Such places had the same facilities as the government-built bathhouses but on a smaller scale. Rex and Geta paid their fee and left their garments with the dressing-room slave. After some exercise in a courtyard to work up a sweat, they oiled and scraped themselves, then settled into the hot pool to relax their muscles and open their pores.

"If we're going to be Romans, we might as well live like Romans," Geta said with a deep sigh. He sank into the pool until only his face was showing. His forehead, nose, and cleft chin were like little islands protruding from the water.

Rex splashed his friend's face, making him sputter and sit up. Geta tried to punch Rex in the arm, but Rex squirmed away, laughing. They assumed positions at opposite ends of the caldarium in a kind of friendly truce. Periodically, each man would ladle a little cool water over his head from a bucket. Since no one else was in the thermal spa, they felt free to talk of the events that had transpired since Geta helped Rex and Flavia escape from Rome to Tibur.

"You'll never guess how we got out of the city after we left you," Rex said.

"I know you couldn't have used a gate because of the guards, so I assume you went over the wall."

"No, *through* the wall."

Geta looked surprised. "The wall has a breach? That sounds like intelligence Constantine will want to know about."

"There's no breach. We crawled through an aqueduct."

"Ew. Sounds tight."

"It was. Wouldn't want to do that again," Rex said.

"So you went to Tibur after that?"

"Yes. Nice little place in the countryside. Lots of waterfalls."

"Why there?"

"Lady Junia has an uncle who helped us." After glancing out the door to make sure they were truly alone, Rex told Geta about Senator Ignatius and the conspirators who wanted to bring down Maxentius. "We need to work with them," Rex said. "Aratus knows about them now, and he approves."

"Good work! That's a strategic connection. It seems your meeting with Lady Junia was predestined by the gods." Geta gave Rex a good-natured smile across the pool. "A lot of benefits came from it, eh?"

"For the mission," Rex agreed.

"And for yourself?"

Rex gave a little *tch* but didn't reply.

"Is she good in—"

"She's a Christian," Rex broke in. "They're not like us."

"Too bad. She's a beautiful woman." Geta clasped his hands behind his head and gazed up into a corner of the room. "I bet she'd really look good—"

"Hey!" Rex sent another splash across the pool. "Enough with that."

Geta brought his eyes back to Rex and sat up straight in the water. "You keep talking like she means something to you! Are you falling in love?"

"Well, I wouldn't put it like that. But we've spent a lot of time together the past few months. You know, visiting her at the palace and sharing a meal, things like that. I've gotten to know her in a different way—not like the girls around the camps, the girls who follow us around. Lady Junia is actually my friend. We talk like equals and discuss things. It's strange. But I like it."

"That is strange. To be friends with a woman is weird."

Rex shrugged. "And yet it happened."

"So she's not your lover?"

"I told you, Christian girls aren't like us. They only sleep with their husbands."

Geta snorted at this news. "Too bad for you, then! You'll never get to enjoy that curvy little body. Her rich father would never let her marry the likes of you."

"I might be young, but I'm on the rise," Rex said defensively. "Provincials are everywhere in the army these days. Sometimes they even rise to the rank of general! Italians have been known to marry Germani who've made it big in life."

"Not Italians from old aristocratic families like that one. Senator Junius isn't going to let his only legitimate child marry a barbarian soldier unless you can bring something extremely valuable in return. And you're poor. You don't have anything that valuable."

"True love is valuable!" Rex replied, then realized what he had just said. "I mean . . . if I had true love, it would be valuable to Flavia."

"Oh, she's Flavia to you now?" Geta teased. "Why don't you just admit you're in love?"

"I'm not in love!"

Or am I?

Another bather entered the caldarium then and settled into the hot pool. Rex and Geta agreed they'd had enough of the heat, so they retired to the tepidarium to cool down. After a good half hour in its pleasant warmth, they took a cold plunge in the frigidarium, then redressed and went back into the street.

"I guess I'll see you around the barracks," Geta said. He leaned close and spoke in Rex's ear. "We only get a little leave time from camp, so we need to use it wisely. Let's meet at this bath once a week to discuss what we've learned and share intelligence. And sometime soon, I need to meet your friend who's leading this conspiracy. Things are starting to come together. I wouldn't be surprised if either Constantine or Licinius shows up in Italy this spring as soon as he can get an army over the Alps."

"I hope it's Constantine," Rex whispered.

Geta stared at his feet for a moment. Finally, he looked Rex in the eye. "Listen, I used to serve under Licinius when I was a new recruit in the infantry, before I started speculator training. That man is an excellent soldier. And he gives more generous donatives than any other general I've ever heard of."

"What are you saying, Geta? We're here to help Constantine, not Licinius."

"I know. And we will! But you and I, we have to watch out for each other. We're just swords for hire. Nobody really cares about us. It's good to keep our options open, you know?"

Rex shook his head as he patted the tau-rho amulet under his tunic. "Not me. I've cast my lot with the man who gave me this."

"Me too," Geta said, pointing to the tiny lump under his own collar. "But things can change. People die in battle. Sometimes there are rebellions, and emperors get executed. If the situation evolves, foot soldiers like us need to be ready to adjust."

"I suppose you have a point."

Geta grinned and clapped Rex on the shoulder. "Alright. Just keep an open mind. And as for the current mission, one week from today let's come here again and share what we've learned."

"Good plan. You got it."

"In the meantime, if there's anything I can do for you, let me know."

"The same for you." Rex looked his friend in the eyes and offered his hand for Geta to clasp. Geta pulled Rex to himself. There on the street, the two men embraced.

"Brothers, always," Rex said.

"To the death!" Geta agreed. And then, with a nod of mutual respect, the two Roman guardsmen parted ways and headed in opposite directions.

<hr />

Chloe found she slept better now that she was rooming with Flavia in Gelotiana House. Flavia had insisted on a stop to the stream of male visitors to Chloe's bed. Until that point, she had always assumed the enjoyments of the flesh would put her in a more relaxed state for sleep. But Flavia was right; it was better to protect the boundaries of one's own body. Chloe had decided it was nice to have the bed all to herself again. Of course, being seven months pregnant was another good reason to bring the nocturnal visits to an end. Sleep was a precious commodity these days.

A late-night stillness had descended on the house when Chloe was awakened by a loud banging on the outer door. Several of the boys shouted for quiet, but whoever was knocking outside kept up the racket. Flavia was awake now too.

"Who could it be?" she asked Chloe.

"I don't know. I'm sure Alexamenos will take care of it."

The sounds intensified into an argument. When the visitors came inside the house, Chloe began to grow concerned. She could hear the metallic sound of scale armor clinking as the men moved around. At one point, she thought she heard a sword being drawn. The men were demanding to search the place, while Alexamenos was insisting they had no right.

"Chloe!" Flavia murmured. "I've got to get out of here! It's me they want!"

But she was wrong.

Four Praetorians burst into the bedroom, causing both Chloe and Flavia to shriek. "That's the girl! Right there!" shouted a sallow-faced scullery maid whom Chloe knew from her daily work. "The pregnant one!"

"Very good. You can go now," the tallest of the four soldiers said to the maid.

A second man marched over and grabbed Chloe's arm. "You're coming with me. Don't struggle, or it will go worse for you."

"Why? What have I done?" Chloe asked, playing ignorant, though a deep fear had seized her soul. She knew exactly what this was. *The augustus wants me whipped!*

Alexamenos was in the room now, trying to intervene, but it was pointless. When he attempted to wedge himself between Chloe and the soldier who gripped her arm, another one of the Praetorians simply threw the slender man aside. "Stay put," he growled to Alexamenos on the floor, "or

I'll have to draw my blade. It can go right through armor, so it'll surely go through you."

"Please, sirs," Flavia said, trying a different tactic. "We have funds at our disposal. I'm sure we could settle this in a way you'd like."

The tall leader now whirled on Flavia. "You think you got some money, slave? There ain't enough gold in all of Rome to pay us off! What good is a bribe if you're dead? Failure ain't an option for us. This order comes from the top. And I mean the *top*." He turned to his squad. "Come on, boys. We got the girl. Let's go."

"Please!" Chloe begged. "Tell the augustus I'm sorry! I love him!"

"You can tell him yourself!" the leader snarled.

Chloe's body sagged, and her legs felt weak. *Great Artemis*, she prayed, *let it be brief. And let it be plain leather—not the scourge!*

The men yanked Chloe into the main street outside Gelotiana House. The long avenue ran parallel to the Circus Maximus, but the soldiers started her toward a different path: the steep one that climbed to the palace atop the Palatine. Chloe let out a little groan.

"Wait!" a voice cried.

A dark figure ran toward the soldiers, prompting all of them to draw their swords.

"Stay back, man!" one warned.

The stranger stopped a few paces away. From his mop of curly hair, Chloe discerned it was Alexamenos again, though the Praetorians might not have recognized him on this moonless night.

"Chloe!" he shouted. "Do you remember what I've been telling you about?"

"You mean—religion?"

"Yes!"

"We're on imperial business," the leader of the squad said. "Go back to your home, or we'll have you flogged."

Alexamenos ignored the threat. "We don't know what will happen tonight, Chloe! You have to decide! Do you want him?"

For a year or so, the Greek schoolteacher had been urging Chloe to consider the catholic faith. She had been reluctant to abandon the old gods—but now, in this desperate moment, she realized those gods had abandoned her. Alexamenos was asking her to believe instead in the risen Christ.

"Keep going, men," the leader commanded. "Up the hill. Double time." The squad started to move again, dragging their prisoner along.

"Chloe! Do you want him? Now is the time to decide!"

"I want him! I believe!" she called over her shoulder.

Alexamenos darted forward. *"Ego se baptizo en hudati!"* he cried in Greek, then doused the whole group with a bucket of water.

Shouts of anger burst from the Praetorians. "Stick him!" one of them yelled, but Alexamenos had retreated into the shadows.

"Forget him," said another. "He's gone."

The men started the uphill climb to the imperial palace. Chloe plodded along in their midst, more terrified than she had ever been in her life. Only one thing gave her comfort. Although these soldiers were local thugs who didn't speak anything but Latin, Chloe was an immigrant from far-off Macedonia. Her native language was Greek, so she knew the meaning of Alexamenos's shouted words.

"I baptize you with water," he had said to her—which meant Chloe was now a Christian.

⸺◦◦◦⸺

Rex struck the fire-starter, causing a spark to land on a scrap of charcloth nestled inside a wad of tinder. The little flame that sprang up was sufficient to light an oil lamp. Soon Rex had five of them burning, and from them, it was a simple matter to light two torches. Now a lively glow illuminated the entrance stairwell to the place that the Christians called the Cemetery of Callistus.

"Thank you, friend," said a distinguished middle-aged man. He wore a long-sleeved tunic of plain black wool. The medallion around his neck was marked with a simple cross. Rex only nodded in response, for he didn't know what was proper to say to the catholic bishop of Rome.

Two of the religious men called deacons followed Miltiades down the stairs, and after them came Flavia. Though her face was covered by a black veil, Rex could tell it was her by the way she moved. Behind her followed an aristocratic lady whom he had never met. Even so, her features were similar enough to Flavia's for Rex to be certain she was Lady Sabina Sophronia. The last person down the stairs was Alexamenos.

Rex handed the Greek schoolteacher one of the torches and kept the other himself. "I'll lead," he said, "and you bring up the rear."

The Christian procession made its way down the hallway of the underground cemetery, with each person holding a source of illumination. The walls on the right and left were pockmarked with burial niches sealed by marble slabs. The names of the deceased were carved on them, along with hopeful prayers for peace and rest. Rex stopped in front of a large wooden box that sat on the floor next to an empty niche. A marble slab leaned against the wall.

"We shall stop here," Miltiades said, "so that I may read from the scriptures."

The bishop placed his lamp in a little nook and received a codex from the deacon's hand. By the glow of the lamp, he found the place he sought and began to speak. "The passage is from *The Gospel according to Matthew*," he said. "It is the parable of the laborers in the vineyard."

He proceeded to recite a story that had been told by the god Jesus. In it, a landlord hired workers in shifts throughout the day. Though some laborers worked long hours while others started late, all were paid the same at sundown. Those who had worked in the heat of the day were angry, but the landlord reminded them he had paid what was mutually agreed. "Is it not lawful for me to do whatever I wish with what is mine? Or is your eye envious because I am generous?" the landlord asked the complainers. Jesus concluded the story with the saying, "Thus shall the last be first, and the first last."

Miltiades closed the book and handed it back to the deacon. "Our sister who lies at our feet is a fulfillment of the Lord's word. Many receive the Savior early in their lives, sometimes even as little children. Others come as adults, and still others at old age. Although our sister was not an old woman, nonetheless, she came to God at the end of her life—the last hour before sunset, as the parable describes. In this we learn that our God is a merciful God, showing us his favor even unto our final moments."

The bishop paused, and Rex heard Flavia stifle a cry. She reached beneath her veil and dabbed her eyes with a kerchief.

"Alexamenos, bear witness to what you know," Miltiades ordered.

"Chloe had been listening to the gospel for some time. Though she was resistant at first, she was growing open to it, like soil softening to the seed. In the end, she accepted the saving Name—and I watered the soil with the washing of an improvised baptism."

"It was irregular, but I declare it valid," Miltiades said. "In desperate situations, we must recognize the intent of the heart, as God certainly does, even when a proper ritual is not observed."

At this point the bishop asked the second deacon to lead the mourners in a doleful hymn. Rex did not know the words, so he merely listened as the Christians sang. When they were finished, the two deacons bent down and opened the wooden box. A body lay there. Even in the dim light, Rex could see a rust-colored stain on the graveclothes. It ran across the corpse's belly.

Her baby was taken.

Rex had chatted with Chloe on a couple of occasions when he stopped at Gelotiana House to check on Flavia. She was a nice enough girl—a little bawdy yet always cheerful. Now here she was, a mangled corpse about to be interred in a Christian tomb. Maxentius had not wanted to whip her after all. Instead, he had murdered her.

The horrified page boy ordered to discard the body said Chloe had been killed and cut open. And the boy knew why, for he had seen Maxentius's secret guest. A haruspex—a priest who inspected entrails for the purpose of divination—had been invited to the palace that night. Usually the sooth-sayers looked at the livers of sheep and chickens. Yet it was rumored that sometimes, in moments of dire need, they could make inquiries into the entrails of the most innocent. And who could be more innocent than an unborn human child?

The deacons lifted Chloe's body from the box and respectfully laid it inside the grave niche. Next they raised the marble slab and pressed it into place. Eventually it would be sealed with cement and inscribed with Chloe's name. The words *in peace* were already written on the slab, alongside a depiction of a fish and an anchor.

With the body interred, the mourners proceeded back to the surface. Everyone squinted as they emerged into the bright sunlight. Rex remained off to one side as Flavia and Sophronia earnestly thanked their bishop for coming out to preside at the funeral. An atrocity of this sort, they said, seemed to require the presence of the church's foremost leader. Emperor

Maxentius was already known to be cruel and vindictive, but this crime was a horror of an entirely new kind. The bishop assured the women he concurred with their feelings. Even Rex, though he did not share the Christian faith of his friends, felt a sense of moral outrage and pointed grief at what had been done to Chloe and her baby.

After the bishop and his deacons left, Rex approached the two women and Alexamenos. He had never met Flavia's mother before. Though the circumstances right now were less than ideal, he thought he should at least make her polite acquaintance. He introduced himself with all the respect and deference that a lady of her station deserved. She evidently knew who he was as well, for she greeted him warmly in return.

Yet despite the pleasantries, Rex could tell his three Christian friends were still disturbed by the savagery of the crime. They talked quietly among themselves, visibly upset. None of them had ever seen this sort of thing up close. Rex had been around battle and bloodshed before—its suffering; its rawness; its cold, still death. He had even inflicted wounds on enemies in war, so he had a certain capacity to tolerate what he had just witnessed. But his friends had no stomach for it. Besides, what had happened here was far worse than warfare. Chloe was an innocent woman, not a soldier fighting under the accepted rules of combat. This wasn't noble death on the battlefield. It was gross injustice. And what made it all the worse was that the highest representative of Roman law had committed the crime.

"Maxentius has to be stopped," Sophronia said, her voice quivering. "No matter who you are, you shouldn't be able to kill a mother and slaughter her unborn child. It is bestial, and unworthy of a just society." The others nodded along with her, and Rex joined them, for he wholeheartedly agreed. It was why he was here in Rome, working on behalf of Constantine, a ruler who wasn't a tyrant like Maxentius. Replacing a bad emperor with a good one was the mission for which he had been sent.

A mission, Rex realized, *that could be aided by a powerful aristocrat like Lady Sabina Sophronia.*

As his three friends grieved for Chloe and mourned the evils of Maxentius, Rex debated whether he should enlist Sophronia in his cause. Her brother-in-law, the senator Ignatius, was already part of a strategic conspiracy to depose the sitting emperor in Rome. Would the wife of the city prefect also be interested in joining the plot? Rex decided to test the waters, saying just enough to see if she responded. If she was open, he would draw her further in.

"It truly is bestial to do such a thing," Rex said. "A man like that should be stopped somehow."

Sophronia sighed. "He is a terrible ruler. A tyrant if ever there was one."

"Have you ever considered what you could do about such a tyrant?"

"The emperors are all-powerful," Sophronia said glumly. "God raises them up, and only God can bring them low."

"That is your faith, I know. But do you think your God sometimes wants his servants to act as instruments of his will?"

Sophronia gave Rex a thoughtful glance. "What do you mean?"

"Well, you know . . . sometimes people pray. Sometimes they use the law. And sometimes certain people even form conspiracies."

"Rex, do not say too much," Alexamenos cautioned.

"Yet say enough to make it matter," Flavia chimed in.

"All I am saying is, people are often motivated to take action when a ruler turns evil. Sometimes those people are far from us. Other times they are much closer than we suspect, perhaps even in our midst, and we could join them if only we knew. Not everyone is brave enough to join such a plot. Yet some are." Rex locked eyes with Sophronia. "Are you that type of person, my lady?"

The little foursome fell silent for a long moment. No one wanted to speak. At last Sophronia broke the stillness. "I am such a person," she declared.

"Then keep your ears open, Mother," Flavia said quietly, "and be ready to act if the opportunity should arise."

The hint of treason had made everyone feel nervous. They instinctively glanced around the suburban cemetery, looking for anyone who might have overheard. Although they saw no one nearby, they all agreed it was time to go. Sophronia had come by carriage from the Aventine Hill, while the other three had proceeded by foot along the Appian Way, which ran straight from the Circus Maximus into the countryside. As they began to disperse to their respective destinations in the city, Sophronia pulled Rex aside before he could leave.

"My daughter tells me you have saved her life many times. She says you are a man of courage and honor. As you can probably guess, Flavia means the world to me. When she slipped me that note and let me know she was alive, I can't tell you the joy and relief I felt! It seems I have you to thank for that. And so"—Sophronia put her hand on Rex's arm and gazed directly at him—"you have my profound gratitude and respect. I deeply appreciate all you have done."

Sophronia's words were so earnest and heartfelt that Rex felt a little choked up. He blinked his eyes a few times and swallowed the lump in his throat. "I was happy to be of service. It was my privilege to help." He thought for a moment, then added, "Flavia is a lovely girl."

Lovely? Why lovely? Stupid! What is her mother going to think of that?

Though Rex kicked himself for his inept remark, he was relieved to see Sophronia smile. "I certainly think so," she said sweetly. "You've noticed it too?" She arched her eyebrows at him.

"Oh, yes, ma'am. She's definitely lovely. I mean, she has a lovely character. Full of virtue."

Shut up, Rex. Just stop now.

"As you get to know her, I think you'll find she is lovely in many ways. Of course, she has her rough spots too—though nothing a good man couldn't help her overcome."

"I . . . um . . . I hope she finds that someday, my lady."

"Me too, Rex." Sophronia began to head toward her carriage, smiling as she backed away. "Me too," she said again. After giving Rex a little wink, the aristocratic lady turned her back and left Rex mulling her words in the Christian cemetery of Callistus.

———————

FEBRUARY 312

The Royal Hall atop the Palatine Hill was an architectural space designed to awe its visitors. As Senator Neratius Junius Flavianus walked down its length, his expensive red slippers softly slapping the marble floor, he couldn't help but be impressed by what he saw. The ceiling was a huge barrel vault, so high and perfectly arched that Neratius felt he wasn't in a man-made building but some kind of supernatural cavern. Magnificent statues of the gods lined the walls on either side, such as svelte Bacchus with an effeminate tilt of his hips, or mighty Hercules with bulging muscles that would make any man jealous. At the far end of the hall was the imperial throne itself, situated in an apse beneath a bronze chandelier. And on that throne sat Maxentius—though why he had summoned Neratius today, the senator did not know.

He bowed deeply at the waist as he stepped into the presence of the augustus. "I honor you, my lord and savior," he said with his arms swept wide. A few years ago, Emperor Diocletian had taken up the habit of making his subjects call him "lord," and he even demanded they prostrate themselves and kiss the hem of his robe. Although Maxentius had embraced the title *dominus* as well, at least he did not require the weird Eastern practice of groveling on the floor.

"Ah, look who it is! My childhood playmate, now serving as the city prefect. The second most powerful man in Rome! You seem so obedient as you bow before me, Neratius. Such a man could never be a traitor, eh?"

A chill ran through Neratius at the ominous words. Nobody wanted to be associated with the word *traitor* in Maxentius's mind. It usually resulted in a death sentence, just in case it might be true.

"I do not know what you mean, Excellency. But I can assure you, the evil connotations of that word have never entered a heart like mine, so enraptured am I with your greatness."

"The omens suggest otherwise, *my old friend.*" The way Maxentius emphasized the last words had a definite ring of sarcasm. Neratius was scared now.

"Any soothsayer who says my loyalty is in doubt has misread the omens. Either his ritual was errant or the spirits have given confusing signs."

"The entrails of the most innocent do not lie," Maxentius said with a cryptic smile. Neratius remained silent as the emperor rose from his throne and took a step closer, though he did not leave the apse of the hall. "Nevertheless, the omens are open to different interpretations," he went on. "Therefore I propose a test for you. A true test of your loyalty."

"Name it, my lord, and it shall be yours."

"I want to lay with your wife."

Neratius's knees went weak. He started to take a step back, catching himself only because proper senatorial protocol required him to stand firm and speak with confidence no matter what troubles assailed him. Yet it was all Neratius could do not to stagger under the weight of these words and flee the room. *Maxentius wants to disgrace me!* The choice before Neratius was stark: deny the direct request of the Divine Augustus or allow him to take Sophronia to his bed.

"Your Highness, I . . . uh—"

"You would deny my wish?" Maxentius asked through clenched teeth. "Others have agreed to it. So should you, if you are truly loyal to me."

Though Neratius wanted to capitulate and make this problem go away, he found himself unable to agree to the emperor's demand. It wasn't a matter of love for Sophronia; an aristocratic marriage wasn't about romance. What bothered Neratius instead was the great shame attached to such a weak and undignified action. Disgrace would haunt him forever if he so easily handed over his conjugal rights. Adultery was a theft of the most intimate sort: the invasion and conquest of territory that was solely one's own to command. No stranger was allowed to have that property, and a nobleman certainly didn't give it up for the asking! Try as he might, Neratius couldn't ignore such an ancient and inviolable principle of Roman matrimony. And as he thought about it, he also didn't want to deal with the anger and criticism Sophronia would throw his way if he said yes. There was no way around it. He was going to have to evade this imperial demand.

Perhaps I can make a counteroffer, he reasoned. *Neratius, old boy, you have dodged opponents all your life with your smooth words. Now is the time for your best show!*

"Your Excellency," he said, "I can assure you, there is no delight to be had from my wife in comparison to your many courtesans. But my loyalty to you is of the strongest sort, nonetheless! Do you not remember, Maxentius, how we used to throw leather balls back and forth? You always managed to catch more than I! Do you ever wish for those simple, carefree days"— Neratius waved his hand at the great hall—"before all this?"

"I often do," Maxentius admitted.

"Look at me, my dear friend, and behold that I am loyal."

Neratius dropped to his knees, then allowed himself to fall forward on his stomach. He inched ahead until he could kiss Maxentius's foot. "You are my great lord forever," he said quietly, pressing his lips to the jewel-bedecked shoe.

"Prove it, Neratius. I need to know."

"A million denarii will be delivered to your palace, to aid you in combat preparations." *A million! Ouch! But there's more coming in every day from the Sardinian estates. I'll make it back within a year or two. It's money well spent.*

"That is very generous," Maxentius said, "but mere silver isn't enough to assure me of your loyalty."

"Then I will give more, Your Highness." *How much is it going to take? A million and a half?*

"Stand up."

Neratius rose to his feet, afraid now that Maxentius's price would be the ultimate one. *Surely he wouldn't kill me.* Neratius swallowed and waited for his master to speak. *Put your life before your dignity,* he told himself. *Hand over Sophronia if you must. Better alive and cuckolded than virtuous and dead!*

"I accept your offer of a million denarii," Maxentius said, "in combination with something else of great value to you." The emperor picked a bit of dirt from his fingernail, then flicked it away and looked Neratius in the eyes. "I shall expect your letter of resignation from the office of city prefect by tomorrow. As supreme ruler of Rome, I require the most unquestionable loyalty in that position. This is my final decision. And now"—the emperor waved at Neratius with the back of his hand—"be off with you, Senator, before I decide to add anything further to my test of friendship."

⸺◈⸺

MARCH 312

Flavia was on her knees, scrubbing the floor of the imperial kitchen. "Why does a floor that the emperor never sees have to be clean?" she muttered to herself. She was alone in the room, so she felt she could complain. But to her surprise, a voice answered.

"It's so we don't slip. A dirty floor can be a slick floor—and there goes the emperor's dinner."

Flavia sucked in her breath as she heard the reply. "Oh, sorry! I was just thinking out loud." Fortunately, the speaker was one of the younger page boys, a cute little fellow of about ten or twelve. "Where did you come from, anyway?"

The lad smiled mischievously. "Emperor's mistress wants a pastry."

"But . . . you didn't come through the kitchen door."

"Not the main one." Again the impish smile.

Flavia rose to her feet. "There's a second door in here? Where?"

The boy hemmed and hawed for a moment, unwilling to give away the pages' secret. Only after Flavia pressed him did he finally cave. "This whole palace—maybe the whole hill!—is full of hidden tunnels," he bragged. "We can get anywhere without being seen. It's one of the first things they teach us. The older boys say new kids sometimes get lost and never find their way out. They say you can find skeletons in the dark corners."

"Take me into the tunnel."

The boy pursed his lips and shook his head. "I can't. It's not allowed."

"Well, then, show me the door."

"I guess I can do that."

Flavia followed the page into the larder. The walls were lined with wooden cabinets whose shelves were stacked with sealed jars, wheels of cheese, and dry goods. Yet one cabinet at the rear protruded from the wall a little more than the rest—something Flavia had never noticed before. It would be easy to miss.

"See here?" said the boy, slipping behind a cured ham dangling from the ceiling. Flavia peeked around the side of the cabinet to see where he was pointing. A tiny keyhole was camouflaged in the grain of the wood. Apparently, the cabinet had a false back that was actually a small doorway.

"Open it. Let me look in."

"No! The keys are for the pages only. We each have one, and we have to keep it hidden or we'll get a hard beating."

Flavia sighed and nodded. "Okay. Run along, then." She didn't want the little tyke to get in trouble. But privately she vowed to discover a way into the secret passages.

By early afternoon, Flavia had finished her scrubbing duties. Back at Gelotiana House, she found Alexamenos in the dormitory's little library. All the Latin classics were there: Virgil, Cicero, Tacitus, Seneca, Livy. But Alexamenos was reading a more recent writer: the Christian apologist Tertullian, who had lived in Carthago about a hundred years ago. Sophronia admired him greatly, so Flavia had grown up reading his fiery and audacious works. Though he could be harsh at times, nobody gave it to the pagans like Tertullian. He was a complex man with a brilliant mind.

"Which volume do you have, Magister?" Flavia asked, adopting the title all the schoolboys used for their teacher.

"It's his *Apology*. He proves Christians aren't immoral, nor any threat to our society. Even so, the pagans still persecute us. But that just leads to more believers. 'The blood of Christians is seed.'"

"I remember that slogan! I once heard Bishop Eusebius shout it against a heretic who denied the sanctity of the martyrs."

"Do you know what it means?"

"I think so. He's saying when the persecutors kill us, many people see our faith and come to Christ themselves."

"That's right. It's an agricultural reference. When you harvest a field of wheat, some grains fall behind and start to grow. The more stalks you cut down, the more new wheat springs up. Remember what the Lord said about this? Until the seed falls to the earth, it remains a single seed. Only when it dies and is buried does it bring forth fruit."

Flavia recalled the passage from *The Gospel according to John*. "He who loves his life will destroy it," she quoted from memory, "but he who hates his life in this world preserves it for eternal life." She looked at the wise Greek teacher—a man who had become her own mentor as well. "Are we really supposed to hate our lives, Alexamenos? Does God want us to throw them down the sewer like waste?"

"God values life and never wants us to waste it. Consider what Maxentius did to Chloe. It was a horrific deed, a thing utterly against the will of God. Life is precious to him! Yet neither should we cling to our earthly life so closely that we never take risks. We Christians are free to sacrifice our lives when necessary, because we know the rewards of heaven are far greater than anything earth can offer. That is what the martyrs understand better than anyone."

"Like Agnes. Or Perpetua. Women who were willing to give up everything for God."

"Maybe like Flavia too, in her own way."

The words were sobering, and the two friends fell silent. "The blood of Christians is seed," Flavia said to herself, turning the words over in her mind. It didn't seem far-fetched that bloodshed would be required of her. Persecution was still happening in other parts of the empire and could easily start here again. Mortal dangers had already come her way, and now the city of Rome was on the brink of war. Not since the Celts of Brennus seven hundred years ago had the city fallen to an invader. But once again, Rome was under assault. Two generals were rumored to be closing in on Rome, each leading an army. Flavia's new friend Chloe had just been brutally murdered, and Flavia herself had no more rights than any other imperial slave, whose body could be violated at will. Danger lurked all around, so the notion that she might be required to shed the blood of testimony was not an abstract thought. *Make me worthy if that day should come*, she prayed. *Thanks be to God!*

A bloody martyrdom did not come that day, however—only the boring routine of a scullery maid. Flavia went to bed that night as tired as always, yet not unhappy. One by one, the days slipped by with little to differentiate them—until the Ides of March, when Flavia found the opportunity to inspect the secret passage.

A holiday for the war god Mars was coming soon, and the kitchen was busier than normal in preparation for the festivities. Flavia was helping Zoticus transport some amphoras of wine into the imperial residence, when he abruptly held up his hand. "You can just leave them there," he said, pointing to the floor at the entrance of a storeroom beneath the palace.

"I might as well take them into the pantry for you, Zoticus. I'll just put them on the shelves and leave you alone."

"The floor outside is fine."

Flavia scanned the hallway in both directions, then stepped close to the page when she saw they were alone. "I know about the tunnels, if that's what you're worried about."

Zoticus narrowed his eyes. "What tunnels?"

"The ones opened by that key around your neck."

"How did you find out?"

"Doesn't matter. Look, I won't tell anyone. Let me help you carry these jugs all the way to where you're going. They're heavy. It would save you a trip."

"Alright, come on. But keep it quiet." Zoticus darted into the storeroom.

The entrance to the secret corridors here was a low door hidden behind a row of heavy stone barrels. Zoticus crouched and withdrew a key on a long string from his tunic. The key slipped into the lock and made a clicking sound as it turned. Pushing the door aside, he stooped and went through.

"Hand me the amphoras," he said from the opening.

Flavia passed him the four wine jugs. On the other side of the door, the hallway was high enough to stand erect. She picked up two jugs and followed Zoticus through the maze.

"How do you keep from getting lost?" she asked.

With his foot, Zoticus tapped two stones set into the floor. "White stones always point toward the imperial residence. Black stones point back to the slave quarters. Just follow me."

After twisting and turning through the narrow passageways by the glow of oil lamps and an occasional skylight, the pair finally stopped at a staircase. "That goes straight up to Maxentius's new baths," Zoticus said. "He soaks there every day and drinks chilled wine to refresh himself. Look at this."

Squatting, the page grasped the ring of a trapdoor and yanked it open. A rush of cool air billowed out.

"An icebox?"

"Aye. Lined with chunks of ice brought down from the mountains. And packed with straw to keep it from melting. Quick—pass me those jugs. We don't want to let the cold out."

When the wine was safely stowed for later consumption, Flavia glanced at the staircase. "Take me up, Zoticus," she urged, then put her hand on her friend's arm. "Please? For me?"

"Fine. Just this once. But we have to be quick."

The stairs led to another long hallway. Soon it started to feel uncomfortably warm. When Flavia reached out and touched the wall, she found it was heated.

"We're at the baths," Zoticus announced. "Peek through here." Flavia put her eye to a tiny peephole. It offered a view into Maxentius's private bathing facility, a marble-lined room with comfortable benches and massage tables in the center. Large floor-to-ceiling windows looked across the cityscape of Rome. As Flavia twisted her head and craned her neck, she caught a glimpse of the turning post down in the Circus Maximus. Apparently, after a good soak, the emperor could relax in his tepidarium and watch the chariots go charging around the bend. And if he cared to look, he could probably even see Flavia's family mansion atop the Aventine Hill on the other side of the stadium. The thought was a little unnerving.

"I'll show you something else," Zoticus said. "Stay here and watch this." He darted around a corner. A moment later Flavia spotted him through the peephole, down in the empty tepidarium. He reclined on one of the benches. "Boy!" he called, "I'm thirsty! Bring me wine!"—and Flavia could hear him perfectly. Evidently, the room's shape was designed to bring the emperor's commands within the servants' hearing. Excited at what this might mean, Flavia filed the secret discovery in her mind, though she was unable to suppress a smile at the advantage her sleuthing had just uncovered. *Rex is going to think I'm the best female speculator ever!*

Zoticus returned to Flavia's side. "Come on. We've been gone long enough. We need to get back." He paused. "Hold still—you have something in your hair." After taking a closer look at Flavia's head, he reached out and extracted a pink strand of ribbon.

"Girls love pink ribbons," Flavia said. "My new roommate was playing with my hair last night."

The remark made no impression on Zoticus, who cared little for such things. He had just started to walk down the hallway when he spun around and faced Flavia. "Hey! Now I know where I've seen you!"

Flavia stepped back from him. "What?"

"I recognize you now! I knew you looked familiar! You're the girl in pink who escaped the amphitheater!"

"N-no, Zoticus, I think you're mistaken. That wasn't me."

"Yes it was! I saw you right after the show, running through the streets. You were with that soldier Rex who visits you at the house. You had a pink ribbon in your hair."

"I . . . I don't know what you're talking about."

"You're a terrible liar, Flavia. I remember it clearly. There was a blacksmith who thought you were a harlot. Rex fooled him and took you away. That was you, I know it. And now I can see you blushing."

Flavia realized there was no use protesting further. Zoticus had identified her. Besides, she could feel that her face had a guilty expression like the boy said. No way around it—she'd been caught.

"Don't tell anyone," she warned. "We're friends, remember? I bring you goodies from the market. So you just keep your suspicions to yourself."

"Hey, don't worry, kitchen girl," Zoticus said with a smirk. "Your secret is safe with me."

⚬⚬⚬

April 312

Neratius knew he didn't have a great record as a churchgoing man. Usually it was Sophronia who gathered with the local believers when they met in his home each week. To Neratius, it had always seemed sufficient to provide a meeting room for the neighborhood Christians, along with burial space in his vault for the deceased and a regular bag of coins for the poor. After all, he was an important man whose time was in demand. Did he really need to show up for the religious rites every single week?

Lately, though, he had been much more faithful to his duty of church attendance—ever since the emperor had stripped him of high office and kicked him to the side. As far as Neratius knew, Maxentius might still be coming after his wife, his estates, or even his life. Therefore it seemed like a good time to start going to church again.

Since Father Miltiades had his own flock down at the Hall of the Church in Trans Tiberim, the bishop rarely got involved with the Aventine congregation anymore. Yet the young priest named Felix who now led the house church was quite a prominent leader within the catholic hierarchy. Neratius thought the fellow was likely on the rise in his clerical occupation. Now the handsome priest sat on the high-backed chair that Neratius had provided, delivering a rather boring sermon about the allegorical significance of Sarah and Hagar. A low altar was situated in front of Felix's chair in the little exedra that defined one end of the church. The gathered faithful stood on either side of the hall, men on the right and women on the left as usual. This former sitting room in Neratius's mansion had been enlarged into a meeting space by knocking down the wall of an adjoining storeroom. Now it could easily accommodate a hundred worshipers and their priest for the preaching of the holy scriptures and the sacrament of the Eucharist.

After the sermon, but before the liturgy of bread and wine, a time was set aside for corporate prayers. Saint Paul had commanded the people to "pray without ceasing," so Felix asked everyone to stand and face east. With arms outstretched, Neratius did his best to carry out this important obligation of his Christian faith. Certainly he had a lot to pray about now. "Holy Jesus in heaven," he whispered, "I have given you two sacks of coins today, and some of them were even gold! Notice it, please, and reward my faithfulness by guarding me from the hand of—" Not wanting to say the name out loud, even at a whisper, Neratius fell silent and finished the prayer in his heart: *Maxentius.*

When at last the service was over and the faithful were beginning to disperse, Sophronia approached her husband. A tall, muscular barbarian was at her side. He had fuzzy blond hair and a noticeable dimple in his chin. Sophronia introduced him as a new visitor—not yet a Christian, nor even a catechumen, yet a seeker dissatisfied with paganism and wanting to learn about the catholic faith. The man bowed his head to Neratius and introduced himself as Geta.

As it turned out, Geta had been newly enlisted into the Emperor's Personal Cavalry. He had attended the church a few times already, and each time, he had asked Sophronia about her husband yet had never been able to meet him. After some polite conversation, Geta looked at Neratius and posed a direct question. "Senator, might I talk with you in private? I have learned some relevant things about the emperor in my duties with the army."

Neratius didn't know what the term *relevant things* might mean, but he was interested in any intelligence he could obtain about Maxentius. He excused himself from Sophronia and invited Geta to step into the garden. After asking one of the house bodyguards to check Geta for weapons— senators should always be wary of assassins—he took a seat in the shady garden across from his visitor. Though Geta was found to be unarmed, the bodyguard took up a stance in the corner, nonetheless. The stocky slave had a dagger on his belt and a heavy staff that could double as a club, so Neratius felt reasonably secure.

Geta began by explaining that he knew Flavia personally because he was a friend of the gladiator who had helped her escape the amphitheater. While Neratius didn't know exactly what his daughter was up to these days, it was abundantly clear she couldn't come back to the Aventine mansion while Pompeianus was out to get her. If he learned of her whereabouts, he would just arrest her again. Apparently, Flavia had found refuge with some soldiers who opposed the Praetorian prefect; and under their care, she was quite safe. Even Sophronia thought so, and that was enough for Neratius. He didn't need to know more.

Having offered his credentials to prove he was an ally of the Junius family, Geta reached for the satchel draped over his shoulder. Though the bag had already been searched, the bodyguard immediately stepped forward with his hand on his dagger. Geta only smiled and calmly brought forth a little scroll. The guard eyed him suspiciously but stepped back.

"This, Senator, is something I think you will want to read for yourself," Geta said as he handed over the document. It was sealed with a glob of red wax.

When Neratius caught a good look at the mark in the seal, he immediately stood up. Taking the scroll into a shaft of sunlight, he examined the impression in the wax more closely. *The imperial insignia of Licinius!* Thoroughly intrigued, he unrolled the scroll and scanned the text. Only a few words were there—but they were significant.

"It says you are an agent of the Augustus Licinius, authorized to deal on his behalf," Neratius said, glancing over at his guest. "That would be quite interesting if it is true. But of course, this could be a forgery."

Geta held up a ring. "Yes, it could. But a forger couldn't have obtained the emperor's signet."

Neratius took the ring from Geta and inspected it in the sunshine. Everything about it looked real, though only a jeweler could be absolutely sure. "I will have the gem evaluated. If the engraving is not authentic, I will know."

"Of course, sir. But you will see that it is real. In fact, that is the augustus's own handwriting. I was there when he wrote it, and sealed it, and handed me that parchment along with his ring."

Neratius took his seat again. "How is this so? Who are you, Geta?"

"Hmm, that's a bit of a story, so let me summarize. A few years ago, when I was just a kid, brand-new to the legions, I found myself fighting for Licinius. I distinguished myself in battle, so they tapped me to be trained as a speculator. Around that time, Licinius was made augustus of Italy at Carnuntum, and that put him against Maxentius. For a while their armies fought over Histria, though they're in a stalemate now. But the two hate each other, sir. *Hate* each other! I don't know where Licinius is right now—I think over in Dalmatia somewhere. What I can tell you is, he's coming to Rome soon, and he's coming for conquest. Obviously, he will be seeking allies in the city—men who might recognize his merits over the current regime. So in light of that, my mind went to you."

Neratius knew such talk was treasonous and so felt the need to distance himself. He gave a shrug and a nonchalant wave of his hand. "Why me? I've always been faithful to Maxentius. I can't imagine anything else."

"Because, sir, you were just dismissed as city prefect! Surely you must feel you have no future with Maxentius. Your life might even be in danger! Shouldn't you ally with Licinius instead?"

"I can understand your logic," was all Neratius was willing to say.

"It will seem even more logical when Licinius shows up here at the head of a vast army."

"Do you think he will arrive before Constantine?"

"It remains to be seen. But Maxentius is weak. He cannot hold this city, and his growing tyranny only makes that more certain. Rome will be captured by either Constantine or Licinius. And make no mistake, only one of those two is going to end up as ruler of the West. Maybe even the whole empire."

"If I were interested—which I am not!—but if I were, could you, theoretically, put me in contact with Licinius when he arrives?"

Geta chuckled and shook his head. "You senators sure know how to guard your words." He paused before going on. "Yes, I could do that. The augustus is my . . . well, for now, let's just say he respects me. I could arrange an alliance with him on your behalf. But only if you had something to offer him."

"And for the sake of conversation, what would a man like Licinius want?"

"He wants the ancient and respected Senate to vote him the sole Augustus of the West—and to back that up with the force of the Praetorian Guard."

"Who else knows of your allegiance to Licinius?"

"No one in Rome, sir, and it would be best if we kept it that way."

"I agree." Neratius rose from his seat, signaling that the meeting was over. "So then, Christian seeker, I am glad you could visit our little church today. I invite you to come again. Perhaps we can discuss the holy scriptures and the things of Christ. Or who knows? Maybe our conversation will once again delve into these imaginative politics that do not, of course, have any basis in reality."

"Perhaps that might happen," Geta agreed. "If so, I hope you might have some new ideas about Licinius. Topics we could discuss, you know, in abstraction."

"We'll see, Geta. Keep checking in with Lady Sabina. Good day."

When the Germanic soldier was gone, Neratius immediately retired to his study. He withdrew a map from his desk and examined the itinerary down to Puteoli. A sea route existed from Ostia, but sailors didn't like to ply the seas during the stormy month of April. Neratius decided he would have to take the Appian Way. There was someone in Puteoli he had to see right away.

<hr />

The preparations for the trip and the advance notice, plus the travel itself, took three weeks. Fortunately, the weather was good, with only a little rain to hinder the caravan's progress. The worst of it was at Three Taverns, where a mule broke a leg in the slippery mud. But at last, after six days on the road, Neratius and his retinue arrived safely at Puteoli.

For as long as the empire had existed, this coastal area had been the fashionable retreat of emperors, senators, and the richest businessmen of Rome. The isle of Capreae, the thermal springs of Baiae, and indeed the whole bay of Neapolis—these stunning places were renowned for their luxury and decadence. Gazing out at the lush beauty of the craggy shoreline and the dark blue sea, Neratius could see why so many wealthy and prominent people owned seaside villas here.

Yet not every visitor to Puteoli was rich. According to the *Acts* of Saint Luke, the apostle Paul came through here and traveled up the same road that Neratius had just come down. *I hope he didn't have to go by mule caravan,* Neratius thought as the scripture came to his mind. Puteoli was a natural harbor, making it a better place to dock a ship—at least until a great harbor was built near Ostia by Trajan—than anywhere between here and Rome. For that reason, it used to be a major entry point for anyone coming by sea to the capital, including a Christian prisoner from Hierusalem on his way to be tried by Nero. As Neratius's caravan pulled up in front of his friend's luxurious villa, he offered a little prayer to Saint Paul for the success of this important endeavor.

The friend Neratius had come to see was the consular governor of Campania, Publius Valerius Urbicus, a man whose greed was outsized only by his even more expansive belly. Yet greed was a vice that tended to bother one's victims more than one's friends. Neratius had never been the object of Publius's land grabbing or price gouging. Quite to the contrary, he had often enjoyed the fruits of those rapacious business practices. Publius was actually generous to those in his inner circle. On many occasions he had said there would always be a place for Neratius at his table—and if you liked tasty and exotic food, that was the table at which to recline.

"Welcome, my friend! Welcome!" Publius exclaimed, smiling warmly as Neratius alighted from his coach at the villa's main entrance. An entourage of butlers and porters had spilled out with the governor to help the guests get situated. One young slave carried an umbrella to shield Publius's bald head as he waddled about in the sun. A second umbrella bearer ran over to offer shade to Neratius, but he waved the boy away.

"I have come far to see you, dear Publius, yet the journey was worth it. I see you haven't changed a bit—still handsome, still cheerful, and still surrounded by the most beautiful things."

"You should see my new wife," the governor said with a wink.

After the initial greetings, the visitors were shown to their rooms and given time to rest for a while. An evening meal was planned for the two aristocrats on Publius's pleasure yacht. Neratius took the opportunity for a quick bath and afternoon nap. Upon awakening, his personal valet helped him dress in a fine woolen toga, then escorted him to the villa's dock, where they boarded the luxurious ship.

The yacht was a typical merchant sailing vessel, but since it wasn't being used for commerce, attention had been devoted to leisure instead of pragmatics. Decorations covered the craft from prow to stern—little ornaments and frills that no merchant would ever allow on his ship. The available deck space was occupied by extravagantly appointed seating areas, while the hold was filled with fine food and drink. Neratius and Publius reclined on couches around a burnished wood table under a silk canopy. Potted plants, trickling fountains, and songbirds in golden cages made Neratius feel that he was visiting an island paradise in the middle of the sea. Below deck was a fully functional kitchen, private bedrooms, and even a marble latrine with pumped seawater to keep it flushed clean.

"Splendid little boat you have here, my friend," Neratius said once they were out in the bay.

"I like to come out and get some fresh sea air. Nice views too. That's Mons Vesuvius in the distance there."

"The one that buried Pompeii?"

"Yes, and also Herculaneum. Two and a half centuries ago, those were busy Roman towns. They were destroyed by the volcano in a single day."

Though Neratius briefly considered the tragedy, the smoke and fire of his own life were a much more pressing concern. He decided it was time to broach the subject he had come to discuss.

"Since we are alone out here on a ship, Publius, I think we may speak freely about the latest activities of our Divine Augustus. You have probably heard that he has grown cruel. Several senators have even been executed on trumped-up charges, and their lands confiscated."

"Their wives taken too, I've heard."

"It's true. However, the real problem isn't Maxentius's need for women—it's money. His building projects are hugely expensive, and now he has to garrison northern Italy against invasion as well as shore up Rome's defenses. To pay for all this, he discovers some supposed treason in an innocent senator. Suddenly that man finds himself banished or killed, and his lands are forfeit to the imperial treasury. It's a disgrace."

"We can't let that happen to us, Neratius."

"No, indeed. We need to think about protection."

"From whom? People are saying Constantine is coming down from Gaul."

Neratius swirled the wine in his goblet, admiring its color and clarity. He took a sip, then looked up at his host. "I think another ally might be better. I am referring to Licinius. It is said he will soon make a bid for Rome as well."

"Whoever arrives first will scoop up the prize. Maxentius is the most inept emperor ever to command the legions. He will not be able to withstand either Constantine or Licinius."

Leaning close to the governor, Neratius set his goblet on the table. "That is why we must join with one of them. And I suggest Licinius."

"How? Are you in contact with him?"

"A spy of his recently approached me—one of his favored warriors. He had the emperor's signet, so I know he is legitimate. Through him, we can reach his master."

"We would need to let Licinius know we belong to him as soon as possible. Then when he arrives, we'd be first in line to receive his favors," Publius said.

"Exactly. And in the meantime, we must guard ourselves against Maxentius."

"That won't be easy."

"But we can do it, Publius! Listen to me. You control a huge voting bloc in the Senate. Everyone with business interests in Campania will vote with you. And my allies in the capital are extensive as well. Together we can keep Maxentius's greedy fingers off our property. Let him pillage other senators who aren't in our alliance until he's defeated. Then, once Licinius is in charge, we'll vote him the sole Augustus of the West and take our cut of the spoils of war."

The governor raised his goblet in his pudgy hand. "I'll drink to that!"

Neratius returned the toast, then called for more wine. The meal continued as more courses were served and the conversation turned to less political matters. After dinner, Publius's daughter came up from the cabins to provide the entertainment. Though she was only fourteen, she had the sensual moves and skimpy outfit of someone much older. Neratius marveled that such a young girl could learn to dance so provocatively. When she finished her strutting, she bowed to the men in a way that accentuated her developing body, then disappeared below deck.

"That's a marvelous daughter you have!" Neratius exclaimed to his host. "She's quite an attractive little lady."

Publius shook his head with a chuckle. "Vulcacia got her natural beauty from my ex-wife, but I think she must have learned those dance moves from one of my courtesans!"

"It was truly breathtaking," Neratius agreed. "You say her name is Vulcacia?"

"Mm-hmm."

"Sweet little thing. You are a blessed man, Publius."

The two men lapsed into a congenial silence. At last the sun began to set on the distant horizon, sending a red glow across the glassy surface of the sea. Neratius rose and went to the deck rail, gazing toward the west. He knew his own estates on Sardinia lay directly across the water, though at a distance too great to see.

Publius joined him at the rail. All was quiet as the two men stared at the sunset. Finally, Neratius glanced toward his friend. "So we have a deal, right?"

"You have made a strong case for Licinius. Yes, I'm with you. But to make it official, let's take an oath by the gods to bind our fates together."

Neratius frowned. A warning voice in his head told him, *Don't invoke any pagan gods and risk angering Jesus. He's your strongest patron. Stay on his good side.*

"My word is enough of a bond," he said out loud.

"Did you know, Neratius, that some people say you are Christian?"

"What? No I'm not!"

"Good. Then by Jupiter the Highest and Best, I swear to join with Licinius against Maxentius." The governor gripped Neratius's shoulder. "Do you join me in this?"

"Yes, I join you."

"By what god? Jesus or Jupiter?"

"J-Jupiter, of course."

Publius reached to a potted fern and dipped his finger in the soil, then dabbed a cross of dirt on the ship's deck. "Spit on it," he ordered.

"What?"

"If I'm going to enter into treason with you, Neratius, I need to know I can count on you. Just two old pagans doing a backroom deal like senators have been doing since they threw out Tarquinius the Proud. I don't work with Christians. I have to be sure about this. If you're not one of that cult, bend over and spit on the sign of the cross."

"Publius! Come on, my friend! You know me. We don't need to make silly gestures."

"Probably not. But humor me."

"Fine. As you wish."

Neratius looked down at the crisscrossed smears of mud and gathered saliva in his mouth. *It means nothing, right, God? This isn't a sacred cross—just a smudge of dirt!*

He let a gob of spittle drop from his mouth. It spattered onto the cross.

"Excellent! I knew I could count on you," Publius said.

"Of course you can," Neratius replied, still contemplating the dirty mess at his feet.

Lord God, what have I done?

—⟪ɷɷ⟫—

Zoticus had never had a massage. He thought it must feel nice, because men in power always got them. They lay there on the table, oohing and aahing as some huge slave worked out the knots in their muscles. *Someday,* he vowed, *I am going to get a massage.*

Staring through the peephole into the new Palatine baths, Zoticus realized he could identify all the important officials who had gathered today, for it was his job to know who was who in the palace. Maxentius was uncharacteristically late, but no doubt he would soon show up, for he never missed his daily bath and rubdown. Several other senators and high-level bureaucrats were there already. The most powerful among them was Ruricius Pompeianus, the prefect of the Praetorian Guard and commander of the Emperor's Personal Cavalry.

Down in the circus, the charioteers were getting ready to practice. A race was coming up soon and the whole city was talking about it. The Blues were expected to win, though Zoticus had always favored the Greens, and he hoped they might pull it out. When the men in the bath were finished with their massages, they made the slaves arrange their padded resting benches so they had a good view of the turning post. The most spectacular crashes always happened as the charioteers rounded the spine of a circus. Although they wouldn't be going full speed today and nobody was likely to crash, the gilded turning post at the far end of the track was still the most exciting place in a chariot race. Maybe something interesting would happen. At the very least, the watchers could get a sense of how the four factions were likely to perform.

As the chariot practice got going, the group of rich, naked men in the bath began to make wagers on who could turn the bend first. Pompeianus was foremost among them, shouting the loudest and laying the highest bets. Soon the relaxed camaraderie of the tepidarium gave way to the competitive frenzy of the racetrack. When Pompeianus's Green chariot rounded the post behind the White, he leapt from his couch and kicked over a side table. "Curse the Whites!" he cried.

"Fortune will smile on you another day," the winning senator said.

Pompeianus only made a guttural sound in his throat. "Boy!" he shouted to the ceiling. "Bring my purse!"

That was Zoticus's cue to move. He darted from the peephole and ran to the dressing room. Under the watchful eye of the attendant, he retrieved the prefect's purse and started toward the bath. "Don't try anything with that money," the attendant said, but Zoticus ignored him.

The purse was bulging with coins, and the young page couldn't resist a peek inside. He found not only an abundance of common bronze nummi washed with a silver coating to give them value but also many gold coins: the brand-new solidi, and even a few of the old aurei. *So much wealth right here in my hands! Where did he get it? What does he do with it all?* It just didn't seem right. This man had a sack of money he wasn't even using, while Zoticus had to scrimp and save to buy one votive offering to Aesculapius. The injustice demanded to be rectified.

Do I dare take a coin? Maybe one little nummus?

Zoticus couldn't do it. All these rich men had accountants who kept track of their funds down to the penny. No doubt the current value of the moneypouch was recorded somewhere. Any discrepancy would be attributed to the page boy who retrieved it, probably at the loss of his right hand. It wasn't worth the risk.

If only I had something to sell him! Perhaps I do . . .

The air in the tepidarium was warm and pleasant as Zoticus approached the bathers. He bowed before Pompeianus. "Your purse, my lord."

"Wait here until I get what I need. Then return it to the attendant for an accounting."

The prefect rummaged in the sack and withdrew the amount he owed— enough to buy ten sacrifices to Aesculapius. *It's so unfair! He throws money away on stupid betting, while I can barely get by!* Zoticus gritted his teeth but said nothing.

"Take it back and put it where you got it," Pompeianus said, jingling the coins in one hand as he extended the purse in the other. "Then go fetch me a cup of chilled wine."

Zoticus received the bag with a subservient bow. Pompeianus began to move away.

Now or never, Zoticus. You have to do what you must to survive in this world!

"Sir?" he asked, trying to keep the quiver out of his voice.

The prefect turned and stared down at the page with an imperious glare. "What is it?"

"Would you grant me a small reward if I brought you important information?"

"Depends on the information. I don't really care which imperial page has become a senator's latest boyfriend."

"It is . . . it is a substantial matter, sir."

"Speak. I will decide if it's worth something."

Don't think. Just do it.

"I have learned the whereabouts of a missing person," Zoticus declared. "Who?"

"The woman you sentenced to death by the beasts. Lady Junia Flavia."

Pompeianus's face was unreadable. "She's dead," he said at last. "I have it on good authority."

"With respect, sir, she is alive. And I can lead you to her."

The Praetorian prefect simply glared at Zoticus—stern and unmoving, like the naked idol of some furious Olympian god. Only when Zoticus had stared back at his face for an unbearably long time did he notice his master's jaw muscles twitching. Suddenly Pompeianus's hand shot out toward the waiting boy.

Zoticus yelped and jumped back. But the prefect wasn't trying to strike him. He simply held out his open palm.

"Give me the bag," he ordered. "That information deserves some gold."

11

Though the morning dawned cold, clear, and windy, Constantine ordered the firemen not to heat the furnace in the Palace Hall of Augusta Treverorum. Better, he thought, to start doing away with the little comforts of civilized life. It was time to get ready for war.

Unfortunately, the bishops and lesser clergy gathered in the throne room hadn't come prepared for the lack of heat, so they stood shivering and rubbing their arms as they awaited the arrival of their leader, the Spanish bishop Ossius of Corduba. Ever since last October, he and the elderly professor Lactantius had been working on a special item. Today it would be revealed—the great day for which it had been made. Constantine believed the momentous occasion required the presence of all the churchmen from the region, even if it meant they had to shiver through the presentation ceremony.

"Lactantius told me the flag is very grand," said the boy sitting on a stool at his father's feet. "I believe it has great magic power. Some people are saying rays of light will shine from it and blind the troops of Maxentius."

Constantine dipped his chin and regarded his firstborn son by his former concubine Minervina. The handsome youth had big brown eyes and a mop of reddish hair like his mother. Although Constantine had set Minervina aside when he married Fausta five years ago, he still doted on Crispus, who was just coming into manhood and had all the makings of a good future

328

emperor. "I don't think it shoots any brilliant rays," he corrected the boy, "but it is certainly powerful against the enemy."

"I can't wait to see it, Father."

Constantine raised a finger toward the rear of the hall. "You won't have long to wait. Look—here it comes now."

Bishop Ossius entered the reception hall through the grand middle door, accompanied by four deacons carrying a long wooden case with handles on both sides. Just behind the bishop was Lactantius, the esteemed Christian rhetorician and tutor of Crispus. Royal guardsmen with plumed helmets and upright lances lined the central aisle as the guests approached the emperor. A trumpeter played a brief military fanfare. When the party reached the imperial throne, they bowed low at the waist with their eyes closed and their palms held out.

"I greet you all as friends," Constantine said. "The priests of the one true God are always welcome in my hall."

The assembly of churchmen murmured. It wasn't the kind of treatment they were used to receiving from the government.

Ossius lifted his gaze to meet the emperor's. "Your Highness, we are honored to bring you a mighty gift today, just as you commanded. May it be a sign of the coming victory in your righteous war against tyranny."

"I shall be pleased to receive it. You may bring it forth."

While the deacons held the case, Ossius opened the latches. The box was lined with purple fabric, upon which rested a spear that had been turned into a military standard. Constantine motioned over his shoulder to his general Vitruvius, who was standing behind him. "Go get it," he said.

Vitruvius removed the spear from its case and lifted it into one of the sunbeams that streamed through the high windows. As it caught the light, a collective gasp went up from the room, and even Constantine couldn't help but marvel at the quality of the workmanship. The entire length of the spear's shaft was covered in gold. Affixed to its top, instead of a blade, was a gilded wreath interspersed with gems. The Greek letters χ and ρ had been superimposed inside the wreath to form a chi-rho: ☧.

Beneath this, a beautifully embroidered cloth hung from a transverse bar, giving the whole banner a cross shape. Attached to the square flag was a gold medallion that depicted Constantine's face with an air of tranquil confidence. Truly this was a magnificent battle standard, a worthy object with which to lead men into war.

"Well done!" Constantine exclaimed. "Be sure the jeweler receives a generous bonus from the imperial treasury for such fine work." The emperor tilted his head, examining the standard more closely. "But why the chi-rho? I seem to remember a tau-rho in my dream."

Lactantius stepped forward, gathering the folds of his robe with his forearm like a distinguished senator about to give a great speech. "We debated the merits of both symbols, Your Highness, for both are found in our scriptures. The tau-rho is used whenever the scribe writes the word *crucify* or *cross*, so of course it is very important. Since it is composed of a ρ on top of a τ, it even looks like a small figure of a crucified man." Lactantius paused and used his finger to trace the shape in the air: ρ.

"However, the chi and the rho are the first two letters of *Christ*," he went on. "Our scribes use the chi-rho when they write the name of the Savior in the holy scriptures. Because there is victorious power in that name, we thought this symbol must surely be put upon the banner."

It sounded reasonable enough to Constantine. "You are the experts in the things of God. So be it." He thought for a moment, then added, "But I believe I shall mark my soldiers' shields with the tau-rho, for that is what I recall from my dream. I want to follow the instructions of the Christ exactly."

"As you wish, my lord," Lactantius said. "And does the banner have a name?"

Now it was Ossius's turn to speak again. "Military flags are not mentioned in the books of God, so we do not find a divine word for it. Yet we must call it something. Therefore I have proposed to name it a *labestauros*."

Constantine smiled at the new term. "A Greek word?"

"Yes. It means 'a cross taken up and held in the hand.'"

"I do speak Greek, Bishop Ossius."

"Oh! Of course you do! Your Highness, I did not mean—"

"Be at peace," Constantine interrupted. "I know what you meant. My concern is that my soldiers will not adopt such a Greek-sounding word. Let us give it a more Latinized name. How about *labarum*?"

"Behold the labarum!" Ossius said, sweeping his hand toward the beautiful banner. Vitruvius lifted it high again, drawing a cheer from the clerics and soldiers in the Palace Hall.

Constantine, however, felt a twinge of concern. Signaling to Ossius, he asked, "Did I hear you say that banners like these are not mentioned in the writings of the Christians? How then can you be certain it will have the intended effect?"

"Do not fear, my lord," Ossius answered. "It is true, no such banner is named in the sacred pages, but you may know for certain that the cross is indeed a mighty sign."

Lactantius held up a book for all to see. "These are the scriptures of the Jews that we call the Old Testament," he explained. "Listen to the story of Moses and the fiery serpents." The wise philosopher then read a passage in which the wandering people of Israel were afflicted by venomous snakes, but the prophet Moses made a bronze serpent and set it on a pole. Anyone who looked at the pole after being bitten would live.

"So the mighty pole had God's magic in it?" Constantine asked doubtfully.

Bishop Ossius shook his head. "No, Augustus. The pole of Moses was not magic. Even the cross of Christ was not magic! It is not the device itself that has power but the God to whom the sign points. He alone brought healing to those people in the wilderness. They only had to show that they were looking to his divine sign. And in the same way, he gives victory to those who look to him in battle—for he is a God who trains the hands of his kings for war."

"Listen also to this scripture," Lactantius put in. He turned to a deacon and exchanged his book for another. After opening it, he said, "Hear now the words of Jesus from Saint John the Evangelist! 'Even as Moses lifted up the serpent in the wilderness, so the Son of Man must be lifted up, so that everyone who believes in him might have eternal life. For this is how God loved the world: he gave his only son, that everyone who believes in him might not perish but have eternal life.'"

Lactantius closed the book and looked straight at the emperor. "Let it be known today that this labarum has no power in itself. Instead, it is a symbol, a marker of spiritual intent. He who looks to the cross of Christ for salvation can be sure his prayers will be heard. He who receives the Son of God has entered into the light and favor of the only Father in heaven and earth."

"What more can I ask than that, professor? Such favor is exactly what I seek."

"Seek and you shall find, O great Augustus."

Constantine mused on that exhortation for a moment, then rose from his throne. "Friends, with this banner in hand, the time has come for us to depart beneath the good eye of the Christian God. Let us be quick about it! General Vitruvius, meet me at the northern gate in one hour, ready to march."

After leaving the throne hall, Constantine proceeded along a private walkway to the palace a few blocks away. He went immediately to his personal chambers, where his valet was waiting with a beautiful yet fully functional set of armor. Its crested helmet, coat of bronze scale, and shin greaves all glittered with gold ornaments and bright trim. With the help of the valet, Constantine donned the armor over a long-sleeved tunic of traditional legionary red, along with the sturdy leather trousers worn by all the soldiers along the northern lines. Over his shoulder he fastened a baldric, from which his ivory-handled sword hung close to hand. A luxurious fur-trimmed cape was fastened at his throat with a Roman brooch shaped like an eagle. However, in keeping with the Germanic origins of his troops, Constantine also wore a gold torque around his neck like a tribal chieftain who had been successful in war. In this gesture he hoped to show he was not a decadent emperor like Maxentius, living a life of pleasure and ease in sunny Rome, but a frontier general who fought alongside his men and bestowed on them the spoils of victory.

A magnificent Persian stallion awaited the emperor in the palace courtyard, its coat entirely white and unblemished. Though a groom had placed a mounting block next to the horse, Constantine disdainfully kicked it away, then mounted his steed like the equestrian he was. "Follow me, men, and stay in formation," he said to the assembled riders of his elite cavalry.

Proceeding up the cardinal street of Augusta Treverorum at the head of his troops, Constantine rode along a grand thoroughfare with colonnades on either side. All the city had turned out to wish him well as he passed. He exited through the massive northern gate with its pair of four-story towers, then immediately found himself in a necropolis, the tombs of which lined the road outside the walls. Soon a little trail branched off between two mausoleums. Constantine followed it and climbed a low rise. As he topped out and emerged from the trees, he could see the entire army encamped on the field to the north of the city.

Most of the soldiers had already packed up their gear and goatskin tents, ready to depart now and let the baggage handlers follow behind. Though the equipment would be floated up the Mosella River and down the Arar, a host of fast riders would turn south with the emperor and take the Agrippa Highway to Lugdunum. Near that city was the turnoff to Mons Matrona Pass, which General Vitruvius had advised using due to its relative warmth and ease of passage through the snowy Alps. Constantine couldn't help but chuckle at the historical irony. *I'm just like Hannibal and his elefanti, five hundred years ago—except I'm coming to Rome as a liberator, not an enemy!*

Out in the encampment, the army awaited their emperor's command. Constantine gazed at the battle-hardened men, their heavy traveling cloaks drawn tight around their shoulders. Although the sky today was clear and blue, an early spring crispness lingered in the air. The wind whipped at the mane of Constantine's stallion and blew his cape to one side. All the soldiers stared back at their lord, pushing close to gather before him in a turbulent mass of eager anticipation and martial splendor. Like a good cavalryman, Constantine sat erect in the saddle as he surveyed his faithful army. General Vitruvius joined him atop the low hill. In his hand, hidden by his horse's flank, he gripped the labarum.

"Soldiers of the Germanic lines, I greet you!" Constantine shouted to a roar of acclaim. When the crowd had quieted again, he continued. "Today we ride out to war! As you know, the tyrant Maxentius calls upon the dark arts of magic. Yet there is a Supreme Deity in heaven, one who is stronger than any spell. And you shall ride out under his protection, led along by his saving sign!"

At this cue, Vitruvius stepped his mount forward and raised the battle standard in both hands, waving it back and forth. All the legionaries fell back at the sight of such a dreadful totem. Though religious devotion had long been given to military standards and the spirits in them, this vexillum was especially magnificent.

Constantine cupped his hands around his mouth. "Behold the labarum— the emblem of the God of victory!"

"Victory!" the soldiers shouted in unison.

"This is the sign I witnessed in the sky!"

"Victory!" the soldiers repeated.

"This is the sign given to me in a dream!"

"Victory!" came the cry once more.

"Vitruvius?" Constantine whispered. "Do you remember that speculator named Rex who confronted me in the hall? What was the slogan he used when he handed me the flag that time?"

"In this sign, you shall conquer."

"Yes, that was it! Raise it up high, General. Follow my lead and stay by my side."

Vitruvius thrust the banner toward the sky, holding the shaft by its butt and waving its golden length in the sun.

"In this sign, you shall conquer!" Constantine bellowed to the troops, then spurred his horse down the face of the little hill. With a boisterous cheer, the men mounted up and surged to get in line behind their commander and his flag.

"I hope you know what you're doing, my lord," Vitruvius said with a shake of his head.

Constantine glanced over at his general, a man who had served him well for many years. "The horse is prepared for the day of war, but the Lord bestows the victory."

Vitruvius gave his master a quizzical look. "Frontinus?"

"Solomon," Constantine said with a laugh. "Come on, my old friend. Let's go conquer Rome."

———◦◦◦———

MAY 312

The frontier legions always mocked the permanent forces of Rome as decadent and lazy soldiers. According to the common wisdom along the Germanic lines, the Praetorians' idea of combat was brawling with the neighborhood drunk, while a foreign expedition meant visiting a suburban garden.

But Rex had found just the opposite to be true in his time with the imperial horse guard. These were crack troops, drilled in combat maneuvers and accustomed to physical exertion under the hot sun. In every way they were the equal of the northern army. Even so, they had a few unique approaches to warfare, the knowledge of which would benefit Constantine.

Everything Rex observed as he played the role of a cadet at the New Camp learning cavalry skills for the first time—things Aratus had already taught him several years ago—he filed away in his memory for future use. At night, by the glow of an oil lamp, he even made a few notes about the guards' tactics and combat readiness. Such valuable intelligence would be incorporated into his eventual briefing to the emperor. Of course, these records were encrypted so no one could read them, should they ever be discovered. Although the espionage was stressful and physically exhausting, Rex loved what he was doing. This was covert reconnaissance at its best, just the way he had been taught.

Despite the cadets' rigorous training schedule, they were allowed an occasional day of leave from camp. Rex often used those opportunities to meet with Geta at the local balneum, yet he had also taken up the habit of checking on Flavia at Gelotiana House. Since he hadn't seen her for a few days, he was on his way there now, which gave him ample time alone with his thoughts. His conversations with Geta had prompted him to consider more deeply whether a future with her might be possible. Many soldiers were married, especially horse guardsmen, with their higher status and better pay. These days, it wasn't uncommon for wives and children to escort the troopers on expeditions. A good marriage was certainly possible for a member of the Emperor's Personal Cavalry. *But not to the aristocratic daughter of one of Rome's most ancient families. Face it, Rex, you're just a barbarian soldier with a spear, a horse, and a small sack of coins to your name.*

The thought was depressing, and it gnawed at Rex until another consideration occurred to him as he walked along the never-ending length of the Circus Maximus. Right now, Flavia was just an imperial kitchen maid with very few friends and even fewer romantic prospects. *For the time being, we're both down and out—a perfect match!*

Except in our religion. Rex grimaced as he considered that obstacle. *Something will have to be done about that.*

The Gelotiana House was unusually quiet when Rex entered. It was afternoon, and most of the boys—like virtually all the free males of the city—had found their way to a bathhouse. It was a perk not many slaves could enjoy, but the imperial pages were exceptions, for their rich masters wanted them clean and smartly dressed. Since the rowdy boys would be elsewhere right now, Rex had decided the afternoon peace that descended on Rome every day was his best opportunity to be alone with Flavia.

She was resting on a couch in the house's shady atrium when he came through the door. Her eyes were closed as she lay on the divan with her head on a cushion. The garment she wore wasn't a long, silky gown like she had grown up with, but the rough-spun tunic of a slave. Her pale legs and bare feet protruded from the hem of her dress. Although her calves were shapely, it wasn't physical attraction that struck Rex immediately but a powerful sense of admiration. There was a very long distance between Flavia's former life and this one, yet she had embraced it with fortitude, perseverance, and no complaints. Rex found her courage deeply respectable.

"Flavia!" he whispered, trying not to startle her.

Her eyes fluttered open. "Rex!" she cried, jumping up as soon as she saw him to give him a jubilant hug. Such affection would have been unthinkable for an aristocrat, but slaves could be more familiar, and Rex found himself glad for the temporary change.

They exchanged small talk for a while, then decided to go outside and find something to eat. Although the length of the racetrack across the street was lined with the stalls of food vendors, most of them had closed for a few hours while the city took its collective rest break. Fortunately, one enterprising merchant was still selling hot sausages on a stick.

"I'll take two," Rex told the man behind the grill. He thought it would be gallant to pay for Flavia's meal, even though her family was fabulously rich. He knew how much she enjoyed sausages. Though it was only a small gesture, Rex liked to do what he could.

"Oh, Rex, meat is so expensive," Flavia said. "Bread and oil will be fine."

"It's alright. I'm happy to buy it for you," Rex replied as he held out some money.

"Not with that coin," the sausage vendor said.

Rex was taken aback. "What's wrong with it?"

"It's fake. There are gangs of counterfeiters working in Rome. That's not a real nummus."

"How can you tell?"

"I was a slave in the imperial mint before I bought my freedom. I know the difference. Let me see your other coins." The man glanced at the rest of the nummi that Rex brought out and held in his palm. "Those are all good," he declared, "but that one doesn't have any silver in it. You might as well throw it away. Unless you think you can pass it off on someone less observant than me."

"You should stick to your new job," Rex said irritably. He paid the man with one of the good coins and received his change without another word.

An umbrella pine nearby provided a pleasant spot out of the sun to stop and eat. The meat was hot and zesty, and its juice ran down Rex's chin when he bit into it.

"Eek!" Flavia cried as she encountered the same problem. Rex looked up to see her standing with her neck craned forward and grease dripping from her delicate lips. She had an embarrassed look on her face. When Rex made a motion to suggest she use her tunic, Flavia shook her head.

"Why not?" he asked, gesturing at her clothes.

Flavia looked down at her cheap garment with patches sewn on it, shrugged, and wiped her collar across her face. The two impoverished diners burst into laughter.

"Being a slave has its perks," Flavia observed.

"I suppose—for now, anyway. But I wouldn't want it for you long-term."

Flavia glanced up at Rex, a little twinkle in her eyes. "That's interesting. I didn't realize you wanted anything for me long-term. Good to know."

Although Rex sensed a little flirtation in Flavia's voice, he wasn't inclined to reveal too much about his own feelings. "I just want you to be happy long-term," he said blandly.

"What do you think that would take?"

Rex chewed his sausage and swallowed the bite before answering. "Not a slave's life, that's for sure. I can imagine a nice home on a Roman hill, and a church nearby, and children."

"And a gentle husband. So many women are mistreated by their men. I want someone gentle."

It was a surprisingly honest statement, one that caught Rex off guard.

Am I gentle? he wondered. *Probably not. I'm a soldier—the opposite of gentle!*

Flavia took a step closer to Rex. "Don't worry," she said, reading his expression. "I think you're gentle."

337

"*Pfft!* I'm a fighter."

"Never against me. Always for me."

"Yes, I'm for you, Flavia. I always will be."

"Rex, I think—"

"That's the girl right there!" someone shouted.

Rex and Flavia spun toward the sound. The voice had come from a scowling Praetorian leading a group of four. "Stay where you are, woman!" he commanded as he marched over, followed by his three comrades. He was clearly the decanus of his little squad.

"My cohort's insignia is on my tunic," Rex whispered to Flavia, "so I can't fight them. They'd be able to identify me. Let me try and talk our way out of this."

Flavia nodded and moved to stand behind Rex.

"No need for any trouble here," he said to the decanus. "I'm a soldier too—imperial horse guard. What do you want with this woman? She's mine."

"We have orders from the Praetorian prefect to arrest her. Stand back."

"Come on! Why would Pompeianus care about a menial slave like this girl?"

"We have reason to believe she's actually an aristocrat the prefect is looking for."

Though he didn't show it, the words hit Rex like a punch in the gut. *Gods! She's been discovered!* Behind him, he felt Flavia's grip tighten on his tunic. She, too, evidently understood that her spying days in the palace were over. Pompeianus was after her again.

Rex's mind was working fast now. *What next? Fight? Lie? Run?*

Whatever you do, you've got to stand between Flavia and these men. She's in serious danger.

I'll kill these four guys before I let them take her back to the Carcer!

Yet despite his protective instincts, Rex knew if it came down to a fight, his mission would be over, and he would be in prison instead of her. No longer could he melt into the immigrant crowds of Rome and disappear. Now that he was a recognizable trooper of the imperial cavalry, too many people knew where to find him.

"I can assure you," Rex said, raising his palms in a soothing gesture, "this girl is no aristocrat. She's just a slave. Born into bondage for three generations. I've known her all her life—and bedded her for almost half of it! Know what I mean?" He gave the Praetorian a friendly soldier's guffaw.

The decanus was in no mood for joking. "We were told she's a highborn lady hiding in the imperial palace as a kitchen slave."

"What? Who told you nonsense like that? What kind of rich girl comes here and scrubs floors? She's just a plain slave. Look!" Spinning around, Rex grabbed Flavia roughly by the elbow and drew her into the men's view. "Her hair is ragged and ugly. Her hands are calloused. And have you ever seen a noble lady with bruises on both knees from kneeling all day on a kitchen floor?" Rex lifted the hem of Flavia's tunic to reveal that, indeed, both her knees were faintly blue.

"Maybe it is the wrong girl, sir," one of the Praetorians suggested to his leader. "The page boy could have been mistaken."

Rex nodded emphatically. "That's right! But I'll tell you what *isn't* mistaken. This wench of mine is the favorite of one of the senators up on the hill. He calls for her after every banquet. You bother her and you'll have made a very powerful enemy. If I were you, I'd get my facts straight before I arrest a senator's favorite girl. You know how those rich old men can be about their little sweeties."

"She has to come with us," the decanus insisted, though he was more tentative now.

"If you take away my woman, I'm going straight to the senator to get her freed. And when that happens, as it surely will, I hope you like the cold rain, because you'll find you've just been reassigned to Hadrian's Wall at the edge of Britannia."

"Sir . . . let's just make sure first," the second Praetorian whispered.

"This is all based on the word of one boy," said a third.

The decanus frowned. "Don't leave the vicinity until we get back," he spat.

"We won't need to," Rex scoffed, "because you're about to find out that this common hussy is no aristocratic lady."

The soldiers moved off to do their investigation. As soon as they rounded a corner, Rex turned to Flavia. "Your cover is blown," he said. "You've got to get out of here right away."

"I know," Flavia said softly. "And I think I know who betrayed me."

"Doesn't matter now. Let's start walking."

"I need to collect a few things from my room first."

"I'll send for them. You're never going into Gelotiana House again. We have to clear the area immediately."

"Can I go home?"

Rex shook his head. "That would be the first place they'd look."

"So then . . . where? Tibur?"

"No, that's dangerous as well. But it gives me an idea. Are there any Christians who would put you up?"

Flavia thought for a moment. Suddenly her face brightened. "Bishop Miltiades would hide me!"

"Good idea. Let's go before those Praetorians return."

"They ordered us to stay put until they get back," Flavia said.

"That sort of threat works on most people, but not on us. We have more to lose by staying than leaving."

"Good point. Lead the way, then. Make for the Bridge of Probus. We have to cross the river to get to the bishop's house."

It was a long walk to Trans Tiberim, but the sun was out and the spring afternoon was warm and pleasant. For a while they hurried along in silence, each lost in thought. Rex's mind was troubled. At last he gathered his courage and apologized for the rude way he had spoken about Flavia. Although it was a ploy, he had insulted her honor and treated her like a harlot.

"No, it's okay," she said. "I knew it was either that or the Carcer. You were just trying to get us out of there." And with those words, Flavia did something surprising: she reached over and slipped her arm into Rex's as they walked.

"If I have to be somebody's wench, I might as well be yours," she said, looking up at him with a tentative smile.

Rex pursed his lips and gave a little shrug of agreement. "I'll take ya," he replied.

The two friends couldn't help but meet each other's gaze, which caused them to break into embarrassed laughter. Rex patted Flavia's forearm where it was entwined with his, and they both lapsed into a comfortable silence again.

It was near sunset by the time they reached the domus of the bishop. A doorkeeper escorted them into the atrium and gave them cold water from a jug. While they waited for their host, Rex examined the niche in the wall for the household gods. Instead of idols, the niche held some books; but since they were in Greek, he could make out only a few words. From the writings' theological nature, he guessed they were probably some of the Christian scriptures.

When Bishop Miltiades arrived, he greeted Flavia with a chaste kiss and bowed his head to Rex. Quickly, they explained their plight to him. The stately priest with oiled silver hair listened as if no one else in the world mattered. "We have some hidden rooms for situations like this," he told Flavia with a sly smile. "The catholic church bought this house in a time of persecution. We know how to hide our own if we need to."

"So you can take care of her until this is all sorted out?" Rex asked. "It won't be long. Pompeianus is about to be stopped."

"Are you so certain, my young friend?"

"I'm going to make it certain. Permanently."

Flavia put her hand on his arm. "Rex! What are you saying?"

He turned to meet her eyes. "Look, it's Pompeianus who's driving all this hostility against you! You'll never be safe until he's dead. It's either him or you! At least that's the way I see it."

"Murder is no solution, Brandulf Rex," said the bishop.

"But he would murder her in cold blood. He's already proven it by trying!"

"And do you aspire to be like Prefect Pompeianus—or something better?"

Rex had no answer to that, for he certainly did not want to be a filthy brute like the man who constantly pursued Flavia's life.

"That is not the kind of man I wish you to be," Flavia said gently.

"I know," Rex muttered. "You prefer gentle."

"Yes. Mighty like David, yet gentle and loving like the Son of David. Is that so hard?"

"Harder than you'd think, Flavia."

"Perhaps instead of killing," she replied, "we could ask God to protect us."

Miltiades took Flavia by the hand. "Yes, daughter. You have spoken wisely. Let us do that now, together, just as I often have prayed with your mother in this very room."

Folding his arms across his chest, Rex listened to the two Christians pray. They faced the compluvium in the roof, their heads tilted toward the evening sky, their eyes closed, their palms upraised. Though he did not disdain their faith, neither did he think their supplications would be effective. He kept putting his hand to his hip, feeling for the comfort of a sword hilt that wasn't there. Because he was off duty today, he had left his weapons at the fort.

When the prayers were finished, Rex committed Flavia to the bishop's care. She said goodbye to him at the door—rather awkwardly, he thought, since several deacons were standing nearby. Outside, the streets were busy with wagon traffic, for vehicles could be driven in the city only after sundown. As he made his way back to the New Camp, Rex dodged all the carters, petty thieves, drunks, and prostitutes that made up Rome's after-hours crew. Reaching his barracks block, he tumbled into his bunk and fell into a fitful sleep.

The next morning, Rex rinsed his face with water and combed through his hair, then he spent the morning polishing his armor and washing his best tunic. Upon joining the guard he had been given an allowance with which to purchase his own equipment—except for his spear and shield, which were standard issues. Since one's gear could make the difference between life and death, Rex had invested the full amount—plus some of his own funds—to obtain a high-quality kit. He had bought an old-style rounded helmet with neck and cheek guards, a long-sleeved chainmail tunic, a cavalry sword with an eagle's-head pommel, an undertunic and leather trousers, and a fine pair of army boots. Good boots, he had found, were an often overlooked necessity.

When Rex was dressed and ready, he left the fort by the main gate and headed to the adjacent Lateran Palace. The ancient building had first been given into the hands of Maxentius's sister, Fausta, but she was far away now and hadn't seen it in years. Since Maximian's execution, the emperor had assigned it to his favorite general, because Maxentius bitterly despised Fausta for betraying their father. It would be interesting to see what would happen to the mansion once Constantine arrived and captured the city. Fausta might even insist that she and her husband take up residence there. But until then, it was home to Rex's foremost enemy: his supposed commander, Ruricius Pompeianus.

A guard stopped him at the palace entrance, blocking his way with a spear. "What business?"

Rex showed the man a wax tablet with a clasp on it. "An important message from the tribune to the prefect," he said roughly, though the tablet was actually blank. "I was ordered to deliver it personally to our master in his private quarters."

"Wait here," the doorman said.

Rex stood in the palace atrium for a long time, his heart beating fast. *Can I really get away with this?* As a speculator, he had been trained in infiltration, assassinations, and poisons, though he had never actually carried out such a mission. Yet if he got the chance, all he needed to do was rely on his training. *Be ready for whatever opportunity presents itself. Don't think. Just react.*

When the sentry returned, he shook his head and waved Rex away. "You are not expected by anyone. Be off quickly, or I'll write you up."

"But the Praetorian prefect—"

"Is right behind you."

Rex spun and was shocked to discover who had spoken. Pompeianus stood there with a gruff expression. Behind him were the two tribunes of the Old and New Camps, along with a gaggle of other officers. All the men were wearing expensive ceremonial arms, clearly on their way to some important official function.

"What do you have for me, soldier?"

"A secret message. But it's one you should only read privately."

Pompeianus snatched the tablet. "I'll read it whenever I want." He lifted the clasp, flipped open the cover, and glanced at the blank wax, then he raised his eyes and glared at Rex. The scar on his cheek wrinkled as a scowl came to his face. "What is the meaning of this?"

"I . . . I don't know. I was told it was a message for you."

"Looks like you were told wrong."

Rex nodded.

"Listen, boy, I have no time for foolishness. As you're about to find out, things have just gotten serious. Draw your sword."

Rex immediately recoiled. Pompeianus slid his gilded weapon from its sheath. "I said, draw your sword!" he snarled.

If he comes at you, go for the head. This is your chance to kill him!

However, no sooner had Rex armed himself than he realized the prefect was only playing with him. He moved slowly through the standard swordsman's positions. One . . . two . . . three. Rex responded with the proper moves—briskly and efficiently. Parry and thrust. Parry and thrust. Parry and thrust. At last Pompeianus took a step back, his blade held wide and out of action.

"You're quick," he said. "You'll do nicely."

Thoroughly confused now, Rex could only respond by asking, "For what?"

"For our expedition." The prefect jerked his thumb toward the officers behind him. "When was the last time you saw all of us gathered in one place? We're about to make a big announcement to the troops. The augustus is sending us out."

"He . . . he isn't leading us himself?" *That's strange,* Rex mused. *Riding out with the troops was what emperors did. The very word* emperor *originally referred to a military commander.*

"Maxentius received a divine oracle commanding him to remain in Rome. He's sending me instead to lead the campaign. Or should I say, sending us. We can use a good swordsman like you on that mission. Tell your centurion I said to include you on the deployment list."

Rex frowned. Though this wasn't what he had expected when he came to the palace today, he was getting important intelligence and wanted to keep pressing with questions. "And what is our mission, sir?" he finally asked.

Pompeianus shoved his spatha back into its scabbard. With a flick of his head, he indicated to his entourage that it was time to keep moving. The party of officers began to head toward the door. "We're deploying to northern Italy at dawn tomorrow," the prefect declared, "and I'll be thrown to Hades before I let any false emperors get into my peninsula!"

"Keep that edge sharp, boy," the tribune of the New Camp called over his shoulder. "You're going to need it."

And with that stern admonition, the leaders of Rome's most ancient cohort left Rex alone with his thoughts in the atrium of Fausta's house.

———⟨∽∾∽⟩———

Constantine's troops made the trek to Lugdunum in three weeks and caught two days of rest while they waited for the supplies to arrive. Resuming the march, they continued south, then turned off toward the Alps. The men left Brigantium at dawn and traveled up a river valley with a gradual incline. By midmorning they were facing their first true challenge: the steep switchbacks that climbed up to Mons Matrona Pass. *If Hannibal and his elefanti could do it, so can I*, the emperor told himself.

Patchy snow clung to the shady places and north-facing slopes, but the road itself was clear. That was good, because a lot of men and horses would be using it today. The centurions had taken a census of the troops at Brigantium, and the numbers were fairly good. Forty thousand men were about to make their attempt at the pass, and a quarter of them were cavalry. Unlike in the age of Scipio and Hannibal, warfare these days wasn't won by infantry in massed formations. The age of the mounted warrior had dawned.

By the time the sun was declining, Constantine had topped out into the pass—a wide, flat place with grassy meadows just starting to emerge from winter's icy grip. A few tribunes and centurions waited for their commander on the Gaulish side of a milestone at the highest point of the highway. Constantine met them, then rode past the marker and dismounted. A tiny yellow flower poked up through the snow, which he plucked and took back to his officers.

"Look, men," he said, holding out the flower. "Spring has already come to Italy. By summer, the peninsula will be ours." The statement brought a patriotic cheer. Constantine glanced around at the Mons Matrona Pass. "Set up camp over there," he said. "We'll give man and beast one day of rest. After that, we descend to make war."

The day of departure brought a cold drizzle. Grumbling a little, the troops followed the long, narrow valley of the Duria River as it flowed down from the Cottian Alps toward the city of Augusta Taurinorum in the plains. Yet before Constantine's forces could attack that citadel, the fortified town of Segusio stood in the way. It would be the first true test of the Italian army's will to resist invasion. Maxentius would surely have garrisoned the town, though probably not too heavily. Because he didn't know which pass Constantine might use, much less the entry point Licinius might choose from the east, Maxentius had to spread his troops all across the northern Italian landscape.

"There's no way he can hold the whole Padus plain against two invaders,"

Vitruvius had declared. Constantine agreed with that military assessment, though he found his brother-in-law rather bold for trying.

Segusio, nestled in a lovely mountain vale, had closed its gates when Constantine's vanguard pulled up before the walls. A few brave souls were taunting the soldiers from the ramparts.

So they want to fight? Then let's give it to them.

"Shall I draw up the engineers and ballista men, sir?" Vitruvius asked.

"I think not. Array the whole army before the towers. Let's make a frontal assault with fire and ladders and see if we can break their spirit."

The strategy worked beautifully. Bundles of sticks and flammable oil were spread against the wooden gate while archers and slingers on the ground kept the defenders on either side occupied. Once the kindling was lit, the gate quickly caught fire and the defenders retreated. Ladder men swarmed the walls. Then suddenly the burning gates were pushed open from inside—a sign of capitulation.

"I'll lead a party of raiders," a junior tribune volunteered. "Let's strip this city of everything we can use for the march ahead. We'll need it."

"No!" Constantine's voice was stern, even angry. "This is an Italian city, and I am its rightful ruler! I am here not to oppress it but to free it from tyranny!"

"But it's aflame, sir. We just attacked it."

"Necessary at first. But now they have surrendered, so we will treat them as loyal subjects. Have our men help put out the fire, and prevent them from looting or raping. I am the rightful Augustus of the West, and these are my people."

Within hours, the people of Segusio, who had just been hurling threats and missiles at the besiegers, were cheering their arrival and hailing Constantine as lord and god. They brought out supplies of wheat, wine, and oil. Blankets and horse fodder were donated too. The city fathers even sent out doctors to tend the wounded soldiers, though there were relatively few since the attack had been brief. Yet while the acclaim felt good, Constantine did not linger in the pleasant valley. Taurinorum awaited.

The city of Augusta Taurinorum sat at the edge of the alpine foothills where the lively stream of the Duria Minor emerged onto the wide plain of the Padus River. This ancient Celtic settlement of the Taurini tribe had been conquered by Caesar Augustus and turned into a Roman colony. Today its towering walls made a nearly perfect square around the city, with the amphitheater being the only major structure outside. The strength of Taurinorum's fortifications and the manpower of its garrison meant victory here would be much more difficult than at Segusio. And it certainly wouldn't be decided by a siege, Constantine realized. It would come down to a pitched battle on the open field.

General Vitruvius could see it too. "I'll line up the cavalry three deep," he said as he sat astride his horse next to Constantine.

"The scouts are reporting they have the riders called 'oven men.' They're fully armored, along with their horses."

"With respect, Your Majesty, we have men like that too."

"Yes, but not nearly as many."

"Sir, let me tell you something about those oven men. The Persians love heavy infantry like that, and we Romans have picked it up from them. And it's true, those riders can be devastating in a straight-on charge. Every bit of them is covered in armor—their faces, their arms, their legs. Even their horses are helmeted and draped in scale. They look like bronze statues come to life! But those troops were nicknamed oven men for a reason. It's got to feel like they're fighting inside iron cookstoves—sweltering and exhausting. Every movement takes an effort to lift all that metal. After the first charge, they're nearly spent. And their horse armor means they can't wheel and turn with ease."

Constantine stroked his chin for a moment. Normally he was clean-shaven, but now he had a few days of stubble. "Let's put our heavy cavalry across from them," he said. "Lure them into a direct charge but let them break straight through. Then outflank them with light, fast skirmishers. Arm our men with shepherd's crooks and long hammers. Blades aren't effective against that armor, but you can swarm the riders from the sides and behind. You don't have to breach their armor, just smash it hard. Or hook them and pull them from the saddle. Once the oven men fall, the rest of the troops will be demoralized."

"It shall be done, my lord."

Though Constantine knew the tactics were sound, when he saw the size of the enemy army, he immediately called for his chaplain Ossius and asked him to say a prayer. The field scouts estimated fifty thousand fighters stood in opposition to Constantine's men. It was a fearsome array made all the more terrifying by their magical empowerment from demons.

"Remember the power of the one true God," Ossius urged the emperor when his prayer was done. "It is said in our scriptures that Jesus himself is a rider on a white horse. His robe is dipped in blood, and a sword of iron shoots from his mouth."

"I should like to see a warrior like that charging into battle ahead of my army," Constantine said wryly.

"He'll be there, Your Majesty, even if he can't be seen."

Ossius's bold prediction was proven true: the rider on a white horse must have been fighting for Constantine, because the battle was a total rout. It happened just like the emperor had planned. When the opposing oven men came thundering across the field in a pointed wedge like the tip of a spear, Constantine opened his ranks and let them charge through. Then the skirmishers galloped in from the sides, swinging their hammers at the enemies' heads and inflicting crushing blows on the horses even without piercing their armor. They dragged the oven men down with crooks until they were helpless and thrashing on the ground. Once un-horsed, destroying them took no more effort than squashing an overturned beetle underfoot. At the sight of this disaster, the rest of the enemy broke and ran—and praise be to God, the people of Taurinorum acknowledged their true emperor. They closed up the gates and gave no refuge to Max-entius's fleeing troops. The men were slaughtered before the walls while the citizens watched and cheered from the ramparts. When the bloodshed was complete, the city fathers welcomed Constantine inside as a liberator and hero.

But despite the great victory, the emperor allowed himself no time to rest. That night, as the field camp rang with the songs of his celebrating men, an aide arrived at the commander's tent to announce a visitor. "There's a centurion here who says you'll want to meet with him, sir."

"Can't you see I'm busy? I'm writing up terms of surrender for Medio-lanum. Once they hear about today, they're going to fold, no question."

"I know, sir. I'm sorry to be a bother. He insists on seeing you. He's a defector from the other side, but he knows all the right watchwords."

"Who is it?"

"He says his name is Aratus."

"Ah! My Roman spy! Send him right in."

Moments later, the tent flap opened again. The battle-hardened Greek speculator looked just as tough as the day he was commissioned. With him were the two Germanic spies, Rex and Geta, now shorn of their long barbarian locks. According to Aratus, the fourth man, Hierax, had been injured and could not complete the mission.

"What news of my enemy?" Constantine asked.

"Maxentius has remained in Rome and seems prepared to withstand a siege like he did twice before. The northern campaign is being waged by Ruricius Pompeianus. He's well entrenched in Verona and Aquileia, with a large body of troops in both places. He has some new Italian levies and the African legions, along with the Second Parthica, the Praetorians, and the Emperor's Personal Cavalry." Aratus pointed to his two protégés. "These men have won appointments into the imperial horse guard, so they have learned much about its tactics."

"Well done! That is important information. Some people say the old Batavi are weaklings nowadays, but I know better."

"They're good fighters, my lord," said the speculator named Rex, "but I know you can take them."

"We shall see," Constantine mused. "I suppose you've deserted from their ranks to come here?"

"It wasn't hard. When the Maxentian lines broke today, the three of us bolted for the woods. After we met up at a rendezvous point, we came straight to your camp and hailed the sentries with the passwords."

"Very good work, men." Constantine rose from his field chair and pulled an amphora from a cabinet. "Take this wine as an expression of my gratitude and go celebrate. Centurion Aratus, I'll want a full intelligence report from you within three days. Then stay near me at all times in case I need to consult you."

Aratus put his fist to his shoulder and bowed. "I'll have the report delivered to you in two days, sir! And what of Rex and Geta?"

Constantine approached the two men. Though still young—perhaps not even into their twenties yet—they were tall, handsome, and self-assured.

He put out his hand and gripped Rex's upper arm. The feel of it was not like flesh, but marble. Constantine was impressed.

"You know about the so-called oven men?" he asked.

Rex nodded right away. "Of course, Your Highness. Fully armored heavy riders. Their horses are clad in scale and chamfrons. They carry no shields. Their weapon is the two-handed lance. Devastating against infantry, and always disruptive against cavalry."

"Can you fight like that?"

Rex and Geta exchanged excited glances. "Definitely, sir," Rex replied, unable to suppress a smile.

"Good. I need some oven men of my own. Strip the dead of their armor and find suits that fit you both. You're back in the service of the true Augustus of the West."

"We never left it, my lord," Geta said with a bow.

"Are we headed straight to Rome?"

Constantine grinned at Rex's question. "One thing at a time, my eager young speculator. You have two tasks to accomplish beforehand."

"What are they, sir?" Rex asked.

"The first is to enjoy that amphora of wine. You earned it through some excellent Roman espionage."

"We will. And the second?"

Constantine turned and snatched a clay pitcher from a stand. He smashed it against the wooden edge in a spray of water and shards, then held up the broken handle before his three startled men.

"We're headed to Verona," he declared with a stern gaze, "and there we shall shatter the army of Ruricius Pompeianus."

—◦◦◦—

JUNE 312

With Segusio and Taurinorum defeated, Mediolanum capitulated just as Emperor Constantine had predicted. Though the negotiations took several weeks, the delay presented no strategic problem, for it gave the men ample time to rest and resupply. Yet Rex couldn't help but feel impatient, for he didn't need to relax. Unlike the rest of the army, he hadn't marched down from the German frontier, nor crossed the Alps, nor fought in any battles. As time wore on, he grew more anxious for some action.

Yet at least it wasn't all boring: he and Geta were occasionally sent on scouting forays toward Verona. A few times they encountered detachments of Pompeianus's troops from a distance, though they always managed to stay back and avoid capture. Now Rex believed he had a good feel for the terrain around that formidable city. It was locked up tight, and Pompeianus was lodged inside like a bear sleeping in his den.

Of course, the fact that Pompeianus was in Verona meant the pressure on Flavia in Rome would be eased. Was that an answer to her Christian prayers? Rex had to admit, it was remarkably coincidental. The same day that she and Bishop Miltiades prayed for relief from Pompeianus, Emperor Maxentius received some kind of divine omen telling him to stay put in the city. Therefore he decided to send his favorite general to defend northern Italy from invasion. For the time being, Flavia was safe from Pompeianus's murderous intent, since the prefect had his hands full preparing Verona for a siege. Maybe Jesus was a more powerful god than Rex first thought.

It was the Ides of June when the army finally moved out from Mediolanum. They took the Gallican Highway to Brixia, where they ran into a cavalry contingent that quickly fled at the first charge. Rex was somewhat disappointed not to see action in that engagement. Though Constantine was grateful for the advance warning about the nearby troops, Rex had wanted to do battle against an enemy. But for now, all they would do was run away.

The city of Verona lay at the end of the Gallican Highway where it joined the Postumian Way. It was strategically located in a large bend of the Athesis River, so only its western side could be approached by land. Constantine drew up his army there, effectively sealing off this western entry point. In every other direction, however, the swift, rocky, and deep Athesis protected the city from invasion.

A bridge carried the Postumian Way across the river toward the east, and beside it was a second span of white stone called the Marble Bridge. The twin bridges were guarded by a strong surrounding wall at their far ends, as well as a natural hill at that spot. Until Constantine had total control of

Verona, the eastern side of the river and all its connecting roads belonged to Pompeianus. That meant resupply of the city and armed reinforcements could easily come from that direction. The first order of business, then, was to traverse the Athesis and set an army across those eastern roads, creating a complete encirclement—but the only nearby bridges were the two inside the city's fortifications. Another crossing point would have to be found for the troops.

While the regulars helped the engineers set up the siegeworks, Aratus gathered a squad of scouts in a tent at the edge of camp. A map on the table displayed the full length of the Athesis. "I want those of you going downstream to be on the lookout for a pair of matching docks," he said. "If the locals have a good spot for a ferry, we might be able to get an army across on rafts." He turned to Rex and Geta. "You two take your men upstream into the mountains. The river might narrow or get shallow for a time. I doubt there's a ford we can wade, but our boys can swim their horses across if the flow isn't too swift for too long."

The next morning, a party of ten scouts with Geta in the lead followed the Athesis upstream into a long, narrow valley with mountains on either side. The main highway between Verona and the Alps, the Via Claudia Augusta, was visible on the far bank—tantalizingly close, if only a decent crossing could be found.

"What about that gravel spit up there?" Rex asked as he reined up next to Geta. "It sticks halfway into the river. We'd only be submerged a few moments."

"There are rapids beside it. They would be tough to negotiate."

"Yeah, but look closely. Those rapids are mostly caused by that one boulder and all the brush that's snagged against it."

"You think we could clear it?"

"We should at least try."

In short order, the men roped their horses to the larger logs that had created the snag. It only took a few pulls to make a big difference. Then, once the branches were cleared, the horses dislodged the boulder with a tree-trunk pry bar, enough to sink it. The whitewater at the surface immediately dissipated.

"You think it's swimmable now?" Geta asked.

Rex grinned. "Let's find out."

The two men prompted their horses into the swift Athesis. Their strong Celtic ponies walked into the current as far as they could. As soon as their hooves left the bottom, Rex and Geta slid into the water on the upstream side. They clung to the mane with one hand and guided their mounts with the other. Once the horses touched the gravel bottom again, the riders were back astride. They came up out of the Athesis like fierce hippocampi, secure in the saddle and ready for war.

Geta whooped as he emerged onto the far bank. "I'm ready to take on Pompeianus myself!" he exclaimed.

Rex pointed south on the wide, smooth surface of the Via Claudia Augusta. "Good, because he's just a few miles that way. But first let's go back and give our emperor the news. He probably ought to send a few more troops with us before we take on Verona."

Over the next week, twenty thousand soldiers forded the stream, each carrying enough supplies and rations to sustain him for a month. The troops proceeded down the highway and promptly encircled the twin bridgeheads that lay behind Verona's walls. Now the city was invested on all sides.

With this development, the two armies fell into a pattern of watching and waiting. Not even taunts were exchanged, much less arrows or stones—just a kind of dreadful silence and brooding anticipation.

Then, three days before the Kalends of July, around sunset, the eastern gate burst open and a sortie exploded onto the Postumian Way. The besiegers were caught unaware as they cooked their evening meal. The clash was brief, consisting mostly of javelins and arrows rather than swords or lances. Since the Constantinian forces were clustered so densely around the gate, the attackers were forced back inside by the hail of missiles. But just when the sortie seemed to be rebuffed, a smaller group made another attempt under heavy cover from archers on the walls. Rex killed one of them, but in return he caught an arrow in his chainmail sleeve that left a gash on his left bicep. Unfortunately, most of the sally got away in the chaos.

"No matter," Geta said after things had settled again. "It was what? A hundred? That's a hundred fewer to defend the walls."

"Our guys are saying that Pompeianus was among those who broke through."

"Hmm. That's not good. If he returns with the legions from Aquileia, we'll have to abandon the siege on this side of the river to face them."

Rex puffed his cheeks and blew out a breath. "I hope not," he muttered with a little shake of his head. "The garrison would empty from Verona too, and we'd be under attack before and behind."

"Yeah. Squeezed like a pair of pliers. Certain death."

"Nothing is certain in war."

Another week of boredom passed. The men ate their porridge and kept watch on Verona's silent walls. But at dawn on the eighth day after the breakout, a scout galloped into the eastern camp with urgent news. He rode straight to the emperor's tent, and within an hour everyone was preparing for battle. Pompeianus was approaching across the Venetian plains at the head of a mighty column. It was rumored to be thirty thousand strong. The Aquileian legions had been summoned to break the siege of Verona.

By late afternoon, the rumble of countless hooves could be heard reverberating through the earth itself. Rex and Geta had donned the oven-man armor they had scavenged at Taurinorum. In addition to his chainmail shirt, Rex's arms and legs were now protected with overlapping bands of iron that flexed as he moved. Even his warhorse, a gray Andalusian stallion, wore armor: a coat of scale hung below its abdomen, and a bronze chamfron left only its eyes and nostrils exposed. Rex could see how such an array would give the heavy cavalry a feeling of invincibility.

The only thing he was unsure about was his helmet. He had chosen one that covered his face with a steel plate adorned with a scary expression. All the oven men similarly armored themselves from head to toe, for it was part of their strategy to charge into a hail of missiles without concern. But Rex was unaccustomed to wearing a helmet that gave him sight through two small eyeholes and breath only through the faceplate's downturned scowl. It felt limiting and constrictive. And he quickly discovered that the nickname for such troopers was exactly right: it really was as hot as an oven inside this thing. Nevertheless, if Constantine wanted Rex to be an oven man, that is exactly what he would be.

Pompeianus arrayed his soldiers on the far side of a grassy meadow east of Verona. A sunset glow cast a red sheen across a battlefield that was about to grow even redder with the blood of fallen men. As General Vitruvius formed up his own lines, he put Rex and the other oven men in the center. Unfortunately, Rex could see right away that the enemy's front was longer. Constantine must have seen it too, for he rode up to Vitruvius, accompanied by the standard bearer who carried the labarum. "Stretch us out so they don't outflank us," he ordered. "We'll have to sacrifice depth for length."

"We could lift the siege and use those troops to lengthen the line," Vitruvius suggested.

"No! That would leave us vulnerable to a rear attack from the city. We've got to divide our forces. I understand it thins us out, but I believe even one rank of our brave men can turn back a charge."

"It's hard for a single line to withstand a direct assault by heavy cavalry," Vitruvius observed. "The textbooks consider that foolhardy."

"Our boys can do it! They're rested and well fed. The enemy has been on quick march for several days. It's late in the day now, so no doubt they're tired and thirsty. And the sun will be in their eyes. If we engage them tonight, our lines will hold no matter how thin they may be. This is the day we break Pompeianus."

"Are you sure, Your Majesty?"

Constantine pointed to the labarum fluttering in the breeze above him. "Yes. The Rider on a White Horse goes before us. Prepare your men."

Vitruvius saluted, then turned and gave the order to redeploy into a single line with the oven men still in the center. Rex tightened his helmet with the faceplate, wishing the armorer had designed it with bigger eyeholes and a wider scowl. But nothing could be done about that now. It was time to fight or die. He reached out and knocked his lance against Geta's. "Brothers always," he said.

"To the death!" came the muffled reply, then the cavalry started to move.

The troopers trotted across the meadow at first, but when they reached the quarter mark, the oven men rose to a canter, and the ends of the line sped up to stay in formation. From across the field, the enemy battle cry was now a monstrous roar, echoed by the angry shouts from the long, thin line of Constantinian riders. The high-pitched whistle of flying slingstones added their deadly whine to the din. Arrows sliced the air alongside the stones, and even a few javelins arced across the field. But the body armor did its job, and the cavalry moved up to a gallop.

Hooves pounded the earth and churned up clods of dirt. The low sun at Rex's back bronzed the faces of the oncoming troops. He could see them now, snarling and gnashing in their furious bloodlust. And then, like two wolves leaping at each other's throats, the lines engaged.

The colossal impact nearly knocked Rex from his horse. The sound of it was like a thousand blacksmiths hammering their anvils at once. Only by squeezing his thighs in a fierce grip against the flanks of his mount did he keep his place in the saddle.

Yet as the cavalry surged ahead, Rex found that his two-handed lance, impelled by the speed of his charge and the sheer weight of horse and iron, couldn't be stopped by the pitiful armor of his foes. He was mighty, invincible—a god! Not by human hands did he fight, but by the divine strength of Hercules Victorious. The Constantinian line ripped into the three-deep enemy front and came hurtling out the other side. Rex's spear had impaled two men at once. He cast it aside with its skewered corpses and drew his spatha as footmen ran to engage him.

The maelstrom where the two armies clashed now became a monstrous snake pit of roiling, writhing, death-dealing fiends. Here the real world disappeared; only violence existed. Every sound faded but the clang of murderous arms and the screams of anguished souls leaving the body. Rex hacked and chopped at the men who attacked him right and left. Their blades glanced off his plated legs, and in return he shoved his steel down their throats. When enemies rose up in front, he spurred ahead and mowed them down under the sharp hooves of his Andalusian steed. Many soldiers fell beneath his onslaught.

A trumpet call rang out across the battlefield, the signal to rally at the imperial standard. Rex had managed to break free from the melee, so he was able to wheel his horse toward the banner. At first he couldn't believe what he saw; yet there it was, unmistakable even in the twilight. Constantine had entered the fight, resplendent in his golden armor as he fought beneath the labarum. And a horde of enemy troops was converging upon him.

Somehow Rex's exhausted horse found the strength to gallop toward the emperor. All the cavalrymen were hurrying to protect their lord. Yet the enemy was growing thick around him too, attracted like moths to a torch. A hail of leaden darts rained down on Constantine's defenders as the

Maxentians sought to end the battle by slaying the opposing commander. He was no doubt a great warrior. Even so, it was a foolish choice on Constantine's part to join the fray; for without his charismatic personality and confident leadership, his troops would be utterly demoralized.

Rex reined up near the labarum, sword in hand, just as Geta arrived too. Though Geta's helmet also had a full faceplate, he was instantly recognizable because his plumage was a yellow horsetail like the braid he used to wear. His armor was dented and his sword bloody, but he seemed uninjured.

"Behind you!" he screamed, and Rex whirled just in time to deflect an attack from a footman's club. Before the soldier could bring his weapon into action again, Rex dispatched him with a backhanded slice across his unprotected throat. A fountain of blood sprayed up, then the man disappeared into the mud.

Yet for every opponent killed, it seemed that two more arrived. The larger army of the Maxentians was beginning to exert its will. Now Constantine's defenders had to pull back, pressed hard by their foes. One by one, the emperor's troops went down into Pluto's shadowy realm. "Victory!" the enemy began to cry, sensing conquest within their grasp. If Constantine fell, the battle would be over.

At that moment, a new force exploded into the fight, a mounted warrior with a scorpion on his shield and a glittering breastplate of gold. Rex knew that armor well. *Pompeianus!*

The prefect and his bodyguards forced their way into the whirlpool of death that swirled around the labarum. After trampling several of the emperor's defenders, Pompeianus turned hard and charged at Constantine from behind, his oaken lance trained upon his enemy.

Though Rex spurred his horse to intercept him, the crush of infantry prevented the speed he needed. Instead of blocking Pompeianus's advance, Rex was only able to come alongside him at an angle. His warhorse knocked all attackers aside, striving to catch up. Yet the prefect was still a few steps ahead, and his path to the emperor was clear. He held his lance low, its razor-sharp blade aimed at the small of Constantine's back. Pompeianus was about to run him through.

"Jesus Christ, save him!" Rex screamed as he watched the hope of victory collapse.

357

A gap appeared among the footmen. Rex dug his heels into his horse's flanks, and the noble Andalusian responded, surging ahead in its final act of bravery. Somehow it summoned the speed to close the distance to Pompeianus. Sword in the air, Rex leaned forward in the saddle, hanging alongside his mount's thrusting, pumping neck as it gave its life on the field of war.

The two enemies converged. The prefect's eyes were transfixed on Constantine, lusting for impalement.

Rex's blood-drenched blade swept down from on high.

And his mighty blow severed the hand of Ruricius Pompeianus.

—◦◦◦—

JULY 312

It was dark now, and strangely quiet. Constantine tried to make sense of the sudden change. *How could things have calmed so quickly?* One moment, there was the ear-splitting clamor of mortal combat. It rose to a crescendo of screams and shouts. Then it melted away. The enemy trumpets had called for a retreat. Now the only sounds were the wails of fleeing warriors being run down by the victorious horsemen.

"Your Majesty! Where are you?" cried an urgent voice.

"Over here," Constantine shouted back, waving his arm because he was unable to stand. The weight of too many corpses pressed him down.

Vitruvius ran to the pile of dead soldiers and began rolling them aside.

"Careful!" Constantine warned him. "Those are the bodies of the honored dead!"

When at last the emperor was freed from the tangled mass, Vitruvius helped him stand. For several moments Constantine panted to regain his breath. He wiped a glob of mud from his eye and flicked it away.

"Are you hurt, sire?" the general asked.

"It seems not," Constantine replied as he examined his torso in the pale moonlight. "And that is only because of these great warriors." He gestured toward the slain legionaries—men with severed arms and crushed skulls and arrows protruding from their chests. Even in the darkness, Constantine could see the glossy black blood smeared across their contorted faces. He saluted to one of the corpses, acknowledging the man's courage even in death.

"You should not have rushed into battle, my lord!"

"Nonsense, Vitruvius. It is an honor to fight with soldiers like these. They surrounded me and fought to the last drop of their blood . . . all but one."

"What happened?"

"I ordered my men to stand and defend the labarum. You should have seen them, Vitruvius! They were worthy of the great days of glorious Rome! Caesar himself would have been proud to fight alongside such men against a host of Celts. But one of them—*a traitor!*"

"What did he do?"

"After he attacked Pompeianus and injured him, the fighting grew fierce around us. Death drew very near. Then this coward grabbed a horse and fled like the accursed son of a gutter wench. I want that man found and brought before me! I will administer his capital punishment with my own hand."

"Did you get a good look at him?"

"He was helmeted, and it was dark. I could not see his face."

Vitruvius grimaced. "If we ever find him, sir, I will sharpen the headsman's sword myself. Rome has no need of soldiers who flee in battle and fail to defend their lord and god."

Constantine glanced around the churned-up turf, then spotted what he wanted. Picking his way through the bodies, he stooped and withdrew the labarum from the mud. Although the standard bearer lay dead on the holy ground, the flag itself was intact and untorn.

"I am no lord and god," Constantine declared. "Can you not see what happened today? Those titles are reserved for Jesus of Nazareth."

—◈◈◈—

Rex was awake and on the Via Claudia Augusta at dawn—the last sunrise Pompeianus would ever see. He had saddled up by the light of the morning star after leading his horse to the river to drink, then giving it a cup of barley. The animal, although nowhere near as fine as the Andalusian, was, nonetheless, a good scout's pony whose master must have met an untimely end. From the gear strapped to the saddle, Rex thought the horse was probably from one of the Maxentian legions, though it was hard to tell because soldiers tended to amass their own kit wherever they could get it. Standardization in the Roman army was a thing of the past.

After an hour of lonely riding, the clip-clop of hooves from behind signaled the approach of a rider at speed. Rex turned into a thicket to let the man pass. He was surprised to discover it was Geta.

"I'm glad I caught up to you!" Geta exclaimed after Rex hailed him. "I thought you'd be farther ahead."

"I would be, but I'm watching for side trails that Pompeianus might have used. So far, he hasn't turned off. It helps that I only have to look on the right. He's in no shape to swim the river." Rex jerked his thumb toward the Athesis, which ran parallel to the road on the left. Suddenly he craned his neck and looked a little closer at Geta. "That's a big dent you have there, my friend."

Geta put his hand to the back of his head. Like Rex, he had shed his oven-man armor on his arms and legs, but he was still wearing the excellent helmet, though without the faceplate pulled down. "Yeah, I'm probably alive only because this thing is as hard as an anvil," he said.

"What happened to you after we got separated? Last I saw, you were mowing down legionaries like winter wheat."

"I wish that were how it ended. But I think we lost."

Rex grimaced and uttered a curse. "Tell me everything."

"I watched you take out Pompeianus. That was a fine piece of horsemanship, brother! You stopped that spear just before it pierced Constantine's spine. Somehow Pompeianus stayed in the saddle even with the loss of his hand. I wanted to follow and help you chase him down, but when the Divine Augustus ordered us to stand, I couldn't leave his side. It was our . . . you know . . ." Geta's words trailed off.

"Duty?" Rex finished.

Staring at the ground, Geta inhaled through his nose, then let out the breath. Finally, he glanced up. "Yeah, Rex. Our duty."

"So keep going. What happened next?"

"I killed two men near the stream beside the flag, but someone got me from behind with a club. This thick iron kettle"—he rapped his helmet—"saved my life. I tumbled into some brush, and when I came to, it was quiet and dark. I couldn't tell if we had won or lost. Everything was unclear and chaotic. A riderless horse passed me, so I grabbed it and decided to follow you up the Via Claudia Augusta. These mountains are Pompeianus's only hope of escape, so I knew you'd both be here. After two hours under the moonlight, I got down and slept a little, then remounted at daybreak and kept riding until I spotted you."

"What about the augustus?"

Geta shook his head sadly. "The Second Parthica was pressing us close. Those boys know how to fight. And they had the numbers on us. So many arrows! I don't think Constantine could have survived."

"All the more reason we must kill Pompeianus."

"Why do you say that?"

"Because who else is going to stop him from going after Flavia if not Constantine?"

"Rex! That's not what this war is about! Don't you see? If Constantine is dead, it's over!"

"Until I know for sure, I'm going to stay on mission. And that means killing the Praetorian prefect."

"Since when is that our mission?"

"It's my mission!" Rex spat. "Are you in or not?"

Though Geta grunted in exasperation, he still collected the reins and rode up next to Rex. "'Brothers always' means *always*, I suppose."

"Right! 'To the death.' But today, it won't be ours. Let's go."

The Athesis valley ran due north, with the river alongside the road the whole way. Rex and Geta soon reached the churned-up area where they had cleared the ford that allowed Constantine's troops to swim across and reach Verona's eastern side. Although Pompeianus might have tried to cross here, hiding his tracks in the remains of all the others, to do so would have put him back into enemy territory. *No*, Rex decided, *that's too risky. A wounded animal always crawls back to its den. He's heading north to Tridentum. From there he'll take the road to his base at Aquileia. It's all he has left.*

Shortly after noon, however, the arrival of an army scout altered Rex's theory. The man was riding down from Raetia and had just passed through Tridentum. "My lord Licinius is on his way to Italy," he declared, "and his forces are moving along every available road."

"How soon will he be here?" Geta asked eagerly, but the scout would divulge no more information.

Rex and Geta now realized that Pompeianus would be forced to turn west, following the only branch out of the valley between Verona and Tridentum. Since the prefect surely knew he was being followed, he had to keep moving ahead; yet the last thing he'd want would be to run into Licinius's oncoming troops. The western turnoff would therefore be his only escape route from the Athesis valley, and he would no doubt take it. The ferryman at the road junction confirmed this hypothesis when, in exchange for an excellent dagger, he stated that he had rafted an injured Roman officer and his manservant across the river earlier that day. After crossing on the same raft, Rex and Geta led their horses onto the western bank of the Athesis and thanked the ferryman before hurrying on.

The western turnoff rose to a low pass and descended to the shores of beautiful Lake Benacus. The oblong body of water was nestled in the embrace of the steep Alps. A fishing village lay on the lake's still, aquamarine waters—a charming little settlement with snug cottages and a few sailboats in the harbor. Rex hailed one of the sailors at the pier.

"You have a doctor in town?" he asked.

"We're too small for that," the man replied. "A witch woman does our healing. That's her house there."

As Rex had surmised, the healer confessed she had treated Pompeianus only two hours ago. "He was pale and in a lot of pain," she said. "There wasn't much I could do. That stump of his needs cautery, not my herbs. Maybe an amputation at the elbow. He's running out of time."

"Where did he go?" Geta pressed.

"Paid a fisherman to sail him to the other end of the lake. To Sirmio, I believe."

Rex and Geta glanced at each other, obviously thinking the same thing. At Sirmio, the lake was pierced by a thin peninsula, the tip of which was adorned with a lavish villa. Some people said it once belonged to the famous poet Catullus. Any house as luxurious as that, with so large a crew of slaves, was bound to have a doctor on staff.

"Does anyone else in town have a boat for hire?" Rex asked the healer.

"Just ask at the pier. Any of 'em will take you. We're always short on money."

The sun was about to dip behind the mountains when the fisherman dropped Rex and Geta at a lonely spot half a mile from the Sirmio villa.

Having left their horses back at the village, they proceeded on foot through the thick undergrowth. Approaching the tip of the peninsula, they found the villa to be more imposing than they had imagined. The whole thing was raised on a gleaming white terrace, which rested on tall stone arches. The situation offered splendid views from the terrace deck, but it provided no easy way inside from ground level.

Yet as the two warriors drew closer, they quickly realized the villa was abandoned. No one stirred in its long colonnades, and the landscaping around the place had become overgrown and brushy. Some of the villa's red roof tiles were missing. A doctor wouldn't be found here after all. Rex was about to leave in disgust when Geta knelt and picked up a scrap of linen bandage stained red with fresh blood.

Rex drew his sword and closed his faceplate. "He's here. He's ours now."

The main door was unlocked, so the soldiers entered and crossed an audience hall into the courtyard at the villa's heart. They found no one there, so they continued to the deck out back. The wind stirred the shreds of what used to be a yellow awning. Beneath it, Ruricius Pompeianus sat in a chair, alone and unarmed, gazing at the whitecaps that ruffled the surface of the lake. His back was to the soldiers.

"So you have found me at last," he said without turning around. His voice was noticeably weak.

"It is time to pay for your crimes," Rex declared, though he did not yet approach.

"Perhaps one man's crime is another man's law?"

"You bent the laws to your own advantage! Sentenced the innocent to death! That can only be a crime."

"Come arrest me, then. I surrender to you and cast myself on Constantine's mercy."

"Constantine is dead," Geta said.

Pompeianus flinched at the news. For a long moment, the deck was silent. At last he whispered, "It matters not. I surrender to whichever augustus claims this land. Under the laws of Rome and the rules of military engagement, I turn myself over to the judicial process."

Rex and Geta now circled around to face the prefect. He gazed back at them—pale, unshaven, sweaty, and disheveled. His stump of a wrist lay in his lap, wrapped in dirty linen. The pain caused him to clench his jaw in a constant grimace. He was a pitiful sight.

"As you can see, gentlemen, I need a doctor." Pompeianus's words were gravelly and thin. "If you will take me to your camp, I can receive medical care. Though I am weak, I assure you, I can stay with you until we reach the nearest encampment."

But Rex had a different idea. He placed the tip of his sword at the base of Pompeianus's throat where his two collarbones met.

Pompeianus stared up at him. "You would kill me, in violation of your honor as a soldier of Rome?"

"You think I should let you go?" Rex snarled. "To twist your laws and your courts, and pay your bribes, and then in one year be exactly where you were before? I think not."

"You have no other choice if you claim to be a just man." Pompeianus held up his oozing, crusty stump. "I am no threat to you. I have surrendered on the field of war. It is your duty to arrest me and take me to your commander—whoever that may be at the moment."

With his left hand, Rex opened his faceplate. Pompeianus's eyes widened in recognition. "You! I met you at my palace! You're a good warrior, son. You have a bright future. Why are you threatening me?"

"I am not what you think, Pompeianus."

"No? Then what are you?"

"A killer," Rex replied, then plunged his blade into the Praetorian prefect of Rome.

ACT 3

ACQUIESCENCE

12

The Hall of the Church was crowded tonight for the all-night prayer vigil before the feast day of Saint Cyprian. The building was lit by many lamps, making its interior warmer and stuffier than usual. Flavia reached inside her veil and wiped sweat from her brow, then fanned the fabric to create a small breeze. *Make me worthy of holy Cyprian*, she prayed, aware that her minor discomfort had ancient precedent.

A lector had just read Cyprian's biography. The story described how the African bishop had been worked up to a sweat as he was marched through the streets of Carthago on the way to his execution. The martyr had been offered a change of clothes by a Christian officer who observed his need.

Now, of course, no one was offering Flavia any garments besides the plain woolen tunic and linen veil that all the sisters wore. But she didn't mind. In recent weeks, she had come to feel at home among the young women who had devoted their lives to God. It was an honor to kneel beside the nuns and participate in their liturgy. A sweaty forehead was a small price to pay for the privilege.

When the second watch of the night arrived, the sisters finally left the hall. Some of the monastic brothers remained to spend the night praying and chanting psalms. However, since it wasn't right for women to pass an entire night under the same roof as men—even in the holy occupation of prayer—a few of the more robust monks escorted the sisters to their private house nearby. Though the streets of Rome weren't safe at night, especially in Trans Tiberim, such a large group, which included several strong men, probably wouldn't be bothered.

The Christians walked in silence and passed no one on the streets. Once the nuns had reached their house and were safely inside, Flavia turned toward the bishop's home, a mere three blocks away.

"Do you need a guardian, sister?" a monk asked.

"No, my destination is close. Thank you for your kindness."

Flavia bowed politely, then hurried to leave, for she wanted as few people as possible to know she was staying in the secret room at Miltiades's house. Aside from any scandal it might cause, one never knew who might be an informant. The point of staying there was to hide from the government's prying eyes. Rumors that Maxentius's army had been routed at Verona had recently reached the capital, so any whiff of treason was being treated with swift reprisals from the agitated emperor. Flavia had no desire to be thrown into the Carcer again. *Don't forget, you're still under a death sentence*, she often reminded herself when she was out in the streets.

Miltiades's house was in sight, its front lamp ablaze in anticipation of her return, when Flavia spotted a squad of four Praetorians loitering across the street. She halted. There wasn't a good reason for them to be there. Another more private door gave access to the home, so Flavia turned down an alley to reach it—then immediately regretted her action. A man stepped from the shadows behind her and began to close the distance.

His boots were hobnailed. And he was in chainmail. A soldier.

Picking up her pace, Flavia moved briskly toward the secret entrance into the bishop's domus. Unfortunately, the soldier was even faster. He caught up to her from behind.

"Leave me alone," Flavia warned as the man drew near. "I have friends nearby, and I'll scream."

"Don't scream," the soldier said. "It's me."

Flavia knew that voice. "Rex!" she exclaimed, dashing to meet him. He beamed back at her.

"Sorry for the scare," he said. "I had to get close. I didn't want to speak your name out loud."

"That's alright. I'm just so glad it's you!" Flavia started to throw her arms around his neck but checked herself. What might have been appropriate for a slave girl in Gelotiana House seemed less fitting for a Christian nun in a veil. She pointed to the cloth over her face. "Maybe I shouldn't . . . you know . . ."

"Oh, right. Of course not." Rex held up his hands in a compliant gesture. "I understand. The sisters would disapprove." A warm smile spread across his face again. "But it's great to see you, even from a distance. I really mean it! I missed you *so much*."

As Rex spoke, Flavia caught the tone that sometimes emerged in his voice—an intensity of feeling that lay under his words. She sensed their reunion was as meaningful to him as it was to her. Of course, Rex was returning from war, so there was no telling what he had just experienced. Many things might make him glad to be back in Rome. Clearly, he was moved right now, but by what emotion? Relief? Friendship? Gratitude? Maybe . . . love? It was hard to say. Perhaps Rex himself didn't even know.

Probably not love, Flavia decided.

Even so, she looked him straight in the eyes to signal that whatever the affection was, it was mutual. "I prayed for you every day, Rex. Prayed for your victory over"—she glanced around and leaned close—"Maxentius," she whispered with a sly smile. "And I often prayed for your safe return. Now here you are! We must thank God for it."

"Your God was definitely watching over me," Rex agreed. "Things got a little dangerous at Verona." He paused for a moment, thinking, then changed the subject. "I was hoping maybe we could talk for a bit. I know it's late, but I don't want to separate yet. You want to go for a walk?"

"After dark?"

"You'll be safe with me."

"Yeah," Flavia said with a grateful nod. "Of that I'm quite sure." She took the risk of giving Rex's arm a soft pat to say thank you.

"So you'll go?" he asked.

"Sure. Where to?"

"Just stay beside me, and I'll show you. I think you'll like it."

The pair made their way across the Trans Tiberim neighborhood in the direction of the river. Just as Flavia had observed at the bishop's house, an unusually large number of soldiers seemed to be lurking about. When her father had served as city prefect, he was in charge of the Watchman

Cohorts, the guardians who put out fires by day and policed Rome at night. Though another man commanded those troops now, the sight of soldiers patrolling the dark city wasn't anything strange. Tonight, however, it wasn't the normal watchmen who were on the streets, but Praetorians. Rex had noticed it too, making a point of avoiding them.

"The city is in turmoil," Flavia told him. "Maxentius imposed a tax in gold on all the aristocrats and businessmen for the city's defenses. He's digging a new ditch and strengthening the walls, but everyone still resents the tax. And there's a terrible food shortage. Prices have gone way up, and the bread supply has been cut to almost nothing."

"The grain is being diverted to feed the army," Rex said. "And the supply never really got going again after the rebellion in Africa, so we were already short."

"People are angry and upset, from beggars all the way up to the Senate. They blame the emperor. Just yesterday, some men in this neighborhood rioted. They made a straw figure of Maxentius and set it on fire. One brave soldier from Moesia tried to stop it. He went up and doused the flames with a bucket."

"How did the crowd take it?"

"The rioters killed him."

Rex's head swung around. "The people *murdered* a Praetorian in broad daylight?"

"It's awful, I know."

"It's more than awful. It's the kind of thing that doesn't go unpunished by a nervous emperor. Letting people kill Praetorians without consequences is what leads to a coup. The mob starts to get too confident." Rex glanced around, then took Flavia by the hand. "Come on, let's get out of here. I think I know why so many soldiers are around tonight. Retaliation is on the way."

Rex led Flavia toward the Bridge of Probus, though at several points he had to turn aside because the number of soldiers was growing. They emerged from inconspicuous buildings or were dropped off by covered wagons. Unlit torches were in their hands, and they all wore armor and helmets.

"Stay close," Rex whispered. "It's about to start."

A trumpet blast ripped through the night. One by one, the torches blazed into life as the men passed the flames to each other. Swords drawn, they began to move through the streets, kicking down the doors to the apartment buildings and setting smoky fires to drive people out. Angry commands, squeals of fear, and the wails of the grieving filled the streets as the massacre began.

Though Rex carried a sword and wore armor, he didn't have on the distinctive garb of a Praetorian. Several soldiers ran up to him, their blades bloody from the slaughter. "Back off, friends!" Rex barked, thrusting out the heel of his hand. "Imperial horse guardsman! This is my woman, and we're not part of your operation!" Grunting, the men headed off in another direction to fulfill Maxentius's lust for vengeance.

After leaving Trans Tiberim by the Bridge of Probus, things quieted down, though the shouts and tumult could still be heard in the distance. A memory flashed through Flavia's mind: she and the "Christian boy" Magnus had escaped a pursuer across this bridge about a year ago. *Rex is more my type of escort*, Flavia thought, then immediately realized that in the most important way, the statement wasn't true. The recognition made her sad.

The night air became cooler and more pleasant as Rex and Flavia ascended the Aventine Hill. Though Flavia longed to glimpse her home, even if just from the outside, Rex had other plans. He took her instead to the Temple of Ceres, located on the brow of the hill with a stunning view of the city.

"It's so lovely!" Flavia exclaimed, gazing across the moonlit cityscape. Below her was the full width of the Circus Maximus, and just beyond it, she could see the top floor of Gelotiana House. Above that rose the Palatine Hill, crowned by the massive imperial palace. The marble façade of Maxentius's brand-new baths glowed white in the light of the moon.

The couple sat down on the temple steps and remained silent for a long time, simply enjoying each other's company in a tranquil setting—something Flavia had experienced all too rarely in her time with Rex. Eventually they began to discuss their respective activities since they had parted ways at the beginning of the summer. Flavia explained that since the day her secret identity was uncovered, she had been living in peaceful retreat at the bishop's house. Only on rare occasions did she leave it to join the Christian sisters in their ministry to poor widows and orphans. Although such behavior was incomprehensible to most Roman citizens, Flavia had come to hold the girls' lifestyle in high esteem.

For his part, Rex had experienced just the opposite. The first battle at

Taurinorum had turned into a slaughter of Maxentius's forces. In the chaos of that moment, Rex, Geta, and Aratus had reestablished contact with Constantine and fought for a while on his side. But when it was time to go back undercover in Rome, they joined up with some ragtag Maxentian legions retreating down the peninsula toward the capital. The spies' cover story was that they barely escaped the massacre at Taurinorum and had to make their way across the countryside on foot, sleeping in barns and stealing food to survive. In reality, they had been fighting against the very legions they were now joining, though no one would have believed such a preposterous idea.

"That's the double life of the speculator," Rex said with a grin.

"It's so scary, what you do." Flavia shuddered a little as she spoke. "You face so many dangers. I thought about you every day while you were gone." She glanced over at him quickly. "Thought about your safety," she clarified. "In my prayers, like I said."

"Well, thank you for that. I suppose I can use all the divine help I can get. Actually, I've come to realize Jesus is more powerful than I thought at first."

"Really?" The statement was intriguing to Flavia, for it was something she had never heard Rex admit. *God, help him see your truth!* "What makes you say so?" she asked in a casual tone.

"At the siege of Verona, I wore the Christian amulet around my neck. And then at a crucial moment of the battle, I invoked the name of Jesus. I don't know why. The words just burst out of my mouth. But your Christ helped me even though I'm not baptized. I defeated my enemy, and I could feel the help of a god as I did it."

"Our scriptures say, 'The Lord trains my hands for war, and my fingers for battle.' So it must have been God strengthening you. He gave you victory. That's what I believe, anyway."

Rex fell silent as he stared out at the temple of Jupiter, pale and luminous atop the Capitoline Hill. Though he was normally so confident, Rex now seemed nervous, fiddling with the leather of his belt. Flavia examined his face from the side. His jawline was well-defined, turning sharply beneath his ear in a knot of muscle, then jutting into a strong chin like the prow of a ship. Where barbarian whiskers once grew, now there was just a smooth Roman cheek. Though Flavia sensed a certain turmoil in Rex and wanted to provide comfort, she resisted the urge to put out her hand and touch his face. The gesture, she knew, would be far too intimate. Instead, she simply rested her hand on his forearm.

"Is something wrong?" she asked gently.

"You said your god helped me. Maybe he did. But the truth is, I also did something evil that day. Something no soldier should do."

A twinge of fear caught Flavia by surprise. Somewhere deep in her mind, a tiny voice whispered that Rex was violent at heart, but she brushed it away. *He's a good man*, another voice countered. *He just needs a friend at his side. Someone to listen to him.*

"You can talk about it if you want," she offered.

Rex picked up a pebble and inspected it in his fingers. "Pompeianus was the general at Verona," he said at last. "I made a vow that I would kill him in war if I could. And I got that chance. He was the enemy that I just described—the one I fought in the power of Christ. I drew first blood from him on the battlefield."

"I don't know if that can be called evil, Rex. Our theologians are divided about warfare. Some say you should never shed blood. Others believe war can be just, like it was for the Jews of the Old Testament. They were clearly doing what God had commanded."

"Warfare wasn't the evil I was referring to. I fought Pompeianus nobly out on the field. It was what happened next that . . ." Rex grimaced and resumed his silence.

"You can tell me," Flavia said softly. "I'll still respect you."

"*Tch!* Not likely."

"Yes, I will! What happened, Rex? You're scaring me."

"I abandoned Constantine to die."

Flavia involuntarily shrank from her friend. "But you're no coward! Why would you do that?"

Rex sighed, tossing the pebble down the temple steps. "Only one thing would make me abandon my commander to death. As it turned out, he didn't die. But only because many brave men gave their lives for him. Men that didn't include me."

Rex's expression was so guilty that Flavia felt tears of compassion gather in her eyes. Clearly, this warrior, this man of action who took pride in his courage and military virtue, was bearing a heavy burden. For a soldier to abandon his post at the emperor's most desperate hour was a crime worthy of death. To any honorable legionary, such cowardice was abhorrent. Dereliction of duty was unforgivable. Those accused of it often committed suicide rather than endure the shame.

"It's not the worst thing," Flavia said, trying to inject hope into her voice. "I know you weren't afraid out there. I'm sure you must have had a good reason for fleeing."

"I didn't flee!" Rex said bitterly. "I chased down my enemy. I had already wounded him on the field, so I pursued him and caught him. By the end of the chase, Pompeianus was at my feet, helpless and asking for mercy."

"He must have been badly injured to stoop to that. He's such an arrogant man."

"I had severed his hand, and he was exhausted, so he gave himself up to arrest and requested a trial."

"Where did you take him?"

"Nowhere."

Flavia gasped. "You let him get away?"

"No. Of course not."

"Then what? You left him to be captured by someone else?"

Rex shook his head.

A creeping horror began to take hold of Flavia. She turned and looked at Rex, uncertain that she knew him like she thought she did. "Surely you didn't . . ."

"Yes. I executed him like the criminal he was. And I don't regret it. Now he will never be able to hurt you again."

"Oh, Rex," Flavia said in a trembling voice. "That wasn't battle. Nor was it self-defense. It was murder for vengeance! The worst sin a man can commit!"

"I don't believe in sin," Rex declared.

"God does," Flavia replied, and burst into tears.

─⊰♦⊱─

OCTOBER 312

Constantine had been to Rome only once before, and on that visit, a decade earlier, he had come by sea. Now he had just spent the better part of three weeks descending the Flaminian Way, the main artery between northern Italy and the capital. It was a rugged road that crossed two passes in the Apennines. At one point it even pierced through an archway carved out of the mountain itself. Yet by the end of the highway's course, as it approached the capital city along the Tiberis River, the surrounding countryside was a flat upland. And it was there, just a few miles short of the walls, that Constantine ordered his soldiers to set up camp. It would be their last field bivouac. The next tent that each man occupied would be within sight of Rome's walls. The final battle with Maxentius was coming soon.

Several of the senior officers rode with Constantine down to a monument called the First Gate. On his previous visit, the emperor recalled being unimpressed by it; and seeing the gateway once more, he found no new reason to feel a sense of awe. It was just a nondescript place where an aqueduct crossed the road to supply water to an ancient villa. As the arches spanned the highway, they formed a kind of portal.

"Not much to look at, is it?" the emperor remarked to Vitruvius.

"I suppose it's mostly symbolic—the first entry point to the vicinity of Rome. But it's not symbolism that matters to me. I care about battle plans. See that cliff?" The general pointed to a low bluff of rust-colored tufa. "It's called Red Rocks. The terrain here narrows, so we'll have to be careful. Maxentius isn't likely to come out and give us a good fight, but he might send a detachment to try and ambush us in a tight place."

"He'd be a fool to leave the walls for a pitched battle," Constantine agreed. "He's survived a siege twice before. It's his best defense now."

"Yes, sir. That's why I've already ordered the men to start constructing catapults and towers."

"Good. Looks like it's going to be a long siege." The emperor reined his horse around. "Let's get back to camp and keep an eye on things."

The scouting party returned up the Flaminian Way to the encampment at the thirteenth milestone. Constantine's men were well trained, each knowing his job. Some were already digging defensive ditches, while others erected orderly rows of the eight-man tents used by legions on the march. The commander's tent, much larger than these, occupied a prominent spot on the highway at the center of the camp. It served as the official headquarters of the temporary fortress, and an open area lay next to it for assembling the troops.

"Today is the Ides of October," Constantine reminded Vitruvius as they shared cups of wine in the privacy of the tent. "You know what's happening down in the city?"

The general had to think for a moment before responding. "Ah, yes! The October Horse is being sacrificed. The race must have just finished. The blood of the winner is probably still warm."

"That's right. On the Field of Mars, that ancient god always gets his blood. It's all rather primitive, don't you think? I mean, this slaughter of animals to appease the deities. Doesn't it strike you as archaic, Vitruvius?"

"It seems traditional and time-honored to me, sir."

"So the priests always say. But I'm beginning to think the spiritual rituals of the Christians are more noble." Constantine snapped his fingers to a bodyguard standing outside the open tent flap. "Go summon my chaplain," he said.

In short order, Ossius of Corduba arrived. He was an old man, probably near sixty, so the rigors of marching with a field army had taken a toll on him. Yet despite his obvious fatigue, his eyes shone with purpose and determination. "You called for me, Augustus?" he asked with a dip of his chin.

"The men of Maxentius are down in Rome sacrificing to their god of war. I believe our troops need to feel they are supported by an even higher God—the Highest Divinity, who created the world. Can you give a speech to the men at the morning assembly?"

"Indeed I can, Your Highness. It would be my honor to do so."

"Good. We will hear from you tomorrow at the third hour."

At the appointed time the next day, the entire officer corps, down to the rank of centurion, gathered at the assembly ground outside the emperor's tent. An elevated podium had been erected from planks laid across the bed of a wagon. Ossius climbed up and stood before a flag-draped crate that served as a makeshift speaker's pulpit. The Spanish bishop was looking much better this morning, wearing a respectable tunic and, in solidarity with the men, the same kind of cloak and boots the officers themselves wore. Even his normally long and wavy hair had been cropped close. He carried a book under his arm, which he placed on the pulpit before he began his speech.

The oration was a rousing one. Clearly, these Christian preachers were well-trained rhetoricians, skilled in the art of teaching, delighting, and motivating their audiences. Ossius captured the men's attention with colorful illustrations and references to classical history that everyone knew. When he began to expound the Christian scriptures—texts with which the men were unfamiliar—he explained the background of the stories and recounted them in a way the audience could understand.

His chosen passage was from the *Book of Exodus*, a Greek word meaning "the way out." Long ago, the ancient Hebrews had fled from the tyrant Pharaoh in Aegyptus. When he chased them with his fearsome chariots, God opened a path through the sea.

"In the same way, O mighty warriors, you must cross the waters of the River Tiberis!" Ossius thundered at the gathered officers. "At the Milvian Bridge, you will cross safely by the hand of God, just like the Hebrews walked on dry land in the midst of the sea. Then you shall come into the promised land of Rome, where the new Moses, our glorious emperor seated before us, will lead us in the divine law after coming down from the high mountains!"

Surveying his men, Constantine could tell that the bishop had convinced them to cast their lot with the Christian God. They nodded among themselves, and no one dared scoff at the oration. Any god was a thing to be feared, but the one who had created everything, and who had been around for so long, was especially dreadful. The Christian religion now had three centuries of proven success. It had survived terrible persecution and come out stronger. It possessed sacred books, mysterious rituals, an effective leadership structure, and some brand-new buildings, though not very impressive ones. Yet even without magnificent temples, Christianity was a force to be reckoned with. Constantine could see that now was the time to put into motion the final part of his plan.

He rose from his ornate folding chair and climbed up beside Ossius on the podium. "Men of valor, I salute you!" he cried, and a cheer rose from the assembled soldiers. "You already know your augustus has been marching under the powerful sign of the cross. You have seen the glorious labarum at the head of the column since we departed on this expedition. But now, my brave soldiers, each of you must receive the heavenly help that the cross affords. And that is why I have arranged this!"

Constantine swept his hand toward a small tent next to the assembly ground. A handful of army slaves came forth, carrying pots of paint and horsehair brushes from a nearby villa. The paint was bright white, so it would show up well on any surface.

"Centurions!" Constantine barked. "Your emperor commands you to mark each man's shield in your century with the holy sign. It must look like this." One of the slaves held up a placard with a circle drawn on it to indicate a shield. Inside it was the tau-rho figure, with its perpendicular arms intersecting at the boss of the shield.

"Soon we will conquer Maxentius by this saving sign," Constantine went on, "the wondrous sign that I saw written in the sky long ago by the hand of the Highest God. And this very sign, which I was told in a dream to accept, I now bequeath to you! Let Hercules and Apollo and Mars be set aside. It is time to let the Lord Christ fight our battles!"

A single voice rose above the hubbub of the crowd. One of the centurions, a devout Christian, was first to run to the pots of paint. "Jesus Christ the victor!" he cried. Snatching a brush, he dabbed a crisscross stroke on his shield, then finished the sign with a curved arc at the top to form a tau-rho: ☧.

The action provoked a powerful response. The other centurions rushed to the paint and enthusiastically marked their own shields.

Ossius let out a long breath as he stood at Constantine's side. "After so much persecution and bloodshed, it is hard to believe I am seeing this, Your Highness. I can only believe it is the handiwork of God."

"I pray that God will also show us his handiwork before the walls of Rome."

"He blesses his followers and hears their prayers. That much, at least, is certain."

Constantine put his arm around his chaplain and gestured to the busy soldiers with his other hand. "You are witnessing a unique event here, Bishop Ossius. Never before has a Roman army fought by any other power than the traditional gods. Yet I believe it is time to revere only one God— and to have one emperor again as well."

Ossius glanced over at Constantine, his eyebrows arched in surprise. "You won't share power with Licinius?"

A mischievous smile came to the emperor's face. "My future brother-in-law has his eyes on Rome—of that we can have no doubt. But we shall have to wait until another day to discover what unfolds within the Imperial College. For now, it seems I am the first to reach the capital. Soon I'll be master of all Italy. And when I defeat Maxentius by the mighty hand of God, I will order a triumphal arch to be erected right here, at this camp."

"A fitting way to mark the beginning of your great conquest."

"Yes. May it stand as a monument to the day the empire claimed the power of Christ. From now on, Bishop Ossius, the legions of Rome shall conquer in the sign of the cross!"

―――⟐⟐⟐―――

Lady Sabina Sophronia signaled for her serving maid to approach with the tray of sweet dates and cheese. The girl set it before the guests and quickly exited, for the household slaves had been told to stay away from the dining room during the meeting. Only faithful Onesimus was allowed to remain nearby, standing guard at the door to prevent any listening ears from coming too close.

Sophronia's brother-in-law, the eminent senator Titus Junius Ignatius, had arrived at the Aventine mansion earlier that morning. But despite his presence, the person Sophronia rejoiced to see most in the room was Flavia. It had been such a surprise when Flavia showed up a few nights ago with the handsome guardsman who watched out for her. Rex claimed to know for certain that Ruricius Pompeianus had fallen in battle at Verona. Now it was safe, Rex declared, for Flavia to return home. The house seemed to have gained a new liveliness with Flavia's return. Sophronia caressed her daughter's arm as they reclined on a divan beside the dining room's central table. *She's home! I praise you, Holy Christ, for your mercies!*

Senator Ignatius, the man with the highest status of the group, reclined alone at the head couch and presided over the meal. To his left were Sophronia and Flavia, while on his right were Rex and the Greek schoolteacher Alexamenos. Fortunately, the master of the house was away on business in Puteoli. Neratius seemed to be going there a lot these days, though Sophronia didn't know why.

"As you are aware, this is not a pleasure banquet but a strategy meeting," the senator said, getting straight to the point now that the food had been brought and the slaves were gone. "It is time to make plans. We shall not leave this table until some specific strategies have been determined." The others in the room nodded but said nothing, deferring to Ignatius's leadership. When he saw that he had their full attention, he continued. "I think we all realize Rome is on the brink of civil war. Maxentius was once popular, but the citizens have turned against him. And why not? His arrogance, harsh taxes, and ravishing of aristocratic wives have angered the people."

"Not to mention his brutal vengeance," Rex put in. "Six thousand peasants were massacred in Trans Tiberim the other night because one soldier was lynched. And most of the people who were slaughtered had nothing to do with it."

Alexamenos grimaced as he shook his head. "It's shameful. But it also reminds us to be careful. Right now, Constantine is out in the countryside somewhere to the north. The Praetorians are here with us, inside the walls. It's risky to take a public stand against Maxentius."

Flavia, who had been quiet so far, finally spoke up. "I agree it's risky, but I think many people are starting to take those risks. I've been hearing open grumbling and complaining. Once Constantine has control of the city, everyone will go over to him gladly. The people are convinced Maxentius will lose. No one wants to be remembered as having sided with him. The whole city is afraid of what is about to happen. Rome hasn't been invaded for seven hundred years. The idea is terrifying."

Senator Ignatius's hand shot into the air, his finger pointing upward in an emphatic gesture. "Yes! You just said it, my little niece. *Fear* is exactly what we need here. It can run through a city like a wildfire. Our job is to be the arsons. Throw sparks of fear among the citizens and fan them into flame. This will bring Maxentius down faster than anything else. Any ideas on how to do it?"

Rex was the first to reply, and since he was a recognized expert in tactics, everyone listened closely to his words. "I think the strategy we want here is to plant one simple idea and spread it from person to person. Just as a fire spreads more easily in a dense neighborhood, we need to go where people are packed tightly together. In Rome, that means one obvious location."

"The slums?" Alexamenos suggested.

"No, even tighter than that. Shoulder to shoulder, in fact."

"Ah, of course," Senator Ignatius mused, "the circus! It holds thousands of spectators."

"Two hundred and fifty thousand, to be precise." Rex made a flicking motion with his fingers. "We only need to cast our sparks among a few of those thousands, then sit back and watch the fire spread."

"I have an idea," Sophronia offered. "Many years ago, I remember a magistrate who advertised his candidacy by hiding medallions in the free bread at the races. He had the little coins washed in silver to give them some value. Each one had his portrait on the front and an election slogan on the back. The people loved it! Even I ripped into my bread looking for a coin, though I didn't get one. But some did, and they were the envy of the city. Everyone was talking about it for days afterward. And the magistrate was elected easily."

"That would be expensive," Alexamenos observed. "We'd need several thousand medallions to influence the whole racetrack."

Ignatius waved his hand. "Money is no object when it comes to bringing down Maxentius. It's a worthwhile investment for me. I'd rather lose some funds than have my estates confiscated by a tyrant."

"Then the way to do it," Rex said, "is to get in touch with some counterfeiters right away. I think I can do that. We'll imprint the medallions with the message that Constantine can't be defeated. Once we have them, we'll need to bribe someone high up in the imperial bakeries to let us insert them in the dough. The coins will bake into the loaves, but no one will know which ones have them inside. The crowd will be interested already because bread is so scarce these days. The money will just add to the interest. It's a simple plan. All we need is high-level permission to do it."

"A close friend of mine was recently brutalized by Maxentius . . ." Sophronia's somber words trailed off for a moment, but she collected herself and continued. "She's the wife of the prefect of provisions. A very dignified lady who was horribly mistreated in the palace. Obviously, her husband is furious and seeking revenge against the emperor. He supervises the imperial bread dole. I'm sure he'd cooperate with our plan."

Rex gave Sophronia an affirming nod. "That will work. So if he says yes, where should we take the coins?"

"There's a bakery on the Palatine that supplies the racetrack," Flavia said. "It also makes bread for banquets in the palace. I'm a familiar face around there, so I could pass by unnoticed. The kitchen maids go there often."

Alexamenos looked doubtful. "I think that's dangerous now that some people know your real identity, Lady Junia. I would have to go with you for protection. The workers all know me in those tunnels. If anyone bothers you, I could insist you're one of my slaves. It's the only way you'll be safe."

The room fell awkwardly silent. No one wanted to insult the brave yet slender-framed Alexamenos after his generous offer of "protection." Finally, Senator Ignatius took the lead. "Rex, you should go with them too," he instructed. "Pose as a porter. There are plenty of stout Germanic slaves carrying loads through the passages beneath the palace. You'll fit right in."

"Yes, sir, I agree," Rex said. "A wise plan."

"So there we have it, everyone! Do we all know our roles?" Each of the conspirators nodded their assent to the senator.

"Very well," he concluded. "Lady Sabina, would you please pass me the dates? Let us take some refreshment in these perilous times."

Although the food was delicious, the rest of the meal passed with none of the guests savoring the delicacies. Too much was at stake, and the conspirators knew all too well what would happen if Maxentius got wind of the conspiracy before he was ousted. At last the meal broke up in a kind of grim farewell. Rex and Alexamenos left the house to attend to their duties, while Flavia retired to the rear garden. Sophronia followed her.

"It's wonderful to have you home again, my love," she said, trying to lighten the mood.

Flavia's lips curled into a little smile as she basked in the waning sunshine of autumn. "Mother, you've told me that a thousand times over the past two days."

"Well, I'm just so happy to have you home again."

"A thousand and one," Flavia said. The two women looked at each other for a moment, then burst into laughter. For now, at least, the fearsome burden of carrying out high treason was forgotten.

When their giggles had subsided, Sophronia sat next to Flavia on a sun-washed bench. "I love you, sweet one," she said, patting Flavia's knee.

"I love you too, Mother."

"I have to admit, I wasn't sad when I heard Pompeianus had fallen at Verona. He was an evil man."

Flavia remained silent, fiddling with the decorative fringe on her mantle.

"It meant you could come home," Sophronia went on. "That soldier Rex takes good care of you. He won't let you go anywhere unsafe."

"Yes. He's very protective. It's one of his positive traits."

Sophronia gave her daughter a sly glance. "Alongside many others, yes? He certainly has more than one."

"I suppose."

"Oh, he definitely does. Older women can see these things. He's a man of high character. Lots of potential in life. And he's remarkably good-looking."

"Mother, stop! You know he's not in our catholic faith. Why are you putting ideas in my head?"

"But what if he converted? He seems open to it. He visited church with you several times."

"Even if he got baptized tomorrow, he's not of our social station."

"I know. But I talked with your father about that. Neratius said it's much easier to enter the knightly class these days. Any aspiring and well-connected young man can do it, especially if he's completed a good tour in the army. He comes out of the ranks with an honorable discharge and has a nice government post waiting. After he puts in a few years in the provinces, he comes back to Rome and works his way up the bureaucracy. Lots of talented Germani are doing it these days. In fact, it has become quite fashionable for Roman girls to marry barbarians."

"Marriage? Since when are we talking about marriage?"

"You're eighteen, Flavia! What else should we be talking about? Once Constantine takes over this city, it's going to settle down again. We need to think about your future."

"My future is to marry a Christian."

Sophronia sighed. "You know I share that intent, my love. I protected you from your father several times when he wanted to form alliances with pagan families. I even stopped him from making you marry Magnus, although that would have helped our fortune. So, yes, I want you to marry a Christian. But I also want you to marry someone you *respect*." Sophronia paused, staring up at the sky. "Marriage is hard if you don't have that," she said quietly.

"I do respect Rex. Very much, to be honest. Unfortunately, I don't think he's close to converting. I mean, he's a warrior. He kills people."

"War can be a noble part of manhood. And even when it isn't noble, it's often necessary."

"I know. But in Rex's case, I fear his warlike spirit keeps him from bowing to Christ."

"Don't give up hope, daughter. Soldiers have been turning to the true faith ever since the centurion came to Jesus to get his servant healed."

"It's a nice story, I guess."

"It's more than a story. It's the truth."

"Sometimes even the truth is hard to believe."

Flavia rose abruptly from the bench and walked to a decorative fountain on a stand. She rested both hands on its rim and stared into the water. It took several moments before Sophronia noticed her daughter's shoulders quaking.

"My love, you're crying!" Sophronia hurried to Flavia's side and tried to stroke her hair. Flavia averted her eyes and pulled away.

"What is it?" Sophronia pressed. "You can share it with me. I'm your mother."

Flavia spun, her face a mixture of anger and despair. Tears had smudged the makeup around her eyes. "All this talk of marriage is foolishness!" she cried. "Haven't you read the scriptures? Saint John's letter says no murderer has eternal life abiding in him. Or if an apostle isn't enough, let the Lord himself speak! He says anyone who murders is of his father the devil. Such a one has no truth in him at all!"

Taken aback by the vehemence of the outburst, Sophronia needed a moment to collect her thoughts. At last she leaned forward and put her hands on her daughter's shoulders. Flavia could only stare at her feet.

"Keep your faith strong," Sophronia urged. "The grace of Almighty God is powerful."

"Yes, I know. But do you know what else is powerful?"

"What?"

"The bloodlust in Rex's heart."

Sophronia shook her head defiantly. "There are other scriptures you're forgetting, Flavia. Don't you remember your favorite one from the *Book of Proverbs*? 'Like a rush of water being diverted, so is the heart of a king in God's hand.' If that is true of a king, how much more of a mere soldier? God can turn your friend's heart in any way he chooses. He can cause Rex to become a Christian."

"Oh, Mother! I want to believe that so much! And I would give anything

384

to see it happen. I mean *anything*! But I fear it never will." Flavia put her hand to her forehead and covered her eyes. "I know it's wrong to despair," she whimpered. "I just have a terrible feeling that Rex and I can never be together, no matter how hard I pray."

"God can do all things. He can certainly do this."

"No, I don't think so." Flavia pursed her lips and shook her head. "I believe Rex's heart is the one kingdom that can't be conquered."

"Flavia! Why are you so fearful?"

"Because this is what I desire more than anything else in the world. I don't know if I can live without it!"

"My sweet daughter!" Sophronia exclaimed, drawing Flavia into a hug. "It sounds to me like *your* heart is the one in need of conquest."

"That's what I'm afraid of," Flavia whispered as she rested in her mother's arms.

⸺◈⸺

OCTOBER 27, 312

Rex gripped the handles of the wheelbarrow and lifted the heavy load. He was nearly naked, wearing only a waistcloth like the most menial slaves in the imperial palace. Such attire was far beneath his station as an elite warrior of the horse guard, but he accepted the disguise as a necessary contrivance. *Flavia endured a much lower drop in social class when she came here for several months*, he reminded himself. *You can do it now for the sake of the mission.*

The mission on which Rex had been sent to Rome—gathering intelligence and destabilizing Maxentius to pave the way for Constantine—had taken on new meaning in recent weeks. Rex had found himself unable to shake his burden of guilt for having abandoned the emperor at Verona. His flight that day had been seen by all. Though Constantine didn't know the identity of the cowardly deserter or he would have had the man arrested, Rex still had to live with the awareness that the emperor now despised him. Ever since that day long ago at Eboracum, when twelve-year-old Rex was spared from execution and sent to military school, the great Emperor Constantine had been a hero of his. Now Rex believed only a major contribution to the downfall of Maxentius could atone for his despicable treason. Fortunately, each step he took as he rolled the wheelbarrow along the tunnel was one step closer to redemption. Senator Ignatius's clever plot was in motion, and if all went according to plan, Maxentius would soon be on his way to ruin.

"Greetings to you, miss," a slave said to Flavia as they passed in the hall. "Haven't seen you around lately."

"Just so busy," Flavia replied, shrugging as she held up her bucket and mop. "So much to do."

Although the passageways that burrowed into the Palatine Hill had the complexity of an anthill, Alexamenos knew his way through the maze, and Flavia seemed to have a good grasp as well. Rex followed them, rolling his cart full of casks—none containing water or oil, as the casual observer would assume. Instead, they held silver-washed medallions purchased from an illegal counterfeit ring.

"Feel that heat?" Alexamenos asked as the threesome turned a corner. "The bakery is just ahead."

Flavia closed her eyes and inhaled through her nose. "Mmm! It smells so good."

"I know. Everyone is craving bread. The bakers had to post guards because people have been stealing loaves and selling them on the black market."

The bakery was located on the outer edge of the imperial complex at a spot where the chimneys from its ovens could be vented outside. A burly slave in a flour-covered apron met the visitors at the door. "Who are you?" he demanded.

"Bread makers with a special recipe," Alexamenos told him.

"What's it for?"

"A bread so good, it will make you rich."

The slave nodded at the use of the proper password and admitted the threesome into the bakery, then shut the door behind them.

Rex set down his heavy wheelbarrow and arched his back. A rivulet of sweat made a ticklish sensation as it ran between his chest muscles and down the middle of his stomach. He brushed it away with his hand.

"Do you, um, need a rag?" Flavia asked.

Rex glanced over to see Flavia offering him a cloth. Strangely, she was staring at her feet as she held it out.

"Thank you," he said, taking the rag and wiping his drenched body. He started to give the rag back to her, but as soon as he looked up after drying off, Flavia averted her eyes and darted away. Rex pitched the wet cloth into a corner.

The bakery was large, designed to produce a high volume of bread. One entire wall consisted of a countertop for kneading the dough into balls. Another was lined with empty cooling racks to receive the freshly baked loaves. The third wall held the ovens, their fiery mouths opened wide.

"Listen up now, men," Alexamenos said to the gaggle of slaves gathered around him. "You have been instructed by your master to participate in a plan that could get you killed. You know how Rome treats its rebellious slaves. If word ever gets out about your involvement, it will mean a long, slow death for you on a cross."

Though the slaves remained silent, Rex could see they understood all too well that the warning had merit. The treasonous nature of what was being done today had made an impression on the workers. They shifted their feet and waited for Alexamenos to continue.

"The medallions are here," the teacher said, sweeping his hand toward the wheelbarrow. Rex reached into one of the casks and extracted a heavy sack that jingled as he held it up. "All we want you to do is place a single coin inside each of the loaves. Once they're baked, you'll mix them with baskets from other bakeries so no one will know where these came from. You must be very secretive about this. Am I understood?"

The slaves nodded, so Alexamenos dispatched them to their task. The three conspirators joined them, sliding the coins into the dough balls with the help of a knife, then smoothing the surface to make the slit invisible. Rex found that the work proceeded quickly. At the end of an hour, four thousand coins had been inserted, which meant sixteen thousand coins still remained to be implanted in the upcoming batches of dough. It would be a big job, but there was plenty of manpower. And it was only the third hour now. The chariot races wouldn't take place until the late afternoon.

"Try this one, Rex," Alexamenos said. He picked up a bun from the cooling rack and tossed it across the room. Rex caught it but had to bobble it in his hand because it was so hot. Finally, he speared it with his knife and held it up before his nose, savoring its wheaty, yeasty aroma. He risked a nibble to let some steam escape, then followed with a big bite. On the second bite, he found the coin protruding from the loaf.

"Let's see it," Flavia said, coming to his side.

Rex showed it to her in his palm. The medallion displayed the triumphant face of Emperor Constantine with radiant sunbeams shining from his head. Flavia flipped the coin over. A slogan was there:

Constantinum Vinci Non Posse

"Constantine cannot be defeated," Flavia read aloud—an expression of her hope. And perhaps a prayer?

"That's our essential message," Rex said. "It'll only take one person shouting it to get the crowd going. Even though Maxentius's army is bigger than ours, Constantine is viewed as a military genius. Everyone believes he's going to win. No one wants to say so out loud. But they might if they're not alone."

"Well, I'm going to make sure—"

A sudden knock interrupted Flavia's boast: three hard raps on the door followed by two more, the signal that the visitor was a friend. The doorkeeper let him in. "Praetorians are snooping around," the visitor, another bakery slave, announced. "We're going to be arrested!"

"Not likely," Rex replied. "Nothing noteworthy is happening here if we keep the casks out of sight." He turned toward Alexamenos. "It's possible that someone has recognized Flavia," he whispered so the slaves couldn't hear. "Bringing her to the palace might have been a bad idea. I've got to get her out of here. Can you stay and supervise the operation?"

"Absolutely. The bread will be ready for the afternoon races. Go now—quick!"

Rex peeked out the door. Seeing no one, he flicked his head to tell Flavia it was time to leave. She came up behind him and peered around his shoulder at the empty hallway. They were about to go when Rex pulled back. At the end of the hall, a squad of soldiers had just rounded the corner. They stopped a kitchen maid and started harassing her as she protested her innocence.

"We'll never get past them, Rex! They're looking for girls my age. And there's no other way out of this bakery!"

Rex put his hand on Flavia's shoulder. "You worry too much for a Christian. Calm down and let me take care of it." He gave her a wink to reassure her. "Now squat."

"What?"

"Squat down," Rex repeated, pointing to the ground. "Make yourself into a little ball. Hold your knees to your chest."

Flavia complied. Before she could protest, Rex pulled an empty grain sack over her entire body and scooped her into his arms. She squealed as Rex lifted her.

"Don't make a sound. Wheat doesn't cry out like that. Just hold still."

"Okay," came a muffled reply from the bag.

After depositing Flavia in the wheelbarrow, he arranged several full sacks of grain around her, then pushed the cart into the hall. The Praetorians had abandoned the girl they were questioning and now were headed toward the bakery. As they approached, Rex could see they were the same bunch he had encountered the day he purchased sausages with Flavia. However, Rex had been in uniform that day, a prestigious cavalryman. The Praetorians would hardly expect him to be here, months later, shirtless and performing manual labor. Besides, the Romans often said that all the blond Germani looked the same. They would probably just pass him by as irrelevant. Rex put his head down and kept rolling.

The soldiers approached. Rex stared at the floor like slaves always did in the presence of troublemakers.

"Stop where you are," one of the men barked. Rex halted but did not look up.

"You trying to run us over, slave? Your stupid cart takes up the whole tunnel."

The soldiers slipped past. One of them bumped Rex with his armored shoulder but Rex didn't respond. When they were behind him, he picked up the wheelbarrow's handles and started moving again.

"Stay still until I say otherwise," he whispered to Flavia.

After a few twists and turns, he took the nearest exit he could find. Out in the sunshine, a crowd was gathering, for the bakery was adjacent to the Circus Maximus and people were arriving early to get a good seat. Unlike the gladiator matches in the amphitheater, the chariot races were free and open to the public. The earlier you arrived, the better the seat you could find.

Rex rolled the wheelbarrow into a shaded alley. He loosened the string on Flavia's sack and her feet popped out. She gratefully slithered out and stood up.

"I thought rich girls put flowers in their hair," Rex said as he plucked a stalk of wheat from her locks. "Is this the new fashion?"

"I thought soldiers wore armor," Flavia shot back, pointing at Rex's loincloth. "Is this the new fashion?"

The saucy rejoinder made Rex burst into laughter. Flavia laughed too, sharing the humor of the moment. Finally, Rex came close to her, looking down at her face with a mischievous grin. "Do you remember the day we dined together in Tibur, Lady Junia?" The playful use of her formal name caught her attention.

After a moment's pause, Flavia mimicked the game. "Why, yes I do, Guardsman Brandulf Rex," she replied. "Why do you mention it?"

"I'd like to offer a second invitation."

"Perhaps I might consider it. Go on."

"What if, instead of sitting down to an elegant meal, a shirtless porter and a kitchen maid went on an outing together?"

Flavia's face lit up—then a strange expression clouded her face. She seemed to become more reluctant than her initial response would have suggested. Even so, she offered a gorgeous smile. "Where is this kitchen maid being taken?" she asked, still playing the game, but with less heart now.

Rex pointed over her shoulder, and she turned to gaze at the immense height of the Circus Maximus. "To watch the downfall of a tyrant," he declared.

"Now *that* should be a good show."

Rex extended his arm like a gentleman. "So might I escort you there, my lady?"

For a long moment, Flavia stared apprehensively at Rex's outstretched elbow. *These Christian girls really are shy*, he thought. Finally, she slipped her arm into his, then cuddled closer to his side than he had expected. She even tipped her head to lean against his shoulder. His arm was clutched tight in her grasp.

"Lead me on, brave warrior," she said, " because I have no idea where I'm going."

—◦◦◦—

At the end of the hunting portion of the circus show, Flavia decided that the variety of animals God had made was indescribable. Ostriches, hippos, panthers, baboons, zebras—each strange creature was too exotic to comprehend. But the animals Flavia marveled at most were the giant spotted camels without humps. These strange beasts, imported from Africa, had such long necks and legs that they towered even above the trees. Their coat was a remarkable patchwork of brown and white blotches, and they had two stumpy horns on their heads. Eight of these tall, loping creatures had been killed by hunters with spears. Fortunately, no men had died in combat with them, though several gladiators did perish in their fights with the elefanti and rhinos. Though most of the beast hunts in Rome were held in the amphitheater, blood sport was also one of the attractions of the Circus Maximus, and today was no exception.

"I'll be glad when the chariot races begin," Flavia remarked to Rex, who sprawled next to her on one of the circus's risers. Since it was a public venue, he had donned a slave's tunic over his loincloth. "I'm not used to watching the hunts. Too much bloodshed for me."

Rex pursed his lips. "I think you'd better brace yourself. The races might not put an end to it."

Flavia shuddered at the remark and vowed not to look if a bad crash happened.

Tomorrow would mark the sixth anniversary of Maxentius's coronation, so all of Rome was being offered bread and entertainment in honor of their great ruler. By now the people had grown sick of the man who wore the royal crown. Nevertheless, if he wanted to put on a good show in the circus, they weren't averse to turning out for it.

"Look up there," Rex said, pointing to the imperial box in the stands. It was a lavish affair with painted columns and a shady porch from which to watch the spectacle. "People are starting to arrive. Mostly soldiers, it looks like. The emperor will be here soon. Then the races can begin."

Rex was right about the emperor's entrance. It wasn't long after his prediction when, accompanied by a trumpet fanfare, Maxentius strode into view and took a seat in his box amid the idols of Rome. His arrival was followed by a long parade that entered the circus through an arch at one end. Priests, musicians, horsemen, jugglers, and dancers followed one another around the track's central spine. After a single raucous lap, the procession exited by the same archway. A curtain closed the portal behind them.

Now a tense silence descended on the thousands of spectators. Charioteers had taken up their positions in six of the starting gates. Maxentius rose from his couch, holding a white cloth above his head. The crowd held its breath. And then, like a single snowflake, the cloth fluttered to the emperor's feet.

The chariots burst from the gates with a collective roar from the crowd. This was the first of twelve races today, a preliminary match between several new drivers for the Blues and Greens. Flavia tried to imagine what it must be like to guide two galloping horses around the sandy track—not to mention four horses, like several later races would feature. "Have you ever tried doing that?" she shouted into Rex's ear over the clamor of the mob.

"What?" he yelled back.

"Have you ever driven a chariot?"

"Once or twice. It's hard!"

It must be very hard if Rex had difficulty with it, Flavia thought.

The chariots thundered around the track seven times, losing only two teams in a colossal smashup before the winner crossed the finish line. The victory went to an up-and-coming Spanish driver for the Blues. Flower petals rained down on him as he received his victory palm. Many of the spectators cheered for him, while others harrumphed at the money they had lost in their betting.

Rex nudged Flavia. "Here it comes. The bread is being brought out. See the baskets?"

"What do you think will happen?" Flavia asked, feeling the butterflies in her stomach. "I'm so nervous!"

"Just watch and see."

And pray, she reminded herself.

Several drivers-in-training rode onto the sand with baskets hanging from their chariots. Drawing close to the stands, they started tossing buns into the lower tiers. Other slaves descended the aisles with baskets of their own. They began to distribute the fresh bread into the upper rows of the circus, one loaf per person. The bread was made with good wheat flour, much better than the barley or rye the commoners usually ate. It was a lavish imperial gift in this time of shortage.

Flavia tore her loaf in half and poked around inside it. "Nothing," she said.

"Me either. But we know it's coming."

The crowd enjoyed the free treat while waiting for the next race. Many people had brought their own flasks of olive oil, or soft cheeses wrapped in cloths, in anticipation of the delicious gift. Unfortunately, nothing seemed out of the ordinary. No one was finding the hidden medallions. Flavia had begun to suspect the secret bread had not yet been distributed when someone yelled, "A coin!"

"I got one too!" someone shouted down the row.

A stir of excitement buzzed through the crowd. People began to rip their bread apart. Across the tiers, shouts of triumph erupted from the lucky few who had found the money. With its coating of silver, the little medallion was worth about a day's wage—no small sum for a working man. Yet in all the excitement, no one seemed to be paying attention to the coin's message.

"They must not be able to read it," Flavia whispered urgently.

"The common people are more literate than we think. They might not write poetry, but that doesn't mean they can't read advertisements or graffiti."

Flavia clutched the skirt of her tunic in both hands. *Please, God, let them get the message! Make them recognize that tyrant for who he really is!*

Most of the audience was standing up now. They clustered in small groups, examining the medallions. Rex rose to his feet. He had donned one of the cheap straw hats that the spectators used to block the sun. Its brim was pulled low, shading his face. In his hand was one of the silver coins. He raised it up.

"*Vinci . . . non . . . posse!*" he declared in a slow, deliberate voice. A moment later, he repeated the slogan. After the third time, a man two rows away joined the defiant cry.

The crowd didn't need further prompting. Flavia's whole section burst into a unified chant. "Can't . . . be . . . defeated!" they shouted over and over. People began to stamp their feet and shake their fists. The taunt spread down one side of the circus and up the other, its energy growing to a deafening roar.

"Look!" Flavia cried. "The emperor is furious!"

"And none of his military men know what to do!" Rex added.

The generals and tribunes in the viewing box were urging Maxentius to leave, but the petite man in the purple toga couldn't tear himself away. He could only stare at the angry crowd, his eyes bulging, his mouth agape. At last his new Praetorian prefect, a tall ex-soldier who dwarfed the diminutive emperor, gathered some officials around their lord. The gaggle of men conversed with agitated gestures.

Now a rumor began to race through the stands. Apparently, someone in the audience had declared—whether accurately or not, who could say?—that Constantine had broken camp and was on the march. He would arrive before the walls of Rome tomorrow. Dread seized the crowd at the prospect of invasion. Would Constantine be merciful, or would he punish Rome for tolerating Maxentius so long?

Flavia glanced at the imperial box again, then shook Rex's arm. "Something's happening up there. See? All the men are leaving."

Rex watched a junior officer relay a message to the high-ranking officials. The Praetorian prefect nodded his agreement, then ordered everyone out of the box.

"Are they going to retaliate, Rex? Should we get out of here?"

He shook his head. "It's something else."

"What?"

"Those men are all in Maxentius's inner circle. It looks like his advisers are being summoned to a council."

"What should we do?"

Rex turned and looked Flavia in the eye. His face was surprisingly stern. "I think it's time you showed me your secret passage," he said.

—◦◦◦—

The door to Maxentius's bedroom burst open and slammed against a wall. Though the sharp bang startled Livia, she managed not to cry out.

It wouldn't do for a noble lady in mourning to make such undignified sounds.

She turned and faced the emperor. Even through the black veil that draped her face she could see he was livid. A slave had already warned her of the thunderstorm that was coming, yet words couldn't do justice to the depth of Maxentius's fury. It was a fearsome thing to stand before such terrible rage from someone so powerful.

Watch your step, Livia warned herself. *You're on a knife's edge here.*

"They shamed me!" Maxentius shouted. "The people of Rome shamed me in my own circus! How dare they!"

Livia glided toward Maxentius with her head bowed. "The rabble shall pay for their sins against their rightful augustus. The gods will take vengeance on them."

"I will take vengeance on them!"

"And they will deserve it, my lord. You are a great man, worthy of respect. The people should love you."

Livia's soothing words had their usual calming effect on Maxentius. He stood silent for a moment, collecting his thoughts. The emperor seemed to enjoy Livia, unlike his many courtesans, as an actual human being. Since the night he first brought her to his bed, he had been summoning her often. Though he did have a legal wife, the truth was that Maxentius despised her. Livia believed a divorce from that annoying shrew—if not an execution on some trumped-up charge—was imminent. And when that happened, Maxentius would need a respectable new woman at his side. Now that Pompeianus had fallen at Verona, the widowed Livia was ready and willing to be the next empress of Rome.

But only if I play him right.

Maxentius took a seat in a cushioned chair and gazed out the window at the circus far below. Another race was being run, though not yet the grand finale with twelve chariots, each drawn by four stallions. All of Rome had money riding on the outcome of that contest. Maxentius had even wagered one of his estates in Corsica on a Green victory. But now he turned away from the window.

"Bring me wine, dear Livia," he said. "Then come rub my shoulders. I am tense."

Livia unstopped a pewter decanter and poured the honeyed Falernian into a crystal goblet. She crossed the room and handed the glass to the distraught emperor, then went around behind him. "Drink it slowly, Your Highness. Savor the taste while I rub your tight muscles."

Livia proceeded to administer a gentle massage while Maxentius closed his eyes and uttered murmurs of contentment. Periodically he would sip the wine, at which times Livia tickled the back of his neck with her fingernails. She knew it was intimate moments like this, even more than sex, that drew a man's affections. When enough of those interactions had accumulated, men would start to think about marriage.

But matrimony wasn't on Maxentius's mind right now. "The people believe Constantine can't be defeated," he said bitterly, staring into his cup. He swirled the wine around as he spoke. "I'm tired of being viewed as a political emperor, Livia! I want the people to see me as a field general like Marcus Aurelius and Trajan and all the great ones."

"But you are a great general, my love."

I called him, "My love!" O Holy Venus, guide me.

Maxentius swiveled his head and glanced up at Livia. A smile that appeared to be appreciative came to his face. "Well, I am glad you think so, at least."

"I do, Maxentius."

"Unfortunately, not everyone does." The emperor grimaced and shook his head. "There was a coin hidden in the bread. It said 'Constantine can't be defeated.' Those coins didn't get there by accident! Somebody put them in the loaves. I want the traitors found!"

Now is the time, Livia realized. *Use what you know. But be careful!*

"I believe, my lord," she ventured, "that I may have a way to help you get your revenge."

Maxentius was instantly intrigued. "Really? What is it?"

"There's a page boy who was supplying palace gossip to my late husband. Lately, he's been doing the same for me. His name is Zoticus—a watchful little fellow who always seems to know what's happening behind the scenes. The boy just left here a while ago. He gave me some valuable information about your enemies."

"Tell me!"

"Zoticus noticed that the bakery slaves were up to something. He got one of them drunk and learned that someone bribed the prefect of provisions to allow the medallions into the bread supply."

Unable to contain his anger, Maxentius leapt to his feet and faced Livia. The red flush had returned to his cheeks. "Curse him!" he shrieked. "I'll have the prefect dismembered and fried in oil! Along with the man who put him up to it!"

"Believe it or not, Your Highness, the instigator wasn't a man."

"*What*? A woman is behind all this?"

Maxentius stamped his foot on the marble floor with such force that Livia took a step back. A fierce look had come into the emperor's eye, a gleam she had never seen before. It was a vicious, almost serpentine expression of insane evil and lustful revenge. "I'll use that woman like a common harlot before I strangle her!" Maxentius roared. "Who is she?"

"That haughty *canicula*, Sabina Sophronia."

"Argh!" Maxentius spun away from Livia and hurled his cup against the wall, shattering it in an explosion of glass. "I want her in my chamber by tomorrow! She escaped me once, but Neratius can't shield her this time. He'll be a widower by this time tomorrow, or may the gods slay me!"

"The gods would never slay you, Augustus!" Livia parted her veil of mourning and looked Maxentius in the eye. "You are under the watchcare of almighty Hercules."

A subtle grin came to the emperor's face, then widened further as he let out a satisfied cackle. "Your words are truer than you know. I am the god's beloved son. And with power like that behind me, whom should I fear?"

"There is no one to fear in all the heavens," Livia declared.

Rex knelt behind a row of stone barrels. Just as Flavia had promised, a door to the secret passages beneath the imperial palace was there, though it couldn't have been seen except from a crouching position. "Hand me the key," he said over his shoulder.

Flavia gave him the key, stolen from one of the pages' rooms. The latch turned, and Rex shoved the door. After crawling inside, he helped Flavia through, then shut the portal behind him. He heaved a sack of potatoes onto his sweaty shoulders—his excuse for being in the tunnels if anyone asked. As for the scullery maid, Rex reasoned this probably wouldn't be the first time a girl had been sneaked into the secret hallways. He'd make up an excuse about a tryst if he needed to.

"You know your way around?" he asked Flavia.

She tapped her foot on a white piece of marble set into the floor. "These show the way to the emperor's residence."

Rex nodded and followed Flavia's lead. They ascended a staircase and, after a long walk, came to a heated part of the palace. Rex touched the walls. "The furnaces must be on the other side. We're at the baths."

"That's right. And Maxentius *always* comes here in the late afternoon. He'll probably watch the final race while he gets his massage."

"And then go to his war council. But let's hope the generals start talking early."

"Here it is," Flavia said, pointing to the peephole that gave a view into the baths. "You can hear every word they say. It was designed that way."

"The page boys stand here and watch?"

"Mm-hmm. And jump into action whenever they're summoned."

Rex gestured to a door at the far end of the hall, which controlled access to this wing of the palace. "Does our key work in that latch? We're going to need some privacy."

"Yes, the older boys have that key. Ours should work."

Rex locked the door, then returned and pressed his eye to the wall. "Looks like some of the lesser officials are already in there. The servants are passing out drinks."

"Anything else?"

A smile came to Rex's face. He turned and gestured toward the peephole. "No. Just ten naked old men. Do you want to see for yourself?"

"Thanks, but I'll take your word for it."

"You Christians are so prudish," Rex said with a little laugh.

For the next hour, he stood next to the peephole and eavesdropped on the men's conversations. Over that time, more bathers arrived, along with the emperor himself. Though all of them were military officers, including the new Praetorian prefect, their banter with Maxentius was the ribald talk of the baths, not battle planning. And of course, the final chariot race captured the bathers' attention for a time. The Greens must have won, for Maxentius leapt from the warm pool, stark naked, and danced like a madman at this one bright spot in his otherwise troubling day.

The sun was starting to set, and the men were lounging on divans, snacking on fruit and cheese, when the conversation finally turned to military affairs. Rex signaled for Flavia to be silent. Every word now could be vital intelligence to relay to Constantine.

"The enemy has indeed broken camp," the prefect said. "He's coming down the Flaminian Way, and we expect to meet him at the Milvian—"

"Flavia!" a voice shouted. "You're spying!"

Rex whirled to see a handsome youth standing at the far end of the hallway. A large amphora was in his arms. The boy began to edge away.

"Zoticus, wait! We're friends!" Flavia cried.

The imperial page started to run, but Rex knew he wouldn't get far. Grabbing Flavia's arm, Rex pressed her to the peephole. "Don't miss a word!" he ordered, then darted after Zoticus.

Rex snatched the boy's tunic just before he started down the staircase. "Hold still, runt, or I'll take you out!"

Despite the warning, Zoticus continued to struggle, so Rex spun him around and clasped the boy's throat in the crook of his elbow. Though Rex didn't clamp down, it would only take one hard flex of his biceps to cause a faint.

Zoticus heaved the amphora down the stairs, where it shattered with a loud crash. "Help me! Over here!" he screamed. "Someone call the Praetorians!"

"Oh, gods," Rex muttered, and squeezed hard.

In the span of a few heartbeats, Zoticus went limp. Rex let him drop to the floor, then returned to Flavia. "We're out of time. Did you hear anything important?"

"Yes! The battle is set for the Milvian Bridge. They cut the real bridge and built a temporary one on pontoons. And Rex—it's trapped!"

"Trapped? What do you mean?"

"They're going to flee before Constantine, but only to lure him onto the span. Then they're going to pull a pin that holds the whole thing together. He'll surely drown!"

Shouts sounded from down the hallway. Men were coming. Probably soldiers, though Rex couldn't be sure.

"We've got to get out of here," he said. "I need to be at the river tomorrow by first light. I have to figure out how the trap works, then tell Constantine. We can't let him onto that bridge."

At the top of the stairwell, Zoticus was moaning as he awakened from his stupor. He struggled to sit up. "Praetorians!" he yelled again. "This way!"

"What is it with him?" Flavia wailed. "Why does he always do that? He already betrayed me once!"

Rex's head shot around. "That was the kid who turned you in to Pompeianus?"

"Yes! Even though I'd never been anything but kind to him."

Rex pointed down the hall toward a remote area with no voices or footsteps. "Start that way. I'll catch up."

"Where are you going?"

"To silence that kid again. Hurry!"

Flavia ran down the hall like she was told. As soon as she rounded the corner, Rex returned to the dizzy youth on the floor.

"The soldiers are coming," Zoticus spat. "They'll catch you! And get Flavia."

Rex didn't bother to reply. With a quick crisscross of his arms, he grasped the boy's collar and put him in another chokehold. The supply of blood through the vessels behind his ears was cut off. Once again, the helpless victim went limp after a brief squeeze.

But this time Rex moved from a blood choke to a stranglehold. Now Zoticus's air was cut off—not just the circulation to his brain.

Rex tightened his grip and waited.

Zoticus's face drained of its color. His eyes fluttered and rolled back in his head. At last, even his chest stopped moving up and down.

"You made your choice, boy," Rex said. "You compromised the mission." He shoved Zoticus's corpse down the stairs, then rose to his feet and started after Flavia.

13

OCTOBER 28, 312

Though few men dared to stare into the face of a god, Maxentius, as an augustus of the Roman Empire, considered himself worthy. He stood at Apollo's feet inside his great temple on the Palatine Hill, letting the god gaze back at his beloved son. The idol's expression was benign, placid, all-knowing. The early morning twilight and the flickering glow from a bronze lampstand illumined Apollo's delicate features and long, feminine locks. A silence born from holy awe—the dread of mortals standing in the presence of a capricious god—had settled on the fifteen senators who accompanied Maxentius this morning. Dawn was near, and Apollo was basking in adoration. No moment could be more propitious to make a request. Surely the god would reveal his will on a morning like this.

Maxentius stooped and kissed the sandaled foot of the idol, then turned and faced his companions. "On this day six years ago, I donned the purple robe of an emperor," he announced to the senators who served as custodians of the Sibylline Books. "Now I come as protector and guardian of the city, seeking wisdom from one of our most ancient patrons."

A senator stepped forward, the leader of the priestly college called the Fifteen Men for Performing Sacred Duties. He offered a slight bow before daring to speak. "Your Majesty, our city's first emperor was the son of a god. Caesar Augustus himself built this temple! Now you are worthy to be his successor. We believe Apollo will hear you and speak forth a divine word."

"Then let the chests be opened and the books be brought forth. I shall retire outside and await the oracle."

The senator withdrew a key from the folds of his toga and unlocked a golden box at the base of the sacred idol. Maxentius watched him remove a heavy, brittle scroll. It was one of the Sibylline Books, a collection of ancient prophecies hidden in Greek poetry. For centuries, the Roman Senate had consulted these texts in times of crisis. *And now is such a time*, Maxentius thought. *Surely an invasion army at the gates of Rome counts as a crisis!*

Once the scroll had been unrolled on a table, the emperor exited the marble temple and waited on the porch. A breeze, gusty and chilly, wafted among the columns. Maxentius tightened his fur-trimmed cape around his shoulders. Although the weather the past few days hadn't been unpleasant, the biting wind suggested an autumn cold snap was coming. Even so, he wasn't about to go back inside. The reception of oracles was a priestly function, a divine task to be carried out by the Fifteen Men. Surely the god would look with no favor on any breach of protocol.

At last the leader of the Fifteen Men emerged from the temple. His face was grave, though not discouraged or downcast. "We have received a word from heaven," he declared.

Maxentius remained aloof as befitted an emperor, though inside he felt jittery and his heart began to race. "Speak it, then."

The senator lifted a slip of parchment, squinted at it in the dim light, and said, "Hear the word of the sibyl! 'On this very day, the enemy of the Romans shall perish.'"

Yes! A prediction of victory! Lust for vengeance surged through Maxentius's body. By sundown tonight, Constantine's bloody corpse would lie at his feet. This enemy who had dared to attack Rome would perish. It had been prophesied long ago. *The gods be praised!*

Now the fourteen other senators emerged from the temple and assembled before Maxentius. He raised both hands to them, taking on the aspect of a general addressing his troops. "Send heralds into the streets!" he barked into the early morning stillness. "The great Apollo has told us what to do. Today the legions of Rome ride to war. Let the people of Rome come out of their homes and rejoice in their salvation!"

"Long live Maxentius!" the leader of the Fifteen replied, joined immediately by the rest of the priestly college. "Long live Maxentius!" they shouted in unison.

Those jubilant words were still ringing in the emperor's ears when his armorer finished dressing him an hour later. Although the armor was recognizably that of a Praetorian, the protective scales were covered in gold leaf, so the tunic's weight was far greater than what a normal soldier would bear. Yet Maxentius didn't mind. His job today was not to fight but to inspire. The sight of the great augustus riding around on the battlefield—as dazzling as Apollo himself—would surely encourage the men.

The emperor shuffled to the stable and stepped onto a mounting block with the help of his groom. A spirited charger stood beside the block, pawing the cobblestone floor with its foreleg. The stallion's white coat provided sharp contrast to its tack of red leather and shiny brass. The horse was a specimen to admire: a rippling and masculine beast with lively eyes, a proud neck, and great, bulbous testicles. A glorious thought popped into Maxentius's mind: *What this creature is among horses, I am among men!* The emperor swung his leg over his mount's back and settled heavily into the saddle. The royal groomsman grasped the halter and led the horse into the streets of Rome.

Accompanied by hornblowers and pipers, a martial parade made its way along Broadway toward the Flaminian Gate. Crowds lined the wide avenue and cheered the imperial horse guard and other cavalrymen riding in ranks behind their glorious leader. The sky was overcast now, and a chill was settling in, but on a day like this, nothing could stop the people of Rome from turning out to behold such a splendid sight.

Maxentius spun in the saddle and spoke to his field commander, the lanky general who had taken Pompeianus's place. "Where are all the traitors now?" he sneered. "See how the people love me! That outcry in the circus yesterday was just an aberration."

"Of course it was, Your Highness! You have the people and the ancient gods on your side. What more could you need in battle?"

"There is one more god whose favor I would seek," Maxentius replied, then turned his back to the general and watched Rome's gates swing open onto the Flaminian Way.

Outside the city walls, Maxentius reined up and the parade came to a halt. The groom rushed over with the mounting block and helped him reach the ground. Instinctively, the cavalry formed a protective semicircle around their leader, keeping the emperor's sacred body safe from the crowd of curious plebeians.

Like the heroic generals of old, Maxentius understood that now was the time to offer inspiring words to the troops. Throughout Rome's history, the leaders of her armies had been rhetoricians as well as warriors. But today Maxentius intended to surpass even the great Julius Caesar. He had decided to give an oration—punctuated with a dramatic action—that would never be forgotten as long as the empire lasted.

"Men of valor, I salute you!" he bellowed to the accompaniment of enthusiastic cheers. "Let it be known that today we ride out to a much greater contest than you might imagine. We are destined for a glorious battle—one fought not only by the strong arms of men, but a battle fought in the heavens among the gods themselves!"

The men cheered again, though less robustly this time. Maxentius could see his words had caught their attention, making them wonder as to his meaning. The troops were puzzled, yet they clearly wanted to hear more. So he gave it to them.

Using the eloquence that all aristocrats had been taught in their schoolboy training, Maxentius proceeded to paint a picture of a great heavenly conflict. The new god, the foul Jesus of the Christians, was a recent intruder into the Roman pantheon. This mangled and impoverished criminal draped naked on a cross surely didn't belong there. He was despised, defeated, crowned with thorns instead of gold. What power could such a god have? Maxentius urged his troops to consider instead the muscular glory of Hercules. Here was a hero worthy of worship! The great Hercules had performed twelve mighty labors, including slaying the Nemean lion with a club.

"Could the pitiful Jesus do that?" Maxentius demanded, his taunt drawing guffaws from the gathered riders. "With what weapon, I ask you? The bloody nails in his own wrists?"

Maxentius turned and received a book from his servant. He held it up in the morning light. In his other hand he grasped an iron-bound club. "Behold the book of the Christians!" he cried. "This is their so-called gospel, a book of fables and legends! The Crucified One supposedly rose from the dead, but who can believe the testimony of peasants and dirty Jews?" After letting the scornful laughter subside, Maxentius continued. "Now look here! In my other hand I hold the club of Hercules—a weapon of war, a tool of conquest! Which will it be, men? Do we fight with mighty weapons or Jewish lies and myths?"

"Weapons!" the soldiers thundered.

"Let me hear it again! Weapons or lies?"

"Weapons!"

As the rowdy troops gave vent to their fierce aggression, Maxentius realized the moment had arrived for his unforgettable demonstration. He threw the Christian book to the ground and stamped it into the mud. Then, with slow and deliberate motions, he lifted his armored tunic, dropped the waistband of his trousers, and exposed himself to the onlookers. Raucous cheers erupted from the crowd, signaling to Maxentius that his men were suitably impressed by his male anatomy. With a cocky grin, the emperor let loose a stream of urine onto the sacred scriptures of the catholic church.

No sooner had Maxentius started urinating than a commotion arose. Shouts and a couple of empty-handed grabs from the troops couldn't prevent a commoner from darting into the circle of riders. The interloper threw himself onto the book, covering it with his body to prevent further desecration. He remained still, awaiting whatever fate would befall him.

Maxentius gestured toward the man on the ground. "Look here, brothers! We have a fine example of a Christian! Behold this fool groveling in the mud like a pig!"

"Kill him, Majesty!" a soldier shouted.

"Crush his skull!" added another.

Maxentius stared down at the man's back. The worthless fellow was dressed in the coarse woolen tunic common among the lowest classes. His sandals were cheap, and his belt was just a scrap of leather. It would be easy to club him to death. But Maxentius had a better idea.

"Pick him up!" he ordered the nearest Praetorian, who wrestled the man to a standing position. Though his face and chest were covered in mud, his eyes were defiant as he clutched the book.

Maxentius marched to a nearby tree. Several Praetorians followed, dragging the Christian along. Enraged by the man's brazen fearlessness, Maxentius seized the captive by the tunic and slammed him against the trunk.

He grabbed the man's wrist and pinned it above his head—then shoved his dagger through the Christian's hand.

Though the man's face crumpled, to his credit, he stifled his cry of pain. Snatching a dagger from the belt of a nearby Praetorian, Maxentius repeated his action with the captive's other hand. "Now do his feet," he ordered the guards. They impaled the Christian's ankles, then stepped back and left him squirming and bleeding against the rugged wood. The muddy, bloodstained scriptures lay at his feet.

Maxentius spit in the man's face. "Behold the follower of Jesus!" he cried. Curses and jeers rained down on the helpless victim.

The emperor returned to his stallion and mounted again. "Do not be afraid of your fate today, mighty warriors!" he shouted. "The outcome of the battle is already decided! Victory is ours! We ride out to meet Constantine, who fights under the sign of the cross." Maxentius swept his arm toward the man hanging on the tree. "As you can see, my brothers, you need not fear! That feeble sign has no power in it!"

"To war!" the lanky general yelled with his sword lifted high. All the men took up the battle cry, for an ancient bloodlust had seized them now.

"To war!" they shouted in unison. And then, with a collective roar like a living beast, the army of Maxentius turned its back on the crucified man and surged north onto the Flaminian Way.

Rex blew into his cupped fists to warm them, though the action didn't do much to take away the dawn chill. A cold fog lined the banks of the Tiberis River as it ran west to east at this quiet spot two miles north of the city. Countless Maxentian troops—Praetorians, horse guardsmen, and regular infantry from the Italian and African legions—milled around on the near side of the river. Across the water, somewhere not far to the north, Constantine's forces were readying their attack. This meant the two armies would have to meet at the ancient Milvian Bridge, a stone crossing built four hundred years ago in the time of the Republic. However, while the famous bridge had stood there ever since, neither of the armies would be using it to cross the Tiberis today. Emperor Maxentius had ordered it cut it in two.

Rex stared at the ruined bridge, procrastinating because of the unpleasant task he was about to perform. Several of the stone arches had been demolished, rendering the bridge impassable. All traffic on the Flaminian Way had been shunted to a makeshift wooden bridge that rested on a row of boats anchored to the riverbed. The crazy-looking thing wouldn't be a long-term solution, but it didn't have to be. It only had to be sturdy enough to last through the battle.

"Maxentius did the job right," Aratus observed. "Nobody's getting across the Milvian today. Even the best horse couldn't jump that crack. It'll take a hundred stonemasons a month to repair it."

Rex nodded. "He's desperate to get Constantine onto that pontoon bridge. Flavia heard him say it's the core of his plan. He thinks drowning his enemy in Rome's river would be symbolic."

"Real generals care more about winning than symbolism."

"Apparently, Maxentius believes he can get both. He rigged that bridge to fail."

"You think he intends to spring the trap himself? *That* would certainly be symbolic."

"I doubt it. He'll probably put another man in charge. Whatever he has in mind, we can't let it happen."

"Then you'd better get going." Aratus gestured to the sky. "The sun is up, and this fog is thinning already. I'll keep everyone away while you're out there."

"Still no sign of Geta?"

Aratus shook his head, grimacing and uttering a curse. "He's supposed to be here. That stinking German! He'd better have a good excuse."

"I'm German too, you know," Rex said with a chuckle.

"Of course I know. You stink like the rest of 'em! It's us Greeks who invented bathing. Now get out there before the fog lifts. If we don't figure out how this trap works, our whole mission will be a failure."

Rex shed his armor and undertunic and slipped into the river wearing only his leather trousers. The fog provided good cover, and no one was paying attention anyway, so he felt certain he hadn't been seen. As expected, the river's icy chill took his breath away. Yet there was nothing to do but swim. Rex knew the exertion would warm his body, and he would grow accustomed to the frigid temperature.

The pontoon bridge consisted of thick wooden planks nailed to a line of identical boats. Each boat was held in place by four anchors, making the edifice sturdy enough for horsemen to cross. Rex swam to the middle of the span and slipped under the planks between the center two boats. Though the gloom made it hard to see details, when he reached up and felt around, his hand closed on a rope. It was taut against the underside of the planks, running back toward the riverbank on the city side. Rex kicked his feet and slid through the water, following the rope to its other end.

The line terminated at an iron pin. Here the planks formed a critical juncture between the northern and southern halves of the bridge—yet the only thing connecting them was the bar of iron. Though Rex was no army engineer, he could see that more nails and another pontoon should be at this spot. The bridge's stability depended on its being a single unit whose ends were secured on the riverbanks. Sever the two halves, and the whole structure would become unstable. Certainly it wouldn't be able to bear the weight of an army.

Rex jiggled the lynchpin, expecting it to be tight, but it was surprisingly loose. *The cold probably shrunk the metal,* he surmised. One hard yank on the rope would free the pin and bring the bridge down. The engineers had done their job well. If Constantine were to mount this bridge in full armor, he would be in deadly peril. Pulling the pin would send him into deep water. He had to be warned right away.

Rex could hear low voices on the riverbank as he swam back to the place where he had left his clothing. He ducked in the water and held still. One of the speakers was Aratus. The other, unfortunately, wasn't Geta.

"You aren't supposed to be here," Aratus barked to the intruder. "I was ordered to watch the bank and keep everyone back. Move along, guardsman!"

"But I'm thirsty!"

"Orders are orders. Get going!"

After a few more complaints about his empty canteen, the soldier grunted and left. Rex emerged from the river, dripping and shivering. The centurion handed him an old saddle blanket. Rex toweled off and quickly redressed.

"It's a dangerous setup," he told Aratus. "There's just one lynchpin holding the whole thing together in the middle. It should be strong enough for us to cross. But that bridge can be collapsed at any time by a lone man tugging a rope."

"Then we have to get across and warn the augustus. Can you swim it in armor?"

"Not without holding on to a horse. And that would certainly draw attention. I'd get a javelin in my spine for my effort."

"What if I created a diversion while you galloped across the bridge?"

Rex shook his head. "Stakes are too high, sir. Too much chance of failure in that scenario."

"I know. I was just testing you." Aratus clapped Rex on the shoulder and gave him an approving wink. "It looks like we'll have to slip away as soon as Maxentius leads his army across the bridge. I expect a lot of confusion. You know how it is—everyone milling around and forming ranks. There's some thick brush on the far side. We can disappear and make a run for Constantine's lines as soon as we get out of sight."

"I'll have to get rid of my shield first," Rex said, pointing to the insignia from the imperial horse guard, "or I won't exactly receive a warm welcome."

"I don't care if you run naked into their camp waving a white flag. You've got to reach Constantine before he advances to the bridge."

"I will, sir. You can count on me."

"I wish Geta were here," Aratus muttered.

"He'll show up soon. I'm sure of it. You know better than anyone how we like to compete and trade insults. But the truth is, we're brothers forever. He'll come, even if at the last moment. He's always ready for a good brawl."

"Yes, he's a good man, and a great fighter. But Rex—you are his superior in battle." The centurion conveyed with his expression the sincerity of the compliment. Aratus didn't do that often.

Rex turned the idea over in his mind. "Why did you tell me that, sir?" he asked at last.

"To give you confidence. The best warriors believe they're invincible. They believe they can't be stopped. They charge into combat with no expectation but total victory. Constantine is like that. And so are you."

"And so is Maxentius."

"Perhaps. What's your point?"

Rex shrugged. "Self-confidence isn't necessarily a virtue. A man like that keeps pressing until he wins. He stops at nothing. And I mean nothing, Aratus."

"So what? Such a man will always triumph, simply through sheer determination."

"Over everyone but himself."

Aratus frowned at this. "Winning feels good no matter how you achieve it."

"Maybe. But is that what I want—to win at any price?"

"You should try it and find out. Listen to me, Brandulf Rex! You're the kind of person who can reach the top. Not many people can. You might like it up there."

Rex remained silent for a long time. Finally, he said, "I probably would."

"Good. I'm glad you recognize it. Now let's get back to the lines. We've been away long enough."

The two men fell into step and trudged up the steep riverbank toward the Maxentian encampment. Rex's hand rested on his sword's pommel, its eagle's head firm and comforting in his grip. Today he would thrust that weapon into the flesh of other men, draining the life from them. Aratus was right—Rex would charge into combat without the slightest expectation that anyone on the field could defeat him. His skills were too sharp. His moves were too quick. He was truly invincible. If he wanted to, Rex knew he could kill his way to the top. Yet even as that thought struck him, his own question flashed into his mind again. *Is that what I want?*

Yes, Rex admitted. *Yes, it is.* The realization immediately prompted another, more sobering question. *Is that who I really am? A killer? A tyrant?*

"If that's what it takes," Rex whispered aloud, forcing the grim truth to become real.

Yet you can choose a different way, countered a delicate voice in his head.

A trumpet sounded in the distance, piercing the morning fog and dispelling Rex's thoughts like mist. It was the signal to mount up.

"Here we go," Aratus said with a cocky grin. "Remember, now—we disappear into the forest as soon as we cross. Whatever you do, find Constantine before he hits the bridge."

"The mission has come down to this. I won't fail you, sir."

The centurion reached out, and the two men clasped each other's hands as brothers-in-arms.

"No one can defeat you, my son," Aratus declared.

He's right, Rex thought. *But can I defeat myself?*

⸺◦∾∾◦⸺

In the end, it wasn't Emperor Constantine who started the great battle. It wasn't even a general, nor a knight, nor even a common foot soldier.

It was a pheasant.

When the bird exploded out of a patch of dense foliage near the Red Rocks cliffs, the scouting party from the Twenty-Second Firstborn—one of Constantine's favorite legions—knew exactly what had caused it. Pheasants didn't flush without reason. The enemy was in the field.

"Form up, men," Constantine ordered. Unlike most emperors, who stayed in the rear, he liked to ride out with the vanguard. He considered himself a good commander, experienced in war and at home on the battlefield. Yet this wasn't a fight in which he should personally engage. The elite scouts of the Twenty-Second Firstborn would destroy whatever Maxentians were lurking in the underbrush.

In short order, the horsemen were rumbling across the grass, drawing out the enemy like the bird they themselves had flushed. The Maxentian riders emerged from their hiding places and began to advance toward their attackers. A hail of javelins flew across the battlefield, crisscrossing in midair as each side bombarded the other. Though a few of the horses took hits and tumbled to the ground, most of the spears missed. For a long, tense moment, the two forces careened toward each other with a throaty battle cry. And then the riders engaged.

Even from a distance, the impact of the clash was a tangible, physical force. "Fight well, brave warriors!" Constantine shouted from the saddle as he watched the confrontation. Enthralled, he stared at the melee. There was no sound but the thunder of sword against shield, the clang of blade on blade, and the unquenchable screams of men releasing their souls into the waiting sky.

"We're taking them, sir!" exclaimed the tribune at Constantine's side. "Look! They're falling back. It's about to turn into a rout. Shall I call for the rest of the army to head for the bridge?"

"No. The Firstborn can chase down this rabble and finish them off. But we won't let Maxentius dictate the terms of our advance. I have no intention of letting battle lust upset our well-laid plans. We will proceed at a measured pace."

"Ho! Ambush from the right!" yelled one of the emperor's bodyguards.

A party of light cavalry—African Moors from the look of their dark skin and long-legged horses—had just burst from the craggy red cliffs. Every soldier feared these auxiliaries for their rapid-fire archery and hit-and-run tactics. The Moorish riders were on an interception course with the Twenty-Second Firstborn, whose flank was exposed and undefended. The Moors' hail of arrows, unreturned by the forward-facing riders who were chasing down the enemy, would be deadly.

"We go now, men!" Constantine cried. "We won't abandon our brothers!"

"No, stay here, Your Highness!" the tribune urged. "We'll handle it!" But Constantine was already on the move.

He cantered onto the field, then immediately rose to a gallop. The stallion between his thighs was a splendid creature, a battle-hardened warrior who responded to even the most subtle commands. Constantine's armor, though decorated, wasn't the ornamental nonsense that military pretenders liked to wear. Other than the trim, it was the same light, strong scale that real cavalrymen wore. His shield was thick, and his spear was stout. No one was going to defeat the Augustus of the West today.

"Archers, give them a volley!" he shouted.

A moment later the sky above and ahead was filled with deadly missiles arcing toward the Moors. The whispering danger in the air and the awesome sound of thundering hooves made the enemy horsemen look away from their quarry. Only a few Moorish arrows had been released toward the Twenty-Second Firstborn. Now the ambush party of mounted archers was forced to wheel away. Since speed was their primary tactic, they weren't armored for close combat. The Moors knew they couldn't withstand a charge from heavy horse. Escaping on their fast African steeds was their only hope now.

But God and his green earth had different plans. Surveying the terrain ahead, Constantine could see the Tiberis River swerve toward the rust-colored bluffs, creating a narrow place unsuitable for a fast escape. The ground was too rough for a gallop, so the fleeing Moors bunched up and began to panic as the heavy cavalry bore down on them from behind.

"Press on!" Constantine cried, urging his stallion forward. "Spears down! Hit them hard!"

The climax of a full-out cavalry charge can be appreciated only by men who have experienced it. Though Constantine had participated in many such charges, each time he was shocked by its raw force and the sudden explosion of violence. Like a blacksmith's hammer on an anvil, or like a woodcutter's ax on a tree, the cavalrymen smashed into the Moorish enemy with devastating effect. Blood, bone, and pulp created a rosy haze around the furious warriors. Horses screamed as their forelegs snapped and they tumbled to the earth. Men wailed as spears impaled them or hurled them from the saddle. Death was king now, and hell was hungry for fresh meat.

Constantine gripped his lance in two hands and aimed for the spine of a terrified Moorish rider. The spear burst from his enemy's belly to bury its blade in the horse's neck. Constantine released the weapon. Though the Moor and his mount went down, the emperor's stallion sidestepped the obstacle and barely broke its stride as it surged toward the next foe. The sharp edge of Constantine's sword severed an arm and a head in two mighty blows. A red mist clouded his vision as he burst from the melee. Wiping his eyes, he circled around to assess the situation, ready to reengage wherever he was needed most. But the battle was over as quickly as it had begun. The elite force of imperial bodyguards had annihilated the lightly armored Moors, all of whom lay dead on the field of battle.

"Victory!" Constantine cried, raising his bloody sword. "Victory for us, and salvation for the Twenty-Second!"

The bodyguards circled around their leader. "How valiant you are, Your Majesty!" one of them gushed.

Constantine lowered his sword and raised the shield on which the tau-rho had been emblazoned. "The cross is a mighty sign indeed," he said, striving for proper Christian humility lest Jesus be angered. "Surely the Highest Deity helped us today."

"Shall I call for a full advance?" the tribune asked again.

The emperor paused, truly reconsidering his battle plan this time. Though he hadn't wanted to be drawn into combat too quickly, the rout had emboldened him. The early victory at Red Rocks would demoralize Maxentius's troops once news of it spread. Perhaps a swifter attack was called for after all. A sudden, hard strike might finish off the tyrant with a definitive blow.

"Make haste to the rear lines," Constantine instructed the tribune. "Tell General Vitruvius to set out at once, marching double time. Foot in the center, horse on the wings. It's seven miles down the Flaminian Way to the river crossing. I'll be waiting there."

"Very good, sir. And what then?"

"Pull out your sword and start swinging. I intend to meet Maxentius at the Milvian Bridge under the sign of the cross. And may the gods of old be damned."

———※———

Rex gripped the saddle horn and swung into the seat with the effortless dexterity of an experienced equestrian. The riders of the imperial horse guard had been assigned to protect the right flank of the infantry as they marched across the plain to confront Constantine. While the orders were clear, everything was confusing now, for the Maxentian army had just crossed the pontoon bridge and was mustering on the northern side of the river. Centurions were barking commands here and there, trying to organize the men into the desired battle formation. Rex managed to find Aratus, who, although mounted on horseback as an officer, was deployed with the foot soldiers.

The grizzled Greek speculator leaned close to Rex from the saddle. "See that bunch of trees? When the battle starts, try to work your way over there. I'll do the same. The bushes are dense. You can disappear in the thicket, and if you come out the back side, you'll be near Constantine's troops. He won't be hard to pick out. He's a fighter, that one. He'll be out front. Just get to him somehow."

Rex nodded his agreement, then spoke in a low voice. "Sir? What about the Constantinian soldiers? It looks like we won't be able to defect until after the fighting has started. Are you going to kill them? We're actually on their side."

"This is war, son. You have to be willing to kill anyone to get the job done. Don't hold back. The other guy surely won't."

"Are you sure?"

"Trust me, Rex. Trust me like you have since the first time I handed you a sword."

Rex slid his spatha from its sheath—not the wooden sword of his youthful training but the deadly weapon of a grown man. He extended its tip toward his beloved mentor, the proud Roman officer who had accepted him as a boy and turned him into a warrior. "Victory or death," Rex said, his voice heavy with emotion.

Aratus drew his own sword, touching the blade to Rex's. "That's right. Victory or death, just like I taught you. Never forget."

The two men parted on the battlefield like soldiers always do, confident in their training yet resigned to a fate beyond their control. Rex took a position at the end of the line, as close as possible to the copse of trees. The overcast sky—finally deciding to deliver on what it had been threatening all morning—had begun to spit sleet on the grassy plain. Tiny ice pellets bounced off Rex's armor and tinkled on his helmet. He reached into his saddlebag for a lump of sticky resin, which he rubbed on his sword's hilt and the grips of his lance. Things were going to be slippery today, and he didn't want to take chances.

A trumpet sounded from across the river. All heads swung toward the pontoon bridge as Emperor Maxentius, resplendent in his golden armor, rode his charger onto the wooden span. Although the animal was too big for such a petite man, it was well trained and surefooted, so it was able to negotiate the crossing despite the deficiencies of its rider. Rex thought about his own traverse across that bridge a few moments ago. The troops had been ordered to ride single file lest they overburden the structure. The makeshift contraption had seemed solid enough for the job, yet Rex thought he could sense a certain shakiness at the spot where the lynchpin was hidden beneath the planks.

The emperor's arrival on the northern riverbank galvanized the men, giving them a rallying point around which to form up. At last the ranks and files came together in a double-square formation, with the Praetorians making up the first block and the conscripted African and Italian legions marching in the second. The Praetorians were experienced veterans, brave men who wouldn't fold at the first enemy charge. Clearly, they should serve in the front line. As needed in the flow of battle, they could receive support from the second block of legionaries. The infantry's flanks were protected by the cavalry, spread out like wings on either side. At the rear, Maxentius and his bodyguards would occupy a low hill from which the generals could survey the battlefield.

"Move out at a walk!" the cavalry commander shouted. "Stay in line with me, and prepare to raise your gait on my order!"

Rex's horse was a good one, a stocky chestnut pony out of the Sardinian stud farms. The creature was old enough to have seen battle yet still young enough to have some spring in its step. Rex stroked his mount's neck and bent to whisper in its ear. "When I ask for it, little friend, give me every-thing you have." The horse's only response was a toss of its head and a flick of its flaxen mane.

Across the plain, a dark smudge indicated the front line of Constantine's men. The visibility was poor because of the wet weather, and the damp-ness must have had a muffling effect too, for Rex couldn't hear the distant rumble that normally accompanied an army on the move. Yet sight or sound wasn't necessary. Everyone knew the Constantinian horde was on its way.

The cavalry commander blew a shrill blast on a whistle. "Enemy riders approaching from the northeast! Rise to canter!" The troopers of the impe-rial horse guard complied at once, each man responding to his comrades as if connected by an invisible thread. Rex couldn't help but marvel at what an effective fighting force these soldiers were. *But today they will meet their match!*

To the northeast, the detachment of Constantinian cavalry drew closer. They rode hard and clearly were eager for battle. Each man's shield was marked with a tau-rho in bright white paint. Rex reminded himself that this was the sign of Flavia's chosen god, and Emperor Constantine's too. He vowed not to kill a man who fought under that emblem if he could help it.

"Spears down!" the commander bellowed. "Full speed now, brothers! And may the strength of Mars be yours!"

The imperial horse guard closed the final distance and crashed into the line of Constantinians like two great ships ramming each other at sea. Rex steered his pony through the enemy riders without engaging them as ag-gressively as he could have. He took a few glancing blows on his shield and used his spear to unseat a rider without running him through. Daylight showed ahead, so he headed for it and burst from the melee not far from the thicket Aratus had identified.

The imperial guardsmen in the initial wave began circling around to reen-ter the fray, but Rex edged his mount away from them. "Line up! Line up!" the commander screamed. Instead, Rex pointed his spear at a pair of enemy scouts lurking near the trees. "I'll take care of those two first!" he replied.

Without waiting for permission, he urged his mount toward the scouts— a justifiable action in the tumult of war, though perhaps skirting the line between courage and insubordination. Yet common military wisdom said any attack from the flank was dangerous and had to be prevented by countermeasures. That would be Rex's argument, at least, if anyone ever questioned him about riding away.

The lightly armed scouts melted into the forest as Rex approached. He entered the dense stand of trees, grateful to get out of the cold rain. No trails pierced the thick undergrowth, but the sturdy pony from the scrubby Sardinian highlands could pick its way through the tangle while Rex kept a lookout for ambush.

Despite his vigilance, though, he was unprepared for the attack when it came. The scouts had dismounted and taken up positions away from their horses to conceal their location. When they rose from the brush and loosed arrows, Rex was barely able to bring his shield around in time. One of the missiles pierced the wood with a loud *thunk*, while the other glanced off his helmet with a force hard enough to snap his neck backward.

But no harm was done, and now the men were exposed and on foot—a dangerous predicament when facing an experienced cavalryman. Rex's horse leapt over a fallen log and knocked one of the footmen sprawling into a patch of briers. The second man dove aside as Rex swiped at him half-heartedly with his lance. These were Constantinian soldiers: fellow comrades in theory, though still mortal enemies until Rex could give up his undercover identity and rejoin the true emperor's side. Right now the men viewed him as a deadly foe who ought to be killed, and Rex had no desire to give them what they wanted. Yet he was mounted, and they were not. He could easily leave them behind. Instead of turning to finish them off, Rex simply kept riding.

The Sardinian pony squealed at the same moment Rex heard the sickly smack of an arrow piercing its flesh. The animal jumped awkwardly, then its rear haunches gave out. The collapse sent Rex tumbling from the saddle, and he lost his grip on his lance. He scrambled up to see a feathered shaft protruding from the pony's rump as it squirmed on the ground. *Useless now*, Rex realized, then turned his attention to the lone scout closing on him with an arrow nocked in his bow.

Since he possessed no ranged weapon, Rex could only raise his shield and charge at his foe, letting out a ferocious scream as he ran. The incoming arrow whisked past Rex's head, but the archer was quick and had another on the string before Rex could reach him. This time, he could hardly be expected to miss.

Rex snatched his shield from his left arm and gripped it in two hands. Like an Olympian hurling the discus, he sent the shield spinning toward his enemy, forcing him to lower his bow and dodge the heavy oaken missile. The action gave Rex the delay he needed. Lunging with his arm fully extended, he plunged his sword into the archer's belly just as the man brought his bow back up. The arrow fell harmlessly away as the archer realized he had gambled and lost. His face contorted into a tight grimace, and he dropped his bow. Rex put the heel of his hand on the man's chest and shoved him backward into the dirt. Bright red blood soaked the blade of Rex's sword, dribbling crimson droplets from its tip.

Yet this was no time to linger. Another scout was out there, perhaps maneuvering for a shot of his own. Rex recovered his shield and ducked behind a tree trunk, then made his way to where the other man had gone down. But this enemy was no threat. He was flat on his back in a fierce-looking thornbush. The thick briers had ensnared him, snagging his armor and holding him fast. Upon seeing Rex, he thrashed violently but couldn't break free of the thorns. At last he sank back and stared up at Rex with a hopeless look in his eye. He knew his end had come.

"Where's your horse?" Rex demanded.

"Why should I tell you?" the man spat back.

Kneeling, Rex wiped the blood from his blade on a clump of thick grass, then slid the weapon back in its scabbard. "Because we're on the same side. We both fight for Constantine."

"Liar! I see your uniform! You're in the horse guard!"

"Not everything is as it seems. Throw me your helmet."

"Get your own helmet."

Rex scowled. "Throw me your helmet," he roared, "or I'll change my mind about sparing you!"

The surprising words made the man more cooperative. Though his arms were constricted, he managed to get the helmet off and toss it onto the grass. Rex removed his own and strapped the replacement on his head. It was the new conical kind made of riveted plates like most of the Constantinians wore. The fit wasn't too bad.

"Your shield is with your horse?" Rex asked.

"Aye." The man flicked his head over his shoulder. "About a hundred steps that way, under the big elm."

Rex approached the mess of brambles that had ensnared the soldier. He used his sword to hack one of the thick branches that anchored the tangle to a tree, then another. At last the thorny vines sagged a little. "Wriggle around a bit, and you should be able to get out," Rex said. "In return, I need your horse and shield."

"Take them. I'll gladly trade them for my life."

"A fair bargain, I would say."

Rex turned to go, but the soldier hailed him from behind. "Guardsman! Why did you do that?"

"I told you. I fight under the sign of the cross."

An excited expression came to the captive man's face. "You fight for Jesus? I'm a Christian too!"

"I didn't say that." Rex withdrew the tau-rho amulet from his collar. "I fight for the man who gave me this."

"Well, my friend, you should know that's a powerful sign."

"So I'm learning. Farewell, Christian."

Rex found the man's horse where he said it would be. It was a spirited dapple gray that shied at first but quickly grew accustomed to its new master. Rex discarded his own shield and took up the important one: the one with the tau-rho painted on its face. Fortunately, the horse's tack was also distinctive to the frontier legions. With that mount and the new helmet and shield, everyone on the battlefield would immediately identify Rex as a Constantinian.

Which is what I am, he reminded himself as he swung into the saddle.

As soon as Rex emerged from the thicket, the sounds of battle confronted him again. Yet most of the action was away from him now, much farther south than he had expected. A chill ran through him as he realized what that implied. Constantine was having quick success—which meant he was pressing hard toward the Milvian Bridge, the focal point of the day's attack. Perhaps he had already reached it?

"Let's see what you've got, little fella," Rex said as he called for a canter from the gray. He wished he had the Sardinian chestnut between his legs, but warfare had a will of its own and a good soldier had to be ready to adapt. Rex set his eyes on the distant bridge and asked for a gallop from his mount.

The fighting was thick at the bridgehead. The Maxentians were in desperate retreat, yet they hadn't turned their tails and run. Though they were giving up ground quickly, they were extracting a price for it in blood. A barrage of javelins and arrows filled the air as both sides converged on the bridge.

Where's Constantine? Rex scanned the clashing armies, trying to find the most important man on the field. The emperor could usually be found at the forefront of any battle. *But where is he now?*

At last Rex spotted him. The Augustus of the West wore no ceremonial plumage or impractical armor—at least not today, when he actually expected to fight. Other than some gold trim, his kit was essentially what a top field officer would wear into battle: high-quality armor and light, strong weapons meant for real war. Yet despite such normal attire, Constantine was readily identifiable once Rex's eye fell on him. The imperial standards were clustered nearby, inspiring the troops and calling them to rally behind their glorious leader.

From across the river, a Maxentian hornblower sounded the call for a retreat. Now a huge mass of soldiers scrambled onto the bridge. For the first time, a spirit of panic began to strike them. The Maxentians were all trying to flee at once, and the temporary bridge was their only means of escape. Constantine could see it too. Like an avenging angel, he surged forward, eager for final victory.

"No! Stay back!" Rex screamed as he galloped on an intercept trajectory. Though he knew the warning couldn't be heard above the din of battle, the words burst from his lips nonetheless.

The gilded and gleaming Maxentius was visible on the far end of the bridge, seated on his white stallion in the midst of his retreating soldiers. He jabbed his finger toward his enemies, hurling curses at the advancing forces. The wind whipped his cape around his shoulders and sent the horsetail crest on his helmet flying behind him like the tail of a dragon. Arrows and javelins rained down near the emperor, splashing left and right in the Tiberis, yet a divine hand seemed to protect him. He refused to leave his end of the bridge—a bitter loser shaking his fist and snarling with rage.

The perfect lure for a warrior like Constantine!

A Maxentian cavalryman from one of the Italian legions caught sight of Rex as he sped toward the bridgehead. The two riders raced beside each other, each striving to beat the other to the goal. Though the Italian's long-legged mare had a bit of a head start, the dapple gray proved the faster of the two. As Rex pulled alongside the man at a full gallop, he leaned over and grasped his enemy's shield. Raising his sword, Rex swept the blade down in a devastating blow that severed his opponent's arm at the shoulder. The man squealed and fell away. Now Rex had a second shield. He extracted the bloody limb from the straps and cast the ghastly thing aside, then set the newly acquired defense on his right arm.

With his two shields raised above his head, Rex squeezed his thighs and guided the courageous gray into the hail of missiles hurtling across the space between the opposing armies. The horse was fast, yet it was also nearing the end of its strength. One . . . two . . . three arrows struck the shields above Rex's head. "Jesus Christ!" he cried. "Protect me!"

A gap opened among the troops, and the bridge emerged into clear view. Aghast, Rex could see he was too late. Constantine had reached it first and was preparing to cross. "It's a trap!" Rex screamed, but nothing could stop the emperor's advance. The experienced commander could sense victory was about to be his, and he intended to claim it without hesitation.

Now Rex changed strategy. Yanking both shields from his arms, he tossed them aside. He flipped the helmet off his head, then hiked up his chainmail tunic and started to wriggle out of it. Though he easily withdrew his arms from the sleeves, the tunic caught on his chin as he tried to pull it over his head. Blind for a moment, he could only trust the dapple gray as it churned forward, expending the last of its strength for its master.

Something smacked Rex hard on the skull, stunning him with the force of its impact. He shook away the dizziness and freed his face from the armor. As he hurled the tunic to the ground, he noticed an arrow snagged in the strong iron links. Apparently, both Jesus and the blacksmith had done their jobs well.

More arrows and javelins pierced the earth around the galloping horse as it raced along the riverbank. Constantine's own mount had arrived at the pontoon bridge and was seeking entrance. Maxentius was at the other end, taunting him. Between them was a horde of panicked soldiers.

A javelin fell from the sky and stabbed the dapple gray in the throat.

Its forelegs collapsed. The noble beast began to tumble headfirst into the mud. Rex leapt sideways from the saddle, hurtling through the air like a human missile.

For a long moment, everything was silent. Rex closed his eyes and braced himself.

And then, with a tremendous splash, the muddy Tiberis swallowed him whole.

⸺◈◈◈⸺

Dawn had come to Rome at last, but its light was thin and pale as it filtered through the high windows in the house church at the Aventine mansion. Flavia pulled a woolen shawl around her shoulders and stirred the coals in a brazier, for the day had turned colder than expected and the room was chilly and musty. The church meeting hall had been closed for a while because the recent upheaval in the city had interrupted the regular services. For the time being, the handsome priest Felix who led the congregation had been transferred to a different location. Yet Flavia still liked to come to the hall when she felt an urgent need to pray. And with Rex fighting in a colossal battle out by the Milvian Bridge, this was definitely a time for prayer.

The scriptures of God were stored in a wooden cabinet at the rear of the hall. Since the mansion was well fortified and safe from intruders, the cabinet was typically kept unlocked. Flavia withdrew the Old Testament, written in large Greek letters, and laid it on the lectern. It was an expensive book that few churches could afford. Flavia had pestered her father for a year before he finally gave in and purchased a copy. Yet it had been worth it, for the congregation had been blessed by God's holy words ever since. *And now, Lord,* she prayed, *give a frightened girl some encouragement on a scary day!*

Though Flavia was tempted to turn straight to the psalms—knowing they would speak about war since so many were written by King David—she sensed the text to which God might lead her lay somewhere else. She flipped parchment leaves again and again, seeking solace, but her anxious heart couldn't find rest. Today either her city was going to be liberated or its horrible dictator was going to win and become entrenched for many years to come. And if that prospect weren't fearful enough, Flavia knew Rex was out there among thousands of men who wanted to kill him.

Sure, Rex was vigorous and skillful in battle. But it would take only a single arrow hitting him in the wrong place, and the man she—

Flavia paused. *The man I what? Finish that thought*, she ordered herself. And when she did, it surprised her. *The man I love. Yes. It's true. I love Rex more passionately than I ever could have imagined. And now I can't live without him. I would marry him if he asked!*

The realization terrified Flavia, yet was also freeing in a certain sense, for at least the idea had become concrete and existent. She didn't have to bottle up this fact anymore, pretending it wasn't true. She didn't have to keep playing the game that Rex was merely a friend. The reality was that she, Lady Junia Flavia, was madly in love with an incredibly handsome, generous, cocky, winsome, tenderhearted, protective man—who also happened to be an unbelieving barbarian killer.

"God!" Flavia screamed, throwing up her hands. "How did this happen?!"

The sudden outburst caused a dove to burst from its roost on a high windowsill. The bird fluttered into the gray sky, leaving behind a puff of dust and down. Flavia watched a single fluffy feather drift from the rafters in a maddeningly slow back-and-forth tumble. But the feather did not touch the floor. It came to rest instead on the page of the holy book.

Flavia approached the scriptures slowly, uncertain if she should take the dove's feather as a random event or a divine sign. *There are no accidents with God*, a voice in her head reminded her, so she decided she had better accept whatever words she found as a special message from the Lord.

The codex lay open to the *Book of Jeremiah*. Flavia bent to the page in the dim light and began to translate the Greek from where the text picked up after the feather: "I will look after you, and confirm my words to you, to return your people to this place. And I know my plans for you, plans of peace and not of evil, that I might bestow on you these things. So pray to me, and I will hearken to you! Seek earnestly for me, and you will find me, when you search for me with your whole heart."

My whole heart. Flavia stared at those words a long time, pondering their significance. Her finger caressed the soft, smooth page as she considered what the words might mean. *God wants my heart to be united with his*, she realized at last. *But what does that require of me? And if I figure it out—can I do it?*

Footsteps sounded in the hallway. Flavia closed the book, then a man stepped into the church: the kindly doorkeeper Onesimus.

"My lady?" he said. "A visitor has arrived at the house. He seeks an audience with you."

"Who is it? I was not expecting anyone. Certainly not at this early hour."

"The man would not give his name. But from his looks, I could see he was a Germanic soldier in our army. He was tall and fair-haired. He said he knows you well."

Rex! You're alive! And you came to me!

Though Flavia's body churned with sudden desire, she kept her voice calm. "Tell the visitor I will greet him shortly," she said with aristocratic dignity. Onesimus bowed and turned to go, but Flavia grabbed his sleeve, pulling him close. "And send the ornatrix to my chamber right away!"

The doorkeeper gave his mistress a little wink. "Of course, my lady. Right away. I was young once. I understand."

Hurrying as much as seemed appropriate, Flavia returned to her bedroom. The ornatrix arrived soon afterward and did a quick job of applying rouge to Flavia's cheeks, pink gloss to her lips, and dark thickener to her lashes. When all was ready, Flavia drew a lovely silk mantle around herself, dabbed some perfume on her neck, and glided to the atrium where Rex was waiting.

Little pellets of sleet tumbled through the skylight and ruffled the pool's surface. Flavia's heart skipped as she sensed movement in the far corner of the room. Though she had intended to walk slowly and gracefully, she couldn't help but break into a run when she glimpsed the tall man in a military uniform standing in the shadows. A smile of uncontainable joy crossed Flavia's face as Rex turned to greet her.

But then he turned fully around.

Geta!

Flavia sucked in her breath and pulled up short. Geta did not stop, however, but closed the distance until he was standing very close.

"Good day, Lady Junia," he said smoothly. "As always, your beauty is like that of a goddess."

"I . . . I don't believe in goddesses."

"Of course you don't. What I meant was—"

"Geta, why are you here?"

"That is what I've come to explain."

"Where is Rex?"

"Fighting at the Milvian Bridge, obviously."

"And why aren't you there?"

"Ah, that is truly a complicated matter. But it relates to the politics of men. Trust me, you don't need to trouble yourself with it."

"Try me. I'd actually like to know. I'm, uh . . . I'm rather surprised to see you here."

Geta sighed. "Fine, I'll tell you. The simple truth is, I can't be seen publicly supporting either Constantine or Maxentius."

"Why not? I thought you fought for Constantine."

"No," Geta said with a shake of his head.

Flavia narrowed her eyes and recoiled. "Surely not Maxentius?"

"Of course not."

"Who then?"

"I have cast my lot with Licinius."

Licinius? Isn't he far across the Alps? What's happening?

Sensing Flavia's confusion, Geta smiled warmly. "Don't be afraid, Lady Junia," he said in a gentle tone, raising both hands in a gesture of consolation. "You'll soon see the wisdom of what I have in mind. Licinius is the emperor who can take us the furthest."

Us?

A cold knot of fear seized Flavia's gut. Something terrible was going on. She couldn't help but shrink away from the tall warrior with the strange look in his eye.

"Let me explain," Geta said, moving toward her.

"Stop!" Flavia exclaimed with a sudden thrust of her palm. Immediately, she realized the command was too intense. "Just give me a moment to think," she added more politely.

"As you wish."

Flavia's head was spinning now. Everything was strange and confusing. "I want to see Rex," she said at last.

"I can't go near him."

"But he's your best friend! You should be fighting at his side!"

Geta wouldn't—or couldn't—hold back any longer. He closed the final distance and almost grabbed Flavia by the shoulders, though he stopped at the last moment and lowered his arms. Even so, he towered over her and implored her with his eyes.

"Are you able to consider new ideas, Lady Junia? Can you open your mind? There are good reasons why I should be here with you!"

"L-l-like what?" Flavia stammered.

"Like the possibility of a very nice life. The best you could imagine."

Flavia's tongue was so dry she could hardly speak. "Geta," she finally gasped, "what are you *saying*?"

A stern and commanding voice interrupted the conversation from the doorway. "He's saying he intends to marry you, daughter," Neratius boomed. "And I intend to make sure it happens."

At these ominous words, Flavia's knees buckled, and she staggered backward. Only Onesimus's quick intervention kept her upright. He cradled Flavia's trembling body and helped her regain her footing. She clutched the servant's sleeve and stared into his eyes.

"Run to the stable," she said in a barely audible whisper. "Take the fastest horse and get to Constantine's camp. Wherever he is, Rex will be. Find him and tell him . . ."

Flavia's voice caught, and she had to swallow hard to continue her sentence. "Tell him I love him," she finished at last, "and I need him now more than ever."

Rex clawed his way to the surface of the icy Tiberis, desperate for air not because he had been under too long but because the frigid river had snatched his breath away. He burst from the water and inhaled deeply, then immediately swiveled his head toward the pontoon bridge. Maxentius was astride his horse on the southern side. At the other end, Constantine and his men were fighting their way onto the bridge, though the panicked Maxentian legionaries were blocking further access by their haphazard retreat. A steady drizzle of freezing rain made the whole scene a slippery mess. Many of the soldiers had already tumbled into the river, flailing around in a futile attempt to stay afloat despite their armor.

"Your God is pitiful!" Maxentius yelled, his shrill voice rising above the grunts and shouts from the soldiers. "Your Jesus rotted on a cross! Filthy Jews made up fables!"

Rex didn't know if Constantine could hear the insult—or how much he would have cared if he did—but either way, the emperor was pressing hard onto the bridgehead. It wouldn't be long before his men had cleared a space and the emperor was out on the planks.

Diving under the water to avoid being seen, Rex swam toward the middle of the span using the powerful strokes he had developed as a boy in the rivers of Germania. Arrows and javelins pierced the water here and there, and Rex knew that without armor, a hit would surely kill him. Yet he kept swimming. Only the luck of the gods could protect him now.

He surfaced not far from the bridge, its beams shaking and groaning under the strain. Along its entire length, Maxentian legionaries and cavalry were trying to push their way across. From his earlier reconnaissance, Rex knew the lynchpin holding the structure together lay under the center span. Somewhere at the end of the rope, a man was waiting to spring the trap and send Constantine to a watery death. *But not if the rope can be cut!* Rex was determined to give it a try. Though he had shed his armor and shield, his cavalry sword remained strapped to his side. It would be a hack job, but the blade could chop through the line—if he could reach it.

"Stop pushing!" someone screamed from above. "Make room!"

A terrified whinny and an unmanly scream combined to tell Rex that a mounted soldier had just fallen from the bridge. The flailing animal landed near Rex with a giant splash, casting its rider into the murky Tiberis. Rex pulled away, trying to dodge the frightened horse—

Wham!

Bright lights exploded in Rex's brain, then blackness washed over him, followed by an ocean of pain. His head pulsed with stupefying agony.

Groggy and disoriented, he let himself slip beneath the waves. The cold water seemed to help.

Just drift down . . . go to sleep . . . it will stop . . .

No! Get up! Fight!

Rex pushed away the dizziness and surged to the surface. Though the darkness faded as he emerged into the air again, everything was still confusing.

427

A hammer seemed to pound the base of his skull. When he put his hand to his scalp, his fingers came back slick and red.

Not far away, the horse thrashed in the river, its iron-shod hooves roiling the water as it fought against the weight of its saddle and tack. Rex realized that he had been kicked. He was about to swim clear when, from beneath the water, a hand grabbed his tunic and pulled hard. Rex barely had time to snatch a breath before he was dragged under again.

The rider who had fallen into the river was wearing chainmail—a death sentence to all but the strongest swimmers. Even so, death hadn't claimed this man yet. With the desperate strength that drowning men always seem to find, he tugged on Rex's clothes, dragging him deeper in an effort to climb up his back and break the surface. For a moment the soldier did manage to grab air, and Rex caught a sputtering breath as well. Then the two enemies plummeted beneath the waters again.

Now it was hand-to-hand combat as each warrior sought the advantage over the other. They tumbled deeper into the blackness, locked in a deadly embrace. Rex tried to pry loose his enemy's fierce grip, yet the man knew that relinquishing his hold would result in a free fall to the bottom. Neither fighter could disentangle himself from the other, so the pair writhed in the murky depths like a two-headed Leviathan.

Rex could feel his breath running out. He released one of his opponent's wrists, allowing the man to gain a much tighter hold; yet now Rex could grope for the sword on his belt. He found the hilt and pulled out the weapon—but in all the thrashing, he lost his grip on it.

Lurching and groping in the darkness, Rex found the blade. He closed his fist around the sharp edge, ignoring the hot sting across his fingers. To release the blade and try for the hilt with his one free hand would probably mean losing the weapon again, so Rex did what he had to do. He gripped the blade hard, pulled it back, and plunged it into the neck of the drowning man.

The wound was mortal. The soldier's body stiffened, then went limp. From the sudden response, Rex guessed he had severed his enemy's spine. The man's fierce grip on Rex's tunic finally relaxed.

But when Rex tried to push himself away from the doomed soldier, he was horrified to discover his own garments had become entangled in the chainmail. The man was now dead weight, dragging Rex into the depths like a ship's anchor. Down he plunged into the weedy gloom. His feet touched the riverbed, sinking into the squishy mud as he struggled to yank his tunic free of its snag. His air was running low, and the urge to breathe was strong. Rex fought against the panic that assaulted him as he found himself pinned to the bottom of the Tiberis by an iron-clad corpse. *Not here!* he told himself. *Not like this!*

Then he realized he still had the sword's blade in his hand. He shifted to a grip on the hilt, dimly aware that his fingers were sliced open. Grabbing a wad of his tunic, he shoved the sword under it and sawed upward. The cloth finally broke free. Rex jerked his feet from the mud and pushed toward the surface. Dark dread seized him, for he knew the top was very far away. He wasn't sure his lungs could resist the urge to spasm and inhale.

The frantic upward swim used the last of Rex's air. His chest ached, and everything in his body demanded that he open his mouth. The light was still far above. He gagged, and muddy water filled his nose and mouth.

No! This can't be happening!

Rex's field of vision narrowed. He stared as if through a tunnel at the light above. Now his movements were weak and listless. His brain lacked clarity; his body lacked desire. It was over.

A face appeared in the halo of light: a beautiful young woman with long eyelashes and high cheekbones. Her lips were a tiny pink rose. Chestnut hair framed her face. She reached out her hand, imploring Rex with her hazel eyes.

"I need you, my love," she said. "Fight for me." And those words made all the difference.

Rex kicked his legs hard, propelling himself to the surface in a final burst of strength. Light and air welcomed him to the land of the living. He retched as muddy water and spent breath exploded from his mouth.

And then he inhaled. A rush of wind flooded his chest like a cool, sweet, life-giving elixir. The world came into focus again. He had survived.

For a long time Rex could only pant. Each breath was a bodily pleasure so intense it rivaled anything he had ever experienced. A cold, hard rain was falling now, but Rex paid it no mind as he floated in the middle of the Tiberis. He greedily gulped down air.

At last he turned and looked at the bridge. Constantine's mount had ventured a few steps out. At any moment, the man holding the rope would pull the lynchpin and send the emperor plummeting into the thick sludge from which Rex had just escaped.

Gripping his sword in his bloody hand, Rex resolved to make for the bridge. Yet even as he began to move, he knew it was too far. Before he could get there and sever the rope, the trap would be sprung—probably on top of his head. The evil Maxentius had won after all. Rex couldn't stop him now.

But he had to try.

He had just started forward when a great squeal assaulted him: the sound of overstressed wood finally giving way. A timber snapped with a loud *crack*, then the two halves of the bridge peeled apart. The middle of the span collapsed as the rain-swollen planks tumbled into the roiling waters. Something must have caused the iron lynchpin to fall out early—but what? The shaking of the stampeding troops? The cold weather shrinking the metal? The icy-slick rain?

Or was it the hand of God himself?

Whatever it was, the bridge began to splinter across its length now that its structural integrity was gone. Chaos erupted as a horde of terrified riders toppled into the river. Though the horses managed to stay afloat, their armored masters immediately disappeared into the brown depths.

"Get back!" Rex screamed to Constantine, but the emperor didn't need the admonition. His light-footed warhorse had already backed up from the danger and found purchase on the slippery riverbank. Constantine could only stare in disbelief as the enemy disappeared before his eyes into the Tiberis's hungry maw.

At the other end of the bridge, Maxentius's horse was doing its best to find its footing, but it was a lost cause. The more the bridge's timbers gave way, the more unstable the whole thing became. Convulsing outward from the center to each end, the entire structure broke up and collapsed, spilling its occupants to either side. A look of terror crossed Maxentius's face as his white stallion lurched to the edge. It remained there for a long moment, its head thrown back, its eyes rolling.

"Welcome to hell, Maxentius," Rex said.

And with those words, the horse toppled from the Milvian Bridge, sending its golden rider into the abyss from which there is no escape.

14

OCTOBER 28, 312

Neratius and Geta loomed over Flavia like a pair of marble columns, immovable and cold in their masculine dominance. Clearly, they had conspired to arrange the repugnant marriage. Flavia drew back from them as much as she could, taking a seat on a divan in the corner of the atrium. Although social constraints dictated that she couldn't flee these men, at least she could increase her distance.

But what I really need is someone to stand between us. Please God, send Rex! Hurry!

"You'll see it all eventually, my dear girl," said Neratius in the patronizing tone that aristocrats so often used. "In time you will come to appreciate the wisdom of my decision. The days aren't like they used to be, when the rule of law prevailed. Today, strong men take what they want. Husbands have to be vigorous fighters—like this man here."

Geta bowed at the flattering words. "I am honored, Senator. I promise to protect the noble name of our family and the reputation of my future wife."

You are not my family! Flavia wanted to scream. *And I will never be your wife!*

But instead of screaming, she forced herself to remain calm and respectful. A violent argument was the last thing she wanted now. Folding her hands in her lap, she said, "Father, I do see the wisdom in what you're suggesting. But my heart belongs to another man. I cannot marry Geta."

"You will do what I say!" Neratius barked, his eyes flaring. "As you will soon learn, Geta is much more than what he seems to be. I'm making alliances here that will set up our family for the new regime."

"Alliances? Father, is that all I am to you—a political tool?"

"Wake up, Flavia! Do you think politics have no consequences? You have no idea what powers are moving against us, even as we speak!"

"I have no false impressions about my safety. Perhaps you forget I spent time in the Carcer. I know exactly how harsh the rulers of Rome can be."

"That's right. Harsh and swift." Neratius waved his hand toward the mansion around him. "You see all this? They can take it away from us, you know. Just like *that!*" He snapped his fingers to emphasize his point.

"Who? Who is fighting against us? Pompeianus is dead."

"But Maxentius isn't—nor the tramp at his side."

"You mean Livia? The widow? It is rumored she is to become the next empress."

"She is. And she's coming after your mother for treason."

"Treason? No! It's untrue!"

Neratius stomped over to Flavia's couch and wagged a finger in her face. "Don't play the actress with me, daughter! Neither of you is innocent! Maxentius learned all about your absurd little conspiracy with your mother. And now I know about it too!"

The emperor knows about the coins in the bread? A hot flush of panic came to Flavia's cheeks as the reason for Neratius's fear became apparent. *Maxentius will attack us for sure! We've got to get out of here!*

Before Flavia could form a response, Neratius spun away and went to the door that led from the atrium to the rest of the house. "Boys!" he shouted, although the young men who did physical work around the mansion were hardly children. "Hurry up with those trunks! We're running out of time!"

Flavia abandoned the safety of the divan, aware now that some kind of action was required. The first order of business was to get out of Rome. Evidently, someone in the imperial palace had divulged information about the conspiracy—and when Maxentius felt threatened, he always lashed out with vicious reprisals. Even if he lost the battle today, his henchmen still had their marching orders, and those thugs took delight in cruelty. Rome was going to be in chaos for a while. During times like that, anything could happen. It would be wise to leave the city before it went crazy. Later, in some safer refuge, Flavia would work with Sophronia to thwart the ridiculous marriage plans.

Two slaves arrived with a heavy trunk on hardwood poles. They set it on the floor of the atrium. "Very good," Neratius said. "Wait here for the next three to arrive."

"Where are you taking us?" Flavia asked.

"Puteoli. I have a friend down there. Soon to be a family member."

A family member? The statement was strange, so Flavia dismissed it, saving her strength instead for a final plea on her mother's behalf.

"Father, listen to me," she said in a gentle voice. "Whether you agree with our conspiracy or not, you need to know that Mother acted bravely. You would have been proud of her."

Neratius whirled around. The rage in his eyes was like nothing Flavia had ever seen in him. "I take no pride in an act of treason against a sitting emperor!" he roared. "Sophronia was a fool! A cursed fool!"

"No! Don't say that. Don't curse your own wife!"

"Why not? She cursed our family when she started plotting against Maxentius."

"He's a tyrant. Someone had to stop him!"

Neratius snorted and swatted his hand. "Well, my little revolutionary, it seems you failed. Now your mother has been summoned to the emperor's bedroom. Execution is likely to follow. The procurers are on their way. Why else do you think I'm packing so quickly?"

"Wh . . . what?" Flavia's mouth fell open, and she lost her voice. She felt as if her father had punched her.

"You heard me. Rape and execution."

No! Lord Jesus! Have mercy!

The awful news sent Flavia reeling. With one hand she clutched the fabric of her gown, and with the other she steadied herself against a statue next to the atrium pool. Sleet was falling hard through the skylight now, disturbing the water and bouncing off the marble flooring. Flavia stared at it absently, trying to comprehend the fact that rapists and murderers were coming to abduct her mother—and Neratius was packing the household treasures in trunks.

"Wh . . . where is she?" Flavia managed to say at last. She turned to go find Sophronia and warn her.

"Around the house somewhere. But don't run off. We'll be leaving soon."

A burst of rage exploded in Flavia's soul. She stormed toward her father, gripping the folds of his toga in both hands. "Fight!" she yelled at him. "Fight for your wife like a real man! Don't let Maxentius do this!"

Neratius could only stare back wide-eyed. Flavia had never confronted him like this before. At last he swept his hand toward Geta, pointing with his finger. "I am fighting! Look! I'm marrying you to the best warrior I could find. Geta will protect our family."

"That's your job!" Flavia screamed in her father's face.

"Not any longer," he replied.

A fist pounded on the mansion's outer door. All heads swung toward the sound. "Open up in the name of Maxentius!" called a rough voice.

Flavia and Neratius turned back to each other, locking their eyes in fierce opposition.

"They're here," Geta said.

Although the Maxentian legions from Italy and Africa fled the battlefield like cowards, Rex had to give the Praetorians credit for their bravery. The fighters of this historic unit, founded in the ancient days of the Republic, remained in combat array until they were completely surrounded by Constantine's troops. Only when all hope was lost and the order to surrender was given did they lay down their arms. It wasn't clear yet what would happen to them. Demotions and transfers to the distant frontiers were likely. Constantine had even talked about disbanding the Praetorian Guard altogether, after more than three hundred years of continuous service. "Too loyal to Rome," he had said.

Rex stumbled out of the frigid Tiberis on the city side of the river. Most of the Maxentians who had fallen into the water when the bridge collapsed were at the bottom now. Only a few had managed to overcome the weight of their armor and reach dry ground. They sat in a dejected huddle, shivering and wet, under the watchful eye of a detachment of Constantinian guards.

A soldier pointed his spear at Rex. "Ho, you there! Your tunic is from the imperial horse guard!" he accused.

Rex straightened his shoulders and rose to his full height, which was quite a bit more than his accuser. He rested his hand on his sword's pommel and looked the man in the eye. "This is a disguise. I am Brandulf Rex, a speculator of the Second Italian Faithful Legion of Divitia and a servant of the true Augustus of the West, His Majesty Flavius Valerius Aurelius Constantine." It felt good to speak the truth again after so many months of undercover secrecy.

"So you say," the soldier muttered with one of his eyebrows cocked.

Rex approached the man until the spear point was against his chest. He slipped the back of his hand against the iron tip and diverted it. "So I am, comrade. Now, stand aside. The emperor is crossing on a boat. He will not be pleased to find you harassing a member of his espionage corps."

The soldier grunted at this bold assertion yet relented. Rex left him standing alone in the mud with his spear and his suspicions.

He made his way to a spot along the river as close as possible to where Maxentius had fallen in. A few horses were still in the water, struggling toward one bank or the other, but all the human swimmers had either reached safety or died in the attempt. Rex walked out until he was knee deep. He had an unpleasant job in mind, yet it was one he knew Constantine would want. Perhaps this worthy deed would compensate for the shame he had earned at Verona when he abandoned the emperor in the heat of battle. "Jesus in heaven, protect that secret," Rex whispered. The prayer caught him by surprise, and for a moment he marveled at how often he was praying to Flavia's god these days. Yet this was no time for reflection on religious matters. Instead, he waded farther into the Tiberis and dove beneath its waters once again.

Inky blackness enveloped him as he kicked toward the bottom. Fortunately, the water wasn't deep here. Rex's hand probed along the riverbed, feeling for anything but thick mud. His hand soon closed on the forearm of a corpse, but the armor was chainmail so Rex left it alone. He found two more corpses before he had to surface to breathe. Both of them also wore the wrong kind of armor.

On his third dive, Rex found a corpse wearing a coat of scale armor. He felt the helmet: conical, richly decorated, and sporting a horsetail crest. A fur cape was fastened around the shoulders of the dead man. It could only be Maxentius.

Rex hauled the body out of the water and dragged it onto the bank, letting it flop like a child's doll on the muddy grass. The ghoulish pallor of Maxentius's face stood in stark contrast to his purple lips. His tongue lolled out one side of his mouth, and his unblinking eyes stared at the overcast sky. Cold rain pelted his cheeks, but the dead emperor no longer cared.

"You deserved your fate," Rex said, feeling no pity for the man who had murdered so many innocent people.

Stooping next to the corpse, he grasped an arm and a leg, heaved the burden to his shoulders, and stood up. Though Maxentius had been a man of small stature, the weight of his golden armor was ridiculous. Rex approached Emperor Constantine, whose boat had landed not far away. A squad of imperial bodyguards now encircled the great man as he prepared to enter Rome in triumph.

"Stay back," one of the guardsmen warned, thrusting out his hand.

"The grave pit is over that way," said another with a flick of his head.

Rex didn't budge. "I need to speak to the augustus. He knows me well."

"He knows you? *Tch!* I doubt it." The first bodyguard waved his hand dismissively. "Move along, kid."

"You sure you want to anger Constantine on the day of his victory? It'll probably mean a demotion for you."

"What?"

"When the emperor finds out you blocked his direct order, he won't like it."

"Coleos Jovis! What are you talking about? What direct order?"

"Quit wasting time!" Rex snapped. "I'm here on the official business of the augustus. Go ask him yourself! Tell him Brandulf Rex has completed his mission—and I have the body of Maxentius to prove it."

The bodyguard took a closer look at Rex's burden. Recognition came to his face as he noticed, beneath the dripping cape, the golden scales. He took a step back. "I'll check with the emperor," he said.

Moments later, Constantine himself came striding over with a huge grin on his face. "Rex!" he boomed. "You did it! You stirred up the people against our enemy. I heard they mocked him in the circus!"

"They did, Your Highness." Rex dipped his chin, unable to look Constantine in the eye. Despite the praise, he couldn't shake the feeling that the augustus was going to recognize him as the man who ran away at Verona.

But the emperor seemed unaware of those events. He gestured to the corpse on Rex's shoulders. "So that's my great enemy, eh? Lay him down and let's have a look at him."

Rex complied, dumping the body on the ground. He winced and rubbed his shoulder, glad to be relieved of the heavy weight.

"Ugly fellow, wasn't he?" Constantine said with a curl of his lip.

"Even more so in death."

"I need the head. It has to go to Africa so they know he's truly gone. Until then, his loyalists will fight on."

"You want me to hack it off, sir?"

"No. Show me some swordsmanship." Constantine bent over the corpse and grasped the horsetail crest on Maxentius's helmet with both hands. Since the helmet was strapped on tight, the emperor was able to elevate the body by its head. "Take it off nice and clean, soldier."

Rex grasped the hilt of the cavalry sword on his belt and made sure he had a firm grip. Then, in a single fluid motion, he drew the weapon, swung it around in a wide arc, and cleaved Maxentius's head from his body. The sharp blade never stopped moving as Rex put all his strength into the slashing blow. The headless corpse collapsed to the ground, and Constantine was left holding the decapitated head.

"Nice work, young man!" the emperor exclaimed. "I knew from the first time you challenged me to a fight that you had the makings of a great speculator."

He remembers! Holy Jupiter and Jesus, please never let him find out about Verona!

Rex couldn't contain his smile. "Thank you, sir. Aratus taught me well."

"Indeed he did. Your stroke is powerful and accurate." The emperor turned to go. "Mount up, Rex. You can ride with my parade into the city. I'm entering the sacred precinct as the savior of Rome, and you had an important role in that victory."

I even killed Pompeianus, Rex thought, *but that's not an honor I want you to know about.*

The vanguard formed up with Constantine at the head of the mighty column. The emperor's most elite officers and bodyguards were positioned around him, many still in their bright uniforms because they had seen little combat today. Although the horse Rex had been given was arrayed in a gaudy military style suitable for a parade, as he looked down at his tunic, he couldn't help but feel out of place. The thing was muddy, wet, bloodstained, and marred by a hole in the chest where he had cut away the fabric in his underwater battle. He tried to wring out some of the water and wipe away the mud, but it was hopeless. The tunic was ruined.

Constantine must have noticed Rex's futile attempts to clean up. "Apparently, you're the only real fighter among us," he joked. "You're the only one with enemy blood on his shirt."

"I'm not fit to ride next to the Augustus of the West," Rex said sheepishly.

"Nonsense! You look like a true warrior. But let's see what we can do for you." The emperor beckoned to a quartermaster from the rear lines. "Take off your tunic and give it to me," he ordered.

The supply officer complied immediately, stripping to his loincloth and handing over the soft woolen garment with crimson piping. Constantine held it up and inspected it, then tossed it to Rex. "It's quite a nice one. I hope this man isn't embezzling funds from the imperial treasury."

The nearly naked quartermaster's eyes widened. "No, sir! Definitely not!"

Constantine threw Rex a wink and a grin. "Even the men who didn't fight need to taste some fear today," he said with a little laugh.

"Of course. Aratus always says fear is a good motivator."

"Wise centurion you have there. Fall in behind me, son, and let's go claim the capital of the world."

The victorious emperor rode in triumph down the Flaminian Way for two miles. Rex followed close behind, holding the standard of the Second Italian Legion with its banner of Rome's famous she-wolf and twins. At last the parade arrived at the same gate through which Maxentius had ridden out earlier today. A jubilant crowd had developed, spilling from the city to line the road or cheering and waving from the high walls. Just as the parade was about to pass through the gateway, Constantine signaled for a halt.

"Who is that man on the tree?" he demanded. When no one answered, he repeated his question more urgently. Finally, a peasant stepped forward.

"He is a Christian who protected the holy scriptures, Majesty," the man said. "Maxentius mocked him and crucified him this morning."

"He still lives?"

"Yes, Majesty. He is . . . he is my cousin."

Constantine turned in the saddle and called for his personal surgeon to come forward. "Take down that poor fellow and attend to him with the very best care. Spare no expense. I shall expect him to make a full recovery."

"Yes, my lord. Count on it, for it will be done." The surgeon saluted and hurried toward the impaled victim.

The parade now entered the city of Rome to the raucous acclamation of the people. Clearly, they viewed Constantine not as an invader but as a liberator. Rex knew how much the citizenry hated Maxentius. Everyone was glad to be rid of the tyrant. The sight of his decapitated head on a spear brought jeers and ridicule as the standard bearer carried it through the streets.

A massive throng was gathered in the Forum when Constantine entered the historic town square, the beating heart of ancient Rome. The cheering onlookers parted to let their new ruler pass. He stopped in front of the partially constructed New Basilica on Sacred Street, just a few steps from where Rex had first met Flavia as she was being dragged in chains to the amphitheater. Maxentius had been funding the basilica as a monument to his own greatness. A giant statue of himself, seated on a throne like a god, had been planned for the apse of the enormous hall.

"I hear there is still much work to be done," Constantine observed as he gazed at the lofty structure.

A gaggle of politicians had emptied from the Senate House when Constantine arrived, and now they surrounded the triumphant emperor as he surveyed his city. "Your Highness, the evil usurper Maxentius commissioned this building," said an oily-voiced senator, bowing low as he spoke. "But now the funds will surely dry up. Where will we obtain the needed resources to finish it?"

"I shall pay for its completion," Constantine said gallantly. He paused, as if thinking about something important. "There is a great statue inside, yes?"

"It was to be of Maxentius," the senator agreed. "But it is not complete. The head is still being made."

Constantine let out a hearty laugh. He beckoned to his standard bearer, then took from him the head of Maxentius on a spear and held it up. "If the statute was supposed to represent the former tyrant of Rome," he cried, "then I believe it is now complete!" The witty remark caused all the senators to burst into boisterous applause.

The emperor swept his hand toward the New Basilica. "People of Rome, forget the face of your oppressor Maxentius! It is I who sit on the imperial throne now. Let the statue be crowned instead with the bust of Rome's true defender. And let my new statue hold in its hand a trophy of mighty power!"

"Hurrah!" the crowd exclaimed.

"What trophy, Highness?" called another senator.

Constantine turned to Rex and took from him the military standard of the Second Italian Legion. "Like this," he said, elevating the pole with its crossbar from which the legion's banner hung. "A normal army flag, a traditional sign of victory—but one that, by the providence of the Highest God, also forms the sacred sign of the cross."

Clever, Rex thought. *A double meaning for Christians and the old pagans.*

A minor disturbance made Rex look down at the crowd from the saddle. A common slave was pushing his way through the mob. With a final shove, he broke into the open and approached Rex's mount. His face was red and his brow was sweaty. "You are Brandulf Rex, are you not?" he asked.

"Do I know you?"

"No, but you were pointed out to me. I am Onesimus, doorkeeper of Senator Neratius Junius Flavianus."

"Ah, right. I have heard of you. Lady Junia is very fond of you."

"And it is because of her that I have come. Please! You must go to her house immediately. The matter is urgent!"

Rex gestured to the victory parade. "I can't leave now. Look! We're celebrating the triumph of the Augustus of the West."

"But you have to come," Onesimus insisted. "Lady Junia says she needs you now more than ever."

"Rex!" the emperor called. "What is this disturbance? Leave it behind, and let's be going. The men wish to sacrifice to Jupiter on the Capitoline. No more delay."

"I'm sorry," Rex told Onesimus. "I can't leave my duties right now." He reined his horse around and rejoined the formation as it moved away.

"Wait!" the doorkeeper cried. "Lady Junia calls you to her side. She is in terrible danger! She needs you!"

Danger? Rex halted and sat up straight in the saddle. A fierce debate now raged within him. *The emperor will despise me and crush my aspirations if I gallop away. But how can I say no to Flavia in danger?*

"Come on, soldier!" Constantine barked. "I said to get moving!"

Onesimus rushed forward and gripped Rex's forearm. The look in his eye was desperate. "Brandulf Rex, listen to me!" he hissed. "Lady Junia told me something else. Something very important—a thing she has never said before."

"What?"

"She confessed that she loves you—you and you alone, with all her heart."

For a long moment, Rex said nothing as he grappled with the momentous choice. Competing voices clashed in his mind, each making its case, vying for his future. Suddenly Flavia's voice rose above the others, repeating what she had told him long ago when they had just met: *love becomes real when the feeling becomes an action.*

All at once, the turbulence in Rex's soul dissolved. Clarity of purpose settled upon him. The way forward was clear.

"I will come," he declared, "for I love her in return." With those words, he turned his horse out of formation and spurred it toward the Aventine Hill.

<hr>

Like a breach in a sewer pipe, the front door to Flavia's house gave way and a flood of filth oozed in. About twenty of Maxentius's thugs—not proper Praetorians but the kind of street toughs that worked as the city's pimps—rushed into the atrium of the Aventine mansion. Their leader was a long-haired man with an eye patch and a greasy beard. "We're here on imperial business," he proclaimed, obviously proud of his status.

"We know why you're here," Neratius said.

"Good. Then there won't be no problems."

Flavia noticed Geta move to Neratius's side, ready to resist, but her father cautioned him with a quiet word. "Not now," she saw him whisper.

If not now, when? she wondered.

The leader of Maxentius's procurers strode up to Neratius with a belligerent

441

look in his one good eye. "Go get the mistress of the house." His face widened into a yellow-toothed grin. "I hear she's frisky. Likes to play."

"Not often enough! Know what I mean?" Neratius said with a wink to the man.

Father! That's disgusting!

Flavia recoiled even deeper into the shadows of the atrium. She could only assume her father was stalling for time while pretending to cooperate and befriend the invaders. Any other explanation was too horrible to accept.

"Who's this guy?" the greasy leader asked, jabbing his thumb at Geta. "Looks like a soldier boy."

"My future son-in-law. He won't give you any trouble."

"Better not. We're here on imperial business."

"Yes, so you said."

The Maxentian procurers had spread themselves around the atrium, and now a few of them began to wander toward other parts of the house. Neratius halted them with a sharp command. "Your jurisdiction does not extend to my whole property," he barked.

"Fancy words, Senator! But you're right—as long as you cooperate." The one-eyed leader turned to the rest of the men. "Boys! Get back here. It's just the lady we're after. This ain't a full proscription."

Flavia blew out a breath, relieved that at least the entire house wasn't about to be destroyed. Enemies of the state who were put under proscription were subject to execution and the confiscation of their property. Apparently, Maxentius was restricting his punishment to Sophronia alone. With the rest of the mansion off-limits, perhaps there would still be a chance for her to sneak out.

"Hey, boss!" one of the procurers shouted. "Who's that girl? Maybe the augustus wants her too?"

"She's probably guilty of somethin'!" another man chimed in. "Let's take her along."

"She is to be my wife!" Geta shouted, moving close to Flavia. "Lady Junia is not part of this arrest."

"You're not in charge here, kid!" the leader with the eye patch shot back. "We can do whatever we want."

Geta thrust out his chin. "By what authority?"

"By this authority!" Eye-Patch drew his sword and held it up. Several of his fellow procurers surrounded him, clearly spoiling for a fight.

"Get out of here, quick!" Geta whispered in Flavia's ear.

Flavia darted toward the exit but wasn't fast enough. One of the thugs grabbed her by the arm. "Where ya goin', little pretty?" he said with a leer.

"Enough!"

The room fell silent. All heads turned toward the speaker. Lady Sabina Sophronia stood in the entrance to the atrium, wearing the distinguished gown of an honorable Roman matron. Her face was tranquil, and her voice was steady. "There is no need to run around this house like wild beasts. Be still and show some respect. I am resigned to my fate."

"No, Mother! Don't give in!" Flavia wrenched her arm from her captor's grasp and ran to Sophronia's side. "You can't let Maxentius win!"

Sophronia looked into her daughter's face. Flavia thought she could see deep sadness in her mother's eyes. "My dear, sweet child," Sophronia said, stroking Flavia's cheek. "All things are in the hands of the Lord. Even life and death."

"Please! Don't say that!"

"It is true, my love. Believe it."

"That's the lady we're after," Eye-Patch announced to his gang. "Arrest her and let's go."

Flavia whirled toward Neratius and Geta. "Do something!" she pleaded. But Neratius remained aloof, which meant Geta could only shrug in helpless impotence.

One of the procurers was about to seize Sophronia's wrist when she stopped him with a firm rebuke. "Wait!" she commanded with such force that the man stepped back. "Do you dare touch the one who has been devoted to the glorious Maxentius? Shall I tell him how you pawed the emperor's lover?"

Despite the ruffian's tough appearance, his face turned scared. "N-no ma'am," he sputtered. "I didn't touch you. See?" He raised his hands as if to protest his innocence.

Sophronia pointed her finger at Eye-Patch. "You, sir! Are you the leader of this band?"

"Yeah. What of it?"

"Maxentius is famous for his jealousy, is he not?" When Eye-Patch gave a little nod, Sophronia pressed her point. "If any of you dares touch me, do you think his rage will be light? Far from it. He will take his vengeance upon you all!"

Flavia could see the men believed it. They looked uneasily at each other, waiting for their leader to decide what to do. Sophronia's bold words had them completely off balance.

"We won't touch you," Eye-Patch said at last. "But you have to come with us." He turned toward the front door. "Follow me, lady."

Sophronia let out a high-pitched laugh—the last thing the men were expecting to hear. They had anticipated fear and cowering, not derision for their social ineptitude.

"What's so funny?" Eye-Patch demanded. Though he spoke roughly, Flavia could sense his confusion.

"You fools!" Sophronia scoffed. "You know nothing about women, nor how to please an emperor!" She gestured to her face and clothing. "Do you really think this is suitable attire to meet the great Maxentius? Does not every courtesan come to him after at least an hour with the ornatrix? How much more should a senator's wife make herself presentable? It will take some time before I am made worthy to be seen by such a great man."

A trick! Mother can hide in the house and slip out a window! Brilliant!

Unfortunately, Eye-Patch was thinking the same thing. "Fine," he agreed. "Go put on your paints and perfumes. You have one hour to get ready and come back. But I got twenty men here—enough to surround this place. If you try to sneak off, I can put you in chains. And the lash is allowed on runaways too."

"That will not be necessary. As I said, I am making a decision of my own free will. I know there is no way to escape this house. I will not flee like a criminal, as if I could somehow evade notice on the streets of Rome. In one hour, you may do as you wish."

"You'd better be back on time, lady! We're keeping your girl here just to make sure."

"My daughter isn't subject to any reprisals from Maxentius. Your orders are for me alone. Anything else will be a violation of the emperor's will."

The truth of the remark seemed to make Eye-Patch nervous. Everyone knew how volatile Maxentius could be at even the slightest hint of disobedience. "The girl stays here until you get ready," he muttered. "Then we'll leave in peace."

"Very well. I shall retire to my room now," Sophronia said gently. After a polite dip of her chin, she turned and left the atrium with aristocratic dignity.

The one-eyed leader went to the mansion's front entrance and looked around, then shouted over his shoulder, "I want fifteen of you out here now! Circle this place and watch every window." His assistants shuffled outside, leaving the atrium much less crowded yet no less threatening. The six men who remained were a sufficient reminder of Maxentius's evil intent.

Geta sat down on one of the trunks that the household slaves had brought. After a short wait, he said, "I suppose we might as well have a drink." He beckoned to the servant girl Daphne trying to sneak past the door. "You there! Bring me a jug of wine."

The timid maid nodded, then returned promptly with an amphora. Geta unstopped it, tipped it back, and guzzled from it. He glanced over at the six procurers milling around the atrium. "Want some?"

Eye-Patch raised an eyebrow and stared back at the German soldier offering him wine. His face displayed only suspicion.

"Go on," Geta insisted. "Have a drink. There's plenty for everyone."

"Why not, boss?" urged one of the thugs. "It's safe. He's drinking it himself."

The exhortation was enough to break the leader's resolve. He accepted the jug and took a swig from it, then passed it around to his men. "Pretty good stuff," he admitted with a loud belch.

Neratius stepped into his study and returned with a goblet. "Pass it over here when you're finished. That's a quality vintage, and I'm thirsty."

The utter insanity of the scene disgusted Flavia. She felt like she was trapped in a terrible nightmare—naked and exposed or falling from a cliff or stuck in clingy mud or struggling to escape a monster. Yet any one of those scenarios would make more sense than the bizarre events unfolding before her. *This can only be a ruse*, she told herself as she sat on the divan in the corner. *It has to be some kind of stalling game. Yes, that's it. Surely my father isn't drinking wine with my mother's pimps and my future husband!*

Eye-Patch took another draught from the jug, then wiped his greasy beard with the back of his hand. He spotted something in Neratius's adjacent study and went to retrieve it. Moments later, he returned with an hourglass. "We'll start it now," he said, setting it on the rim of the atrium's pool.

The sleet and rain had finally stopped falling, and the sky had brightened a bit. Now that it was midday, Flavia realized she was hungry. At one point she rose from the divan and tried to step into the kitchen for something to eat, but the procurers immediately stopped her. "You stay put, little girl!" one of them said roughly. Rather than anger the men, she complied.

Slowly yet dreadfully, the trickle of sand slipped through the hourglass's narrow waist. Flavia felt the tension in the room increase as the pile grew at the bottom. At last the final grains dribbled through the aperture. Flavia prayed her mother had managed to climb out a window and make good her escape.

Eye-Patch snatched up the hourglass and swaggered over to Neratius. "Where's your wife?" he demanded.

"She's coming soon," Neratius replied, his voice slurred from too much wine. "You know how women can be."

Eye-Patch was drunk now, too, but the wine had made him irritable instead of relaxed. He scowled at Neratius. "I'm ready to get this over with! Why isn't she here?"

"How should I know? I don't care where that treasonous hussy is!"

"Father!" Flavia exclaimed, rising to her feet.

"It's true," Neratius said. "I've got no use for her anymore."

"You're lying!" Eye-Patch accused. He drew his sword and waved it around to emphasize his point. "You're just trying to buy her time! No man betrays his wife like that."

"Sophronia is no longer my wife," Neratius declared.

What? Another ruse? Is he serious? God help me!

The bewildering announcement caused Flavia to sink onto the divan again. Even the procurers were taken aback. Neratius walked into his study and returned with a pair of legal documents, each impressed with a wax seal. "Can you read?" he asked the leader.

Eye-Patch shook his head. He signaled for one of his helpers to inspect the parchments. The man looked them over, then glanced up. "They're real," he confirmed. "The first is a divorce paper for Lady Sabina Sophronia. Second is a betrothal agreement."

"To who?"

"A girl named Vulcacia. The fourteen-year-old daughter of a politician in Puteoli."

No!

"A new family member," Father had said . . . His friend Publius! This can't be happening!

Everyone stared at Neratius. The procurers didn't know what to say. Even Geta's mouth was agape. But the senator only shrugged.

"She got old," he said simply. "I got tired of her. It happens to a lot of men."

Flavia could stand the tension no longer. The urge to flee overwhelmed her. She had to warn her mother . . . escape this evil house . . . defy the insane world her father had inflicted upon her. She bolted for the exit—but was snatched by one of the pimps before she could take three steps.

"Let me go!" she screamed.

Flavia struggled in the man's cruel grip, but he was much stronger. His fingernails dug into her upper arm. "Hold still, wench!"

"No! Get out of my house, you fiends! Maxentius has lost already. The battle is over! Constantine has won!"

Neratius's response was immediate: "Silence, daughter!"

"That's treason!" Eye-Patch accused. He grabbed Flavia by the back of the neck and hurled her onto the divan. "Stay right there! Now you're coming with us too."

Geta rushed to the couch and tried to slip a protective arm around Flavia. "I'll get you out of this, my love," he whispered.

Flavia wriggled out of his grasp and shrank away from the disgusting German soldier. "Leave me alone! I am not your love!"

Eye-Patch pointed his sword at Flavia. "Keep an eye on that girl," he said to one of his henchmen, then turned toward the others. "The rest of you, draw your weapons and follow me. There's been enough fooling around here. I'm going upstairs to find that lady. It's time to take Maxentius his prize."

One of the men paused uncertainly. "Hey, boss? What if the girl is right? What if the emperor has already lost?"

The yellow-toothed smirk came to Eye-Patch's face again. "Then I guess the prize is ours to enjoy instead. Come on, boys! Let's go and claim it."

———•❀❀❀•———

The mansion on the summit of the Aventine Hill was surrounded by foul-looking ruffians when Rex arrived. They lurked near the front entrance and lined the alleys on either side. The sight of such rough men at Flavia's home made him want to charge into the fray and find out what was going on. Yet the military tactician in Rex made him hold back from any sudden moves. At least ten thugs—Maxentius's city pimps, Onesimus had said—were visible in the streets, and there was no telling how many more were inside. A lone man couldn't defeat so many opponents. If Rex was Flavia's only hope, he had to play this one just right. Secret infiltration of the premises was required.

He scanned the mansion with the eyes of a trained speculator, looking for the easiest access points. Most city houses had few doors and no windows at ground level, since wealthy residents considered it wise to conceal the opulence of their homes from the jealous masses. Yet the lack of entrances wasn't necessarily a problem. Back in his cadet days, Rex had been instructed in housebreaking by some of the best burglars ever to pilfer the jewels of Rome. He recalled the words of one expert thief, a wiry little Scythian saved from crucifixion on the condition that he pass on his knowledge to the imperial speculators: "Doors are for guests, and windows are for birds, but a burglar uses the roof." The trick wasn't getting through the roof, for the tiles were easy to remove. The real difficulty was getting onto it.

Rex frowned as he evaluated Flavia's house. On a planned mission, the use of ladders or grappling hooks by night could give access to a building's roof. But this was no planned mission. Rex felt a growing urgency as he realized he needed a much more immediate solution, one that didn't require any special gear. Climbing up from the street wasn't an option. Only a descent from a higher point would work. He glanced around, checking for nearby heights. *Adjacent roofs? All too far. The umbrella pine? Perhaps.*

It grew near the back corner of the mansion: a gnarly and misshapen tree, probably two hundred years old. Such a large specimen wouldn't be found in the crowded urban lowlands, but up here on the luxurious Aventine, many houses were still shaded by greenery. *That drop from the canopy looks a little long*, Rex thought, but he decided to worry about it later. It was probably just an illusion. Either way, the tree was his best choice under the circumstances.

Now the mental steps for his infiltration began to fall briskly into place. *The guards around the perimeter require a diversion. Get them good and distracted, then drop to the roof from the pine. The diversion will provide cover, but I'll have to be quick. Lift a few tiles, and I'm in. Simple as that. Time to move!*

The Aventine Hill was crowned by the Temple of Ceres, and next to it stood a popular new tavern that celebrated one of the grain goddess's most bountiful gifts to men: beer. Although grape wine had long been the beverage of choice in Rome, the recent influx of barbarians had opened up a market for the grain-based drink too. The tavern's typical patrons were immigrants and slaves, fair-haired men of the north who longed for the taste of the yeasty, sludgy brew of their homelands. Rex entered the crowded barroom and immediately saw it was full of his kind of people: gregarious and excitable Germani seated at benches with big cups in front of them. *Perfect.*

"Maxentius is dead!" he shouted into the tavern's busy hubbub. "Hail Constantine Victorious, our new emperor!"

The dramatic words immediately silenced the room. All eyes turned and stared at the intruder who had just thrown out the life-changing news. The quiet pause seemed to build until it reached its breaking point—then the room exploded into a frenzy of whoops and acclamations.

"The tyrant is gone!" one man shouted in a booming voice that rose above the general celebration.

Another fellow was more skeptical. He hurried over to Rex. "Are you sure about this?" he asked through his bushy mustache.

"Definitely. Look at my tunic." Rex gripped the fabric. "I'm in the army, and I just came from the Forum. Constantine brought in Maxentius's head on a spear!"

A crowd had developed around Rex now. "You're sure it was him? He's really dead?"

"I saw the decapitation with my own eyes. All the people of Rome are rejoicing. Come see for yourself!"

Everyone spilled from the tavern and thronged the front steps of the temple. Down below, the Circus Maximus was visible, with the Palatine rising behind it. A mob had gathered in the racetrack, waving Constantinian military banners and cheering wildly.

"The Praetorians would never allow that if they were still in control," someone observed.

Rex nodded vigorously. "It's time to spread the word, friends. Let the people know they are free!"

The idea appealed to the half-drunk Germani. They bolted from the temple steps and began to ramble through the maze of streets atop the Aventine, shouting the good news to anyone they encountered on the sidewalks or in the balconies. "Maxentius is dead!" they proclaimed again and again. "Hail, Constantine!"

"Look there," Rex said, pointing to the nervous-looking procurers outside Flavia's house. "I think those men served the tyrant!"

"Hey, pimp!" yelled a husky Goth wearing a blacksmith's apron. "Are you with Maxentius?"

When the man's only reply was a crude curse, a couple of the Germani stormed over to confront him. A scuffle broke out, and Rex decided the diversion was sufficiently in place now. He headed for the back of the mansion where the old tree was growing.

Fortunately, the twisted pine had some knobby branches below its first major fork. Rex managed to shimmy up the trunk to the crook of the tree, then followed a side branch into the canopy. He was so focused on his handholds that he didn't notice how high he had climbed until he stopped for a breather. Although Flavia's roof was below him now, the drop was much farther than he had hoped it would be. To make matters worse, the roof was pitched steeply toward an inner courtyard.

I need a rope, he thought. But, of course, he had no rope.

One of the tree's branches drooped farther than the rest over the mansion's roof. It was slender, yet it looked like it would support a man's weight. Rex guessed if he could dangle from it and make it sag, the drop wouldn't be too far. He stretched for the branch, leaning out as far as he dared, but the limb was just out of reach.

Should I jump?

He examined his right hand. Two deep gashes crossed his fingers and the heel of his palm where he had gripped his sword blade underwater. He flexed his fingers, hoping they would be strong enough to hold on. It wasn't a sure thing, yet he had no other option if he wanted to get into Flavia's house. Fixing his eyes on the target branch, he made sure his stance was steady, then leapt into empty space.

Rex caught the limb easily and clutched it in both hands. Now he hung from it like an African ape. His heartbeat was rapid as he stared between his feet at the roof below. Yet there was no point waiting in one place. Every moment wasted would increase the fatigue in his arms. Hand over hand, Rex began to move out onto the branch.

He quickly discovered that his plan was working. The farther he advanced from the trunk, the lower the limb sagged and the closer the roof became. By the time he was out near the tuft of needles at the branch's end, he thought he would probably—

Snap!

The branch broke, and Rex plummeted to the roof. He hit the tiles hard and began to roll down the incline. A few of them shattered, cutting his side, but he had no time to think about that as he tumbled toward the eaves. A fall over the edge into the marble courtyard of the rear garden would surely break a bone, or worse. He swiped frantically at any protuberance he could find but couldn't arrest his fall. The pitch was too steep. Aghast, Rex reached the edge and went over.

And caught the gutter as he fell.

Truly scared now, he dangled from the trough that channeled rainwater into the garden's central cistern. Glancing over his shoulder, he could see that a second-story gallery ran around the interior perimeter, forming a balcony that overlooked the garden. Fortunately, its balustrade wasn't far away. Rex swiveled his body and stretched his foot but missed the railing. On his fourth attempt, however, he made contact.

Stabilized now, Rex was able to get his other foot onto the railing as well. With a push from his hands and a swing of his body, he dropped safely onto the gallery that circled the garden. *Gods in heaven, thank you!*

If that was you, Jesus, I hail you!

Rex put his hand to his side and felt warm blood where the broken roof tiles had sliced a gash. The wound was deep enough that a surgeon would have sewn it closed, but that kind of care couldn't be had now. Rex's right hand was also bleeding where he had grasped the tree branch. Yet at least he was inside the house and on solid footing again.

This part of the mansion, with its secluded and pleasant view into the garden, housed the bedrooms of the master's family and his most esteemed guests. Rex didn't want to be noticed by anyone, so he ducked into one of the rooms with a curtain over its entrance. Shouts and commotion still rang from the streets, though the noise was dampened by the thick walls. A flurry of activity also seemed to be happening in the front of the residence, leaving the rear garden relatively quiet. If any of Maxentius's pimps were still in the house, they would probably be gathered in the atrium.

Rex was about to make his way to the front of the mansion when his eye fell on a ladder that a servant had been using to prune a cherry tree in the garden. Reaching over the gallery's railing, he snagged the ladder and pulled it up, then took it into the empty bedroom and laid it on the floor. If the pimps were guarding the front door, that would leave no other option for escape. Standard battle tactics called for never conceding such an advantage to the enemy. With the ladder, Rex knew he could escape the house at the time and place of his own choosing. It was just the kind of strategic foresight that often tipped the battlefield conditions in a speculator's favor.

He exited the guest bedroom and was at the top of the stairs when he caught the sound of female crying. *Flavia?* Cautiously, Rex approached the bedroom from which the muffled sobs were coming. Instead of being partitioned by a curtain, this elegant room was closed by a hardwood door. Yet its bronze pivot wasn't precisely flush with the jamb, leaving a small gap. Rex leaned forward and peered into the slim opening.

Lady Sabina Sophronia sat on the edge of her bed with a book in her lap and a kerchief in her hand. She read aloud as she traced the words with her finger, but the book was in Greek, and Rex knew only a little of that language. He thought he caught something about commending one's spirit into the hands of the father, but otherwise he couldn't make out what she was saying.

Should I knock? he wondered. *Call out to her? What if someone hears? Is she safer in there than anywhere else?* Rex blew out a breath of air. Nothing in cadet school had prepared him for a situation like this.

Sophronia put down her book and dabbed her eyes with the kerchief. Turning toward the rumpled blankets at her side, she found an object and gripped it in both hands.

What is that? What is she holding?

The noble lady raised the object above her head. It glinted in the light from the window. Rex's heart lurched as he realized what it was.

A dagger! She's killing herself!

"No!" he screamed, smashing his fist on the door.

But it was too late. The deadly deed was already done. Lady Sabina Sophronia's hands swept down to her breast, and she let out an agonized cry as the knife pierced her flesh.

The greasy man with the eye patch led four of his pimps from the atrium toward the upstairs bedrooms that overlooked the rear garden. "You don't have jurisdiction!" Flavia cried, echoing her father's earlier words, but the thugs ignored her and hurried toward the back of the house.

A sour stalemate now settled on the atrium. The lone guard left behind scowled at Neratius, Geta, and Flavia, and they stared back at him with the same level of disdain. The man was stocky and foul, as if a wild boar had risen up to walk on two legs. He loosened his sword in its sheath. "Don't get any ideas," he growled. "I'm handy with this thing. You just sit still—all of you."

Geta turned to Neratius. "Sir, these men are getting out of hand. And things are turning strange outside. There's yelling in the streets. I think we've reached a dangerous point here."

Flavia let out a frustrated *tch!* but suppressed any further response. *Dangerous? Didn't you think it was dangerous when you let in a horde of pimps?*

A cry of "Open up!" resounded from upstairs, followed by the sound of someone trying to kick in a door. Though it was sturdy, it wasn't designed to take that kind of abuse. The men would break into Sophronia's bedroom eventually. Only God knew what would happen next.

That's it, Flavia decided. *I'm going. Christ, help me!*

She leapt from the couch and sped from the atrium. "Hey!" the guard yelled, lunging for her. But this time Flavia had caught her enemy by surprise and was able to evade capture.

Geta finally sprang into action, too, though not with the devastating impact he could have had as a speculator. He merely spun the guard around and immobilized him with a chokehold. "With your permission, I can easily take him out," he said to Neratius.

Flavia didn't wait to see if her future "husband" received permission from Neratius to defend his family. These men had wasted too much time already. She turned a corner and bounded up the stairs toward her mother's bedroom.

The four thugs led by Eye-Patch were just about to knock the door off its hinge when Flavia arrived. The thing was nearly ruined already. By now the lintel was cracked and the hinge pivots were bent from repeated blows. A final kick from the beefiest of the pimps was enough to finish the job. The door banged onto the floor as the men stared into the room.

"Run, Mother!" Flavia screamed. "Jump out!"

Eye-Patch whirled to face her. Though he seemed surprised to see her, a lusty gleam quickly came to his eye, the universal look that only men can display. "I'm taking you for myself," he announced with a bestial grunt, "right after I take your mother!"

He swiped at Flavia, but he was still tipsy and she was much more agile. Dodging his lunge, she dashed into her mother's room—and into a nightmare.

Sophronia lay on the floor. Eyes closed. Covered in blood.

The handle of a dagger protruded from her left breast.

"What have you done?" Flavia shrieked. Rooted in place by sudden horror, she could only stare at her mother's corpse.

"We didn't do it, canicula!" growled one of the pimps. "We just now found her like that."

"No, you did it! You killed her!"

"She killed herself," the man replied. "Look! Her own hand is on the hilt."

Flavia began to rush to her mother's side, but Eye-Patch grabbed her arm. Wrenching it behind her back, he twisted it so hard that Flavia had to cry out in pain. "Hold still!" he ordered, then addressed his men. "What's this all about? The lady's dead?"

"Yeah, boss. Watch this." The man hauled back his foot and kicked Sophronia's thigh. His boot toe made a dull thud against the soft flesh, yet she did not flinch. He knelt and lifted the matron's arm. It flopped to the ground when he released it—lifeless and unmoving.

"A noble suicide," Eye-Patch declared. "Christian ladies are famous for it. They'd rather die than have sex with pagans, I hear."

"Maxentius won't want a corpse, boss."

Eye-Patch shrugged. "Looks like our job here is done, then."

One of the pimps had moved to an exterior window and was gazing out. He beckoned his leader to come close. "Look at this! There's a mob in the streets. They're all saying Constantine killed Maxentius today."

Eye-Patch shoved Flavia into another guard's hands and rushed to the window. He watched for a moment, then turned toward the man who had alerted him. "It's ugly out there. Why didn't you say something before?"

"Just noticed it, boss!"

"This isn't good," the leader muttered. He stroked his greasy beard, formulating a plan. "We've got to scatter," he said at last. "We aren't uniformed like the Praetorians. People won't recognize us if we're not together. They won't know we worked for Maxentius. We can disappear in the streets."

"So we don't bring the old lady with us?"

Eye-Patch cuffed his stupid henchman. "She's dead, and so is the emperor, you idiot! Our mission is over! It's time to survive now."

The man nodded slowly, comprehending at last. "But . . . can we take the girl with us?"

Eye-Patch glanced at Flavia, and the sick look of carnal desire returned to his face. "I think we could get away with that in all this chaos." His grin widened. "Why not, eh, boys?"

A cheer went up from the pimps. Eye-Patch swaggered toward Flavia, and her captor gave her a shove in the boss's direction. He reached out to caress Flavia's face. "Come here, my lovely," he said, his breath like rotten eggs.

"Here I am," Flavia whispered—then kneed him hard in the groin. He howled and doubled over. Flavia sidestepped him, dodged another lunging hand, and darted out to the gallery that encircled the garden.

"Get her!" Eye-Patch cried through his pain.

But the men were distracted by their own predicament and responded too slowly. Flavia reached her bedroom and slammed the door before they could catch up. A hook-and-eye latch served as a lock—strong enough to guarantee privacy from accidental intrusion, but not strong enough to keep out a determined assailant.

"Open it!" the ruffians clamored as they banged on the door.

"Listen to the streets!" Flavia yelled back. "Maxentius is dead! The people want revenge! On you!"

Mercifully, the banging soon stopped. Flavia couldn't quite hear the conversation on the other side of her door, though she could tell the men's debate was vigorous. She grabbed a water pitcher to defend herself, then backed to the window and glanced out, trying to decide if jumping from so high would cause injury. By the time she decided it almost certainly would, silence had returned to the walkway outside her bedroom. She snuck to the door and peeked through the space between the hinge and jamb.

The men were gone.

Flavia set down the pitcher and collapsed onto her bed, exhausted by all that had happened. Tears burst from her now, the sudden release of burdens too great to contain any longer. It was all too much—the rejection and betrayal by her father, the bloody death of her mother, the threat of rape and abuse that she had so narrowly escaped.

O Jesus! I cry out to you. Help me!

A gentle knock sounded on the door. "Flavia? Are you in there?"

"Y-yes," she said, breathless from her crying. She wiped her eyes with the heels of her hands. "Who is it?"

"It's me—Rex."

Rex!

At last, you're here!

Flavia exploded from her bed and dashed across the room, desperate for the safe refuge and comforting strength of the man she loved. She lifted the latch and flung aside the heavy wooden door as if it were made of parchment.

But it was only Geta who stood there, tall and imposing. "Sorry for that," he said, "but I knew it was the only way to get you to open."

The deception, the trickery, the sheer disappointment at not seeing Rex—these hurts brought new levels of pain to Flavia's already wounded soul. She staggered back from Geta, a man she now considered as bestial as the pimps who had just fled the house. Tears wouldn't come, for they were all spent, so Flavia was left only with the numbness of utter abandonment. She was bereft, unsure that even God regarded her anymore. Silence filled the room, the silence of the derelict and the forlorn.

Geta did not take long to break the silence. His words—his very presence— invaded the secret places where Flavia's crumbled walls had left her vulnerable. He took her by the hand and led her back to the bed. Unable to resist any longer, Flavia let it happen. The pair sat together on the soft mattress, side by side in body, though not in spirit. The German warrior draped a thick arm around her shoulders. The weight of it was oppressive: a yoke too severe to bear yet too heavy to shrug off.

"My sweetest Flavia," he cooed. "Take rest beside me. Those evil men are gone." Though the news was welcome, Flavia was too exhausted to respond, so Geta just kept talking. "We can get on with our lives now," he continued. "We can build a new life together. Think of it!" He gestured expansively with his free hand, as if imagining a glorious future. "The glorious Licinius is the emperor who will ultimately prevail. And I am"—Geta paused while choosing his words—"I am one of his favorites! When he comes into his kingdom, I will be at his right hand—and you too, my pet! You are an important part of our future. I'm likely to be regarded as lowly without a noble wife. Your good family name will provide the bloodline our children will need. With my skills and your heritage, our future is guaranteed to be bright."

Flavia's shoulders drooped. "Nothing is guaranteed," she whispered at last. "The will of God is strange and mysterious."

Geta turned his head to gaze at her. Strangely, he did not look away. When Flavia finally glanced at him from the corner of her eye, she was horrified to see the same possessive gleam she had witnessed earlier in the dirty pimp. The look was really no different. Both men wanted Flavia's body. They had not earned it. They did not deserve it.

But they would take it if they could.

Though Flavia pulled away, Geta's arm was like an iron chain. Instead of granting freedom, it enclosed her, tightened down on her, drew her inexorably to his side.

"Y-you are not my husband yet," she stammered. "I w-want to leave." Fear had finally awakened Flavia from her stupor. With dawning horror, she realized this Germanic warrior might try to force his attentions on her prematurely. Geta might be brash enough to take a noble daughter's virginity in her father's own house. The thought was repugnant—and utterly terrifying.

"I wish to leave," she repeated more forcefully.

"Why, my bride?"

"We . . . we must wait, of course. It is the only right way."

Geta yanked Flavia close, nuzzling her hair, gushing hot breath into her ear. "No one has to know. I will close the door."

"God will know."

"Your God doesn't even exist, Flavia. He was made up by the filthy Jews."

The blasphemy gave Flavia the final strength she needed. She wrenched herself from Geta's grip, tearing her gown in the process. Backing away, she pointed her finger and glared at her assailant. "My God is the only true God," she declared with resolution in her voice and spiritual fire in her veins. "He is Lord of heaven and earth."

Geta chuckled and swatted his hand. "Fine! Believe your silly myths. Keep your old-fashioned morals for now. But when you are my lawful wife, I can promise you I won't be so patient."

Flavia subtly edged toward the door. "And I can promise you something too, Geta," she said sternly. "I will never be your wife!"

She was out the door and on the gallery walkway before Geta could grab her. Though she wanted to go left, Neratius was there, eavesdropping. Sickened and disgusted by everything in the house, Flavia spun right to take the longer way around to the stairs. If she could gain access to the city streets, perhaps she could blend into the craziness outside.

Find Bishop Miltiades, she told herself. *He'll shelter you!*

"Stop, daughter! I command it!" Neratius shouted.

Geta merely laughed as he stood in the bedroom doorway, his arms folded across his chest. "She can't get away, sir. I locked the front door after the pimps left. Let her run around the house a bit."

Apparently, Neratius didn't want even that much resistance from Flavia. "Slave!" he barked to the gardener. "Hold my daughter when she reaches the bottom of the stairs."

Flavia halted midway between the staircase and her two tormentors. Her mind was spinning as she tried to form a plan. *Play nice with my father and escape later? Dash down the stairs and try to shove past the gardener? Or jump from a window and take my chances on the pavement?*

The door to a guest bedroom lay only a few steps away. Flavia knew its window looked toward the street. The shopkeeper's awning below it might arrest her fall.

Yes. That could work.

Or at least, it offered the best chance of success amid terrible options. She ran to the bedroom and flung open the door. Too late, Geta and Neratius realized their mistake and bolted into action.

"Someone grab my daughter!" Neratius yelled. "Seize her! Anyone!"

But almost all the servants had fled this part of the house. After latching the door behind her, Flavia crossed to the window yet was hesitant to look down. She stared instead at the sky, focusing her attention on God. Determination mingled with fear as Flavia tried to summon her resolve.

There's nothing else to do. Just go! It's your only chance!

She put one leg out the window and sucked in a deep breath. The shouting and the fists banging on the door were angry now. Flavia swung her other leg out so she was sitting on the sill. For several long moments she sat motionless, eyes closed, gathering her courage for the jump.

Dear God, be with me!

"Open up!" Neratius demanded with venom in his voice.

"Never!" Flavia yelled over her shoulder.

A hand grabbed her ankle as it dangled from the window. Though Flavia tried to break free, the grip on her leg was too strong. "Let go of me!" she cried.

"Not when you need me most," said a strong and manly voice.

Flavia finally looked down. Rex stood there on a ladder, smiling up at her. He had come for her at last.

⁓•⁓

Rex could tell from Flavia's tear-streaked face that she had reached the limits of her endurance. She yanked her feet from the window and allowed Rex to follow her into the bedroom. As soon as he clambered over the sill and stood up, she tumbled into his arms. Like a castaway clinging to driftwood, she encircled his waist and buried her face against his chest. "Oh,

Rex, finally, you're here," she whispered. "I needed you *so much*." He could feel her body trembling as she spoke.

"I'm here with you now," he soothed, stroking her back with the palm of his hand. "I'll take care of you."

"Where were you?"

"I came as soon as Onesimus found me in the Forum. It's a long story, but I managed to get inside your house. When the pimps came upstairs, I climbed down to the street to try a different window. I didn't know where you'd be. Then those nice-looking calves appeared out the window. That's a sight that will always draw me closer."

Rex heard Flavia utter a surprised giggle as she leaned against his chest. She separated and glanced up at him. "Even in a time like this, you can still make me laugh."

He smiled back as warmly as he could, reassuring Flavia with his eyes, sending his brash self-confidence into her battered soul. "Those legs will always be worth fighting for," he said with a wink.

Again a fist pounded on the door, interrupting the moment. "Daughter! Open this door immediately! Open it now, or you'll never see one penny of your dowry!"

"I don't care about that!" Flavia shouted back.

"We could climb down the ladder and run," Rex said in her ear, "but is that our best choice? Can we always keep running? How about if we open the door and face your father? I'm not afraid of him. Let's end this once and for all. Then I can get you out of this house and take you where you want to go."

"Just take me far away—anywhere in the world, Rex, as long as I'm with you."

Now it was Rex's turn to be surprised by unexpected words. He drew back upon hearing the heartfelt plea and looked at Flavia's face more closely. She smiled up at him, tentative and demure, yet hopeful and trusting too. Something had changed since he had seen her last. Underneath her tears, underneath her obvious distress, Rex could see a new firmness of resolve in Flavia's features. Everything she had counted on before was gone. She had made her decision to cast her lot with him. Rex found this intensely beautiful—the thrilling recognition that such a radiant woman would put herself under his care and protection. It was time to give her exactly what she needed.

"Open the door this instant!" Neratius bawled, punctuating his bossy commands with insistent banging.

"It's time to do it," Rex said quietly to Flavia. "Stay close by me." He squeezed her hand, then went and unlatched the door.

Neratius stood there with a sour expression, and beside him, to Rex's surprise, was Geta. The unexpected presence of Rex's best friend threw him off for a moment, though he did not let it show. Instead, he broke into a warm smile. "Well, there you are, brother! We have some stories to tell, I'm sure!" Though Geta returned the greeting with equal affection, Rex thought he sensed confusion on his friend's part too. Each man was trying to assess the reason for the other's presence in the mansion.

Not wanting to be trapped in the guest bedroom, Rex stepped through the doorway and went out to the gallery that ringed the rear garden. Since the walkway made a full circle, he could go right or left and still reach the stairs. He looked over his shoulder at Flavia and flicked his head to indicate she should stay near. The other two men were keeping a wary distance until they discerned how things would play out.

Neratius started to reprimand his daughter, but Geta put up a soothing hand. "Sir, if you will allow me to speak, I believe I can bring some clarity here."

Though Geta's tone was congenial, Rex recognized his friend's approach as the classic tactic of special forces operatives. It was always better to talk one's way out of conflict than resort to violence. Geta was stalling for time. Even so, Rex actually was interested in what he would say. "I think some clarity would help," he agreed.

Geta looked Rex in the eye. "I'm a double agent," he said flatly.

Rex didn't flinch at the announcement. "For who? Maxentius? He's dead, you know."

"Give me more credit than that, my friend."

Rex thought for a moment, then quickly realized there was only one plausible alternative. "So it's Licinius, eh? You did once tell me he gives the most generous donatives. 'We have to keep our options open,' you said. Sounds like you're doing that."

"Of course. If we don't look out for ourselves, who will?" Geta took a step closer to Rex. "Join with me, brother," he urged. "Think about it! Licinius's army is bigger, and he's an excellent strategist. His provinces are full of good mercenaries too. Eventually he's going to beat Constantine. It's inevitable. And when he does, we'll be at his side. He's looking for good men like you. It's an opportunity you shouldn't miss."

Rex could only throw back his head and laugh. "Were you even out there at the Milvian Bridge today? Constantine just crushed a much larger army of elite Praetorians. He captured Rome! Nobody has done that for seven hundred years. I don't think Licinius will be taking his place anytime soon. Geta, you and I just need to go have a drink. Then tomorrow we can get to work for the new Augustus of the West."

"No! Constantine does not deserve that title. It rightfully belongs to another man. The man who is my—"

"Your what, Geta? Your patron? Your benefactor who throws you some gold coins every so often? Can you be bought so easily? I thought more highly of you than that."

"Licinius is my father."

The astonishing news caused a sudden silence to descend on the foursome. Staggered by the implications, Rex could find no words to respond. For a long moment, he struggled to gather his thoughts and form a coherent reply. Finally he said, "I don't believe it. You're Germanic."

"And so is my mother—a tall, blonde Saxon like me. She is one of Licinius's favorite courtesans. For that reason, the augustus wishes to see me prosper, though he knows I can never rule the empire after him."

"When Licinius is finally in charge of Rome," Neratius put in, "Geta's economic future will be as bright as can be imagined. He is a man on the rise."

Geta took another step forward, his demeanor urgent and intense. "Please listen to my words, Rex! You have only one good option here. Join with me! Be assured, we will take good care of you when our day of victory comes."

"No! I will never betray Constantine," Rex declared.

"Then you have no place in my home, young man." Neratius jabbed his finger toward the staircase. "I order you to leave right now."

Rex turned to face the senator. Though Neratius had once been a man of influence, Rex now viewed him as a tragic and pitiful figure. Despite his money and connections, he was no longer the formidable powerhouse he once was. Flavia didn't need the senator's riches; she needed a man who loved her enough to lay down his life for her. It was time to free her once and for all from this sad excuse of a father.

He took Flavia by the hand. "I will leave now," he said, his tone firm and unyielding. "But your daughter is coming with me, and you will not prevent it."

Neratius's response wasn't what Rex expected. His reputation suggested he would fly into a rage, but he only touched his fingertips together, dipped his chin politely, and offered an oily grin. "You are right," he said in a level voice. "I cannot prevent it. However—"

The senator paused for a long time. No one dared speak, knowing that whatever words came next would require drastic action. Flavia sidled closer to Rex, and he encircled her with his arm to reassure her.

At last Neratius broke the tension. "My son-in-law will stop you," he announced, then turned toward Geta. "Do not let your bride leave this house."

Rex's jaw dropped. His glance shot first to Geta, who was wearing a pompous grin, but Rex immediately whirled to face Flavia.

"Y-you're married?"

"No, Rex! I love *you*! It's just their crazy plan!"

A molten wave of anger surged through Rex. *Geta made a play for my woman!*

Although the revelation brought an instant urge to fight, the rage Rex felt was much more than battle lust, for it included the pain of betrayal and a desire for revenge.

He's not just a double agent. He tried to take Flavia from me . . . connived with her father . . . stabbed me in the back!

Brothers, always?

To the death!

Rex noticed Geta's hand resting on the pommel of his sword. He dropped his hand to his own weapon, though he did not draw. "Do not try to stop us from leaving here, *brother*," Rex said, spitting out the last word like poison. "We're getting out and never coming back."

"Unfortunately, I can't let that happen."

Blood is going to be spilled today, Rex realized. *Some of it probably mine. But I will die before I let any man claim Flavia as his own!*

Using the same tactic Geta had employed earlier, Rex decided to talk first and buy some time to enhance his position. He began to chastise the two men; yet as he did, he subtly shifted his stance so that he stood between Flavia and danger. Her pathway to the staircase was clear.

"Your arrogance is disgusting!" he accused the evil conspirators. "You think you can make Flavia do whatever you want. And when she was alone, you could! You're too strong for her. Together, you could beat her down and defeat her. But no more! I'm here to defend her now. I will stand against you forever and never let your plans for her life prevail!"

"Impressive words, little orator," Neratius sneered. "Nice speech for a barbarian."

Geta's hand moved from his sword to the pouch on his belt. He reached into it with his fingers and withdrew a parchment, which he held up with smug self-assurance. "Well, Rex, I assumed it would come down to this at some point. You love Flavia—I can see that. I've known it since you snatched her from the lion's jaws in the amphitheater. That's why I had this document drawn up."

"What is it, you snake?" Flavia demanded angrily, though Rex could also hear apprehension in her voice.

"An eyewitness affidavit of something I saw on the battlefield." Geta intensified his gaze and met Rex's eye. "Your so-called augustus isn't going to hold you in such high esteem once he learns of your cowardice and treason at Verona!"

Flavia sucked in her breath and recoiled deeper into the safety of Rex's side. She gripped his tunic in her fists. "No, Geta! That will be Rex's death!"

"So be it. Cowards should get the fate they deserve."

With haughty confidence, the tall Germanic warrior turned away from the horrified couple and bowed deeply to Neratius. "I will come tomorrow for your daughter's hand. I believe under the present circumstances we should be quick about the nuptials and leave the family celebrations for later."

"I agree," said the senator. "By noon, you shall be wed."

"By noon," Rex countered, "Flavia and I will be far away from this house of death. I'm taking her now."

"As I told you before, young man, I forbid it."

"And as I told you before, I'm doing it anyway."

Metal scraped against metal as Geta drew his sword. "Then today is the day you die," he said.

"Today is the first day of my new life," Rex answered, and the battle began.

The two warriors had no shields, so they didn't immediately spring to close quarters. Rex knew that good footwork would matter most here. He held his sword low and circled around Geta, thrusting, feinting, and parrying his opponent's attacks. Both fighters were consummate swordsmen, evenly matched and highly trained. The first one to make a simple mistake would be the one who died.

"You're tired from battle," Geta taunted. "I can see it. Your grip is weak. And you've been wounded in your side."

"I fought an army today while you were taking your rest. I think I can handle you."

Geta tried a low stab of his spatha. Rex sidestepped the attack and deflected the blade with his own. The loud *clang!* made Flavia squeal, and as Geta recovered his stance, he glanced toward her. Before Rex could stop him, he grabbed Flavia and put his blade to her neck. "Throw down your weapon!" he demanded.

"Hiding behind a woman, Geta? Now who's the coward?"

"Do it! Or I'll slit her throat!"

Rex's heart pounded at the thought of the great risk he was about to take. Geta was unpredictable; yet Rex believed he wouldn't kill the woman who guaranteed his alliance with a powerful senator. He fixed Geta's eyes with a malevolent stare and began to advance toward his enemy.

"Throw down your sword, Rex! Do it now!"

But Rex kept coming, never breaking his fierce gaze.

Flavia squirmed in Geta's arms, her eyes wide with fear. The sharp steel edge was at her neck. "H-h-help me, Rex!" she said in a shuddery voice.

"I surrender," Rex proclaimed. "Look!" He raised his sword above his head, then hurled it in a high arc over the gallery's railing to the garden below. Everyone watched it tumble end over end, waiting for it to clatter onto the marble terrace.

And as they watched—mesmerized by the whirling blade—Rex lowered his shoulder, exploded from his stance, and barreled into Geta and Flavia at full speed.

The three of them crashed through the flimsy railing and went over the edge into empty space. Flavia's piercing scream was the last thing Rex heard when he hit the water of the garden's cistern.

Unlike the shallow decorative fountain in the atrium, the cistern here was deep—an ample reservoir of rainwater to be used throughout the dry season. Rex plunged into the cold depths but immediately surfaced and grasped the pool's rim. He scrambled out and spun toward his opponent. When he turned, he saw exactly what he had hoped for. Victory was about to be his.

Taken by surprise at Rex's audacious move, Geta hadn't been as quick to prepare his body for the fall. He had surfaced after Rex and was just now crawling from the cistern. His body was splayed out on the pavement while his lower legs were over the water. For an instant, he was completely vulnerable.

Rex seized the opportunity, knowing the stakes of the battle were too high to pass up any advantage. He dashed over to Geta. Raised his boot high. And shattered his enemy's shinbone against the rim of the pool.

"Argh!" Geta cried at the top of his lungs. He writhed in agony and clutched his leg with both hands.

But Rex felt no pity for the man who would betray him to Constantine. Treason was a capital crime, which meant Geta was essentially planning Rex's murder—not to mention a life of misery for Flavia. This fight was to the death. Geta himself had made it so. Now he would die, and his terrible secret would perish with him.

A few steps away, Rex's cavalry sword lay on the marble patio. He retrieved it and stood over his enemy. A dreadful hush descended on the garden.

Rex pressed his sword's point into the base of Geta's neck. Bright red blood welled up. "You started this battle," he said evenly. "Now I'm going to finish it."

"You aren't brave enough," Geta mumbled through the grimace that contorted his pale face.

"I've always been braver than you."

"Make it quick, then. I'm not afraid."

"You should be. Hell is waiting." Rex raised his sword for a clean blow to the heart.

And that was when Lady Junia Flavia—not even twenty years old, yet as noble and heroic as any great matron in Roman history—did something Rex would never forget.

She darted to Geta and draped her body over his. "No, Rex!" she cried. "Please! Don't do it."

Rex staggered backward, stunned by what he was seeing. "You love him?" he exclaimed.

"Of course not!"

"Then get up and let me finish it. Why are you protecting him?"

"Because I love you! Not the killer the army has tried to make you. Not a savage barbarian and murderer. I love the *real* you, Rex. Who you are now . . . and who you could be!"

Rex clenched his jaw and gripped his sword's hilt in his strong, sweaty hand. He wanted to believe he could be someone else, someone who didn't kill to solve his problems. Yet peace wasn't in his blood. Violence was.

"You . . . you can't change me, Flavia."

"Perhaps not. But I know someone who can."

"Your Jesus?"

"Yes! Bow the knee to him, Rex. He's worth every sacrifice you can make."

Rex towered over Flavia as she lay across Geta's body. He showed her the crimson droplet that stained the tip of his sword. "See this? This is who I am. No one can change that."

"There is one in heaven who can."

"I don't believe it."

"Try him, Rex. Just try, I beg you."

"Don't you understand? If I don't kill Geta, I'll lose you—and probably my life!"

"But if you do this, you're lost anyway! I refuse to believe you could slay your best friend in cold blood. It would change you forever. You would cease to be the man I love!"

Rage had a deep hold on Rex now. "Stop this nonsense!" he roared. "Are you trying to ruin our future together? Get up! Get up, Flavia, and you'll see who I really am! I'm a killer, and I have been since I was a child. I took

467

my first life when I was twelve. If you want me, you have to accept that. It's who I am. It's *what* I am!"

For a long moment, Flavia said nothing. At last she arose with great dignity. She stood over the helpless Geta and stared hard at Rex. "I do want the real you, my love. But that man is not a murderer." She took a step back without breaking off her gaze. "Now do what you will."

Rex held his sword in both hands and raised it above Geta's body. The weapon dangled over the crippled warrior like the fang of some hideous beast. *As soon as this is finished, you can build your life with Flavia. Just get it over with!* The blood on the blade's tip oozed down the point and dropped onto Geta's tunic.

"Do it," Geta snarled with a curl of his lip. "I dare you!"

Twice Rex raised the sword high. Twice he did not follow through.

But on the third time, he did what the whispering voice in his head told him to do.

He hurled the sword away and withdrew to Flavia's side.

"You're a coward," Geta scoffed.

Flavia took Rex's hand and interlocked her fingers with his. "You are the bravest man I have ever known," she whispered as she laid her head upon his shoulder.

⟞ ᧞᧞᧞ ⟝

After all the turbulence and violence of the day, a welcome silence came to Flavia's house at last. The evening sky had been set ablaze by a distant sunset, and now its light washed the mansion's garden in a ruddy glow. The servants had found deep hiding places to ride out the storm. Neratius had escaped to some unknown refuge. Even Geta had left the maelstrom, stumbling away like a wounded animal with the help of a garden rake as a crutch.

But Rex was still there, and Flavia clung to him—the one sure and solid fixture in an ever-shifting world. Both of them were wet from their plunge into the cistern, yet neither cared. Rex's strong arms held Flavia close, providing at least the temporary illusion of safety and well-being. Of course, she had to admit, the feel of his muscular chest against her cheek gave her other feelings besides safety.

"I love you so much, Rex," she murmured. "I need you with me forever."

"It turns out I needed you too," he replied as he played with a loose strand of hair at the back of her neck. "You helped me find myself. I'm glad you believed in me."

"You aren't a murderer. I knew it. You had the chance to kill Geta—but you did the right thing."

"I believe so. But it will have its consequences."

"At least you have the affidavit! Burn it, Rex! Make it disappear."

"I will. But what is to keep Geta from writing another? I believe my fate is sealed."

Flavia sighed deeply. "Only God knows what will happen."

"Listen to me for a moment. We need to talk." Rex separated from Flavia so he could look into her eyes, though his strong hands held her waist, keeping her near. "I will do my best to stand between you and harm. You know that, right? I'll take care of you as long as I'm able, even when no one else will. Everyone has abandoned you except me. I would never do that. However . . ."

Flavia waited silently. Though her heart was screaming, *Don't say it!* she knew the terrible words needed to be voiced.

"I fear I will be torn away from you," Rex finally admitted.

"I know."

The sad reality overwhelmed Flavia. Sensing the depth of her sorrow, Rex brought her close again. Something intuitive seemed to drive him—a heart-to-heart connection that allowed him to read her emotions and anticipate her needs. His arms enfolded her, drawing her back into an embrace. One of his hands caressed the small of her back in a comforting way. She laid her head on his shoulder, and he rested his cheek against the top of her head. *He always takes care of me, no matter the cost*, Flavia realized with aching desire. *But what will tomorrow hold?*

"Oh, Rex!" she cried, her agony too intense to contain. "Who will take care of me if they drag you away? My father is a beast. And Mother! She's gone!"

"No!" Rex said. "Take comfort in this! Your mother is alive."

Flavia gasped, then pulled away just enough to look up at his face. A glimmer of hope had just illumined her dark future. "How can that be?" she exclaimed. "I saw her dead on the floor!"

"It's true that she tried to kill herself with a dagger. But people don't realize how hard that is. It's much harder than what you read in tragic stories. At that angle, it's difficult to generate enough force. Beyond that, the mind stops you, even when you think you want to do it."

"So what happened?"

"Lady Sabina had merely wounded herself when I came to her door. She let me in, and I gave her a better idea. I knew Maxentius's men would leave only if they thought she was dead, so I mixed wine and mandragora from your healer's kit. Enough of that potion will make you like a dead person—and I gave her a lot! Then I broke off the blade and put the shard in her wound. She will feel sick when she wakens, and her injuries will have to heal. But they are flesh wounds. She will live for a long time, untouched by filthy Maxentius."

Flavia glanced up at Rex, awed by what he had done. His warrior's strength, his quick thinking, his confident boldness—all of it constantly deployed for Flavia's advantage. She locked eyes with him, searching those blue Germanic depths. Rex stared back, long and hard, unwilling to look anywhere else. Clearly, this man wanted her. Yet Rex's intense gaze was communicating something more than his obvious masculine desire. Though Flavia could sense his powerful sexual attraction, her heart melted when, with sudden clarity, she recognized the softness in Rex's expression for what it really was: true, abiding love.

Yes. The real thing. Love for her as his only beloved. His chosen one.

It was all there in his gaze. Rex was shouting it with his eyes. Mere words could never have said it so profoundly.

"Ohhh, Rex," she sighed. "My love for you is like . . ." Flavia hunted for the right image. "Like a great ocean wave," she said at last, "so powerful and impossible to hold back!" She lifted both hands to the back of his head, savoring the tickle of his soft military stubble against her palms. "I am yours, Brandulf Rex. Yours forever and ever."

"And I receive you, Flavia. I return your love with everything I have. With my body and"—he pounded his chest with his fist—"even more, my soul. I've loved you since I first saw you in the Forum. The whole world was against you, but in that moment, I fell in love. Flavia, do you understand me? Do you know how I feel? *Ach!* I'm sorry. I'm not a man of great eloquence. How do I say this right?"

470

Rex paused, struggling for words, which Flavia found sweetly attractive in someone so otherwise capable. "It has been my greatest happiness," Rex went on, "an honor, a true privilege, to care for you. To look out for you, to stand between you and harm. But I made a choice just now. And I can't stop the forces that will tear us apart. I don't see any way for us to spend our lives together. I'm about to be condemned as a criminal. They might even execute me."

"No! Rex, don't say that!"

"It has to be said because it's true. We have to recognize what just happened. Your God asked something of me, Flavia. And I gave it to him because of you. It was the greatest gift I could ever give, because it came at my own greatest cost."

Flavia hung her head, nodding slowly. Tears welled up in her eyes and rolled down her cheeks. "I understand that, Rex. It's what the Christian faith is all about."

"I know. I see it now. Your God is true and good."

"He's your God too."

"Yes. And I'm going to need him in whatever future I have left."

They fell silent then, holding on to each other for solace and comfort because there was no one else to give it and nothing else to do. For a long time they remained like that, savoring one another's quiet presence.

But as their emotions roiled within them, their embrace abruptly intensified into something more. Flavia felt it happen, and she opened herself to it.

Pressed up against Rex—body to body and heart to heart—Flavia found that her desire had become more than she could contain. Though she didn't intend to abandon her morals, neither did she intend to remain an unkissed innocent any longer. If this was to be her only intimacy with Rex, she would make it worthy of remembrance forever.

"You're shaking, Flavia," Rex whispered in her ear.

"Yes. You make me weak."

"I make you strong, my beloved."

It was true. And so sweet.

Rex bent down his head. With the lightest possible touch, his lips caressed the soft skin behind her ear.

"Just kiss me, Rex," Flavia said. She had never felt like this before, never experienced a feeling so intense.

"We Germani value the art of romance," he replied. "We believe a man should take his time with the woman he loves."

"Ohhh, Rex! You love me? You really do?" She tipped back her head and closed her eyes. He cupped the back of her head and drew her face toward his.

"Always and forever, I am for you," he declared.

He kissed her then, for the first and maybe the only time. The affection was so real, the exchange of love so true, that Flavia gave herself to the purity and rightness of this moment—and gave her heart to this man.

When at last they parted, Flavia stayed in Rex's embrace, and he in hers, and they refused to let the moment go. A day of reckoning would surely come. Suffering was no doubt on its way. But that was then, and this was *now*, and the present was unspeakably good.

15

FEBRUARY 313

Sitting down on the jewel-encrusted throne, Constantine couldn't help but appreciate its fine craftsmanship and ornate beauty. He glanced around the throne room, marveling at the high quality of its architecture. *Maximian did a good job with this palace,* he thought. *Too bad he tried to kill me. He was an effective ruler and a good ally for a time.* Now, of course, Maximian was dead—hung from the rafters by Constantine's bodyguards in Gaul a few years ago. His son Maxentius was dead too, killed at the battle last October. And yet, while the family line of Maximian was broken, his legacy lived on through the splendid palace at Mediolanum.

It seemed strange to Constantine that this northern Italian city was, technically speaking, the capital of the Western Roman Empire. Perhaps some purists would insist that Rome should always retain that distinction, and in an informal way, it still did. Yet when the enemies of today were crossing the Alps with their armies of barbarian mercenaries, they weren't hitting Rome first. They were attacking cities like Mediolanum, situated in the center of the Padus River plain that swept across northern Italy. And that meant Mediolanum had taken on new imperial significance.

Though Constantine had been only a boy at the time, he remembered when Emperor Diocletian made Mediolanum the new western capital because of its strategic location. As part of the honor, the city was updated with the imperial palace under a gorgeous dome, a new racetrack, magnificent baths dedicated to Hercules, and imposing defensive walls.

Mediolanum has plenty of imperial glory, Constantine decided. *It will make a fitting venue for my sister's wedding.*

The emperor turned to his secretary, a pale-skinned eunuch with a shock of red hair that signaled his northern origins. "How are the wedding plans coming along?" he asked. "I haven't heard anything about it."

"The plans are proceeding, Your Highness. It's going to be a grand affair. Very lavish."

"Excellent! A royal wedding doesn't happen often. Let's hope it forms a strong enough alliance to keep Licinius and me together for many years."

The emperor gave a little chuckle, knowing how quickly rivalries could develop between powerful men. *Will my new brother-in-law always be on my side? Not likely!* Constantine shook away the question as a topic for another day.

"So when does my sister arrive?" he asked the secretary.

"We expect Lady Constantia to reach Mediolanum sometime next week. The nuptials can happen soon after that."

"Very good. Licinius told me yesterday he's anxious to get it over with. Our enemy Daia is riding out against us, and Licinius must confront him. Tell the bishop he has two days after my sister gets here to make final plans. On the third day, he will perform the wedding."

"You are referring to Bishop Ossius? The Spaniard?"

"Yes, that's the one. It is to be a Christian wedding."

Though the secretary nodded, his face was perplexed. "No pagan priest? It might be more auspicious to include at least one."

"Absolutely not! Licinius and I follow the catholic faith now. It was the mighty sign of Christ that gave me the victory in Italy. I intend to honor my obligations to the Christian God." Constantine shifted in his seat, signaling his readiness to do business. "Speaking of that religion, I believe it is part of our agenda today, is it not? Let us proceed with the day's duties."

The royal secretary called for his assistant to come forward with a dossier of imperial documents. Constantine affixed his signature to the ones he accepted and ordered corrections for those that still needed work. Most of the items were perfunctory. After about an hour, the list was whittled to the final two. The secretary had declared these to be the weightiest matters. The next to last topic was the new imperial policy toward Christians.

"We have drafted the letter of toleration to be dispatched from you and your brother-in-law," the red-haired eunuch said. "It will go out to the governors of the Eastern provinces as soon as you approve it."

"Read it to me," Constantine commanded. "It has to be worded just right. No room for other interpretations by those who might wish to disregard it."

The secretary bent his head closer to the wax tablet that served as the rough draft of the important letter. He cleared his throat and began reading:

When I, Constantine Augustus, as well as I, Licinius Augustus, met on a happy occasion at Mediolanum, we took the opportunity to consider everything that related to the public's best interest and security. We thought that, among the many things we perceived would be profitable for the majority of the people, the first order of business was to secure proper reverence for the Divinity. Thus we granted to Christians and everyone else the freedom to follow the religion each one preferred, so that whatever Divinity is seated in heaven might be favorable and well-disposed toward us, and to all who have been placed under our rule.

In light of this beneficial strategy and completely logical way of thinking, we believed it appropriate that absolutely no one should be denied the right to devote himself to the observance of the Christian faith, or to whatever religion he might deem most fitting. Thus the supreme Divinity, whose religion we follow with free minds, may be inclined to show us his usual favor and benevolence in every way.

Therefore it has pleased us to cancel every one of the regulations about the Christian faith formerly sent to your office in various letters. Now anyone who has the desire to observe the religion of the Christians should hasten to do so freely and openly without any disturbance or molestation. We thought this should be commended to your care with utmost clarity, so you might know we have granted to those Christians an unhindered and unconditional right to practice their religion. And when you see that we have awarded them this freedom, you will understand that others, too, have been given the same open and unrestricted right of religious observance, as is fitting in our peaceful times.

Thus every person shall have free opportunity to engage in whatever religion he has chosen. We have decreed this so it won't seem we have discriminated against any form of worship or religion.*

"Stop there," Constantine interrupted. He turned and signaled for his adviser, the brilliant orator Lactantius, to approach. "Listen to the rest of this. Tell me if it is what the Christians will need." The emperor motioned for the secretary to continue.

The remainder of the letter dealt with the restitution of church properties that had been confiscated by the state. Although most of the western provinces had already returned them, not all the Eastern governors had complied. The joint letter from Constantine and Licinius made it clear that every ruler in the provinces they controlled was obligated to do so right away. The letter was to be proclaimed in the streets and posted where all could see it. At last, the catholic church throughout the empire was going to get its lands back.

"How does that sound to your Christian ears?" Constantine asked Lactantius. "Is it sufficient?"

"It is gracious beyond measure, Your Highness. The one true God will certainly be favorable to such an obedient servant. It is as though you are an instrument for good in the hand of the Almighty."

"Perhaps that is what I am," the emperor mused. He considered the idea for a moment, then brought his attention back to the present. "Lactantius, I want you to personally deliver this letter to Nicomedia. When you arrive, you shall resume your chair of Latin rhetoric as a professor serving the imperial court."

A wide smile broke out across the eminent scholar's face. "Thank you, Your Majesty!" he gushed. "I am greatly honored!"

The red-haired secretary received Constantine's seal of approval on the letter of toleration, then gave it to his assistant for copying and dissemination. Turning back to the emperor, he folded his hands behind his back and

---

*This is the famous "Edict of Milan" that ended Christian persecution. The words are my own translation of Lactantius's Latin text, and it appears in my book *Early Christian Martyr Stories: An Evangelical Introduction with New Translations* (Grand Rapids: Baker Academic, 2014), 163–66.

lowered his eyes. "We have one final item to address, Your Highness. I am afraid it is a somewhat distressing matter."

"Let's get it over with, then. It is almost time for my bath."

"I have a legal document here from a respected speculator in the Second Italian Legion. It is his sworn testimony from the battle at Verona."

"About the man who fled?"

"Yes. This affidavit declares who it was. And it gives the kind of details that only an eyewitness could know. There can be no doubt that it's authentic and accurate."

Constantine's eyes narrowed, and he made fists with both hands as he attempted to control the sudden burst of rage that coursed through him. He thought back to that deadly moment when Pompeianus's forces were pressing close—and one lone speculator went galloping away while the rest laid down their lives for their commander. *If we have found that man, he must certainly die!*

"Speak his name," Constantine ordered.

"It was Brandulf Rex."

Rex! How could you? You were one of my best! I gave you a second chance when you were just a boy! And you threw it all away.

The emperor puffed out his cheeks and blew out a breath of air. Though he felt deeply disappointed and betrayed, he knew that throwing a temper tantrum in the throne room would be unworthy of an emperor. "Where is Rex now?" he asked in an artificially calm voice.

"He was arrested soon after the battle at the bridge, based on the evidence of this affidavit. The authorities put him in the Carcer in Rome. They have been holding him there until you could dispose of this matter personally."

"Well, there's nothing else we can do. He's a traitor. Have him strangled to death and dispose of his body down the sewer. That is all for the day. You are dismissed."

The secretary nodded and turned to leave. Constantine drummed his fingers on the armrest of the throne. It was always a hard business being an emperor. He had genuinely liked Rex. But a crime was a crime, and it had to be handled as such.

"Your Highness?" inquired a tentative voice.

Constantine turned toward the sound. It was the rhetorician Lactantius who had spoken.

"What is it, professor?"

"You mentioned the Christian God a moment ago. He is a God I know well. His ways are often difficult for us mortals yet good and beneficial. He asks hard things of his followers—and blesses us when we do them."

"And what is your point?"

"I think . . . perhaps . . ." Lactantius paused, fiddling with the folds of his toga.

"Just say it. I want to learn about this God. You may speak freely."

"I think perhaps your order just now came from a spirit of revenge. But vengeance belongs to God alone."

Constantine pursed his lips and stared at the floor, trying to consider the matter fairly. "One of my soldiers abandoned me in the thick of battle," he countered. "That is treason, a capital crime. It must be punished under the normal rule of law."

"Wouldn't he at least be due a trial, Your Majesty?"

"There is no time for that. I'm leaving Italy within a few weeks, and I have no idea if I'll ever return."

"Have you known Rex to be a good man in other respects?"

"Yes. I liked him a lot. I'm drawn to manly fellows like him. He was a highly skilled speculator and a likable kid. I foresaw good things from him before he became a coward. And it's not just cowardice—he's also rebellious. He rode away from the parade in the Forum when I told him not to. He's unpredictable."

"Perhaps there were extenuating circumstances?"

"What circumstances could justify a warrior abandoning his lord in battle? It's an absolute moral travesty. He ought to pay for his actions with death. The world doesn't need people like him in it."

"The ways of the Lord are mysterious," Lactantius said. "You never know what might happen someday. The speculator Rex might have an important role to play in the great plans of God. In any case, vengeance is never the right motivation for our decisions. Might you choose a lesser punishment?"

After a long moment, Emperor Constantine let out a heavy sigh. "Secretary!" he shouted.

The man was just about to leave the throne room, but upon hearing his master's voice, he turned back. "Yes, Your Majesty?"

"Do not have Brandulf Rex strangled. Have him enrolled in the imperial navy as a common oarsman. Strip him of his rank and give him no hope of advancement. Station him permanently at the remotest edge of the empire."

"Yes, sir. It shall be done."

"I think that is wise of you," Lactantius declared.

Constantine grimaced. "I think being a Christian is going to be hard work," he muttered to himself.

—⟨ɷⱨɷ⟩—

MARCH 313

Trunks and boxes lay strewn around the atrium of Bishop Miltiades's house, but Flavia paid them no mind. Her heart was so heavy that details like these hardly registered in her consciousness. Though on some level she under-stood the bishop was moving into Empress Fausta's former house in Rome, it seemed irrelevant in light of everything else. She ignored the clutter and stepped around a stack of crates to find Miltiades waiting for her.

"Come along, dear one," he said, lightly grasping Flavia's wrist. "We can find a quieter and less hectic place to talk."

He led her to a little sitting room with a view into the garden. Flavia took a seat in a wicker chair, and Miltiades pulled up an identical one beside her. A sparrow perched on the shoulder of a marble statue, cocking its head and examining the pair with its beady eyes.

"It hurts, child," the bishop said. "I understand. It hurts greatly."

"So much! I don't know if I can cope with this pain. I can't stand the thought that I'll never see Rex again. They're sending him far away forever."

"Have they moved him from the Carcer yet?"

"Yes, to Ostia. I'm preparing to have daily rations sent there like we've been doing here."

"God's Spirit will be with Rex. His infinite love and mercy will overcome all evils. Even if Rex is beyond your reach, he is not beyond God's."

Flavia cupped her forehead in her hand as she tried to gather her thoughts. Finally, she found the courage to look the kindly bishop in the face and ask the theological question whose answer would determine her future. "I know God will be with him," she acknowledged, "but will God deliver him? If we

479

pray harder than ever before, will God find a way to free Rex before they ship him away?"

Miltiades shook his head slowly. "God never stops loving us. Yet that doesn't mean he always grants our heart's desire."

"I wish he would this time," Flavia said sadly.

She closed her eyes and tucked her chin to her breast. "Please God," she whispered in heartfelt prayer. "Please. Just do this thing for me. I'm desperate for Rex in my life."

For a long time she could not speak. Bishop Miltiades waited quietly beside her, wordlessly offering the full riches of pastoral love. Although various thoughts and ideas swirled in Flavia's mind, none would crystalize into a concrete utterance. Her emotions were too raw. She had just expressed her heart's deepest longing. It was a request she couldn't help but make. Yet something told her she needed to say more.

At last she looked up and met the bishop's eyes. "Even if . . ." she started to say, then her courage faltered and her words tumbled away.

The bishop placed his hand over hers. "I know your heart, Lady Junia, and I know what you are about to say. God knows it too. Nevertheless, I encourage you to voice it aloud."

Power came to Flavia then, a sudden strengthening that fell upon her like a divine anointing. It could only be the Holy Spirit, the Comforter of God, the white dove from on high. Finding her voice, she said, "Even if God takes this man from me . . ." Yet no sooner had she uttered those words than her strength evaporated again like morning dew and she couldn't continue.

"Press on and speak," Miltiades urged. "Search for your voice and send forth the truth."

Flavia clutched the folds of her gown in her fists. "Even if God takes this man from me," she repeated, "I will follow my Savior no matter what."

"When you are conquered by Christ, you have to make hard choices and do hard things," said the bishop. "Wise people learn it early. I declare you wise, my daughter."

Flavia had no response, so Miltiades patted her hand and smiled gently. "Perhaps I may cheer you with some good news for a change." He clapped his hands, and a deacon hurried over. "Send in the lady," the bishop said.

A few moments later, Sophronia entered the sitting room. A cry of joy burst from Flavia's lips, for she hadn't seen her mother in many weeks. "You're healed!" she cried, rising to offer an exuberant hug. "You look so good!"

"Careful," Sophronia said, easing away from Flavia's embrace. "The wound is much better now, but it's still mending."

The deacon brought a third chair and a tray of light snacks. The threesome gathered around the small table with the food on it. "Mother, tell me everything," Flavia said. "All I know is that you were sent someplace safe to recuperate."

"I've been up in the mountains at a remote cottage. It was a quiet and restful place, away from watching eyes. It has taken me quite a while to come to terms with . . . that terrible day."

Flavia nodded glumly. "I'm sorry you despaired to the point of death."

"I did. I saw no way to avoid being violated by Maxentius. Death was preferable to me. However, God had other plans. God and Rex, actually."

"So what happened?"

"I did try to stab my heart, but as Rex told me afterward, it is nearly impossible to accomplish such a thing. All I did was give myself a painful wound. But then everything changed. Rex was so confident and strong! He knew exactly what to do, then did it. He immediately had things under control. I knew I was in good hands."

Flavia tried to utter a sigh, but it came out more like a shuddery whimper. Her mother glanced at her, and their eyes met. Sophronia winked at her daughter, giving her a tiny smile. The two of them shared an understanding that only women can know.

"Rex went straight to the medicine cart," Sophronia continued when the moment had passed, "and mixed up a potion to deaden my senses. He learned all about poisons and drugs in his speculator school. I just let him take over. For some reason, I wasn't worried at all after he arrived. He's such a capable man."

This time, Flavia didn't even bother trying to hold back her lovesick whimper. Sophronia smiled knowingly again.

"After your mind went dark, did you feel anything?" Miltiades asked.

"Nothing at all. Rex broke off the blade and thrust it into the flesh of my bosom where it would harm no vital organs. Though it bled greatly and had the appearance of a dagger to my heart, it was just a superficial wound. As you know, the news of Maxentius's death arrived then, so his men fled. I woke up sick and in pain, and immediately went into hiding."

"Onesimus came to my house that night," Miltiades explained to Flavia. "It was I who arranged to have your mother removed from the mansion in a coffin. We let the servants assume she had killed herself. Now the rumor has spread among the Christians that she preferred a noble death to being ravished by Maxentius. Only the three of us, and Rex, and Onesimus know the truth."

"I am a woman with an open future," Sophronia said, "because I no longer have a past."

It took Flavia a few moments to comprehend the ramifications of this strange new reality. Over the past few months, she had become resigned to the fact that Neratius had moved to Sardinia to frolic with his fourteen-year-old bride. Normally that would leave his first wife as a disgraced divorcée. But the bishop's quick thinking had opened up a different opportunity: Sophronia could start afresh. As far as wider society knew, she was dead. Therefore, if she wanted to, Sophronia could begin an entirely new life.

"What's next?" Flavia asked, bewildered by the possibilities. "Do you intend to reveal yourself to everyone again?"

"I do not. Our mansion is being sold to the catholic church. After that, I intend to disappear."

"To where?"

"There is a convent at Tauromenium in Sicilia. I have decided to take up holy orders there, living with the Christian sisters as a woman of prayer and celibacy." Sophronia reached out and took Flavia by the hand. "And I ask you to consider joining me."

What? Go to Sicilia? As a nun?

Flavia withdrew her hand from her mother's grasp and ran her fingers through her hair. A jittery sensation had overtaken her. Terrified, she realized she was being asked to give up everything she had dreamed of since she was a little girl.

No! This can't be right. What about my life here in Rome? What about the house I will share with Rex? Surely he will escape his sentence eventually! Then he will come back and find me! And then we'll . . . we'll—

"My dear Flavia," Miltiades said with great tenderness. "This might be your best option. Please consider it. The man you love cannot be in your life. You have to find a way to go on."

But . . . to be a nun means no husband! And no children! And of course, never having . . . ! Not ever!

"I don't think I can do that," Flavia said.

"What else is there?" asked the bishop.

And the answer was clear: *nothing.*

At that moment, Flavia felt it happen. She gasped aloud as her heart broke inside her breast. The pain of it was as intense as her mother's stabbing must have been. It hurt deeply and completely, overwhelming her body with a tangible, visceral ache. The searing agony of her loss was like swallowing broken glass. Never again would Flavia be a carefree Roman girl with a happy dream.

Life was utterly different now.

"I am so sorry, my love," Sophronia said quietly.

"We are here with you in this unimaginable suffering," Miltiades added.

Flavia stood up, her motions listless, her body numb. A heavy weight seemed to rest on her shoulders. Yet despite the physical toll this terrible fate was taking, her mind had clarity of purpose.

She stared into the faces of these two beloved people: her pious, devoted mother and the kindly bishop who was now essentially her father. They looked back at her with nothing but compassion in their eyes. For a long time, no one said a word.

At last Sophronia broke the silence. "So, my daughter . . . will you go with me?"

Flavia exhaled a deep breath.

She raised her palms to heaven.

"Jesus is Lord," she said.

━━━━◦◦◦━━━━

APRIL 313

"Brother, it's going to take twenty additional clergy to run a big mansion like this," Bishop Miltiades said to his deacon, a capable man named Quintus. "Where are we going to put so many new men?"

"There will be room for them after we sell all of Pompeianus's luxuries," Quintus observed.

"Yes. Let's do it quickly. And be sure to keep good records. I want all that money going to the poor, not to some dishonest servant who knows how to hide funds."

"Yes, Your Holiness," Quintus said with a bow.

Miltiades glanced around the palace's reception hall. It was lavishly decorated with expensive statues and fine wall hangings. The palace's former occupant, Prefect Ruricius Pompeianus, had been killed on the field of war at Verona. Yet in truth, the home hadn't been his in the first place. It had belonged to Fausta, the sister of Maxentius and wife of Constantine. When Maxentius controlled Rome, his choice of occupant was the arrogant prefect. But now that Constantine was in charge, he preferred that the city's bishop live there.

This is far too much luxury for me, Miltiades had decided immediately. *We'll sell off whatever we can, then find a better way to use this grand house for the purposes of God.*

"Get rid of anything remotely pagan," the bishop instructed. "In fact, anything lavish or prideful should be removed. Sell it all to the highest bidder. Use some of the proceeds to have a nice altar made, something suitable for the size of this hall. And keep those candlesticks"—Miltiades pointed to them—"because they're beautiful, and we'll want them in here during the sacred liturgies."

Quintus's face lit up, for he knew what the instructions meant. "You're turning this reception hall into a church?"

"Yes. It will be the special church of the bishop of Rome."

"Do you have a name for it, Your Holiness?"

"I think we can determine the exact dedication later. For now, we'll just call it by the name of the neighborhood: the Lateran Church."

"Since it is Christ who saved us from the treachery of Maxentius and Pompeianus, perhaps it can eventually be dedicated to Christ the Savior," Quintus suggested.

Miltiades rubbed the whiskers on his chin. "Not a bad idea."

A thunderclap sounded outside, prompting the bishop to wander over to a window in the grand reception hall. A deluge was coming down, filling the cisterns of Rome with fresh, spring rain in anticipation of the dry season to come. Instead of a beautiful vista, a muddy field lay before Miltiades's eyes, strewn with chunks of rubble and a few discarded pieces of equipment.

"Can you believe that?" Quintus marveled as he came to the bishop's side. "Just a few months ago, that was a barracks full of troops. The New Camp, they used to call it! Now it's completely gone. Not so new anymore."

"Leveled to the ground by Constantine," Miltiades said. "I suppose that's a fitting punishment for opposing the rightful augustus in war. The Emperor's Personal Cavalry is destroyed."

"And so is the Praetorian Guard. I heard they were disbanded forever, and the men sent to the frontiers."

"Emperor Constantine is generous to his friends and ruthless with his enemies. Anything in Rome connected with Maxentius is being blotted from public memory."

"What will the augustus do with that empty land?"

A sly smile came to Miltiades's lips. "I have requested that he give the deed to me, since the property is attached to my new palace."

"Will he do it?"

"I think so. Constantine is in the mood to show gratitude to the church."

"What will you use the land for? Gardens?"

"Perhaps. But I can imagine a day when a truly great church could be built on this site. A grand hall, as big as a civic basilica. Right here at the Lateran Palace."

"A church the size of a basilica! Now that would be a church to remember through all the ages."

"Let it be so, for your glory, Lord Jesus," Miltiades prayed.

The palace doorkeeper approached the pair as they conversed by the window. Though the man had served Pompeianus, he was secretly a Christian, so Miltiades had decided to keep him on staff. He knew every detail about the inner workings of the great house.

"The lawyer has arrived with the documents," he said with a bow.

"Very good. Send him in."

Quintus cocked his eyebrow and glanced at the bishop. "Is it the deed to the former barracks? Soon to be a basilica?"

"No, that is still in the works," Miltiades replied with a laugh. "It is a different deed."

The lawyer arrived with another man behind him. The second figure was a slave wheeling a large rectangular object on a handcart. Clearly, it was heavy, but since it was wrapped in cloth, its exact identity was hard to determine.

"Would you care for wine?" Miltiades asked the men. The lawyer responded with a grateful nod.

The bishop poured a glass for the lawyer from Pompeianus's old wine cart. The wine was a beautiful golden color, an excellent Falernian that shouldn't go to waste. Miltiades turned and offered a second glass to the slave, whose expression of surprise was rivaled only by the shocked look on the lawyer's face. After a moment, the thirsty slave snatched it and greedily gulped it down.

"All God's children can enjoy good wine," Miltiades said with a gentle smile.

After some initial pleasantries, the lawyer finally brought out the deed. It was written on fine parchment instead of a wax tablet. "My client, Senator Neratius Junius Flavianus, does not know who the buyer of his mansion is," he said. "I think it's best if we don't make it widely known. He considers the price a good one. That is all he needs to know."

"Rumors will not reach him?"

"Unlikely. Now that poor Lady Sabina has perished, he has left Rome for Sardinia with his new wife."

The scoundrel took that little girl as a wife before his true wife "perished," Miltiades thought, yet he refrained from comment. Many true things, despite being true, were better left unsaid.

"I am ready to sign," the bishop announced.

Quintus handed him a reed pen, then offered a jar of ink. After dipping, Miltiades scratched his signature onto the deed for Neratius's mansion on the Aventine Hill. Quintus signed it as a witness. When the lawyer took it back and put his seal on it, the transaction was complete. The catholic church in Rome now owned the hilltop property where a house church had been meeting for many years.

Miltiades found the transaction especially gratifying. The old mansion would be the perfect place for the neighborhood priest Felix to live, along with some deacons and perhaps even some monks—a relatively new vocation that many young men were taking up with enthusiasm. There would be chambers to store charity for the poor and a dining room with a kitchen for love feasts. The household baths could be used for baptisms. And of course, the senator had already consented to some modifications that created a spacious worship hall, thanks to the urgings of Sophronia and Flavia. Surely this property would serve as a beautiful house of God for many years to come.

A thought occurred to Miltiades as he reflected on church houses and basilicas. *Domestic buildings, for all their many uses, limit the number of congregants a church can hold. But if a great basilica could be put up here at the Lateran, why not also on the Aventine? And for that matter . . . why not the many other house churches around the city? Perhaps the influx of converts would soon require larger buildings?*

The bishop resolved to get wise counsel about this matter. The necessary supply of funds was in place now that Constantine favored the church. Perhaps it was time for a new sacred architecture to arise in Christian Rome.

The lawyer tucked the deed into his satchel and turned to the slave behind him. "Take the wrapping off," he instructed. The slave began to untie the strings on the heavy object.

"What is it?" Miltiades asked.

"I don't know. My client's daughter instructed me to bring it to you. I believe it's an inscription. She commissioned the epigraphist herself."

"Do I owe you for it?"

The lawyer shook his head. "Lady Junia paid for everything."

"Let us have a look."

The slave removed the covering to reveal a milky-white slab of marble. It was a *titulus*: a large placard to be mounted above a door as a means of identifying the building. Words had been carved into one face of the slab:

Sanctae Sabinae Sophroniae Domus Ecclesiae

"The house church of holy Sabina Sophronia," Quintus read aloud. "That is a fitting memorial for a Christian woman who gave up her life rather than lose her chastity."

Miltiades pursed his lips. *Though she was willing to give up her life, she was actually spared—thanks be to God!* It was a wonderful truth, but here indeed was another secret that didn't need to be uttered aloud. Yet since the deacon's observation required a response, Miltiades said diplomatically, "That noble lady showed great virtue and courage as a disciple of the Lord. May the church that is marked by this sign honor Saint Sabina for many ages to come."

"Amen," Quintus replied.

A sudden sadness overcame Bishop Miltiades. He dismissed the lawyer, then turned away from the deacon and stared out the window at the steady rain. Lady Sabina Sophronia was alive, yes—but her life had taken a terrible turn. Her husband had divorced her, her household had been shattered, and she had lost the high social position she once possessed in Rome. Now she would take up the simple life of a nun in distant Sicilia, accompanied only by her daughter, who herself was bereft of the man she loved.

It is a great sacrifice you are asking of them, Lord. Grant them strength!

Quintus approached his bishop and put a comforting hand on his shoulder. "You seem downcast, my friend," he said.

"I am."

"How come? Everything is going so well for the catholic church. At last, Jesus is defeating the pagans who serve the devil."

"Many good things are happening now. Yet many people still suffer."

Quintus sighed and gave a little nod. "Wise words. A good reminder."

"You know what I have come to realize?"

"Tell me."

Instead of answering right away, Miltiades looked down to his hand and caressed the gemstone on his ring. It had been incised with a cross. On either side of it were an alpha and omega—the beginning and the end.

"The cross is the glorious emblem of our great Victor," Quintus observed.

"Yes. He is Lord of all. And I repeat: *all.* He leaves no stone unturned in his conquest. It is total."

"What does that mean, Your Holiness?"

A grim smile crept to Miltiades's face as he shook his head in contemplation. At last he looked up and met the deacon's eyes.

"It means you have to do hard things when you are conquered by the cross," said the godly bishop of Rome.

A steady rain had been falling all morning. It was a gray day in the port of Ostia—a day for deep sorrow.

Rex sat below deck on a wooden bench about halfway from the front of the ship. The light in the Roman galley was dim. Fore and aft, all the other rowers were contemplating their grim fate. Across the aisle, many more dejected men did the same. And directly in front of Rex was the bloodstained oar that would bedevil him for the rest of his life.

He stared at the cruel wooden shaft, knowing the labor of a navy oarsman was long and hard. A rower's muscles would burn like white-hot flames. Hands would turn raw and red. Thirst would torment parched throats. Skin would crack and peel in the salty air. Total-body exhaustion would set in. Under such a load, the strength of men would often fail. But Rex didn't care. The torture of the oar was nothing compared to the eagle talons of grief that raked across his soul.

Absently, he touched the coarse wood of the oar's handle. *Ohhh*, he moaned, unable to form coherent words. The aching bite of despair gnawed at Rex and refused to subside. Though he tried to push his heartache away, every thought, every imagination, every attempt at self-distraction quickly failed. No sooner would a daydream begin than it would collapse, and his mind would turn back to the woman he loved.

And the cycle of pain would begin all over again.

Flavia! He could see her lovely face. She had chestnut hair . . . long-lashed hazel eyes . . . the high cheekbones of a regal queen. Her smile was gentle and inviting. Her body was soft and slim.

And she could not be his.

Forever and always, she would be out of reach.

Argh! It hurts!

Rex let himself slump forward, his forehead resting on the oar. Like the mythological figure of Tantalus, he felt trapped in an eternal punishment: condemned forever to stand in a pool that receded when he bent to slake his thirst, and to gaze upward at a branch that lifted its fruit when he reached to satisfy his constant hunger.

Always longing. Ever denied.

"Hawsers free!" cried a voice from the pier. Rex felt the warship move.

"Prepare to row!" the overseer barked to the men below deck. "Forward strokes on my command!"

Sweat broke out on Rex's brow. His breath began to come in rapid pants. Desperate to escape, he looked around for a way out, but there was none. He was trapped forever. Nothing would free him from this terrible fate.

I can't do this! Flavia! I love you! Who will take care of you? Stand at your side? Provide you a home? Clasp your body in the warmth of the night? Give you children and raise them up? Love you until the end of time? Who will do this, if not me?

"Forward strokes!" shouted the overseer.

In unison, the crew began to row. The pinewood shaft began to move, turned by the other man on Rex's bench. The ship lurched ahead. Yet Rex's arms hung by his side. He couldn't bear to row away from Italy into the vast unknown.

The Christian amulet was around his neck. Rex clutched it and pressed it to his chest, more panicked than he had ever been in his life. "Jesus!" he cried. "I'm in agony! Have mercy on me!"

A hand touched Rex's shoulder from behind. He turned to see the earnest eyes of a handsome young man staring back at him.

"I am Stephen," said the youth. "A priest of the Lord Jesus Christ." The man reached out and grasped Rex's wrist, then placed his hand on the oar. He did the same with the other hand. The pole shivered against Rex's palms, buffeted by the sea outside.

"Wh . . . what . . . what do I do?" Rex whimpered.

"Be strong and courageous, brave warrior," Stephen said. His smile was gentle and kind. "Row now, and keep rowing, and wait to discover the plans of God. Forward strokes, one after the other."

Rex turned back to the oar. He gripped it hard in his fists and let its revolution carry him forward.

Flexed his powerful muscles.

And began to row.

———❧———

MAY 313

The snow-capped mountain sent a plume of smoke and ash into the blue Sicilian sky. *Volcanoes are deceptive things*, Flavia thought as she stared at

Mons Aetna from her seat in the open-air theater at Tauromenium. *They look so peaceful on the outside, but great turbulence lies within. Fire and ice— two mortal enemies locked in a stormy embrace.*

Will Aetna erupt one day? Perhaps. Until then, it lies dormant, its bubbling lava buried under earth and stone.

Buried deep, Flavia reminded herself. *But can such seething devastation be contained forever?* It was a question for another day.

Sophronia drummed her fingers on the stone riser next to Flavia. The theater was empty now, for it was only the Kalends of May and the summer production season had not yet started. "It is quiet here, my love," Sophronia said. "I like it."

"Yes. I have found it a good place to be alone. Today, though, I am glad you are with me."

The rugged, windswept coast around Tauromenium provided the perfect seclusion for the convent of devoted Christian sisters. Since arriving two weeks ago, Flavia had made it a house of urgent prayer. Yet because the convent was tucked into a ravine, she sometimes felt the need to break out of its isolation, to reach up to heaven, to ascend a hillside where she could see the ocean. She stared at it now, that boundless expanse behind the theater's stage. A bitter curse against the sea's vastness sprang to Flavia's lips, but she did not utter it aloud. She had learned the hard way that blasphemous ranting provided only temporary relief. It was not the way ahead.

A harbor was visible below, almost empty at the moment, though a few fishing boats rested alongside the pier. "Ships come and go quite often," Sophronia said wistfully.

"I cannot look at them."

Sophronia covered her daughter's hand with her own. "I know." Tears came to Flavia's eyes then, gushing up from the deep well of desire. She didn't wail, nor shake, nor even raise her hands to wipe away the tears. Instead, she let them flood her eyes and spill over her lashes and dribble down her cheeks.

"It hurts," she whispered, dropping her chin to her breast. The utterance was so mournful that Sophronia began to cry softly too. Flavia accepted her empathy, though it brought no relief from the gnawing ache.

Rex! Where are you, my most beloved? We could have been so happy together—and now you are lost! Will the Lord of all let me see you again? Could he be so kind?

Have mercy on me, my God! Remember me in this endless night!

Oh, Rex! I miss you! Will you come to me again when I need you most?

A little moan escaped Flavia's lips, and with it, her silence was broken. "God! I don't want this!" she cried. "This is not how I thought my life would turn out!"

Sophronia put her arm around her grieving daughter, pulling her close. "God sees your suffering, my darling girl. He crowns your faithful obedience. The blood of the martyrs is precious to him. And so are the tears of the faithful."

"This is a living martyrdom," Flavia replied. "The death of a dream. Every . . . single . . . day."

"Some say martyrdom is joyous."

"I do not feel it."

Flavia covered her face with her hands and groaned with an agony that could not be contained. Sophronia cradled her daughter as she wept until she could weep no more. After a long time, her tears slowed. At last they ceased. A heavy silence descended on the two women.

Flavia's body felt numb. She raised her chin and cast her eyes across the ocean.

"I am completely broken," she said.

But the heartless sea did not respond.

Bryan Litfin is the author of the Chiveis Trilogy, as well as several works of nonfiction, including *Early Christian Martyr Stories*, *After Acts*, and *Getting to Know the Church Fathers*. A former professor of theology at the Moody Bible Institute, Litfin earned his PhD in religious studies from the University of Virginia and his ThM in historical theology from Dallas Theological Seminary. He is currently an acquisitions editor for Moody Publishers. He and his wife have two adult children and live in Wheaton, Illinois. Learn more at www.bryanlitfin.com.

MEET BRYAN

Follow along at

BRYANLITFIN.COM

to stay up to date on exclusive news,
upcoming releases, and more!

  Bryan.Liftin

Be the First to Hear about New Books from Revell!

Sign up for announcements about new and upcoming titles at

RevellBooks.com/SignUp

@RevellBooks

Don't miss out on our great reads!

a division of Baker Publishing Group
www.RevellBooks.com